The Mermaid's Pool

Detective Inspector John Smithdow
things to deal with.

It's 1988 and ecstasy is flooding the

The Second Summer of Love is her

Tell that to the locals on DI Smithdown's patch.

Over one weekend, Smithdown is faced with a missing single mum, machete wielding gangs in Oldham, simmering racial tensions across communities and a mutilated body found at the edge of a remote lake with a mythical reputation.

People say bad things happen at the Mermaid's Pool.

They're dead right.

Black Moss

In April 1990, as rioters took over Strangeways prison in Manchester, someone killed a little boy at Black Moss.

And no one cared.

No one except Danny Johnston, an inexperienced radio reporter trying to make a name for himself.

More than a quarter of a century later, Danny returns to his home city to revisit the murder that's always haunted him.

If Danny can find out what really happened to the boy, maybe he can cure the emptiness he's felt inside since he too was a child.

But finding out the truth might just be the worst idea Danny Johnston has ever had.

The Ballad Of Hanging Lees

In Manchester, vigilantes are setting traps online to expose sexual predators and once they have a suspect in their sights they're taking the law into their own hands, acting as judge, jury and executioner.

When the suicide of a troubled woman near to Hanging Lees Reservoir implicates an old friend, reporter Danny Johnston has no choice but to investigate.

As more bodies are discovered Danny finds himself being pulled deeper and deeper into a case whose roots date back decades, and as he tries to uncover the truth he begins to be haunted by horrifying dreams of his own.

A terrible secret, kept for than 40 years is about to change everything.

In the final act of David Nolan's Manc Noir trilogy, *The Ballad of Hanging Lees* will play us out... then fade to black.

"The King Of Manc Noir" – Altricham Word Festival

"Dark but compelling novels very much rooted in fact" – I LOVE Manchester

"David Nolan has used his memories of the 1990 Strangeways riots as a backdrop to his debut novel and channelled his anger about a Manchester murder that shocked the nation" - Manchester Evening News

"Dark, brooding, angry - very angry at times. A compelling mystery with a social conscience." - itsanindiebookblog.com

"Gripping from the outset. This is a stark, desolate book – stunning." - The Irresponsible Reader

"Manchester is a location that's been underused in fiction but David Nolan is keen to claim it - this is Manc Noir" - Northern Soul Magazine

The books in this edition were first published 2018, 2020 & 2022 by Fahrenheit Press.

This edition first published 2024

ISBN: 978-1-914475-51-1

10 9 8 7 6 5 4 3 2 1

www.Fahrenheit-Press.com

F 4 E

Cover Design & Manuscript Typesetting by www.SkullStarStudio.com

RAIN FALLS DOWN

(The Manc Noir Trilogy)

By

David Nolan

- *The Mermaid's Pool*
- *Black Moss*
- *The Ballad Of Hanging Lees*

Fahrenheit Press

Manc Noir: A Glossary of Terms

For those outside the Greater Manchester area, the following explanations of expressions used in all three books might prove useful:

And all	As well.
Any road	Anyway.
Chuffed	Pleased.
Conk	Nose.
Cordial	Dilutable juice, often orange or blackcurrant.
Dead (aside from the obvious meaning)	Really. For example: 'I'm dead chuffed.'
Dob you in	Tell on you.
Effing and jeffing	Swearing.
Ginnel	Alleyway between or behind houses.
Gob	Mouth.
Keks	Trousers.
Kinnell	Shortened version of 'fucking hell'.
Mam	Mother.
Mard	Person who is easily upset. Not to be confused with the Yorkshire 'mard' which means moody.
Mard arse	Person who is VERY easily upset.
Mither	To bother or cause trouble.
Mucky	dirty.
Nora	A woman's name often attached to a swear word. For example: 'Bloody Nora.'
Nowt	Nothing.
Odd	Added to other words when approximating something. For example: 'It's worth fifteen-odd quid, no more than that.'
On the knocker	Turning up unannounced at someone's front door.
Owt	Anything.
Piffy on a rock bun	To waste time or be of no use. For example: 'Stop standing there like Piffy on a rock bun.' Yes, it is a very odd expression.
Proper	Really.
Right	Very. For example: 'That's right tasty.'

Soft Mick	A mysterious Mancunian character who has a great deal of everything. So, to have 'more shoes than Soft Mick' means you possess a huge number of shoes.
Ta	Thanks.
Tea	Evening meal. Teatime is rarely much later than six pm.
Tight	Mean, unwilling to share.
Un	One. For example: 'You're a wrong un, you are.'
Vimto	Mysterious Mancunian fruit cordial (see above). No one knows what's actually in it.

MAP OF MANC NOIR

1 Pennine Way Footbridge
2 Windy Hill Transmitter
3 Bull's Head Pub
4 Maggie Ormrod's House
5 Hanging Lees Reservoir
6 Hunter's Hollow School
7 John Smithdown's House
8 Black Moss Reservoir
9 Royal Oldham Hospital
10 Oldham Athletic F.C.
11 Oldham Police Station
12 Kate Smithdown's House
13 Danny Johnston's House
14 Alexandra Park

The Ballad Of Hanging Lees

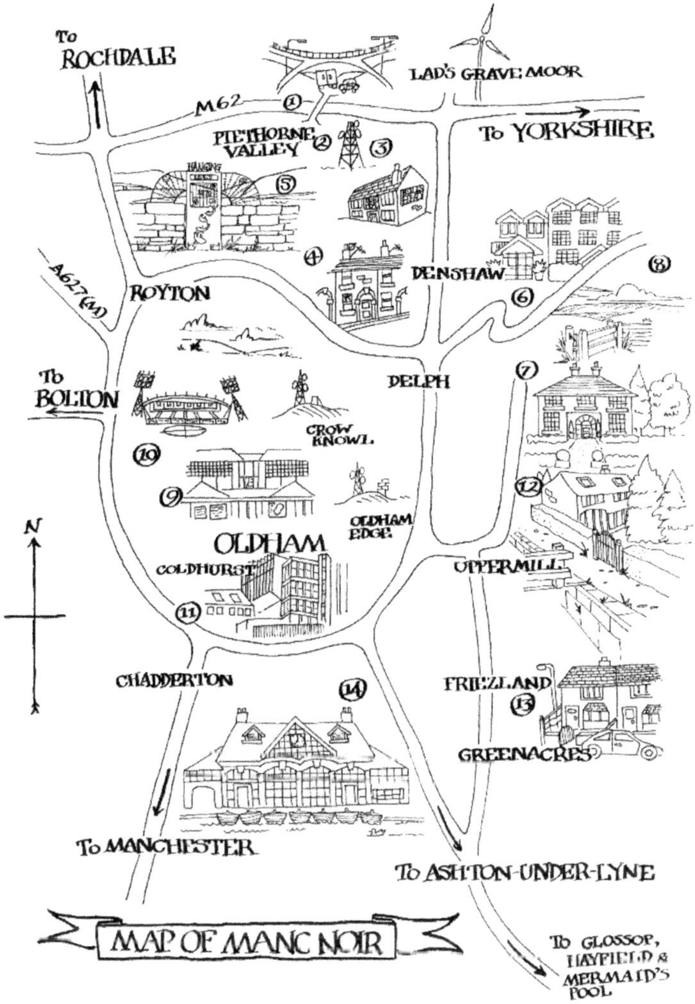

To my mum, Margaret Nolan. I wish I'd known her a little better.

Introduction

Anger, as a great man once said, is an energy.

Some people need candles and mood music to write. I just need to be really angry about stuff.

I wrote *Black Moss* in a fury because a publisher had cancelled a factual book I'd been writing about historic child abuse. When they told me the deal was off, I took my anger out on my keyboard. I don't even remember writing it, to be honest. I just sort of spat it out. That's how furious I was. It wasn't until much later I realised that I had sort of written the factual book I'd originally started - it's just that it came out disguised as a crime fiction novel. All the issues that journalist Danny Johnston and Detective Inspector John Smithdown confront in *Black Moss* are the same ones that I would have tackled in the original factual book.

The Mermaid's Pool came about because I was angry about the rise of the far right in the UK - and in particular the terrible murder of British MP Jo Cox. I was also angry about my wife having breast cancer. God, I was furious about that. I can remember being at the Christie Hospital in Manchester thinking… why won't they take it out of her and give it to me? Apparently, they can't do that. Bloody NHS…

I started writing *The Ballad of Hanging Lees* when it was my turn to be in hospital after a routine operation I had undergone went horribly wrong. The first chapter was written when the hospital went into gradual lockdown as Covid took hold. Scary. What scared me even more was finding out that during lockdown the online grooming of children rose by 70 per cent. That's just the cases we know about. Everyone should be angry about that.

But you need more than just anger to write a trilogy of books that has become known as Manc Noir. You need help, specialist knowledge and a lot of patience from people who might be baffled about why this strange (rather angry) man is asking them all these odd questions. I literally contacted Kinder Mountain Rescue Team in Hayfield and asked them: 'If a dead body was found up at Kinder Scout, how would you get it down?' They would have been perfectly within their rights to call the police, but rather charmingly they didn't. Instead, they helped me. So, thanks to KMRT, especially Jim Harries. Thanks also to Station Manager Dave Swallow (Greater Manchester Fire and Rescue Service), Tom Dowse (local politics guru), Parminder Paul (BBC Bengali) and all my friends at BBC Urdu in Islamabad, Pakistan. Former Detective Constable Phil Selley's knowledge meant that our view of Oldham Police Station in the 1980s is an accurate one. Dee Graham and Katherine Macfarlane assisted me greatly by sharing their personal knowledge of cancer treatment; Neil Summers did the same, but his specialist subject was in a rather different pharmaceutical area. Paul Lockitt helped with the radio stuff, David Prior gave me guidance when it came to hyper-local journalism, and Police Coroners Officer Emma Campbell advised me on crime scene stuff. Thanks also to Maureen Carnighan, OU Distance Learning Co-Ordinator for HMP Manchester (Strangeways) and Amy Jenner of Partners of Prisoners, along with Prison Officer Russ Kenyon. Cheers to Matt Keyes for making sure the Oldham vibes were right and to Lucy Milburn for her Map of Manc Noir. Thanks especially Nicola Graham, former Detective Constable with Greater Manchester Police who was there for all three. I owe you a hug, as you once said to me outside Manchester Crown Court…

For *Rain Falls Hard* the three Manc Noir books are presented in a slightly different way than when they were first published. *Black Moss* (2018) was originally a stand-alone book, *The Mermaid's Pool* (2020) was a prequel and *The Ballad of Hanging Lees* (2022) rounded everything off. They now follow the actual chronology of the interconnected stories of Danny Johnston, DI John Smithdown, and his daughter Kate, rather than the order that the stories were originally published in. So, for *Rain Falls Hard*, we start in 1988 with *The Mermaid's Pool*, move to 1990 with *Black Moss* and then to the present day with *The Ballad of Hanging Lees*. Makes sense. I think.

I never intended to write a novel, let alone three. I didn't set out to 'invent' Manc Noir and certainly didn't mean to become the 'King' of it. I was just angry about stuff.

Anger.

It's an energy.

David Nolan, Manchester, England
March 2024

The Mermaids Pool

PROLOGUE

9.30 pm Thursday 31 March 1988

When they came for her, she fought.

Hard.

She kicked, scratched, screamed and spat at the men, grabbing at their balaclava masks… trying to find a way out.

But there were five of them. And there was no way out.

She shouted too, of course. And tried to scream. But the hand that covered her mouth and the forearm that cradled her neck were both strong and practised.

The leader - she instinctively knew he was in charge - put his covered face next to hers. He put a finger up against the wool of his mask, where she imagined his mouth was.

'Shhhh now,' was his advice.

She nodded. A moment of silence.

'It's time,' he stated.

The grip on her mouth loosened.

Slightly.

She said something in a language the men didn't understand. 'English!' another man screamed. He poked her hard in the face once with the flat, handle end of the baseball bat he was carrying. Then he hit her again after every subsequent word: 'This. Is. England. Speak. Fucking. English.'

As they took her, bare toes dragging on the carpet, she dared speak one more time: 'Where are we going?'

The leader replied: 'Swimming.'

PART I

'Manchester Radio News at six - this is Beth Hall. Police are investigating a series of apparent race hate attacks in Oldham last night. White paint was splashed on houses, restaurants and a mosque in the town centre as Robert Crane reports…'

'Police were initially called in the early hours after the owner of a restaurant in the Glodwick area said his premises had been targeted during the night.

White gloss paint had been thrown at the restaurant's windows. The front door, walls and even the pavement outside had been daubed with swastikas and what appeared to be paintings of a wolf's head.

Several homes in the area were also targeted, and white paint was also thrown at a mosque in Coldhurst. One local man whose home was vandalised - but who didn't want to be named - says the police aren't interested in attacks on the South Asian community:'

> *"We are on our own. They don't care about our homes, our businesses or our kids. If it happens around here, the police don't want to know. It's scary right now, I mean it. These are frightening times and the authorities don't seem to be on our side."*

'Police believe the incidents are linked but say they're keeping an open mind as to whether they were racially motivated. They're urging anyone who saw anything suspicious in the area at the time to come forward. Robert Crane, Manchester Radio News in Oldham.'

CHAPTER ONE

9.45 pm Thursday 31 March 1988

Looking closely at the little girl's swollen and bloodied lip, Detective Inspector John Smithdown sighed, rubbed a hand across his unshaven chin and shook his head. 'It's nasty,' he conceded. 'I'm not saying it isn't, because it is. It's definitely nasty. But it's not nasty enough, that's the problem.'

He looked again, his tired, grey face just inches from hers. Nearly everything about Smithdown seemed tinged with grey - grey hair, grey bog-brush moustache, grey suit, even blue/grey eyes. There were some tonal differences in his appearance - light grey to dark grey - but it was all pretty much grey.

As he continued to look at her lip, she stopped crying - largely because she was so puzzled as to what the policeman was up to. She lay still on the examination table.

The girl's lip was slightly split, just to the right of the bow. Again, Smithdown looked hard at the cut. 'Fuck,' he muttered, after much deliberation. Then he remembered the girl was just ten years old. 'Sorry, love,' he said by way of an apology. 'But, honestly. It's just not fucking nasty enough.'

'I don't follow, Mr Smithdown,' the young photographer said, looking at the girl's face and then at the detective. 'Sorry. Am I being thick? I was just told to take some snaps of her injuries. That's all I know. I have to say, it looks pretty nasty from where I'm standing.'

Smithdown motioned for the photographer to come with him to the rear of the examination room, one of several at Oldham's brown, pebble-dashed police station. The detective looked at him. *Twenty-two. Twenty-three, tops. Straight out of Manchester Polytechnic. Streaked-blonde hair and wearing jeans and his dad's old suit jacket. Fucking Nora.*

The detective placed a hand on the young man's shoulder, then subtly moved it so he cupped the nape of his slim neck. Smithdown then pulled the photographer ever-so-slightly towards him. 'So, you're the new staff snapper… What's your name, lad?'

'Paul, Mr Smithdown. Paul Rees. I'm new. Yes. I only started this week.'

'Look, Paul,' the DI said in a whisper, turning his head away from the girl. 'It's like this. The doctor will be here any minute. He'll take one look at that kid's lip, see straight away it doesn't need stitches, wipe her face, give her a lolly and send her home. Straight back into the hands of the twat that did that to her in the first place. The same twat that probably did it to her last month. And the month before that. And that is unacceptable in my view. Un-acc-ept-able, Paul. Let me give you an alternative scenario. Instead of that happening, we could get her into the Royal Oldham Hospital for the night. Then - are you following all this, Paul? Then, social services can work a bit of their hippy bollocks magic, get her made a ward of court and then get her out of that shit pile she calls her home - and away from that shithead she calls her mum's boyfriend. Me and you. We could do that, Paul. We could make that happen. So - are you with me, or against me?'

'I'm very much with you, Mr Smithdown,' the photographer replied after a few moments. 'I think.'

DI Smithdown gave the young man a hearty double slap on the back of the neck. 'Absolutely top notch. Now, put your camera down, Paul, face the wall and shut the fuck up.'

'The wall?' the photographer asked.

'The wall,' DI Smithdown confirmed. 'It's the big pile of bricks over there.'

Paul lifted the strap of his Hasselblad camera over his head and carefully laid it onto the table in the corner of the room. Then he turned to face the examination room's yellowy-white wall.

'Cracking,' said the detective. He checked the paperwork connected to the case then walked over to the young girl. He popped a mint into his mouth, aware that the two pints he'd had earlier in The Old Bill bar next to the police station were probably still wafting about on his breath - it was the favoured drinking spot for Oldham detectives and hard to resist of an evening shift. Smithdown bent down so that his eyes were at the same level as hers and spoke quietly to her, his hands deep into the pockets of his grey suit trousers. 'Hi, Rebecca.'

'It's Becky,' she said in the quietest of voices.

'Sorry… Becky. Hello there. Can I ask you something?'

She nodded. Her hair was greasily dark. There was dirt underneath her fingernails and her eyes were underscored by dark semicircles. She was wearing a Mel and Kim t-shirt, jeans that were too small for her and scuffed, pink plastic sandals. Smithdown recognised them. He saw a lot of kids wearing them in his line of work. *Woolworths' sandals. Bless her. She's wearing plastic sandals from Woolies. Never a good sign. The cheapest shoes in town and probably second-hand. Poor, poor little Becky.*

'Right then,' the detective said. 'Do you want to go back home tonight? Back to your mam's?'

A pause.

'And back to her boyfriend? Or would you rather stay the night somewhere else? Maybe with some nice nurses at the hospital? They could look after you while we get this all sorted out.'

The girl looked at him – her dark brown eyes were locked onto Smithdown's - but she said nothing.

'Home? Or somewhere else?' he reiterated.

There was silence as Becky continued to think. She seemed slightly embarrassed to give the DI a reply and looked away for a minute. But eventually she answered: 'Somewhere else,' she said. Then she looked directly at the policeman and added: 'Please.'

Detective Inspector John Smithdown nodded. He turned to check that Paul the photographer was still looking at the wall. He was. 'Right then,' the DI sighed. 'Sorry, love.'

With one quick move he slid a finger into the girl's mouth, yanked his hand back and split the child's lip a third of the way up to her nose. A thin squirt of blood jetted onto his overcoat. *Shitting hell, it'll have to get its annual clean a little earlier this year.*

'You can take your photo now,' Smithdown said to the photographer. But the girl was screaming so loudly, the young man couldn't quite make out what the detective had said. Paul made as if to turn around several times but was clearly nervous about seeing anything that he wasn't supposed to see.

'I said you can take your photos now lad!' Smithdown said loudly as he crossed the room and leant against the far wall. He folded his arms and watched as the photographer took a reading with his light meter and bent over, looking into the camera's reverse image viewfinder. He held the electronic flash over his head - his hand was still shaking - and took four pictures of the girl's face. He turned to look at DI Smithdown. 'Okay?'

'Perfect, Paul,' the detective replied, just as the on-duty doctor came into the room. He was a slight man in his late fifties, his hair scraped across his head in an inelegant combover. He looked at the blood on Smithdown's coat. 'Christ Almighty, John. I can remember the days when you at least tried to be a bit subtle about these things.'

'I can remember the days when I didn't have to do such things at all, Clive. I'll ring the hippies and get her booked in. Then I can start rattling a few bins to find the twat that did it to her. Pint later?'

'Absolutely, John. I'll just clean up your fucking mess and I'll see you for last orders.'

CHAPTER TWO

11.45 am Friday 1 April 1988

Smithdown stood on the steps of the children's care home and thought for a moment. *What's the best way to play it? Doesn't really matter, Brenda will give me a gob full either way.*

The large, red brick house on the semi-rural estate of Alt on the south eastern outskirts of Oldham would have looked out of place and lopsided to anyone looking at it from the road. It was actually two, semi-detached houses that had been knocked into one large property. Three separate strains of dance music could be heard coming from the open windows of the upstairs rooms. The detective recognised at least one of the songs as something his daughter listened to, but they all sounded the same to Smithdown. *Car alarm music. Wah-Wah-WahWah. I bloody hate it.*

He popped open the glove compartment and rummaged through the cassettes that filled it: Kilburn and the High Roads… Brinsley Schwarz… Dr Feelgood. Meat and two veg pub rock - that was Smithdown's kind of music. He'd lost interest after the mid-70s. *You'll never improve on 'Surrender to the Rhythm' by the Brinsley's, so what's the point?*

He opted for Dr Feelgood's *Down By The Jetty* and shoved the tape into the car's player in readiness for his return. *I'll need a bit of Lee Brilleaux after the bollocking I'm about to get.*

Smithdown locked his dusty, dark blue Ford Escort then checked it was secure by pulling up the door handle. *Can't be too careful around here.* The detective liked to use his own car; he hated the pool vehicles that were provided for detectives at Greater Manchester Police – beige Morris Marinas, mainly. There was never enough of them to go around and on one occasion Smithdown had to resort to catching the bus to get to an incident. Never again.

Using his own car also meant he wasn't at the beck and call of the 'GK' radio fitted as standard in the police pool cars. And that suited him just fine. Especially when he accidentally forgot to take a portable PF1 Pocketphone unit with him too. He was always doing that.

Smithdown walked towards the front door of the care home; it opened before he could ring the bell and a woman in her 40s wearing a baggy, brightly coloured jumper put her finger close to the detective's face, held it there and began shouting. 'You absolute fucking lunatic, John Smithdown!' Brenda Graham shouted, a twist of south west Ireland in her accent. 'The state of that girl's face when she arrived this morning. Like she'd been mauled by an animal. Which she fucking had been, by the way… You! I said give her lip a squeeze, not tear it in half, you useless fucker. Anyway, how are you? Come in.'

Head down, Smithdown walked through the hallway into the large, open-plan kitchen which acted as the central hub of the care home. Although it was nearly lunchtime, the kitchen was humming with chatter as a dozen youngsters ate cereal, made toast, chatted, laughed, bickered and smoked. Smithdown noticed how the older kids – aged about 15 – helped the younger ones without any fuss or complaint. 'Too noisy in here,' Brenda shouted to the detective. 'Outside.'

The detective nodded, followed Brenda through the house and stepped outside into the warm, late-Spring breeze that eased across the large, overgrown garden. There were so many bikes, scooters and outdoor toys scattered about the lawn that they seemed to be growing out of the long grass. Brenda sat on the back step as Smithdown offered her a John Player Special cigarette from a battered, black pack pulled from the inside pocket of his grey suit jacket. He'd dropped off his overcoat at the cleaners on the way.

She took the cigarette, tucked it behind her ear and then rolled one of her own from a pouch attached to the belt of her red, corduroy trousers. She lit it with a Micky Mouse Zippo lighter - offered the flame to Smithdown - then flicked it shut with a loud clack. 'Anyway,' she sighed; her voice was much quieter now. "Thank God you got that girl out of that house. I don't care for the way you did it, mind, but you got it done. Fair play. You're still a fucking animal, though.'

'I had to make sure that Dr Clive would definitely sign her away,' Smithdown explained. 'He's half-pissed most of the time. It had to be a dead cert. Black and white.'

'Black and blue, more like,' Brenda pointed, her voice going up a few notches again. 'The state of her this morning after she'd come back from the Royal.' She shook her head slowly from side to side to make sure that the detective was in no doubt about how annoyed she was.

'It could have been a lot worse if she'd gone back to her mum's bastard boyfriend,' Smithdown offered quietly. 'Dread to think what he would have done to the poor little mite.'

'Becky,' Brenda stated. 'Her name is Becky.'

'Right. Becky. Yes. Is she okay? Apart from the whole lip thing, obviously.'

'She's okay. Just about. It's her mam I'm more worried about.'

'I see. So, there's more to you asking me here than just the mere pleasure of bollocking me, then?'

'The bollocking is just a bonus, to be honest, John. Her mam's not been seen for at least 24 hours.'

'Right,' said Smithdown, searching for his notebook. 'That's... what day is it today?'

'Friday, John. It's Friday. Good Friday, to be precise.'

'Okay. Of course.'

'Little Becky says there was trouble at the house yesterday teatime - and that's all she'll say. The neighbours rang social services because they were worried about her, but your lads ended up getting there first because of all the screaming and shouting.'

'Her mum's Naomi Wells, right?' the detective asked rubbing the side of his nose with the end of a betting shop pen. 'I know her. Christ. She's not had the greatest life so far, but she's more sinned against than a sinner, I'd say.'

'She's a good person, John. And a good mam to Becky.'

'Have you seen her boyfriend about?' the detective asked, the ash from the cigarette dangling from his lips landed on his notepad as he wrote. 'Jimmy Todd isn't it?'

'That's him. Thankfully, I haven't seen him, no. He's a piece of dirt. Describes himself as a DJ but he's basically a drug dealer with a big record collection. He's only been with Naomi for about a year. She's been known to do a bit of sex work on the side, as you know, and I think he encourages it. Probably got his eye on little Becky too, the shit bag.'

'Don't suppose you have a photo of mum, do you?' Smithdown asked.

'I don't,' said Brenda, squeezing off the end of her roll-up and popping the tiny dimp down the backyard drain. 'But little Becky has one. It's in her room by her bed. Perhaps you could pop upstairs and ask her for a lend of it? Seeing you is sure to bring a smile to her face. Oh no. She can't smile just now, can she? I forgot.'

'Kinnell,' sighed Smithdown, jabbing his JPS out against the back wall, causing a small tumble of sparks to fall into the grid. 'Okay. Lead on.'

The detective felt the angry stares of at least a dozen pairs of young eyes as he followed Brenda and walked back through the kitchen and then up the stairs. They passed several doors – all with customised variations of KEEP OUT signs on them - before stopping outside the last door on the first-floor landing. Brenda knocked. Nothing. She tried again, louder this time. 'Becky. It's Brenda. I've got a policeman with me. I'm afraid it's the same one you met last night. He wants to talk with you. You don't have to talk to him if you don't want to. But he wants to try to find your mum. That picture of yours will definitely help.'

Silence.

'It's up to you Becky,' Brenda continued. 'I'd completely understand if you don't want to see him.' She looked at Smithdown and shook her head in disapproval. 'I wouldn't blame you in the slightest, I really wouldn't.'

Silence again. Brenda was about to try one more time when the door opened. A little. Becky Wells' bruised face could be seen through the small gap. There were stitches in her lip. Her hair looked clean and shiny. She was wearing what looked like a new, plain white t-shirt and clean but clearly second-hand jeans. Smithdown looked at her feet through the opening. *Woolies' sandals.*

Becky passed a photo to Brenda through the gap, caught John Smithdown's eye for the briefest of moments, then closed the door. Music started from the room: Mel and Kim's '*Respectable*'. Brenda motioned for the detective to follow her back down the stairs. When they got to the hallway Brenda stopped, took a look at the photo and handed it to the DI. It showed a woman in her late 20s punching the air and laughing in what looked like a nightclub. She was wearing a black vest top and army-style grey and white camouflage trousers. The red date stamp on the bottom right-hand corner of the photo showed that it had been taken just two months previously: 11.2.88.

'Yep, that's Naomi. Quite the party girl,' offered Smithdown.

'You can be a good parent and have a good time as well, John. I'm sure your mates down at the Old Bill will agree with that. How's your daughter doing, by the way?'

'Point taken, Brenda. Point taken. She's doing great, thanks. Still at uni. She's quite the party girl too.'

The pager on Smithdown's belt buzzed an interruption. It was his one concession to being contactable as he could very easily just ignore it. The display's message wasn't the usual instruction to ring a phone number.

<ALEX PARK NOW>

The detective looked at it with a frown. He didn't like carrying a pager at the best of times, but he liked it even less when the messages sounded like he was being shouted at. He re-attached the pager to his belt and placed a hand on Brenda's upper arm, giving it what he hoped was a reassuring squeeze. 'Right, I'll get this circulated and do some digging. My presence is required at Alexandra Park, apparently.'

'Thank you, John,' she said, placing her hand on his and returning the squeeze. 'You're still a massive fucking arsehole, but I'm glad you're on our side.'

'Beautifully put, Brenda. I'll be in touch.'

Smithdown walked back to his car then paused. He took another look at the photo - it still had a yellowed curl of Sellotape stuck to the back. He looked at Naomi's happy face then tucked the photo into his jacket pocket. He got in the car and pushed the Dr Feelgood cassette he'd found earlier into the slot. As he switched on the engine the tape mechanism kicked in and '*She Does It Right*' wowed into life.

It took him just a few minutes' drive to get to Alexandra Park; it ran along the south western edge of the town. As he drove past uniform roads tightly packed with corner shops, takeaways and terraces he wondered exactly where in the park his presence might be required. He quickly got an answer; half of Oldham's police force seemed to be swarming around the park's boating lake. Smithdown pulled into the car park, nodded to the uniformed constables herding afternoon school kids out of the main gates and headed down the sloping path, past the tennis courts towards the main lake. In between the main boat house and a separate launch building was a slipway that led into the shallow, brown water. There were two police officers already there, talking to a very distressed looking man with a red setter dog. The dog was also extremely agitated, yanking and straining in the direction of a plastic bag by the water's edge. *A man out walking his dog. It's always a man out walking his dog.*

He caught the eye of Detective Constable Bob Donaldson as he approached the lake's shoreline. Donaldson, in an old blue suit, light blue shirt and a dark blue tie had an unusually cheery face for a police officer. He looked more like a friendly butcher than a detective. But his face was currently set to 'very stern indeed.' By pursing his lips, exhaling and shaking his head, Donaldson managed to tell Smithdown a great deal about what was going on as he approached the scene. Essentially, it was along the lines of: 'This is grim and you're not going to like it one little bit'.

The red setter was barking loudly now. Smithdown spoke to one of the PCs who was trying to calm down both the man and his dog.

'Could you get this pair away from here for the time being, please?' he told one of them. 'Tell him to take the dog up behind the boathouse, to wait there and to say nowt to anyone. Wait with him until we're done here. And tell him to shut that fucking dog up - I can't hear myself piss here with all that racket.'

He turned to Detective Constable Donaldson. 'Bob. On a scale of one to ten, how badly are the contents of that placcy bag going to put me off my tea?'

'What are you planning on having for your tea,' the DC said. 'If you don't mind me asking, boss?'

DC Donaldson was in the habit of being overly curious about things that most people wouldn't ordinarily bother with. A good trait for a policeman to have, some might say – but an annoying one, nonetheless. Smithdown knew it was quicker to indulge him. 'Chippy tea, Bob', he replied. 'Steak pudding, chips, peas and gravy. And a can of dandelion and burdock.'

'No fish? Not like you. It's Friday…'

Smithdown took a look across the lake and back down to the bag. There was a puddle around it where the lake water had seeped from the bag's holes. The water was speckled with what looked like soot. 'I'm off fish today, Bob, if I'm honest.'

'In that case,' Donaldson offered, 'I'd say a good strong nine.'

'Cracking...' Smithdown said. 'Absolutely cracking.'

Smithdown pulled a pen from the inside pocket of his jacket, squatted down and eased apart the handles of the bag with the pen's tip. Inside, somewhat puffy and wrinkled from the lake water it appeared to have absorbed, was a human hand. The detective did what he always did in these circumstances and followed the advice he'd been given by a senior detective he'd worked with in the late 70s: think with your eyes open and your gob shut.

DI John Smithdown looked long and hard at the contents of the bag. And kept his gob shut.

It was a left hand. The cut at the wrist was neat. The fingers were slender. The nails had chipped traces of dayglo nail varnish on - the colours alternated between orange and lime green on each fingernail. Smithdown didn't feel that he was jumping to a conclusion by considering it to be a young woman's hand. But he was, as ever, prepared to be convinced otherwise. While the main, fleshy part of the hand was blanched white - not unlike tripe from Oldham market - the tips of the fingers were blackened. Smithdown, again not unreasonably, felt they could well have been badly scorched, as if a harsh flame had been held to them. Three of the fingertips had been burned so badly the skin and flesh had flaked away. The thumb and forefinger got his attention - they seemed to have had less time in the flames.

'Fucking Nora,' Smithdown sighed, sensing that his chippy tea was now looking increasingly unlikely.

'I know,' offered DC Donaldson. 'Not nice. Not nice at all. Any missing-from-homes that might fit the bill? Or indeed, fit the wrist.'

'Brilliant Bob. You've been waiting half the afternoon to use that line, haven't you?' said Smithdown. 'Let's see if we can get some dabs off those fingers that haven't been totally barbecued and take it from there, shall we? We're not in the business of jumping to conclusions.'

'I reckon you know whose mitt that might be, don't you, boss?'

'Potentially. Get them to do a check against a Naomi Wells. Age 26. One of our regular clients. I hope I'm wrong, but it might save time. In the meantime, go and take a statement from the bloke that found it and tell that twat if he breathes a word of this to anyone, I'll drown him and that noisy fucking dog of his in the lake myself. Okay?'

'I'll tell him that word for word, boss.'

CHAPTER THREE

3pm Friday 1 April 1988

Smithdown was at his desk listening to the radio, when DC Donaldson approached with a file under his arm. The DI held up his hand for a moment as he monitored what Manchester Radio was saying about the find.

'…Murder squad detectives in Greater Manchester are investigating after a human hand was found at a park in Oldham.

The grim discovery was made by a man out walking his dog in Alexandra Park yesterday afternoon. Robert Crane has more.'

'It's always a GRIM DISCOVERY, boss,' Donaldson said. 'Ever noticed that? Always.'

'Shush.'

'The hand, thought to be that of a woman, was found wrapped in a plastic bag in the boating lake at the park yesterday. Brian Sharples was out walking his dog at the time and became suspicious when his red setter spotted something in the lake.'

> *"Me dog… it were going mad. Barking and that. Barking at this bag in the water. So, I let him off the leash and he dragged it out. Wish I hadn't now, when I saw what were inside. Horrible. Never seen anything like it in all my days. You just don't expect it, like, do yuh?"*

'Forensic tests are now being carried out to try to identify the victim. In the meantime, police are trying to reassure local residents who say they're fearful that more remains will be found. Robert Crane, Manchester Radio News, in Oldham.'

'Fucking Nora, Bob,' Smithdown said, turning the radio off. 'Didn't you tell that bloke not to speak to the press?'

'I absolutely did,' Donaldson replied.

'I was hoping to keep some of those details back. We don't actually know it's a woman's hand. It could belong to a bloke with a sensitive disposition for all I know.'

'That's what I wanted to talk to you about,' Donaldson said, standing in the doorway. Smithdown's office was so tiny it was more comfortable to stand outside it than to try to squeeze into it. 'We've got a preliminary ID on the hand. It'd been torched alright, but not quite torched enough. They manged to get a fingerprint match from the thumb and the pointing finger.'

'Forefinger, Bob,' Smithdown said with a sigh. 'That's what we tend to call it. Not pointing finger.'

'Aye, that as well. Looks like you weren't wrong boss. Prints seem to match those of a Naomi Laila Wells, D.O.B 12th of the second 1962. Half-caste girl…'

'Mixed-race is my preferred option here Bob, we have spoken about this.'

'With respect, boss,' Donaldson replied, 'Half-caste is still the term used by the GMP press office in their descriptions.'

'I think we can aim higher than the GMP press office, don't you Bob?'

'We can but dream, boss. Any road, she was known to the Manchester Criminal Records Office, so her dabs were in the system: theft, soliciting…'

'… I know she had a MANCRO number, Bob. It was me that did her for most of the crimes in question.'

'Can't say I'm surprised. The boyfriend is top priority now, I'm guessing.'

'Your guessing right, Bob. Cancel your plans for tonight, because we need to get that dickhead into custody, sharpish. We can get him in on suspicion of murder, but without the rest of her, technically speaking she's still just a missing person. That's what we say to the outside world and that's what I'll be saying to her daughter - for the time being, at least. I've upset that little girl quite enough so far this week, without having to tell her that her mum's probably in bits across half of Oldham.'

'Can't blame you there, boss.'

'We need a press statement for now, saying that we're growing increasingly concerned for Naomi's safety - the usual holding line - that'll see us through the weekend. Then we'll need to get a press conference on the go for first thing Tuesday morning…'

'Why wait 'til Tuesday?' asked Donaldson.

'Monday's a Bank Holiday, Bob. Glance at a calendar from time to time, will you?'

'Will do. In fact, I'll make a note in my diary to do it…'

'I'll tell DS Pym about the presser. We need to have a total blackout on any mention of her previous convictions. Public sympathy goes right out the fucking window as soon as you mention it, especially soliciting.'

'Aren't you supposed to check with the DS before you organise a press conference?' asked Donaldson. He was smiling. He knew the score between Smithdown and James Pym, their Detective Superintendent.

'Of course, Bob,' Smithdown said, his tone of voice bone dry. 'How remiss of me. I'll get right on it.'

'He'll be wanting to buy himself a new suit if he's going to be on the telly at Tuesday teatime.'

'I'll call ahead to *Stolen From Ivor* and let them know he'll be round for a fitting.'

'Very decent of you.'

'Right,' said Smithdown, waving the DC away. 'I've already rung the landlord of Naomi's flat. He's dropping the keys off any time now. Let's give it an hour to get everything else on the go, then meet me out front.'

DC Donaldson's eyes darted to his left by way of a signal - Smithdown immediately understood. 'Good stuff DC Donaldson. Well done. First things first - let me appraise the DS of the situation and I'll be with you shortly.'

'Looks like I've arrived at just the right time then, doesn't it?' said DS James Pym, approaching from Donaldson's left. The DS, five years younger than Smithdown but looking at least ten, was smartly dressed and looked like he'd just come from the barbers. He smelled strongly of Aramis. 'Always good to be kept abreast of the latest developments,' he said. 'Especially where it comes to body parts being left in the grounds of our local leisure spaces.'

'Vital, I'd say,' agreed DC Donaldson. 'I'll see you downstairs Mr Smithdown.'

'Looking forward to it, DC Donaldson,' Smithdown responded, switching from dry to sarcastic. 'Take a seat, Jim,' the detective offered with a smile, knowing full well that there wasn't a seat in his office other than the one he was already sitting on. Pym didn't move.

'Hand. Lake. Bag,' stated DS Pym. 'Appraise me. Now.'

'Of course. The hand belongs to Naomi Wells - known to us but nothing earth-shattering.'

'Prossie, wasn't she?'

'Soliciting is how I tend to refer to it. Occasional sex worker at a push.

Bit of theft, handling stolen goods, low-level dealing. A bad life rather than a bad person. I think we should have a presser on Tuesday if nothing else has turned up. Her daughter's currently in care up at Alt. She's only little. Nice kid. She's had a time of it too. We were called out to a domestic yesterday. The daughter had certainly taken a knock. We think that Naomi's boyfriend banged the kid against a few walls at their flat over in Glodwick. Jimmy Todd is his name. He's a dealer. And a DJ. And a dickhead. So, we are looking for the boyfriend for assault on the girl and he's clearly a person of interest in terms of the hand and Naomi being missing. We're off to their flat, now.'

'So, we've a DJ who likes chopping up bodies and beating up little girls? Lovely little town this, isn't it? Well, you'd better find him, John. Sharpish. We like our murdering dickheads in custody, not running around Oldham on an Easter weekend. Never mind a presser on Tuesday - I want to be on the telly saying we've caught the bugger before I have my Bank Holiday lunch on Monday. Clear?'

'Of course, Jim. You've never been clearer.'

'And please remember to take a fucking radio out with you.' Pym said as he walked away. 'If I didn't know better, I'd say you were doing it on purpose.'

CHAPTER FOUR

4.25 pm Friday 1 April 1988

The address the detectives had been given for the house that Naomi and Becky Wells shared with Jimmy Todd was a flat above a South Asian sweet shop, barely a mile from Alexandra Park. Smithdown knew the owner, who'd dropped off a small set of keys to the flat at the police station reception half an hour earlier. He'd also left the DI a small, neatly wrapped box of mixed barfi, his favourite. Nice touch, Smithdown thought, as he popped the key into his pocket and slipped his thumbnail through the round sticker that sealed the box. The sticker featured a drawing of a friendly-looking man with a huge moustache winking, with "Mr Aleem's" written underneath it. The cardboard lid popped open and a sweet waft of condensed milk and cardamom was released. A pretty reasonable consolation prize for missing my chippy tea, he thought, taking an oblong of cake and popping it into his mouth. Making inroads with the local South Asian community was one of Smithdown's ongoing projects, but the DI was under no illusions about how long this was likely to take. He knew the kind of language some of his colleagues used about the ever-growing Pakistani and Bangladeshi presence on the east side of town; was it any wonder that many of the local South Asian youths mistrusted the police to the point of hatred?

'You drive, Bob,' Smithdown said. 'Get us there in one piece and I'll save you a bit of barfi.'

'I don't like it, boss, as you well know,' the DC said as they pulled out of the car park and cut across the town centre to the sound of Ian Dury's '*What a Waste*' on the cassette player. 'I like a nice Eccles Cake. Or an Iced Finger. Or a Manchester Tart. Not up my street that Asian gear.'

'Bob, you're in The Raj for a lamb biriyani at least once a week. You talk shite.'

'That's different, boss. Savoury is fine. It's when they do sweet that I don't approve of. A cake that smells like pilau rice? It's not right.'

'You're not right, Bob. Just drive.'

It took a matter of minutes for them to get to Naomi Well's flat. It was on the corner of a terraced cul-de-sac off the main road between Oldham and neighbouring Ashton. Identical streets stretched out in every direction, featuring identical houses: same red stone front doorsteps, same two-up, two-down design. Many had windows that were boarded up with metal sheeting. Smithdown could see one street where only one or two houses remained occupied.

Naomi's flat was above Mr Aleem's sweet shop which, unlike many of the surrounding houses, was very much occupied. There was a queue out of the door as people waited to be served. Through the shop window Smithdown caught the eye of the owner, who was chatting to people as they made their purchases. The staff serving wore green and white hats and tabards with "Mr Aleem's Sweet Centre" written on them in an extravagant, signature-style script. Aleem himself wore a three-piece suit; his tie pushed out by a gold pin. His moustache wasn't quite as huge and lustrous as the cartoon suggested, but it wasn't far off. He was in his early 50s like Smithdown, but his hair and his moustache were matching jet black. The detective gave him a thumbs-up, waived the two keys he had been given, pointed to the flat upstairs and held five fingers up to indicate how long he would like the shop owner to wait until he joined them. Mr Aleem smiled and returned the thumbs-up.

'Business is booming for Mr Aleem, I see,' Donaldson commented as Smithdown opened the door next to the front entrance of the shop that led to Naomi Wells' flat with the larger of the two keys.

'Big noise in the local Tory party, isn't he?' Donaldson added. 'Running to be a councillor soon, I believe.'

'So I hear,' Smithdown acknowledged, struggling with the lock.

'Everyone calls him Mister Aleem, don't they? Even you. Mister Aleem this and Mister Aleem that. Don't get me wrong – smashing bloke and all that. But, he always gets the Mister treatment. What's his full name?'

'Mr Aleem,' Smithdown replied.

'No, but what's his actual first name?'

'Mister,' confirmed the DI, pushing open the door and shifting a small pile of free newspapers, takeaway menus and general post in the process.

The two detectives climbed the steep stairs which led to a small landing and another door. Smithdown opened it with the smaller of the two keys he'd been given, and they walked straight into the flat's main living room. It was a plain affair - largely clean but not particularly tidy. There was woodchip wallpaper throughout; some of it darkened with scuff marks and crayon. Several ashtrays - the metal kind often found in pubs - were full of dog ends on the low slung, smoked glass coffee table. Some of their contents appeared to be legal. Some weren't. The rest of the furniture seemed to date from several different decades - mainly the 1970s. It looked as if the items in the flat had been cobbled together from junk shops and relatives having a clear out; they even included a coffin-sized radiogram with records piled up in matching towers either side of it. A dark brown settee dominated the room - it sagged in the middle and one of the seat cushions had been stitched in several places. The TV and accompanying video recorder were both huge by 1988 standards - dating from the start of the decade. There was a mantlepiece framing a log-effect gas fire with at least a dozen photos on the top of it. Some pictures were in frames, some were loose, propped up against the wall. Most were of Becky Wells. Several were of Naomi, Becky and Jimmy Todd. Smithdown looked at Todd's face. Late 20s, slim face. Nice white teeth. Hair cut short at the sides, streaky blonde on top. *Half the lads in Manchester have that haircut.*

Smithdown zeroed in on one photo: little Becky was in the middle of the shot - her eyes were closed - and she was laughing. The faces of her mum and of Jimmy Todd were pressed against her cheeks, one either side. They were laughing too. Smithdown looked. He said nothing.

Eyes open, gob shut.

Smithdown took the picture and eased it into the inside pocket of his jacket. He felt the corner of the other photo - the one of Naomi nightclubbing that Becky had given him - with the edge of his fingers.

He walked into the kitchen. There was a similar feeling here as there had been in the living room - a hodgepodge of items that looked like they'd been begged and borrowed from friends and relatives. Smithdown opened one of the drawers. It held a mix of knives, forks and utensils. He looked at them then rummaged for a moment. He found a tin opener, looked at it then tossed it back in. Smithdown turned when he heard a knock on the kitchen door. Mr Aleem was trying to get the detective's attention rather than asking for permission to enter. It was his property after all. 'I'm not disturbing you am I, John?' Aleem said. His voice was clear, his diction crisp; only the elongated vowel sound in *disturrrbing* gave him away as being Oldham through and through.

'No, no. Just looking, Mr Aleem.'

'And thinking, John,' Mister Aleem added. 'That's you to a tee. Always thinking.' Aleem walked across the room and shook Smithdown's hand. It was a perfect handshake, just the kind that the detective approved of. *Not too firm - a bullshitter's handshake, no thanks. Not too weak – like a wet lettuce, a vicar's handshake, no thanks either.*

'Well, I think that I'll definitely have to get some more of that barfi before I leave,' Smithdown said. 'Paid for this time, obviously.'

'Obviously, obviously,' Aleem said, with a wink.

'Tell me about Naomi Wells, Mister Aleem.'

The landlord sighed and put out his hands in a gesture that suggested disappointment, resignation and slight regret all in one. 'So nice. A nice, nice girl. Dotes on her daughter - little Becky. She's okay? Please tell me she's being well looked after.'

'She's being very well looked after,' confirmed Smithdown.

'Naomi didn't have much,' Mr Aleem continued. 'But Becky was her top priority. Number one. Always. Sometimes she was late with her rent, but I knew she'd pay at some point, so I let it pass. She always paid eventually. Always. Then that boy moved in and things went downhill, seriously downhill.'

'In what way?' chipped in DC Donaldson, who'd been quietly taking notes.

'Noise. Parties. Complaints. Big trouble the other night,' Aleem said. 'Rent not paid… at all. He treated her badly, I believe. Very badly. And now there's this terrible business over in the park. Please tell me they're not connected John. Please.'

'We're anxious to trace the boyfriend Mr Aleem, put it like that. That's our priority. The boyfriend.'

'I'm told he sells drugs. He goes from nightclub to nightclub on a bike. Demand is so high, he uses a racing bike, John. Can you imagine? A racing bike like you see on the Olympics so he can get around at double speed. Imagine.'

'What's his favourite spot?' Smithdown asked.

'The new place in the town centre. It used to be a regular club, now it's changed. Kingdom it's called. Different music, different drugs. Changes, John. Big, changes.'

Smithdown had seen the changes first-hand. The old-style white shirt, slacks and loafers crowd were morphing into a new type of clubber. There was less need for the police outside the clubs at the moment because there was much less drunken fighting. Former hard cases were coming out of nightclubs hugging people they'd been punching in the face a few months earlier. Beer sales were down, water sales were up. Ecstasy had come to town and Oldham's's nightclub bosses were having to adapt accordingly. A bottle of water now cost nearly as much as a pint of bitter. A bottle of Lucozade cost even more. There were rumours that cold-water supplies to the toilets at Kingdom had been cut so people couldn't slake their E-fuelled thirsts for free. Smithdown had heard that the owner of Kingdom - one Richard T. King - was raking in cash by selling ice pops worth pennies for the price of a cocktail.

Smithdown didn't like Richard T. King - he insisted on being called that - one little bit. Most of the town's troubles seem to inevitably snake back to him. The local press liked to call King a 'flamboyant businessman'. That was just a euphemism for 'crook who likes to show-off' as far as Smithdown was concerned. When asked what the T stood for, King was in the habit of answering: 'The'.

'Yes, Mr Aleem,' Smithdown said. 'You're not wrong. Big changes.'

CHAPTER FIVE

9.45 pm Friday 1 April 1988

'These balaclavas are itchy as fuck,' the masked man said as he waited in the orangey glow of the street near an unkempt set of deck-access flats. He wasn't alone. There were six of them - at least five seemed to be having a competition as to who could look the most suspicious. Mr Itchy Face was currently the clear winner. Tapping out a beat on his thighs, accompanying it with a tsk-tsk-tsk noise of exhaled air through his teeth, he stared up the road, then down, then back again. Unable to bear it anymore, he pulled up the balaclava exposing the lower half of his face, removed one glove and scratched both cheeks.

'I swear there's nits or something in them,' he carried on. 'Were they second hand? They're itchy as fuuuuck, I tell ya. These gloves are just as bad.'

'Shhhh now,' the tallest of the group said. 'We'll be done soon. Until then keep it shut.' The tall man alone seemed in control of his movements. Like Itchy Face, the others jogged on the spot or stepped from one foot to the other - not to keep warm, but to drain off the excess energy that seemed to ripple around them. As they waited, they scanned the area. One spotted a youth crossing the street about 150 feet from where they were standing. He was wearing headphones and had his head down. 'Him there,' Itchy Face said. 'The lad in the white hoodie. He's a Paki. He'll do.'

'He's supposed to be from Bangladesh,' the leader said. 'That's the point. Bangladesh. Not Pakistan. That's the whole point. That's why we're here. I think his family run a business on Coldhurst Street. A restaurant, yeah? You know him don't you, Tariq?'

There was silence. Tariq Shamsi - also wearing a balaclava - was staring at the pavement. 'Tariq?' the leader shouted, 'Do you, or do you not know that lad?'

Tariq glanced in the youth's direction for the briefest of moments. Then his eyes returned to the pavement. 'I think so, yes,' he confirmed.

'And does his family run the restaurant on Coldhurst Street, or do they not?'

'Yes. I think his name is Musta.'

'And where are they from? The family, where are they from?'

A pause. 'They're Bengalis.'

'So, he's a Bengali Paki then?' asked Itchy Face.

'His family are from Bangladesh, yes,' Tariq confirmed.

'Right then. If that's the kind of Paki we're after, let's get cracking.' He pulled the balaclava back over his chin. 'Itchy as fuck,' he reiterated. The leader gave a nod. A red and white Adidas holdall was produced, and weapons were handed out. One each. Tariq shook his head when he was given his.

'Take it,' he was told. He did. The group headed down the street - the leader and one other member of the gang hung back a little. Itchy Face raced ahead.

Sixteen-year-old Mustafizur Rahman hadn't been paying much attention to what was going on ahead of him. But a blur of peripheral movement made him look up slightly. He saw the gang framed under the curved upper edge of his hoodie. A group of lads walking towards him was a fairly serious worry at the best of times. The fact that they appeared to have baseball bats meant that it was time for him to make the swiftest exit possible.

Go.

Go, go, go.

Go now.

Go!

Still moving at walking pace, he turned sharply into a passageway between two blocks of flats. The moment he was out of sight, he ran. Hard. The sound of several pairs of feet immediately followed him. He heard a shout too: 'Yeees! Here we go. The thrill of the chase - fookin' brilliant.'

The boy ran harder. Across the square, through the passage, up the stairs. Flat 24. He'd be home in a minute. If he ran really, really hard. Halfway across the square he risked a glance back. He was pulling away from the group.

Yes.

But keep going. The greater the distance, the safer you'll be. Nearly home.

He faced forward again, entered the final alley and ran straight into the balaclava-clad leader. He'd pulled away from the main group and gone another way into the square. 'Hi,' the big man said. He pointed the end of his baseball bat directly into Mustafizur's face. The bat was tilted down slightly - the man was nearly a foot taller. The others were there now, buzzing around them. The teenager could hear their laughter, smell their beery sweat, see their breath hissing from the mouth holes of their balaclavas.

A moment of stillness. The bat's tip inched forwards and touched the young man's forehead. The big man winked. The teenager grabbed the end of the bat and shoved it away from him, hitting the big man in the eye.

Mustafizur turned to run but one of the gang swung his bat hard into the boy's stomach. A second bat then smacked across his shoulders and he hit the pavement. He was surrounded now. In turn, each took two swings with their bat. The boy instinctively put his hands over his head, but the blows all connected with his arms, legs and torso.

All but one of the gang took a swing. Tariq was at the back, several feet away, until the leader pushed him forward. As he did so, his balaclava was pulled off by one of the group exposing his face. 'No! Why would you do that?' Tariq shouted.

'So you can see better,' said Itchy Face, handing him a weapon.

Tariq tried and failed to avoid the boy's frightened eyes as he took it, his fingers flexing around the handle. The leader leaned in. 'Say it,' he whispered.

A pause. 'Say. It.'

'Fuck Bangladesh.'

'Again. And put some life into it.'

'Fuck Bangladesh!'

'Now do it. Do it! Fuckin' do it!' Itchy Face screamed.

Tariq pulled his balaclava back over his face, as if it somehow made the situation better and afforded him some protection from Mustafizur's hurt and hateful stare. He swung once at the top of the teenager's arm. Despite the slightly half-hearted way it was done, the boy screamed.

'Proper! Do it proper!' Itchy Face screamed.

He swung again. This time the machete - because that was the weapon he'd been given - cut right to the bone.

CHAPTER SIX

11.15 pm Friday 1 April 1988

Smithdown and Donaldson made absolutely no effort to blend into their surroundings as they walked slowly - very slowly - around the dancefloor of the Kingdom nightclub that evening. It was as if they had gone out of their way to stand out even more from the club's Friday night clientele. Most were young, late teens, early twenties, and were far too busy earnestly concentrating on their repetitive dance moves to pay the two detectives much notice. The heat inside the club was intense. Overwhelming. Kingdom was in an old, art deco-style bingo hall and despite the post-modern, industrial stylings that had been added to the interior, it had retained many of its original fixtures and fittings. The DI placed a hand on an ornate iron radiator that had been painted grey and gold; it was hot. To Smithdown's eyes, the clubbers clothes looked strangely uniform yet practical: baggy tops mixed with cycle shorts; vests and combat trousers; bandanas and sweatbands. *They're not here to fight and pull like normal. They're here to dance and try to stay cool while they're doing it. And Richard T. King is making it as difficult - and probably expensive - for them to do that as possible. The sly twat.*

As Bang The Party's '*Release Your Body*' segued into '*Voodoo Ray*' by A Guy Called Gerald, the two detectives approached the bar. Smithdown leant in to speak to the barman; he was in his late 20s with a black polo shirt, shaven head and a beard. Ornate, animal-themed tattoos could be seen across his arms, neck and head. Nearly all the staff seemed to sport a similar look. The staff at Kingdom seemed to be exclusively male; the only females Smithdown had seen were on the dancefloor.

It took Smithdown three attempts to make himself understood. The barman nodded, held up a finger indicating he'd be one minute, flipped up the counter and walked briskly down a corridor to the left of the bar. Smithdown looked at the pained expression on his colleague's face. DC Donaldson was more of an ELO man and the music and its eardrum-rattling volume was visibly distressing him. Donaldson mouthed two words to Smithdown, 'fookin' shite'.

The barman reappeared and indicated that they should follow him. Smithdown and Donaldson made their way down a grey and gold corridor. It was lined with exhausted clubbers, sheened with sweat, taking a break from the dancefloor. Some were still performing tiny dance steps as they chugged on bottles of water. Others were in small groups of two or three, with their arms around each other, glassy-eyed and smiling.

They reached a door marked PRIVATE - STAFF ONLY. The barman punched a four-digit code into a keypad on the wall, pulled the door open and invited the officers to take the stairs. As the heavy-duty door closed behind them the noise level dropped by 75 per cent: 'Absolute bliss,' sighed DC Donaldson as the two detectives climbed the stairs. Each step they took reduced the decibels from the dancefloor. As they reached the top of the stairs, another door was opened by a tall, well-built man in a smart, well-cut black suit, shirt and tie. He seemed different to the other members with their shaved heads, polo shirts and tattoos. His hair was short and neat with a side parting. 'Evening officers,' he said in a soft Oldham accent. 'Please, come in.'

Smithdown recognised him. The detective knew a lot of people in Oldham and he had been at school with Tom Lennon's mum. 'Evening Tom,' he replied.

The room opened out into a huge office. The walls were bare brick and the wooden floors had been stripped and oiled to an expensive-looking finish. Framed posters and prints lined the walls, each hung with exacting precision at exactly the same distance from its neighbour. They highlighted pop culture moments that reflected the tastes of the man at the end of the office: films (*Battleship Potemkin*), music (*Solid Air* album cover, signed by John Martyn) and gigs (Slaughter and the Dogs + Sex Pistols, Lesser Free Trade Hall, Manchester, 1976). The centrepiece of the room was an oblong granite table that seemed to be floating in mid air. As Smithdown got closer he saw that it was suspended from the exposed beams in the ceiling by thin black wires. Behind the desk sat Richard T. King. He was eating. Mixed tandoori grill with salad and a nan, Smithdown noted. *Christ, I'm fucking starving.*

King stood up, motioned to the bouncer that everything was fine and wiped his hands and mouth with a baby wipe from a pack on his desk. He bounded across the room and offered both the detectives an overly firm handshake. His dark blonde shoulder-length hair bounced slightly as he greeted them. He was wearing a dark blazer with white piping that appeared to be modelled on the style favoured by Patrick McGoohan in the TV show *The Prisoner*. Underneath the jacket he wore a Mickey Mouse t-shirt, knee-length multi-coloured Bermuda shorts and light blue flip-flops. His toenails were painted black. 'DI Smithdown!' he cried. 'Welcome, welcome. So very pleased you've decided to spend your Bank Holiday weekend with us. Soy contento. Please, please… won't you and your colleague take a seat.'

In the space of four sentences King's accent had pinballed between Manchester, London and New York with a little touch of Spain for good measure. Smithdown had read that the nightclub owner was in fact from Tintwhistle, to the east of Manchester just over the Derbyshire border. King liked to boast that he was the second most famous person to come from the village, after clothes designer Vivienne Westwood.

The detectives both ignored King's offer of a seat and Smithdown produced the two photographs that were in his jacket pocket. He placed them one after the other on King's floating desk as if he was playing pontoon. The desk wobbled slightly. 'Naomi Wells. Missing person. Known to frequent this club. Jimmy Todd. Person of interest in said missing person case. Also known to frequent this club. Any information gratefully received, Mr King.'

One of the wires holding up King's desk was close to Smithdown's face. The detective reached out and gave it a twang. It made a satisfying noise, not unlike a harp. King didn't look at the photos. 'I know them both. They've set up home together across town, I believe. Naomi is a regular; she sometimes dances on the podiums. Really lovely girl with an equally lovely daughter. Jimmy pretends he's a DJ but he's not. He's a scumbag and a dealer and I won't have him in the club. He's barred. I don't allow drugs in my club therefore I won't allow drug dealers in my club. I told Naomi to have nothing to do with him too. She ignored me, of course. Quel dommage.'

'What a shame indeed, Mr King,' said Smithdown, quietly pleased that he'd managed to dredge up a little O Level French to understand what King was talking about. 'Because if I find out that you know where either of them are, I'll have the licensing authority close this sweaty shithole down so fast it'll make your flip-flops spin. Capisci?'

'Naturalment', replied a smiling King, his hands apart in a wide, peaceful gesture. He leant back in his chair and put his hands behind his head.

The detective picked up the two photos and returned them to his pocket. He turned to leave. DC Donaldson glared at the nightclub owner for a few seconds, then followed. 'And turn the fucking heat down on that dancefloor you money-grabbing bastard. Some kid's going to die of exhaustion while you're selling ice pops at 20 times the usual price.'

As the two detectives left, Smithdown nodded to the tall man at the door. 'Give my regards to your mum, Tom.'

'Will do Mr Smithdown. Have a good evening.'

With jackets over their arms to ease the effects of the heat, the detectives made their way down the stairs and around the edge of the dancefloor in silence. They nodded to the bouncers on the door and were relieved to feel the night air cooling their faces. They both took out a cigarette each - John Player Special for Smithdown, Benson and Hedges for Donaldson - and lit up. 'What do you think?' asked DC Donaldson.

'I think he's full of shite,' replied Smithdown. 'The flip-flops, nail polish and cod French don't fool me. You don't get your hands on as much money and property as Richard T. King has without being a hard-faced fucker. He knows more about this than he's letting on, but he's saying nowt. What I want to know is why he's saying nowt.'

'Good to know that he won't allow drugs in his club though,' Donaldson observed, as he passed a small group of young men walking arm in arm down the street.

'It's a weight off my mind, it really is,' Smithdown replied.

The two detectives walked through the town centre as they smoked and watched as the local pubs emptied. The further they got from the Kingdom club the more a grumbling sense of trouble increased in the air. Their night shift police colleagues were maintaining a quiet presence at the periphery of the precinct, waiting for the older, pub crowd - mullet haircuts and moustaches for the men, mini-skirts and heavy makeup for the women - to start the inevitable Friday night fighting sessions. Having been a night-time PC himself, Smithdown knew that there'd be just as many fights among the women as the men. He compared the atmosphere outside the town square pubs to that around King's nightclub. Outside Kingdom there were smiles and hugs, laughter and dancing. 'Maybe if the pubs served ecstasy on draught there wouldn't be all this mither at the weekend,' offered DC Donaldson, pulling on his cigarette from a cupped hand.

'An interesting suggestion Robert,' replied Smithdown. 'I'll raise it with the Chief Constable next time he's buying me a pint in The Old Bill. Now, shall we have a crack at a few of these delightful pub-goers and ask them if they've seen our missing Romeo and Juliet?'

Donaldson looked directly at his senior officer: 'Look. you get yourself off. I think I can handle chatting to a few drunks. Go home.' A pause. 'How's Jean doing?'

Smithdown looked at the pavement. It was studded with a grey carpet of dried chewing gum. He didn't look up. 'Okay, I suppose. But she's tired, mate. Dog tired. This chemo… it's worse than the cancer, I swear it is.'

'Get home then,' Donaldson said quietly. 'Look after her. It'll be right; you know what they say…'

'If you're going to get cancer, get it in Manchester,' Smithdown cut in, saying the words in a sing-song voice. He'd heard this particular pep talk so many times, but still found it strangely comforting. The Christie Hospital in South Manchester was world-renowned as a cancer treatment centre and it was just a 40-minute drive from their house. *We're lucky really. Really lucky.* Smithdown dropped his cigarette, put his shoe to it and popped a mint into his mouth. *She'll kill me if she knows I'm still smoking. I wish cancer was transferable, like money in a bank account. I'd ring the hospital and say, take it from her and transfer it to me. All of it.*

'Spot on, boss,' Donaldson confirmed. 'Yet another reason why we live in the greatest place on earth. Now, give me those snaps and get on your way.

Within half an hour Smithdown had returned home. Jean was half asleep and squeezed his hand when he got into bed beside her. He carefully placed his arm around her surgery-damaged chest. He looked at the knot on the brightly coloured paisley-patterned bandana she wore to cover her hair loss. She had quite a collection now.

He stared at the bandana and thought about what the cancer - and the treatment for it – was doing to his wife. Smithdown had lost count of the number of times he'd sat with her at the Christie as the red chemotherapy liquid was fed into her. He'd smile thinly at the other couples that shared the treatment room, but inside he was furious at the reasons for their enforced confinement. He hated the proximity of the other couples and families and the self-consciously comfortable chairs they were provided with - not like the hard, plastic ones in a normal hospital. As the chemo liquid went in, he would read a book and chew half-heartedly on one of the pre-packed sandwiches the staff had handed out. He remembered that there was a choice of three sandwiches that first day they'd attended. The choice had remained unchanged: cheese, ham, or cheese, and ham. He'd never eaten a cheese, ham, or cheese and ham sandwich outside of the hospital since.

He remembered how sick she'd been after that first cycle - and the reasons why. The doctors wanted to know how she'd react to the chemo so they had withheld any anti-sickness medication, which coincidentally was very expensive. Unsurprisingly, she had reacted very badly.

There'd been hours and hours of tears and vomiting. Then more tears.

Jean Smithdown's hair had gone after the first cycle. She had bought a bandana in time for the second and third sessions. The start of her collection.

She was probably fully awake now - the steroids kept her from sleeping. But she stayed still and silent.

Please. I'm begging. Give it to me. Not to her. Anyone but her. I'll do anything. Give it to me.

CHAPTER SEVEN

11.55pm Friday 1 April 1988

'Fuck! Paki! Stan! Fuck! Paki! Stan!'

The gang kicked the door of the house with each syllable. The chant continued as petrol from a small plastic bottle was squirted through the letterbox of the impressive, three story townhouse overlooking Alexandra Park.

The liquid was followed by a burning, rolled up copy of the *Oldham Messenger* newspaper. Voices - screaming and shouting, male and female, young and old - came from inside the house. The door opened and the burning paper was kicked outside. The homeowner shouted to people inside the house as he stamped on the paper at the doorstep, pulling his dressing gown around himself as he tried to put out the flames. The gang stood either side of the door on the wide porchway. As the man came out, one slammed the door behind him. Another two hit him with their bats. But he didn't go down. It took a third hit to do that. Once he was on the floor, the machete came down: once to the upper leg, then another to the arm just above the wrist. Instinctively, he put his other hand in front of his face to protect himself. The third blow hit his hand between the second and third fingers and split it in two. He was screaming now. They didn't understand what he was saying but they could tell that he wasn't begging – he was cursing them, furiously defying them. A baseball bat swung in from the right and connected with his head, the second swipe knocked him unconscious.

'Go. Go. Go,' commanded the leader and the gang ran down the driveway, crossed the road and shot into the park.

'Fuckin' 'ell, did you see his paw?' Itchy Face shouted. 'Did you see it? Fuckin' 'ell, it split like a kipper! Like a big, brown stinkin' kipper. Fuckin' ell!'

The leader ignored him. 'There are bins near the lake,' he said as they ran. 'Head there. Go!'

They ran past the tennis courts, down the winding path past the boathouse and arrived at the lake. There was a concrete bin sunk into the ground near the lakeside toilets. The gang stripped off their masks, jumpers and trousers and shoved them into the bin, pressing down the chip wrappers and aluminium cans that half-filled it. Underneath they were wearing jeans and t-shirts. It was a warm evening and they wouldn't look out of place. The leader produced a tin of lighter fuel, doused the pile and then set it on fire.

They stood for a moment around the bin as the flames caught hold. Their breathing was rapid - partly from the run, partly from the adrenaline hit of the second attack. All were tall and well-muscled with hairstyles that ranged from short to shaven. All were white. Apart from one. Tariq Shamsi was staring at his feet rather than the burning bin. 'Give me your gear, then fuck off, Tariq,' the leader said. 'Do nowt. Say nowt. A word about tonight - a single word - and we'll dob you in to the cops.'

'It was you what did the nasty stuff, anyhow,' added Itchy Face. 'Not us. That swing is really coming along, by the way. What a swipe that last one was!'

'You do understand, don't you, Tariq?' the leader said. 'Tell me that you understand this simple instruction and that you won't say anything.'

'Course I won't say anything,' the young man said. 'How can I?'

'Exactly,' Itchy Face said. 'We'll have done your mum and your sister in before you're halfway to Oldham nick anyway.'

'I know.' Tariq said. He pulled off the balaclava and gave it to the leader.

'After the lads have all had a crack at them, obviously,' Itchy Face added. 'One at a time. Maybe two at a time. We'll see.'

Tariq pulled off his trousers - he had a track-suit on underneath. He started to take off the jumper, but it got stuck as he tried to pull it over his head. The gang laughed at him as he struggled. Itchy Face pulled it off him, sending the young man staggering around the burning bin. He was crying now.

There was a growing swell of noise and light around the park. The sound of sirens came from the police station to the north of them; ambulances came from the west. A set of fire engines appeared from the east - the gang could see the crews stop at the edges of the park, so close they could hear the firemen's voices.

'You'd better get off home Tariq. Make sure your mum's alright,' the leader said.

'And your sister,' added Itchy Face. 'She's sweet. For a Paki.'

Tariq headed east though the park. The leader nodded to one of the gang, who quietly peeled off from the group and followed the teenager down the path on the south side of the lake. Tariq was crossing a small bridge that separated two sections of the pool when he was hit across the back of the head with a baseball bat. He fell to the floor. The bat came down again and again.

Such was the force of the blows that the deadly assault mercifully lasted only a few moments. When it was over, his attackerused the baseball bat to push Tariq's now lifeless body towards the edge of the bridge where it slipped silently over the side and into the water below.

It would lie there undiscovered for almost a week.

The gang dumped the last of their clothes into the flames but left Tariq's by the side of the bin. They went north, keeping their distance from the commotion outside the house, but remaining close enough to see and hear snatches of what was happening. Pockets of noise were springing up around the park. The voices of young men could be heard, shouting. Swearing. Making threats. Some of the voices spoke in English, some didn't. Windows were being smashed. Security alarms began ringing out. A wave of violent energy was sweeping across the town centre. The gang seemed pleased with their work.

There were streetlamps in this section of the park. Itchy Face caught sight of the leader's face, his eye in particular. 'You'll have a shiner there tomorrow, Tommy lad,' he noted.

CHAPTER EIGHT

2.15 am Saturday 2 April 1988

When the trimphone chirruped a double ring next to his bed, Smithdown wasn't sure whether he'd actually slept at all. He still seemed to be staring at the knot on his wife's bandana. He turned and his hand shot out to grab the receiver, to stop it ringing again. 'Smithdown…' he whispered.

'So sorry to disturb,' said Bob Donaldson, 'but I've two bits of news that I thought you ought to know about.'

'Go on,' Smithdown said, as quietly as possible. His wife stirred next to him.

'We've got Jimmy Todd in custody. He's saying nowt at the moment but I'm sure we can soon change that.'

Smithdown sat up in bed. 'I'll be right there.'

'No. Your services are required elsewhere. We've got a body, out at Kinder Scout near Hayfield. Not my decision, it's down to you - but I reckon you'll want to go there.'

Jean Smithdown was looking at her husband through the half-light now. He mouthed the word 'Bob' to her. She switched on the bedside light, put on a pair of reading glasses and took out a paperback book. It gave Smithdown the go-ahead to speak in a normal voice: 'I'm assuming,' he said, 'that you're going to give me a compelling reason why I should give a shit about a body that is not only outside our division, but outside our county? Hayfield is in Derbyshire, Bob, as you well know.'

'I do indeed, boss. The thing is, the body has got a hand missing.'

'I see,' said Smithdown, getting out of bed and looking for his trousers. 'To be fair, that is a fairly compelling reason.'

CHAPTER NINE

2.40 am Saturday 2 April 1988

Smithdown knew how to get to the village of Hayfield without looking at the crumpled A-Z map he always kept in the glove compartment of his car; at this time of night it was barely a half-hour drive south east of Oldham. Marooned in the green folds of the Derbyshire countryside between Glossop and Chapel-en-Le-Frith, he remembered coming to the village on days out as a kid. Indeed, he'd taken his own daughter here when she was young.

She was at university now, studying journalism of all things. *Bloody journalism.* In London, of all places. *Bloody London! God, I miss her.*

Hayfield was easy enough to locate, but Smithdown wasn't quite so sure about finding his way to the Hayfield Mountain Rescue Centre. The directions that he'd been given seemed simple enough though: turn right into the village. Big pub on left. HMRC is in the pub car park.

Smithdown had heard that the rescue teams liked a pint - particularly after a hard night pulling idiots off Kinder Scout - so positioning their HQ behind the Old Ship Inn was clearly good planning on their part. *I like these lads already.*

The village seemed largely unchanged from the mental image his childhood provided: two pubs, a fish and chip shop, a boutiquey antiques place and an all-purpose corner shop. Kinder Scout was the big attraction that drew people to Hayfield. The moorland plateau looked, from a distance, like someone had taken a giant tenet saw to a normal mountain and cut it in half, creating a bizarre table-top oddity that could be seen by half of Manchester. And, as every student of North West England history knew, it had a way of drawing people to it, like a truncated beacon.

In 1932, disaffected young ramblers and communists from Manchester and Sheffield had taken it upon themselves to organise a mass invasion of the moors around Kinder Scout, a place that they were forbidden to walk on by moneyed landowners. Their act of youthful class warfare had ultimately opened up the British countryside - thanks to those brave souls woefully ill-prepared townspeople could now come freely to places like Kinder Scout and be rescued by the volunteers of the Hayfield Mountain Rescue Centre.

The HMRC was set in a strip of stables at the rear of the Old Ship Inn. Volunteers of all ages and shapes were to-ing and fro-ing from the stables with vital-looking pieces of outdoor equipment like a team of industrious, bearded bees. Their headtorches sent wobbly beams of light across the early morning darkness of the car park as they loaded gear, checked kit and quietly chatted. Smithdown checked his watch as he parked up. *2.45am. Fuckin' Nora.*

He had to dip his head to get through the main door of the centre. 'Detective Inspector John Smithdown, Oldham Police,' he announced as volunteers squeezed past him to get out into the night. 'Which one of you extremely energetic gents are in charge, please?'

A man who looked to be in his early 40s - slim as a stick of liquorice and wearing tight-fitting dark blue running gear - leant back slightly from the huddle of people he was involved with so he could see who was asking. 'For tonight's purposes, that would be me,' he said with the flat hint of a Derbyshire accent. He put out a hand to Smithdown: 'Brian McIntyre,' he said, giving Smithdown's brown shoes and suit the once over and smiling slightly.

'I believe there's been a spot of mither up on your moors,' the detective said.

'You could say that,' McIntyre replied. 'One of your lot?'

'Potentially,' Smithdown nodded. 'I believe there's a Detective Constable from the local Con-stab-u-lary about too?' the detective added, pronouncing every syllable of the archaic sounding word for the local Derbyshire force. It tickled him to think they still held onto the title of Constabulary.

'DC Seddon is unavailable,' McIntyre said, the smile subtly easing itself from his face.

'Well,' Smithdown sighed. 'While I'm waiting for the DC to find a moment in their busy schedule, maybe you could fill me in?'

'With pleasure,' McIntyre offered, gesturing for the detective to come over to a map of Kinder Scout and the surrounding Dark Peak area that covered most of the far wall of the rescue centre. 'The body was spotted from up here at Red Brook,' he said, jabbing his forefinger at an area of the map three quarters of the way along the v-shaped rim of the plateau. Smithdown struggled to see so McIntyre shone a torch onto the map and wiggled the beam over Red Brook. On the map it looked like a stream, but the contour lines showed it was almost vertical.

'A guy walking the edge of Kinder saw it lying right next to the Mermaid's Pool,' McIntyre continued. 'It's a small lake tucked away under the Kinder plateau below the edge. I've got four volunteers up there already. They've staked out the area, taped the scene off and they're making sure no one gets near. They'll stop there with the body for as long as it takes.'

He knows his stuff this guy.

'Are you in radio contact with them?' he asked.

'After a fashion, yes,' McIntyre said. 'There's no point-to-point comms from here to the pool, so we've sent two of the team up to an adjoining area to set up what we call a repeater. We talk to them; the repeater relays the message to the team at the pool and vice versa.'

'And where exactly are they?' the detective asked.

'Here,' McIntyre said, punctuating his words with another jab on the map. 'On Mount Famine.'

'Of course,' said the detective, peering at the map. 'The Mermaid's Pool. Mount Famine. Does everywhere around here have a weird name?'

'Pretty much, yes. They don't call it the Dark Peak for nothing.'

'I'm beginning to realise that. And the body… it's definitely deceased?'

'Oh yes,' McIntyre nodded. 'Most definitely deceased.'

'What makes your lads so sure?'

'A couple of reasons. One, because they all have a reasonable degree of medical training. Two, because the body was on fire when they got the call out - it took them nearly an hour to get to it and it was still smouldering when they got there...'

'Fair enough...'

'...and three, because DC Seddon from the local Con-stab-u-lary based at Glossop is already at the scene. DC Seddon also happens to be one of our rescue volunteers and is currently at the pool, keeping the site secure.'

'And I'm sure he's doing a grand job,' Smithdown offered with a weak smile.

'Yes. She is. Jenny's doing a proper grand job.'

Smithdown felt that a change of tack was called for: 'And the body has got a hand missing, I believe?'

'Yes, that too; gets better all the time, doesn't it?'

'Do you know which one?'

'Does it matter?'

'Yes. It does.'

'Let's ask the team up at the pool then, shall we?'

McIntyre reached across the detective and pulled a handset from its cradle on a sturdy-looking radio set. It looked old and took up a considerable amount of space on the cluttered desk tucked into the corner of the rescue centre. 'Kinder Link, Kinder Link this is Kinder Base. Over,' said McIntyre.

A pause. Then a crackly click; a voice came from the set's speaker: 'Kinder Base, this is Kinder Link. Over.'

'Kinder Link, please ask Kinder Jenny at Kinder 2 the following. Which hand is missing from the deceased – left or right? Over.'

The voice came again through the speaker: 'You want to know which hand is missing from the deceased – left or right? Over.'

'Affirm. Out.'

McIntyre waited. 'They'll relay the message up to the Kinder 2 team at the pool. Everything is double-checked to make sure nothing gets lost in translation. Simple, but effective.'

After about ten seconds, the radio crackled back a reply: 'Kinder Base, Kinder Base. This is Kinder Link. Kinder 2 confirms that the deceased's left hand is missing.'

McIntyre double-checked the message: 'I understand - Kinder 2 confirms that it's the left hand on the deceased that is missing? Over.'

'Affirm. Over.'

McIntyre looked directly at Smithdown; his expression suggested he was checking that the detective was satisfied with the answer. Smithdown nodded his approval. Without breaking eye contact with the detective, McIntyre spoke again: 'Kinder Link. This is Kinder Base. Please tell Kinder Jenny at Kinder 2 to take care. And that me and the kids love her very much. Base Out.'

He returned the handset to its cradle and smiled at Smithdown. 'Right then, looks like we need to get you up to the pool, doesn't it?'

'And get that body down,' added the detective, feeling the heat of embarrassment around his collar.

'Well, that's where the fun will really start,' McIntyre stated. 'It'll take 18 volunteers to bring that body down to Hayfield. Minimum.'

'Eighteen volunteers to carry one person?' queried Smithdown. 'Who's up there, the fucking Pope?'

'No, Mr Smithdown,' McIntyre pointed out. 'Not the fucking Pope... at least, as far as I'm aware. It's only the early stages of the enquiry though, isn't it? So, no - probably not His Holiness. Just a poor soul that deserves care and respect to get them back off those moors. That's fair, isn't it?'

'Yes, it is - perfectly fair,' Smithdown said, quietly.

'It's a bit wet out,' McIntyre continued. 'And we have a saying around here: the wetter it is, the harder it is. Every time you put a foot down, there's no telling where it could end up. There are peat hags, dykes, rocky gritstone cliffs, steep piles of scree, boulders the size of Mini Cooper's, hidden streams and gaps in the rocks to trap and snap your ankle - all the fun of the fair around Kinder Scout. It takes an eight-man team to operate a stretcher safely - plus short and long navigators to look out for hazards and plot a safe course through the terrain. The first team will need relieving at some point. They'll be exhausted. So, another eight will take over the stretcher. So, 18 souls in all. It's not a Sunday stroll through Oldham up there, you know. That corpse has decided to set up camp in one of the trickiest spots in the Dark Peak to get to.'

'And the weirdest,' said another rescue volunteer, taking a metal Bell Tangent stretcher from a rack on the wall and smiling at the detective.

'What do you mean,' asked Smithdown. 'The weirdest?'

'I'll tell you on the way up,' McIntyre smiled. He glanced at Smithdown's scuffed brogues with a small shake of his head. 'Like I say, this won't be a stroll through Oldham, Mr Smithdown. What size boots do you take?'

CHAPTER TEN

3.45 am Saturday 2 April 1988

After leaving the rescue centre, Smithdown had taken a ride in the mountain rescue team's Land Rover along a service track near to Kinder Reservoir, in the shadow of the plateau. The vehicle had then begun the much bumpier job of tackling the uphill lower slopes of the moors. The detective was jammed into the vehicle with Brian McIntyre and three other rescue team members. He held onto an internal strap to stop his head banging onto the ceiling of the vehicle. There was silence as they made the journey. 'Go on then,' Smithdown said. 'I know you're dying to tell me. What local cross-eyed country crap are you going to give me about this Mermaid's Pool, then?'

McIntyre was driving. He looked into the rear-view mirror at one of the men squeezed up against the detective. 'Go on, Barry,' McIntyre said. 'You tell him.'

'Well,' Barry said, rubbing his beard and smiling. 'It's believed that the ancient Celts would carry out water worship rituals in this area…'

'Here we go…' muttered Smithdown.

'… and that this pool we're heading for was a particular favourite with the Celts because the water is salted. Like the sea. And no-one's quite sure why. They also liked it because of the mermaid that's said to swim in it.'

'Jesus Christ,' muttered Smithdown, folding his arms.

'It's said that once a year, if you visit the pool on the right day and the mermaid appears - and if she takes a shine to you - she'll grant you eternal life.'

There were smiles and quiet laughter from the other members of the rescue team. 'Is this the bit where I ask what happens if she doesn't like you?' Smithdown said.

'Yes, it is,' Barry confirmed.

'Okay. What happens if the mermaid doesn't like you?'

'She'll rise up out of the water and kill you,' Barry stated.

There was silence. 'Ooooooooooh,' howled another of the team. The rest laughed.

'Brilliant,' Smithdown said. 'I'm so glad I came. Just for fun, which day of the year are you supposed to visit the mermaid to test this story this out?'

McIntyre spoke this time. 'Joking aside, this bit is actually rather weird. Easter Eve. The day before Easter Sunday. Which given the time right now, is technically, today.'

Smithdown looked across the moors. The ridge of Kinder was getting closer now, a huge black wall of moorland rock blocking out the stars. The yellowy light of the dawn was just starting to pick out its shape against the Dark Peak sky. 'Fuck off,' Smithdown said, closing his eyes. 'Wake me up when we get there.'

'No need,' McIntyre said. 'This is as far as we can go. The rest will be on foot.'

'Fantastic,' grumbled the detective.

The Land Rover had stopped next to an identical mountain rescue vehicle. They got out and Smithdown felt his boots - which were a size too small - sink slightly into the wet, mossy peat. The detective found himself in a large group of mountain rescue volunteers. They flicked on their head torches; four of them began walking up a barely visible path that led up the moor in the direction of Kinder Scout. 'Follow them,' said McIntyre. 'Do exactly as they say. Nothing more, nothing less.'

Smithdown did as he was told. The mountain rescue team members walked just ahead and just behind him. McIntyre and Barry were by his side. Occasionally the volunteers in front would offer advice about hazards that were approaching. *They're protecting me from the moors.*

The path initially followed the left-hand line of a stream, then crossed the water back and forth several times. The detective tried to keep his boots dry as he went, but soon gave up and just splashed his way across the water as the mountain rescuers did.

Then the path peeled away from the stream and cut though a walled plantation of pine trees. It became darker, the light of the stars extinguished by the density of the small forest. They picked their way carefully through, stepping over logs and negotiating their way around fallen branches; the floor of the plantation was thick with a soft carpet of fallen pine needles. Then the stars reappeared as they cleared the plantation - the landscape opened up again to wide, rolling moorland. To Smithdown's eyes, the path had disappeared, but the rescuers seemed to follow a route only they could see.

McIntyre pointed up to his left. There was a deep scar in the vertical landscape that disappeared into the night. 'That's the Downfall. It has a waterfall that sometimes goes up instead of down, depending on the wind.'

'Course it does, muttered the detective, tripping over a small hole in the moor and finding himself briefly in the arms of a burly, bearded volunteer.

'It's true,' McIntyre offered. 'I'll take you there sometime, if you fancy coming back.'

'I think that's unlikely, but I'll bear it in mind.'

After a further fifteen-minute walk across the upper moors they crested a small hill. 'There it is,' McIntyre said.

In front of them was the Mermaid's Pool. It was strangely unimpressive to Smithdown's eyes - brown and shallow-looking, with a few rocks and reed banks scattered around the perimeter. It was about 40 feet long and less than 20 feet wide in the middle. It was uneven, shaped not unlike a map of Ireland. Behind it, the ground rose up sharply to meet the edge of the plateau above. Blue dragonflies flitted and swooped around the water's edge and Smithdown could hear a light chakka-chakka-chakka sound. A series of metal stakes had been pushed into the soft ground around the pool, connected by tape. The sound was the tape fluttering in the moorland breeze. There were four mountain rescuers stood in a line at the far end of the pool, guarding the area marked out by the tape.

The dawn air smelled foul, like a rotting butcher's bin that had been set on fire. At the far end of the water, steam rose from what appeared to be a tangle of blackened sticks, laid out as if someone wanted it to look like a body. *There were some recognisable shapes: legs, torso, arms, the notion of a head - but too burnt, too wrecked, too alien to have ever been a human being. Surely?*

Any chatter among the newly arrived rescue team members petered out and then stopped entirely. At first, they stared. Then they looked elsewhere, the lights on their head torches slowly dipped and pointed away from the Mermaid's Pool as they turned their eyes to look somewhere - anywhere - rather than at the remains in front of them.

There was pity in their faces; pity for the poor soul at the edge of the pool. But pity also for their friends and fellow rescuers who had been standing guard at this terrible scene for the best part of five hours. Smithdown looked at their faces. Some were holding hands. Several were in tears. He caught the eye of one member of the team. She wasn't crying - from the look on her face, she seemed to be in a fury. *DC Jenny Seddon,*

Derbyshire Con-stab-u-lary. Fucking Nora.

Smithdown nodded at her and dipped under the tape. As he did so Brian McIntyre leant in and spoke quietly to her, their conversation was silent yet clearly heated. As they spoke, Smithdown approached the body. The ground around it was scorched, like a small bomb had gone off. One hand was stretched out, as if the victim had been reaching to grab a fistful of the peaty brown water of the Mermaid's Pool. The fingers looked like black twigs. *Jesus. She was trying to save herself… trying to get to the water to douse the flames.*

The other hand was missing. The body was wreathed in mist now, as the sun began to heat the ground around it.

Smithdown wasn't sure how long he'd been silently staring at the body when he was joined by one of the mountain rescue team. 'DI Smithdown?' she stated, in a clear, no-nonsense tone. Smithdown knew what was coming. 'Detective Constable Jenny Seddon. Glossop CID.' A pause. 'Derbyshire Con-stab-u-lary.'

Smithdown turned and looked at her. 'Morning DC Seddon. You must be starved.'

'Not heard that expression for a while.' the Derbyshire detective said. 'Starved instead of cold. My dad used to say it. He was a Manc. Wonderful man my dad. But very, very old-fashioned. Know what I mean?' Seddon's Derbyshire accent slid the words into each other: norwharramean?

'I do,' Smithdown said, trying to sound apologetic. 'Message received. Let's start again, shall we?' He put out a hand. DC Seddon removed a glove and gave Smithdown a firm handshake. Her hand was red with cold. Smithdown's fingers left white marks where the grip of his hand had been. She was about 30 with round gold-rimmed glasses; her dark blonde hair was cut into a smart, short style. She was small but looked extremely fit. She also looked completely at home there in the hills. 'How are you doing, DC Seddon?'

'I am tired, hungry, wet, cold and a bit pissed off,' she replied. 'But things could be worse. I could be her…'

'Her?' Smithdown queried.

'Well, you've been fishing female hands out of your local boating lake - a left hand, I believe. And you've got a female missing-from-home. And we've got a body with no left hand. And you're here. Plus, there are female belongings scattered over there on the other side of the pool. So yes. Her.'

'Belongings? Okay. Can I see?'

'Sure.' DC Seddon leant sideways to see around Smithdown. 'Brian. I'm taking the DI to see the personal effects. Get one of the lads to cover my spot, please.'

A shout of 'will do' came from a huddle of rescue volunteers. 'Brian's your bloke, is he?' Smithdown said, trying to make conversation.

'He is,' confirmed DC Seddon.

'Kept your maiden name, though.'

'I said he's my bloke, not my husband, DI Smithdown. Christ, you really are like my dad.'

'I'm fucking glad I'm not your dad,' he muttered with a smile, just loud enough for her to hear. 'Let's take a gander at this gear then, shall we?' he added. The two detectives gave the steaming body a wide berth and walked towards a spot behind a clump of reeds at the far end of the Mermaid's Pool. Several items were there: an inside out canvas shoulder bag was first. Close to it was a Williams & Glyn bank card with "Miss Naomi Wells" embossed on it. Next to it was a photo of Becky Wells – she looked a few years younger than when Smithdown had seen her at the children's home and her front teeth were missing. She was smiling for the camera, showing off the gap with pride. Sundry items of makeup were also scattered about, along with a lip balm and some green Rizla papers. Next to the papers was a small plastic pouch with several bright pink pills inside.

Smithdown looked long and hard at the items. Then he looked at DC Seddon. She said nothing; she just looked, taking in the scene.

Thinking with her eyes open and her gob shut.

A voice came from behind them - it was young and scared-sounding. 'Mr Smithdown?' said Paul Rees. 'I suppose I need to photograph those items, don't I?'

The photographer was wrapped in a snorkel parka. His face was peering out through a ring of synthetic fur around the hood. The DI saw the young man had tears in his eyes. 'Yes lad,' Smithdown confirmed. 'You do.'

'I've already done the... is that technically still a body?' he asked. 'Yes. Course it is. A body. A very, very burnt body. Is it burnt with a T or burned with ED on the end? I can never remember. Either way, I've snapped it. Didn't like it one bit, but I did it.'

'It's never easy, Paul. Yes, these items by the water too, please. Just do your best.'

Paul wiped his nose with the sleeve of his parka. 'Christ Almighty, what a way to die, Mr Smithdown. What kind of fucking wrong 'uns would do something like that?'

'I don't know, Paul. I really don't. Just take the pictures and get yourself off home.'

'Right, yes,' Paul said with a sniff. 'I'll do these last pictures. The items. Then I can go. Go back down. Away from here. Yes. Okay. Right. Snaps.'

'Yes please, Paul. Snaps. Then you can go. Then we can all go. Including that poor soul by the side of this… Mermaid's Pool. Fucking stupid name.'

Paul nodded, took his camera from his shoulder bag and began by taking wide shots of the scene, before picking out the individual items for more specific shots. The two detectives watched him. Eventually, DI Smithdown spoke. 'What do you make of it then, DC Seddon?' he asked, quietly.

'Christ Almighty,' she sighed. 'To do that to another human being, all the way out here. Fucking animals. I've never known anything like it.'

'Neither have I,' Smithdown agreed. *What had the victim done to generate that kind of hate?*

CHAPTER ELEVEN

7.05 am Saturday 2 April 1988

Sitting in the snug bar of the Old Ship Inn, eating a second bacon roll and contemplating a third, DI Smithdown thought about what he'd witnessed coming down from the Mermaid's Pool.

He'd watched as the mountain rescue team had eased what was left of the victim into a body bag. At least two charred limbs had snapped in the process; the rescuers had carried on despite the distress several of them were clearly in. He'd seen the care they'd taken in keeping the metal stretcher straight and level, despite the up and down unpredictability of the Kinder terrain. He'd waited as a second team took over as the first became exhausted. And he'd seen them slowly push the body into the waiting Land Rover, then wait until the vehicle had been driven away and crested the hill on its journey down to Hayfield, before allowing the emotion to take over. There were hugs and quiet tears. Now he saw them sitting quietly in the Old Ship Inn, clearly unable to process what they'd just been party to. Some had curled up into any available seating and gone to sleep. Others stared at the walls. *These are volunteers, Plumbers and teachers and shopkeepers. They shouldn't have to deal with this.*

'Can I join you?' asked DC Seddon. She smiled at Smithdown and offered him a plate. She'd bought him another bacon roll.

'Please do,' he said, shifting his jacket to make a space next to him. *She looks younger in the daylight, tough as anything though this one. Took her turn on the stretcher for as long as any of those big, bearded bastards on the rescue team. Good on you, our kid. We could do with a few more like you back at Oldham.*

Despite his approving internal monologue, what actually came out of Smithdown's mouth was: 'Good butties these. This'll be my third.'

'So I see,' she noted. 'We'll need a stretcher for you too at this rate - straight to coronary care.'

Brian McIntyre brought over two mugs of tea - he smiled at DC Seddon then left the two detectives to it. 'They're good people, this mountain rescue lot,' Smithdown said. 'Your lot, I should say. Really good people. How do you find the time to volunteer for this as well as being a detective?'

'Well,' she replied. 'Working for the Con-stab-u-lary largely consists of sheep rustling incidents, mint cake theft and the odd bit of rambler disorder, so I have bags of time on my hands to do other things - like drag smouldering bodies down the side of Kinder Scout.'

Smithdown winced at her response. 'Fair enough, I deserved that. I'm sorry. I really am. What you and these people did tonight was amazing. It really was.'

'I should think so, you cheeky old bastard. Apology accepted.'

There was silence now between the two police officers. The small shoots of respect that were growing between them were still tempered by caution. DC Seddon spoke first. 'They must have watched her burn. Chucked petrol on her, set her on fire and watched as she tried to drag herself towards the pool to try to put out the flames.'

'Did you notice how the head was more badly damaged than any other part of the body?' Smithdown asked.

'I did,' she replied. 'That's where the fire burned the hardest - where the accelerant was most concentrated. It was probably petrol - they made her swallow it, didn't they?'

'Yes,' said Smithdown. 'I think they did.'

'So - no teeth.'

'Definitely no teeth.'

'Christ Almighty,' sighed DC Seddon, finishing the last of her bacon roll.

'Did you read about that case the other month?' Smithdown asked. 'The double rape and murder in the Midlands solved by DN whatsit genetic evidence?'

'DNA - yes I did,' DC Seddon replied. 'Colin Pitchfork - he was sentenced in January. Good job that by the Leicestershire Con-stab-u-lary.'

'Okay, okay. No more,' Smithdown said. 'They're talking about setting up a national DNA database, you know. That'd make life easier, wouldn't it?

'Don't hold your breath for it to arrive in Oldham. Let alone Glossop.'

Both detectives sipped at their tea. 'What happens now?' DC Seddon asked.

'We've got the boyfriend of our missing person in custody,' Smithdown stated. 'I'm going home to freshen up and then I'll go and have a chat with him. Can't see him taking long to cave in and that'll be that, I suppose.'

‘Really? That’s that?’

‘That’s that. Why? What’s on your mind, DC Seddon?’

‘I can’t stop thinking about what we saw up there,’ she said.

‘That’s understandable. It was a distressing thing for anyone to see.’

‘I didn’t mean that,’ she cut in. ‘I meant the whole scene; the body, yes but the belongings, the bag, the bank card. The whole bit.’

‘What about it?’ Smithdown asked.

Detective Constable Jenny Seddon of the Derbyshire Con-stab-u-lary pulled at the sleeve of her fleece, took off her glasses and cleaned the lenses by pinching them through the material between her thumb and forefinger. Then she put her glasses back on. ‘I thought it was the biggest load of stage-managed bollocks I’ve seen for quite some time.’

'Manchester Radio News at seven - this is Beth Hall. Murder squad detectives are investigating the discovery of a badly burnt body close to a Derbyshire beauty spot. Officers from Greater Manchester Police and the Derbyshire Constabulary are thought to be linking the find to an incident in Oldham where a woman's hand was found in a local lake. Henry Matthews is at the scene and sends this report.'

'The body was found next to the Mermaid's Pool in the early hours of this morning. The remote spot lies underneath the edge of Kinder Scout close to the village of Hayfield.

Local officers and mountain rescue volunteers have been at the scene since the alarm was raised by a walker late last night. Now, detectives from Oldham police have also become involved in the case - it's thought they're investigating a connection between the body and the discovery of a hand at Alexandra Park. It's understood the body at the Mermaid's Pool had a hand missing but is so badly burnt that a positive identification is thought unlikely.

Mountain rescuers spent the night carefully removing the charred remains from the scene. This morning the area around the Mermaid's Pool is still sealed off.

The pool is a notorious part of local legend. It's said that anyone who goes there the day before Easter Sunday risks the wrath of the mermaid that lives in the water. By a grim coincidence, today is Easter Eve. Henry Matthews, Manchester Radio News, Hayfield.'

CHAPTER TWELVE

7.45 am Saturday 2 April 1988

Smithdown's head nodded slowly downward as the need to sleep tugged at him. He snapped back awake. It happened again. Sleep was pleading with him now. Then a third time and just for a moment his eyes shut fully. *Just a little kip. That's all I want. Twenty winks will do me. Ten, maybe.* Then his head jerked, the steering wheel of his car jarred to the right and he was suddenly very awake and aware of the steep drop to the left of the moorland road that twisted its way to his house on the outskirts of Oldham. *Just another mile. That's all. Then home. And sleep.*

He wound down the driver's window and the car flushed with cold, clear air. He switched on the fan and set it to cool. He turned on the car stereo and put the volume up as high as he could bear: '*What a Waste*' by Ian Dury drifted across the moors. He slowed the car right down, crawling the last half mile at less than 30 miles an hour. Finally, he turned into the short gravelly drive of the detached cottage that had been the Smithdown's home for 20 years.

He killed the engine and rested his head on the steering wheel. Sleep was coming again. The detective banged his head twice on the steering wheel, widened his eyes and made a "baaah" sound. He shook his head until his lips flapped and stepped out of the car.

The front door was unlocked. Jean liked to leave it open. Friends from the nearby village and the wives of other officers were in the habit of calling in, often with homecooked food in Pyrex bowls - food she rarely ate but that Smithdown was very grateful for.

He saw that his daughter Kate's rucksack was lying in the hallway.

The house was quiet. He went into the living room. His wife was sitting on the sofa with her legs tucked up to one side. Smithdown's daughter Kate had her head in her mother's lap. Jean Smithdown was stroking her daughter's hair. It was shorter and spikier than when Smithdown had last seen Kate at Christmas. She also seemed to have more piercings in her ears, though he couldn't be sure. One thing the detective did know - both his wife and his daughter had clearly been crying.

'Where have you been, Dad?' Kate Smithdown said, in a quietly furious voice. 'I mean literally, where the fuck have you been? Mum shouldn't be on her own. Not now. Not ever. But definitely not now. In case you hadn't noticed, she's sick.'

Jean Smithdown looked at her husband and shook her head. *Don't. Not today.*

The detective toyed with the idea of telling his daughter about the hand in the lake; about the trek to the Mermaid's Pool; about the steam coming off the body; about the haunted faces of the mountain rescue workers. But he decided against it. 'Bit of trouble down at Alex Park. And then I had to go out Hayfield way. Couldn't be helped. You're here now, Kate. All three of us are here. That's the main thing.'

'You should sleep, John,' Jean said, continuing to stroke her daughter's hair. 'You look absolutely awful. Your trousers are filthy too, what have you been up to?'

'Classic mum,' Kate said, raising her head from her mother's lap and wiping her nose on the sleeve of her baggy red top. 'Looking after everyone else. Looking after you while you're out being The Great Detective.'

'Not fair, Kate,' Smithdown said, quietly. 'You're not here. You've got university. That's just not fair.'

'Well I'm here now and I'm staying,' Kate said, running her hand through her black hair and making it stick up even more. 'I'm packing in uni. I want to be with mum. Someone needs to be.'

'I don't want that, Kate,' Jean stated, taking her daughter's hand. 'Really. I don't. If you want to help, then finish your course. It's important. The first person in our family to go to university! Please. Make me proud. That's the kind of support that'll keep me going.'

'Christ,' Kate said, tears appearing in her eyes. 'Hear that, Dad? You're so fucking brave, mum.'

Smithdown was about to speak when his wife cut in: 'It's not fucking brave, Kate. Trust me. It really fucking isn't.'

The detective and his daughter were surprised into silence. *She never swears. She's really upset now. Shit.*

'Brave is choosing to do something that's really hard,' Jean Smithdown said, adjusting her bandana as she stood up from the sofa. 'I've got no other bloody option. I'm not sick from the cancer - they've cut that bit of me out. I'm sick from the chemo - it's the price I've got to pay to stop it coming back. I'm going to be fine. Just fine. It was a decent cancer to get. I can recover from it. But I need your help. Both of you. Together. Will you do that? Will you help me? Both help me?'

Smithdown and his daughter looked at each other for the briefest of moments, then nodded. They both independently decided that the best option right now was to just stare at the carpet. So that's exactly what they did.

'The best thing for me would be a house with no angry voices in it,' Jean Smithdown said, quietly. 'If they could bottle a bit of niceness and inject that into me, I'd be right as rain.'

Silence again. And carpet staring. 'Kate, make me some toast. John. Go to bed.'

Kate did a mildly stroppy walk to the kitchen. Smithdown headed for the stairs. He kissed his wife on the way. He was aiming for the side of her face but connected with the edge of her bandana. 'Just let me sleep for an hour,' he said quietly. 'An hour and a half, tops. No more. Okay?'

'Okay.'

Four hours later, the phone rang. It was DC Bob Donaldson. 'Boss. I know you've earned that kip, but I think you need to get down here to the station quicksticks. The place is going mad.'

'The news from Granada Television this Saturday lunchtime, I'm Hazel Barrett, good afternoon. Community leaders in Oldham have hit out at the local police force, saying not enough is being done to stop violent attacks in the area. They claim people from both the Pakistani and Bangladeshi communities have been subjected to a growing number of violent incidents, culminating in two separate machete attacks late last night. They've accused the police of turning a blind eye as Andy Gill reports.'

'At around 10 o'clock last night a 16-year-old boy was attacked by a gang wielding baseball bats and a machete. He sustained serious injuries to his arm and a concussion.

A man, described as wearing dark clothing and of Asian appearance, was seen running from the scene. Burnt clothing - including a balaclava mask - was later found in Alexandra Park.

In the second incident, a 52-year-old man was also set upon by a machete gang at his home on Queen's Road, which overlooks the park. The attackers had started a fire at the man's home before the attack took place. Detective Superintendent James Pym of Oldham Police says the two incidents may be connected:'

> *"We're keeping an open mind but in both attacks, inflammatory anti-Pakistani and anti-Bangladeshi statements were thought to have been made. In both incidents the attackers are thought to be Asian, so we'd ask that anyone with information from either community contact us immediately."*

'The attacks follow the death of Naomi Wells earlier this week. The 26-year-old year mixed race woman had been dismembered - part of her remains were found in the boating lake at Alexandra Park. Meanwhile, a body found near Kinder Scout in Derbyshire that had been set on fire is believed to be that of Miss Wells.

Community leaders are this morning calling for calm but are accusing Oldham Police of losing control of law and order in the area. Andy Gill, Granada Newss, Oldham.'

CHAPTER THIRTEEN

1.05 pm Saturday 2 April 1988

Smithdown wasn't in the habit of entering Oldham police station through the public entrance but given the amount of noise that was coming from the front desk area he decided to make an exception.

He lit a cigarette and took in the scene. 'Fucking Nora,' he muttered as two men in their late 50s tumbled through the swing doors and aimed wild punches at each other outside the main entrance. They were being egged on by a group of about a dozen noisy bystanders, making threats towards each other in a language – or maybe two languages – that Smithdown didn't understand. The feelings they conveyed were very much universal ones, though. Anger. Mistrust. Fear.

The detective could have intervened. But he chose not to. Instead, he eased his way around them and walked into the main reception area. The scene outside the station was relatively calm in comparison. Six more arguing men, plus two middle-aged women in tears; a white woman in her late 40s who looked like she'd been out all night, was being restrained by what appeared to be her husband and her son; a reporter from the *Oldham Messenger* was going amongst the various factions with a pad and pen, asking questions and being shouted at.

Sitting quietly in a scooped plastic chair in the corner was Richard T. King. He was, rather ostentatiously in Smithdown's opinion, reading a paperback copy of *The Consolation of Philosophy* by Boethius. King gave the detective a smile, saluted him and carried on reading. Next to him was Tom Lennon. He had a round, red mark over his right eye. 'Morning, Mr Smithdown,' King said. 'Have you been having a lie in? Don't blame you - but look what happens when you're not around. Pandemonium ensues!'

'So it appears,' the detective agreed. 'What's happened to you, Tom? You been messing with your catapult again?'

'He was assaulted last night in an unprovoked attack, weren't you, Tom?' King offered.

'I was asking him,' Smithdown pointed out.

'I was assaulted last night in an unprovoked attack,' Lennon stated.

'That's unfortunate,' Smithdown noted.

'All fortune is good fortune,' King said, gently shaking his paperback in the detective's direction to make sure Smithdown was aware that he was quoting Boethius. 'We've come to report the matter,' added King. 'These people can't be allowed to rule our streets. Tom's bravery in coming forward will benefit the wider community when the aggressors are apprehended.'

'You can count on it,' the detective added, muttering another quick, 'fucking Nora,' under his breath.

The Duty Sergeant buzzed him through and Smithdown took the stairs to the first floor CID department. As he pushed open the double doors from the stairwell the noise of the area was released: typewriters, telex machines, ringing phones, shouting, laughing, swearing, distant furious banging from the cells. *All human life. God, I love it.*

He spotted DC Donaldson walking towards him: 'An appraisal of the current situation, if you'd be so kind, Bob,' said Smithdown.

'Right. Kinnell. I'll do me best. Here we go: the Asians are up in arms because a Bengali lad got battered and macheted up round Coldhurst way last night. They reckon a Pakistani gang done it. The lad's family are currently going spare out front.'

'I've just seen them. How badly hurt is the lad?'

'Broken tibs and fibs, concussion and a couple of machete wounds you can get your fist into, but he'll live.'

'Next?'

'Report of a similar incident in reverse. Looks like a gang of Bengali lads have macheted a Pakistani bloke on his doorstep at one of those big houses near the park in the early hours.'

'Revenge attack?'

'Sounds like it - classic tit for tat. Neighbours heard anti-Pakistan chanting. Fuck Pakistan - all that. They did a spot of arson with intent for good measure.'

'Not helpful that, is it? What are his injuries like?'

'Similar. Less broken bones, but his machete wounds are worse - absolute shocker apparently, might lose his hand. Waiting to hear.'

'That's going to play badly on both sides of the fence.'

'Yes indeed. Multiple reports of Pakistani and Bengali lads tooling up ready to do more of the same tonight. Bengali community leaders are going barmy about it. Pakistani community leaders are going barmy about them going barmy about it. And vice versa.'

'Inevitably. Next?'

'Got a missing-from-home - also an Asian lad, as it happens. Seventeen-year old Tariq Shamsi. Mum's distraught. She's also in reception. Totally out of character for him to stop out all night, apparently. Last seen yesterday evening in the Coldhurst area.'

'I've a feeling there's more,' sighed Smithdown.

'You would be correct. Richard T. King is also out front. Says one of his lads was attacked by a big gang of Asian lads last night. Hardly on the same scale, clearly, but a crime number is being generated as we speak. It's Tom Lennon, Maureen's lad. Big fucker. Tom, that is, not Maureen.'

'I assumed that,' Smithdown said.

'Anyway, looks like he's poked himself in the eye with a teaspoon quite frankly. Flimsiest Section 47 wounding I've seen for some time, but the "King of Clubs" is demanding action.'

'He was quoting Greek philosophy to me at the front desk. King, that is, not Tom.'

'I assumed that,' replied DC Donaldson.

'That it?'

'That's just your starters. Main course?'

'Jesus wept. Go on.'

'Jimmy Todd, noted disc jockey and drug entrepreneur is currently in a cell, right here, right now. While you were taking a well-deserved rest, he confessed to the murder of Naomi Wells. He has refused the offer of legal counsel on multiple occasions. All other enquiries - beyond "yes, DC Donaldson, I did it" - are getting a firm "no comment" from Mr Todd. DS Pym wants him charged as soon as possible, probably so His Lordship can get his gob on the telly at teatime and deliver at least one piece of good news to the good people of Oldham. Apart from that, fairly quiet.'

'Where did they find Todd?' Smithdown asked.

'He strolled in while you were hibernating. Looked a right mess, by all accounts. Waited his turn at the front desk like a nice, polite lad, coughed to the murder, then sat back down again. Never seen anything like it. You don't get people queuing politely like that round here, do you?'

'No, Bob. You don't. I need to see Jimmy, sharpish.'

'DS Pym says no one is to see him. We tried to get Todd to see the Custody Sergeant, but he refused to come out of his cell, so we charged him through the hatch. He seemed frightened to death. His 330 paperwork's all boxed off ready for court. Done and dusted, essentially.'

'I might just pop in to pay Jimmy my regards. The DS doesn't need to know, does he?'

'Know what?'

'Precisely. I'm just gathering intelligence, DC Donaldson. No more than that. Perfectly legit.'

Smithdown knew Jimmy Todd by reputation rather than via a great deal of first-hand knowledge. He was aware of him around town and he'd seen him in the photos he'd seen at Naomi's flat: good-looking with a big smile and that shock of blonde hair. *Got the look of a German holiday rep. Eager to please. Charming. A bullshitter but relatively harmless. A wannabe, yes - but a murderer? That's a surprise.* The person he saw in the cell looked very different to the man in Smithdown's photo. Todd's handsome head of hair was plastered onto his forehead with dirt and sweat. His left eye was swollen shut. His hands were filthy. He was digging dirt from under his fingernails when Smithdown came in. He didn't look up. 'Jimmy, my name's DI John Smithdown. I believe you've confessed to the murder of Naomi Wells, is that right?'

'Yes,' he said, still looking at his fingernails. 'I've made a statement. Nothing more to say.'

'Mind telling me what happened?'

'We had a row,' Todd said, he gently touched the desk with the edge of his hand as he spoke. 'I strangled her in the flat. I started to cut her up, but it was too hard. So, I dumped part of her in the lake and the rest up in Derbyshire.'

'At the Mermaid's Pool...' the detective said, leaving an opening for Jimmy to speak further.

'No further comment to make, Mr Smithdown.'

'This isn't an official interview, Jimmy,' the DI said. 'There's no tape going. We have to tape all interviews now, it's a new thing. Did you know that?'

'I didn't,' Todd said.

'Not required here, though. This isn't going to be used in evidence. It's just you and me. Go through what happened for me, if you don't mind.'

'No further comment to make, Mr Smithdown.'

'I'm trying to help you, Jimmy. Honestly, I am. What were you rowing about?'

'No comment to make, Mr Smithdown.'

'I knew Naomi. I liked her. She had it hard, but she was making a life for herself. And for Becky. I don't get it, Jimmy. It just doesn't fit. Why did you do it?'

'No comment.'

'We've plenty of lakes and reservoirs of our own round here - why drag the rest of her all the way up to Hayfield and beyond?'

'No comment.'

'You burned her beyond recognition yet left her personal effects scattered about for all to see - makes no sense, does it? Why would you do that?'

'No comment.'

'I don't think she died in the flat. She was still alive when she got there, wasn't she, Jimmy? At the pool, I mean. Still alive. She must have been begging and screaming all the way up the hill. I've been up there; it took me ages and I was in a Land Rover for half the journey. She must have been bleeding all over the shop too, but still fighting, I'll bet. Right to the end. But why burn her like that? Domestics that get out of hand don't end like that. She suffered. Really suffered. If it was a moment of madness, why prolong it like that? It. Makes. No. Sense.'

'No comment, Mr Smithdown. No comment. No fucking comment.'

'And you'd been knocking her daughter about too, hadn't you Jimmy? Little Becky. She was here with her face all bashed in. The neighbours heard you smacking her about and found her all alone in the flat above Mr Aleem's. You were obviously busy setting fire to her mum up at Kinder...'

'Please, Mr Smithdown. Please, please, please. No fucking comment.'

Smithdown looked at Todd. He'd closed his eyes, dropped his chin to his chest and folded his arms. *Shutdown. I'll get no more from this lying twat.*

As he left the cell, the first person Smithdown saw was DC Donaldson, who was pulling his 'warning' face. Again. Detective Superintendent James Pym was a few steps behind him. 'John. Morning. I could have sworn I'd told DC Donaldson that Todd wasn't to be disturbed. I must be going mad. Any road - Todd is all sorted and ready for shipping to court - special weekend sitting first, then off to the Stangeways Hotel on remand, I expect. We've got too much on our plates to be wasting time on a domestic. Albeit a fucking nasty one. One less drugged-up DJ to worry about I suppose. And one less prossie girlfriend.'

Smithdown sidestepped DC Donaldson and stepped directly in front of his senior officer. His face was just a little closer to Pym's than normal work etiquette allows for. 'These are people Jim,' he said in a quiet voice. 'They might have fucked up in the course of their lives but they're real people. Naomi was a good person. A good mum. Now what's left of her is in the morgue over at Stepping Hill. And that lad in there isn't telling us the truth about it. Call me an old fusspot, but I'd quite like to find out why he isn't telling us the truth - what with me being a police detective and all.'

'He's confessed, John,' Pym pointed out. 'End of. She's dead and he's coughed to it. We've got too much shit to deal with right now to be dwelling on the whys and wherefores. Plus, we'll never get an ID from that pile of burnt sticks you recovered from Kinder. So, you need to get down from your high horse, get your sleeves rolled up and do some policing. We've got two Section 18 Assaults in the Royal and two sets of community leaders going spare about it. One will probably end up as attempted murder. Our priority right now is to bring a bit of calm to the streets before things really kick off. Oldham was on the verge of serious disorder last night while you were admiring the view up at Kinder Scout. So, let's have you down the hospital sharpish and find out what the victims are saying. Okay?'

The two stared at each other, their noses just a few inches apart. 'The daughter,' Smithdown said after a few moments. 'Someone needs to tell the daughter. Don't send some faceless constable. She knows me. I'll do it, then I'll go to the hospital. Have you got names for the two machete victims?'

'I've written them down for you,' Pym said, offering Smithdown a piece of paper. 'Wouldn't want you to get them tricky Asian names wrong now, would we?'

Smithdown looked at the piece of paper. He could have sworn that he saw the briefest of smiles on DS Pym's face.

CHAPTER FOURTEEN

2.15 pm Saturday 2 April 1988

'That,' Smithdown said, sitting on the back step outside the care home smoking with Brenda Graham, 'Went as well as could be expected.'

'That poor little girl,' Brenda agreed. 'That's no start in life, is it? Bless her. She didn't even cry. Saving it up until we've gone, I'll bet.'

'Maybe, deep down, she knows she'll be better off without her mum,' the detective offered. He regretted it almost as soon as the words had left his mouth, but it was too late.

'John Smithdown, you heartless shite!' Brenda shouted. She immediately realised that with the back door open, her voice could be heard across the house. So, this time, she whispered it: 'You heartless shite! Naomi adored that girl, doted on her. They had it tough and maybe weren't everyone's idea of the ideal family unit, but that little girl was happy. People who live in nice houses like you don't have the monopoly on happiness, you know?'

It was Brenda's turn to regret saying something now. 'Sorry, sorry, sorry. You've got me at it now, talking shite. Sorry. How is Jean?'

'Again, as well as can be expected,' the detective replied in a quiet voice.

'Will you hug her from me. I mean it. A proper hug.'

'Yes, I will.'

'Promise?'

'Promise.'

She squeezed his arm, jabbed out her roll-up on the wall and stood up. 'Time to be changing Becky's status on the system, I suppose. She'll be needing a more permanent temporary home, if you know what I mean. It would be good to get her away from around here, that's for sure.'

'Her mum's inquest will be all over the paper's before you know it,' Smithdown pointed out. 'Every grisly detail of the whole business there for the whole of Oldham to see.'

'I know. This town right now, John. Jesus wept, it's gone mad. Lads with machetes wandering the streets. A mini-riot last night. Communities that have lived peacefully alongside each other for years at each other's throats. The old guard, the 1970s racist fuckers saying: "I told you so." Absolute madness. How are the people that were attacked - a Pakistani and a Bengali, I hear.'

'You hear correctly. I'm on my way to the hospital now. I thought I'd come here first. Just one long cavalcade of fun today, isn't it?'

CHAPTER FIFTEEN

2.45 pm Saturday 2 April 1988

'Mr Aleem. How are you doing?' asked Smithdown. He'd bought some flowers and a small box of After Eights. He'd managed to work himself into a mild state of worry as he entered the Royal Oldham Hospital, concerned as to whether there were any issues with the ingredients in After Eights that might make it an inappropriate gift for Aleem. Maybe for religious reasons?

Then he realised that he had no idea what Aleem's religion actually was. And even if he did, he had no detailed knowledge as to how that affected his chocolate choices either. Then he saw the state his friend was in and he forgot all about the After Eights.

Mr Aleem 's face was so swollen he looked like he'd had air injected under the skin around his cheeks, forehead and eyes. The redness of the bloated skin was in the early stages of turning purple. His left hand and arm were criss-crossed with cuts, scratches and sutures. His right was bandaged so heavily it looked like a white boxing glove. There were two pillows under his upper arm - three under his lower arm and wrist. Aleem's arm was pointed upwards, like a power salute. His eyes followed Smithdown as he entered the open ward and pulled up a seat next to Aleem's bed. The detective placed the After Eights on the small, brown bedside cabinet next to the bed. Aleem looked at them. 'You know, John,' he said, speaking while moving his jaw as little as possible and glancing at his hand. 'I might struggle to open a wafer-thin mint just now. I'll save them for later if that's okay. But the thought is very much appreciated. Very much indeed.'

'Yes, you might find it little tricky just now, but they're something to look forward to, I suppose,' Smithdown said, trying to sound as encouraging as possible. 'Bloody Nora, what a mess, mate. I don't know what's happening to this town - the place is going insane.'

'Something stinks in Oldham right now, John. Something bad has arrived. The hand in the lake; then Naomi goes missing; I hear you've found something terrible over Derbyshire way, too? Now this.'

Smithdown was reluctant to ask Mr Aleem questions but he knew that he had to: 'Look, I know this isn't a great time, but I want to find who did this. The neighbours heard anti-Pakistani chanting outside your door. Were they Bangladeshi lads? Is that who did this?'

'I don't know,' Aleem sighed. 'I heard something. Shouting. Banging. It's what made me go to the door. Then there was the fire too. I don't know. It's hard to remember. My family were in the house. They could have died. Why would these people target us?'

'Revenge?' Smithdown offered. 'A Bangladeshi lad was done over earlier in the evening. There's been multiple reports through the night of attacks from both communities. We've got teenage lads from either side in custody. The attack on the lad in Coldhurst… then you? It kicked off a whole load of trouble right across the town. Fighting, criminal damage. All sorts.'

'I heard. But, baseball bats? Machetes? That's not our town, John. That's not our youth. There's a kind of poison in the air. Poison.'

'It's like someone's put something in the water, alright,' the detective agreed. 'There's too much for us to cope with right now and all of it is off the scale. And it's involving communities that… I don't claim to be an expert in these matters, put it like that. I'm a bit embarrassed about how little I know, to be honest.'

The two men were silent for a moment. 'I came here with my family 15 years ago after the Liberation War,' Mr Aleem said. 'It's not been easy, let me tell you. Abuse? Yes. Violence? Sometimes. Vandalism and graffiti? Sure. Almost constant. You know where that has all come from, John? Of course you do - a tiny minority in the white community. But nothing like this. There's a boy down the corridor with machete wounds too. A boy from a good Bengali family. I know them. They walked past the ward earlier - they turned away when they saw me. Like it was somehow my fault.'

'I know there's always been this undercurrent of animosity between the Pakistanis and Bangladeshis in Oldham. Separate parts of town, worshipping at different mosques. Were they Bengali lads? Did they attack you because you're from Pakistan?' the detective asked.

'Maybe. Maybe not. I don't know. Sorry.'

'It's okay. I'll leave you be. Get well, okay?'

'Sure. I'll be out of here by teatime I reckon.'

'I bloody well doubt it,' Smithdown said.

'John? Can I ask… How's Jean?'

'She's just like you, making life difficult for the good folks of the NHS.

But, also like you, on the mend. Take care, mate.'

Smithdown gave Mr Aleem a thumb's up, headed towards the reception and was directed to where he could find Mustafizur Rahman. The 16-year-old was upright in bed talking to another young man, who looked about 20. *A friend? Maybe his big brother. Probably very pissed off.*

'Hey look, it's a man in a grey suit,' the older one said. 'Must be one of Oldham's finest - here to ask some stupid questions instead of being out there trying to find the animals that tried to chop up my brother.'

'And a very good afternoon to you too,' Smithdown replied. The detective turned his attention to the young man in the bed. His arms were bandaged, and his face was bruised. He looked tired too, but overall, he seemed in better shape than Mr Aleem. 'Mustafizur Rahman? I'm Detective Inspector Smithdown from Oldham Police. I'd like to talk to you about what happened. Do you feel up to it?'

'Hey, hey,' interrupted the older of the two. 'He's my bother and he's only sixteen. Our parents have just left. Mum was too upset. I mean, can you even do that? Can you question a kid of his age without them here? Is that even legal?'

'I'm not questioning him,' Smithdown pointed out. 'I'm trying to find out what happened so we can catch the people responsible. And, for your information, I can talk to him if it's in the presence of a responsible adult. Do you know any?'

'Oh wow. A comedy cop. Nice. Just what we need right now.'

'Look. We're all on the same side here…'

'Are we, though? Are we really?' Smithdown looked at Mustafizur's brother. The young man was sporting a floppy centre-parting and his hair was cut very short up the back and sides. He was wearing a brightly coloured top and baggy jeans. He looked about the same age as his daughter, Kate. *Got a right gob on him too - just like her.*

'Yes, we are. Absolutely,' Smithdown said and put out his hand. 'Sorry, I didn't get your name. I'm John.'

The young man waited a few beats, looked out of the window, then glanced at his brother, before reluctantly shaking the detective's hand.

'Mohiuddin,' he said.

'Sorry?'

'Uddin. Call me Uddin if all those brown syllables are too much for you to handle.'

Fuckin Nora. 'Right you are, Uddin. I just want to get a few details from your brother, that's all.'

'Okay with that, Musta?' Uddin asked his brother.

'Sure,' the teenager replied. 'But I already gave a statement to a uniformed officer,' Mustafizur said. 'I told them what I know. I don't remember much.'

'Did you recognise any of the people who attacked you?' Smithdown asked.

'They were all masked,' the young man replied, occasionally glancing at his brother. 'Gloves too. They hit me with baseball bats. One guy lost his mask at one stage. Not sure how. He was definitely a South Asian kid. He said something anti-Bangladesh. Then he hit me with the machete.'

'What about the others - were they South Asian?'

'I don't know. The masks, you know? And the gloves.'

'Did the others… well, sound Asian?'

'Oh wow!' exclaimed Uddin, placing both hands on his head with a look of disbelief. 'Mate. Comedy cop. Listen to yourself. You need to go on a course or something. Listen to yourself.'

'I don't know,' Mustafizur replied. 'Sorry.'

'Maybe it was hard to hear because of the sound of the baseball bats and machetes hitting him!' Uddin offered.

Smithdown carried on: 'The lad who spoke. Did you recognise him? Do you know him? Would you know him if you saw him again?'

'I don't know him, but I've seen him about town.

'Is he Pakistani?'

'Whoah, whoah, whoah mate,' interrupted Uddin. 'What's this all about?'

'Not sure yet. We're keeping an open mind.'

'That's a copper way of saying, "we haven't got a clue", I reckon,' Uddin said.

'Well, there was, what appears to have been, a revenge attack on a man from Pakistan shortly afterwards,' Smithdown said. 'He's in a room down the corridor with his hand hanging by a thread. Then there were attacks on shops and businesses from both communities. During the second attack, a gang were heard shouting things that were anti-Pakistan. During your incident… anti-Bangladesh stuff was shouted. That's the line of enquiry because that's where the evidence is leading. That okay? Where were you last night, Uddin when it was all kicking off?

'Brilliant. Try to pin something on me rather than find the people who did this to my brother. Classic.'

'It's not a secret that the Pakistani and Bangladeshi communities don't always exactly see eye to eye around these parts,' the detective offered.

'That's fair isn't it? Different parts of town, separate mosques...'

'Oh, wow listen to the expert - Mr South Asia here - explaining how things work in downtown Oldham.'

It took a lot to agitate Smithdown, but Uddin was doing a pretty good job of it. Mainly because he was right. Smithdown didn't really know what he was talking about: South Asian people accounted for almost a third of the population in the town centre of Oldham, yet he knew next to nothing about the differences between the communities.

'Okay, Uddin. Who do you think was responsible?'

'The Pakistani lad said something against our community. Then hit a kid from our community with a machete. That's all I need to know.'

'It wasn't quite like that, though,' Mustafizur said, pushing himself upright in his bed. 'It was weird.'

'How do you mean?' asked Smithdown, grateful to hear from him rather than his brother.

'There was something about the way he hit me…'

'…with a big machete…' added his brother.

'Like he didn't want to do it. Like he'd rather be doing anything… be anywhere… rather than be there doing what he did.'

'But he did it anyway,' added his brother.

'Why do you think that was, Mustafizur?' Smithdown asked.

'Like… It's weird, really. It was like if he didn't do it, something much worse would happen.'

CHAPTER SIXTEEN

4.50 pm Saturday 2 April 1988

Several weeks earlier, Jean Smithdown had been fitted with a semi-permanent cannula to allow the next cycle of chemo to be pumped in. The treatment was wrecking her veins and it was becoming increasingly difficult - and painful - to put a needle into her.

The fixed cannula meant the discomfort of trying and failing to find a vein was one less thing for her to dread about the process. She'd lost her hair almost straight away; her appetite had followed soon after and her weight had plummeted. Everything tasted like iron filings, she said, and yet she couldn't face anything more flavoursome than vegetable soup. Thanks to the chemo, her urine had gone red too. The steroids she was taking made sleep almost impossible, so she was tired all the time. What's more the pills made her feel spacy and not-quite-there - or 'off her tits' as her daughter liked to put it.

Kate Smithdown was holding her mother's hand - the one that wasn't receiving the chemo cocktail. Both were reading a book with their spare hands: *McNae's Essential Law for Journalists* for Kate, her mum had Stephen King's *Misery*.

John Smithdown watched them from his seat a few feet away. Both had to use a chin, the edge of the chair they were sitting in or even a tongue to help turn a page. It was clearly an awkward and inefficient way to read a book for both of them, but it preferable to the alternative - because that would have meant letting go of each other.

For no apparent reason, Kate turned away from her book. Father and daughter looked at each other for second, maybe two. The detective felt his eyes become warm and itchy and he was worried he was going to cry. Then his daughter jutted her chin at him and gave him the cross eyes - just like she had done since she was tiny. He smiled and the need for tears fell away.

Kate returned to her book. Smithdown shifted his weight in the scooped plastic hospital chair and thought. He should have been thinking about the attacks on Mr Aleem and Mustafizur Rahman. But instead he was thinking about Naomi Wells. He was running through a list in his head:

Alex Park Lake - just a hand? MNFS

Distance from Naomi's flat to the pool? MNFS

Murder scene at the Mermaid's Pool. MNFS.

Destroy body but leave ID? MNFS

Jimmy Todd confession? MNFS

The problem with this whole Naomi Wells business is most of it Makes No Fucking Sense.

'Dad,' hissed Kate. 'Stop muttering and swearing to yourself, you weirdo. You're not at work now.'

'Sorry,' he said with a small smile. 'I was miles away,' Smithdown stared at the chemo drip attached to a stand near his wife. She'd dozed off

Kate gently extricated her hand slowly from her mother's, checking constantly that she was still asleep. She stood up from her chair and carried it over to sit next to her father. They both looked at Jean Smithdown. She looked peaceful; her fine features and naturally pale skin were set off by the sheer white of the hospital pillows tucked behind her head. She'd chosen a pale yellow and white scarf today, as if it had been specially picked to match the light in the room. 'She's the only person who can take the whole no-hair-and-bandana cancer look and carry it off,' said Kate with a sniff. 'She's so beautiful.'

'Yes, she really is,' agreed Smithdown. 'That's one thing we can definitely agree on.'

'Sorry for being a dick the other day,' Kate said. It was time for holding hands again - this time, it was her father's. 'The hospital is looking after mum, mum's looking after me and no one's looking after you. Sorry.'

'It's alright,' John Smithdown said. 'All forgotten about. Though you are a bit of a dick, to be fair.'

'Were you thinking about Naomi Wells?' Kate asked.

'Yes, I was, did you know her?'

'Are you questioning me, Dad?' Kate said, folding her arms across her '*Meat Is Murder*' t-shirt.

'I'm gathering intelligence,' Smithdown pointed out. 'Perfectly legitimate…'

'I did know her,' Kate said. 'Sort of. If you went clubbing in Oldham or Manchester, you knew Naomi. They say she was first through the door on the opening night of The Haçienda in '82. She was one of those people who seemed to be able to be at two different club nights in totally different places at exactly the same time. She was Ms Manchester.'

'And Jimmy Todd?'

'Similar situation. If you go to clubs - and you take drugs - you know Jimmy.'

Smithdown shifted in his chair: 'Well that's comforting for a father to hear, I must say. Probably best not to say anymore. You do know I'm a police officer, don't you?'

'It has cropped up a few times in conversation, Dad, yes. Look, drugs aren't my thing if that helps. Even if they were, I'd be so wary right now. Things are very different right now. It's all too new. No one has any idea what they're swallowing and they're practically giving out ecstasy for free in the clubs - carrier bags full of it.'

'Bob Donaldson reckons that if they served it in pubs, we'd have less people in the cells. Big gangs of lads hugging outside the clubs instead of fighting.'

'Maybe he's right,' Kate said, nodding in agreement. 'Did you know, the original name for it was empathy not ecstasy?'

'I didn't know that. Why did they change it, do you think?' the detective asked, genuinely interested.

'Marketing, I suppose. Why buy empathy when you can buy ecstasy?'

'Good point well made,' Smithdown conceded. 'This is a really weird conversation, by the way.'

'I know. Shall we pretend it never happened?'

'Yes please.'

'Seriously, though,' Kate said. 'The whole thing is bizarre. First the hand in the lake - then taking Naomi all the way up to that weird lake near Kinder. The press is having a field day with that. All the Mermaid stuff. It's a journalist's dream. Then Jimmy coughing to it - just strolling into Oldham nick with his hands up.'

When she was younger, Kate had talked about wanting to join the police force. As she grew older, the idea of being a journalist took over. A good cop and a good journalist are cut from very similar cloth, he'd told her on many occasions.

'So, what do your journalistic instincts tell you about all this, then?' Smithdown asked.

Kate thought for a moment. She glanced over at her mother, then looked at her dad: 'It makes no fucking sense, does it?'

'Language, Kate,' murmured Jean Smithdown, stirring from her nap.

'Sorry, Mum,' Kate said, winking at her father.

'Dad?'

'Yes, Katie.'

'I do love you.' She leant over and kissed his cheek.

'Not as much as I love you,' the detective replied. 'You're still a bit of a dick sometimes though.'

CHAPTER SEVENTEEN

8.35pm Saturday 2 April 1988

After calling her from the hospital, DC Jenny Seddon had agreed to meet Smithdown at the Star Inn, in Glossop. The detective felt that as he'd been so rude to her last time they'd met, the least he could do was to buy her a drink on her patch, and it was him who wanted to see her, not the other way around.

The Star was perched on a corner, tucked between the train and police stations at the top end of the town. It had a rounded front, etched glass windows and as Smithdown noted as he stepped inside, dim lights and reassuringly low ceilings that gave it a warm, orangey atmosphere. A fug of cigarette smoke clung to the room. Plus, they sold Big D peanuts behind the bar - Smithdown's favourite.

Dressed in a tracksuit, DC Jenny Seddon was standing at the bar talking to a group of men - every one of them was at least a foot taller than her. She glanced at Smithdown, nodded and pointed to her glass to ask if he wanted a drink; the detective nodded back and mouthed the word 'bitter' as he squeezed through the crowd to get to the bar. Jenny Seddon gave him a thumbs up, then said something to the group; whatever it was it caused all of them to laugh. Loudly. *My punishment continues.*

'Alright?' she said, handing him a pint whilst taking a sip of foam from the top of hers. 'Find it okay?'

'Yeah. My wife's from near here, so we did a fair bit of courting round this way.'

'Courting?' Jenny said laughing and shaking her head as she pointed to a small, copper-topped table in the corner. 'That's another blast from the past. Are you sure you're not related to my dad?'

'What's up with the word courting? It's a good Manchester expression is that.'

'In 1965, it quite possibly was, yes.'

'Never thought I'd be lectured on the modern way of doing things by someone from Glossop. You lot still stop and point at the planes when they're flying over to Ringway Airport.'

'Manchester International Airport, grandad. It's not been called

Ringway since 1975.'

'Don't start...I come in peace.'

'Sorry.'

They sat quietly for a moment. The jukebox kicked in. Someone had selected '*How Long*' by Ace. Smithdown smiled - Jean loved this song - and he instinctively reached for his cigarettes but then thought better of it.

'The girl's boyfriend coughed to the murder then?' DC Seddon asked.

'Jimmy Todd? Yes. He was in court first thing this morning. Special sitting. Back again on Tuesday,' Smithdown replied.

'Did you talk to him?'

'I did.'

'And?'

'He was scared shitless. Not of me. Not of being charged. Not even of going to jail. He was a wreck, but beyond admitting he'd killed her with the bare minimum of detail, it was no comment all the way. But a confession is a confession as far as the boss is concerned. All sorted now, I suppose.'

'I get the feeling you're still not happy,' Jenny stated.

'Not especially,' Smithdown offered, being cautious with his responses. 'The scene up at the Mermaid's Pool - you weren't happy about that either, were you?'

'No. I wasn't. But it's GMP's case not ours. It's not for me to say.'

'Well, I was interested in what you said afterwards. "Stage-managed bollocks" - that was the expression, I believe?'

'That was the expression, yes,' she agreed.

Smithdown waved his hand in a rolling motion: 'Care to elaborate?'

Jenny put down her pint: 'It looked like the pool had been dressed by the local amateur dramatics' society. Other than hang a big sign up saying HERE LIES THE BODY OF NAOIMI WELLS - HER HAND IS IN A PLACCY BAG IN THE BOATING LAKE IN OLDHAM TOWN CENTRE... I don't know what more they could have done. I mean it must be her – obviously it's her - but why go to all that bother?'

Smithdown made a "hmmm" noise and took a drink of his bitter.

'What do you mean, "hmmm" what does "hmmm" mean? Don't start being a pillock again, or I'll set the lads on you.'

Smithdown looked at the giants standing at the bar. 'No need for that. You're right. It stinks. Why take her across the border into another county and then kill her? It would have been far easier to do it the other way around. Why all the attempts at spooky bollocks by dumping the body at this Mermaid's Pool - on Easter Eve as well. Someone's been doing their Kinder Scout shit-we-tell-the-tourists research, haven't they? Why dress the scene? It was properly over the top.'

'It really was, wasn't it?' DC Seddon said. 'Also, why go to the bother of making sure her teeth were burned to avoid identification if you're then going to leave a pile of identifying personal effects lying about the place? It…'

'…makes no fucking sense,' Smithdown agreed.

'Exactly!'

Silence for a moment. 'I had to go and tell the daughter that her mum had died,' he said. 'Not nice.'

'No. It's never nice isn't that,' Jenny agreed.

'Didn't cry. Said nowt. Just took it. Tough little kid.' Smithdown reached into his pocket and took out the photo of Naomi Wells that he'd had since his first visit to the children's home. He showed it to DC Seddon. 'She gave me this. I forgot to give it back to her.'

'That's Naomi? She looks like she's having such a great time,' she said. 'Poor, poor girl.'

'Indeed,' confirmed Smithdown. 'Here's a thing, see what you think.' Slightly self-consciously, the detective raised his left arm into the air and made a fist, imitating Naomi's pose in the photo. Jenny Seddon looked at him, looked at the photo, then glanced around the bar to see who was watching.

'Bit inappropriate, under the circumstances, DI Smithdown. Can't say I approve.'

Smithdown held his pose. Other people in the pub were staring at him now. Slowly he put his arm down. He pointed at the photo. 'The hand we found - Naomi's hand - was a left hand. Naomi was kippy-handed. Look at the way she's punching the air.'

'Kippy what?'

'An old Manc expression. Kippy-handed. She was a lefty.'

'It's probably been a while since you were out clubbing…'

'…I was in one the other night, actually…'

'… but people in nightclubs have been known to punch the air with either hand, DI Smithdown.'

'You're right. Of course you are. Thing is, I've been in her flat. I looked in her kitchen. She had a left-handed tin opener in her drawer. Unimaginative people give them to kippies as presents when they don't know what else to give them. Every kippy-hander has one. My daughter is left-handed. She has one. I gave it to her before she left for uni.'

'Okay,' said Seddon not quite sure where the conversation was going. 'But that matches, doesn't it? You found a left hand in the lake at Oldham and the left hand was missing from the body at the pool.'

'Yes, but that poor creature up at the pool was reaching out to the pool with her right hand.'

'Hate to spoil your flow, but it was the only one she had, Detective Inspector,' Jenny pointed out.

'I know, I know. Hear me out. With her last breath - on fucking fire, mind - she instinctively reached out with her right arm.'

This time, Smithdown stretched his right arm out in front of him, again generating a few looks from the pub regulars. 'I don't know. That just doesn't feel right. Naomi was kippy-handed, but that I think that poor soul up at the pool was right-handed. Maybe whoever did that to her wanted us to think it was Naomi.'

Jenny took a drink. Then she took off her glasses and cleaned them.

'Go on. I'm listening,' she said.

'That body up at the pool was torched beyond recognition,' Smithdown continued. 'Yet the hand we found - it's definitely Naomi's - had been selectively burned to leave a usable fingerprint. That's handy.'

'Poor choice of words Mr Smithdown…'

'I can only apologise,' the detective offered. 'The way the scene was dressed is one thing. That's weird in itself. The thing with the hand, that's potentially weird too. Both together? I'm not having it, Jenny. You don't mind if I call you Jenny, do you?'

She shook her head. 'As long as you don't ask me to call you John. I'm not quite at that stage yet.'

'Fair enough. Here's a thought: maybe they want us to think it's just one murder. But what if it's actually two.'

'Buy one murder, get another one for free?' Jenny said.

'Exactly - I fancy some nuts,' Smithdown said, getting up from the table. 'Do you want some?'

'Go on then.'

Smithdown rummaged in his pocket for change. 'Right then, two packs of Big D coming up. So, here's the plan. We need to get back on Jimmy Todd's case and find out what really happened in that flat. We need to work out where the rest of Naomi's body is; and we need to find out who the fuck is really in that smoky body bag in the morgue at Stepping Hill.'

'How do you mean,' DC Seddon asked. 'We?'

CHAPTER EIGHTEEN

8.45pm Saturday 2 April 1988

It was dark now at Strangeways Prison in Manchester. Lights out soon. The 19th century red brick jail, with its imposing balconied ventilation tower, dominated the skyline just north of the city centre, close to the border with Salford.

The jail currently housed five hundred more prisoners than it was originally designed for. Earlier in the day that figure became five hundred and one.

That morning, one of the more puzzling elements in the murder of Naomi Wells had been summoned from his cell at Oldham police station and taken via an underground corridor to the magistrates' court next door.

Head down, he had quietly answered 'yes' when asked to confirm his name, address and date of birth. He had then been asked if he understood that he was being charged with murder. Again, he'd given a quiet 'yes'. Then he'd been told by the chairman of the bench that the charge was too serious to be heard in a magistrates' court, so he was to be remanded in custody until it could be dealt with at the City Police Court on Minshull Street after the Bank Holiday Weekend.

He'd then been taken from the court and driven through Failsworth and Collyhurst to Strangeways. There, he'd been processed and told that although, as a remand prisoner, he had different rights to a regular prisoner as he was presumed innocent, there was currently no room in the remand area of the jail. So, he was to be housed in the main body of Strangeways as a provisional Category A prisoner.

Next, he was taken across the jail's noisy, clanking stairwells and shown his cell. There was another prisoner already there, who greeted his new cellmate by name. The new inmate couldn't understand how the other prisoner could possibly know who he was. When the cell door shut, Jimmy Todd became very afraid indeed.

'BBC Manchester News at ten, this is Richard Hemmingway. An investigation is underway after the death of a remand prisoner at Manchester's Strangeways Jail earlier today. Jimmy Todd was facing a murder charge after his girlfriend's body was found at a Derbyshire beauty spot in the early hours. Vince Hunt has more.'

'This morning, 28-year-old-Jimmy Todd had appeared in court in Oldham, charged with the murder of Naomi Wells. The 26-year-old mum of one's body had been found next to the Mermaid's Pool near Kinder Scout at Hayfield. It's believed she'd been set on fire - her body burnt so badly that a positive identification was deemed impossible, until Todd himself confessed to the killing.

The previous day, Naomi's severed hand had been discovered in Alexandra Park boating lake near Oldham town centre.

Todd had been sent to Strangeways straight after his court appearance and had only been at the jail a matter of hours before his body was discovered. It's thought there are no suspicious circumstances in connection with his death and that no one else is being sought in connection with the incident. Vince Hunt, BBC Manchester News, Strangeways.'

CHAPTER NINETEEN

10.05pm Saturday 2 April 1988

After leaving Jenny Seddon in the Star Inn, Smithdown had headed home via the town of Mossley. The road hugged the hills through the small towns and villages that peppered the route home to Oldham. '*Born to Be With You*' by Dave Edmunds was on his cassette player. Edmunds' *Subtle as a Flying Mallet* was one of the detective's favourite albums.

As he drove, cigarette sparks flying out of the barely open window as he flicked his ash, Smithdown noticed that the sky to the east of his route looked odd. There was normally an orangey glow to the view from here - the kind of hazy, urban hum of light that would be expected to hover over a town the size of Oldham. But tonight, the sky seemed to flicker and dance like the fake coal effect of an old gas fire. It looked alive.

The detective took a slight detour via Grasscroft and drove down Oldham Road towards Grotton, an area, he always like to note, that was far more pleasant than its name suggested. As he travelled through the village, he saw dozens of people standing outside their houses. They were pointing, talking and shaking their heads. As he rounded a bend that had the advantage of a small layby, Smithdown pulled in and stopped. He stood at the gentle ridge edge that swept down towards Oldham town centre. Several other drivers had also parked up. One of them, a man of a similar age to Smithdown, looked at the detective and nodded down the valley. 'Absolute fookin' madness,' he said.

Smithdown had to agree. The intermittent illumination of orange was fire. Oldham was burning.

'D'ya know who I blame?' the man asked. 'Do ya? I'll tell ya exactly who I blame…'

Smithdown didn't wait to hear the answer. He got back in his car and headed for the town centre. Noisy bursts of trouble flashed past his window as he drove: a fistfight here, a restaurant window put through there. The level of aggravation - and the sour, frightening atmosphere it generated - got stronger as he neared the south-east corner of the town. The road ahead was blocked; a car had rammed into the side of another and had attracted a crowd. The jeering mob managed to look both jubilant and angry at the same time. Smithdown turned off into the terraced side streets and weaved his way through the tightly packed houses. He slowed right down until he was driving almost at walking pace.

More and more people, many carrying improvised weapons, dashed in front of him as they crossed Glodwick Road. Their movements and voices suggested they were young; many of their faces were masked in balaclavas. *The owner of that army surplus store over in Royton must have sold more balas than Soft Mick today. He's probably retired.*

A stone cracked against the driver's-side window of his car and Smithdown instinctively flinched and swerved slightly away from the direction it came from. Hunched over his steering wheel and moving slowly forward, he looked left and right. Ahead of him, on the flat roof of the Turn of Luck pub, half a dozen people were throwing stones, bottles, and half bricks down at a gang of youths at street level. They were returning fire with anything that came to hand. Not all them wore masks: the detective noted that most of the youths at ground level were South Asian. Most of the people on the roof were white.

Smithdown watched as another group of teenagers carried a large wooden dining table above their heads like a rowing team carrying their boat. They picked up speed as they got to the pub's main window and then shoved the table through it. A cheer went up. Then the pub missile throwers responded by rolling a huge metal beer barrel to the lip of the roof and tipping it off, scattering the youths below in the process. It bounced erratically as it hit the ground and rolled across the road, adding to the debris that had already made the road impassable.

The detective pulled his car into the quietest looking side street he could find, locked his car and continued on foot. On the corner across the road from the pub were two men in their 20s with a video camera. It didn't look like the kind that the local television news crews used. He'd seen them many times and knew most of the local BBC and Granada TV cameramen by sight or by name. This camera was smaller, less substantial - the kind you could rent from most high street TV shops or even buy if you had the money. One of the men was filming, the other was directing him towards individual pockets of rioters. He didn't recognise the cameraman - wiry, nervous and aggressive looking with an angry-looking rash on his neck - but the 'director' was clearly Tom Lennon.

Smithdown approached them. 'Documentary maker now, are you

Tom?' he shouted over the noise. 'Don't strain your poorly eye, will you?'

The cameraman muttered 'wanker' under his breath and pointed the lens at the detective and took a few steps towards him. 'We're in a public place and we're not causing any obstruction, Mr Smithdown,' Lennon said. 'Surely your time would be better spent on tackling the feral Asian youth over there who are committing criminal damage and public disorder under your very nose.'

'Any comment to make about the feral Asian youth, Mr Smithdown?' the cameraman asked.

The detective pointed his finger directly at the lens. 'What's your name, lad?'

'Hitchcock,' the cameraman replied, smiling and scratching at his face. 'Alf Hitchcock.'

'Is the camera running, Mr Hitchcock?'

'Yeah, it is,' the cameraman shouted, causing the camera to tilt up and down slightly as he nodded.

'Good. Then stick this in your documentary. Turn the camera off and fuck off home or I'll do you for being a pair of shit-stirring twats.'

Lennon smiled at the detective. He had a light, nut brown suntan and his teeth were unusually white and straight. He was smartly dressed in a black jeans, t-shirt and Harrington jacket. He towered over Smithdown. 'We're going to get a few close ups first, I think,' he said. 'Then we'll be on our way.'

The pair walked towards the Turn of Luck pub. 'Give my regards to your mum, Tom,' Smithdown shouted after them. Lennon began pointing and directing again. Smithdown noted that they weren't filming any of the white rioters.

The detective wound his way through the back streets towards the town centre. Every few seconds a half-brick or bottles clattered against the pavement or a wall. There were shouts and whoops all around him as rioters filled the ginnels and walkways that spread in all directions.

As he walked, he stopped and spoke to pockets of youths dotted around the streets. He identified himself as a police officer, showed his warrant card and advised them to go home and stay off the streets for the rest of the night. He didn't linger or argue - there was too many of them for that - he spoke quietly, listened if needs be, then moved on to the next group. Some took what he said on board and walked away. Others told him in no uncertain terms that they had no intention of going anywhere.

He saw a fresh set of masked youths appear from a block of flats; they were carrying plastic trays, the kind favoured by milkmen. All the trays had a dozen milk bottles in, each with a rag stuffed into its neck. They set them down just as several uniformed officers appeared. The PCs immediately came under fire from a stream of Molotov Cocktails that splattered fire across the pavements around them. One officer's tunic caught fire briefly before his colleagues were able to beat it out. They seemed panicky and ill-prepared for what they'd encountered and began defending themselves with improvised dustbin lid shields.

Smithdown shouted some advice to his colleagues: 'Fuck off out of it before you get barbecued, you dozy twats,' he said. They followed his words of wisdom to the letter and fell back through a patch of wasteland next to a second-hand shop.

The detective crossed the ring road and worked his way around the side of the Town Square shopping centre. Bollards to stop cars entering the area had been smashed and the entrance to a Rumbelows electrical shop had been rammed with a Ford Escort. The double doors hadn't quite given way. Smithdown was heading over to speak to the youths buzzing around the car - they were trying to force the shop's doors open with staves of wood when they suddenly froze, let out shouts of warning and scattered. Smithdown turned; he had more sense to think they were running away from him. He spotted a battered Peugeot 205 heading his way and at considerable speed and managed to turn away just as the wing mirror hit his arm, sending him spinning to the ground. From his vantage point lying on the pavement he saw the Peugeot crash into the back of the Escort, pushing the first car fully through the doors with a metallic crash. There was a rousing cheer as a gaggle of young men dashed forward, clambered over the two cars and entered the store.

Within a matter of moments, a selection of video recorders, radios and cassette players had been liberated. Smithdown noticed that - rather incongruously - one youth had opted for a kettle. *That'll be for his mum, nothing if not considerate that lad.*

A steady stream of people now entered the shopping centre in their wake as the detective got to his feet. *Fair to say things are getting a bit out of hand here, where the fuck are the police?*

Smithdown immediately got his answer; a squad of riot officers in full protective gear headed up the high street, banging their shields as they went. *About fucking time.* A second squad stomped past him from the other direction and formed a barrier across the entrance where the bollards had been. *Right, now I won't have to single-handedly defend the shopping centre, shame really, I could have done with a new telly.*

Then, GMP Tactical Aid Group officers - bigger, stronger-looking and sporting even more protective gear than their colleagues - appeared seemingly from nowhere and began chasing the escaping youths down. One TAG van whizzed past Smithdown; it sent a young man flying by following him at speed down a side street and clipping him with the expertly timed opening of the vehicle's passenger door. He was snatched and bundled into the van by a huge TAG officer. *That lad's going to get a right shoe-ing before he gets to the cells.*

Smithdown - his elbow throbbing with pain - made his way through an alleyway between the shops. He rested against the wall for a moment, the heat of his injury making him feel momentarily faint. The detective heard a voice: 'Hey… It's you… Are you alright, Mr Smithdown?' Uddin Rahman said, running down the alley to where the detective was standing.

'I'll live, lad. What the hell are you up to? After a telly for your mum?'

'That's borderline racist in my opinion, Mr Smithdown,' Uddin pointed out.'

Fucking Nora. 'I'm just sightseeing. Nothing more. There was a bit of trouble here last night, but nothing like this. Unbelievable. Everyone is taking the chance to have a crack at this - white lads, Pakistani youth, Bengali youth. This is an equal opportunities riot, I'll say that.'

'Well, can I suggest that you get out of here as soon as you can, Uddin? Those TAG lads will be delighted to have you in the back of their van, then you'll be in the bed next to your brother at the Oldham Royal all cosy like with a fractured skull. I mean it, lad. Go home, right now.'

'What about you?' Uddin asked. 'You're hurt.' He seemed genuinely concerned.

'I'm fine. Now go.'

Uddin nodded and ran down the alley away from Town Square. 'No heroics, Mr Smithdown,' he shouted as he went. 'You are not a young man.'

'Cheeky twat,' Smithdown muttered and headed towards the rising tide of noise as the alley up ahead opened out into another row of shops. A tight knit gang of youths, most with balaclava masks or bandanas covering their faces, were staging a stand-off in the pedestrianised street. Missiles ricocheted around the high street as the police riot squad spread out across the walkway and began advancing forward. Their presence seemed to have the desired effect almost immediately - Smithdown could see that some of the younger, more slightly built rioters quickly lost heart at the sight of the riot shields and began to slip away down the side streets. TAG officers were there to grab them with only the quickest and most agile rioters able to make their escape.

The detective could see that as quickly as it had flared, the heat was being taken out of the situation. He was now in a position to take in the extent of the damage: every second or third window on the high street was either cracked or smashed; rocks and bottles littered the street and a few fires - the residue of Molotov Cocktails - were being stamped out.

There was one spot on the High Street that seemed to have escaped almost entirely unscathed: the entrance to the Kingdom nightclub. A double semi-circle of men - all of them white, most of them shaven-headed and many carrying baseball bats - had formed outside the club. Richard T. King stood at the heart of the semi-circle; Tom Lennon and 'Alf Hitchcock' were by his side. Lennon spoke to King then smiled and nodded in the detective's direction. The nightclub owner - who was wearing an ornate Oriental dressing gown - gave Smithdown a cheery wave. 'Evening Mr Smithdown. What a night… the atrocious crime of being a youth! Your guys seem to have the situation in hand, though. Very firm. Very fair. About time too, if I may say. What a night!'

'Knowing you're safe and well is a real weight off my mind, Mr King,' Smithdown said. 'You should get yourself inside before you get a chill.'

'Bless you, Detective Inspector,' King said. The detective watched as the nightclub owner rubbed his hands up and down his upper arms with a smile, tied his dressing gown with a flourish and went inside his club. Tom Lennon followed; 'Hitchcock' carried on filming. The guard of protectors outside the club stayed exactly where they were.

You cocky twats, what the fuck are you up to?

'Welcome to Granada News, I'm Hazel Barrett. Our main story this Sunday lunchtime. A major clean-up operation is underway in Oldham after rioting broke out across the town late last night. Gangs of Asian youths - some throwing bricks and bottles - fought pitched battles with police for several hours in what's been described as the worst outbreak of civil disorder Greater Manchester has ever seen. Tim Wyatt was following events for us last night and sends this report from the scene.'

'At the height of last night's violence, as many as 250 youths took to the streets of Oldham town centre. In this exclusive footage, they can be seen fighting pitch battles around the Turn of Luck pub. Bottles and stones rain down and a beer keg is thrown from the roof - narrowly missing the rioters below. Elsewhere the Town Square shopping centre was ramraided, with several shops being looted.

This morning Greater Manchester's Chief Constable James Anderton visited the scene to see the scale of the damage for himself. He's been talking to people from the business community including nightclub owner Richard T. King, who says he believes the police aren't doing enough to stamp out trouble caused by rival Asian gangs:'

> *"Sadly, the growing tensions between various communities and factions in this town just aren't being tackled by the police or the council. We saw it with revenge attacks over the last few days and we've seen it again here overnight. Perhaps they're afraid that it's too much of a hot potato, I don't know. I'm not a politician, I'm a businessman. But it's businesses that are counting the cost of the inaction this morning, I know that much. But we won't be beaten - we'll be open tonight, in defiance of the trouble-causers who are out to spoil this amazing town."*

'Police say that 63 arrests have been made following the disturbances - mainly for public order offences and criminal damage. They're now urging community leaders to call for calm to avoid another night of trouble. Tim Wyatt, Granada News s, Oldham.'

'In other news, concern is growing over the whereabouts of Oldham Councillor Sharmeen Chowdhury.

Councillor Chowdhury - who represents the Coldhurst ward - hasn't been seen since the council closed for the Easter weekend break on Thursday. Colleagues say that for her not to leave word as to where she was going is completely out of character. They're urging Councillor Chowdhury to get in touch as soon as possible to let them know she's safe and well.'

CHAPTER TWENTY

12.15pm Sunday 3 April 1988

Detective Superintendent Pym, motioned DC Donaldson into his office with friendly gestures of hand and head and closed the door behind him. 'Bob, take a seat,' Pym said. 'I won't keep you.'

'No problem, sir. What's it about?'

'It's about DI Smithdown, Bob.'

'Oh yes? Right. And?'

'I'm worried, Bob.'

'I suppose that's understandable, sir.'

'Where is he - I mean right now, where is he?'

'Out and about, as usual. He took it upon himself to get involved in the rioting last night. He was on the streets advising the local youth to go home to their mams. Not all of them took his advice, as the head count in the cells clearly shows.'

'Exactly, Bob,' Pym said, leaning back in his chair. 'That's my point. The Naomi Wells murder, the machete attacks between the Asian communities, now the riots. He seems to be grabbing every ongoing case on our patch, calling them his and then trying to link them all together. I wouldn't be surprised if he starts taking an interest in this missing councillor too. Plus, there's Jean to consider. Any normal person would be off on compassionate leave. Not him. I'm concerned, Bob. Genuinely concerned.'

'He can handle it, I've no doubt,' Bob replied. 'He knows what he's doing and if he stays in holding Jean's hand all day, he'll go mad. More importantly, he'll send Jean mad too. He's better off out and about, doing his job. Getting things done. Just my opinion, sir.'

'Noted, Bob. But I don't want things slipping through the net, do you understand what I mean? His focus should be on these race attacks. The Chief Constable wants results. Barring the inquests, the Wells murder is all boxed off. The post-mortem on Jimmy Todd will tell us what we already know then he'll be off to Hollinwood Crematorium. All sorted. Yet I know for a fact John's been mooching around Glossop with that

DC from Derbyshire, still wasting time on the Wells case. None of us is going to get any medals for poking around a murder that's done and dusted.'

'I suppose not, sir.'

'How about you keep an eye on this missing councillor, get a grip of it before he does. Sharmeen Chowdhury - she's well-connected, fronts up the Scrutiny Committee on the council. High profile but no family around here. Workaholic apparently. Future council leader some say. It'll play very well for you if you track her down. You sort her out and that'll be one less thing for John to worry about.'

'Are you sure?' Bob asked. 'He won't be happy. He doesn't like things going on behind his back.'

'No question of it going on behind his back. I'll tell him. It'll be official. There'll be an Orange on his desk ASAP,' Pym said reassuring DC Donaldson by promising to deliver an official memo in an orange GMP internal envelope. 'Don't worry, there'll be no comeback on you. I just want to lessen his load. I know full well he won't be told how to do his job. And I never would. But I want to help. I've just got to be a bit subtle about it, that's all.'

'Subtle. Right you are.'

'Thanks Bob. Knock on some doors at the council, see what turns up. And keep me informed. Got it?'

'Got it.'

CHAPTER TWENTY-ONE

12.25pm Sunday 3 April 1988

Give it to me. Take it out of her, open me up and give it to me. Then pump all this shit into my veins, not hers. They assumed their usual positions in the Christie chemo unit: Kate sitting next to her mother as the tube was fixed onto the semi-permanent canula in her hand, the DI in a nearby chair, close to his wife and daughter yet slightly distant.

'What's on your mind, love?' Jean Smithdown asked her husband.

'Sorry?' he asked. 'I was miles away.'

'Mind… Yours… What's on it?' his wife said.

'Work, probably,' offered Kate. 'How to single-handedly stop Oldham descending into anarchy and chaos.'

'Something like that,' the detective replied. He had no intention of telling them what he'd actually been thinking.

'I've got an idea,' Kate said. 'They could build a big wall around Oldham town centre, like *Escape From New York*. All the nutters in one place. Sorted.'

'I'll get straight onto Chief Constable Anderton and we'll swing that plan into action,' Smithdown said and pulled a face at his daughter. *Smartarse.*

'Seriously,' Jean said. 'What's on your mind?'

'No place for shop talk, this.'

'I'd appreciate it - something to think about other than this,' she replied, nodding towards the chemo going into her.

'Sure?' he asked.

'Sure,' his wife reassured.

Smithdown pulled up his chair so he was closer to them. He dropped his voice so the other patients couldn't hear him. 'Right. Okay. Obviously, there's been a fair bit going on at the moment…'

'What with the chopped up, burned-to-buggery bodies and the machete attacks and the rioting and all,' said Kate.

'Yes,' agreed Smithdown. 'All the above…'

'A reasonable few day's work,' Jean added.

'Quite,' the detective concurred. 'And that's what's bothering me. Six months of mither just happens to have kicked in over the space of one Bank Holiday weekend.'

'TFC,' offered Kate.

'Exactly,' agreed her father. 'Added to that, Jimmy Todd's mysteriously topped himself and now some councillor has gone missing.'

'Totally TFC,' Kate said.

'TFC?' asked her mother.

Father and daughter said the words in unison: 'That's a Fucking Coincidence.'

'Charming,' Jean said, straightening the blanket she had over her frail legs.

'The riots will keep everyone occupied for months,' Smithdown continued. 'Years even. There'll be inquiries and recommendations and all sorts. It was absolute carnage last night.' Smithdown rubbed his elbow - he hadn't told them that he'd been hit by a car. No need to add to their worries. 'Yet it all felt a bit… orchestrated. Richard T. King seemed well prepared - I'll give him that. No one got near his place. Plus, I saw Maureen Lennon's lad Tom filming it all last night too. The big bastard who works at King's club. Absolutely bizarre. But he was only interested in filming the Asian lads.'

'Maureen Lennon's lad?' Jean said. 'Not seen her for years. I hear she's not been so well.'

'I presume you've spoken to Tom about Naomi Wells?' Kate asked.

'Why would I do that?' her father said.

'Because she used to knock around with him before she hooked up with Jimmy Todd.'

'I don't know why I bother sending DCs out to do house to house enquiries, I should just get them to ask you. Go on then…'

'I told you she was "Party Girl Number One" - they say it was her who first brought E up from Manchester.'

'E? Oh ecstasy - that's what we're calling it now, is it? I'll let the drugs squad know. When did they split up?'

'Start of the year, I think.'

'Any idea why?' the detective asked his daughter.

'Because Tom found out she was mixed race. And that's a no-no as far as he's concerned.'

Smithdown looked at his wife. She'd dozed off. He dropped his voice to a whisper: 'That's nice. He's got no record, I've checked, but the more I find out about this lad, the more I don't like him. Maybe I should go and pay him a visit. I don't suppose you know where he lives, do you?'

'As it happens, I do,' Kate replied, also whispering. 'I'll tell you if you let me come too.'

'Why the hell would I do that?'

'I need a good story for when I leave uni. A calling card to help get me a job. This could be it.'

'You're not coming along. No chance.'

'Then I'm not telling you where he lives.'

'Fucking Nora,' Smithdown sighed, then turned to see the other patients and their families staring at them. 'Sorry,' he mouthed.

CHAPTER TWENTY-TWO

4.35pm Sunday 3 April 1988

'I thought you knew Tom's mum?' Kate asked as they headed back into Oldham after dropping Jean Smithdown off at home and making sure she was comfortable. She was immediately suspicious about her normally warring husband and daughter going out together but had been too tired to ask too many questions.

'From years ago, yes,' the detective said. 'Schooldays. It's that weird thing of knowing someone yet not really knowing them. I'd often say to Tom: Say hello to your mum. It's just one of those things you come out with, isn't it?

'Why don't you ask her where he lives?'

'Like your mum says, she's not so well. Cancer. Like mum. But her's is terminal I believe. She's in a hospice.'

'Christ, I fucking hate cancer, Dad.'

'I fucking hate cancer too, love.'

On his daughter's instruction, Smithdown turned his car into a terraced street. It was bustling with activity: people chatting on doorsteps, going in and out of each other's two-up two-down houses, pushing prams down the street, small groups of residents standing in groups. *Proper community this, makes a change, these days.* In his heart, he knew there were plenty of officers at the police station that would view this part of Oldham very differently. He loved being a policeman, but he hated some of the words and attitudes he heard in the station. The language some of them used about the South Asian community made his skin crawl.

Smithdown pointed at an end terrace that led to a local green space known as Snipe Clough. 'Do I take it that's Tom's house?'

'It is,' his daughter confirmed. 'How did you guess?'

Lennon's house had metal grills covering both windows, upstairs and down. Underneath each window was draped a flag of St George. The front door had been painted white with a red cross - it was also protected by a metal grille. 'I thought all that bollocks had died a death,' Smithdown said to his daughter.

The mill towns around Manchester had seen wave after wave of interest from Far-Right political groups over the years. They'd rise. Then fall. The National Front - seemingly so powerful and dangerous in the 1970s - had worn itself out with ideological infighting and then split into two. The British National Party had emerged as the dominant force. Smithdown remembered seeing their first march in 1982 on the news; it was on St George's Day. *Of course it was.* The following year they'd had enough of a surge to warrant a Party Political Broadcast on TV.

'I see these twats are back again,' Smithdown had commented to his wife, before she'd told him off for swearing in front of Kate.

'Dad's right though Mum,' Kate had replied, 'they are twats.'

Rise.

Then fall.

By 1987 the BNP had decided to sit out the General Election. Their influence seemed to be on the wane, but the attitudes still bubbled under. There'd been talk - second hand, sometimes third - that officers from Oldham Police had links to some of the parties. If that was true, then they'd been very careful to hide their tracks. If Smithdown had found any evidence he'd have reported them in an instant.

In the meantime, here was Tom Lennon; claiming he'd been attacked by a South Asian gang, filming South Asian rioters and sending it to TV stations, dumping a girl after he'd found out she was mixed-race whose body parts start appearing in lakes. Tom Lennon, with his house festooned with English flags, on an almost entirely South Asian street, three weeks before St George's Day.

DI Smithdown's desire to talk to Lennon had just gone up another notch. 'That's weird,' said Kate, staring at the house as they pulled up outside. 'It wasn't like this last time I was here.'

'Can I ask, what exactly were you doing here, last time you came?' Smithdown said as he rang the doorbell next to the metal door grille. The small terraces on the street had no driveways or footpaths - only a small red step separated the doors from the street.

'What's that supposed to mean?' Kate said. 'I'm not supposed to come here because it's a South Asian area? One of my best mates at school lives across the road. Just because the police don't come around here, doesn't mean the rest of us can't.'

'I didn't mean that - and it's not true by the way - I meant what were you doing at Tom Lennon's house?'

Before Kate could answer, the white and red inner wooden door was opened. Smithdown recognised the blotchy face immediately. 'Ah, Mr Hitchcock,' the detective said, speaking through the metalwork. 'Fancy meeting you here. You're a home help now as well as a film director. Well done. Is Tom in please?'

'Nope,' the young man said, itching his neck and yawning. 'He's elsewhere.'

'I see. Sorry, what's your actual name? And think on - if you give me the name of the "Master of Suspense" again, I'll do you.'

The young man hesitated for a moment. 'Griffin. Adam Griffin. Pleased to meet you.' He looked at Kate. 'And you. Especially you.'

Smithdown made a point of finding his notebook, finding a fresh page and then writing down the name Adam Griffin… laboriously checking the spelling too. He looked over Griffin's shoulder; the house had bare floorboards and no wallpaper. There were cardboard boxes piled up in the hallway and all the way up the stairs. 'I know you,' the detective said. 'I've got a very good memory for suspicious-looking fuckers. Almost perfect, in fact.'

'Well, I sometimes work at Kingdom if they're short,' Griffin replied. 'I know you like hanging about there.'

'Nope, that's not it,' Smithdown persevered. 'Where do I know you from? It'll come to me...'

'I mean, this is fascinating, obviously…'

'Hospital! You work at the Royal Oldham Hospital, don't you?'

Griffin's cocksure persona dimmed a little. 'Yes, I do. I'm a porter. Well done. Quite the gift you have there. Anyway, if that's everything…'

Smithdown waved a finger side-to-side, informing him that he hadn't finished yet. 'I see your footage made Granada Reports yesterday,' the detective said. 'Thank goodness you were there to record things. Very civic minded of you. A cynic might think you were deliberately shit-stirring, but luckily I'm a very charitable sort of person.'

'So I'd heard,' Griffin said, again looking at Kate.

'Could we come in and wait?' she said, staring right back at him. *I'm the police officer here, thank you Kate.*

'Ordinarily, I'd have you in as quick as a flash,' Griffin grinned. 'But it's not my place. Sorry. Maybe come back another time?'

'Definitely,' confirmed Smithdown. 'Can I ask where you were between 9.30 and 10.30 on the evening of Friday the 1st of April. A teenage boy was attacked quite near here - Mustafizur Rahman. He was hit with a machete and beaten with baseball bats. Loads of them.' Smithdown took a very deliberate look over Griffin's shoulder at the boxes in the hallway.

'So I believe,' Griffin replied. 'Pakistani lads did over a Bengali I hear. Nasty business. I was here all evening, just relaxing with Tom. Watching videos, chatting. That kind of thing. Nice quiet night in.'

'All night?' the detective asked.

'All night.'

'Sounds idyllic,' Smithdown said. 'Can I leave you my number, so Tom can give me a ring?'

'Of course. I'll make sure he gets it.'

'If I don't hear from him, maybe I'll come down to Kingdom and find him. Maybe see you, as well?'

'Be lovely to see you,' Griffin said. 'We'll get the DJ to play you a request. Something appropriate.'

'That's be nice. Do you like pub rock?'

'What?' asked Griffin.

The detective leant in, pressed his face between the bars so his nose stuck through and spoke to Griffin as if he was stupid: 'Do you like pub rock? I do. I love it. How about *Police Car* by Larry Wallis? Do you know it? "I sit in the shadows waiting for a fight..." Crackin' tune. See you later...' he looked at his pad again, '... Mr Adam Griffin.' Smithdown tapped his pad on the metal bars. Then he and his daughter walked back to their car.

'Are you normally that melodramatic?' Kate asked.

'When required, yes,' her father replied, opening his car. 'What a little turd.'

'Absolute skin crawler. Never seen him before. Did you clock the house? All those boxes?'

'I did. You were about to tell me about how you ended up at Tom Lennon's.'

'Was I?'

'Yes, you were.'

'We were out clubbing last year,' Kate said, reluctantly. 'He offered me a a lift. We stopped off at his house to get something. Didn't invite me in. Off we went, then true to his word, he dropped me off at ours - said he was off up to the hills going camping or some such outdoor bollocks. Nothing happened. Don't get all weird about it.'

'I'm your dad. It's my job to get all weird about things like that. So, no indication he was going off the deep end - with all the Nationalist stuff?'

'He seemed perfectly normal last year. Until he finished with Naomi.'

'Because she was mixed race?'

'That's what I'd heard.'

'You never mentioned it.'

'If I was to tell you about every time I met a racist in Oldham, Dad, I wouldn't have time to do anything else.'

'Point taken.'

'Maybe that's my story for my uni course,' she said. 'About how this town is divided with parallel communities. Whites. Bengalis. Pakistanis. All the fear and suspicion and how it changes people.'

'Tall order,' Smithdown said. 'Stay well away from him in the meantime, okay?'

'Okay.'

'Promise?'

'Promise.'

They got in the car and were quiet for a moment. 'Dad?' Kate asked. 'Is Mum going to be okay?'

'I don't know, Kate. I wish I did. But I don't. Shall I drop you in town?'

'Yeah - I want to see the damage for myself.'

Smithdown opened the glove compartment and rifled through the cassettes.

'Do we have to listen to bloody pub rock?' his daughter groaned.

'Yes. We do,' he replied, fast-forwarding the *Live Stiffs Live* album until he found '*Police Car*' by Larry Wallis.

'Manchester Radio News at five - this is Beth Hall. Council officials say Oldham will need a multimillion-pound re-building programme after rioter's wreaked havoc in the town centre overnight. Many businesses remain closed after rival gangs of Asian youths took over the town last night, fighting with police - and each other - over the course of several hours. But at least one businessman has vowed he WILL be open tonight, in defiance of the rioters. Robert Crane has more.'

'As the clean-up continues and community leaders call for calm, the true cost of the violence is now becoming clear. Insurance assessors have given police and local councillors a provisional report - it's thought that the repair bill will run into tens of millions of pounds. Not to mention the loss of income for businesses that cannot, or will not, re-open today.

Meanwhile Oldham entrepreneur Richard T. King - owner of the Kingdom nightclub - says he definitely plans to open his doors this evening. Mr King wants the gangs to know that he won't be beaten:'

> *"What happened last night was terrible for Oldham, terrible for the town centre and terrible for the way we're seen in the wider community. We don't normally open on a Sunday, but it's a Bank Holiday and we're going to make an exception. In fact, we're going to make a point of opening. To stay shut would be like saying that the rioters have won. So, our doors will be open tonight. We won't let them win."*

'Tomorrow, assessors will turn their attention to the Glodwick area, where several roads were badly damaged by firebombs. It's now thought that many houses, possible even entire streets, will have to be demolished after the riots. Robert Crane, Manchester Radio News, Oldham.'

CHAPTER TWENTY-THREE

5.05pm Sunday 3 April 1988

Smithdown was planning on popping into work and going straight out again but the sound of loud voices from DS Pym's office caught his attention. He changed direction and casually walked past.

Sitting on the edge of Pym's desk, looking at a framed photo of the DS with Chief Constable James Anderton, was Peter Jeffries, Member of Parliament for Oldham North. The Conservative MP was, in Smithdown's opinion, someone to approach with extreme caution. A notorious self-publicist, Jeffries had carved himself a niche as a populist show off, always available to the press if some rent-a-quote outrage about society's latest turn for the worse was required. His apparent fascination with child abuse - he had a weekly column in a Sunday tabloid which he regularly used to sound off on the subject - had earned him the nickname "Paedo Pete." Despite this - or more likely because of it - the people of Oldham seemed to love him. The fact that the town wasn't a traditional Tory heartland didn't seem to matter, the voters of Oldham normally returned Jeffries election after election with a thumping majority. Until last year, that is. He'd won comfortably by most politician's standards, but his majority had been reduced dramatically. The local paper - the *Oldham Messenger* - had been running a series of editorials about the MP, saying he'd lost touch with the issues the town cared about: jobs, housing, unemployment, hospital waiting lists.

Dressed in his usual slightly-too-tight three-piece suit and sporting a "three glasses of wine at lunch" complexion, Jeffries was holding forth to DS Pym and to Bob Donaldson. All three had drinks in their hands. Pym looked annoyed when Smithdown appeared at the doorway.

'John, Mr Jeffries is here to talk about Councillor Chowdhury, one of our missing-from-homes. Her colleagues are very concerned about her. Mr Jeffries here has taken an interest in the matter - she's a C onservative councillor - and wants to know what we're doing about it. I've asked DC

Donaldson to oversee the investigation. I was updating Mr Jeffries about all the other matters that are keeping you busy this Bank Holiday weekend.'

Jeffries stuck out his hand and gave Smithdown a ludicrously firm handshake. 'Of course,' Smithdown said. 'It's very worrying. There's so much going on in this town right now, Mr Jeffries, none of it good.'

'It's like there's something in the water,' Jeffries said, his manner theatrical and showy. 'Utter madness. And now this. You know, it's only people like Councillor Chowdhury who keep this town from tipping right over the edge. She's a real public servant, Mr Smithdown. With all the trouble last night, you can understand why we're so concerned about her.'

'As I say, DC Donaldson will be dealing with it,' offered DS Pym.

'Sorry Bob,' Smithdown said. 'Don't mean to tread on your toes.'

DC Donaldson raised his open palms in a 'it's nothing to do with me' gesture. 'What can you tell me about her?' Smithdown asked, ignoring DS Pym.

'Well,' the MP said. 'She has no family in Oldham. She's from Leicester. She isn't married. Work, work, work that's all she does. When she didn't appear at the council offices on Thursday, that's when people became concerned. Totally out of character. She practically lives at the Town Hall.'

'What does she do at the council, Mr Jeffries. Sorry, local politics isn't my strong point.'

Pym tried to interrupt again: 'John, I'm sure you've other things to occupy yourself with other than a missing person...'

'She represents the Coldhurst ward,' Jeffries continued. 'She's also Chair of the Scrutiny Committee. She makes sure things are done by the book. You've got to keep an eye on these councils Mr Smithdown. Regardless of their political colours, everyone needs to be accountable. And that's what she does. In spades.'

'Could that be connected with her disappearance, do you think?' Smithdown asked.

'We're right across this now, John, thanks,' said Pym. 'I've assured Mr Jeffries that we'll stop at nothing to trace Ms Chowdhury's whereabouts. Bob will be reporting directly to me. I'm taking personal charge of the matter now. I just thought it was a courtesy to let you know.'

Classic Pym. Like flies around shit if there's some sucking up to be done. He'll make Assistant Chief Constable yet.

Still ignoring the DS and his reassurances, Smithdown kept his attention on the MP. 'Is she popular within the council?'

'Oh, our lot think she's wonderful,' Jeffries replied. 'She's an absolute workhorse. It's traditional to have an opposition councillor as head of scrutiny. It keeps the Labour lot on their toes and avoids any whiff of cronyism.'

'How was she seen within the community?'

'Which one? There are many, many communities in Oldham, Mr Smithdown.'

'Any of them,' Smithdown said. 'All of them.'

'John, I think you've taken up enough of Mr Jeffries' time,' DS Pym interjected.

'No Jim, it's fine,' the MP stated. 'Good to talk these things through. Get a fresh perspective. Like I say, the Tories loved her. Nothing got past her. The Labour and Liberal lot begrudgingly respected her. Within the Bangladeshi community she was seen as a role model. The business community thought that she was too harsh on them.'

'Any issues with her race?'

'Oh yes. The usual crowd thought she was an uppity Asian gobshite who had ideas above her station.'

'Which usual crowd?'

'Mr Smithdown,' Jeffries said, putting his glass down. 'I shouldn't have to be telling an officer of Oldham Police that the Far-Right is on the rise in this town. They've been licking their wounds, lying low, but they're re-charging their batteries. Going legit. They've got their sights on winning Council seats. Maybe even getting places in the European Parliament. Quite easy to sneak in and win elections that hardly anyone votes in. We've got to be vigilant, Detective Inspector. History teaches us that. I wrote a piece for the *News of the World* about it the other week. You should read it.'

'Yes. I probably should.'

'And you should probably also get on your way, John,' interrupted DS Pym once again. 'I promised to introduce Mr Jeffries to some of the Tactical Aid Group officers who proved so effective the other night.'

'Of course. Nice meeting you, Mr Jeffries.'

The MP crunched the detective's hand and gave him a business card. 'Give me a call if I can be of help, Mr Smithdown.'

'I will. Thank you.'

'What's your next move, John?' DS Pym asked, clearly annoyed.

'Think I'll grab a bite to eat. And then go clubbing.'

CHAPTER TWENTY-FOUR

7.45pm Sunday 3 April 1988

Many police officers based in Oldham liked to drink and unwind at the private bar and social club situated on the top floor of the police station. It was called, somewhat unimaginatively, The Bar. Smithdown had gone off the place since the Oldham Borough Force had merged into Greater Manchester Police in 1974 and the licensing hours had become a little less flexible than he'd liked.

Other officers preferred the somewhat better-named Old Bill bar and restaurant at the side of the police station - the interior was decked out with police memorabilia. Some ventured across the pedestrianised shopping area outside the station to the Three Tunnes, a straightforward town centre pub favoured by the uniformed officers and civilian support staff.

All of these places had one key drawback for John Smithdown: there were too many cops in them. He preferred his own company - or at least that of people who didn't talk about police work all the time - so he preferred to drink in The Raj restaurant just up the hill.

Most of Smithdown's colleagues knew this, so they tended to avoid the place, unless it was to pick up a takeaway and give the detective a quick nod. Kate Smithdown also knew her dad liked to drink at The Raj, so that's why she headed there.

The front window had a shatter mark in it and was being held together with tape - other than that it was business as usual. 'Pint of lager please,' Kate said, pulling up the one remaining high stool so she could sit next to her father at the tiny bar.

'Aren't halves a bit more ladylike?' her father asked.

'Fine, I'll order two halves then.'

'Hilarious. Pint of lager and another bitter for me.'

The drinks arrived. Smithdown sipped his and took a handful of Bombay Mix from a bowl placed next to his pint. He offered some to his daughter: 'No thanks,' she replied. 'I don't want to deprive you of your evening meal.'

'Very gracious of you,' Smithdown replied, saluting his daughter with his pint.

'This is a restaurant you know,' she pointed out. 'You could order some actual food.'

'Not hungry. Maybe later.'

'What's on your mind, Dad?'

'Everything. Everything is on my mind. How about that?'

'Come on. Might work with Bob and the lads at the station this, but it doesn't work with me.'

Smithdown pushed the last of the Bombay Mix around the bottom of the bowl with his index finger. 'I've just been given a lesson in things-I-should-have-been-aware-of by Peter Jeffries. Peter Fucking Jeffries! The Member of Parliament for Self-Promotion. The guy everyone dismisses as a buffoon knows more about what's really going on in this town than the cops do. We should have been across this Far-Right, neo-Nazi stuff but we've missed it by a mile. I feel embarrassed about how little I know about the different communities in this town. Just because I'm matey with Mr Aleem so I feel like I'm doing my bit. It's all bollocks. I know nowt. And what's worse, I believe there's cops in that police station who are out and out racists and that's a disgrace.'

'You're doing your best, Dad.'

'No, I'm not. I'm doing enough to get by. Enough to keep up appearances. It's not on.'

They were quiet for a moment. Father and daughter, drinking at the tiny bar of a restaurant with a smashed window. 'So, what's the plan?' Kate asked.

'I need to find Tom Lennon. And you need to go home.'

CHAPTER TWENTY-FIVE

11.15pm Sunday 3 April 1988

Walking into the Kingdom club to the clicks and pulses of *'151'* by Armando, Smithdown noted that security was considerably tighter than the last time he'd visited. There seemed to be at least twice as many shaven-headed young men dressed in black outside as well as in. The detective quickly tired of getting a shake of the head and a shrug from the security staff as he asked: where's Tom Lennon? Plus, the noise level as he entered the main body of the club was so intense, he could barely hear anyway. So, he thought he'd head straight for Richard T. King's office instead.

He got as far as the end of the bar when he noticed that King wasn't in his office, he was in the main body of the club. Dressed in a baggy, psychedelic hooded top and very roomy jeans, he was standing by a plastic bin filled with ice and bottled water. King was handing the bottles out to the young clubbers. One, a young woman about the same age as Kate Smithdown, touched King's face and smiled at him. She stood for a moment and stared at the bottle, then danced away, shaking her head as if the gift was the single greatest act of generosity the world had ever seen.

The thunderous volume meant it was easier for the detective to mime at King rather than attempt to speak. He pointed to the nightclub owner, pointed to himself, made a talking motion with his hand and pointed upstairs. King smiled; he touched a bouncer on the shoulder, pointed to the water, then at the crowded dance floor. He then indicated that Smithdown should follow him.

Adam Griffin was already in King's office, standing almost to attention as if he'd been expecting them. 'Good evening Adam', Smithdown said as he passed. 'Lovely to see you earlier. Hope that house is spic and span.' The young man scratched at his face and silently mouthed 'fuck off' at the detective. Smithdown pulled a face at Griffin as if he was mortally offended, then winked at him.

'Water, Mr Smithdown?' King asked.

'I will, thank you. It's baking in here.'

King tossed a bottle to him and Smithdown drank half of it in one go. 'You're giving it away, I see. Not like you.'

'Well I'm concerned about what some of these kids could have taken before they arrive in my club,' King said, taking a seat behind his floating table. 'There's a lot of ecstasy about, no one knows where it's coming from and it can cause severe dehydration. Although, ironically, we can't be handing out too much water because over-hydrating can cause brain damage, apparently. You can't win, can you? Anyway, I've put my admission charge up to cover any costs, so don't feel too sorry for me.'

'I wasn't planning to. Down to business then. Tom Lennon - I want him. Where is he?'

'He's on a rest day,' King said in a helpful voice. 'Do you know Mr Smithdown, that guy gave his all protecting this place during the riots. Literally put his life on the line. So, he's taking a well-earned break.'

'I've been to his house and the only person there was Syd Little here,' Smithdown sighed, nodding towards Griffin, who held his ribs and silently mimed uproarious laughter, before his face dropped to a blank canvas again.

'Why so keen to track down Tom, may I ask?' King said.

'I want to talk to him about Naomi Wells.'

'All stowed away that case, isn't it?' asked King, casually rubbing an invisible mark off his snow-white trainers that now rested on the suspended desk.

'There's a few blanks I'd still like to fill in,' replied the detective, resisting the urge to give the desk a good kick.

'Jimmy Todd's the only person who could do that, I fear,' said King. 'And he decided to take the other route. The thought of suicide is a powerful solace, Mr Smithdown.' He left a few beats of silence. The bwomp-bwomp of the music downstairs filled the space. 'Nietzsche,' King added.

'Tell Lennon to present himself to Oldham police station, Mr King,' replied the detective. 'Or I'll close you down until he does.' A pause. 'And that's a direct quote from me. Same goes for you, Little Ern,' he added, giving the side of Griffin's face two gentle taps as he passed. 'Front desk by 10am. Clear?'

'Absolutely,' King responded. 'Thank you so much for coming.'

As Smithdown left the office, another one of the seemingly interchangeable security staff passed him on the stairs: shaved head, black clothes, powerful build, just like all the others. He smiled at the detective, adding a cheery wink too. *Don't know what you're so jolly about - you'll be out of a job tomorrow.*

King and Griffin waited until they heard Smithdown clear the stairs and open the door to the dancefloor, momentarily increasing the noise level ten-fold. The door closed and the noise dropped.

'I will fookin' do that cunt,' Griffin said. 'Swear to God.'

The bouncer who'd passed Smithdown on the stairs spoke. He was still smiling. 'His daughter's in.'

'Whaaaat?' Griffin said, clapping his hands. 'The little brunette. Serious? Oh man!'

'She arrived a few minutes ago asking for Tom. Says she wants to interview him for a journalism project. I don't think Columbo there knows she's here. She even asked if her dad had been in.'

'Fook me!' added Griffin, raising his fists as if he'd just scored a winning goal. 'I mean seriously, fookin' fook me.'

'Perfect,' said King, taking a bottle of water from a small metal filing cabinet near his desk and tossing it to Griffin. 'Just perfect.'

CHAPTER TWENTY-SIX

1.25 am Monday 4 April 1988

Smithdown was at home when he got the call that Kate had been taken to hospital. He was just sitting quietly with his wife, holding her hand as they read and listened to a radio phone-in show when DC Bob Donaldson rang.

'Boss. Is Jean there?' the DC asked.

'Yes,' Smithdown replied. *That's an odd question, even by your standards, Bob.*

'Take the call in another room, will you?' the DC asked.

'Okay.' He went through to the hall then asked his wife to put the receiver down when he'd picked up the extension, making it seem like he didn't want to disturb her listening. The radio host - James Stannage - was taking a caller to task about his opinions on repatriation after the weekend riots. Smithdown waited for the sound of the other line being closed until he spoke: 'I'm here, Bob.'

'Right. Straight to it. Kate's in the Royal and she's in a bad way. She was taken in after being found collapsed in the street.'

'Christ Almighty. Where?'

'Outside Kingdom in the town centre. They think its ecstasy-related.'

'No fucking chance,' Smithdown responded, manging to shout and whisper at the same time. 'Absolutely. No. Fucking. Chance. That's not Kate. We both know that.'

'All I know is you better get down to the Royal quicksticks,' Donaldson said. 'I'm sorry, boss. I really am.'

Jean Smithdown was so used to her husband getting late night phone calls and slipping out of the house that she didn't question why he was putting on his shoes and coat. She just asked him to take care. 'I will,' he replied.

With no thought to speed limits, one-way systems or red lights, Smithdown was at the Royal Oldham Hospital within 20 minutes. He left his car on a space reserved for doctors, found out where Kate was from a receptionist in double-quick time by flashing his warrant card and headed straight to the ward she'd been taken to. He grabbed - literally grabbed - the first doctor he came across: 'Smithdown. Katherine Mary. Date of birth: ninth of November '67. Brought in after a suspected drug overdose. I need an update. Can you give it to me? If you can't, then I need you to take me to someone who can. Right now.'

'She's in ICU,' the doctor said. He looked so young to Smithdown's eyes. The detective had to gulp in air to stop the overwhelming need to cry. *Not my girl. Not my Kate. Not you, too.*

'What can you tell me?' asked the detective. 'I'm her dad but I'm also a police officer - a crime may well have been committed here.'

'She was brought in unconscious,' the doctor said. He had a similar haircut to Jimmy Todd - same blonde good looks. 'Temperature and blood pressure were sky high. Seen a few like this in recent months - looks like MDMA overdose. Ecstasy. Probably laced with LSD too for a bit of added bite. She'd been drinking too, so that didn't help. Quite the mixture. She has a swelling on the brain - looks like she worked out what was happening to her and was trying to counteract the dehydration that comes with ecstasy by drinking a huge amount of water. Too much water, as it happens. The water did as much harm as anything. You know that old tale that you can die by drinking too much water? It's true.'

'You know what I'm going to ask…'

'Is she going to be okay? I don't know. I'm sorry I can't be more positive. We're bringing her temperature down and the swelling seems to be subsiding - but I really can't say yet. We're still feeling our way with MDMA but it's fair to say she had enough in her system to stop a double-decker bus. She's very lucky. Tough girl.'

'When can I see her?' Smithdown asked.

'Soon. Wait here. I know it's frustrating but bear with us for a little while.'

'Okay. Sure. I understand. Please let me know as soon as you can. Thank you.'

Smithdown sat down in the waiting area and saw a young girl about Kate's age in the chair opposite him. She was wearing dayglo, baggy clothes and her hair was in two high bunches on her head. She was quietly crying. It took him a few moments to recognise her: 'Sandra? Christ, I didn't recognise you.'

Sandra Charles was a girl from Kate's school. The detective hadn't seen her for several years and still had a mental image of her as a ten-year-old at Kate's birthday party. He'd always made sure that, despite his job, he'd never missed any key moments in his daughter's life. *Looks like you've got yourself another key moment right here, John lad.*

She caught the detective's eye; for the briefest moment he thought she was going to run away. But she didn't. She stayed still, shook her head and wept. Harder this time.

Smithdown crossed over to the chair next to hers, put an arm around her and was about to say a few comforting when she spoke first: 'Oh, Mr Smithdown, I'm so sorry. So very, very sorry. You've got to believe me, nothing happened. She did nowt wrong. We'd just had a few drinks, that's all. A few pints, I swear to God. You've got to believe me.'

The detective held her as close as the scooped back plastic chairs would allow.' Of course I believe you Sandra. It's okay. Trust me. Everything will be alright. But you've got to tell me exactly what happened. Don't leave anything out, even the tiniest detail. Not a single thing, do you understand?'

Sandra wiped her eyes with the back of her hand. A smear of glitter was left behind. Smithdown pulled a small packet of Handy Andy tissues from his pocket - he nearly always carried them - split the cellophane wrapping and gave Sandra several sheets. 'Everything. You must tell me everything. Okay?'

She nodded. 'We went to the Turn of Luck. The damage from all the trouble was still pretty noticeable but they were open. She was asking people questions about the riot and the trouble they'd had. We had two drinks - two, I swear. Then she said she wanted to go to Kingdom. They were having a Ravers Versus Rioters night. Never misses a trick that Richard T. King, does he? Anyhow, she wanted to talk to Tom Lennon about…

'Christ Almighty, she promised me she'd stay away from him,' Smithdown interrupted. 'Sorry, love. Carry on.'

'Tom's gone proper weird since his mam got cancer, draping his house in flags. Dumping that girl… the dead girl… when he found out she was mixed-race. Filming stuff around town. Kate thinks he got it in his head that his mam would have been treated quicker if they weren't so many Asian people in front of her on the waiting list. Pretty out-there shit. Sorry, Mr Smithdown. I know Kate's mum is proper poorly with cancer too.'

'Yet, strangely enough, we aren't draping our house in the flag of St George,' Smithdown pointed out. 'It's bollocks, love. It was bollocks in the 70s and its bollocks now. What else?'

'So, she wanted to talk to Tom and sure enough he was at Kingdom…'

Fucking Nora.

'… but not on the door. He wasn't in uniform, neither. He was just hanging about, handing out water. It was baking in the club last night. Absolutely sweltering. The radiators were on full blast too.'

'Go on.'

'They talked. That was it. He didn't seem to want to know. He was smiling, like it was all a big joke. Like what she was saying was the daftest thing in the whole world. Then he left. We stayed in the club and talked a bit, then that's when Kate started… whooshing.'

'How do you mean, whooshing?'

'She went to the toilet and she said… Sorry. It's a bit embarrassing.'

'Please. Tell me.'

'She told me she'd just had the best shit she'd ever had. Sorry Mr Smithdown. Such a weird thing to say, but that's what she said. The best ever. Then she kept saying… I feel like I'm whooshing. I'm coming up. I'm really whooshing. She was grinding her teeth - her jaw was jittering so much she pressed her head against the wall of the club to stop it from going side to side. When she started hugging people and crying and telling me how much she loved me, that's when we figured she'd been spiked. She was panicking then; necking water like there's no tomorrow, frightened she was going to die of dehydration. She'd researched it for uni. She was burning up. That's when we went outside and called an ambulance from a phone box. She'd made me carry a load more water out with us. Bottles and bottles of it. She went unconscious just before the ambulance arrived. And that's it. I heard the doctor say he didn't know if she's going to make it. They wouldn't tell me owt. Oh, Mr Smithdown. This is mad.'

'It is, Sandra,' the detective conceded. 'It really is. I'm sorry to keep asking questions…'

'It's fine, honestly.'

'Did you drink anything else in the club? Another few pints?'

'No, just water.'

'Did you leave the drinks unattended?'

'No. They were in our hands the whole time.'

'Was the water identical?'

'Yes. I think so. I don't know. Oh God, I'm not sure. We both got them from Tom Lennon. I didn't really check. I'm sorry. It was so hot. It was just water.'

'Looks like it was a bit more than just water, love.'

'But we both drank it Mr Smithdown. How come I'm okay?'

'Because fortunately for you, Sandra, you're not my daughter. This was targeted against my Kate - they used those drugs like a weapon against her.'

'She was just asking questions, Mr Smithdown. For her uni project! Why would someone dose her just for that?'

Smithdown squeezed the girl tightly. 'Because this town is going mad, love. That's why. Absolutely mad.'

'Manchester Radio News at eight, this is Beth Hall, good morning. A young woman is fighting for her life in hospital after being found unconscious in Oldham Town centre. The 20-year-old, who hasn't yet been named, is thought to have collapsed after taking the drug ecstasy. Robert Crane has more.'

'An ambulance was called to the scene at just before midnight after a friend of the woman raised the alarm.

They found the 20-year-old in the street close to the Kingdom nightclub, though a spokesman for the club says they believe that neither of the women had actually visited the nightspot.

She was treated first at the scene and then taken to the Royal Oldham Hospital, where she's believed to be in an induced coma.

It's thought that she may have taken the drug ecstasy, which is becoming increasing popular among revellers involved in the dance music scene in clubs across Greater Manchester.

If toxicology tests show that she did take ecstasy, it could prove to be the first case of its kind in the Oldham area. Robert Crane, Manchester Radio News at the Royal Oldham hospital.'

CHAPTER TWENTY-SEVEN

9.10 am Monday 4 April 1988

Smithdown slept in Kate's room until a new doctor came on shift. He quizzed the doctor relentlessly about his daughter's condition *no change… a good sign… keep hoping for the best* then he headed for Oldham Police Station.

Officers and support staff quietly gave him their best wishes, shared their hope that everything was going to be alright or just placed a hand on his shoulder as he passed them. He acknowledged each with a thin smile or a nod of the head as headed for DS James Pym's office. He went straight in, closed the door and sat down without being asked. His lit up a cigarette, despite knowing that Pym didn't care for smoking in his office. 'John, I'm very sorry to hear about what happened to Kate. We've made sure her name has been withheld from the press. In the meantime, if there's anything we can do…'

'I want to raid the Kingdom nightclub and Tom Lennon's house as soon as possible,' Smithdown said, staring out of the window at the ring road traffic. 'Simultaneously, obviously, so word doesn't get out. They dosed my daughter with ecstasy, used it as a weapon just as much as someone used machetes against Mr Aleem and Mustafizur Rahman, that lad over at Coldhurst. I want Lennon in custody before lunchtime. I want to question him about what happened to Kate and about all the other shit that's been stirred up around here over the last few days.'

'John, there's no way I can allow you to do that,' Pym said. 'There's no evidence that Lennon's involved. There'll be a dozen members of staff at Kingdom who'll swear blind he wasn't even there last night. Even if we arrested him, your involvement will have his brief rubbing his hands with glee. Lennon would be out before teatime. I'll get a different team to look at what happened with Kate, but it can't be you. It's got to be separate.'

'That's what they want, Jim,' Smithdown responded, quietly. 'Separate everything. Different teams looking at different things. A murder here. Maybe another there. The machete attacks, the riots, that missing councillor. Our lot scurrying around on different treadmills instead of seeing the bigger picture. Everything smells like Tom Lennon and he's away somewhere laughing at us. Laughing at what he did to my Kate.'

'John, I know you're upset. I totally understand. But I need you as far away from this as possible. You shouldn't even be here. You've barely slept since Thursday. Kate needs you. Jean needs you. Go home.'

'No. You don't see it do you? It's more than my Kate. More even than the machete attacks and the riots. It's bigger than all the parts put together, Jim… and Tom Lennon is at the fucking heart of it. Christ Jim, he tried to kill my girl…'

'You cannot be involved in any investigation into what happened to your daughter while you're still on this force, John,' the DS stated. 'It's as simple as that.'

The detective continued to look out of the window. Then, without a word he got up and left Pym's office. He headed straight for the photographic unit. The red light was on outside the dark room; the detective ignored it and walked in. The bright white harshness of the fluorescent strip lights in the corridor flooded the dark room, cancelling out the dim red glow in the tiny room and getting an immediate reaction from Paul Rees. 'Fuck me! The red light's on! No fucking entry, it says so on the bastard door,' the photographer shouted.

Smithdown put a hand on the photographer's slim shoulder and led him out of the darkroom as if he was being arrested. 'Sorry Paul. I need you. Now.'

'What do you want, Mr Smithdown?' the photographer said, rubbing his eyes as they adjusted to the shift in brightness.

'I want you to tell the truth, lad. Nothing but. Trust me. It'll be right.'

Smithdown led Rees up the stairs and back to Pym's office. 'Right Paul. Take a seat. I want you to tell Detective Superintendent Pym here exactly what happened the other night - just before you photographed the domestic injuries on that young girl. Do you remember? Dark hair? She was called Becky Wells. Little thing with plastic sandals on.'

'Yes, I remember her,' Rees said, speaking cautiously, clearly concerned he was about to do wrong whichever way this went.

'Tell Mr Pym what happened,' Smithdown said reassuringly. He was looking straight at the DS as he spoke.

'I really don't know what I'm supposed to say…'

'Just tell him,' Paul. 'It'll be fine. I promise.'

Still wary, Rees began to speak: 'Mr Smithdown asked me to snap the little girl's injuries. She'd been in some sort of incident at home. Mum's boyfriend I believe, the guy who topped himself in Strangeways.'

'That's right Paul,' coaxed Smithdown. 'I did ask you that, didn't I? How would you describe her injuries?'

'She'd been knocked about a bit, that's for sure. Bit of bruising…' Paul hesitated for a moment.'

'Go on,' the detective encouraged.

'Split lip. She had a split lip.'

'And what did I ask you to do before you took the snaps, Paul?'

The photographer looked back and forth between the two detectives, baffled as to what to say next. 'Mr Smithdown, I don't understand.'

'It's fine, Paul. What did I ask you to do?'

'You asked me to turn around and look at the wall, Mr Smithdown.'

'I did. But you sneaked a peek, didn't you? It's okay. Tell the truth, that's all I'm asking.'

A pause. 'Yes. I did.'

'And what did you see, Paul?'

'Mr Smithdown, please…'

'Paul. It's very important that you tell DS Pym exactly what you saw.'

'I saw you pull the girl's lip open to make it worse,' Rees said, quietly. 'There was blood everywhere.'

'Christ Almighty,' sighed DS Pym.

'That's right, Paul,' agreed Smithdown. 'I split her lip right open, didn't I?'

'I know why you did it,' the photographer said. 'It was to stop the girl going back home and getting more of the same. You might have saved her life. I completely understand why you did what you did, Mr Smithdown. Completely.'

'Much appreciated, Paul,' Smithdown said. 'Sorry to interrupt your work. That's all I need. On your way.'

DS Pym waited for the photographer to leave. 'You'll be suspended on full pay pending further investigations, DI Smithdown,' he said, making notes as he spoke. 'You're to have no contact with anyone involved in this case, or anyone from the Greater Manchester Force. You'll receive notification shortly about when you'll be interviewed under caution by the Y Department.'

Smithdown allowed himself the tiniest of smiles on hearing the name of the dreaded Y Department. Every officer despised GMP's internal complaints division based on the 11th floor of the force's headquarters at Chester House in Old Trafford. Such was the stigma attached to being summoned to see them, there was a separate staircase so other officers didn't have to look at you as you entered their interview room. It was known as the Walk of Shame. It wouldn't be the first time John Smithdown would do that walk. It might be the last though.

'I need your warrant card and I need you off the premises immediately,' Pym continued. 'Don't go back to your office. Just go. I'm very sorry John.'

'Right you are, Jim.'

Smithdown did as he'd been asked and left the building. He walked to the nearest phone box, pulled out a handful of two pence pieces and made a neat pile of coins on the phone box casing.

First, he rang his wife and explained what had happened to Kate. There were tears.

Then he rang directory enquiries for the numbers of all the local hospices.

Finally, he rang DC Jenny Seddon of the Derbyshire Constabulary.

'BBC Manchester News at noon, this is Richard Hemmingway. A senior Oldham police detective has been suspended over allegations of assaulting a child. Detective Inspector John Smithdown was relieved of his duties earlier today after the alleged incident at the town's police station. Vince Hunt has the details.'

'The young girl, thought to be aged nine, was being cared for at Oldham Police station after an apparent domestic incident.

While she was there it's claimed that she was deliberately injured by an officer who was supposed to have been looking after her. Greater Manchester Police has declined to name the person involved, but senior sources within the Oldham division have confirmed that the officer is in fact Detective Inspector John Smithdown.

He'd recently been involved in the investigation into the murder of 26-year-old Naomi Wells. The Oldham single mum's body was found at a Derbyshire beauty spot on Saturday. Her hand had previously been found in a plastic bag in Oldham's Alexandra Park. It's thought that the injured child may be her daughter.

DI Smithdown has been suspended and will now face a disciplinary inquiry into what happened. That could be followed by criminal charges. Vince Hunt, BBC Manchester News, Oldham.'

PART II

CHAPTER TWENTY-EIGHT

2.30 pm Monday 4 April 1988

Working his way through his pile of two pence pieces, Smithdown got what he wanted. The third hospice that he rang had reluctantly confirmed to him that they did indeed have a Maureen Lennon in their care. It was in neighbouring Rochdale and the detective was there within half an hour.

Maureen Lennon was sitting up in bed chatting to a woman in a tabard who was pushing a drinks trolley; it was fully stocked with beer, wine, mixers and sprits. Maureen was debating whether to have a Bacardi and Coke or a vodka and orange. She was pointing a finger - a grey, desperately bony finger - at a bottle of Vladivar when she spotted the detective: 'Johnny Smithdown. Good God. Will you take a drink? Or is it not allowed when you're on duty.' There was Irish in her accent but there was a lightness to it. Some words were from across the water, others were pure Oldham. Smithdown had known her from primary school but they'd lost touch when he had gone to Oldham's Blue Coat School and she had gone the more traditional comprehensive route. Their lives had intersected lightly over the years - in the street, at a christening or wedding - but being a policeman meant that some people kept him at arm's length. He knew this and accepted it.

He leant in and pressed his cheek against hers. Her skin felt like baking paper and there was a sour smell in her hair. 'I'm not technically on duty, Maureen' he replied. 'So, why not?' He scanned the cans of beer on offer. 'I'll have a Long Life, please.'

'Wish I could fookin' have that too,' Maureen said. There was a beat of silence, then she and the woman staff member wailed with laughter.

Smithdown had never been in a hospice before, but it's fair to say that this wasn't what he was expecting. *Let them have a drink, why not? No harm at this stage of the game, is there?*

The hospice assistant passed Smithdown a small can of the unfortunately named light ale and handed Maureen her vodka and orange. She held the glass in both hands; it seemed to take all of her strength to just lift it to her lips as she took a tiny sip. Then she settled the drink back into her lap. Smithdown leant over, tapped his can against the rim of her glass and pulled up a seat. He could see her skin stretched hard and tight against the roundness of her cheekbones; the outline of her eye sockets was clear and stark. There were only a few light strokes of her old features left - Maureen Lennon was almost unrecognisable. 'How's your Jean?' she asked. 'Still the best-looking woman in all of Oldham?'

'I can confirm that she still is. No question about that, Maureen. Not so well at the moment, though. She's been pretty poorly, in fact. But she'll come through,' he regretted the insensitivity of his words immediately they'd left his mouth.

'I'm sure, Johnny. I'll be praying for her.'

'Given where we are, I feel daft for asking,' Smithdown. 'But, how are you?'

'I'm close, Johnny. I'm very close to it now. Remember when we were kids? We never thought of the future, did we? Never ever. Now all I think about is the past. I was thinking of you the other day too. How strange is that? Probably seeing all this mither on the telly news and thinking… Johnny Smithdown will need an extra-large mop to wipe all this shite up.'

'It's this shite I want to talk to you about, actually, Maureen. Maybe you can help me mop a bit of it up.'

There was silence. Maureen took another sip. 'It's not about my Tom, is it?'

'It is about your Tom, Maureen,' the detective said. 'I need to find him and I don't think I'll get an honest answer from anyone else - but I might just get one from you.'

'Maybe. Maybe not.'

'I don't want to upset you, Maureen. Really, I don't. Let's just say I need to find Tom as soon as I can.'

'What do you want with him, Johnny Smithdown?' she asked. 'What has he done that's brought you all the way out here?'

'It's best if I don't say…'

'You'll have to say, I'm afraid Johnny.'

'Maureen, my daughter Kate is in hospital and I think Tom helped put her there. She's in intensive care. Please.'

She heaved the glass of vodka and orange to her lips, took a bird-like sip and let it rest again. 'For God's sake, Johnny. I'm so sorry. I didn't know. How could I know?'

'Please, you need to help me, Maureen. All the recent trouble - all the shite - seems connected to him. I've got a smashed-up town, people missing, people in the hospital, people dead. Things are bad in Oldham, Maureen and it feels like they could very easily get even worse. Please. You must help me.'

Maureen thought for a while, rubbing the rim of her glass with a stick-like finger. For a moment the detective thought she might nod off; her eyes dropped for a moment, then she jumped slightly. 'They never bothered me,' she said, finally. Quietly.

'Sorry?'

'The Pakis. The Asians. They never bothered me. I know what it's like to be discriminated against. No Irish, no dogs and all that. No, they never bothered me. But by God they seemed to upset our Tommy. Him and his mates take to the hills anytime they can, to get away from 'em. He said they couldn't bear the sight of them anymore. Like I said, I've no problem with them, but our Tom, well that's a different matter altogether.'

'Could he be up in the hills right now, Maureen? Is that where he could be?'

'Sure. Anytime he can, him and his mates head up there. It's an old hunting lodge out near Hayfield. Right out in the sticks. Do you know where it is?'

'No,' Smithdown said. 'But I know someone who will.'

'There's a group of them. The Wolves they call themselves… The English Wolves, that's it. Daft name, isn't it? Irish Wolves would be better, don't you think? They get lads from Stockport, Salford, Huddersfield, all over joining them some weekends. I don't know what they're up to and I don't ask. But they're better off up in the hills than causing trouble down here, I suppose.'

'Maureen. I've got to go,' the detective said. 'If you hear from Tom, I want you to get one of the staff here to call me. I'll leave a number.'

'I'm not stupid, Johnny. I know he's been up to no good. But, my God, if he's harmed that beautiful girl of yours, I'd never forgive myself. Or him.'

'I'll be in touch, Maureen and I'll come back when I can,' Smithdown said, finishing his drink and then touching Maureen's hands, still clasped around her vodka and orange. Her fingers felt deathly cold and as he looked in her eyes he could see they both knew that this was probably the last time they'd meet.

'Right you are,' she replied. 'There's always a drink and a welcome here for you, Johnny. You know that, don't you?'

'Yes, Maureen. I do.'

'Wish Jean all the best from me,' she said. There were tears in her eyes now.

'I will, Maureen. Bye. And thank you.'

CHAPTER TWENTY-NINE

4.50 pm Monday 4 April 1988

'Mum, where's my football kit?'

'In your drawer - all washed and nicely folded,' Jenny Seddon shouted up the stairs. 'Wonder who did that?' she added - a little more quietly - to her unexpected guest. 'Come through to the kitchen, Mr Smithdown. Tea? Wine? Beer? Bit early, but it's a Bank Holiday, isn't it? These things are allowed.'

'I'll take a beer please Jenny, thank you,' the detective said, removing his wet mac and folding it over his arm. 'Please, call me John.'

'I'll try, might be tricky, you're just such a… Mr Smithdown,' she explained, placing a tin of Thwaites beer and a dimpled pint glass in front of the detective.

'Wine, love?' asked Brian McIntyre as he stirred a large pot of chilli on the stove. He was wearing running gear, very similar to the outfit he'd been wearing at the mountain rescue centre. *Bet he doesn't actually own any other kind of clothes.*

'Yes. A small vase-full please,' Jenny replied, standing on her tiptoes, kissing her partner on the cheek and then taking a seat at the large pine table that dominated the kitchen. Jenny and Brian's three-storey terraced house was in the Old Town area of Glossop and was exactly what Smithdown had expected it to be: noisy and messy with a huge pile of muddy walking boots in the porch. The kitchen had a huge collection of children's artwork covering every available space. Two children - or maybe three, it was hard to tell - ran in and out of the kitchen, grabbing snacks and drinks as they went. All were boys aged ten and under, all said HI! to the detective in loud, confident voices and all had bright red hair. 'Right you horrors,' shouted Jenny. 'Go and watch a video in the front room and leave us to talk to Mr Smithdown.'

All three children did as they were told and dashed to the next room in a blur of red hair and biscuits. Smithdown could hear them arguing about whether to watch *Ernest Goes to Camp* or *Spaceballs* as Jenny closed the kitchen door.

‘So,’ Jenny said, taking a seat next to Smithdown and making very deliberate direct eye contact with him. ‘First things first. Serious question.’ She matched it with a serious expression and glanced at the closed kitchen door. ‘Can I pinch a cigarette, please?’

‘Jenny!’ Brian cried, waving his wooden spoon in her direction. ‘I thought we agreed!’

‘From the look on Mr Smithdown’s face I’d say this was an emergency,’ she replied, pulling a JPS from the detective’s battered packet and sharing a light with Smithdown from the equally worn box of Bryant & May matches. ‘Fire away, Mr S.’

‘I’m not one for big, long speeches,’ he said. ‘So, this is the state of play: I reckon I’ve got two murders on the go; one suicide that might not be a suicide; two… sorry three probable attempted murders. I’ve got missing-from-homes and so many public disorder and criminal damage charges that the magistrates court won’t know what’s hit them after the Bank Holiday. It’s madness. The connecting factor is one Thomas Robert Lennon, aged 26 of Snipe Street, Oldham. Occupation: security supervisor. Current whereabouts, unknown. No previous convictions but has all the hallmarks of extremist, possibly neo-Nazi beliefs. I think he is, at the very least, involved in some way. At worst, he’s behind the whole fuckin’ lot.’

‘Is that it?’ Jenny asked. Her eyes wide as she inhaled luxuriously on her cigarette, then wafted away the smoke with quick, guilty movements of her hand.

‘Almost. One of the attempted murders is on my daughter… she’s in hospital right now. Oh, and I’ve just been suspended from GMP. I think that just about covers it, yes.’

‘Fucking hell…’ Jenny responded, looking at her partner and blowing smoke from the corner of her mouth to send it in the other direction. ‘Is that why you’re this side of the border, because you’ve been run out of Oldham?’

‘I sort of banished myself, in a way,’ admitted Smithdown.

‘We heard about your suspension on the radio,’ Brian said. ‘Nice of someone at Oldham nick to provide the press with your name. It’s almost as if someone’s got it in for you, isn’t it?’

‘Looks that way, doesn’t it? To be fair, that’s the least of my worries. The reason my girl is in an intensive care unit is because someone spiked her with ecstasy and LSD. They targeted her to get at me. Now I want to get at them. It’s going to be easier to do that without my boss breathing down my neck. So, I decided to go freelance for a bit. Now…

this is where you two come in. I'm told Lennon and his mates are in the habit of heading for the hills near an old shooting lodge close to Hayfield. Do you know it?'

Brian McIntyre came away from the stove, reached up to a shelf and pulled out an Ordnance Survey map from dozens that were stashed there in a disorganised pile. He unfolded the Dark Peak map and spread it out on the table. The satellite towns of Uppermill and Diggle on the outskirts of Oldham were at the top left of the map, along with the Pennine Way route past Black Moss reservoir close to Smithdown's house. Brian's hand traced a line across Stalybridge, Tintwhistle and Glossop before finding Hayfield.

The detective saw the flat moorland plateau of Kinder Scout; it was rendered white on the map because of its lack of contour lines. 'There's two that I know of,' said Brian, plucking the cigarette from Jenny's hand, taking a drag and handing it back to her. 'One's here at White Brow - it's marked on the map. You can see it from the Glossop to Hayfield road.' He pointed to a black dot marked Shooting Cabin in an area designated for grouse shooting.

'Seems a bit obvious to be a hideout, love,' Jenny said. 'You're a massive hypocrite by the way,' she added as she smoked the cigarette down to the filter.

'Absolutely,' Brian agreed. 'But there's another lodge here.' His finger circled an area of moorland called Burnt Hill. 'It's not on the map. Maybe that's what you're looking for.'

'Jesus Christ,' said Smithdown. 'Burnt Hill. There's another one for the weird name list…'

'Maybe that's your spot, John?' Brian said.

'Could be,' the detective agreed. 'I'll go and take a look. Thank you. Can I borrow the map?'

'You'd never spot it at the best of times,' Jenny said popping her cigarette end into an empty wine bottle with a sizzle. 'It'll be dark soon and it's raining pussycats. You've got absolutely no bloody chance of finding it. I'll take you.'

'I can't ask you to do that,' Smithdown said.

'I know you can't,' Jenny said. 'Because you're a stubborn old sod. That's why I'm offering. Brian? Get some boots and waterproofs for our guest - we're going for a yomp.'

CHAPTER THIRTY

7.55 pm Monday 4 April 1988

Brian McIntyre's boots almost fitted Smithdown. But not quite. Barely a hundred yards up the farm track from the Glossop road the detective could feel them pinching his heels and digging into the top of his feet. It didn't help that he was walking at least 20 per cent faster than he normally would as he tried to keep up with Jenny Seddon. She strode seemingly without effort up the incline as it took them up onto the moors. The orangey glow of Hayfield began to fade behind them as the dark slopes and bends of the landscape began to make themselves known. So did the noises: the bird cries, the wind across the coarse grasses, the sounds of multiple brooks and streams in all directions filling with light, misty rain. This was the second time that Smithdown had been in the shadow of Kinder Scout at night and he had come to a conclusion that he didn't like it - not one little bit.

As they progressed up and through the clough, there was an added atmospheric touch that seemed almost designed to unsettle them: a faint waterfall of smoke that tumbled down the sides of the narrow valley and snaked towards them like a white magic carpet. It smelled like steamed vegetables. 'What the fuck is that all about?' Smithdown asked, as the smoke approached them and began to curl around their boots.

'This is grouse country,' Jenny replied, maintaining the pace up the track. 'The moor managers will have been burning back the sphagnum moss - the stuff you see on top of the peat. They control the moorland vegetation to make it easier for the knobs to shoot the grouse. It's getting pretty cold now. The smoke that's been rising all day is falling back and it's making its way down the moors. Bit spooky, isn't it?'

Their head torches lit up the top of the smoke as they watched their footing; the path began to give way to open moorland. 'I fucking hate this place,' Smithdown muttered. "It's like fucking Scooby Doo. When this is all done with, I'm never, ever coming back to Derbyshire ever again.'

'You big soft get,' Jenny laughed. 'It's just a bit of smoke.'

'I mean it. There's too much weird bollocks going on around here for my taste.'

As they crested the brow of the next hill, Smithdown could see the lights of Stalybridge and Oldham in the distance across the top of the next ridge. Then they dropped down, the detective slipping a few times but just about managing to keep on his feet. In the tight valley below, he could see the murky outline of a single-story brick building. The two windows and the doorway at the front were covered in metal shutters and there were signs warning that this was a DANGEROUS BUILDING and that people should KEEP OUT. Smithdown looked around. The smoke from the moors rippled slowly past them, following the contours of the route they'd just taken. 'I was here a few years ago,' Jenny said. 'I don't remember it being like this.'

Smithdown touched the nearest shutter and ran a finger around it. He did the same on the second front window and the door. 'All the fixings look pretty new,' he said.

The two detectives circled the lodge. There were more shuttered windows behind the building and a plastic barrel of builders' debris. Again, Smithdown touched the windows - one was fitted slightly less snugly than the rest. He kicked over the barrel and, without prompting, DC Seddon began to dig through the contents. Her search produced several pieces of two by four wood and some metal offcuts from the shutters. Smithdown worked the metal piece behind the loose shutter and bent it back far enough to slip the wood inside. They both pulled back and down, hanging their combined weight onto the wood; the metal shutter's fixings popped off and the window covering clanged against the side of the lodge as it tumbled down. 'Nice one, DC Seddon,' Smithdown said. 'I'll be putting you forward for a commendation.'

'Unlikely,' she pointed out. 'You're on suspension.'

Smithdown emptied the remaining bits of rubbish from the barrel onto the ground and upended it, placing it near the exposed window to act as a step. He went first, putting his hand through the window frame as he took a quick glance around the inside. The light from his headtorch scoured the interior: some boxes, a barrel with wood in it, nothing much to a report. He climbed in then turned his back to the inside of the lodge and helped DC Seddon through the gap. He felt a shudder of discomfort - fear - as he did so.

With the combined light of both head torches they could see a little better. The detectives started to look slowly around the inside of the lodge, their sweep starting just to the right of the main door. The inside was clean - as if it had been recently swept. Thirty or forty folding metal chairs were stacked neatly in one corner. In the next corner were the boxes. Very similar to the one's at Tom Lennon's house.

They continued to turn their heads slowly in unison, trying to keep their light beams together. The light dimmed as it went far into the lodge. Then the light seemed to stop suddenly as it hit the broad figure of a man, standing so close they could touch him. 'Fuck me!' cried Smithdown, instinctively pushing both hands out and stepping back sharply, almost losing his balance.

The figure rocked backwards, then lunged at them. Then back again. Then silence. It was broken by a whispered voice: 'Dummy,' DC Seddon said, holding the yellowy gaze of her head torch onto the dark, inanimate figure on a sprung stand. 'It's a martial arts practice dummy. Try and keep it together Mr Smithdown.'

The DI stared at the figure. It wobbled slightly where he'd struck it and the spring below the main torso squeaked. It was pitted with dents and marks and the head was being held together by electrical tape. 'Try to swing your punch a bit more from the hip next time, she added.

'I'm going right off you, DC Seddon,' whispered Smithdown.

In the third corner of the lodge was a tub of wood, similar to the one they'd found outside. Their headtorches revealed the wood to be baseball bats, a dozen or more. Finally, their torches came full circle and illuminated the door. Painted on the inside of the metal shutter was the white face of a wolf. It was a simple design that looked like it had been spray-painted with a stencil - two pointy ears, a triangular face and two slits for eyes. Underneath the face, two long-handled machetes had been mounted on the wall, so the blades crossed. 'Oh, look,' sighed DC Seddon, 'they've got a logo. Very important to have an easily recognised symbol to represent what you're trying to do. It's good for your brand; increases sales.'

'And what exactly do you reckon is being sold here, DC Seddon?'

'Being a racist dickhead, I'd say, Mr Smithdown,' she replied. 'Being a very dangerous racist dickhead, to be precise.'

'I think you're probably right,' he replied.

They approached the plastic barrel; Smithdown pulled out a baseball bat. It was dented and chipped. A closer look revealed that they all were. Then to the boxes. Some were small and shallow, others larger and deeper. 'I saw boxes like this at Tom Lennon's house,' Smithdown said. 'Loads of them.'

The detective pulled at the brown parcel tape that held one of the smaller boxes shut. Inside were stacks of A5 flyers. Smithdown held one up so it connected with the beam from Jenny's headtorch.

ST GEORGE'S DAY UPRISING!

ARE YOU SICK OF IMMIGRANT GANGS RUNNING RIOT IN OUR TOWN? ATTACKING EACH OTHER WITH MACHETES!?

DO YOU FEAR FOR OUR MOTHERS, SISTERS AND DAUGHTERS AFTER THE RECENT SPATE OF SEX ATTACKS ON WHITE WOMEN AND YOUNG GIRLS IN OUR COMMUNITY?

THE RACIST INTIMIDATION OF WHITE, WORKING CLASS PEOPLE (WHO ARE THE BEDROCK OF OLDHAM) MUST END!

THIS IS OUR TOWN… OUR COUNTRY!
FOR TOO LONG WE HAVE BEEN TREATED LIKE SECOND CLASS CITIZENS!

THAT ENDS ON SATURDAY APRIL 23rd
ST GEORGE'S DAY!

JOIN US AT 12 NOON OUTSIDE OLDHAM TOWN HALL!

(Security by English Wolves)

'Christ Almighty,' Smithdown. 'That's what that bastard Lennon's trying to provoke. A full-on fucking race war.'

'I hadn't heard about this spate of sex attacks in Oldham,' said DC Seddon. 'When did they happen?'

'There's a reason you haven't heard about them,' Smithdown replied, causing the light from his head torch to dance back and forward in the dark as he shook his head. 'That's because they haven't happened yet. Because that's the final outrage Tom fucking Lennon has up his sleeve. That's still to come. Kick things off with a few machete attacks to get things going - get the communities turning on each other. That's a cracking start, isn't it? Then some murder. Got to have some murder, haven't you? Then a bit of rioting - film it, obviously, and make sure the telly people get their hands on the footage. Then organise sex attacks on white girls to really stoke things up. Once you've got everyone close to boiling point, put them in one place on St George's Day, then... Boom.'

Smithdown opened one of the larger boxes. Inside were Styrofoam chips; he brushed the top layer aside. Underneath were Stanley knives - sixty at least in the first box. Smithdown pushed out one of the blades then clicked it back into place. 'That's nice,' the detective said quietly. 'Just in case the whole starting-a-race-war thing doesn't work out, they're doing a bit of carpet-laying on the side.'

DC Seddon pulled the boxes away from the wall. Tucked behind them was a folded up Black and Decker Workmate. She pulled it out. The main clamping section was covered in what appeared to be blood. 'And a bit of DIY surgery on the side,' she said.

'Fucking Nora,' Smithdown said. 'Naomi - that poor girl.'

'So, it really was her, then... At the Mermaid's Pool?'

'Maybe. Maybe not. There are so many missing persons on the go, who knows? This thing gets messier by the minute. And I reckon that's exactly what Tom Lennon and his mates want. Mess. Chaos. The more messy and chaotic the merrier. The more he muddies the water, the harder it is for us to see what he's really up to. But now we know. It's war.'

The two detectives stood quietly for a moment. Jenny put several flyers and a Stanley knife into the pocket of her jacket.

'That's great,' Smithdown said. 'But we need more evidence. We need to show the scale of this. But we can't drag this lot down the moors, can we?'

'No, but we can photograph it,' Jenny replied, producing a Boots instamatic camera and a cube flash from her jacket. 'I've got a few frames left from my holidays.'

'Good thinking, DC Seddon. We're just like *Dempsey and Makepeace*, you and me, aren't we? My wife loves that show.'

Jenny attached the flash cube to the camera and checked the counter to see how many frames she had left. 'Mind your eyes,' she told Smithdown.

He took her advice. She took a picture of the bats, then the knives, then the wolf logo on the door. Finally, she took a picture of the bloodied Back and Decker. Each flash dazzled Smithdown despite him covering his eyes with his hand. 'Let's go,' DC Seddon said, as the final frame was taken.

The blinding light from each photo had burned a round shape on the detective's retinas that took a while to shift as they made their back down the valley. The four flashes from the camera had been efficiently contained by the walls of the shuttered lodge, except for the window they'd removed. The light from each of the flashes had escaped through that window, bounced against the side of the clough behind the building and ricocheted across the moors. Four ultra-bright signals that cut through the night.

Tom Lennon and five of his fellow English Wolves saw the flashes from their tents on the other side of the valley. They immediately broke camp and headed towards the lodge.

'BBC Manchester News at seven this is Richard Hemmingway. Firefighters have spent the night tackling a blaze on moorland in North Derbyshire. Fire crews from two counties were called to the scene at around 10 o'clock yesterday evening in an area known as Burnt Hill close to Kinder Scout, as Vince Hunt Reports.'

'Burnt Hill lived up to its name last night as emergency crews from Glossop and Hyde converged on the fire which started on moorland near the village of Hayfield.

The heart of the blaze - which centred on an abandoned hunting lodge - was too far from a water source to use fire hoses, so it had to be dealt with by hand by firefighters using beaters to extinguish the flames inch by inch.

An investigation is now underway into the exact cause of the blaze, but it's thought that it may been started deliberately.

In the meantime, fire chiefs say that during wildfire season - the middle of March to the end of May - the public should take extra care while visiting the moors. And they're advising people to stay away from the area around Burnt Hill. Vince Hunt, BBC Manchester News, Hayfield.'

CHAPTER THIRTY-ONE

7.45 am Tuesday 5 April 1988

Smithdown grabbed an uncomfortable few hours' sleep on Jenny Seddon's sofa before he was woken by all three of her children. They were standing close - very close - to his face and giggling as he opened his eyes. 'He's awake!' they cried, triumphantly. 'He's awake! Mum! The old copper man is awake!'

Sensing that their work here was probably done, the children ran off. Smithdown heard a kettle click on and fire up. A mug of tea appeared on the coffee table close to the detective without comment. He took it and - fully dressed - hauled himself upright.

'Guess what?' Jenny said.

'Go on.'

'There was a fire last night out near the lodge. Must have started after we'd gone.'

'Well that's a fucking coincidence,' Smithdown said, causing a ripple of giggles from Jenny's children. 'Good job I suggested we take some photos, isn't it?'

'What would we do without you?' Jenny offered dryly. 'So - what's the plan then?'

'Shouldn't you be in work?'

'I wish I was. School holidays. This lot are going to my mum's in Buxton for the day.'

Smithdown took another glug of his tea and popped a cigarette between his lips. He noticed that all three children were watching him from the other side of the door frame, so he put the cigarette back in the packet. 'I'd better go home before my wife reports me missing.'

Smithdown took his tea into the kitchen, tipped a quarter of it down the sink, topped it up with cold water and drank the lukewarm brew down. DC Seddon held out the instamatic film cartridge from her camera. 'You'll be needing this,' she said. 'Please excuse the swimwear shots. I might be a bit pissed on some of them, too.'

'I'll get the pics sorted asap,' Smithdown said, smiling. 'Then I'll meet you down at Oldham nick at one o'clock and we'll take them to the DS. I might have to wait outside to start with as I'm not supposed to enter the police station. Then I'm sure the DS will immediately see the light, give me a promotion and a huge pay rise and say no more about it.'

'Hmmm - will he though?' Jenny asked. 'Didn't you rip some kids lip open?'

'Technically, yes, but let's try to look forward rather than dwelling on the past.'

'Didn't it happen, like, a few days ago or something?'

'I'll see myself out,' he offered, heading for the door. He opened his wallet and stuck a ten pound note into the hand of the eldest of the children as he passed, making a circular motion with his finger to indicate it was for all three of them. They cheered their approval and took off up the stairs like a trio of ginger rockets.

'I saw that, DI John Smithdown,' Jenny said as he was leaving. 'Adding bribery to your list of crimes isn't going to help matters. I'll see you at one.'

During the drive back home to Oldham, Smithdown ran through the way he wanted things to pan out over the next few hours. He made a mental list:

Return to lodge - anything left worth salvaging?
Stage simultaneous searches of Tom Lennon's house and Kingdom club.
Eliminate King from enquiry?
Public appeal to capture Tom Lennon.
Arrest TL - multiple counts of murder and attempted murder, abduction, offences under 1986 Public Order Act for inciting racial hatred and of riot. Criminal damage? Probably not worth it but see if it sticks.
Missing-from-homes - poor lad that disappeared after Mustafizur was attacked seems to have got lost in all this. TL connection? Ditto missing councillor. What's Pym doing? Enough? Anything?
Question TL over abduction and murder of Naomi Wells and possibly of Councillor Chowdhury.
Question TL over three attempted murders (including Kate).
Pray. Pray. Pray that Kate is okay.
Check on Jean.

When he arrived home, he could smell toast. *I'm famished. I could murder some toast.* He heard his wife's voice from the living room: 'John!' she shouted. She sounded far cheerier than he was expecting, joyous almost. 'In here,' she cried again, impatiently. 'Quick, quick. Great news from the hospital, love.'

Jean Smithdown was sitting in her favourite armchair, facing the morning sunshine. Her pale face was alive with energy and excitement. The detective knelt by her side. 'It's our Kate,' she explained, grabbing her husband's hand. 'She's conscious. She's talking. She's going to be alright. Oh John, she's going to be alright.'

The detective felt the heat of tears in his eyes. He put a hand around the back of his wife's neck, pulled her to him and kissed her cheek. 'I was going to go and visit her on my way to the station,' he said. 'Did the hospital ring?'

'No,' she said with a smile and a nodded across the room. ''Tom was there this morning. He came straight here to tell us, bless him.'

Standing next to their living room window, with its commanding view across the moors, Tom Lennon saluted Smithdown with a half-eaten piece of toast and popped the remainder in his mouth. 'Cracking toast, Jean,' Lennon said with a grin. Smithdown outwardly returned his smile. *I will fucking kill you, Tom Lennon. I swear to fucking God, I will.*

'So good of him, John,' Jean said in a quiet voice. 'With Maureen being so ill and all.'

'Least I could do, Jean,' Lennon said. 'Mr Smithdown took the time to visit my mam at the hospital, didn't you? I thought it was only right and proper for me to keep an eye on Kate after what some piece of shit did to her. Sorry for the language, Jean.'

'I've said considerably worse over the last 24 hours, Tom,' Jean replied, pushing herself up from her chair. 'Considerably.'

'Tea and toast for you too, John?' she asked. 'Tom can fill you in. Then you can let me know what's happening with you and James Pym. I'm sure you said some things that you didn't really mean in the heat of the moment. Doubtless it can all be sorted out. You two are like a pair of kids, honestly. They've been like this for years, Tom.'

Jean Smithdown walked carefully to the kitchen, occasionally touching pieces of furniture for support as she went. Smithdown waited for her to leave the room and heard the click of the kettle and the twin rattle of two pieces of bread going into the toaster. Smithdown paused for a few seconds until the kettle began to noisily whoosh, then he rushed across the room with a speed that seemed to take the younger man by surprise. The detective put his face as close to Lennon's as the height difference would allow. The younger man reeked of smoke. Smithdown had never felt such hatred for any other human being in his life. He could feel it in his bones. His hands shook and he had difficulty speaking.

'No need to thank me, John,' Lennon whispered, with a wink.

'What is it you want, lad?' Smithdown asked. 'What is all this for?'

'An end to new Commonwealth and Pakistan immigration, a properly financed system of repatriation, voluntary to start with; the repeal of the so-called Race Relations Act and the abolition of the ludicrous anti-white organisation known as the Commission for Racial Equality.' Lennon almost chanted the words as if he'd said them many times before. 'We want Oldham back. And then we want our country back.'

'How much of this is you?' Smithdown asked. 'The murders, the attacks, the missing people. Most of it? All of it?'

'Haven't you heard the news?' Lennon whispered. 'All that stuff is waaaay down the running order. Asian-on-white violence. Asian-on-Asian violence. It's really kicking off but all anyone cares about is the riots and the way immigrant filth are destroying this town. Damage to property outweighs damage to people every time. I did a media degree, John. Did you know that? Or did you just think I was just another bull-necked thicko fired up by what they've read in *The Sun* or heard down the pub? I think not. I've studied the way news cycles work. How they need to be fed. If it bleeds it leads. If it burns, it earns.'

Smithdown pulled a leaflet from his pocket - one of the A5 flyers he'd found with DC Seddon at the abandoned lodge. He pushed it into Lennon's face, then tucked it into the neck of his Fred Perry polo shirt. 'Sex attacks? Is that what's next? Raping girls and then blaming it on other communities?'

Lennon grabbed the flyer and looked at it. He smiled and tutted with mock disapproval at the contents. 'Looks like people are very upset, Mr Smithdown. You and your mates in the police haven't been looking after this town properly. Well, some of your mates have. There are a few good souls in Oldham police. Some genuine people who want what's right for this town. They're alright. In the meantime, thank goodness for the English Wolves. They'll provide protection when and where it's needed.'

'You're fucking thick, lad,' Smithdown spat. 'We saw what was up in that lodge. Saw what you're planning. It's over.'

'No, Mr Smithdown,' Lennon countered. 'You're fucking thick. There's nothing to tie me to the lodge, or the Wolves, or any of it. That lodge was cleaned out spic and span after you left. Then torched. Which leaves you with what? My word against yours. My word against some old soak who's on suspension for abusing a little girl. Some bitter old fuck who's not right in the head over his sick wife and his druggie daughter. No mate. The only person it's over for is you. We're just getting started.'

Lennon pushed his Harrington jacket lightly to one side and put his hand to his hip. He had a leather sheath strapped to chest. In it was the biggest knife Smithdown had ever seen. Lennon wobbled his head and winked at him. 'If you go near my mother again,' Lennon said. 'I'll gut your wife and then your daughter, understand? It's simple. Stay away from me, stay away from the town centre and stay away from the Wolves until after St George's Day. All you need to do is potter about your garden for a few weeks on suspension. That's it. Watch some telly. Go for a walk or two. Take Jean for a nice pub lunch. Keep the fuck out of the way. That's all. No one's going to listen to some mad old cop who abuses children anyway.'

'We've got photos, lad. A detective from Derbyshire saw it with her own eyes.'

'Have you now,' Lennon smiled. Again, the wink. The knife that Lennon had shown him had rattled the detective. But it was the wink that really worried him.

'Will you have another cuppa, Tom?' Jean Smithdown said as she re-entered the living room. The two men stepped slightly apart.

'I'm alright Jean. I'll get on my way. Things to do. People to see. Take care Mr Smithdown. And think on.'

Jean Smithdown touched Lennon's arm as he passed. 'Give my best to your mam, Tom. I'll be thinking about her. And you. All the best.'

'That's very kind, Jean,' Lennon said. 'Will do. All the best to you. I hope your Kate makes a full recovery. I know she will.'

Lennon leaned in and kissed Jean Smithdown lightly on the cheek. 'I'll be seeing you,' he said with a smile.

Jean and John Smithdown watched as Lennon walked briskly up their driveway. Moments later a motorbike whizzed past their front gate. Lennon was still putting his helmet on in the pillion position. The couple watched the bike fade into the moorland road towards Oldham town centre.

'I'd better ring the hospital,' Smithdown said. 'Just to make sure Kate's okay.'

'Yes, you'd better,' she replied. 'Oh, and John?'

'Yes love?'

'Could you also make absolutely sure that piece of shit gets everything that's coming to him?'

'I will indeed, love. Everything.'

'Good. Because he's a bloody wrong 'un.'

Once out of sight of the Smithdown's house, Tom Lennon instructed Adam Griffin to take the road to Uppermill then head for Glossop.

Lennon knew exactly where he wanted to go - before he'd arrived at Smithdown's house a friend of the English Wolves in the Derbyshire Constabulary had given him the address of DC Jenny Seddon's house.

CHAPTER THIRTY-TWO

8.50 am Tuesday 5 April 1988

There was no way that Smithdown would ever let Bob Donaldson see him with even the hint of a tear in his eye. But the sight that met him as he walked into Kate's hospital room made it very difficult for the detective to keep his emotions in order. Kate was awake and she gave him a woozy smile. Next to her, slumped in an uncomfortable looking hospital chair, was DC Donaldson - fast asleep.

"I think he's been here all night," Kate whispered to her dad.

He leant in and kissed her cheek. Her hair seemed to have absorbed that smell that only occurs in hospitals. Smithdown breathed it in like it was the most addictive perfume ever. *Thank you, thank you, thank you for giving me my little girl back.*

Donaldson's head popped up in a way clearly designed to give the impression he hadn't been asleep at all. 'Morning, sir,' he said. 'Nothing to report here. All quiet. Mind you, I'm not supposed to be talking to you at the minute, am I?' He winked at Smithdown. ' This guy is mad, bad and dangerous to know Kate.'

'Bob, what the hell are you doing here,' Smithdown said. 'My God, I appreciate it, but I didn't expect you to be here, let alone be here all night. I'm sure the staff had things under control.'

'Well, you never know, do you?' Donaldson said. 'Open spaces, these hospitals. Anyone could be coming in and out. And we can't have that, can we?'

'You're right. We can't. Have you seen anyone that had no business being here?'

'Tom Lennon was sniffing about early doors. I saw him off, the cocky twat.'

'Thank you, Bob. I mean it. Thank you. You won't believe what that shit's been up to. Now's not the time. I'm hoping to get in to see the DS at lunchtime to show him what I've got. It's chilling. Absolutely fucking chilling.'

'Okay. Christ - the madness continues. I'd better get myself down the road, then. Take care Kate.'

'Thank you, Bob,' she whispered as he headed out of the room. Her eyelids began to close with tiredness.

Smithdown handed the DC the film cartridge he had in his jacket pocket. He whispered, so his daughter couldn't hear: 'Take this to Paul Rees in photographic.' Smithdown checked his watch. 'I need two sets of the last four or five frames by one o'clock. I've got that DC from Derbyshire coming over to back me up. Tell Paul to ignore any holiday snaps. What I'm interested in is the weapons stash we found up at Hayfield. Not to mention the fucking Black and Decker torture chamber they had set up there, too.'

'Just gets worse and worse this, doesn't it?' Bob said. 'Okay. Will do.'

'I'll sit with her for a while,' Smithdown said. He put out his hand. They shook. 'Thanks again for what you've done, Bob.'

'Not a problem. All I did was keep an eye on things. You'd do the same for me, I'm sure.'

'I would, Bob. No question. Though I hope you never find yourself in a situation half as bad as this.'

CHAPTER THIRTY-THREE

9.35 am Tuesday 5 April 1988

'Just a minute,' Jenny Seddon shouted as she put on her dressing gown and ran down the stairs. After rushing to get the children ready to be picked up by her mum, she'd showered quickly and was getting ready for the 25-minute drive to Oldham when the doorbell rang. She could see the outline of the delivery man though the frosted glass of her front door. Bloody nuisance she thought as he rang the bell for a second time. 'JUST A MINUTE!' the DC cried, then stubbed her toe on the small hallway table. 'Christ Almighty,' she muttered as she got to the front door and turned the lock. 'Sorry,' she said, looking at the spilt in her toenail *thanks to that stupid bloody table.* 'I was upstairs. It's not for those lazy buggers across the road again, is it?'

As she opened the door fully, a fist shot forwards, hitting her square on the nose, knocking her glasses from her face. The blood had already begun to pour by the time the second and third blows came in. She saw them land in the reflection framed in the visor of her attacker's motorbike helmet.

Right, left, right. Boxer. Well-trained. Oh shit. Oh shit, shit, shit.

She fell backwards and the back of her leg caught the small table that supported the phone, a few directories and several framed photos of her family.

I'm always banging into that, should have moved it years ago. Too late now.

As Jenny hit the bottom of the stairs the man was on top of her, his hands around her throat. She had trained for situations similar to this many times, but her options right now were severely limited. She couldn't move back because of the stairs and his weight. Left and right were closed off because of the walls either side of the narrow staircase. The cold black helmet meant attacking his eyes was a waste of time. The high-collared leather jacket that he wore protected his neck, collar bones and Adam's apple.

Fuck. This is bad. So very, very bad. Thank God the kids aren't here. Oh Christ, my kids.

Again, DC Seddon's training held firm. She tried to bring her knee up, hoping to connect with his groin. Once, twice, a third time. But he was so close the best she could manage was a few glancing blows against his hip. She felt for the pressure points on the back of his hands and between the thumb and forefinger. The thick biker gloves he wore stopped her getting a firm hold.

Think.

She tried to grab one of his fingers to wrench it back; his hands were quite far around her neck. It was difficult, but she managed to connect with the forefinger of his right hand and pulled hard. He let go of his grip briefly only to punch her again, fracturing her eye socket. Both hands went straight back to Jenny's neck - she knew she was about to pass out.

Last go. Last chance.

The DC grabbed below the lower part of his helmet, her fingers skittered around the strapping until she found the release catch and yanked it. She slowly pulled off the helmet to see the blotchy face of a man in his 20s. Adam Griffin was laughing at her, sticking out his tongue and crossing his eyes, making fun of her distress. 'Like I give a shit that you can see my face,' he whispered. 'Too fucking late now, love.' His grip around her neck tightened.

DC Seddon smashed the back edge of the helmet against his nose as hard as she could. It took a second blow to break it. The hands loosened as he screamed in pain. Griffin pulled slightly away from her; the space this created allowed her a better upward swing and she hit him twice more, the full weight of the helmet creating two small compression fractures either side of his head. He fell backwards.

Yes! Thank you. Yes.

Her training told her that she was far from being free of danger. Was she prepared to kill her attacker?

Abso-fucking-lutely.

She managed to get to her feet, took two shaky steps forward, raised the helmet above her head and was about to drop down and pin his arms under her knees when he rolled to one side, got to his feet and took a few steps back. They looked at each other for a moment. A few beats of silence apart from their matching heavy gasps for air. Then Jenny Seddon looked straight at him, crossed her eyes and stuck out her tongue. Her teeth were covered in blood. 'I will FUCKING DO YOU,' the DC shouted as she ran towards him. With both hands she heaved the helmet at his face. Griffin's head bounced off the wall and then re-connected with the helmet generating a satisfying rat-a-tat sound.

Jenny collapsed onto the muddy hall carpet; she looked up and saw him grab the instamatic camera from the table.

It's empty, you daft fuck.

Then Griffin dragged himself through the door before she lost consciousness.

Good job, Jenny love. Proud of you.

Then, with no more fight left in her, she let go.

It would be nearly an hour before she was discovered by the postman.

CHAPTER THIRTY-FOUR

10.45 am Tuesday 5 April 1988

Kate remembered nothing about what happened to her at the Kingdom club and Smithdown knew that now wasn't the time to push her for more information about it.

Sitting in his car outside the hospital the detective weighed up the options. He had time to kill while he waited for Jenny Seddon and having assaulted a minor, engineered his own suspension and carried out some low-key breaking and entering, Smithdown took the view that he now had very little to lose. He didn't want to cause Bob any more problems by being seen with him as he wasn't supposed to have contact with any officers from GMP while his suspension continued, but no one said that he couldn't go and knock on a MP's door.

Everyone in Oldham knew where Peter Jeffries MP lived. His farmhouse stood high on a hill overlooking the village of Alt, to the south-east of the town centre close to the Tameside border. The slope underneath the house featured a billboard pointing in the direction of Oldham that could be seen for miles. Against a vivid Tory-blue background was a head and shoulders shot of Jeffries, his round face set in a stern frown. One eyebrow was raised in a challenging manner; the photo matched the catchline emblazoned on the poster in white, capital letters:

PETER JEFFRIES: FIGHTING FOR OLDHAM,
FIGHTING FOR YOU.

Jeffries' dogs - two rottweilers and a red setter - came galloping up the driveway to meet the detective. Smithdown waited until the MP shooed them away before he got out of his car. Smithdown's Ford looked rather tatty parked next to Jeffries' collection of classic cars; the MP had been polishing a sky-blue vintage Jaguar as Smithdown arrived. Despite this task he was wearing two-thirds of a three-piece suit. He put down the polishing cloth he'd been using, put on his jacket and set about crushing

Smithdown's hand. 'Come in Detective Inspector - though it's just plain John at the moment, isn't it? Until that small matter of child assault is cleared up…'

'Look, there is an explanation behind that,' Smithdown said as he dipped his head to avoid the beam over the doorway and entered Jeffries' country-style kitchen.

'I know there is. You caused that girl a little bit of pain to save her from a great deal more pain. I understand. And given that her mum's now been murdered, and her abusive boyfriend is dead, it looks like you did the right thing. Tea?'

'I could murder one, thanks.'

Jeffries provided Smithdown with tea in a Margaret Thatcher mug. The MP took a seat at the rustic pine kitchen table and gestured for the detective to join him. 'What's on your mind, John?'

'The Far-Right.'

'There's plenty of people in Oldham that would call me the Far-Right, John.'

'You're a hang 'em and flog 'em Tory, Mr Jeffries. I'm talking about neo-Nazis. What do you know about the English Wolves?'

'I don't know a great deal,' the MP said, choosing his words with care. 'But I've heard quite a bit. All of it bad. Very bad.'

'What have you heard?' the detective asked.

'When we spoke yesterday, I told you the Right were on the rise,' Jeffries said. 'People thought they'd faded away because they didn't fight the last General Election, but they're back under a different guise. They're seeking legitimacy, challenging the mainstream parties for political power. They're shredding the old look - the classic skinhead and bovver boots - and putting suits on. But the new men in suits still need protection. If they're going to go out on the campaign trail, they'll be targeted by Left wing agitators at every public meeting, every speech, every attempt to engage with the public. So, the Wolves are their protection squad.'

'How do you know all this, Mr Jeffries?'

'John. Please. I'm a politician. It's in my interest to know where my next political rivals might be coming from. What do you know about the English Wolves?'

Smithdown rubbed his unshaven face: 'It's more what I think I know,' he said, cautiously. 'I think they've been stoking up trouble between the Pakistani and Bangladeshi communities; I think they're using it to bait the white working class population and stoke up racial tensions; I think they're feeding video footage to the media that backs up their version of events. I think the murder of Naomi Wells - the girl at Kinder Scout - and your missing councillor are tied in too. I reckon these English Wolves have soaked this town in their own brand of racist petrol and I think they're planning to throw a match on it by using rape as a weapon on the run up to St George's Day.'

'My God,' Jeffries said. 'That's insane.'

Smithdown showed the MP the flyer he'd taken from the lodge at Hayfield. 'I also think they dosed my daughter as a warning to me and I've just found their top lad Tom Lennon at my house with a knife as long as the Huddersfield Road.'

'Tom Lennon? I see.'

'Yes, Mr Jeffries. Tom fucking Lennon. Mate of yours, is he?'

'No, Mr Smithdown. No friend of mine. He volunteered as a helper in my office a few years ago. Stuffing envelopes, making tea. That's all. But you could tell he was there to watch. To learn. We let him go when we found out he'd been doing the same thing with the other political parties too. He was spying, of course, but not for anyone else. He was spying on behalf of himself.'

'What, so he could get into politics?'

'No. Not politics as it stands. Something else. He was angry at the apathy of voters, especially what he called the indigenous population. The white working class. He believed that many problems could be traced back to their inaction. He was like any young person who flirts with politics, they always want to do things differently. And it looks like he's found a very, very different way of doing things.'

'I think what's happened so far has just been the warm-up act,' Smithdown said. 'Come St George's Day, with everyone stoked up after these targeted sex attacks, that's when it'll really kick off. A full-on white riot. Then good old Tommy Lennon can stroll in, like the Great White Saviour, and legitimise the Far-Right so they can get a handful of actual political power.

'No, no John. I don't think so. He's too clever for that. There's nothing to link him to the Wolves, I imagine?'

'Not directly, no,' the detective admitted.

'Of course there isn't. I imagine he'll drop the Wolves like a stone once St George's Day is done. He'll step forward as the appeaser, Mr Reasonable, the man who can understand how tensions can boil over but would never, ever condone violence. No - I think he'll stand as an independent in the upcoming council elections as the genuine voice of working-class Oldham and play the man-of-the-people card. He could win by a landslide. Then he'll be onhis way.'

'Didn't you think about coming to the police with your suspicions, Mr Jeffries?' the detective asked.

'They're just that. Suspicions. If I were to head to your police station every time I had concerns about racists in Oldham, I might as well move in.'

'You sound like my daughter,' Smithdown said.

'I heard about what happened. How is she?'

'She's on the mend,' the detective replied, feeling himself getting upset and angry all over again. 'Thank you for asking. And thank you for your time, Mr Jeffries. And the tea. And the information. I'll be back to take a statement from you. If they let me back on the force, that is.'

CHAPTER THIRTY-FIVE

1.20pm Tuesday 5 April 1988

DC Seddon was already 20 minutes late. *Not like her - not her style at all.* Smithdown leant against the metal railings that led to the Oldham Police station entrance and smoked a JPS.

He'd been there since 12.45 and he wasn't particularly enjoying the experience. Colleague after colleague, people he'd known for decades, had passed him with the merest of nods. Some had avoided eye contact with him altogether; several had clearly turned on their heels and gone another way so as not to breathe the same air as him.

One person didn't: Bob Donaldson waved then jogged down the slope from the main entrance towards Smithdown. 'Hi Bob. Is the DS free?' the detective asked. 'I'm still waiting for DC Seddon.'

'Pym won't see you. He says it's for your own good. If you're spotted in the building you've had it when it comes to your disciplinary. It's bad enough that half the force has already seen you hanging around here.'

'Did you show him the photos?' Smithdown asked.

'I didn't.'

'Could you go back in and put them under his nose. That'll change his mind.'

'I wish I could.'

'Bob, please.'

'I can't because there's nothing on them. Some nice snaps of your mate and her kids on the beach but that's about it. The last few frames didn't come out. The lad in photographic says he's tried his best, but they've come out blank.'

'Fucking Nora. Are you sure?'

'Positive.'

'Jesus wept - we're being nobbled here, Bob. Fucking Pym. I knew it.'

The two men stood in silence for a moment: 'Is it true that you got yourself suspended on purpose?' Donaldson asked.

'Who told you that?'

'The lad in photographic says you forced him to grass you up about that Wells kid.'

'He's got a lot to learn that lad.'

Bob put an arm on Smithdown's shoulder. 'Permission to say something that you probably won't like?'

'Go on then.'

Donaldson pointed to the Oldham Borough coat of arms above the door to the police station. The scroll at the bottom said: *Sapere Aude*.

'Dare to Be Wise. Very good, Bob. Never had you down as a Latin scholar.'

'Good advice, though, innit? Clear off, boss. Go back to the hospital. Spend time with Kate. Take Jean out for lunch. Get away from here. You've got more on your plate than anyone should have to deal with at home, let alone all the shit that's been going on here. We're on it: the attacks on the Asian lad and Mr Aleem; the missing-from-homes, all of it. Half of Oldham is already in custody for rioting and as soon as Kate's well enough I'll be round to take a statement from her personally to see if there's anything in this cstasy business.'

'That twat Tom Lennon did it!' Smithdown shouted, attracting attention from passing shoppers.

'You're not going to like this either then…' sighed Bob.

'This should be good…'

'There's half a dozen witnesses that say they saw Kate buy the gear from a dealer outside Kingdom and then necked it herself.'

'Fuck off, Bob. That's bollocks and you know it.'

'I don't know it,' the DC said, raising his voice for the first time. 'I wish I did, but I don't. I'm trying to help you here but you're making it very difficult. Back off, let us do our jobs. For once, do as Pym asks; I know he's a dick, but it's for the best.'

'What about the missing councillor?'

'He's on it. He's got a DC in Leicester as we speak talking to her family. House to house is happening with her neighbours. Media appeals have been done. I think he sees the brownie point possibilities now Peter Jeffries has stuck his oar in. Police work does actually happen in your absence, you know.'

'Of course, I'm not saying it doesn't…'

'Go. Now. Give my love to Jean. And to Kate.'

'I will, Bob.'

'Straight to the hospital, now. I mean it.'

'I will, Bob. You're dead right.'

The two men exchanged a half salute/half wave as DC Donaldson walked back into the police station.

Smithdown thought for a moment as he finished his cigarette, then he got in his car, put on some Dr Feelgood and headed straight for Tom Lennon's house.

CHAPTER THIRTY-SIX

1.45pm Tuesday 5 April 1988

Smithdown decided that the time for subtlety had long since passed, so he made no effort to disguise the fact that he was tying a rope to the metal window grille protecting Tom Lennon's front window. He made even less of an effort to gloss over the small matter of attaching the other end of the rope to the towing hook of his car.

As he went about his work, Lennon's largely South Asian neighbours began to take an interest in what was going on. Net curtains twitched and were pulled aside; some residents came to their red front doorsteps and debated with their neighbours about what the man in the grey suit was up to. A passing postman lay down his bag of letters and parcels, took a seat on the kerb, lit a cigarette and waited. There was a sense that something worth watching was about to happen.

Smithdown didn't disappoint them.

Pausing a moment to advise a young boy on a bike to stand clear, he got in his car, turned over the engine and accelerated. '*Roxette*' by Dr Feelgood whirred into life from the stereo as he eased the Ford Escort forward. There was a satisfyingly loud pang-pang sound as two sides of the front window grille came away from the wall. As a crowd began to gather, the detective got out of his car, calmly untied the rope from the half-removed grille and tied it to the other side.

He nodded at the postman, who seemed largely unfazed - although clearly fascinated - by what was going in. 'You the police?' the postman asked from his prime position on the kerb.

'For the purposes of this exercise, yes,' Smithdown confirmed.

'No need to call them then, is there?' the postman observed.

'None whatsoever.'

'Best crack on, then.'

'Will do,' the detective said with a smile as he got back in his car and again eased into the accelerator. The final two fixings came away more quickly this time and the window was exposed. The detective reversed then parked his car. One of the many reasons Smithdown preferred to use his own vehicle was the easy access it provided to a variety of household items and tools that he stored in the boot. He took out a small axe, a crowbar and a picnic blanket and walked over to the window. A young mum walked by with a pram: 'Afternoon,' he said, placing the blanket on the ground in front of the window. He waited until she'd passed before jamming the blunt, top end of the axe straight into the glass, resulting in a very loud noise from the glass and an ooh of surprise from the crowd. The blow sent most of the glass tumbling inside the front room of the house. The rest went onto the blanket. He then used the edge of the axe to chip away at the remaining fragments sticking out of the frame and tipped the debris from the blanket through the window.

'You're very tidy, aren't you?' offered the postman.

'Can't have glass on the pavement with kiddies about,' Smithdown pointed out.

'Fair dos,' the postie agreed.

Smithdown placed the blanket over the frame to protect himself from the remaining shards and climbed in, pushing aside the thick curtains. He stepped into a sea of empty beer cans, takeaway boxes and crumpled cigarette packets. All of the smells those items generated were joined by an undertow of vinegary, male sweat - as if someone had set up a bar in a boxing club.

The stencilled wolf logo he'd seen in the abandoned lodge was on the chimney breast above a 1970s style gas fireplace. He trudged through the debris and got to the living room door, which was slightly ajar. He touched the door frame with the head of the axe with the intention of pulling it towards him; then he stopped. There was a sound - maybe heavy steps, maybe banging - from elsewhere in the house. Then a whining sound, the kind a fox might make on the moors at night. Then silence again.

Smithdown yanked the door open, using his axe like a hook, and stepped sharply into the hallway, leading the way with the crowbar in his outstretched arm. Again, there was a bang. More whining. *It's coming from the cellar.* The detective knew the layout of these terraced houses. He'd grown up in one. The cellar door was between the back room and the kitchen. The stone stairs would be steep, the headroom low, the light dim and the room to manoeuvre almost non-existent. *No choice in the matter, down we go.*

The back room of the house was a similar mix of cheap furniture and ankle-high rubbish. It was dark, the heavy blackout curtains at the rear window were open but only slightly apart. The graffiti on the walls was bolder than the front room: alongside the wolf stencils the detective had seen before there was also hand-painted NF and BNP signs as well as several swastikas.

Smithdown stood at the doorway to the cellar. It had three bolts holding it shut at the top, middle and bottom. He could still hear whining and banging. There was a mirror attached to the cellar door and Smithdown looked at himself as he hesitated. He saw a grey-faced, tired looking man with an axe in one hand and a crowbar in the other. *This is mad. Absolutely fucking mad.* He tucked the crowbar into his belt and slid back each bolt as quietly as he could. Then, he stretched out his hand to touch the door's handle. Another bang. Smithdown had to admit to himself that he was scared.

The detective decided to count down in his head before yanking open the door.

Three

Two

Then a figure appeared behind him and Smithdown jumped, turned and pulled back his axe ready to swing. Fortunately, he didn't, otherwise he would have put Uddin Rahman in hospital alongside his brother. 'Fucking Nora, lad! I nearly brained you. What the fuck are you doing here?'

'Half of Oldham is standing in the road watching what's going on,' Uddin pointed out. 'I live nearby, and I thought I'd take a closer look. Good to the see the police finally taking a bit of action. Although I heard on the news that you've been binned off.'

'Let's just say I'm acting in a freelance capacity at the moment and leave it at that, shall we?'

'I thought so - axes aren't normally standard police issue, are they?'

'They might be soon, the way this town's heading. I don't suppose there's any point in asking you to fuck off and leave me to it, is there?'

'None whatsoever,' Uddin confirmed. 'This is the best show in town. Plus, this is Tom Lennon's house - and if you're here that means he's probably got something to do with the attack on my brother. If that's the case, I want to be the first to know about it.'

'How do you know it's Lennon's house?' asked the detective.

'Oh my God! Are you the only person who doesn't know what's going on? Have you seen the outside of this house?'

'Okay. Fair point,' Smithdown conceded.

'He's feeling better now, by the way. My brother. Thanks for asking.'

'That's great. Can we discuss it later? I'm a touch busy. Here, grab this, will you?' Smithdown handed Uddin the crowbar and - without the aid of a countdown this time - opened the cellar door. The grating hinges produced a long, loud screeching sound like air being released from a balloon.

'This is just like being in a film,' Uddin said to the detective.

'Shut... Your... Trap,' Smithdown whispered back as he flicked his lighter to provide some light. It gave enough of a yellowy glow for them to see to the bottom of the steps. The detective was surprised to see another door there. *The cellars in these terraces are open plan. There's no door here normally. Not right at all, this.*

The whitewash on the walls crumbled to the touch as the pair made their way slowly down the cellar steps. It seemed to get colder as they got nearer to the door. The only sound was the scrape of their shoes against the stone steps.

Though the entrance to the cellar was old and untouched, the door at the bottom was clearly new. The wooden frame was fresh pine and the padlock and heavy sliding bolt that accompanied it looked like they'd come straight from a hardware shop.

'It's locked,' Uddin pointed out from halfway up the steps.

Smithdown shooed him back and hit the door with the axe three times around the latch: above it, to the left and below. 'No. It. Isn't,' he said, a syllable for each strike. A fourth blow landed straight onto the bolt and separated it from the door. It lurched open, clattering against the wall behind it.

The smell inside the cellar room was harsh and sour - sweat, bleach and urine hit Smithdown and Uddin as the air from their side of the door rushed in. They heard the noise again. Thud-thud. The whine was louder and more insistent now.

The detective stepped into the cellar room and slowly moved his lighter around. 'Let's see what we can see, Uddin,' Smithdown said.

The detective wasn't too surprised to see boxes and tubs of weapons; they were probably the same knives, bats and machetes he'd seen at the lodge. He was quite surprised to see bags of multi-coloured pills piled up on metal shelving units pushed up against two sides of the room. There were a dozen units with four shelves each - and every shelf had twenty or thirty bags of pills, each one the size of a crisp packet.

He was, however, very surprised indeed to see Naomi Wells handcuffed to the frame of a bare metal bed, banging her head against the wall behind her and trying to shout through the thick strip of electrician's tape across her mouth. The handcuffs - which looked to

Smithdown like they were police issue - were attached to both of her ankles and to her right wrist. It would have been pointless putting handcuffs on her left wrist, because her left hand was missing.

CHAPTER THIRTY-SEVEN

1.50 pm Tuesday 5 April 1988

'Shitting, shitting, shitting hell, Tom,' said Adam Griffin as they watched Smithdown climb through the front window of Lennon's house. 'He's going to find her then we're fucked. I mean really fucked. We can't grab them, there's too many people about. What the fuck are we going to do?'

Griffin had two swollen eyes that were starting to purple up. He had blood-speckled toilet paper sticking out of both nostrils. The two stood in a ginnel between two rows of terraced houses that faced Lennon's. 'We're going to stop acting like a big mard girl with bog roll up her conk and we're going to get a grip of ourselves and then of the situation,' Lennon said. 'That's what we're going to do.'

The two stood in silence. They saw Uddin follow the detective through the window, then they heard the banging of Smithdown's axe against the cellar door. 'We need to send someone to see his daughter. Right now,' Lennon said.

'I'll go,' Griffin said. 'I'll fucking do her, right there in the hospital. I done that cow of a copper in Glossop, I'll do her and all. Makes no odds to me.'

'I think you'll attract too much attention, looking like that,' Lennon pointed out. 'We need to be a bit more low-key, for once. Someone else can go. Then we'll see how keen Mr Smithdown is to help out our Naomi. He might just rethink his priorities.'

CHAPTER THIRTY-EIGHT

2pm Tuesday 5 April 1988

'I will fucking kill the bastard lot of them,' screamed Naomi Wells as Smithdown took away the gaffer tape, releasing a toyshop bouncy ball that had been put in her mouth. It made a bizarre poing-poing sound as it hit the harsh stone cellar floor and rolled under an old table. 'Dirty, bastard fuckers,' she added.

Naomi's left arm was neatly bandaged between the elbow and the end of the stump. She was wearing jogging bottoms, a t-shirt that had once been white and her jet-black hair was plastered to her face. 'I know you!' she shouted. 'You're that DI fucking what's-his-face, aren't you?' What are you going to do me for this time? Loitering in a cellar in possession of one fucking hand?'

'I wasn't expecting that response, if I'm honest,' muttered Smithdown as he inspected the handcuffs. 'It's DI Smithdown, that's right, Naomi. We've lots to talk about, but right now we need to get you out of here as quickly and as quietly as possible. Emphasis on the quietly. Do you think you can walk?'

'I'd rather fucking run,' she replied. 'But I'm every-so-slightly handcuffed to this bleeding bed.'

'Uddin,' the detective said. 'Run up to my car and get my bolt cutters out of the boot. If anyone ask you what's going on, say nowt. If anyone asks you who's in the house, say nowt. If anyone…'

'…I get it, I get it. Say nowt,' he confirmed, tucking the crowbar Smithdown had given him through a belt loop on his baggy jeans.

'Correct.'

The young man took a step backwards then hesitated: 'What happened to your hand?' he asked Naomi.

'I sold it,' she said. It was said in a straightforward, matter-of-fact tone. Smithdown remembered it from when he'd arrested her in the past.

'Sold it?' Uddin shouted in response. 'Sold your hand? For money?'

'Yes.'

'Quietly,' Smithdown reminded them both. 'We're supposed to be doing this quietly.'

'You sold your actual, real-life hand? I'm in shock here. Genuinely. Are you being serious? Oh wow - a second-hand hand! That's just... wow. I mean, who buys hands? Serious question. Who buys hands?'

'Richard T. King,' Naomi said. 'He buys hands.'

CHAPTER THIRTY-NINE

2.25 pm Tuesday 5 April 1988

Detective Constable Bob Donaldson gave a friendly nod and a cheery smile to the reception staff as he walked into Oldham Royal Hospital. He chatted briefly to a hospital porter he vaguely knew; his son was applying for a job with the police and Donaldson wished him the best of luck. He jokingly told an elderly man in a wheelchair to slow down as he passed him on the corridor, winking at the nurse who was pushing him. Then he made his way towards the ward where Kate Smithdown was being treated. He waited until the corridor was clear then opened the door of the private room and quietly stepped inside.

Kate was asleep, her normally spiky hair flattened and pressed against her head. It made her look much younger. Donaldson watched her for at least a minute, making sure she was fully asleep. Then he took the sterile mini scalpel that he'd taken from another ward on his earlier visit from his pocket. It was tiny - the kind they used for cutting away stitches or bandages when a patient had recovered.

In his head he ran through the picture he would paint when he filed his report.

Kate must have pinched it when one of the nurses wasn't looking. Only a little thing, but sharp as anything those blades. The shame of it all was just too much for her, I reckon. Plenty of people saw her buy those drugs but she denied it and denied it. You can't blame her, I suppose, being a copper's daughter. But I never thought for a moment she'd do herself in. Terrible. Just terrible. I've known her since she was this big. Watched her grow up. Just awful to find her like that. Blood everywhere. There was nothing I could do. I called for help straight away but it was too late. It was the way she did it that got me. You don't cut up the arm if you're messing about. You mean it. I blame myself. If only I'd stayed longer to keep an eye on her, maybe it wouldn't have happened. I'm so, so sorry.

Donaldson was about to peel open the scalpel, reminding himself to keep the thin, flat handle inside the foil wrapper to avoid getting his fingerprints on it, when he heard a voice from the corner of the room: 'Hello Bob.'

'Fook me Jean, you nearly had me in coronary care.' The blade went back into his pocket.'What are you doing here?'

Jean Smithdown pushed herself up from the chair in the corner of the room and stood deliberately close to the alarm button next to Kate's bed. For someone so thin she looked incredibly strong. 'I'm on mum duty, that's what I'm doing, Bob. Keeping Kate from harm's way. How about you?'

'I promised John I'd swing past. Have you heard from him?'

'I have. He told me to get myself down to the hospital and keep an eye on our little girl. He said there's a lot of trouble right now and that you've got to look out for your loved ones. Keep them close. Keep them safe. Just in case.'

'He's not daft, your husband.'

'He's not, Bob. And neither am I.'

'So, you won't be needing me?' Bob asked, his hand still on the scalpel in his pocket.

'Definitely not. If there's a problem I just need to press this alarm here and a nurse will come running. I tried it the other day. It's amazing. One press and someone was here in an instant. The staff here are wonderful, they really are. So quick. So attentive. God bless the NHS I say, Bob.'

'Can't disagree with you there, Jean.'

They stood for a moment. Both assessing the situation. Weighing it up. Both knowing, yet not saying. 'I'll be off then,' Donaldson said.

'Goodbye Bob.'

'Bye Jean.'

Jean Smithdown stood perfectly still, her hand still hovering close to the alarm button. She waited until the door was closed and Donaldson's footsteps faded away into the general noise of the hospital. Still she didn't move. It was a good three minutes until she allowed herself to sit down. And weep.

CHAPTER FORTY

2.40 pm Tuesday 5 April 1988

'The police station isn't this way,' Uddin said from the passenger seat of Smithdown's car. 'It's literally the other way. I'd have thought that you, of all people, would know where Oldham Cop Shop is.'

'We're not going to the police station,' the detective pointed out. 'I need somewhere safe, somewhere away from anyone who means Naomi harm. And, unfortunately, that isn't the police station right now.'

'Why is he even here?' Naomi asked the detective from her position lying flat on the back seat of the car. 'He's fucking annoying.'

'That's not very nice,' Uddin said.

'He knows you're alive,' Smithdown pointed out. 'Not many people do. I want him near me. He's got a proper gob on him.'

'Again, not very nice...' Uddin muttered.

'Plus,' the detective added. 'I'm not sure I could have carried you up those stairs on my own.'

They'd created quite a stir in the street when they'd emerged from the house. Smithdown imagined someone giving a description to the police about what they saw: a middle-aged white male, grey hair, moustache, wearing a white shirt and grey trousers... Accompanied by an Asian male, early 20s, wearing a brightly-coloured top and loose-fitting jeans. They were helping a third person into a car - possibly female. The third person had a grey suit jacket covering their face. Some eyewitnesses say this person was holding their arm as if injured.

Smithdown hadn't been sure what to do in the street. Despite how suspicious the scene looked, the people stood and watched in near silence. One elderly man even helped them get Naomi into the car by holding the door open. As they'd lifted Naomi into the car, a plastic bag of pills had fallen from the detective's trouser pocket and hit the kerb. The two men's eyes met for a moment, then the older one picked the bag up and handed it back to Smithdown. There had been a ripple of noise through the crowd when this had happened. It was as if the people in the street knew that despite the strangeness of what they were witnessing, there was good at play not evil. Once the young woman was in place, the detective had stood for a moment and looked at the crowd.

He'd nodded his appreciation and then driven off.

'I could have walked,' Naomi said from the back seat. 'I didn't ask to be carried. Can I sit up now? It smells bad back here. Have you been eating chips in this car? I'm starving by the way.'

Smithdown was astonished by her resilience. She'd complained about many things since they'd broken open the door in Lennon's basement, but she hadn't once mentioned the pain she must have been in. *Tough woman. Fuck knows what she's been through.*

'No, you can't sit up - stay put,' the detective instructed. 'Not long now.'

Smithdown's car reached eastern edge of Alexandra Park and turned into Queen's Road. He stopped, told his two passengers to wait - particularly when Naomi swearily complained about the indignity of lying on the chip-scented back seat for a moment longer - and knocked on the door of an impressive, three-story red brick town house.

A minute later, the detective was back. 'Let's go,' he said. 'Quick as you can. Naomi, keep your head covered.'

She did as she was asked as Smithdown and Uddin helped her up the steps and into the roomy hallway of the house. Like a soldier on manoeuvres, the younger man swept the air around them with his crowbar as they walked. He hadn't let it out of his sight since Smithdown had handed it to him in Tom Lennon's house.

Naomi took Smithdown's jacket from her head and looked at Mr Aleem. 'Hello, Naomi,' he said with a smile. His face was purple and bruised and looked as if the smile hurt him. But he did it anyway.

She looked at Aleem's bandaged arm - then looked at her own: 'Snap,' she said. 'Do you have anything to eat? I'm absolutely famished.'

CHAPTER FORTY-ONE

3.15 pm Tuesday 5 April 1988

'Mr Aleem?' Smithdown asked. 'Do you have a recording device of some description that I could borrow?'

'Yes, I do.' He went to another room. The detective heard what sounded like the contents of a drawer being turned out. The house was quiet. Aleem's family had moved out of the house, fearful of more attacks. They'd gone to Longsight to stay with relatives and he was due to follow them but had changed his mind when Smithdown appeared at his door. The detective was glad he was there but concerned about his friend's bruised and battered appearance. *Another tough customer. Not one complaint about his injuries.*

'I bought it a while ago,' Mr Aleem said, returning with a small Dictaphone. 'I planned to fill it with great ideas that would make me a millionaire. I've barely used it.' He tested it with a one-two, one-two and then played it back. Satisfied that it was working, Mr Aleem put it back into record mode and placed it on the kitchen table in front of Naomi. He put two spare micro cassettes next to the recorder. 'You may need these as well,' he offered.

'You might be right there,' Smithdown replied. The recording light on the Dictaphone winked on and off as he spoke, reacting to the detective's voice. He waited until Naomi finished the last piece of a pile of toast that Mr Aleem had put in front of her. Uddin pulled up a chair and leant forward, as if he were about to listen to a master storyteller weave a fantastic tale. Mr Aleem took a chair and leant in too.

'So,' the detective began. 'First things first Naomi. The hand. Tell us about how your hand ended up in the boating lake at Alexandra Park.'

CHAPTER FORTY-TWO

3.30 pm Tuesday 5 April 1988

'I'm just doing what Mr Smithdown told me,' DC Bob Donaldson told Brenda Graham in a quiet, conspiratorial voice. 'He was very particular. Speak to Brenda, get little Becky well away, do whatever it takes to make the kid safe, because she's not safe there. Those were his very words.'

'Okay,' Brenda acknowledged, taking one of Donaldson's Rothman's and lighting it as the pair stood at the back doorstep of the care home.

'Don't let me down, Bob. That was the last thing he said. Don't take no for an answer and don't let me down.'

'But why?' Brenda asked. 'No one knows she's here but the police and social services. I'm here day and night. We're well out of the way here, to say the least. Surely, Becky's best left here? She's had enough to-ing and fro-ing to last a lifetime.'

'I agree with you,' Bob said, his arms outstretched. 'I really do. But he was adamant. There's something going on that's for sure but he's not sharing it with the likes of me.'

She thought for a moment. 'Poor girl. She's been through so much. Now more disruption for her. Bloody John Smithdown. What's he playing at?'

'Who knows? I'm just a foot soldier, doing what I'm told.'

Brenda grumpily tapped the cigarette out against the back wall so she could smoke the rest of it later. A mini waterfall of sparks tumbled down the red bricks. 'I'll get her stuff together,' she muttered. 'Bloody John Smithdown.'

CHAPTER FORTY-THREE

3.35 pm Tuesday 5 April 1988

'Me and Jimmy owed King money,' Naomi began. 'A lot of fookin' money. He'd been flooding the town with E and everyone wanted it. We couldn't shift it fast enough. Actually, we could shift it fast enough… in fact we started shifting it faster than we were getting it. People were eating them like sweets. But then there was a break in supply. Some gangster-shit in Ibiza. The pill heads of Oldham were not happy. We had their money; they had no Es and King had no profit. Probably didn't help that we were necking it ourselves like there was no tomorrow. Any road - we owed King ten grand. That's what he told us, anyway. So that's when he offered me a deal - I give up my hand and me, Becky and Jimmy disappear off to the coast.'

Uddin couldn't help himself: 'Ten grand for a hand? Wow. I mean... wow. That's just off the scale mad that is.'

'Just to be clear,' Smithdown said, holding up a hand to temper Uddin's excited curiosity. 'Richard T. King chopped your hand off in exchange for cancelling your drug debt?'

'The money was a side bet to be honest,' Naomi admitted. Then she let out a long breath. There was a pause. The detective waited. He knew from years of interviewing people that creating silence was a good way of getting someone to say more. 'They came to the flat and that shit Adam Griffin belted my little Becky,' she continued. 'They had Jimmy pinned down. He couldn't stop them. Griffin proper knocked her about. Tom Lennon was there too. Just watching. He said she'd get worse if I didn't go along with the hand thing.'

She paused again. For a moment Smithdown thought she might cry. She didn't. 'Poor Jimmy. He was a good guy. Kind. Great with Becky. She really liked him. Now he's dead and everyone thinks he beat up a little girl.'

'No wonder he didn't want to talk to me when he was in custody,' Smithdown observed.

'He couldn't.' Naomi said. 'He let everyone think that he'd done that to our Becky, and he said nowt. Then he goes to Strangeways and suddenly hangs himself? I don't fookin' think so.'

'Christ. Becky said nothing either, not a word,' the detective said.

'I hear you got her put in care by ripping half her face off.' Naomi responded. 'You're a twat but you probably saved her life.'

'How did you know about that?' Smithdown asked.

'It's amazing what you hear when you're handcuffed to a bed in a cellar,' she replied, pointing to the ceiling. 'Is she okay?'

'She's in a children's home over at Alt,' the detective said. 'She's absolutely safe. So, Jimmy had nothing to do with Becky's injuries?'

'They said they'd kill her if we didn't do what they said. In fact, they said she'd get worse. King said them racist pricks… the White Wankers or whatever they're called... could have her first. Then they'd kill her. My hand was by way of a swap for no more harm coming to Becky. The drug debt was just a bonus. What would you have fookin done? They could have taken both me arms as far as I was concerned.'

'But what did they want with your hand?' asked Mr Aleem. 'Sorry, John. This is your interview, apologies.'

'Not at all,' Smithdown said. 'That was exactly what I was going to ask, to be honest.'

Smithdown, Mr Aleem and Uddin all looked at Naomi, not wanting to seem too eager but all - for their own reasons - wanting to know the answer: 'They wanted it so that your lot would think it was me up at that Mermaid's Pool.'

'So, who was it then?' the detective asked. 'At the pool?'

'That councillor woman.'

'No, no, no,' said Mr Aleem. 'Sharmeen Chowdhury. My God.'

Smithdown thought about the scene at the Mermaid's Pool. The twisted, smoking thing that had once been a person. He remembered what DC Seddon had said: What had she done to generate that kind of hate? 'Because she was Asian?' the detective asked.

'King didn't give a fook what she was,' Naomi said, almost laughing. 'Though it was probably a nice tease in getting Tom Lennon and his mates involved. Nah. Nowt to do with it. She was just in King's way. She was of Head of Stopping Cunts Getting Away With Shit for the Council. And old Richard T. King is literally King of the Cunts Who Try To Get Away With Shit.'

Smithdown and Uddin both looked at Mr Aleem for an explanation. 'I wouldn't quite put it in those terms myself, to be honest,' Aleem sighed. 'But, put another way, Sharmeen was Chair of the Scrutiny Committee. She was one of us…'

Smithdown looked puzzled. 'A Tory, John. It's traditional to have an opposition councillor in charge of overseeing what the Council does. So, Labour-led council, Tory Chair of Scrutiny. Most of her time was spent knocking back housing proposals, particularly ones that involved the mass development of ex-council house stock. Like all those boarded up houses to the east of the town. People tend to think of council houses as being newer houses, built in the last few decades. But a lot of council stock is older mill workers' terraces. A lot of them were badly damaged in the rioting.'

'That's handy,' Smithdown said. He was fairly certain he heard Uddin snigger, but he let it pass.

'Quite,' Aleem continued. 'Now, I'm all for a bit of gentle social engineering via home ownership. You've got a Conservative for life if you've sold someone their council house and they've made thousands of pounds on it - but putting it all into one person's pocket is a no-no.'

'Was King behind all the applications?' Smithdown asked.

'Possibly,' Aleem conceded. 'There's been a flurry of these lately - made in a variety of names not normally known for their interest in housing development. Councillor Chowdhury was making it her business to find out who was behind them. Then she went missing. Caught up in the riots was the way it looked.'

Smithdown was quiet for a moment, processing what he was hearing. Naomi cut in: 'King makes millions on damaged council houses,' she said, as if it was completely obvious. 'Tom Lennon gets to act like a hero and become a fookin' councillor or some such shit…' She glanced at Mr Aleem. 'No offence. And the White Wankers get to fire up a race war and kill some brown people. Everyone's a fookin' winner, aren't they? Is there any more toast?'

'On its way.' Aleem said. He indicated to Uddin that it was his turn to make toast. Reluctantly, the young man headed for the kitchen.

'Did you honestly think they'd let you go?' the detective asked. 'Didn't you think someone would want to know more about what happened to you?'

'You know full well Mr Smithdown, nobody gives a shit about people like me being cut up and burned. Ten a penny we are. Barely gets reported when some no-one like me goes missing. But someone like Councillor what's-her-face? Different matter. So, they do her in. It looks like it's me and then she's just an unfortunate missing person after the riots. No one can prove anything. Bingo.'

'I gave a shit, Naomi,' Smithdown said, quietly.

'Yes,' replied. 'You did, didn't you?'

'We can't prove any of this,' Smithdown pointed out. 'I know you're right and I know that bastard Lennon targeted my Kate too, but we can't prove any of this.'

'Yeah you can,' Naomi corrected. 'That councillor's hand will do the job. Bang that on the front desk at Oldham nick and you've got them by the goolies.'

'But we don't have her hand,' Smithdown pointed out.

'Not yet, you don't...' Naomi said, raising her eyebrows conspiratorially. 'But I know where it is. That sicko Griffin kept the fookin thing. Until Tom found out and made him get rid of it.'

'So where is it now?' Aleem asked.

'It's in that pool.'

'It can't be,' the detective pointed out. 'It was dredged top to toe after the body was found. There was nothing in it apart from a load of old pop bottles.'

'They waited until your lot did their stuff then went back and dumped the hand in it,' Naomi said. 'Pretty clever really. What's the one place you wouldn't think of looking? The place you've already looked. They watched you from that lodge. That hand is still in the pool right now as far as I know. There's your proof, right there.'

Uddin returned with more toast. So far, he'd taken Smithdown's request to heart and kept silent. Now he spoke: 'I don't mean any disrespect by this, I'm not saying I don't believe you, I'm really not. But why keep you alive? Why tie you up in that cellar? It would have been easier to do you in when they were taking your hand. Why keep you alive?'

Smithdown remembered the leaflets at the lodge. The promise of justice after what the Wolves described as 'a spate of sex attacks' in the town. Attacks that, to the best if his knowledge hadn't happened. He realised then why they had kept Naomi alive. And it sickened him. 'Leave it lad,' the detective advised.

Uddin pressed on: 'No, sorry. It doesn't make sense...' he continued.

'Leave it, I said,' Smithdown repeated.

'If I was them, right,' the young man continued, 'I'd have killed you at the earliest possible opportunity. Probably when I was doing your hand. That's when I'd have done it. But they kept you in that cellar. Why would they do that? I'm just asking. Why would they?

'Practice,' Naomi said flatly. She gave Uddin a hard, direct look. 'They knew that attacking young white girls in town and blaming the South Asians would really kick things off, yeah? But they needed someone to practice on. Yours truly…'

There was quiet now. 'I'm so, so sorry,' Uddin whispered.

'Next time I ask you to leave it, just leave it, right?' Smithdown said.

'Sorry. I just. Right. Okay. Sorry.'

Mr Aleem had tears in his eyes. He spoke quietly: 'Naomi. Who cut your hand off?'

'Adam Griffin did it. He's a porter at the Royal and apparently, pushing people around a hospital qualifies you to perform surgery. I can assure you that it don't. It really don't.'

'Mr Aleem, you've helped us no end,' the detective said. 'I appreciate it. I really do. I wonder… could you possibly help a little more?'

'Of course, John. Anything.'

'Naomi here needs medical attention...'

'I'm fine...' she interrupted.

'Christ Almighty! You've been locked in a cellar for days and your hand has been chopped off. I think that's worth a once over with a stethoscope at the very least, don't you?'

'Spose so...' she conceded.

'We can't trust the hospitals around here, especially if the Wolves have mates at the Royal. Can you take Naomi over the border to the hospital in Glossop? While you're there, find Detective Constable Jenny Seddon from the local police. She knows the deal. I trust her, but she didn't show up to the meeting we'd arranged earlier today, so she needs updating.'

'John, of course I want to help, but I can't drive,' Aleem pointed out, lifting his bandaged arm as if proof were needed.

'Good point. Take a taxi.'

'Shall we go now?' Aleem asked.

'No. Sit tight here. Tell no one about Naomi. Wait until we've found what we're looking for at the pool, then I'll call you.'

'*We've* found what *we're* looking for?' Uddin checked. 'I'm coming too?'

'Yes, you are,' Smithdown said. 'Can't have someone with a gob as big as yours, knowing what you know, wandering about. Might as well put it on the news...'

'So rude, honestly,' Uddin muttered.

'Plus, I need a witness. It's my word against half of Oldham at the moment. Being a witness will require you to keep your eyes and ears open and your trap shut.'

'Of course,' Uddin said, 'Mr Discreet. That's me.'

'We need to put Tom Lennon and his mates on the back foot,'

Smithdown told them. 'Naomi here - back from the dead - plus Councillor Chowdhury's hand should do the trick. About time too. Our town's gone very, very wrong this last week or so. We need to start making things right.'

CHAPTER FORTY-FOUR

4.05 pm Tuesday 5 April 1988

'King here…'

DC Bob Donaldson punched three two pence pieces into the payphone and spoke once the beeps had cleared. 'Mr King, it's Mr Donaldson here. Bit of an update, a bit of news, plus a bit of a suggestion. Which do you want first?'

'I want you to tell me what the fuck is going on and what the fuck is being done about it,' King said. 'That's what I want.' His legs swung gently left to right as he rested them on the suspended table in his office. Lennon and Griffin were there too. 'I've had enough surprises for one day, thank you very much.'

'The daughter was a no-go at the hospital,' Donaldson stated. 'Couldn't be done. Maybe another time. So, I improvised and grabbed the little 'un from the care home instead. Told the woman in charge that I was acting on Smithdown's orders. She seemed happy with it. I've tipped off the press to that effect and that'll link her name to his. So, everything is being pushed nicely in his direction now.'

'I thought you weren't supposed to name kids in care…?' King queried.

'Children and Young Persons Act 1933, Mr King,' Donaldson pointed out, in a bad-tempered voice. 'The welfare of the child is paramount. She's under a care order with anonymity, but her safety overrides that. We'll use the law in our favour to link Smithdown to the kid. He's done for. You stick to showbiz - leave the law to me.'

'So where is she now?' King asked.

'Young 'un? In the boot of my car with half a bottle of your electric water down her trap.'

'Well, that's one less thing to worry about.'

'Funny you should say that -we do actually have another problem,' Donaldson said, tapping one his spare coins on the telephone box window. 'According to your man Lennon it turns out that dickhead Griffin kept a bit of Councillor Chowdhury as a keepsake. Is he there?'

'Yes, he is,' King confirmed.

'Tell him he's a fucking tool from me.'

King put his hand over the receiver and caught Griffin's very swollen eye: 'DC Donaldson says you are - and I'm quoting here - a fucking tool.'

'Her hand is in the water up at Kinder Scout,' Donaldson continued. 'And if Naomi knows about it, then you can be pretty sure they'll be headed that way. If Smithdown gets hold of it, we're all fucked.'

'An absolute mess, this is,' King said, staring at Lennon and Griffin.

'No, I reckon it's perfect,' Donaldson corrected. 'We get them all together in the same spot and sort it out in a one-r. Smithdown, Naomi, the Paki lad and the daughter. Bang. Job done and everything lands on Smithdown's plate.'

'That sounds grand but there's one small problem - I DON'T KNOW WHERE THE FUCK NAOMI IS,' King shouted.

'Luckily, I do. I had them followed from Tom's house, she's at Aleem's. Two uniform lads - both true to the cause - are outside the house now waiting on instructions. I suggest the instructions should be to take out Naomi properly. She's already dead as far as everyone's concerned anyway and I'll say Smithdown told me to deliver little Becky to him. Out of his mind with grief over his missus, and all that - ashamed of what his daughter had done. So, he's taken the little 'un up the moors and done her in. There are plenty more good soldiers back at the station who'll back me up and say he was going round the bend. Then it's done.'

'What about Aleem?' King asked.

'Easy. Pakis came back to finish the job, didn't they? More fuel for the fire. As it were.'

'You make it sound so easy,' King sighed.

'It is easy,' Donaldson said. 'It always was. Councillor out of the way, use Naomi as the diversion, stoke up the trouble in town, get a foothold on the council. Easy-bastard-peasy. Too many dickheads with their hand on the tiller - that's been the problem. Not anymore. I'm taking charge now. Tell Cannon and Ball there to meet me up at Kinder. I'll make sure things are done right. I appreciate that you're seeing all this largely as a way of making a fuckload of money. But to us, this is a fucking war. God's on our side. So are a good portion of the Oldham police. So, it's a war we cannot - will not - lose.'

'Manchester Radio News at six this is Beth Hall. There's growing concern this evening over the whereabouts of a nine-year-old girl who's gone missing from a care home in Oldham. It's believed that Becky Wells may be with a middle-aged man who has recently been suspended from Greater Manchester Police. Robert Crane has more.'

> *'Oldham Police and council social workers say that Becky Wells may in real danger after going missing in the Alt area of Oldham earlier today.*
>
> *The child is thought to be in a very distressed state after the recent death of her mother.*
>
> *Police investigating her disappearance believe that one of their colleagues may have vital information about Becky's whereabouts. They want Detective Inspector John Smithdown to contact them immediately. He has been suspended from his job after an incident at Oldham Police station where a child was injured while in his care. Sources within Oldham Police say that Becky Wells is the child that was hurt.*
>
> *Now an appeal's gone out asking local residents in Alt and surrounding areas to look out for the pair. Mr Smithdown is described as white, in his 50s with grey hair and a moustache. He's wearing a grey suit and white shirt. Becky Wells is slightly built and has dark hair. When last seen she was wearing a t-shirt, jeans and sandals. Robert Crane, Manchester Radio News, Oldham.'*

CHAPTER FORTY-FIVE

6.10 pm Tuesday 5 April 1988

'If I'd have known we were going climbing, I wouldn't have worn these trainers,' Uddin said after Smithdown parked close to the dam end of Kinder Reservoir and they took the path up towards the moor. The warm evening wind followed them, pushing the pair lightly along. The sun was dropping now, getting closer to the ridge of Lantern Pike behind them. Soon, the moorland underneath Kinder Scout would be in shadow, then darkness - and so would the Mermaid's Pool.

'I don't think this is technically classed as climbing,' Smithdown countered. 'Though it will be technically classed as bloody dark in about an hour, so we'd better get a shift on. Been here before?'

'Absolutely not,' Uddin replied. 'I don't do countryside. Too many variables. You know where you are in a town.'

'I think your brother might disagree with you there,' Smithdown muttered as they walked past the reservoir overflow. The lack of rain over recent weeks had reduced it to a weedy trickle over the top of the shiny green moss that lined the concrete funnel running from the top of the dam. What little water there was then joined the River Kinder which stretched away down the valley back towards Hayfield.

The detective looked up at the Kinder Downfall as they walked: 'Do you know what's weird about the waterfall up there?' Smithdown asked, waving a finger in the direction of ridge above them. He was trying to make conversation as they walked. He felt awkward with the young man, out of his depth.

'I must confess I don't, Mr Smithdown,' Uddin replied. 'Do I need to?'

'No,' admitted the detective. 'But I'm going to tell you anyway. One of the mountain rescue lads told me about it last time I was here. It'll pass the time.'

'Brilliant,' Uddin said, wiping his trainers on a clump of grass for the third time since they'd started. They passed through a kissing gate - taking turns to swing the wooden gate back then forwards to step through - then began their walk across the open upper moor.

'It's unusual because sometimes the water goes up, instead of down,' Smithdown said.

'Yeah, right.'

'It's true.'

'Absolutely.'

'See that?' the detective asked, pointing up towards the ridge of Kinder Scout. One section had a deep groove cut into it several hundred feet across, bookended by huge slabs of rock. 'It's called the Downfall. It's a waterfall that sometimes goes backwards when the wind is just right. A waterfall that goes up not down. Weird, isn't it? The wind rattles in and if it's stronger than the downward force of the water, the waterfall goes up instead of down.'

'As if things weren't freaky enough right now - what with the whole let's-fish-a-hand-out-of-the-Mermaid's-Pool stuff, you're pointing out further local spots of weirdness. And this one just happens to be called the Downfall. Thanks for that, Detective Inspector Metaphor.'

'I'm not being metaphorical. I was just making conversation. Did it sound like I was?'

'Potentially,' Uddin sighed. 'I can't work you out.'

'Likewise,' the detective grunted. 'Sorry. Just thought it was interesting. You think too much, mate, that's your problem.'

'Okay then - seeing as though you are clearly steeped in local legend... tell me this: why do they call it the Mermaid's Pool?'

Smithdown thought about the story he'd been told about the mermaid legend... and her propensity for killing people she didn't like. 'It's just mumbo jumbo bollocks courtesy of the locals,' the detective said, keen not to pursue the line of conversation any further. 'It's getting dark and as we're about to go paddling looking for the severed limb of a murdered woman... so it's probably best if we skip that one.'

'Shall we just walk in silence, then?' Uddin asked, somewhat sarcastically.

'Of course not. Sorry. Any other non-weird questions?'

'Bit tricky at the moment - everything is weird, to be honest. I saw you looking at those handcuffs on Naomi. They were really hard to cut too. Were those police handcuffs?'

'Have you ever thought of joining the police, Uddin?'

'Absolutely not. I'm going to be a lawyer. Why?'

'Although you're quite annoying, you'd probably make a pretty good policeman. You notice things. Yes, they were police handcuffs.'

'So, the cops could be involved in this too?' Uddin asked, his voice a mix of disgust and disbelief. 'Your mates… in bed with these Nazis? I refuse to use the expression neo-Nazi. Makes it sound fashionable and desirable, like a new nightclub.'

'I think so, yes.' The detective was getting short of breath now, as the land began to rise, and the hags and dips of the terrain became more prominent.

'Wow,' the young man deadpanned. 'Nazi cops. Absolute shocker.'

'Is that how you see it?' Smithdown asked.

'Yes, I do. And it appears that I'm entirely right.'

'This is the bit when I tell you about a few bad apples isn't it? About what a great lot we all are - on the whole; just good people doing a tough job as best we can? But under the circumstances, I'm going to say nowt. I don't know what I know anymore. Or who.' Smithdown looked around the darkening landscape. 'I'm a bit lost, to be honest.'

'Maybe if you got out of the bubble of your own world, your own experience. Your own kind. That would help. That's the problem with Oldham. It's completely compartmentalised.'

'No, I mean I'm literally a bit lost,' the detective pointed out. 'I thought we'd be clear of the open moor by now.'

'I see,' Uddin smiled. 'You're not a great one for introspection are you, Mr Smithdown.'

'Not if I can help it mate, no.'

Once Smithdown had satisfied himself they were indeed going the right way, they carried on without speaking. They walked through a walled plantation of trees, criss-crossed another stream and eased their way up and across the final stretch of moorland.

Then they crested the final hill that hid the Mermaid's Pool from view from the moors below. It looked smaller than when the detective had been here to view what they'd thought had been the body of Naomi Wells just a few days earlier. The water level seemed lower too. One end now had so little water in, it had turned to mud. The pool had a haze of blue dragonflies over it, dancing and darting around the reeds as the last of the sunlight disappeared over the ridge behind them.

A pile of bottles and cans had appeared next to the water; the police divers who'd searched the water had placed them neatly at one end, but none of them had apparently decided that it might be a good idea to take them away. So, there they had stayed, like a bizarre memorial cairn to where Councillor Sharmeen Chowdhury's life had been ended, as she reached out to try to end her indescribable suffering.

'Is this where it happened?' Uddin asked, his voice quiet now, all the confidence and humour scrubbed away.

'Yes,' Smithdown confirmed. 'Right here.' The two were silent for a moment. 'She must have begged,' the detective said. 'Over and over again. All the way here. Begged when they had her hand away, begged when they got the petrol out and begged when they made her swallow it. Then they set fire to her anyway.'

Uddin looked at the blackened patch of grass near to the pool. It had grown a little, the burnt areas where the fire had been now formed the top of the blades where the grass had grown through. 'Are we going in there?' Uddin asked, turning away from the burnt grass and looking across the peaty-coloured surface of the pool.

'Yes, I'm afraid that we are,' Smithdown replied. 'If this all works out okay, I'm sure there'll be some compensation fund that will get you some new trainers. Potentially, anyway. Which end do you want?'

'What?' Uddin replied.

'The pool, the detective pointed out. 'We need to search it methodically. Which end do you want to start at? Then we can meet in the middle.'

'The un-muddy end.'

'Thought you might say that. Right. See you in the middle.'

Smithdown stepped into the water up to his knees and his feet immediately dropped a few inches into the silt at the bottom. He remembered what one of the mountain rescue team members had said to him about the water in the Mermaid's Pool: how it was salted because the lake was somehow connected to the sea. He dipped a finger into the water and put it into his mouth. It tasted a little stagnant and mossy, but there was no hint of salt. *Mumbo jumbo bollocks.*

The detective went in another few feet then bent over and began a fingertip search of the bottom of the pool.

Uddin, meanwhile, was still standing by the water's edge, gingerly poking at the bottom of the pool with his crowbar. 'I can smell smoke,' he said. 'Can you smell smoke? Should we be smelling smoke way out here?'

'Nothing to worry about,' Smithdown said, reassuringly. 'You're in the countryside now, lad. All sorts of weird and wonderful smells out here. Stop being mardy - get in the water and start searching.'

CHAPTER FORTY-SIX

6.25 pm Tuesday 5 April 1988

Aleem had just finished on the phone when there was a knock at the door. 'Good evening sir, sorry to trouble you. It's Mr Aleem, isn't it?'

He looked at the two police officers. Both young, both keen-looking and both smiling. Both white.

'Yes, it is. Good evening. Can I ask what it's about?' Aleem asked.

'We just need a moment of your time,' the first PC said. 'It's in connection with the attack and the injuries you sustained.' He nodded at Mr Aleem 's bandaged arm. 'We've got a bit of news. Could we come in for a moment please?'

Aleem hesitated. He glanced inside the house and immediately regretted it. 'Is there anyone else here with you this evening, sir?' the second officer asked.

'No there isn't - just myself,' he replied. Smithdown had insisted that Naomi stay out of sight until they received a call from him to head for Glossop police station. If anyone else were to ask, he was to deny all knowledge of her.

'Officer, as you know - as you can see - I was quite badly injured a few days ago. I'm not feeling anywhere near well enough to speak to you, though I'm keen to hear the news you have. Could you possibly come back tomorrow? I'd be so grateful.'

The two officers looked at each other. The first one smiled and nodded. 'Of course. We'll come back then. Not a problem. Sorry to trouble you.'

'I very much appreciate it,' Aleem said. He pushed the door to close it just as both the PCs kicked the door, sending him crashing against the hallway wall.

Naomi called out from upstairs. The police officers didn't understand the word Naomi had screamed. Aleem did and as the blows came down it broke his heart.

Daddy.

CHAPTER FORTY-SEVEN

6.50 pm Tuesday 5 April 1988

Bent nearly double, with water up to the tops of their legs and their arms totally submerged, Smithdown and Uddin had been in the Mermaid's Pool for nearly 15 minutes when the younger man did a combined shout and scream, fell backwards and sat down. He immediately leapt up, windmilled both arms, stumbled forwards and waded to the water's edge. 'There!' Uddin shouted. 'Where I just was. There's something there. I'm not touching it. That's your job.'

'Technically, it isn't any more,' the detective said quietly, pushing through the water to where Uddin had been searching and reached under the surface. He felt something soft and round and lifted it up. It felt like a ball of uncooked chicken. It was heavier than he was expecting it to be, but the detective felt there would be a logical explanation for that when he lifted it clear of the water. There was.

The small areas of Sharmeen Chowdhury's hand that he could actually see were just as bloated and puffy as the one he'd looked at on the edge of Alexandra Park boating lake just a few days earlier. Probably more so. But that hand was supposed to be found. This one wasn't. It had been crudely Gaffa-taped to a rock to make sure it sank into the waters of the Mermaid's Pool. The flesh had begun to break down in the water. The detective examined the find more closely. The tape - and the fact that the fingers were pressed into the rock – appeared to have protected the integrity of the fingerprints. Smithdown felt elated. *We've got the fuckers.* Then almost immediately there was a jab of guilt. *These are human remains, John lad. A hard-working, decent person who wanted the best for Oldham. She was the exact opposite of the racist fucks who did this. It's not the time for celebrating.* 'I think our work here is done, Uddin,' he said quietly as he made his way to the shore.

'Is that what I think it is?' the young man asked, hugging his knees as he sat on the grass.

'It's exactly what you think it is,' the detective confirmed.

He looked around for something to wrap the hand in. There was nothing. 'I don't suppose you have an evidence bag on you, Uddin.'

'No,' the young man replied. 'I feel a bit stupid now for not bringing one with me when I left the house this morning.'

Smithdown remembered the care that the mountain rescue team had taken in bringing Sharmeen Chowdhury's body down from the same spot. He felt embarrassed that he couldn't offer the same level of respect with the last of her remains.

He thought for a moment, then took off his jacket, shirt and vest. All three were wet. He carefully - he hoped respectfully - wrapped the hand in his vest and put the hand into his jacket pocket. Then he put his shirt and mac back on. Not ideal, but better than nothing. 'Come on,' the detective said, bone tired but with the end in sight. 'Time to go, mate.' He put his hand onto Uddin's shoulder and gave it an appreciative squeeze. 'Thank you. You've done brilliantly. You didn't have to come, but you did.'

'Well, it was an experience I won't forget, I'll say that,' the young man replied.

'We'll be at the front desk of Glossop Police station in less than an hour. Can't risk going to Oldham. We'll meet up with Mr Aleem and Naomi, tell the local cops what we know, then this will all be over.'

They walked away from the pool and headed downhill. 'I can still smell smoke,' Uddin said. 'And the smell's getting stronger.'

'It'll be the gamekeepers,' Smithdown said. 'They do controlled burning to get rid of the dead vegetation. It's very carefully managed, we're quite safe.'

'How do you know that?' Uddin asked, sounding slightly cynical about Smithdown's confident-sounding display of countryside knowledge.

'A friend of mine told me,' the detective replied. He thought about Jenny Seddon for the first time in a few hours, remembering once again that she hadn't shown up to see DS Pym earlier in the day. 'She knows these hills. I mean really knows them. If Jenny Seddon says it's safe, then that's good enough for me.'

CHAPTER FORTY-EIGHT

7.00 pm Tuesday 5 April 1988

As the sun set behind White Brow, the soft ridge that ran above Kinder Reservoir, Tom Lennon questioned several of the Wolves about the firelighters they'd bought. 'How many did you buy in each shop?' he asked.

'Two packs in each. Like you said,' one replied.

'I actually got three in one shop,' replied another.

'What the fuck did I tell you?' Lennon shouted, his voice carrying across the empty car park they were standing in.

'There was an offer on!' the Wolf replied. 'Buy two, get a third one free. It would have looked weird if I'd turned it down.'

'Fine,' said Lennon. 'Always nice to get a bargain. How many packs in all?'

'I've got twelve,' said one Wolf.

'Thirteen, here,' the second one replied, quietly.

'Twenty-five packs with two dozen firelighter blocks in each,' Bob Donaldson said to King. 'That should send half of Derbyshire up in flames, let alone this moor.'

Adam Griffin, one of his eyes now completely swollen shut, spoke: 'If this moor goes up, we could all go up with it.'

Donaldson stepped forward, grabbed the younger man's face and pushed him backwards. 'If you hadn't decided to keep her hand like a little fucking weirdo, we wouldn't be here in the first place, would be?'

'The wind will be behind us,' Lennon said. 'It'll send the fire in their direction.'

'Sure?' Griffin said. 'I've seen these fires on the telly. They're mad.'

'Fookin hell,' Donaldson said, getting ready to properly hit Griffin this time.

'I know these hills,' Lennon stated, as if trying to show Donaldson he was still in control of Griffin and the other Wolves. 'And I know that if the fire doesn't get them, the panic created by the heat and smoke will send them into a gully. Then the fire and smoke will get them anyway.'

Donaldson pointed at Griffin: 'You. Get the little 'un and let's get cracking.'

Becky Wells was wedged between some rocks close to the path. She seemed to be moaning, crying and laughing quietly to herself all at the same time. Griffin took her arm, stood her up and lifted her onto his shoulder. Lennon addressed the Wolves: 'Right. Listen up. Adam, we'll take the girl up to the plantation. That's where the fire will burn the hardest. Give us 15 minutes head start so we can get clear off towards the side of Kinder Scout, then the rest of you take five packs a piece, spread out in a line at the bottom end of the moor, spark up the firelighters and drop them. Do it all at the same time then fuck off out of it. That'll create a nice strong line of fire. First there'll be a cold burn across the top of the moss. Then when it hits the peat it'll create a hot burn and that's when the fun will start. It could keep burning for weeks - months even.'

Bob Donaldson - there was no question as to who was really in charge now - spoke to the assembled Wolves. There were fifteen of them in all: as well as Lennon and Griffin there were several other members of the Kingdom security team, four members of well-known Manchester crime families and three convicted football hooligans - all the rest were police officers. As Donaldson spoke two more officers arrived - the pair who'd visited Mr Aleem's house.

'Right, I need to get back to Oldham, raise the alarm about Smithdown going crackers and get things in place at that end. This is simple, lads. Dump the little girl. Burn the moor. The evidence disappears. All sorted. Then it's all clear for St George's Day.'

He looked at each of them in turn. Then he asked: 'Who are we?'

'WOLVES!' they shouted in unison.'

'What are we?'

'WHITE AND RIGHT!'

CHAPTER FORTY-NINE

7.45 pm Tuesday 5 April 1988

Heat. Fuel. Oxygen.

The perfect fire triangle was crackling into life at the bottom end of the moor, just as Smithdown and Uddin left the area at the top end close to the Mermaid's Pool.

With heat from the Wolves' firelighters and fuel in every direction, the fire was spoilt for choice as to where it would head, but the wind took control and pushed it up the moor in the direction of the pool. The fire was low-key to start with, the accompanying smoke was white and hissy, producing a steam engine-like smell. As it grew hotter and dug into the peat, the smoke became yellowy brown, taking on the more sweet and smoky flavours of the moor that surrounded it.

The smoke folded itself into the contours of the land as the fire became more confident and reacted to the ever-changing environment the landscape provided. Large boulders made the flames stop momentarily, reassess, then find a way around; tempting, tufted hags - grassy islands of especially combustible vegetation - made it stay a while, burning hard, flaring in the darkened landscape before moving on. Gullies forced it to stop and spread right and left until it found a new route or built up enough intensity to leap the break in the landscape and carry on regardless.

Smithdown and Uddin were halfway through the walled plantation of trees that separated the upper and lower areas of the moor when the smoke, emboldened by the wind, began to flood uphill towards them. It swirled around their legs, which were still wet from wading into the Mermaid's Pool. Through the trees and behind the smoke they saw the orange and red line of the fire moving in their direction. It stretched left and right as far as they could see and seemed to be moving at a sprinter's pace. 'I thought you said it was a managed fire,' Uddin said. 'That doesn't look managed to me. That looks really, really un-managed.'

'Yes, it does look a little unruly, doesn't it?' Smithdown admitted. The detective had picked up a little knowledge from the other emergency services of the years - one thing had always stuck in his mind: never be in front of a fire with smoke in your face. *And that's exactly where you are John lad.*

'We need to go back up the moor,' the detective said. 'Right now.'

The detective turned around and began to walk uphill when he saw something that made him stop and reluctantly go back towards the flames. 'No, no, no,' Uddin cried, pointing back up the moor. 'It's this way. It's totally this way and not that way, which is where the fire is. Trust me, I might not know much about the countryside, but this is the way we should definitely be going.'

'Not any more it isn't,' Smithdown replied, walking downhill through the smoke until he got to the collapsed figure of Becky Wells. The little girl was leant against the broken gate at the low end of the plantation. She was semi-conscious and dressed in just a t-shirt, jeans and plastic sandals - the same sandals that she'd worn when the detective first saw her at Oldham Police station. Smithdown knelt beside her; he touched her face and checked her pupils. They were huge, turning her brown eyes almost black.

'Oh my God!' Uddin shouted. 'Is that Naomi's daughter - the one who was really, really safe in the care home? My God. Who dumps a little girl out here? Seriously. Who does that?'

'People who want all the evidence destroyed in one go, that's who,' Smithdown pointed out. 'These moors could burn for weeks. No will find us and even if they do, they'll be nowt left worth identifying.'

The smoke was rushing and swirling between the plantation trees now, surrounding the three of them. Becky, lower down than Uddin and the detective, was coughing and spluttering, grey mucus flying from her mouth as her airways tightened. Smithdown knew he had to get her off the ground and up the moor.

He was about to pick her up when he heard shouts from the other side of the smoke. Sprinting towards them, with the leading edge of the fire alarmingly close to her, Naomi Wells was shouting something at them, her voice cracked and hoarse sounding. As she got closer, the detective could see that her face was covered in blood. Her saw her bandaged arm swinging left to right as she ran ahead of the flames. Smithdown also realised what it was she was actually saying: 'Pick her up you dozy twats. Pick her up and fookin' run!'

Seconds after she climbed over the gate, the fire hit the outer wall of the plantation, stopped for a moment, then set about burning the gate down. It wouldn't be long before the fire entered the walled-in space fully; dead, dried out trees, pine needles and vegetation all crammed into one space.

Heat. Fuel. Oxygen.

Smithdown watched as the flames began to take their first steps into the plantation. He was afraid now. Really afraid. They were tired, sluggish with hunger, drained from the cold of the Mermaid's Pool and lacking the skills and knowledge to deal with the situation. The detective might not have been an expert in the outdoors - unlike his colleagues from the Derbyshire Con-stab-u-lary - but he had more than his fair share of common sense. He looked around the plantation. *We're in a stone box filled with stuff that burns really well - it's going to go up like a barrel of fireworks. We need to get out of here right now.*

'Come on you pillocks! Shift yourselves!' Naomi shouted.

The detective slipped his hands under Becky's legs and lifted her out of the smoke; she began to scream and shout, hitting and kicking Smithdown and scratching at his face. He tried to pin her arms down as they moved back through the plantation. Every third step he seemed to stumble over a log or a tree root. Naomi tried her best to calm her daughter - but her quiet, soothing words made no difference. 'She's dosed up,' Smithdown said. 'God knows what they've put inside her. She must be terrified. I'm terrified and I'm not on drugs.'

Uddin, coughing, spitting and shouting almost at the same time, had a question: 'I don't suppose now is a good time to ask WHY SHE IS NOT HIDING AT MR ALEEM'S READY TO ALERT THE POLICE IN GLOSSOP SO THEY CAN ARREST EVERYONE!'

'They dragged me over here and gave me a choice,' she said walking quickly alongside Smithdown so she could stay near to her daughter. 'Die down there with them or die up here with my Becky.' She stroked the little girl's hair. 'No contest.'

'Where's Mr Aleem?' asked Smithdown.

'Back at his house,' Naomi said, quietly.

'How is he?' he continued.

'He's dead.' She looked straight into the detective's eyes. 'They beat him with… what do you call them? Batons. Police batons.'

Smithdown slowed a second. 'Jesus Christ. Not Aleem. He was a bloody good man. And he seemed to care a lot about you and Becky.'

'Yes, Mr Smithdown,' Naomi agreed. 'He really did.'

There was brief silence between the two of them. *Was she going to cry?*

'We need to shift,' Naomi said, firmly.

'Yes, you're right, we need to get out of here quicksticks,' the detective agreed.

Smithdown could feel the heat of the fire now as the last sections of the plantation gate gave way, giving the flames free reign to take hold of the trees and dried out vegetation across the forest floor. To their left and right the fire had started to race ahead of them now, matching them either side as they stumbled through the plantation. The stone walls were protecting them temporarily from the flames, but it wouldn't last. Soon they'd be surrounded. With Becky in his arms, the detective began to run as best he could through the trees. 'We need to get to the other end before the fire does.' The detective was shouting now; the flames had leapt over the walls and were taking a grip of the trees inside the plantation one by one. Rising columns of fire that had wrapped themselves around the trees, were appearing all around them.

The carpet of smoke was turning into a wall. The edges of plantation were now lost in the yellowy haze. Smithdown, his eyes streaming and his throat raw and swollen, was losing all sense of direction. Naomi was holding onto his arm - in reality she was dragging him downwards. Uddin was trying to keep up as best he could but was by now on his knees as often as he was on his feet. Becky, through a combination of fear and the cocktail of drugs she'd been given, screamed and screamed until her voice began to dry up.

They were done. And Smithdown knew it.

'GRAB THIS. GRAB IT. NOW!'

The voice didn't belong to Uddin or Naomi; it was muffled by a decorator's-style white breathing mask and came from a figure in the smoke illuminated by a head torch. A pole was wavering close to the detective's face. At the same time another pair of hands took hold of Becky Wells and lifted the child's limp body onto their shoulders.

Smithdown saw that the pole was a fire beater. He took Naomi's right hand and closed her fingers around the end of the pole. He grabbed the top of her bandaged arm and took a fistful of Uddin's collar with his other hand. It wasn't the most elegant human chain ever, but it seemed to work.

'KEEP TOGETHER AS BEST YOU CAN,' the voice instructed. 'WATCH YOUR FEET AND WATCH OUT FOR EACH OTHER. WE NEED TO GET OUT OF THE SMOKE AND GET CLEAR OF THE FIRE'S PATH.'

Smithdown felt himself pulled along by both the pole and the words of someone who seemed to know what they were doing. But then he noticed that they seemed to be heading back down the plantation towards the fiercest line of the fire. He was about to voice his opinion but realised that he didn't have the breath left in him.

The group then veered off to the left towards a break in the wall where it had been damaged. Fallen stones lay scattered either side of the gap and, by starving it of fuel, had made a small gap in the fire which created a way through.

Their rescuers dragged them through the opening and out of the plantation, extinguishing any remaining snatches of fire with their beaters.

They stepped into a triangle of moor that was a respite from the fire and the worst of the smoke. Behind them the plantation was now fully ablaze. To their right, the main line of fire was still approaching; to their left was the imposing edge of Kinder Scout.

Brian McIntyre dropped the fire beater and pulled off his mask. His face was blackened from the smoke save for an oval of white skin where the mask had been. 'Brian, lad,' Smithdown wheezed. 'You big, beautiful bastard. I could kiss you, I really could.'

'Something for me to look forward to for when we're properly safe,' Brian replied.

'Agreed,' the detective said, hawking up a big glob of phlegm and spitting the blackened mass onto the grass. 'But thank you anyway. I'm glad to see you. What brings you out here on this fine evening?'

'To be fair,' Brian replied, 'You can see this fire from Manchester city centre, but it was your friend Mr Aleem who told us you'd be out here. He called the Glossop cops.'

'It must have been the last thing he did before they got to him,' the detective said. 'I told him to wait. Thank God he didn't.'

'They've already rounded up a gang of nutcases heading out of the village,' Brian explained. 'Fucking neo-Nazis, apparently. In Hayfield! They say some of them were off duty cops from Oldham. Whether they got them all, I don't know.'

Smithdown looked at Naomi. She was too busy being sick to hear the conversation. 'I was worried for Jenny,' the detective said, quietly. 'She never showed up at Oldham nick.'

'You were right to be worried,' Brian replied as Jenny pulled off her mask to show her bruised and heavily swollen face. 'She shouldn't be here, she should be in hospital, but since when did she ever listen to me?'

'I was the nearest,' she said, her voice barely registering from the injuries to her throat. 'It made sense for me to come with you when we got the call. Now shut it and let's get moving. I assume that is Naomi?'

Wiping the sick from her mouth, Naomi nodded. 'Well, we don't want her dying a second time, do we?' Jenny said. She turned to Brian. 'We can't go back the way we came, and the fire has cut us off from the Mermaid's Pool.' She pointed up at the dark groove that stretched up to the edge of Kinder Scout. 'Our best bet is Red Brook.'

CHAPTER FIFTY

7.45 pm Tuesday 5 April 1988

'You can fuck right off,' Smithdown said to Jenny and Brian, looking up at the cluster of giant boulders and scree that formed the base of Red Brook, an intimidating upward gash in the landscape. 'Red Brook? That's not a brook, it's a fucking waterfall.'

'It's a dry waterfall - a smaller version of the Kinder Downfall,' Brian explained, trying to sound reassuring. 'There's hardly been any rain for weeks - by usual standards around here anyway. It's a fire-proof escape route and we are going up it.'

'What about this lot?' Smithdown said, indicating towards Naomi, Becky and Uddin. 'They're half dead as it is.'

'They can stop here and be 100 per cent dead if you'd prefer,' Jenny replied in her dry, whispery voice.' How about that?'

'Upwind and downhill is the safest place to be right now,' Brian added. 'But that's not going to happen. We can't go sideways so we've got to go up. Apart from the fire there's 150 years' worth of industrial pollution in the peat on these moors and the fire is releasing it. This is not a good place to be for a lot of reasons. We need to get out of this smoke and away from the path of the fire.'

Smithdown was about to speak again when Jenny leant in: 'Just for once, you stubborn bastard, just accept that someone else might know a bit more than you do. It's possible, isn't it?'

'Of course, I wasn't saying that...'

'Good. Glad to hear it. Time to go, then.'

'We will get you all off this moor, John,' Brian added. 'I promise you. You're in good hands.'

'Okay, understood,' Smithdown conceded. 'Thank you both. But little Becky there has been dosed. God knows what drugs she's got rattling around inside her. She's still hallucinating and even more frightened than I am. And I'm fucking terrified.'

'We'll have to tie her up,' Jenny said, looking to where Naomi was trying to comfort her daughter as the little girl feebly kicked out and continued to hoarsely cry. Exhaustion seemed to be overcoming the child as her struggles became weaker and less aggressive.

Jenny went to them: 'I'm sorry about this… it's Naomi, isn't it? And Becky? I'm Jenny.'

The women looked at each other's damaged faces for a moment. 'Alright?' Naomi said. 'You look worse than me.' Naomi waved her bandaged arm in the air. 'In the face department, anyway.'

Jenny allowed herself the smallest of smiles, then regretted it with the pain that it caused. 'I know it sounds harsh, but we need to tie little Becky up. It's the only way to ensure her safety - and ours - on the way up. I'm sorry. I hope you understand.'

Naomi nodded as she stroked her daughter's face. Becky struggled a little as Jenny and Brian tied her hands and then her feet with light cord. Brian put her over his shoulder then Jenny tied a third cord between her hands and feet across Brian's chest. She was becoming more still now; the fight seemed to have all but gone from her.

Brian and the Becky led the climb as the fire edged towards the lower slopes of Red Brook. It had easily jumped the small stream that came from the downfall and was now approaching them from both sides. Smithdown had seen moorland fires on television before, but the local news crews always filmed them from above - aerial shots from a helicopter to give an impression of scale. To be this close to the fierce, orangey heat was a very different experience - it was frightening, choking and overwhelming.

Uddin was next to climb, moving left to right on the giant rocks at the base of Red Brook - he was silent now, all his chatty bravura gone. Next came Naomi helped by Smithdown with Jenny at the rear, her headtorch providing a little light for them to find their way. They zig-zagged their way slowly up the vertical split in the Kinder landscape. Apart from the occasional instruction as to where best to place a hand or foot, the group were largely silent. The more they climbed, the larger the rocks they scrambled up seemed to become. What started as small steps were now wider, more difficult stretches; soon they became jumps as they cut left and right up the dry waterfall. To Smithdown's eyes the edge of Kinder Scout was no closer now than it had been when they started.

There was something hypnotic about the repetitive moves - Smithdown realised he had lost all sense of time. Had they been climbing for twenty minutes or two hours? He ached from his shoulders to his ankles - but wasn't about to admit it - as he tried to keep his eyes on his hands and feet. It was a difficult task, made worse by the fact that the fire was matching them step for step, catching hold of the moss and heather either side of them. The detective could feel the heat and taste the smoke but despite how close it came as it darted in and out of the rocks alongside Red Brook, the gully protected them. The sheer volume of rocks either side of them deepened, putting more and more distance between the group and the fire. *This might just fucking work.*

Brian - despite having Becky strapped across his shoulders and back - pulled ahead as the others helped Naomi navigate a particularly large set of moss-covered boulders. Jenny scaled them first - making it look easy - then pulled Uddin, Naomi and Smithdown up one after the other.

'I can see the ridge,' Brian shouted from above them. 'Not long now. Then we can take the Pennine Way path down to Kinder Low End and come down around the other side of the fire. We can beat it! You okay down there?'

'Oh yes,' gasped Smithdown. 'We're having an absolute hoot.'

'You're nearly there, John,' Brian cried. 'We'll sign you up as a mountain rescuer when this is done.'

'You fucking well won't,' the detective muttered, taking hold of another slab of rock and pulling himself upwards.

'Can we stop, please?' Uddin asked, sitting on a square, level boulder. 'Just for a minute?'

'You big mard arse,' Naomi said. 'I'm doing this one-handed.'

'One minute,' Jenny responded. 'Literally. I'm going to time it.'

The two detectives, the young man who wanted to be a lawyer and the single mum everyone thought was dead, rested for a moment and looked out across Greater Manchester and beyond. In the distance they could see the centre of Manchester. To the left was Stockport, the runway lights of Manchester Airport and then the Cheshire Plains; to the right, Ashton and the southern edge of Oldham. Below them were huge, curved fire walls that cut the moors into a series of impassable, blazing sections. They could see a mix of fire, plus ambulance and police flashing lights, scoping and illuminating the area behind the fire. More were arriving from all directions, heading for the car park where the White Wolves had gathered earlier in the evening. The four of them looked at the scene and then each other. 'Mad,' Uddin stated in a quiet, flat voice. 'Just... mad.'

'We need to go,' Jenny said, her voice now just a cracked whisper. 'Brian and Becky will already be on the Kinder edge path. Not long now.'

By now, Jenny and Uddin were helping Smithdown as much as they were helping Naomi. The detective was hurting. Hee was more than 30 years older than Uddin - the youngest of the group - and the detective's arms and legs burned with pain. But the ridge was now was almost in sight; the end point of Red Brook was just ten feet above them - two sides of the gully that came together in a V shape, with a tiny trickle of water going over the edge. Crossing it left to right was the Pennine Way path. Sheer black rock was behind the thin walkway.

Naomi went over the edge first, then Uddin. Smithdown was next, then Jenny. The detective was hoping to rest for a while to ease the searing ache the climb had created.

He immediately saw that wasn't going to happen.

On an outcrop of rock 20 feet from the edge of Red Brook, Adam Griffin was holding Becky Wells; his arm was across the little girl's mouth with the point of a machete touching the side of her head. She didn't seem tired and woozy now - her eyes were wide with fear and her body shook.

Next to them was Tom Lennon, standing over Brian McIntyre's body with a machete held above his head. He hacked at Brian's neck and shoulders once, then twice. A third machete blow came down. Lennon's legs shielded them from the worst of what had happened, but the detective could see that Brian's head was now resting on his shoulder at a sickening angle, the light from his headtorch stretched out into the night. Lennon turned, looked directly at Smithdown - then Jenny - and pushed Brian's body off the edge and down into the Red Brook gully.

Uddin's eyes flickered then closed; he swayed, fell against the rocks to the side of him and bounced off them, falling towards the edge in a dead faint.

Smithdown was surrounded by shouts and screams - he didn't know which belonged to Jenny, Lennon, Griffin or Naomi. Some were probably his own. Into the mix of noise came distant sirens, the sound of the fire below and the wind scraping across the rocks of Kinder Scout.

The four of them clung to each other on the ledge. 'If you move,' said Lennon. 'The little 'un goes next,' he said. He traced a finger through the air in an arc and made a descending whistling noise.

The screams and shouts dipped a little, but not by much. Smithdown's head was reeling from what he saw; he tried to focus on a way out, a resolution, a plan of action. *That's what detectives do, isn't it? Sort it out? Make it right?*

He tried to think of something - anything - that could bring a halt to the madness that was around him. For once he had nothing. There is no way out. All the detective could do was plead. 'Tom, please. This is madness, lad. Please. I'm begging you. No more.'

Lennon stood next to Griffin and Becky and pointed his machete at Smithdown and the others. The smoke from the moor fire was creeping over the edge now, snaking around their feet. 'SHUT THE FUCK UP,' Lennon shouted. 'Not fucking interested. You don't get a say any more. Your time is up. Your generation had your chance and you fucked it. This is not the time for talking. It's time for action. St George's Day is when things will really start. Then nothing will get in our way.'

'You bastards killed Brian,' Jenny screamed. 'Deprived my kids of his dad - and for what reason? He's a teacher… a fucking mountain rescue volunteer. What possible reason can you rustle up to justify that?'

Griffin, still holding onto Jenny, screamed back at Jenny: 'We are at WAR you stupid bitch. It's a fucking RACE WAR. Our race - your race - is under threat. This swarm of filth, drowning our people, ruining our way of life, has to end. It's a battle to the death and we are going win it.'

'You're not the same race as me,' Jenny shouted back. 'You bastards aren't even the same fucking species.'

Lennon spoke more quietly now: 'We'll wipe the slate clean in Oldham, then across Greater Manchester and then the whole country. But first we need to clean things up right here.'

He nodded to Griffin who loosened his grip on Becky and pushed her downwards until she lay on the path. He placed his foot onto the small of her back and raised his machete. The little girl seemed to have shaken off the last of her drug-induced lethargy. She turned her head and looked up at Griffin who laughed and let out a wolf-like cry. Becky matched him with a terrible scream.

The crowbar whooshed across the gap and hit Griffin square in the face. No one seemed more surprised than Uddin that the piece of metal he'd doggedly kept hold of since they were in Lennon's house had found its target and then clattered and clanged down Red Brook. Uddin's arm was still outstretched, frozen in time, as the blood spurted from Griffin's already battered nose. He lowered the machete slightly, wavered a little, then two seconds later raised the machete again over his head. Griffin had both hands on it now and was ready once again to bring it down on the little girl.

Naomi saw her chance the moment Uddin let fly with the crowbar. She ran, jumped the small V at the top of Red Brook, hit the path on the other side and kept on running. A moment after the blood had hit Griffin's jacket, she hit him straight on, wrapping her arms and legs around him in a crab-like grip. Griffin held firm, fury in his face but fear in his eyes. Then he staggered. Then fell. The momentum, plus Naomi's weight, took them both straight off the edge and down into the darkness.

'Look after Becky,' Jenny said to Smithdown in her sandpaper voice as she sprinted after Tom Lennon who had turned and run the moment Griffin and Naomi went over the edge.

The path at Kinder Edge was in total darkness now, the only light came from the flames below and Jenny's headtorch. Despite her injuries, she moved at astonishing speed, vaulting over rocks and deftly following the swerve of the path until she was within six feet of Lennon. Sensing she was behind him, he stopped, swung his machete back like a baseball bat, aiming it at Jenny's head as she hurtled towards him. She skidded to a halt and bent her neck back, allowing the blade to whistle past her face. As Lennon's weight followed the machete, she landed a kick to the side of his knee that unbalanced him. His leg buckled and he was brought low. The DC punched him in the throat. Lennon dropped the weapon, put his hands to his neck and wheezed for air as he dropped to his knees.

Smithdown could see them from Red Brook, their shapes highlighted by the glow of the fire below. Jenny grabbed Lennon by his jacket collar and looked as though she was readying herself to push him off the path. She leant him right out over the edge, letting him see the drop. For a moment she caught a flash of colour and light from the rocks below - it was Brian's jacket and torch.

Lennon saw it too.

Jenny swung him back from the edge and smashed his head against the wall of rocks that ran alongside the path. Then she pulled him back and did it again. 'Once more for good luck,' Smithdown whispered quietly, as he held Becky in his arms on the other side of Red Brook. 'Go on, girl.'

There was no way that Jenny could have heard him. But she did it once more anyway.

'Manchester Radio News at eleven, this is Beth Hall. Emergency crews from several counties have descended on a tiny village in north Derbyshire after a huge moorland fire broke out earlier this evening. It's thought the fire may have been started deliberately and several arrests have already been made. Mountain Rescue Teams have also been searching for the bodies of at least two people who are reported to have fallen from the edge of Kinder Scout - the highest point in the Peak District. Robert Crane joins us live from the scene and has the very latest.'

'The village of Hayfield is in chaos tonight as fire crews from several counties try to bring the blaze under control. It's thought to have started on moorland close to Kinder Reservoir and quickly spread up through a small plantation of trees and then on to an area known as Red Brook.

At least ten people have been arrested at the scene - they've now been taken to Glossop Police Station.

Meanwhile, Hayfield Mountain Rescuers - who've been searching for two people thought to have fallen from the edge of Kinder Scout - say they've now recovered a total of three bodies at the scene. At least one of the dead is thought to be that of a local rescue volunteer. Another is believed to be that of Naomi Wells. Bizarrely, the same woman who is thought to have already died at Kinder Scout several days ago.

It's not yet known how many of the fatalities died as a direct result of the fire, but I understand the moor - and Kinder Scout itself - have now both been declared murder scenes. This is Robert Crane, Manchester Radio News, in Hayfield.'

CHAPTER FIFTY-ONE

12.45am Wednesday 6 April 1988

After they'd been treated by an ambulance crew at the base of Kinder Scout - and a call had been made to Jean Smithdown - it was time to go. Smithdown and DC Seddon had both refused the offer to accompany Uddin and Becky to hospital. They didn't want further treatment, thank you. They had other business to attend to; Jenny Seddon had insisted on it. They said their goodbyes then asked to be taken to Glossop Police Station.

They passed a long line of fire engines as they drove away from Kinder Scout. Crews from three counties had answered the call to help put out the fire and the narrow road between Kinder and Hayfield was rammed with emergency workers preparing for one of the biggest fires they'd ever dealt with. Outside broadcast vehicles from Granada TV, the BBC and Manchester Radio were gathered at the far end of the road - police officers were directing the traffic as best they could, but it was a chaotic scene. A cordon had been formed to keep the journalists at bay. Smithdown recognised some of them from the TV. *What a story we have for you.*

Jenny leant her head against the window of the car as they drove away. The flashing lights illuminated her bruised and swollen face. A few dabs of rain touched the window. She waved weakly at one of the police officers who were trying to hold back a particularly pushy reporter with a microphone: 'Derbyshire Con-stab-u-lary,' she whispered and smiled at Smithdown. He took her hand and squeezed it.

As they weaved slowly but steadily through the tide of oncoming traffic towards Hayfield, Smithdown spotted something in the car park close to the mountain rescue centre and asked the driver to stop. Derbyshire Constabulary officers were holding several men ready to be taken away. The detective recognised some of them as Oldham police colleagues, mainly young constables. They were shouting and swearing as they were handcuffed and bundled into the back of a series of police vans. When they spotted Smithdown they directed their anger towards him as they disappeared through the van's rear double doors. One of the arrested men was more still than the others; he stood quietly waiting his turn. It was DC Bob Donaldson.

'One minute, please,' Smithdown said, as he stepped out of the car. 'This won't take long.'

'Fucking Nora,' Jenny Seddon muttered to herself as she watched the detective get out of the car.

Donaldson - handcuffed and being held by two PCs - half-smiled as he saw the detective walk across the car park towards him. It began to rain more steadily as the two men faced each other; a few dots and dashes at first, then it became steadily heavier as grey sheets of rain bounced off the ground around them. Black streaks of soot began to slide down Smithdown's face as the water washed his smoke-darkened skin.

'It's nasty out tonight, Bob,' Smithdown said, lighting up a JPS.

'Yeah,' Bob said, waiting his turn to be loaded into the back of the van. 'And now it's pissing it down too. Grim.'

'The rain's not so bad though,' Smithdown said. 'I don't mind it. It'll put the fire out. I hope so anyway. Wash all the burnt shit away. It looks terrible right now - fucking awful, in fact - but it'll be better by the morning.'

'You reckon?' said Donaldson.

'I reckon,' Smithdown confirmed, 'I spoke to Jean, just now.'

'Did you?'

'I did. She says you paid another call to Kate in the hospital.'

Donaldson was silent for a few beats. 'I suppose I did,' he confirmed.

'I hope you enjoy being in prison, Bob. Because everyone in there will know you're a cop. I'll make sure of it.' Smithdown took a step closer and looked Donaldson in the eye. The Derbyshire officers holding him weren't quite sure what to do. The situation confused them. As the rain came even more heavily, Smithdown gave them a reassuring look. Then he hawked up a gob of blackened phlegm and spat it right into Bob Donaldson's face.

Donaldson said nothing. Smithdown turned and walked back to the car. 'Let's go,' the detective said. This time, Jenny squeezed *his* hand.

Fifteen minutes later they walked through the front doors of Glossop Police Station and asked for the Duty Sergeant. 'Jesus, Jenny,' the middle-aged officer said as he approached the front desk from a back room and looked at the three blackened and bleeding faces in front of him.

'Sergeant,' she began. 'This is Thomas Lennon of Snipe Street,

Oldham.' Jenny pushed Lennon closer to the front desk. His hands were tied with the same cord that had been used to restrain Becky on their climb up Red Brook. His face was a tangle of cuts, gashes and bruises from being slammed against the Kinder rocks. Lennon stared at the ceiling, refusing to engage with what was happening. 'I've arrested him on suspicion of a number of offences both here and within the Greater Manchester force area. It's my belief that, because of the nature of the alleged crimes, it is better for him to be placed in custody here, rather than with the Greater Manchester Police.'

'DC Seddon,' the Duty Sergeant said. 'Are you sure you're in a fit state to do this…'

'Never been surer of anything in my life,' she replied.

'Okay - what have you arrested Mr Lennon in connection with, DC Seddon?' the Duty Sergeant asked.

She paused. 'I've arrested him in connection with the murder of Sharmeen Chowdhury of Oldham, Greater Manchester. She is a local councillor and was recently reported missing-from-home. It's my belief that it was her body that was discovered last week at the Mermaid's Pool near Hayfield and not that of one Naomi Wells. Ms Wells is in fact one of three fatalities that have occurred over at Kinder Scout this evening.

'Right you are,' the Sergeant said, writing the details onto the custody record sheet as fast as he could.

'I've also arrested Lennon in connection with the murder of a Mr Aleem …' she turned to Smithdown. 'Sorry, what was Aleem's first name?'

'Amir,' the detective replied. 'His name was Amir Aleem .'

'… in connection with a Mr Amir Aleem, of Queen's Road, Oldham.'

Just for a beat, Jenny hesitated. She breathed in and out, heavily. Then continued: 'Also, he is under arrest in connection with the murder of Brian McIntyre of number 70, Old Glossop Road…'

The Duty Sergeant looked directly at DC Seddon. For a moment he was silent. 'My God, Jenny,' he finally said. 'Brian? Christ… I mean, I'm so sorry…'

'Brian McIntyre is the second of the three fatalities at Kinder Scout. The third is Adam Griffin, also of Snipe Street, Oldham.'

The Duty Sergeant was struggling to keep up. 'Also,' Jenny continued, 'I'll be speaking to Lennon in connection with offences of attempted murder… unlawful imprisonment… rape… grievous bodily harm and Section 18 wounding. Plus, offences under the Public Order Act of 1986 that are frankly too fucking numerous to go into right now.'

'I've never heard anything like this in all my life, DC Seddon,' the Sergeant said, shaking his head.

'I agree, Sergeant. It really is quite the shopping list, isn't it? There's more. I'll also be seeking to speak to a Mr Richard T. King, a businessman based in Oldham, Greater Manchester and to a Detective Constable Bob Donaldson of Greater Manchester Police, also based in Oldham.'

'And who is this gentleman here?' the Sergeant said, pointing his pen in Smithdown's direction.

'This is Detective Inspector John Smithdown, also of Oldham Police. His testimony will be vital to the case against Mr Lennon and others. I may wish to put Mr Smithdown into witness protection as I believe his life may be in danger from elements within his own force.'

'You're alright, Jenny. I'll be fine. Soon as we're done here, I'm off home to see my Jean.'

'Whatever you say, Mr Smithdown,' Jenny said before addressing the Sergeant again: 'That's your lot, Sergeant.'

'Jesus wept…' the Sergeant said in an exhaled whisper. 'Do you have any pieces of evidence you wish to book in at this time?'

Smithdown dug deep into his jacket pocket and pulled out Mr Aleem's small tape recorder that contained their discussion with Naomi. He placed it on the counter. Then he felt around in his other pocket and pulled out his vest, still bundled into a tight ball. He carefully unwrapped it and placed Sharmeen Chowdhury's gaffa-taped hand next to the tape recorder. 'Just these two,' he said.

CHAPTER FIFTY-TWO

10am Thursday 7 April 1988

'Come in John,' said DS James Pym. 'Take a seat.'

Pym put out a hand and offered Smithdown a handshake. The detective's hands were criss-crossed with scratches from the rocks of Red Brook. He still smelled of smoke despite takings several baths. He took the DS's hand and the two men shook. Pym normally favoured an overly firm grip - what Smithdown considered to be a golf club bullshit handshake. Not today; it was soft and compliant. Maybe Pym was being cautious of his injured hands? Maybe not.

'John, let me be frank,' Pym sighed.

Here we go.

'We've got a balancing act on our hands here. A delicate one. We need you to see GMP's dilemma - and understand it.'

Smithdown said nothing.

Eyes open, gob shut.

'No one - absolutely no one - doubts that what you did was extraordinary. What you've uncovered in this division, maybe in this force, is going to be felt across the land. You've sent a shockwave thought the policing community. No question. You instinctively felt something wasn't right about the Wells case and you went with it. And you were dead right. Fair play to you.'

'I'm sure you would have done exactly the same thing in my circumstances, Jim,' Smithdown said. He was aiming for a low-key tone of deadpan sarcasm and was slightly concerned that he might have underdone it.

'You saved that kiddie, Becky Wells,' Pym continued. 'You saved that lad Uddin too. Though what he was doing out there on the moors with you in the first place is something I'm looking forward to hearing all about. Or maybe I'm not.' Pym smiled. He didn't get one in return. So, he continued. 'This is going to take a long time to… untangle.'

'Is it?'

'Yes, John. It really is.'

Smithdown went silent again. He was in no rush. 'It's going to be in everyone's interest to get this to trial as soon as possible,' Pym continued. 'But it's still going to take time. They're all saying nowt, so far. Bob, King, Lennon… these so-called Wolves… the lot of them. But maybe that will change. It'll be interesting to see if Bob survives being on remand. A cop, facing the kind of charges he's got coming down the pipe? He'll have more targets on him than a Mod's parka.'

'Let's hope no harm comes to him then,' Smithdown offered. 'That would be a bad thing in all sorts of ways.'

'Yes, it would. Absolutely. So, John. What I'm saying is… you're going to have to bide your time. We need to get the trial done before we can even look at your disciplinary. There's obviously going to have be an inquiry into the whole… *infiltration* of the force thing. What went on etcetera. Root and branch, lessons learnt - all that. It could take a year or so to sort out. But maybe the timing's perfect. Kate's on the mend. Jean needs you at home now more than ever. Get yourself off home. You might even be able to stretch this to your retirement. You're not far off doing 30 years, then that's you done.'

'I'm in no hurry to retire, Jim,' Smithdown said. 'Sooner I can get back to work, the happier I'll be.'

The two men looked at each other. 'So that's it, John,' Pym said. 'Sit tight. Wait for the process to work itself out, then we'll take it from there.'

'That it?' Smithdown asked.

'Yes, it is John. Give my regards to Jean and of course we all wish a speedy recovery to Kate.'

Smithdown got up from his chair. He looked at the scratches on his hands. 'Just one thing before I go, Jim…'

'Of course. Anything, John.'

'You knew, didn't you?'

EPILOGUE

9am Sunday 1 April 1990

'Radio Manchester News at nine, this is Beth Hall. A policeman, hailed a hero after his part in exposing the neo- Nazi infiltration of Oldham Police, is set to return to work tomorrow after spending nearly two years on suspension. Detective Inspector John Smithdown was told to step down from his duties after allegations he harmed a child in his custody in 1988. But an internal Greater Manchester Police inquiry has found that there was no case to answer. Mr Smithdown is due back at his desk first thing tomorrow morning. The investigation had to be put on hold untilthe end of the so-called 'Nazi Cops' trial. Several Oldham police officers, including Detective Constable Bob Donaldson were finally jailed on Thursday for their part in a string of murders and racist attacks in Oldham. Danny Johnston reports.'

'What started as a murder inquiry into the apparent death of sex worker Naomi Wells in April 1988, turned into one of the biggest police scandals the UK has ever seen. Officers from Oldham Police were found to have been conspiring with neo-Nazi groups to seize power on the local Council by any means possible - that included murder, kidnapping and inciting a riot. Their aim was to provoke a race war to push an extremist, racist agenda. Nine people are now serving life sentences for their part in the scandal - six were serving police officers, including Detective Constable Bob Donaldson.

Donaldson, along with neo-Nazi activist Thomas Lennon, conspired to stage a series of murders and attacks to further their aim of generating a backlash against South Asian communities in Oldham. Their ultimate goal was grabbing political power and making money from land sales brought about by forced repatriation.

Yesterday a memorial was unveiled outside the town hall, dedicated to those who lost their lives during those tragic events of Easter 1988. Those include murdered local Councillor Sharmeen Chowdhury, mountain rescue volunteer Brian McIntyre, local businessman Amir Aleem and teenager Tariq Shamsi. Oldham MP Peter Jeffries says it's their names - not those of the guilty - that we should remember:'

> *"These evil people used fear to generate hate and divide our communities. But they failed. This town showed it was better than that and rose above their hate-filled message. The Oldham we had before all this was a good place, full of good people. The Oldham we have today is even better."*

The memorial was paid for by local businessman Richard T King - one of ten people originally set to stand trial. He was cleared of all charges after a search of offices above his Oldham nightclub was deemed to have been unlawful. The incident forced a retrial of the remaining accused.

Detective Inspector John Smithdown is now in line for a police bravery award for his actions in exposing the scandal, alongside DC Jennifer Seddon of the Derbyshire Constabulary. Oldham teenager Mohiuddin Rahman will receive a civilian award. Posthumous awards will go to DC Seddon's late partner Brian McIntyre and to Naomi Wells, the woman whose disappearance sparked the initial inquiry.

Detective Superintendent James Pym of Oldham Police, says that he is looking forward to welcoming DI Smithdown back to work on Monday:'

> *"DI John Smithdown exemplifies everything this force and this division is about: honesty, integrity, decency and fairness. We are forever in his debt. The policing community in Oldham have been through some tough times in the last two years, but we are a family. And we're looking forward to welcoming back one of the most important members of that family on Monday."*

'After the initial arrests of DC Donaldson and several of his colleagues, Greater Manchester Police promised what was described as a 'root and branch' investigation into further links between its officers and neo-Nazi groups. So far, no other officers have been suspended and GMP describe the 'Nazi Cops' case as a one-off incident. Danny Johnston, Manchester Radio News, at GMP Headquarters in Old Trafford.'

CHAPTER FIFTY-THREE

5am Monday 2 April 1990

When the phone rang, Jean Shipdown knew full well the call wouldn't be for her and barely stirred. 'Bloody hell,' Jean muttered. 'First day back and they're ringing already?'

She'd enjoyed the peace that her husband's nearly two-year suspension had given them - no phone calls at strange times of the night or morning, no coming and going when regular people were asleep, no aching worry for the harm that might come her husband's way. That, it appeared, was all over, but then Smithdown had received the news confirming he was to be reinstated on the previous Wednesday. The official letter had arrived by recorded delivery first thing on Friday morning. She was happy for him but had cried later when he wasn't in the room.

John and Jean Smithdown had spent that Saturday in nearby Uppermill. They'd had a pub lunch, done a little shopping and called in to see Becky Wells, settled and happy now that her adoption had been confirmed with Mr Aleem's widow and her extended family.

Then they'd walked a little on the Huddersfield Canal that cut gently though the centre of the town, but Jean had tired quickly and he'd taken her home.

After what seemed like real progress with her treatment, the cancer had started to make inroads back into their lives again. The disease seemed harsher this time; fiercer - more determined. The options open to them looked narrower, the words from her oncologist quieter and more final. Smithdown had told his wife that he wanted to take retirement. She'd said no. 'I'm sick of you knocking around this house,' she'd lied. 'You're driving me mad. You should get back to work. You need to walk back into that police station with your head held high. I'm not going to deny you that.'

Reluctantly, he'd agreed.

'Smithdown,' the detective said into the trimphone receiver.

'It's DC Cave, sir. Sorry to ring so early.'

'It's okay, Jan. Strangeways, is it?'

They'd planned to spend Sunday visiting friends but had stayed in to allow Jean to rest and to follow events at Strangeways Prison. A riot had broken out during a service at the jail's chapel. The Smithdowns watched as rioters took control of the prison, then broken through to the roof, taunting prison officers from their vantage points, knowing the authorities couldn't touch them as the drama played on television. 'If they don't regain control today - they've had it,' Smithdown had told his wife.

Bob's in that jail. The other inmates will be gunning for him. He's had it.

After seeing the rioters on the news, the detective had volunteered to come back to work a day early - but Detective Superintendent James Pym had told him to wait, take the day with Jean and arrive fresh on Monday. Perhaps the DS had changed his mind.

The detective had then phoned Kate, but she wasn't in. Then he'd tried the *Oldham Messenger* where she was working, but he'd been told that she was on her way to the jail - several prisoners spotted on the roof were thought to be from the Oldham area. *You've always got to get a local angle.*

'No, you're not required at Strangeways, sir,' DC Cave continued. 'Bit closer to home. Literally close to your home, in fact. We've got a report of body - possibly a child - out at Black Moss reservoir. That's near you, isn't it?'

'It is, just up the Huddersfield Road,' he confirmed. 'Bang on the Yorkshire border, in fact. Are we sure it belongs to GMP? It might be a case for the Tykes not us if the body's on the other side of the Pennine Way.'

'It was called in from the Manchester side, so I assume so,' DC Cave said. 'Mr Pym told me to pass it straight to you as you know the area. Is that okay?'

'It's fine, Jan. I can be there in ten minutes, though it's another 20 to walk to the reservoir down the Pennine Way.'

'There's two uniforms there already, securing the scene. That's all I know. I'll leave you to it.'

'No problem, Jan.'

'Good to have you back, sir,' she said.

'A dead kiddie by a reservoir out on the moors? Who wouldn't want to come back to work to a treat like that? Tell Pym I'm on it. Thanks Jan.'

Smithdown replaced the receiver and got out of bed. He pulled his trousers over his pyjama bottoms and swapped the top for a shirt. He pulled his mac from the wardrobe. He hadn't worn in for nearly two years.

'Straight back to it then?' Jean said, propping herself up in bed. There was barely anything left of her now. The cancer had whittled her away. But her eyes and smile were enough for Smithdown.

'Yes love,' he replied, putting a tie around his neck and rummaging in a chest of drawers for some socks. 'Straight back to it.'

THE END

Postscript

The Mermaid's Pool is a work of fiction but, like all the stories in the Manc Noir Trilogy it has its basis very much in fact. Real-life riots took place in Oldham in 2001. At the height of the disturbances 500 youths were involved and 15 police officers were injured. Here is a section of the Minutes of Evidence from the House of Lords Select Committee on Religious Offences in England and Wales 2002-3. Full details at www.parliament.co.uk

A Case Study On Oldham

The classic example of the nature and impact of Far-Right activities against the Muslim community is provided by the northern city of Oldham. The upsurge in the level of activities by Far-Right organisations in this city, including the BNP and the NF, are at least partly the catalyst for the civil unrest witnessed there in the early summer of 2001. Two reports seek to illustrate the socially divisive and disruptive role played in this city by Far-Right organisations.

The first report, produced by the Black Racial Attacks Independent Network, entitled *The Oldham Riots - Shattering the Myths*, states:

'. . . the result of years of . . . institutional attitudes combined with media hysteria has given legitimacy and created a climate for the racists and the BNP (British National Party) to gain a foothold to propagate and stir hatred... It is important to note the BNP's strategy of blaming Muslim communities for the problems in the northern towns. Articles have appeared on BNP websites and literature, with titles such as: '*The Situation in Oldham: Ethnic Cleansing Muslim Style*', calling for a boycott of Muslim businesses, but not Chinese or Hindu. On the BBC's Newsnight programme, in an interview by Jeremy Paxman with Nick Griffin, Griffin stated that: "It's not an Asian or black problem but a Muslim one". The existence of Islamophobia in society endorsed by Government policies on refugees, asylum, terrorism . . . etc., in conjunction with the media's subsequent portrayal [of these people] further adds to Islamophobic attitudes which the BNP turn into political gain by claiming to disillusioned whites that these fundamentalist Muslims live only up the road from them...'

The second report, produced by the Islamic Human Rights Commission, entitled *The Oldham Riots - Discrimination, Deprivation and Communal Tension in the United Kingdom*, offers similar insights:

'Political leaders in the town have admitted that the riots had been stirred up by right-wing white extremists. Both the Police and the Prime Minster concurred . . . Even [a local] Chief Superintendent highlighted the particular role of the National Front (NF) and British National Party (BNP)… Statements by right-wing groups reveal that their efforts were primarily directed against Oldham's Muslim Community. An article on the race riots on the BNP's website commented that "this is how extremists within the Muslim community in Oldham are repaying the hospitality of the people who built the town and allowed them to settle there by the tens of thousands." Another BNP article remarked on how the Party has been able to use the riots to further exacerbate racist and Islamophobic sentiment to thereby recruit members: 'Media coverage and the personal experience of scores of thousands of white people every year are combining to make gangs of Muslim thugs the best recruiting sergeant the British National Party has ever had… it is a perceived distinction… and one which indicates the current state of anti-discriminatory legislation in the UK.'

BLACK MOSS

PART I

ONE

7.05am Friday 6 April 1990

The location instructions that Danny Johnston had been given by the news desk were odd, even by the standards that he'd come to expect over the last six months: *Take the A62 out of Oldham. Pass through Diggle. Stop at Brun Clough Reservoir car park. Pennine Way sign on your right. Walk PW path until you reach another reservoir (Redbook). Next one is Black Moss Reservoir, with Little Black Moss next to it. Look for a beach and police activity.*

Look for a beach… *Seriously?* It was bad enough being sent this far out of his patch. The radio station Danny worked for as a reporter was supposed to cover Greater Manchester and no more; Danny was almost certain that this far up the moorland A62 road he could practically smell Yorkshire. There was certainly a glow of amber light over the next heather-covered brow and he had a strong suspicion it was coming from Huddersfield. *This isn't our patch – this is wild goose chase bollocks. That's bad enough in itself. But look for a beach? Come on. That's taking the piss.*

Spotting the wooden Pennine Way marker that the instructions had mentioned, Danny parked up the radio car with its distinctive rooftop mast and yellow-and-blue Manchester Radio logos. He turned off the cassette that he'd been playing as he drove – Technique by New Order.

Pulling a can of Coke from his pocket, he popped the ring pull and drank half of it. His head throbbed, and his throat was parched. The shock of sugar and caffeine didn't cure it, but experience told him it would see him through the next twenty minutes or so.

As he got out of the car he pulled a tie out of his pocket – it was already looped into a tight knot – and pulled it over his head and around his neck, tucking it roughly under his collar. *Proper reporters wear ties*, he'd been told on his first day at Manchester Radio. *In some of the places you'll be going, people treat you like God if you're wearing a tie.*

Danny put the strap of a black, Marantz cassette recorder over his shoulder, shoved the microphone attached to it into his trouser pocket and locked the car. You could always tell reporters from independent radio stations from their BBC counterparts by the tape machines they used. The BBC favoured hefty, reel-to-reel German Uher machines. The indie reporters were issued with the much lighter Japanese Marantz units. *The BBC are slow and safe, like their tape machines* – another piece of wisdom he'd been issued with – *we are light on our feet and fast. In and out. No messing.*

Lighting up a cigarette and swearily muttering about the boggy conditions and his inappropriate footwear, Danny set off down the windy Pennine Way path. The gravel soon gave way to paving slabs, which rocked and squelched under his feet – the ground below was soaked through with water. Pockets of icy snow still lined either side of the path, the result of a slightly freakish series of spring-time snow showers earlier in the week.

The path forked right at the first reservoir and then headed upwards, following the soft, rolling flow of the moorland. The slabs that formed the path were drier here, the slope of the route allowing the moisture to drain off the watershed. Danny looked right; down through the valleys he could see the lights of Manchester.

He looked left. More lights, telecommunications towers and buildings, *that's definitely Huddersfield*, he thought. *There's no story out here and even if there is one, it probably doesn't belong to us.*

Danny had never been out here before. He'd heard the moors were bleak, but he wasn't prepared for the sheer unrelenting *nothingness* of the area. It was like the world had been horizontally cut in two – sky at the top, moor at the bottom, with nothing to provide any form of relief from the two themes. *Not even a tree. Not one. In any direction. Bleak.*

As he crested the hill he could see a second reservoir; there were figures there. Activity. There was clearly *something* going on – whether it was happening within the Manchester Radio broadcast area was quite another matter.

The thin blue jacket and off-white shirt that Danny wore gave precious little protection from the wind as it nipped and pinched at his upper body. The situation wasn't helped by the fact that halfway down the front of his shirt, one of the buttons was missing. Every push of wind seemed to find the gap. Danny pulled his jacket together, held it shut around his slight frame with both arms and continued.

The wind pushed his dark brown hair back from his face. Danny's hair had been fashioned into the floppy, fringey haircut adopted by the majority of Manchester males in their mid-twenties over the last eighteen months. The hairdo was so omnipresent it was probably no longer fashionable, but Danny hadn't had the time or the inclination to do anything about it.

He got closer to the second, grey sheet of reservoir he'd been told to head for. The wind pushed tiny, quick waves across the top of the water. The Pennine Way's paving slabs gave way to grit and small stones and then to sand. Danny saw two police officers close to a patch of land between the path and the water's edge of Black Moss. One policeman was waving his arms at the other, shouting at him. Danny looked past the officers and his eyes were drawn to a dark, yellowy strip that separated the mossy moorland from the reservoir. Next to the reservoir – there was no other word for it – was a beach.

The police close to the water spotted Danny approaching and held up a shiny, white sheet to mask something in the sand. The sheet made a plasticky, crackling sound, like something used on a building site to wrap up bricks. 'Morning,' Danny said. 'I'm from Manchester Radio. Is the senior officer about, please?'

'Fuck off mate,' one of the PCs shouted, struggling in the wind with the white sheet. 'We're not supposed to talk to you... But fuck off anyway.' The officer was a similar age to Danny. His face was as pale as the sheet he was grappling with and he appeared to have vomit down the front of his uniform. His helmet was lying on the floor close to his feet. It was speckled with wet sand.

Danny was about to go into his spiel – the one he had been told to trot out in circumstances like these – about how that this was a public right of way and he wasn't causing any obstruction. The usual stuff. As he was about to start speaking the harsh moorland wind whipped hard against the sheet and pulled it from the hand of one of the policemen. One side of the plastic flipped left to right and flew into the face of the other PC, exposing the area of beach they'd been trying to hide. Danny looked down and saw the body of a small child lying face down in the sand. His tiny legs just touched the path. It was a boy. At least, it looked like a boy. A bloated, puffy, white thing, but a boy nonetheless. Nine, maybe ten years old. He was wearing socks, sandals and grey school shorts. His hands were bunched into fists and looked unnaturally dark, like they'd been dipped in black paint. His arms and neck were bare, but his torso was covered with a shiny black strapping that had been wrapped around and around his back and chest. His face was almost entirely buried in the sand, but Danny could just make out the corner of his mouth. It was curled up. Like he was smiling. Danny had never seen a dead body before. Ever. 'Christ Almighty,' said Danny. 'Poor kid. *Christ.*'

'No pictures, you fuckin' vulture,' said a third officer, who ran towards the group as his colleagues struggled to put the sheet back in place. 'Get back to the road. I mean it. Fuck off out of it. Right now.'

Danny half-heartedly waved his microphone in the policeman's direction and stepped back. 'I'm from the radio,' he said quietly. 'We don't do pictures. We do sound. Christ. *Poor kid.*'

Danny began to walk back up the path. Then he glanced back at the scene and again caught a glimpse of the body, this time over the top of the sheet. The officers were still struggling with it against the wind and they were arguing between themselves again. The strapping across the child's back seemed to shine in the early morning light. Then the wind eased, and the sheet began to behave, doing the job it had been commandeered for in the first place: that of stopping people from seeing the body of a little boy, half buried in sand next to a grim, moorland reservoir in the middle of nowhere.

Halfway back to the radio car, Danny saw a middle-aged man in a dirty, fawn-coloured rain mac and crumpled suit walk towards him. *Here's the boss*, Danny thought. *He must be in charge – he has a moustache and he looks pissed off.* Danny recognised him: *Detective Inspector… Smithdown? Yes.* DI John Smithdown from Greater Manchester Police. *Good bloke. Old school cop. Meat and potatoes… as straightforward as his name. Snap out of it and do your job. Talk to him.*

'Mr Smithdown? Danny Johnston from Manchester Radio. Remember me? I interviewed you about a thousand times over the Oldham prostitute murder a few months back. Good result for your team that was.' *Shameless flattery, but it might work.*

'Yes Danny. Morning. Nice bit of flattery there. Well done. It won't work, you know.' The detective stopped and glanced at Danny's tape recorder. 'Bit far away from the bright lights and wine bars of Manchester for you this, isn't it? How are you coping alright with the altitude?'

'I got a mild nosebleed as I drove through Diggle, but it soon passed,' Danny replied. The slightest of smiles appeared briefly across DI Smithdown's face. *Good sign,* Danny thought. The golden rule of Manchester Radio was: *Never Come Back to the Station Without an Interview. Ever.* So, he continued trying to engage the DI in chat. 'This is bloody miles away from anywhere though,' added Danny. 'Where's the border with Yorkshire?'

'You're standing on it, young man,' said the policeman. The two looked at the stone-flagged Pennine Way path beneath their feet. The DI stamped his feet. 'This is the border right here.'

'Terrible business down there at the... well, beach I suppose,' Danny continued. The two men looked at each other. The officer was in his late forties. His face was grey, so was his moustache. And his eyes. Danny suddenly felt very young and inexperienced. Long pause. DI Smithdown said nothing.

'Your lads let the sheet slip for a second,' Danny said, pointing down the path with his microphone. 'Easily done in this wind. Not their fault, I'm sure.'

Danny looked directly at DI Smithdown and made a point of holding eye contact with him. 'I saw the kid's body. Just awful. Couldn't have been more than nine or so, would you say?' Again – the pause. Danny instinctively wound the flex of his microphone in a loop around his hand. This stopped the lead from touching the ground, in case anyone was to step on it and disconnect the mic. *Habit.* 'Could I get a few words, Mr Smithdown? For our next bulletin?' Very long pause. 'I've come a long way. As you yourself pointed out.'

DI Smithdown looked away from Danny and up the path towards the road. There were headlights approaching. Forensics, more officers, scenes of crime personnel – they'd make a better job of shielding the boy's body than two PCs with a sheet. He looked back at Danny and pulled a crumpled, black pack of John Player Special cigarettes from his coat pocket. There was one left. He lit it and again looked directly at Danny – so much so, it made the reporter feel slightly uncomfortable. 'How come you were here so quickly?' the detective asked. 'You journos normally hunt in packs. There's always a huddle of you. You're streets ahead of everyone this morning. How come?'

'We got a tip off,' Danny said. 'An anonymous call about an hour and a half ago. I suppose I was the next person due on shift, so they got me out of bed and sent me straight here. Everyone else has been too busy covering the riot. Just my bad luck, really. And yours.'

The riot that had started at Strangeways Jail on Sunday of that week had electrified the Manchester Radio newsroom. Ever since prisoners had broken through the upper ceiling of the jail and taken up residence on the roof, coverage had been wall to wall and the story led every bulletin. Nothing else seemed to matter other than the latest news on the rooftop protests at the prison. There'd been talk that dead bodies were piled high inside the jail and that the SAS were preparing to go in.

One remand prisoner, who'd been attacked by other inmates on day one of the disturbances, had already died in hospital from his injuries. Danny had gleaned most of this by listening to the radio and reading the *Manchester Evening News*, because he hadn't been near the jail since the riot had started.

'All the proper reporters are covering the riot, I reckon,' said DI Smithdown. *You probably have a point there*, Danny thought. 'Right,' sighed the detective. 'Get your microphone out. But, let's be clear...' The DI took a pull on his cigarette and took a step closer to Danny. He was head and shoulders taller and smelled of alcohol and mints. 'You didn't see the body, did you?' he said, softly but very, very firmly. '*No, I did not, Mr Smithdown*,' the DI said, providing his own answer before Danny could reply. 'Because my lads never dropped that sheet, did they? *No, they did not, Mr Smithdown.* So, you can't ask me anything specific about the body, can you? *No, I cannot, Mr Smithdown.* Clear?'

'Crystal clear, Mr Smithdown,' said Danny. He pressed play and record on the Marantz recorder and held the microphone about six inches from the DI's mouth. 'Could you identify yourself for the tape please?'

'DI John Smithdown, Oldham CID, Greater Manchester Police... tired, hungry, pissed off and eager to get this over with very quickly indeed.'

Okay. Best keep this straightforward, Danny thought. 'DI Smithdown, what can you tell us about the discovery officers have made out here this morning?'

DI Smithdown switched immediately into copperspeak, the bland, verbal autopilot that the police tended to use when they wanted to give as little away as possible: 'At approximately 5.30 am this morning the body of a juvenile male was discovered by a man out walking his dog. The area is currently being sealed off and a fingertip search of the scene will commence shortly. The age and identity of the juvenile male are not yet known, and I have no further details to give at this present moment in time.'

The officer gave Danny a small nod, a semi-polite half smile and walked off towards Black Moss. More vehicles and officers had arrived. *Not the greatest interview ever*, thought Danny, *but it will have to do.* He looked at his watch: 7.45 am. If he could get a decent signal going from the radio car, he'd be able to make the 8 am bulletin. He rewound his tape, turned up the volume on the built-in speaker and pressed play to check that the interview – such as it was – had recorded. He heard Smithdown's words about a 'juvenile male' – all was well. 'Thank you, Mr Smithdown,' he half shouted at the officer as he walked behind him up the path. Then he thought of something. 'Mr Smithdown?' The policeman half turned. 'Who's in charge then, Greater Manchester or Yorkshire?'

'We are,' the DI shouted back. 'The body's lying right across the border but the bloke who found it called it in from Diggle. That makes it GMP.' He carried on walking.

There were more police vehicles gathering now. It looked to Danny like they were setting up an incident room. Soon the scene and the story would be locked down. The police press office would take over and there would be no more opportunities to talk to officers at the scene like this. 'Mr Smithdown? One more thing. The recorder's off by the way – what was that stuff wrapped around the kid's chest?'

DI Smithdown carried on walking but half raised both hands in a universal gesture that anyone would recognise for *how the hell should I know?* He carried on down the path towards the reservoir.

Danny ran the opposite way up the Pennine Way and arrived back at the radio car; he unlocked it and sat in the driver's seat. He had things to do and they needed doing quickly – the eight o'clock news was now less than ten minutes away. He pulled a small pad from his inside jacket pocket, took a green, Pentel pen from the breast pocket and pulled off the cap with his teeth. At the same time, he pushed a large red button on a control panel behind the handbrake. It operated the mechanism that raised the huge, sectioned mast that sat in the middle of the car. The motorised mast groaned, scraped and moved upwards, its sections separating one by one, pushing the mast from the roof of the car and into the bright, moorland sky. Danny had to keep one hand on the button at all times to keep it moving. There was a reason for this: if he had forgotten to check for overhead power lines and was electrocuted, the mast would stop moving upwards, thus reducing any further damage to the expensive radio car.

With his other hand, Danny started to write a rough script for his piece. It came in two sections: first a cue – a few sentences for the newsreader to say to introduce the piece – then Danny's report, with a gap in the middle for DI Smithdown's 'interview'. The words came quickly: murder squad detectives... *that was always a good way of suggesting it's a murder without actually saying it.* Grim discovery... *Dramatic. The station bosses loved that kind of stuff.* He decided to put the name of the reservoir in his SOC – the 'standard out cue' that signified the end of his piece. Black Moss Reservoir: *that sounds spooky.*

When the mast was fully upright it stopped. Danny picked up the chunky mobile phone that was embedded into the dashboard. He uncoiled the spiral lead and dialled the number that was taped to the dashboard of the car and marked 'Master Control Room'.

'MCR, Gary speaking,' said the voice on the end of the line.

'Gary, it's Danny.'

'Danny boy!' yelled Gary Keenan, the radio station's chief engineer.

'The very same. Right, I need to get a signal up to feed a piece for the eight and I'm on the outskirts of fucking nowhere. Or just past Diggle, as it's also known.'

'Telling you now – shit signal from there mate,' Gary responded, in a slightly offended tone, as if Danny had gone there on purpose just to annoy him.

'I don't care, as long as it's audible.'

'Absolute philistine. Right, no guarantees, but let's give it a whirl. Powered up?'

'Yes.'

'Waving your wand in my direction?'

Same chat every time. To get a signal, the head of the fifteen-foot mast had to be literally pointing at the radio station – nothing more technical than that. Once the engineer had located the position, the mast was then twisted and fine-tuned until the best possible feed could be established. Danny put his hand around the mast ready for the engineer's instructions.

'Absolute shit,' Gary said, looking at the signal display in the control room. 'Let's see what we can do. Okay, turn right. Right. Right again.' Danny edged the mast in the direction he was told.

'Stop there,' Gary ordered. 'Stop. *Stop, you twat!* Back a bit. Bit more. Done. Shall I transfer you to the news desk?'

'Yep.' Danny heard a short blast of the station's output – 'Dub Be Good to Me' by Beats International – and the transferred call was answered. One of the curses of working at a radio station was that Danny knew every record in the chart, whether he liked the song or not.

'News desk,' came the answer.

'It's Danny, who's that?'

'It's Beth and it's five to eight,' the voice replied.

'Fully aware,' Danny mumbled. He really didn't like Beth Hall. She was Manchester Radio's morning news presenter. She was ex-network news and everything she said – and the way she said it – was designed to remind you of the fact.

'Cue,' she said. It wasn't a question.

‘Right,’ Danny spoke slowly, giving Beth time to type the introduction to his piece. He heard the clatter of an electric typewriter as he read out the words. ‘A child’s body has been found close to a reservoir on the outskirts of Oldham. The grim discovery was made in the early hours of this morning. Murder squad detectives have sealed off the area close to the main A62 road at Diggle. From the scene, Danny Johnston has this report.’

‘Are there any other journos there?’ Beth asked.

‘Not yet.’

‘This *exclusive* report,’ she corrected. Beth swung her chair around, expertly wound some quarter-inch tape into the Studer reel-to-reel machine behind her and jabbed the illuminated button marked ‘OB’ on the control panel next to it. At his end, Danny knew the drill. He plugged his tape recorder into the mini sound mixer fixed into dashboard and lined up the tape to where DI Smithdown began his brief statement. Danny paused the tape just as the officer took a breath before saying his first words. At the same time, he plugged his mic into the adjoining input. He needed to give a sound level. Without being asked he began speaking: ‘Two, two, one two, I can count, and I am giving you a sound level by counting… Two, two,’ he said as his voice jarred the sound level needle from its resting place. In the newsroom, Danny’s signal should have been wavering around five on the sound meter but was struggling to hit four.

‘The signal’s crap, give it plenty of oomph,’ said Beth. ‘And it’s four minutes to. If you balls it up you’re doing it live. And we both know you’re shit at that.’

Thanks for the confidence boost there, Beth, he thought. *What a cow.*

A few weeks earlier, Danny had lost his way during a live piece outside a local town hall. His words had tumbled into each other and the sense of the piece had been completely lost. Beth had cut his item short and continued with the rest of the bulletin.

‘Okay,’ said Danny. Two minutes to eight now. He prepared to do a count in, so Beth knew when to press record.

Three, two, one... (pause). ‘The body of the child, thought to be around eight or nine years old, was found at the edge of Black Moss Reservoir a few miles outside of Diggle. It’s believed the body had been discovered on the exact spot that marks the border between Greater Manchester and Yorkshire. Officers are now sealing off the scene. Detective Inspector John Smithdown is in charge of the operation...’

Danny released the pause button and played in the recording of DI Smithdown’s brief chat. When the officer finished off by saying, ‘present moment in time,' Danny picked up and continued his voiceover: *'Forensic teams are now arriving, and murder squad officers are now overseeing the removal of the child's body before a post-mortem examination can reveal the cause of his death. Danny Johnston, Manchester Radio News, at Black Moss Reservoir.'*

He heard Beth jabbing at buttons and his own voice play back down the telephone line. It had recorded fine at the other end. He expected a word from Beth that all was well, but the line went dead. He didn't mind. It was nearly one minute to the news. Danny turned on the radio and stepped out of the radio car, leaving the door open so he could hear. He lit a cigarette as the DJ spoke over the outro of 'Loaded' by Primal Scream and introduced the news. The jingle stated that Manchester Radio was 'always first with the news that matters.' Then Beth introduced herself: 'Manchester Radio news at eight o'clock, I'm Beth Hall.' The crabby, bad-tempered tone she had used with Danny was gone. In its place was a smooth, soft and low delivery as she read the first item... about the ongoing riot at Strangeways jail. *She hasn't even led on it! Fucking cow!*

Danny leant into the car and switched off the radio. He looked down the A62 road and saw more vehicles approaching. Other journalists were arriving – the BBC's radio car was bringing up the rear. Looking over his shoulder to the crime scene he saw the boy's body was now covered by a portable white tent. *The professionals have arrived*, he thought. He saw DI Smithdown walking back down the path, briefing a scene of crime officers. The whole area was now cordoned off with 'Police Do Not Cross' tape. *No one else will be getting near the reservoir today*, he thought. *Or the kid's body.*

He pulled on the last of his cigarette. *God, it's freezing.* He thought about what he'd seen, about the little boy, the edge of his mouth curled into a deathly smile. That thought – and the cold bite of the Pennine air – made him shiver. He constantly told himself he wasn't going to become one of those clichéd reporters that didn't care and seemed to take pleasure in boasting about the fact. Those hard cases that let everything just wash over them like it didn't matter. Something truly terrible had happened out here at Black Moss and Danny Johnston cared about it. It mattered.

TWO

9.35pm Friday 20 May 2016

His first thought wasn't... *How badly am I hurt?*

Nor was it... *Have I hurt anyone else?*

No. It was... *I wonder if this is the same tree Marc Bolan crashed into?*

Daniel Johnston leant forward and looked at the tree he'd hit. The shattered windscreen made it difficult to see, but it set his mind at rest on one issue: *Can't be the Bolan tree,* he thought. *It would have flowers and ribbons and messages on it. Definitely.*

Hang on a minute, you daft sod, Johnston thought. *That tree's in Barnes. This is Clapham Common. Thank fuck for that! You're not thinking straight, Daniel... God, you really are pissed.*

He grabbed at his seat belt and tried to find the release catch. Then he realised he wasn't wearing a seat belt. *Good, that'll save some time. Best get out of the car.*

He opened the door of his high-end four-by-four, fell forward, twisted and somehow landed neatly on his back. He looked at the sky. A young couple in their twenties leaned over him and partially blocked Daniel's view of the stars. The woman seemed concerned. The young man with her had an iPhone in his hand and was pointing it down at Daniel. The light from the phone glared white into his eyes. 'Are you okay?' the young woman said, looking down at him.

'He's absolutely wankered is what he is,' the young man said, shaking his head. 'Wasted.'

The woman prodded her friend with her finger. 'It's him, isn't it? The guy off the telly. The documentary journalist guy.'

'The Mr Totally Wasted Guy, more like,' the young man said. 'All self-righteous on the TV and here he is all pissed up, falling out of his flash car. Absolute joke.'

'Hi,' said Daniel from down on the floor. 'I don't suppose I could ask you not to film me at this rather difficult time?'

'You don't ask permission from those guys you chase down the street on the telly, do you?' the man replied.

'Fair point,' Daniel conceded. He tried to get up, thought better of it and decided to stay put. The ground felt cool on his back. Two police officers joined the small group of people now looking down at him. Blue lights danced across the faces of the staring group. One officer was speaking into his radio: 'Yeah, white male, late forties/early fifties, RTA on Clapham Common Southside – junction with Rookery Road. Male is conscious. Just about. Injuries not yet ascertained. Front-end damage to vehicle. Looks like no other vehicles involved. Request ambulance.' The officer paused. 'Drink apparently taken,' he added.

Copperspeak, Daniel thought. *Never changes.* He rolled over and got to his feet with a speed that surprised the people around him. He made a grab for the young man's camera phone but managed to half punch one of the police officers on the shoulder instead. The chatter of the people around him – about a dozen by now – suddenly stopped.

Silence.

'I'm not taking a breathalyser!' Daniel suddenly shouted. The police officers and the group of bystanders all stared at him. He sat down with a dull thump on the grass verge close to his car. The young man with the iPhone shook his head as he deftly topped and tailed the video of Daniel shouting. He then posted the clip out onto five different social media platforms at once.

I am massively, massively in the shit, thought Daniel Johnston. He lay back down on the ground and closed his eyes.

THREE

9.30am Friday 6 April 1990

Danny drove the radio car up the spiral ramp to the first-floor parking area in the city centre slab of concrete that housed the Manchester Radio studios. The City Tower and Piazza was also home to a hotel, shops and a few cafes, all of which had seen better, busier days. The twenty-year-old facade of the hotel was blackened with car fumes and many of the shop units had 'To Let' signs taped to the windows. Rubbish and leaves swirled in the wind across the half-empty car park in a series of rather depressing mini twisters.

The site was being deliberately withered on the vine of the city's commercial property market. The owners wanted a fresh start, so life for the current occupiers was being made as difficult as possible to gently force them out. Many businesses had taken the hint and moved on, but Manchester Radio still had a few years left on its lease, so Danny and his colleagues were stuck here for the time being, regardless of how unglamorous things became for them.

He parked the radio car in the covered space marked RESERVED FOR MANCHESTER RADIO OB VEHICLE. For a moment, Danny stopped and stared through the windscreen at the concrete wall in front of the car. He leant an elbow on the steering wheel, put his hand across his nose and mouth and began to cry. Just two or three big sobs. Then he took a deep breath and stopped. He paused for about ten seconds, again staring at the concrete wall ahead of him. Then Danny got out of the car and plugged the charger cable that hung from a hook into the side of the vehicle. He'd once forgotten to do it after a job and the station's news editor Mike Sharston had made a big deal of telling Danny what an idiot he was in front of the whole newsroom. That kind of thing happened a lot at Manchester Radio: *why have a quiet word in a new reporter's ear when you can shout at them in front of everyone else in the newsroom?*

Danny trotted down the steps from the car park and walked across the filthy, deserted piazza that stretched under the car park towards the Manchester Radio reception. He saw the yellow-and-blue station logos attached to the windows and felt a nervous grind tug at his stomach as he approached the door. The same feeling he'd had every day since he'd started thc job the previous October after three years on a local newspaper. The feeling could be could be summarised along these lines: *I'm shit at this. Everyone knows I'm shit at this. They are currently discussing how shit I am right now, and they'll go suddenly quiet when I walk in. Mike Sharston thinks I'm shit. Gary the engineer thinks I'm shit. Beth Hall KNOWS I'm shit. Why am I putting myself through this? I should pack it in and go back to local papers. Or get a job in PR. Anything but this.*

Then another thought put a stop to his train of thought like a cold, hard slap.

Christ, that kid.

Spotting Danny as he approached the glass door, the middle-aged receptionist smiled and buzzed him through. 'Morning, Danny!' she said. She was wearing a blue blazer with a white, ruffled shirt, her red hair styled into an elaborate bun. 'Terrible business up at Oldham. Just awful.'

'I know, Pauline. Shocking stuff, even for round here.'

The reception was a dazzlingly bright collage of primary colours, lit by rows of spotlights suspended from the ceiling. Framed gold-and-silver albums scrawled with cheery messages from the singers and bands responsible for them lined the walls. Alongside them were photos of the station's main presenters. Most had alliterative names or Christian names for surnames – *Jonathan Jones, Stuart Simon, Mike James.* Their hair, their clothes, their smiles, everything about them was the antithesis of what was happening outside the radio station. Manchester was now *Madchester.* The city was exploding with music, art and nightlife. Little or nothing of that was reflected in the reception of Manchester Radio. It was 1990 outside, but inside things felt distinctly 1983.

Danny kept walking. A few people looked through a small rack of cassette tapes sitting on the counter of the chest-high reception desk. *Billys*, thought Danny. It was what the station staff secretly called the listeners. Billy Bunters. *Punters.*

Pauline buzzed a second door that connected the rear of the reception to the radio station itself. There was a third door, where guests were able to go straight to the studios, but that wasn't for the likes of Danny. 'That was a really good report, Danny,' Pauline said as he walked by. 'No one else got an interview at the scene. Well done.'

'Thanks Pauline.' Danny pushed the door. 'Didn't think anyone would notice with Strangeways still going strong.'

Pauline gave Danny her best sympathetic face then turned to serve someone who wanted to buy a tape. She'd been here since the station opened nearly twenty years earlier. She saw everything and knew everything. *At least Pauline doesn't think I'm shit,* he thought.

Danny stepped through the second door and the bright, pleasant surroundings of the reception instantly gave way to a wash of dirty grey and beige. The carpet was stained with scores of uneven, brown splodges, where endless cups of tea and coffee had been spilt over the years. Plastic cups – most with cigarette ends in them – were everywhere. The edge of every available surface was dotted with scorch marks where lit cigarettes had been balanced on table edges and window ledges – and forgotten about. The building had recently gone smoke-free, but you'd be hard-pressed to know it. There was a smoking room off to the left of the corridor. Two people were standing in the corridor having an argument. Both had lit cigarettes in their hands; their arms were outstretched so their hands were a few inches inside the smoking room, meaning they were sticking to the letter of health and safety law but studiously avoiding the spirit of it. Danny squeezed past them and headed towards the newsroom.

'Danny boy, you little fucker!' Gary Keenan cried as they passed in the corridor. Heavyset, bearded, ponytailed and sporting large teardrop glasses with a sticking plaster holding one of the arms to the frame, Keenan wore a plain grey sweatshirt and misshapen jeans that were being tugged to one side by a huge bunch of keys attached to his belt loop. He was eating a bacon roll. And smoking. He had a plastic cup of tea on the go too. 'Good piece by your standards that was,' he boomed as he walked in the opposite direction. 'Piss poor by anyone else's, but quite good by yours.'

'Stop flirting with me Gary,' Danny replied. 'I'm straight. I've told you before.'

'You wish, Danny boy. You wish. By the way, Sharston's after you.' Gary disappeared into the reception in a cloud of cigarette smoke. Danny could hear Pauline shouting at him for smoking in her reception area as he headed out onto the piazza.

Danny pushed open the door of the newsroom with his shoulder. The noise of the place would have shocked anyone not used to it. A wall-mounted TV was on with the sound of the *Kilroy* debate show underscoring the still image of the CEEFAX news headlines.

STRANGEWAYS' STAND OFF CONTINUES was the lead story. Mixed in with *Kilroy* was the sound of the Manchester Radio station output, plus that of their BBC opposition. Then there were the typewriters: manual and electric. There had been talk of word processors – computers even – but they had yet to arrive at Manchester Radio. Across the top of this wash of noise was the sound of voices – arguing, shouting, laughing, swearing. There were about fifteen people in the open-plan space. Some were on phones, some were talking face-to-face. Some of the voices were on tape, being edited by reporters who should have been wearing headphones but couldn't be bothered. The words and sounds were being pulled back and forward across tape heads on giant Studer editing machines as journalists tried to find the exact point to mark their edit with a chinagraph pencil, before cutting the tape with a one-sided razor. Voices. *Everywhere.*

'Danny! Here. Now.' Danny looked at Mike Sharston though the glass of his office which was separate to the rest of the newsroom. Sharston was a short, wide man in a very tight suit. He was balding with a red face. On several of his fingers were heavy signet rings. No radio reporter in his or her right mind would wear rings like that – they'd bang on the metal microphones as you were recording and ruin the audio. But Mike Shartson never did interviews these days. He never seemed to leave his tiny office. He was there when Danny arrived for an early shift and he was there when Danny finished a late shift. He never seemed to go home. Danny lifted his tape recorder, waggled it in Sharston's direction and pointed at the charging dock where all Marantzs were supposed to go as soon as possible after arriving back at base. That was the rule. It was Mike Sharston's rule.

'Now!' Sharston yelled.

Danny caught Beth Hall's eye. She was typing quickly at the seat reserved for whoever was reading the news that day. Possession of that seat and that typewriter meant she was in charge of the news output too. She looked across the top of her rather unflattering, large-rimmed glasses, poked her lower lip at him and fluttered her eyes, like a child would do when they want to express a sentiment along the lines of, *there, there, don't be a cry baby*. Then she winked at him.

Nice, thought Danny. *What a cow.*

Danny did as he was told but walked slowly towards the news editor's office and casually leant against the door frame. He didn't want to appear as if he was scared of Sharston and was jumping to it. Even though he was. 'Danny. Hi. Right. What was it I wanted to talk to you about?' said Sharston, tugging at the neck of his grubby, off-white shirt.

'A massive pay rise and a shot at reading the morning bulletins?' Danny replied.

'No. It definitely wasn't that,' Sharston replied. He moved some papers around his desk and looked at his notebook. Then he moved the papers again. 'Ah yes. Right. Oldham. The kid's body. That was wasn't too bad this morning. You got on air first too, I'm told. If the post-mortem says it's definitely murder, we may have a story on our hands.'

Oh, it's definitely murder, thought Danny.

'There'll probably be a press conference at Oldham nick first thing Monday morning,' continued Shartson. 'Go along. Stick with this story. Make something of it. Make it your own.'

Danny tapped his fingers on the door frame of Sharston's office. 'I was hoping to get down to Strangeways. Everyone's been covering it except me. It's the biggest story ever. The whole world is there.'

The riot had started on Sunday lunchtime a few days earlier. Trouble had broken out during the lunchtime church service and had spread quickly throughout the jail. After raiding the prison medical centre to get their hands on prescription drugs, the rioters targeted the jail's E wing where sex offenders were housed – in the eyes of inmates, they were the lowest of the low. The chilling, grunting chants of 'Beasts. Beasts. Beasts' could be heard from the road outside the prison as the rioters got nearer and nearer their targets.

The *Manchester Evening News* was busily proclaiming that, according to their sources, Strangeways was filling up with corpses: '20 DEAD' their latest headline proclaimed. There was no actual proof of this yet, so the Manchester Radio reporters had been told to steer clear of such in their reports. It was the UK's biggest independent radio station outside of London and they had a reputation to maintain. They were pushy and fast, but they were also fair and accurate.

After the inmates had taken control of the jail, they'd armed themselves with scaffolding poles and smashed through the ceilings of the upper floors and accessed the roof, where they were currently putting on quite a show for the TV cameras that had taken up residence around the jail. Every aspect of the rooftop protest was being lapped up by the media. As far as Danny Johnston was concerned, the riot was the chance for him to prove himself, prove he was the real thing.

'No Danny,' Mike Sharston said. 'I don't want you at Strangeways. We've got it covered. It'll probably all be over this weekend anyway. There's talk of the SAS going in. Maybe even today. I want you to stick with this dead kid thing. This could be a good opportunity for you. I suggest you take it. Now off you trot.'

'Maybe I could go to the jail after I've finished at Oldham?'

'Got it covered, Danny. On your way.' Sharston went back to the task of moving paper around his desk. Danny returned to the noise of the newsroom, looking for an unoccupied typewriter so he could freshen up his 'dead kid' story.

Beth Hall walked past him, heading towards the small booth next door to the newsroom to read the next news bulletin. She was seven or eight years older than Danny. She was wearing faded jeans and a black polo neck jumper. Her long red hair was a mess, pinned up on top of her head with hair grips and held together with a large elastic band. She was carrying several scripts and a small pile of 'carts' – plastic boxes containing loops of tape that could be played into the news report. 'Haven't you freshened up your piece for this bulletin yet? Shame on you,' she said. And exited in a waft of expensive but intrusive perfume. *She even smells annoying,* thought Danny.

FOUR

10.25am Thursday 2 June 2016

Leaning into the intercom, Daniel pressed the button next to the speaker and waited for his cue to talk. Nothing. He buzzed again.

'Hello?' the female voice said.

'Hi. It's Daniel Johnston. I've an appointment with Jo McGuire.'

'Push the door and come through,' came the reply. Daniel tried to do as he was told but pushed too soon. The door didn't move. After he'd finished pushing, the door buzzed, and the latch was opened. By the time he realised he'd missed his cue, the door had locked again. He pressed the intercom again. 'Hi. It's Daniel again... I... sorry...'

The door buzzed again and this time he made it through and into a tiny reception area with enough room for two people, three at a push. There were two layers of glass between him and the receptionist. A large sign warned that the physical or verbal abuse of staff would not be tolerated. The receptionist – a woman in her thirties with tattoo-covered arms – glanced at him over the top of her large, black-rimmed glasses. 'Are you here for the needle exchange?' she said.

Daniel returned her look. Then he realised that she was talking to him. *Needle exchange?* 'No,' he said. After a pause, he added: 'I'm with the alkies.' He smiled at the receptionist, quite pleased with his attempt at keeping the situation light. It didn't seem to have worked – her face was unchanged. 'Alcohol support,' said Daniel. 'I'm with the alcohol support programme.'

'Alcohol is to the left. Go through, take seat.' A second door buzzed, and Danny went through into the waiting area. *Things are bad,* he thought, *but they could be worse. I could be turning right.*

Daniel sat down. The furniture was dark beige and blocky. The floor was a chessboard of dull, dark brown and light brown plastic tiles. There were framed pictures on the wall that were abstract and bland. One wall was completely covered in leaflets and flyers: self-help, support groups, psychotherapy, yoga, Pilates, massage – all the kind of things that he would normally have given a very wide berth to. He sat very still. Very still indeed. *Don't look right,* he thought.

After a few minutes of sitting very still and not looking right, Daniel was approached by a woman in her forties. She was wearing black, skinny jeans, Converse trainers and a white t-shirt. Her long blonde hair was parted in the middle and looked slightly wet, as if she'd just arrived after a hasty shower. 'Daniel?' she asked.

'Yes,' he replied, getting out of his seat. 'Yes. That's me.'

'I'm Jo McGuire.' A handshake. 'Do you want to come with me?'

Not especially, Daniel thought. 'Yes. Sure.'

They walked towards a series of brown, wood-effect doors that were, much to Daniel's relief, to the left of where he'd been sitting. Jo motioned for him to go into room six and she slid a sign on the door over to one side. IN SESSION, it now said. PLEASE DON'T DISTURB.

Daniel went into the small room and was asked to sit down. More beige furniture and another nondescript framed print. There was a small wooden table and on it was a box of tissues, with a single tissue sticking out of the box, ready to be plucked out and used. Daniel stared at it.

'Right Daniel, can I get some details from you before we start? Full name?'

'Daniel Johnston.'

'Date of birth?'

'July 12, 1966.'

'Big birthday coming up soon then?' said Jo, without looking up.

'What?'

'Big birthday. Coming up. For you.'

'Right. Yes. Big five oh. Can't wait.'

Daniel looked directly at Jo as she tilted her head up from her clipboard. 'Great,' she said.

'I have your address as Abbeville Road, Clapham. Is that right?'

'Yes. *No*. I'm staying at a hotel at the moment. Trying to keep a low profile.'

'Are you currently taking any medication Daniel?'

'Yes. Tons.'

'And what are the names of these items?'

Daniel fished into the pocket of his fashionable black, collarless jacket and produced a series of cardboard strips. He'd torn the lids off the pill boxes before he came to the treatment centre, knowing full well he'd forget the names of them otherwise. He looked at the ripped packaging: 'Prozac, diazepam and some kind of vitamin E supplements,' he said. 'I'm down to half a diazepam tablet at a time now. After today, it's a quarter. Then nothing.'

'The diazepam is to help with the alcohol withdrawal, yes?'

'Yes, indeed.'

'And how have you been getting on with the diazepam?'

Daniel remembered taking the first one just over a week ago. It had knocked him senseless. 'They're refreshingly strong,' he said.

'They're supposed to be,' said Jo, still looking down at her notes. 'That's why they've told you to drop down to a half and then a quarter to wean you off them slowly. They're highly addictive.'

'No point replacing one addiction with another,' said Daniel.

'No. No point in that,' she agreed. 'The vitamin E is to help repair damage to nerve endings that may have happened because of long-term alcohol abuse. The Prozac is, well, to take the edge off any depressive feelings that might occur during withdrawal. It's quite usual to sort of... start looking inwards in these situations.'

She looked through her notes. 'Are you driving at the moment?'

'No. I had a crash. I refused a breath test at the scene. There's talk of challenging it – some loophole lawyer says he can get me off. Some technicality. I'm not so sure it's a good idea. It'll probably make me look even more of a giant twat than I do already. Sorry. No need for that kind of language, is there?'

Jo looked directly at him for the first time. 'Why are you here, Daniel?'

Pause. 'Is this the bit where I'm supposed to say, "because I'm an alcoholic'?" Daniel overdramatically wobbled his head and waved his hands to make his point.

'No. It's the bit where you tell me why you're here in whatever way you see fit.'

Long pause. 'Because I've been pissed for the best part of the last quarter of a century,' Daniel said. 'Because I massively, massively fucked up my life and my career. Because I crashed my car and somehow, miraculously, didn't kill anyone. Because I need help. That's why I'm here. I suppose.'

Jo and Daniel looked at each other. Daniel was breathing heavily. Jo glanced at the tissues. He shook his head. 'So yeah. That's why I'm here.'

'A perfectly good answer. Thank you.'

'Plus, private rehab clinics leak like sieves – the press pay staff for information and pictures. I thought an NHS place would be more discreet.'

'Sure,' Jo said.

'Can I ask something?' Daniel said, leaning forward in his chair. 'Why am I not in a group? Why am I not sitting with a bunch of people in a circle? I thought that's how this kind of thing worked?'

'We thought having you in a group would be... distracting,' she replied.

'How do you mean?' Daniel asked, despite already knowing what Jo was about to say.

'Because you're well known. You're on the telly. There was a lot of publicity about your crash.'

'TV Daniel in Drunk Drive Smash.'

'Exactly.'

'I see.'

'Distracting.'

'Got it.'

Pause. 'So, how can I help?' said Jo, putting her clipboard on the floor and making herself comfortable.

'I don't really know,' Daniel replied. 'I've never done this before.'

Jo put down her paperwork. 'Well, the diazepam will be finished within a matter of days. That basically keeps you pleasantly out of it for a week or so... you're just about high enough that you can't be bothered with drinking, basically. It only takes about 10 or 14 days for your body to be free of alcohol. Amazing really. After what it's been through. Beyond that it's all in here.' Jo tapped the side of her head with her pen. 'If you decide you want to start drinking again, you probably will. If you decide you don't, you probably won't. It's not up to me. It's up to you. You're in control. Drink or don't drink. It's up to you. I've worked with hundreds and hundreds of people over the last fifteen years with drug and alcohol problems. I'm here to talk a bit but mainly listen. That's it. I can't prescribe you more drugs. I am not on call to you. I'm available once a week for an hour at a time. To talk. To help you with this…' For the second time, Jo tapped the side of her head. A pause. The longest one yet. 'Why not tell me about when you started drinking? And why.'

FIVE

10.15pm Friday 6 April 1990

The carnival was in full swing when Danny arrived at Strangeways. He turned off Bury New Road, finding a parking spot alongside a clothing wholesaler, whose window was full of garishly coloured gear aimed at the current *Madchester* market. *Counterfeit,* thought Danny. *Every last stitch of it. No one seems to care though. Criminality that they turn a blind eye to, right outside a prison.*

Music drifted across the road as Danny locked his car, an aging blue Ford Escort. Then he double checked he'd locked it properly. The song was 'Ghetto Heaven' by Family Stand. There were scores – no, *hundreds* – of people milling about in the side roads and wasteland that surrounded the jail. Many were drinking from tins of beer – there was a man selling them from a makeshift stall made from what looked like a decorators table. An additional boozy waft was provided by the Boddington's brewery next door to the jail. It only added to the party atmosphere – as did a heavy smell of weed in the air.

Danny spotted a kid of about 12, selling t-shirts. He had a swathe of them across one arm and he waved one in the air with his free hand. Danny looked at the design as the boy passed him: it was a silhouette drawing of the jail and the words *Strangeways Breakout 1990* written underneath. *Must get one of those*, thought Danny, as he weaved through the crowd, looking for the Manchester Radio outside broadcast car that had been parked outside the jail since the start of the riot on Sunday.

On top of the main roof area of the prison – to the left of the jail's distinctive red brick central rotunda and tower – figures could be seen scurrying about. The hole they had punched through the roof could be clearly seen to the left. One inmate – wearing what looked like a prison officer's uniform – was waving a hand-made sign that said: 'TOLD WE WILL DIE'. A prisoner next to him was shouting into a makeshift megaphone fashioned from an orange and white traffic cone. What he was saying was a mystery, because every time he tried to shout, 'Mr Blue Sky' by ELO would blare out from within the prison compound. Danny had heard that the prison authorities had been using music to keep the rioters awake and to stop them relaying messages to the outside world. It was clearly true; what's more, it was apparent that the Home Office's taste in music was as suspect as their riot containment techniques.

Lights glimmered in the upper windows of a huge warehouse to the right of the jail. The words PAKASTANI UK TRADE CENTRE were written in huge white letters on the gable end. Danny had heard that several news operations had hired out space in the warehouse, so their cameramen could get better shots of the rioters.

On a side street to the right of the jail, Danny spotted the radio car, parked between an ITN satellite truck and a BBC outside broadcast vehicle. Manchester Radio engineer Gary Keenan was standing at the front of the car – the bonnet was up, and he was fiddling with the engine. And swearing. In the driver's seat was Robert Crane, the radio station's chief reporter. Crane was a foot taller than Danny, five years older and twice as experienced. Despite being a radio journalist, Crane was wearing a black suit and a red tie as if he was all prepared for his big TV break. He had the air of a man who didn't think he'd be staying long at Manchester Radio. Leaning through the radio car window and chatting to Crane - with a tin of beer in one hand and a joint in the other - was Beth Hall. Danny was about to turn around and walk back to his car when Gary Keenan spotted him: 'Danny boy!' he shouted. *Fuck,* thought Danny. Reluctantly, he carried on walking towards the radio car.

'Come to check out the party for yourself, have you?' Gary asked, still ferreting around under the car's bonnet.

'Yeah. What are you doing?' Danny knew nothing about cars and wasn't remotely interested in what was going on, but would rather talk to Gary about car maintenance than chat to Beth Hall and Robert Crane.

'Swapping the battery. It's knackered. It needs a drive around to re-charge it, but we can't move from the spot otherwise some BBC bastard will pinch it. So - old battery out, new one in. What you doing here? Thought you were on kiddie murder patrol out in the swamplands of Oldham?'

'I was. I am.' Danny looked at Beth through the radio car windscreen. She was still talking to Crane. They were laughing. Beth caught Danny's glance and he looked away. 'Still waiting on the post-mortem result, but it's a bit of a dead end, Gary, to be honest with you. There's isn't a single house near the scene, so no doors to knock on to see if anyone saw anything. No ID yet on the kid. Cops are stumped. So, I thought I'd come down here and see what all the fuss is about.'

'And what do you think of it so far?' Gary asked, tugging at the battery connections to test they were secure.

Danny looked across the scene outside the prison. With the amount of drinking and drug taking going on, it reminded him of a nightclub, but with no walls or roof. He saw a TV reporter give a young man in a shell suit some cash – about £50 by the look of it – to give an interview. He heard the man, who's back was to the camera, so his face couldn't be seen, describing how his friend had just given himself up and that there were 'bodies all over the place' inside the jail.

'It's a circus,' Danny said.

'It's a fucking madhouse, Danny boy,' Gary said, slamming the car bonnet closed. He tapped on the windshield to get Robert Crane's attention. 'Right, Bobby Boy, fire it up.' Crane started the engine.

'I keep thinking I should be here, Gary. That I'm missing out. Letting Max Headroom there get all the glory.' He motioned towards Crane, who was writing his script and simultaneously checking his hair in the rear- view mirror of the radio car. Again, Danny accidentally caught Beth's eye. She got out and started walking around the car towards them. *Shit.*

Danny started thinking of more things he could talk to Gary about, but didn't manage to think of one by the time that Beth got to them.

'Daniel...' she said. Beth was the only person who called him that. 'Thought you'd been told to stay away from here. The grown-ups have got this covered.'

'I'm on my own time, Beth. I'm not here for work – purely for pleasure.'

Danny looked at her. Her hair – normally piled up on top of her head in a messy bundle – looked freshly washed and styled. Her usual jeans and jumper had been replaced by a leather jacket and short black dress. The glasses that she normally glared at him through at work were gone. *Contact lenses? She's on the pull!*

'How about you - on your way out, Beth?' Danny asked, glancing briefly at Robert Crane as he rehearsed his piece in the radio car.

'Just passing though, Daniel. Very much like yourself.'

'You should take care, Beth. Some right nasty types to be found around Strangeways you know.'

‘I can see that,’ she replied.

Danny smiled at Beth and she walked away. ‘See you on Monday, Gary,’ Danny said.

Gary leaned in. He smelled of oil and cigarettes. ‘Don’t take the bait Danny boy,’ he said, quietly. ‘That’s what she wants. Steer well clear. Do your own thing. You’ll be fine. You’re good.’

‘Cheers Gary.’ Danny walked towards the perimeter mesh fence of the jail and looked up at the rioters. One of them was swinging a makeshift hangman’s noose above his head. Another had taken all his clothes off and was walking tightrope-style across the apex of the main prison building. A fire had started behind him. ‘Mr Blue Sky’ kicked in again. Danny stood and stared. *Gary’s right. It’s a madhouse.*

On the way back to his car he bought a four pack of Red Stripe beers from the man with the decorating table. The man asked Danny for ten pounds. ‘A tenner?’ Danny said, digging into his pockets to find more money. ‘They’d barely be a fiver, ordinarily.’

‘These are extraordinary times, mate!’ said the beer seller, smiling at Danny and exposing missing front teeth. He plucked Danny’s ten-pound note with a flourish.

‘Not all the robbers are in the jail, are they?’ Danny took his beers and got into his car.

The beer-seller shouted after him. ‘Extraordinary times, mate!’

Danny opened one of the beers and drank about half of it. He thought about the men inside the jail. He thought about the circus outside. And he thought about the little boy, face down on the beach at Black Moss reservoir. He put the half-empty beer can into the coffee cup holder near the handbrake. *Yes. No question about it… It really IS a fucking madhouse*, he thought as he drove away.

SIX

10.30am Thursday 9 June 2016

'So, Daniel, before we start. Can I ask – have you consumed any alcohol or taken any drugs since our last meeting?'

'Danny,' he said. Jo looked at him, looked at her notes and looked back. 'Call me Danny. And no – other than the diazepam I was kindly given. I was never really that bothered about drugs. I've tried the lot, been right through the menu, but it never really grabbed me. Not like drinking did.'

'Why do you think that is?' she asked.

'Have we started now?' Danny was aware that his tone was more defensive, more bristly, than he intended. He sat back slightly in his chair and held up both hands in an apologetic gesture. *Try not to be an arse, Danny boy,* he thought.

'Sorry, Jo,' he offered. 'Do you know what? I think it's the people. Drinkers tend to be pretty straight, if you know what I mean. You know where you stand. All the people I've ever met who take drugs have all been quite shocking wankers. They'd pick your pocket to fund a wrap of coke. But a boozer will share his last tenner with you. And buy you a drink with it. And one for himself obviously.'

'Was that important to you, the company of other drinkers?'

Danny thought of his regular coterie of drinking buddies: a few film editors, a director, a photographer, an actor and an accountant. He'd seen them almost every day for years yet couldn't have told you where they lived. 'Yes. We were a like an army unit. A band of brothers. All for one and all that.'

'When was the last time you saw them?'

'The day I crashed the car.'

'Is it worth talking about that?'

'I suppose it must be.'

Again. The bristle.

Danny exhaled, long and hard. 'We'd just finished a show, an expose about dodgy landlords. Hidden camera stuff. Nothing special. We'd finished early, so we went on the medicine – sorry, went for a drink – about 6.30. I'd been in there at lunchtime as well. We tended to drink at an Italian restaurant near the TV studios. It was our place that we'd kind of adopted. We had this idea that no one would find us. Nonsense, obviously. Everyone knew we drank there. Anyway, I put a few hours in there then got off. I'd taken some food with me to eat at home. A bit of seafood pasta. I'd gone back to the studios to get my car. I've got my own parking spot... *had* my own parking spot. Then I headed home. I know that boozers always say this, but my driving was fine. I'm extremely experienced at driving with a few drinks in me. I'm really good at it. I know. We all say that. It's bollocks, isn't it? Anyway. That's what happened. I set off for south of the river and was a few minutes from home...'

A pause.

'Then I saw something.' Danny paused again. 'This is confidential, isn't it? I didn't mention this to the police. Don't know why. I just didn't want to.'

'Of course it is,' said Jo leaning forward ever so slightly.

'Then I saw this little kid. Eight or nine years old. A boy. He ran across the road right in front of me. He was wearing shorts and had no top on – bare-chested like he was on holiday or something.'

Danny Johnston looked at the tissues on the table, as if to check they were still there. They were. There was one sticking out of the oval hole in the top of the box.

'He looked right at me as I was swerving and skidding. *Right at me.* And smiled. The little bastard! Then I hit the tree. Then everything went to shit. Or not. Maybe hitting that tree was the best thing that has happened to me for a very long time.'

'Was the little boy okay?'

'Yes. I think so. Yes. I didn't see him after the crash but I didn't hit him, I'm sure of it.'

'Why didn't you mention it to the police?'

'Not sure. Maybe I... I don't know. I don't want to just make up an answer for you, Jo. I'd just be saying words for the sake of it. No point. I don't know why I didn't mention it.'

Danny and Jo sat in silence for about thirty seconds.

'You look different,' Jo said.

Danny, never particularly heavyset, had lost more than a stone in weight since he'd stopped drinking. He'd had his hair cropped close, which revealed its true colour; underneath the expensive dye job he'd had for the last ten years his hair was a very light grey. He'd also stopped shaving and the developing beard was virtually white.

'I am different,' Danny said.

SEVEN

8.45am Monday 9 April 1990

Danny pulled the radio car up to the barrier of Oldham Police station and wound down the window. There were rarely any spare parking places at Oldham nick, especially when a murder press conference was being held. But today, Danny was waved straight through and told to park in the visitors' section. *That's a first.*

The police station – a grey, pebble-dashed piece of sixties brutalism – formed part of a series of equally grey and brutal buildings that greeted you as you came into Oldham town centre and drove the seven unlovely miles from Manchester city centre. Nothing said: 'Welcome to Oldham' less than Oldham Police station.

Danny signed in at reception and was told to wait. There was only one other reporter there – a woman in her early twenties – that Danny had never seen before, was sitting in the waiting area. She had short, jet-black hair and was wearing what appeared to be a chamois leather skirt. An alarmingly short chamois leather skirt. Danny sat opposite her and made a point of keeping his eyeline perfectly horizontal. She had no technical equipment with her. *Must be a print journo*, thought Danny. *They think they're better than us.*

'Hi. You from *The Messenger*?' Danny asked. The death of a child in these circumstances would make the lead story for weeks for a daily teatime paper like the *Oldham Evening Messenger*. It was always a good idea to keep it friendly with the local reporters. *Especially with Ms Power Skirt here,* thought Danny.

'Yes I am.' she replied in a medium-strength local accent.

'Here for the press conference on the kid?' Danny asked, tweaking his slightly grammar-school accent to mirror hers, a habit he'd developed recently. It was another piece of advice he'd picked up: *blend in, adapt, talk to people in the same way they're talking to you.*

'Correct again.' She glanced at Danny's Marantz. Her attitude towards him became a few percent friendlier. 'Are you from Manchester Radio? We monitor it in the office. You were first there weren't you?

Jimmy something, isn't it?'

'Danny Something. Danny Johnston.'

'That's right. Hi, Danny Something. I'm Kate.' She leant forward and put out her hand. Danny shook it. *No, I won't tell you anything about what I saw out on the moors,* Danny thought. *That skirt has no power over me.*

'Did you see much out on the moors? What do you know that I don't?' she said, leaning even closer to him as she spoke.

'Not really,' replied Danny, trying to make the story sound as dull as possible. 'Bit of activity. Noncommittal coppershit from the local DI. Usual stuff, really.'

'How did you get there so soon? It's way out in the sticks for you lot. Must be nearly out of your patch.'

'News desk got a tip off. Yeah, it's the very ends of the earth for us. Proper *Deliverance* country.' Danny crossed his eyes and played an imaginary banjo to make his point.

Kate smiled at him. Not the friendliest smile Danny had ever seen. 'I'm from near there,' Kate replied, leaning back into her seat.

'Right.' *Bloody hell,* he thought. 'Some really lovely countryside around there.'

A middle-aged man with a clipboard approached them. His name band identified him as Brian Lake – GMP Press Office. 'Right, you here for the press conference. Only two of you? That's a bit disappointing. Ah well. You'd better come this way.'

Danny and Kate followed the press officer through a series of double doors. 'How's your mum keeping Kate?' the press officer said as they walked down a long corridor.

'Not bad, thanks. Keeping herself very busy – you know what she's like.'

Danny felt even more out of place than usual. *No, I don't know what she's like, actually. Do feel free to fill me in. And how come she knows the press office guy so well?*

The two journalists were led into a large conference room with thirty or more chairs – set out like a school play– facing a long-top table. Danny sat a few seats away from Kate on the front row. He felt it might be a bit odd if he sat next to her. At the table facing them sat DI Smithdown. He looked like he'd made a real effort with his appearance, but still looked rather uncomfortable. Danny tried to catch his eye; he was sure the DI would remember him from the moors. If he did, he made no indication of it – he just looked around the room and then out of the window – anywhere apart from at Danny and Kate. Next to the

DI, according to the triangular nameplate that sat in front of him, was Detective Superintendent James Pym. He was a similar age to DI Smithdown but looked altogether more comfortable in his well-pressed suit and bright white shirt. His hair was well-cut and suspiciously dark brown.

The two policemen leant in and spoke quietly to each other. Then DI Smithdown called over the press officer. He looked at the journalists who were currently taking up precisely two of the forty seats and moved his arm in their general direction. His facial expression suggested something along the lines of: *is this it?* Danny couldn't be sure, but he was fairly certain that DS Pym said something back along the lines of 'fucking Strangeways, isn't it?'

Danny left his seat and placed his Marantz recorder on the table in between the two detectives. He gave the DI an awkward smile, like a workman who knew he was slightly in the way. He attached his microphone to a small stand, pressed play and record and went back to his seat. 'So that's you done then?' Kate stage-whispered to Danny. 'Easy job being a radio journo. Just press record.'

'Play *and* record,' Danny corrected. He folded his arms, quite pleased with himself.

Glancing at a few sheets of notes and leaning slightly too far into Danny's microphone, DS Pym began speaking: 'Ladies and gentlemen, thank you for coming this afternoon.' He paused and looked at Danny and Kate. 'Both of you. I'm Detective Superintendent James Pym and this is Detective Inspector John Smithdown. We're here today to issue an appeal on behalf of Oldham Police in relation to the discovery of a young, deceased male. The body was found in the early hours of Friday morning close to Black Moss Reservoir. Those of you who know the vicinity…' the DCI glanced in Kate's direction, slightly annoying Danny… 'will be aware that this is a very remote area, just off the A62 Oldham to Huddersfield Road, beyond Diggle. The body was removed from the scene later that same day. It appears to be that of a male child, approximately nine to ten years of age. The body was discovered partially-clothed. A post-mortem took place over the weekend. The exact cause of death hasn't been one hundred percent ascertained but the boy had suffered multiple catastrophic injuries. I don't want to go too deeply into the nature of those injuries at this stage, but any one of them could have caused his death. Suffice to say, this discovery is being treated as murder. With that in mind, we have an appeal to make to the public today.'

DS Pym put his notes to one side and looked directly at Danny and Kate. *Are we about to disengage from copperspeaky?* thought Danny. 'We urgently need to identify this child,' the DS said. 'We don't know who he is. We don't know how he came to be up there at Black Moss. The one thing we do know is that something has gone horribly, horribly wrong for a young boy to be found in this place in this way. Horribly wrong.'

That's my clip for the next news bulletin, thought Danny.

The DS continued: 'We would appeal for anyone who saw anything suspicious in the Black Moss area over the last seven days to come forward. Although the reservoir is very remote, the nearby road is busy. It has particularly heavy traffic in terms of lorries and HGVs driving to and from Manchester and Huddersfield. I'd also ask if anyone has information about any missing children in the Oldham or surrounding areas to come forward. They can contact us on 856 2220 – ask for the Oldham incident room. Alternatively, they can call Crimestoppers anonymously on 0800 555 111. That ends this appeal. I will answer any questions you have as best I can, but I'm limited in what I can say at this present moment in time.'

Danny hated asking questions in front of other journalists. Fortunately, Kate half raised her hand and asked: 'DS Pym. Has anyone reported a child missing in the area?'

'No, they haven't, Kate.'

'Isn't that unusual? For a child's body to be found without a child being reported missing?'

'Yes, it is unusual.'

'How unusual?' she pressed.

'Very.'

'Are you following any particular lines of inquiry?' In the same way as coppers spoke copperspeak, journalists spoke *journalese.* This was a coded question, meaning: *do you know what happened here and can't actually tell us at the moment?*

'Not at the moment, no,' the DS replied. 'We're keeping an open mind. One matter of interest to us is that the body was found exactly on the border with Yorkshire, so we'll be liaising with our colleagues on the West Yorkshire force who are taking a great interest in this case.'

Kate continued to gently pepper the officer with questions, deftly writing extremely neat shorthand notes into a spiral-bound notepad as she spoke. 'Should we read something into the fact that the body is in that spot?' she asked.

'Again, we're keeping an open mind, but it would be astonishing coincidence that it just happened to have been placed exactly on the county border.'

'Can you tell us the nature of the boy's injuries?'

'I'm not going to release that information at this present moment in time as I feel it might prejudice our inquiries.'

That's copperspeak for 'only the police and the killer know the nature of his injuries and I want to keep it that way' thought Danny. He looked at DI Smithdown, trying to get a sense of whether he'd told his boss about Danny seeing the boy's body. *He hasn't told him,* thought Danny. *That's interesting.*

DS Pym looked across to DI Smithdown, who had sat in silence with his head down and his arms folded throughout his colleague's statement and answers. 'Anything to add, Mr Smithdown?'

'No. I think you've got it covered, Mr Pym,' he said. His arms remained folded.

DS Pym began to get up out of his chair. 'Thanks very much for your time,' he said. 'We've a lot to do as you can imagine and if you don't mind, we need to crack on.'

Kate put away her notebook and took out her purse, foraging for change. 'See you again, Danny Something,' she said as she half ran from the room. She was obviously planning to phone some copy through for the late edition and needed a payphone. She smiled at the press officer and left in a chamois leather blur.

'See you,' said Danny, largely to himself.

Danny was in no such rush. He was way too late for the nine o'clock news so he had another half an hour, at least, to file his report. Not that anyone would notice. *Strangeways, Strangeways, Strangeways. That's all anyone seemed to care about.* He sauntered over to the top table. DS Pym was in a huddle with the press officer a few yards away. DI Smithdown hadn't moved. Danny reached over for his Marantz. 'Mr Smithdown,' he said, quietly. The officer, arms still folded, was looking out of the window. 'Why no mention of the tape on the kid's body?'

DI Smithdown turned away from the window. He looked at Danny. Then he looked at the tape machine – its twin wheels were still turning, and its red recording light was still lit. He looked back at Danny. *He's not daft, this guy,* thought Danny. He pressed the stop button on the Marantz. The wheels stopped turning, the red light faded away to nothing. DI Smithdown looked at Danny and stood up, pushing his chair back.

'Tape? Pure speculation, young man.' DI Smithdown rummaged thought his pockets and pulled out a packet of cigarettes. 'There's a time and a place for speculation.' He leant in slightly. 'And this definitely isn't the time or the place.' DI Smithdown gave Danny a flat smile and walked away.

EIGHT

11.35am Thursday 9 June 2016

'What do you mean... a *kill payment*? What the fuck is that? I've never heard of it.'

Standing outside the drug and alcohol unit after his appointment, Daniel Johnston was shouting at his agent, George Pritchard, via his mobile phone. The ache for a drink had sucked all the moisture from Danny's mouth and the bottom edges of his rib cage throbbed. He wanted to retch but managed to hold it back. Rather stupidly, after all these years, Danny had started smoking again. He pulled a Silk Cut Ultra Light from its white packet of ten and lit it. *I'm only buying them in tens,* he thought. *It's not like I've really started again. Not full-on.*

Then, he continued with the business of shouting.

'But I've already started work on it. It's my big book. My proper book. My fucking take-me-to-another-level serious book. They can't just change their minds and cancel it.'

'They can, and they have,' said George Pritchard on the other end of the line. Pritchard had been Daniel's agent for fifteen years. He'd steered Daniel from jobbing local TV journalist to full-on celebrity righter-of-wrongs. When you thought of campaigning TV journalism, you thought of Daniel Johnston. But since his car crash, work for Danny had been haemorrhaging out of George Pritchard's Soho office.

'But I signed a contract!' Danny shouted, even louder this time. He threw his cigarette into a flower bed outside the unit and lit up another.

'Yes, Daniel,' George said patiently. 'But the publishers didn't. The contract needs both signatures for it to be valid. They hadn't signed – now they don't want any part of the book since your... *accident*.' This was George's preferred word for what had happened: *accident.* A less diplomatic person might call it *driving your car into a tree while pissed out of your mind then taking a swing at a policeman*, but George preferred *accident.*

'Unbelievable,' said Daniel.

'They've offered you the kill payment to not write it basically. It's quite good of them really. They could have just walked away.'

'So, I'm being paid not to work.'

'Correct.'

'To go quietly like a good little boy?'

'In a sense, yes.'

'They can stuff their kill payment.'

'No, they can't, actually,' sighed the agent. 'It'll be received with considerable gratitude, thank you very much. It's the only money you've got on the horizon.'

Danny took a few paces left, then right, the sat down on the steps of the drug and alcohol unit.

'How much is it?' he asked.

'Five grand.'

'Okay. Could be worse. What else have I got coming in? Surely, I've got money owed from *2016*? I've done three episodes for them already this year.' The TV show *2016* – the name cunningly went up a digit every year – had been Daniel's main employer for nearly ten years. ITV's flagship popular current affairs show had made his name. He'd interviewed dictators, exposed con men and changed laws as the programme's best-known reporter. He'd even saved a young girl's life after bullying a regional health authority into changing its mind over her cancer treatment. *Won a bloody BAFTA for that,* Daniel reminded himself. *What was the kid's name? Briony or Bonnie or something.*

'*2015* have been looking at their contracts too,' sighed Pritchard. 'You should have told them you'd been arrested at the scene of the accident. It's in the fine print. You have to tell them if you get in trouble with the police. It affects their brand. There'll be no work forthcoming from them for the foreseeable. They're within their rights to withhold payments too, because you've brought the company into disrepute. You've tarnished their image.'

Oh, come on. Even I can't tarnish ITV's image, Danny thought. For once, he kept the thought to himself.

'But you're technically still an employee, albeit a freelance one,' George continued. 'So, they have a duty of care towards you. They've asked about your treatment. How's it going?'

'Swimmingly.'

'You're not helping your cause you know, Daniel.'

A long pause. 'I won't lose sleep over *2016*. I should have moved on from there years ago. But the book was a big deal.' Danny had made a well-received episode of *2016* about celebrity historical child abuse. It had touched on the connections with the establishment and politicians. Cover-up or conspiracy fantasy? Not hugely in-depth but that was TV half hours for you. But he'd been offered the book deal on the strength of the programme and he'd recently started to work on it. He'd started to structure it, play with it, shape it, finesse the idea. It really had the makings of something very special indeed. He hadn't actually written anything yet, but that wasn't the point.

'I know the book was – is – really important to you,' soothed George. 'Look. Lie low. Maybe go back to Manchester for a while. Let things blow over for a few months, then we can get the PR guys on the case. Do some redemption-type pieces – rehab your image. How the accident was the best thing that ever happened to you... Pulled you from the brink, that kind of thing. Then we can get you some reality TV gigs. Daring-do stuff. Channel Four has a ski-jumping show you know?'

'I'm not standing next to Davina Mc-fucking-Call in a lycra onesie George,' Danny stated. 'Not for anything.'

'Have a think. Look, I've got to go. Got a call on the other line. I'll be in touch. Bye, Daniel.'

'Okay, George. Look – thanks. I mean it. And sorry for being an arse. Thanks for being there for me.'

'That's what I'm here for mate,' said George. 'Take care.'

Danny ended the call. He headed off towards the main road adjacent to the unit and looked for a taxi to take him home. He found one quickly and gave the driver the address. The driver pulled away from the kerb and looked at Danny in the rearview mirror. His face lit up in recognition of his passenger.

'You're that telly bloke, aren't ya? The car crash telly bloke? That's it. Off the telly.'

Danny slid down into his seat. 'The very same,' he confirmed. *This is going to be a very long cab ride,* he thought.

Thankfully, his phone pinged, notifying him of an email. It was from George. The email said that George was terminating their existing terms and agreements as client and agent forthwith, citing an irreconcilable breakdown in their professional relationship.

He'd already drafted it, thought Danny. *Bastard.*

NINE

5.45pm Monday 9 April 1990

Danny stood at the bar of the Three Tunnes pub in Oldham town centre, smoked his third cigarette and started on his second pint. He looked around the pub. It was the kind of pub with horse brasses above the bar and a very regular clientele. Nearly everyone there was male, middle-aged and smoking. *This is the copper-iest pub I've ever been in,* he thought. *DI Smithdown is bound to drink in here.*

Danny may have been a stranger in Oldham, but some things were true wherever you went. Journalists drank in the nearest pub to their newsroom, no matter how rundown, expensive or unpleasant that pub happened to be. The closer the pub, the more time you got to spend drinking. By the same logic, police officers always drank in the nearest pub to their police station. Walk straight out of Oldham Police station and just past the magistrate's courts and you came to the black and white frontage of the Three Tunnes.

Danny had long since filed his piece after the police press conference but had decided to return to Oldham after his shift was done. There was nothing to particularly drag him back to his flat in Didsbury, south Manchester. He didn't have a girlfriend. He had a ragtag gang of drinking mates at a pub near his flat, but he didn't really *know* anyone in Didsbury. He didn't know anyone in Oldham either; in fact, he didn't know anyone who *knew* anyone in Oldham. But still, here he was.

As he continued to search the faces of the early evening drinkers, Danny spotted someone he recognised: Kate from *The Messenger*. She was standing on the other side of the pub with a female friend. They were the only women in the pub, yet strangely they seemed to fit right in. She nodded to Danny, who took that as a signal that he should go over and say hello.

'Hi Kate,' he said. He smiled at her friend. 'This your pub?'

'Kind of. What are you doing here Danny Something?'

'Just having a drink, soaking up the atmosphere,' Danny said in the most casual manner he could muster.

'Rubbish. You're looking for DI Smithdown, aren't you?

'Why, does he come in here?' Danny asked.

'No. He drinks in the Indian restaurant over the road,' Kate said.

'Alright, no need for sarcasm.'

'We don't do sarcasm in Oldham, there's no market for it. I'm deadly serious. It's weird, but that's where you'll find him.'

Kate looked at him and narrowed her eyes. 'This story has got under your skin a bit, hasn't it, Danny Something? You broadcast guys never hang around. Straight in, straight out. Yet, you're still here. Why's that then? What did you see out on the moors?'

'A dead kid,' he said, sipping his pint. Danny looked at Kate's friend. She was the same age, but she didn't look like a journalist. Probably an old school friend. She showed no interest in their conversation whatsoever. 'Just a dead kid.'

'It's terrible, just terrible.' sighed Kate, taking a glug of her lager. She was drinking a pint, Danny noticed. 'It really is. But no one seems interested – it's Strangeways or nothing at the moment. I filed a piece about the kid for tonight's paper, but now I've been told to track down rioters who come from the local area and get their families to talk.' A pause. Danny looked at her. Her eyes were so dark they were nearly black. Very striking. *Bit scary*.

'I'm sure they'll soon ID him,' she continued. 'I've not heard anything weird about the body or how it was found, have you?'

Danny thought about mentioning the tape, then decided not to and shook his head. He finished his drink. 'I'm going to get off home. It's been a long day. See you again.'

Danny smiled at Kate's friend – got nothing in return – and headed for the door.

'Say hello to DI Smithdown for me, Danny Something,' said Kate as he walked away. Her friend said something quietly in her ear and the two young women laughed. Fortunately, they couldn't see his face flush red as Danny walked out of the pub.

Outside the Three Tunnes, Danny looked around the precinct. He quickly saw what he was looking for and headed up the sloped street to The Raj restaurant. As he went in, a customer came out with a takeaway; there was a small bar with two high stools at the far end of the restaurant. There was only one person sitting at the bar: DI John Smithdown. What little colour there'd been in his face earlier in the day had all but disappeared. He looked exhausted. He wasn't drunk, but he was several pints ahead of Danny. He made his way through the tables – all of which were empty – towards the bar. Danny pointed at DI Smithdown's near-empty pint of bitter 'Another one?' he asked.

'Well done for finding me,' the detective said. 'We'll make a journalist of you yet. A large half, please.'

'Why do you drink in here?' Danny asked, ordering himself a pint of strong lager and another pint of bitter for the DI. The waiter seemed to know that Danny wasn't here for food and didn't bother offering him a menu.

'I come in here because all the coppers go in the Three Tunnes, that's why,' the DI said. 'Sometimes you need a break from them. All they talk about is crime.'

'Can I talk to you about a crime, Mr Smithdown?'

'Depends which one.'

'You know *exactly* which one.'

DI John Smithdown shifted his weight on his bar stool. He started peeling apart a beer mat, then spun it away across the top of the bar. 'Didn't think anyone was interested in that kid,' DI Smithdown said. He was looking at the bar top, not at Danny.

'*I'm* interested Mr Smithdown. Otherwise I wouldn't be here.'

'Why Danny? Your radio station covers the whole of Greater Manchester. There's a murder every five days in the GMP patch. Take your pick. Why this one?'

That, thought Danny, was a perfectly reasonable question. 'Maybe it's because I *saw* him. Mr Smithdown,' Danny said, taking the stool next to the detective. 'When there's a murder, we cover the press conferences, interview the officers, do the "emotional appeals for help"… It's the way it works. It's the same every time, a ritual. You do your bit, I do mine. But this is different. I *saw* him. No kid deserves to end up like that.'

DI Smithdown grabbed a handful of Bombay mix that was in a bowl on the bar. 'Ordinarily I wouldn't be seen dead talking to the likes of you Danny,' he said, washing the mix down with a big gulp of his pint. 'No offence – cheers, by the way – but I wouldn't. Truth is, I'm fucked with this case. It's barely started, but I'm fucked. I need the oxygen of publicity, but every bit of it is being sucked out of Oldham nick, across Greater Manchester and straight into Strangeways fucking jail. We have a dead child and the only people we can convince to cover it are you and Kate from *The Messenger*. Pathetic. No offence. I've got no resources, no staff. Most of our cells are full of rioters who've either given themselves up or been dragged backwards out of Strangeways. People are too busy staring at the roof of that prison to realise what's going on around them.'

'What *is* going on Mr Smithdown?' said Danny.

The policeman rubbed a hand across his unshaven face. It was speckled with grey stubble. His eyes were red with tiredness. 'Something terrible happened to that kid. Yet my boss won't release it. Says we should wait. Keep our powder dry, he says.'

'The placing of the body is very telling, isn't it?' said Danny. 'Right on the border...'

'Bollocks. You've been watching too much telly. So has the DS.'

'How do you mean?'

'They panicked,' Smithdown said, staring at himself in the mirror behind the bar. 'Whoever did this was *shitting* themselves. They left that kid there because they got scared and ran off. Must have been pretty weird, carrying a kid across the moors in the dead of night. Fuck me, he might even have been still alive. But I don't think there was any intention to leave him on the border. That's bollocks.'

'How do you know?' Danny asked his question quietly, leaning in,

DI Smithdown took a hefty swallow of his pint and turned to look at the reporter. 'Because of the tape, Danny. The tape that you saw. That tape you weren't *supposed* to have seen.'

'Sorry, I don't get it, Mr Smithdown.'

'Because that little lad had weights attached to his body. Strapped to him with tape. They had no intention of leaving him in the sand on the county border. They probably didn't even know the border was there. They were going to sink him in Black Moss. Maybe they panicked. Maybe they thought they saw someone coming. Who knows? But the idea that he was left on the border as some symbolic act is pure DS Pym bollocks.'

'How did he die, Mr Smithdown?' Danny had no idea why DI Smithdown was telling him all this. At that moment, he didn't care.

'Asphyxiation. He was probably half dead already. After what had been done to him.' DI Smithdown reached across the bar and took back one of the split beer mats. He took out a pen.

'What had been done to him?' Danny asked.

DI Smithdown made light work of the rest of his pint. He nodded to the waiter. 'Everything, Danny. The full fucking works. We won't identify that kid anytime soon unless we accidentally get a DNA match with someone we arrest for something else, or we trace a relative, or someone walks into Oldham nick and tells us who he is.'

The detective was writing as he spoke: 'He had no teeth – they'd been knocked out or pulled out, probably a bit of both. His hands had been burnt – probably with a blow torch or over a fire. So, no fingerprints. For a kid of that age, they were really hedging their bets with that one, belt-and-braces stuff. Christ, I hope he *was* dead by the time they'd got him to Black Moss. Poor little shit.' He took another hefty gulp, finished his pint and leant close to Danny. 'Which is why we can't let this be buried because of Strangeways and my stupid twat of a DS. No way.'

DS Smithdown handed Danny the split beer mat. A number was on it. 'Call me tomorrow. Early doors.'

The waiter handed DI Smithdown a takeaway bag. He took it with a nod and left. Danny watched him leave then turned his attention back to his pint. He was feeling stunned by what had just happened. And very nervous. He was also strangely elated.

TEN

2.20am Friday 10 June 2016

That, thought Danny Johnston, *was a fucking horrible dream. Jesus Christ Almighty.*

Since he'd stopped drinking, the ferocity and realism of Danny's dreams had increased massively. He was feverish and hot, yet the sweat all over his body was already starting to chill him. Maybe it was down to the pills he'd been taking. Or the fact they had run out. Maybe it was because he was actually sleeping now rather than simply passing out after a night's drinking. Blackout boozing doesn't tend to encourage dream-filled sleep. Either way, he was starting to dread going to sleep.

He looked around his hotel room. He swung his legs around and sat upright on the edge of his bed.

He'd dreamt he was back on the common. But this time he was searching for something. He staggered and stumbled as he looked – dream Danny clearly knew what he was looking for; asleep Danny didn't.

He turned around and saw his car was on fire. He didn't care – the search was more important. After what seemed like hours, Danny came across a quieter, more still area of the common. He could hear the sound of rippling water but couldn't see where it was coming from. Pushing apart some branches from a large bush, he saw a small boy lying asleep on a single bed. The boy was tied to it; the bed was filthy – the boy even filthier. He was close enough for Danny to reach out and touch, yet when he tried, the boy seemed to be a hundred feet away.

Behind him, Danny heard the sound of an explosion. He turned and saw a fireball where his car had been. Again, he didn't seem to care.

He turned back to look at the bed.

The boy's face was inches from his. His breath stank of rotting vegetables. He spat wet earth into Danny's mouth then screamed at him.

That's when he woke up.

What kind of a person has a dream like that?

ELEVEN

Noon Wednesday 11 April 1990

Danny had agreed to meet with DI Smithdown at a tiny, side-street cafe close to Oldham Police station. Despite not feeling his best, Danny was bang on time. The cafe was busy with people visiting the nearby market. DI Smithdown put up a hand and waved Danny over to his table when he spotted him.

Smithdown was drinking coffee and screwing a cigarette out into the ashtray. He seemed to be ageing in dog's years – he looked ten years older than when they'd first met out near the reservoir less than a week ago. There was a woman sitting with him. She was dressed in some white shirt and black trousers – not a uniform, but she was clearly a copper. Her dyed blond hair was scraped back from her head and tied back tightly. She was tall and strong-looking, like a PE teacher She also looked rather annoyed at being there. No words were spoken between her and DI Smithdown.

Danny nodded in the DI's direction and ordered a slice of toast and a can of Coke at the counter. The Coke was for caffeine and sugar, to try and wake himself up. The toast was because he felt he ought to eat something. He hadn't eaten properly for days. After finishing his last shift, he'd gone drinking at his local pub; on returning, he'd found half a bottle of malt whisky tucked towards the back of his kitchen cupboard and demolished that too. Then he'd fallen asleep. Or passed out. *Depends how you look at it.* Today was supposed to be his day off.

He took his Coke and toast over to the table where Smithdown and the female officer were sitting. Still no words between them. *Funny old dynamic going on here,* Danny thought.

'Alright Danny,' the DI said. He gestured at an elderly couple at the next table to see if a chair was free and pulled it over for Danny when they indicated that it was. 'Danny, this is Detective Constable Jan Cave.'

'Hi,' said Danny and put out his hand. She shook his hand – the thinnest of smiles appeared.

'DC Cave is the closest thing we have to a child safety expert round these parts,' said DI Smithdown. 'She's been on a course.'

'Oh right. Great,' said Danny and bit into his toast. It made him feel a bit sick. He had no idea why he was here but thought it best to say as little as possible and see where it went. He put the toast down and drank the Coke instead.

'I thought it would be a good idea for you to meet DC Cave and get an idea what we're up against when it comes to unidentified and missing kids. I'd like to tell you that the system is under strain, but the truth is, there isn't really a system.'

'Do you think the kid might have been a runaway? From a kids' home or something?' Danny asked him. The question was more for DC Cave.

'Possibly,' she said. She looked at DI Smithdown. Then back at Danny. 'Not sure.'

'Okay,' said Danny trying a different tack. 'Well, what happens when a kid goes missing? What procedures kick in?'

Again, the female officer looked to DI Smithdown. He nodded, as if to say, *Go on, tell him.* 'You're not recording this are you?' she asked. She had a strong North Manchester accent.

'No, I'm not,' Danny said, smiling in what he thought was a reassuring way. 'I'd have a microphone out and it would be near your face if I was. We're just talking, aren't we, DI Smithdown?'

'Just talking,' he confirmed.

'Sorry,' said DC Cave. 'I've only ever had dealings with the press once before and it wasn't a very nice experience. *The Messenger* printed my picture a few years back. I was on duty outside a house where there'd been a domestic murder. Dad killed two kids with a claw hammer. Absolute horror story. My neighbours on the estate where I lived didn't know I was with the police. After the paper appeared, I got all sorts of hassle. The dad who hammered his kids got flowers outside his house – I got dog shit through my letterbox. I had to move. Not right, is it?'

'No. It isn't,' agreed Danny. 'Are you a child safety specialist, DC Cave?'

For the first time, the female officer smiled. There was almost a laugh. She pushed her cup of tea away and leant on the table. 'Let me tell you how it works,' she said, and the smile fell quickly from her face. 'Missing kids, kids in danger, vulnerable kids – these jobs always fall to female officers. Most of the blokes at the station have kids – I don't, I've never changed a nappy in my life, but I'm supposed to know more about kids because I'm female.'

She looked at DI Smithdown as if to check she wasn't speaking out of turn. 'If a kid goes missing – a kid that's actually *cared* for, in a good community surrounded by good people – there'll be search parties out within the hour combing the streets and parks looking for that child. Children that are cared for – that are *loved* – very rarely go missing. On the odd occasion that they do, they're normally found before the police even arrive at the scene. Because the people that love them will move heaven and earth to find them.'

'So what kind of kid was the lad up at Black Moss, in your opinion?' asked Danny.

'Well, he was almost certainly a kid that *wasn't* cared for – and kids that aren't cared for tend to end up in care.'

'In a care home?' Danny asked. 'Looked after by social workers?'

'No,' said DC Cave firmly. 'The homes are staffed by *residential* staff, they aren't qualified social workers. They're there to do a head count. If the head count doesn't add up, they fill in a missing from home report and hand it to the police. Some of the kids go missing so often, the homes have the forms already filled out to save time. The forms are handed from shift to shift at the police station and that's it. It's just a bit of paper and that can go missing as easily as a kid who wants to hitch a lift into Manchester and see the sights. How much effort goes into looking for a kid that's already gone missing ten times so far this month? Not a lot. You guys from the press aren't interested because they're, well, they're kids in care.'

'Not sure that's true,' said Danny.

'These kids go missing *all the time*,' stated DI Smithdown, jabbing the table with his finger. 'I can show you case after case of kids who've just disappeared into the mist and I can count the column inches we've had about them on one hand. Without using my thumb. These kids aren't a story to you guys. That's not a criticism – it's a fact. Actually, it's a criticism *and* a fact.'

'So, what's different about this case?' asked Danny.

'We've had scores of kids go AWOL in this division over the years, but we've never had a dead one before. Not a dead one we've known about anyway. And not one that had been subjected to serious sexual assaults like this lad was. Attacks that were... *sustained*. It probably went on for several days before he ended up at Black Moss.'

Danny looked straight at DC Smithdown. He'd felt hangover sick when he arrived at the cafe. Now he felt an altogether different kind of sickness.

'Mr Smithdown thinks this boy was snatched – stolen to order,' said DC Cave. 'I'm keeping an open mind, but one thing's for sure: the best way of stealing something, Danny, is to take something that no one will miss. That way, less people will come looking for it.'

'Okay,' said Danny. 'I get it. But what do you want from me, Mr Smithdown?'

'Interest,' said the DI. 'Time. Publicity. I need you to keep chipping away at your bosses to keep running this story. Keep it in the public eye as best you can. I know that all that anyone's interested in is Strangeways at the moment, but we need you to keep it in the news. But I also need to trust you not to release what we know until I say so. Especially about the way the kid's body was found. Hardly anyone knows about that – if it gets out, I'll know it was you that blabbed it. Stick with it and, when the time is right, I'll give you everything. The big exclusive. Young guy like you, it could make your career.'

'I'll need new audio,' Danny said. He saw the slightly puzzled look on the officers' faces. 'A new interview, to freshen things up. Maybe you'd like to do it DC Cave? My recorder's in my car.'

'No chance,' she said. Danny could see there was no point in trying to cajole her.'

'I'll do it,' said DI Smithdown. 'I'll come with you to the car – we can do it there.'

Danny and DI Smithdown both got up. 'You settle up, DC Cave, while I escort this young man to his vehicle. Make sure you get a receipt.'

'Just one thing,' said Danny. 'Can I ask – why me, Mr Smithdown? There's better journalists than me about.'

DI Smithdown looked at DC Cave and back to Danny: 'Because you saw him. You're involved. Tell me you haven't thought about that kid since the other morning out on the moors?'

'I haven't thought about much else,' Danny said.

'Then that's your answer. That's why.'

'What about Kate from *The Messenger*? Can't she help?'

DI Smithdown leant in, so he was close to Danny's face. 'Two things. One: *The Messenger* doesn't have the same reach as you guys. I need to spread my net good and wide. Second – and this is very important – the shit who did this is off the scale. Fucking evil. And I don't want my daughter anywhere near him.'

TWELVE

10.30am Wednesday 15 June 2016

'So, how have you been, Danny?' said Jo McGuire.

'Okay. Not bad,' he replied. 'Lying low. I've moved back into my house. And no, I haven't had any drugs or alcohol.'

'Fine. Good. Thanks for the update.'

Danny pulled some extra strong mints from his pocket and popped one in his mouth. Since he'd stopped drinking he'd had a constant, foul, metallic taste in his mouth. Plus, he was aware of his smoker's breath. He offered a mint to Jo, but she shook her head. 'Actually,' he said, 'there is one thing. I'm having problems sleeping.'

'Insomnia is a very common side effect of alcohol withdrawal,' the counsellor offered.

'I can get to sleep fine, but the dreams – they're waking me up every night. Never had anything like it.'

'What kind of dreams?' she asked, popping out the point of her pen.

'Just the usual sort of thing – car crashes, screaming children, that kind of thing.'

Danny crunched on the mint in his mouth and it made a harsh, cracking noise that sounded much louder because of the quietness of the small meeting room. 'I'm alright, though. A bit of disturbed sleep. A few bad dreams. There's plenty of people worse off than me.'

'Did you check with the police about that boy you saw? It might set your mind at rest. You must know a lot of police officers in your line of work.'

'Not really, no. I used to – I used to be a proper journalist. In those days, my God. The kind of things the police would tell you over a drink or two in a smoky pub. Unbelievable. But I've had people to do that kind of thing for me for years. That sounds crap but it's true. To be honest, I'm just a front man. A presenter. I read things out that other people have written, ask questions that have already been prepared… I'm not a proper journalist. Not like the old days. Anyway, you can just Google it these days, can't you? So, I Googled it. No reports of any kids hurt that night.'

Danny was going to offer Jo a mint – then remembered he'd already done so. He played with the wrapper. 'You've never mentioned your family or relationships,' she said. 'Do you have anyone, Danny? Anyone to help you with all of this?'

Danny paused to think. He knew the answer but was slightly embarrassed to say it out loud. 'Not really. I've been in London for years now, but all I've ever done is work and drink. Very often at the same time. So, no wife, no kids. All my friends are really just drinking friends and I've broken the code of honour by packing it in. I've deserted them, basically. So, I can't see any of them coming round and having a heart to heart about my sleeping habits, to be honest.'

'You're from Manchester originally though, aren't you?'

'Yes, I am. But I haven't been back there for years.'

'Any family? Brothers and sisters?'

'No. No brothers and sisters. My parents died about ten years ago. I wasn't that close to them, to be honest.'

'Do you want to talk about that?'

'Not really. It's not a big deal. Sorry, that sounds a bit harsh, but it isn't. It wasn't then, and it isn't now.'

'This might sound a bit clichéd,' Jo said, 'but were you unhappy when you were young? Is that part of all this?'

Danny shifted in his seat. 'I'm very wary of going down the whole *woe is me* route. It's too easy, isn't it? *I hated being a kid and it made me get pissed for thirty years.* No. You won't get that from me. Maybe I just really liked the taste of alcohol. That's as good an explanation as anything, isn't it?'

Silence for a while. 'Sorry,' Danny said. 'It sounds like I'm getting angry at you, but I'm not. You're just... well, you happen to be in the same room as me, don't you?'

'Is there anyone back in Manchester that you could talk to? Maybe they can help you?'

'Maybe,' said Danny. 'Yeah. I've been thinking about that.'

THIRTEEN

2.30pm Wednesday 11 April 1990

After interviewing DI Smithdown in his car – a couple of copperspeak soundbites, nothing too earth-shattering – Danny decided to take a trip back up to Black Moss. It had only been a few days since he'd first been here, but so much had happened since then, it seemed like months ago.

After saying his goodbyes to the DI, Danny had a swift couple of pints in the Three Tunnes then headed out of town up towards the moors. The sun was shining. The sky was blue, crisp and clear. *There were worse places to be on a Wednesday afternoon.* Danny parked up and headed down the Pennine Way path, moving quickly past the first reservoir and heading up the slope towards Black Moss. He was more appropriately dressed this time around, with boots and a fleece, but the cold still bit at him as he crested the hill.

There was a single policeman standing at the spot where the body had been found. A woman was talking to him. Danny looked to see if there was a route on the other side of Black Moss so that he could bypass the two figures. There wasn't. Plus, it was too late; the woman had spotted him and was running up the path in his direction. *Fucking hell*, thought Danny.

'Danny Something! Hang on!' shouted Kate.

'Ah. Kate from *The Messenger*,' said Danny as she approached. 'Kate *Smithdown* from *The Messenger*, daughter of DI Smithdown, who chose not to tell me that her dad was running the investigation while pumping me for information in a chamois leather mini skirt. *That* Kate Smithdown.'

'He isn't running the investigation, that's half the problem,' she said, slightly out of breath after running up the path. 'Don't be so paranoid.' Danny noticed he'd made her blush. Only a little, but it showed quite strongly across her pale complexion. He was quite pleased with himself.

Kate continued: 'The bad guys are the people who know how that kid ended up dead out here, not me.' Her Oldham accent began to push through as she raised her voice… *owt 'ere.*

'It's bad enough being a copper's daughter round here as it is, let alone when you're a journalist and everyone thinks you're biased towards the police. I wasn't singling you out. I don't tell *anyone* who my dad is.'

'What the hell are you doing out here, anyway?' Danny asked. 'Shouldn't you be harassing the families of Strangeways rioters?'

'I live near here. Remember?' Kate crossed her eyes, reminding Danny of the look he'd given her at the police station. She pulled a packet of Benson & Hedges from her shoulder bag. There were only two left in the pack; she put one in her mouth and offered the other to Danny. He took it. She lit hers then his. 'Look, Dad's really worried. There's something very, very grim going on here. You should be flattered that he is trusting you with this. He likes you. He *trusts* you.' She looked down the path towards the reservoir. 'He obviously sees something in you that I don't.'

'I have no idea what you're talking about,' Danny said. He motioned for Kate to continue down the path towards the water. Despite the sunny sky above it, Black Moss looked greyer than ever, as if deflecting any attempt the beautiful day might make to brighten it up.

'Does your dad know you're here?' Danny asked as they walked.

'I'm not thirteen you know!'

'I know, but he seems keen for you to keep well clear of the case.'

'Is that what he told you?' Kate asked.

'Sort of.'

They walked past the officer on duty at the spot where the boy's body was found. Danny wasn't sure, but he thought that he might have been one of the men on duty the other morning. The policeman wouldn't make eye contact with him but nodded at Kate. They carried on down the straight path alongside the edge of the reservoir. There was a small, derelict jetty halfway long. They stopped. 'Have you been down to Strangeways yet?' Kate asked. 'The inmates are coming out in droves now. Oldham nick is full of them. They say it's a matter of hours until it's all over.'

'They've been saying that since April the first when it all kicked off,' Danny said. 'No one knows what the fuck is going on. It's a riot. The people in charge aren't in charge anymore. The guys on the roof are and they're just making it up as they go along. Anyone who claims to know what's about to happen next is kidding themselves.'

He picked up a stone and was about to skim it across the water. He changed his mind and dropped it in the sand instead. It didn't seem right, somehow. 'The riot will play itself out soon enough, I reckon,' Danny continued. 'I don't care anymore, to be honest. I kept thinking I was missing out by not being there. Maybe I'm not.'

There was silence for a moment, apart from the wind, the birds and the distant burr of cars from the main road. 'What did you see the other morning, Danny?'

He thought for a good twenty seconds before answering. 'Well, the kid was in a bad way, that's for certain,' said Danny. He wasn't sure if he was being too cautious. *But what if this was a test?* What if DI Smithdown was checking to see if Danny really was discreet, could really keep his mouth shut when told to? He might have sent Kate to test his resolve. He couldn't chance it. 'All I saw was a poor little lad face down in the sand. That's enough, isn't it?'

Kate looked back at the lone policeman next to the reservoir. 'Dad said you've been speaking to DC Cave?'

'Uh huh,' confirmed Danny. 'She's not a million chuckles, but she does seem to be trying to help. She thinks the kid was from a home – it could explain why no one has reported him missing. The system's a shambles – just a bit of paper passed from one shift to the next to keep tabs on kids that no-one cares about anyway. If someone loses that paper, it's like the kid never existed. It stinks.'

'So, what happens next?' Kate asked. She hugged herself to keep out the cold.

'Your dad wants me to keep the story on the go – keep broadcasting appeals for information. It's not going to be easy.'

'Well, that's the Strangeways effect for you,' said Kate.

'It's more than that. You know the deal with murders – the police run them to a system. After the initial release of information, the cops put a grieving relative up at a press conference; they make an emotional appeal. We always describe them as an "emotional appeal" don't we? Hopefully, they'll cry a bit and that's the bit we'll use. It keeps the story going. But with this – there's nothing. There are no grieving relatives. There's no one to make an emotional appeal. There's *nothing*. No cares about that kid. Just your dad.'

'You seem to care, Danny Something.'

The two journalists stood silently next to the water. It still refused to take on any hint of colour other than grey. 'Why did you come back up here today?' Kate asked. 'I know you were seeing Dad, but it's not exactly on your route back, is it? I imagine you live in Didsbury or somewhere like that.'

Danny smiled. The south Manchester suburb was well known to be populated by radio and TV types. It would be a terrible cliché for Danny to live there. 'Yes. I do live in Didsbury actually,' he admitted. 'I'm a walking, talking stereotype, aren't I?'

'I don't know what you are, Danny Something. But Dad seems to like you. So that's in your favour, I suppose. Anyway, back to my question. Why are you here?'

'Don't know, really. Just thinking about the kid, I suppose. This seems the best place to do it. Anyway, I'm heading off,' Danny said. 'Back to my fantabulous Didsbury *pied-à-terre*.' He began to walk up the path. 'We all talk like that in Didsbury, you know, it means – '

'I know what it means,' interrupted Kate. 'It's French for dickhead's flat.'

Danny carried on walking. He nodded at the policeman as he approached him. *I'm sure that's the cop who was sick the other morning.*

Kate spoke again, louder this time. 'Why d'you come back up here, Danny Something?' she shouted. Like Kate's father had done the other morning, Danny gave a gesture universally accepted to mean... *how the hell should I know?*

Danny reached his car, a small Renault he'd had for two years and never washed once. If the outside was bad, then the inside was a disgrace. The back seat was covered in newspapers, takeaway cartons, empty Coke cans, notepads and chocolate bar wrappers. *I should probably clean this out,* he thought. *Or get rid of the worst of it, at least.*

Danny leant in and found a screwed-up plastic bag. He filled it with the most unpleasant looking rubbish – not all of it, by any means – and walked across the car park to a concrete bin by the side of the road. He put the bag of litter into the bin. He had to push it down as it was already full. As he did so, a white, Manchester Radio van drove past. It was going very fast in the direction of Huddersfield, but he had time to see the person behind the wheel – Danny recognised him. And he was pretty sure that the station's engineer, Gary Keenan, had recognised him too.

FOURTEEN

10.30pm Wednesday 15 June 2016

In the previous two hours, Danny had managed to walk around the various tree-lined sections of Clapham Common three times. Head down, hands in pockets, he was walking fast as if he had a purpose. Which, in fact, he didn't. An old joke kept circling around his head: *My dad had a problem with his legs… they wouldn't walk past pubs.*

Danny couldn't get the joke out of his head. *Maybe that's what I'm doing – seeing how well my legs will walk past pubs.*

He'd walked past a lot of pubs in the last two hours. And off-licences. And mini markets. And restaurants. *Some people drink in restaurants*, he thought. *People who want to avoid other people – people with a lot on their minds – they drink in restaurants. It's not that unusual.*

Tucked away in the far corner of the common – Clapham Old Town, they called it – was Danny's favourite pub, The Mitre. In the various loops, routes and permutations he'd taken around the common, he'd so far managed to avoid The Mitre. Now, he was very clearly walking down a slim road called The Polygon and could see the pub dead ahead of him. *Fuck. There's a pub my legs haven't walked past very often. Fuck.*

Danny stopped across the road from The Mitre. He sat on a bench and watched. He listened to the thrum of sound that wafted across the road. The *rat-a-tat-tat* of glasses and chatter; the punctuation point created by a loud peel of laugher; the muffly bass of the music. The way the sound changed and wavered as people came in and out of the pub door.

Danny stared at the front door of The Mitre, his favourite pub. *Where everyone knows your name.*

At 11.30 pm, after the last of the drinkers had left, he went home.

Until he'd stopped drinking, Danny had never really noticed how bland his house was. It was a desirable Clapham terrace – the value just kept going up and up – but it was un-lived in and cold. There were no photos, mementos or individual touches. There was furniture and basic practicalities but no imprint of ownership. It was like a house that had been bleached of all personality in order to sell it. Danny had lived there for nearly a decade. It had been like that since the day he moved in.

It took an hour or so for him to get to sleep. It seemed like only minutes for the dreams to come. This time, it was Danny who was on the bed, his hands tied behind his back. The bed was sinking into water – water so dark it looked like black gloss paint. There was relief for Danny as the bed slipped away and left him struggling yet afloat on the surface. Then fear – real, chest-punching fear – as he realised he was chained to the bed and it was dragging him down.

FIFTEEN

7.30am Friday 13 April 1990

Seeing Gary Keenan out on the Huddersfield Road had bothered Danny for two days. He couldn't shake the thought of it. *What was he doing out there, driving past that very spot? That's just so weird. Maybe it's just me being paranoid. I don't know who the fuck to trust anymore. But I'm sure he saw me, and knew I was up there the other morning when the body was found. But he said nothing. Why?*

He needed to settle his mind, and to do that, Danny needed an excuse to talk to Gary. He'd come up with an idea and he was quite pleased with it. He'd arrived at Manchester Radio half an hour early for his day shift. Just before leaving home he'd uncoupled the microphone of his Marantz recorder from the main unit. Exposing the five pins that made the connection, he'd rammed a kitchen knife into it and deliberately bent the pins out of shape. When he tried to re-connect the microphone, it wouldn't fit. *Rather than just marching up to him and asking outright, I can go and see him about my busted Marantz and see if he mentions seeing me. If he doesn't mention it, I will.*

It was too early for Pauline to be on the reception, so Danny punched in the security numbers on the door and let himself in. Station output was piped into the building twenty-four hours a day and 'Real Real Real' by Jesus Jones was ending; then Beth Hall read the 7.30 news headlines.

Because it was Friday the 13th, many journalists seemed to have decided that today would be a convenient time for the Strangeways' riot to end. It would, at least, suit their headlines: 'Prison authorities at Strangeways' prison in Manchester are hoping that Friday the 13th will prove unlucky for the remaining rioters still holding out inside the jail,' he heard Beth say via the corridor speakers.

'Absolute bollocks,' Danny muttered to himself. 'Clutching-at-straws shite. She should be ashamed of herself.'

If he was quick he could sneak past the news booth without having to talk to Beth. Danny saw her through the small square window embedded into the door. *Cow*. All doors into rooms with microphones on the other side had windows in them, so you didn't walk in on someone who was recording or live on air. Danny could see the back of Beth's head as she read the news. Each story was in a separate piece of paper. As she read each story, she threw it away with a flourish.

Despite the heavy door that separated him from Beth, Danny walked quietly. He passed the news booth and headed around the building towards the engineering section where Gary Keenan's office was. There was a sign above Gary's door. It said: THE ANSWER'S FUCK OFF – NOW, WHAT'S THE QUESTION? Danny went in anyway.

There was a fizzy, metallic smell in the room. Gary was using a soldering iron with his back to the door. 'Enter, Danny boy,' he shouted over the sound of complex, progressive rock that Danny thought might be early Genesis. The room was one of the few spaces in the Manchester Radio that wasn't filled with station output. Gary had disconnected it. Instead, the music came from a filthy, double-cassette player perched on a shelf above the wooden work station that dominated the room. There was barely a square inch of the workspace that wasn't covered in tools, tape, wire, screws and the internal workings of tape machines, record decks, CD players and speakers. Danny didn't wonder why Gary had known it was him, despite having his back to him. The engineer had a wing mirror mounted on his desk, so he could see who was approaching.

'Morning, Gary. Sorry to bug you. Got a problem with my Marantz. The mic won't plug in and I don't want to knacker it any more than it already is. Have you got a minute to take a look?'

Gary pushed aside an armful of debris from his desk and cleared a Marantz-sized space. He jabbed at the space with his finger, indicating that Danny should place the offending item right there. 'Bet you a tenner you've fucked up the pins,' Gary said. For a moment, Danny thought he'd been rumbled; then he realised the engineer was talking generally. Reporters were forever breaking the connection pins. Gary looked at the recorder's microphone input: 'Guess what?' he said. 'The pins are fucked.'

'Right,' said Danny. 'Is it up for a swift repair or should I grab another Marantz? I need to get up to Oldham for the kiddie murder.'

Danny waited to see if Gary would chip in about seeing him out on the moors. The engineer swung around in his leather swivel chair and looked directly at him. 'I've just refurbed one,' he said. 'You can have it while I give your one a bit of resuscitation.' He grabbed another Marantz and gave it to Danny. He placed Danny's machine into a heavy-duty plastic box marked with a handwritten sign. It read: 'Fucked'.

'Cheers,' said the reporter. 'I think I might have dropped it out on the moors.' Again, he left a space. It was something radio reporters are taught to do – if you want someone to speak, then say as little as possible. Leave them room to do the talking.

'Serves you right for going out into the arse end of nowhere,' was all that Gary offered.

'Do you know it round there?' Danny asked, trying a different tack.

'No. But I imagine it's a horrendous shithole.'

'It isn't exactly Chelsea, but the countryside around the reservoirs is amazing. Especially near Black Moss.'

Gary looked at him blankly. 'I'll take your word for it, cocker,' he said. 'Now toddle off and leave me to it.' Gary turned back to his work bench and carried on soldering. Danny looked around the room. It was chaos. 'Gary, how the fuck do you find anything in here?'

'It's all for show this,' said Gary. 'People expect it don't they? But it's all smoke and mirrors mate. You only need two things in this game. Because there's only ever usually two problems that need dealing with. Either something isn't moving, or something is moving too much. And you know what they say, don't you, Danny boy? If it won't move and it should do, squirt it with WD40. If it moves when it shouldn't do, you need to bang a load of gaffer tape on it.'

Danny waited. Nothing. 'Now fuck off and let me pretend to work,' Gary said.

Danny turned around, left Gary's office and pushed open the door of the newsroom. No wall of noise this time. It was still early, and the other daytime reporters hadn't arrived yet. The late reporters were probably still at Strangeways. On the wall was a piece of A3 paper with the words '24- HOUR CLUB' scrawled across it in marker pen. Several Manchester Radio reporters' names were on it – it signified those who had worked around the clock covering the riot, which was by now heading towards the end of its second week. At the top of the list was the name of Manchester Radio's chief reporter Robert Crane – his name appeared several more times too. Danny's name was nowhere to be seen.

The appetite for the story hadn't reduced in the slightest, although those initial claims of '20 DEAD' made by the *Manchester Evening News* were now being played down. The inmates had even fashioned a makeshift banner with the words 'NO DEAD' on it and displayed it from the rooftop. After a prison officer had died from a heart attack he suffered while helping inmates to evacuate the jail, the rioters made another banner, this time expressing their sympathy for the officer's family. Not that he had anything to compare it to, but Danny doubted that prison riots usually panned out this way. It was showy and theatrical. It was articulate yet surreal. Danny thought about the party he'd seen outside the jail. The music, the drugs, the t-shirts. *It's a very Manchester sort of riot,* he concluded.

Danny looked at the CEEFAX headlines on the dusty, wall-mounted TV in the corner of the newsroom. NO END IN SIGHT FOR STRANGEWAYS' RIOT was the headline. The newsroom was even more of a mess than it usually was. Pink and white sheets of paper seemed to cover every surface – and a reasonable portion of the floor. Pink sheets were used by newsreaders to read a scripted cue that would be followed by a piece of audio. White sheets were for straight reads, short stories not worthy of a fuller report, like less-serious crime stories, the weather or 'and finally' light stories. Since the riot started, 'and finallys' had largely been abandoned.

Beth Hall came though the door at the other end of the newsroom. She glanced at Danny but said nothing, instead dropping her spare scripts to the floor and adding to the mess in the news room. She lit a cigarette; smoking rules were largely ignored before 8 am. She began clattering on her typewriter and the cigarette wobbled between her lips as she typed. After about fifteen seconds, she spoke: 'Yes, Danny boy? Something on your mind? You're early. You're never early.'

'I got a fresh interview on the Oldham case.'

'What Oldham case?' said Beth over the *pak pak pak* of the typewriter.

'The dead kid at the reservoir,' Danny said, not quite shouting in frustration but getting pretty close. *That stuff you read out on the news… does any of it go in, or does it just pass straight through you?*

'Oh, that. Sharston isn't convinced it's our patch. And he is the head of news, after all.'

'It *is* our patch. It's Oldham Police's case. Oldham is in Greater Manchester. We cover Greater Manchester. Therefore, it's our patch.'

'Wasn't it found over the border?' Beth wasn't looking at him as she spoke. The *pak pak pak* continued.

'On the border. HE was found ON the border. *He* was a boy, not an *it*.'

Pak pak pak.

'You alright, Danny?' said Beth. 'You're being weird even by your standards.'

Danny cleared some pink sheets from a seat close to Beth's and sat down. He was in serious danger of having a proper conversation with her and it felt a little odd. 'It's a little bit frustrating, to be honest,' he said, quietly. 'Actually, it's a *lot* frustrating. It's very, very fucking frustrating, in fact. Every reporter who can hold a microphone and speak at the same time is down at Strangeways soaking up the glory. I can't even get near the place. Instead, I'm sent off to the back of beyond to cover a story that actually turns out to be really important. But, no one cares about it. I feel like I'm really close to something big and serious and fucking awful, yet I'm struggling to get it on air.'

The *pak pak pak* stopped. The silence made Danny drop the volume of his voice by fifty percent. 'Very... frustrating,' he added, one more time. Danny looked at Beth, expecting to get a mouthful. She offered him a cigarette. He took it and lit it up.

Beth looked at him with a slightly offended expression on her face, as if she'd caught a whiff of an unpleasant smell. 'Are we about to have an actual proper conversation?'

'Don't know. Are we?'

Beth dropped her cigarette into a plastic cup of coffee. It hissed as it extinguished. 'Look, Danny. I get it. I understand. But you've got to understand that for a station like us, Strangeways is a once-in-a-lifetime story. Our listening figures have, well, they've gone through the roof, if you'll forgive the expression. We aren't Radio Four, you know? Half of our demographic knows someone inside that jail. That's the kind of station we are – and those people are looking to us to keep them updated. It works both ways too – we're getting scoop after scoop because families are coming to us first with news of what they know. The BBC aren't getting a look in and as long as those scrotes are up on that roof, we are not going to let the opposition off the hook. It's Strangeways all the way.'

Danny rolled up a pink script sheet and put it to his eye like a telescope. 'Yeah, I get it,' he said. 'But there must be space for other news too?'

'Course there is – or there will be. This riot will be over any time now. Maybe even today. Then we'll lead with your kid story every bulletin. Look, do me a copy read for the 8 am and I'll try to squeeze it in.'

'I've got some fresh audio too,' Danny added. 'Of the main cop. Appealing for witnesses, that kind of thing.'

'Like he did last week?'

Danny put down his paper telescope. 'Kind of, yeah.'

'I'll take a copy read for now and maybe some audio for later.' A pause. 'Listen, Danny. Stick at it. Sharston must really rate you to give you this story all to yourself. Maybe the glory isn't out at Strangeways at all – maybe it's out in the wilds of Oldham.'

'Maybe.'

'Do me the calls and that copy read, okay?'

'Okay.'

Beth stuck out her lower lip. 'Now fuck off and stop being such a soft arse.'

Danny found the least messy desk in the newsroom and sat down. He inserted a sheet of white paper into the typewriter. Instinctively he typed the time and date of the bulletin onto the top left corner of the paper and a tagline for the story on the top right – a word or two to describe what it was about to save someone having to read the whole thing. Danny wrote 'Oldham Kid' then quickly banged out two paragraphs about the case: *police still baffled, appealing for witnesses, care home theory*... Not great, but something. Danny pulled the sheet from the typewriter and placed it into a wooden tray marked 'New Copy'. Beth was busy shouting at someone on the phone, so Danny left it at that and returned to his desk.

He turned his attention to the calls. Attached to the newsroom wall were two black display boards covered in white lettering. The pegged letters were stuck on by pressing them into hundreds of holes that peppered the boards. They were the kind you'd normally see in takeaways or pubs to show what the establishment served and how much it cost. Instead of prices, the letters spelt out the names and numbers of police, fire brigade and ambulance contacts across Greater Manchester and the adjoining counties. Reporters had to call them every hour to see if there were any ongoing incidents that might be newsworthy.

Danny never quite understood why a Manchester radio station felt the need to ring ambulance stations in North Wales, but those were the rules. He started with Greater Manchester Police, asking for the duty sergeant. Then he moved on to the fire and ambulance stations. It took him nearly twenty minutes to get through the list; by the time he'd finished, Beth had gathered up her scripts and walked through to the news booth to read the 8 am news. Danny stood up and noticed his 'Oldham Kid' story was still in the tray. He sat down and waited for Beth to start reading the news on the internal feed. Then he rang the *Oldham Evening Messenger* and left a message for Kate Smithdown.

SIXTEEN

10.35am Friday 17 June 2016

'Just to cut to the chase,' Danny said to Jo McGuire as he settled into his seat at the drug and alcohol unit. 'No, I haven't consumed any alcohol since I last saw you. Yes, I'm taking my medicine, though the heavy-duty diazepam ones have all gone. I miss them, they were great. What else? Yes, I'm still dreaming like a bastard. No, I'm not working at the moment. Yes, I think it's a good idea to stay away from my old friends. No, I haven't consumed any alcohol. Yes, I think about it all the time, but no, I haven't consumed any alcohol.'

'Good,' said the therapist, looking at her notes. 'How often do you think about it Danny?' she asked. Her voice was very soft, so was her accent. Danny had never noticed before. *Derbyshire, maybe,* he thought. *Edging towards the east Midlands. But not too 'eh up me duck'… good voice for radio, actually. Late night though, not morning or daytime.*

'About what?' he asked momentarily distracted by the accent issue.

'Drinking. Drinking alcohol. How often do you think about it?'

'Well, during the week after I stopped, about five hundred times a day. Now I'm down to about a hundred.'

'Seriously?'

'Seriously.'

'If you were to rate the level of temptation that you feel out of ten, what would you rate it at?'

'Twenty to twenty-five, I'd say. Even talking about it now sets off a taste in my mouth. Horrible, metal taste like I've been sucking on tin foil. Vile. But it doesn't matter though, does it? Very binary this not drinking game, isn't it? It's on or off – either you have or you haven't. There's no middle ground. And I haven't. So that's good, isn't it?'

'Okay.' She made a note of what Danny had said. A pause. 'You mentioned work. Do you have plans? You were very successful.'

'Being on the telly and being successful are two separate things,' Danny said, slumping in his chair and folding his arms. 'If you put a packet of biscuits on TV people will recognise it – doesn't make it any good. People just assume they're good biscuits – because why would anyone put rubbish biscuits on the telly?'

'Don't you think you were good? You seemed good to me.'

Danny breathed out long and hard. He rubbed his beard – it was more accurate to call it white now, rather than grey. He sunk even lower into his chair. 'I'm not sure I deserved it. I was just a front man, a talking head, a turn, an act. I didn't find the bad guys – I was just plonked in front of them after a team of researchers found them. It's not proper journalism. It's showbiz. Showbiz bollocks. Big, daft showbiz bollocks. The fact that I could literally do it when I was pissed sort of proves that, doesn't it?'

'How are you for money?' Jo asked.

'I'm cash poor. I've got no money coming in. No one with any sense will touch me at the moment. I had a book on the go but that's been strangled at birth. I've been given a few quid to not write it but that won't last long. Do you know what that's called in publishing circles? A "kill payment". Charming. I've got the house in Clapham and a pension pot but that's about it. So, cash poor – asset… okay.'

'So, what's your plan?'

'I'm not sure yet. My agent suggested I go back to Manchester for a bit. Before he stopped being my agent that is. I don't know. I'm thinking about it.'

'You mentioned your parents last time,' said Jo. 'That you weren't that close. Is that right?'

'Yeah. We weren't, really.' Danny pulled at one of the ever-present tissues from the box in front of him. It was a different box from last time. He tugged it slightly so it began to rise up. Then he stopped.

'Thing is, they weren't actually my parents. I was adopted when I was pretty young. My real parents couldn't look after me – didn't have the skills I suppose someone in your line of work might say. The folks who adopted me were perfectly decent people, but when I left Manchester for London in the nineties I just sort of drifted away from them. I came back less and less. Just Christmas for a while, then not even that. They died a few years back. Shame, really. Decent people.'

'So, who would you go and see if you went back to Manchester?'

Danny looked at the therapist. And thought. He tugged the tissue out of the box and put it in his back pocket.

SEVENTEEN

5.30pm Friday 13 April 1990

Danny walked through the front door of the Three Tunnes and spotted Kate ordering a pint at the bar amongst a grim-looking gaggle of teatime drinkers. She caught his eye and pointed to her drink with a questioning look. Danny raised a thumb and a pint of lager arrived at the bar at the same time as he did. He took a sip – it was what Danny referred to as 'cooking lager', the weak kind, Carling or Skol. Danny preferred stronger stuff like Red Stripe or Stella Artois. *It's the thought that counts, I suppose.*

'Not to your taste, Danny Something?' Kate said, pulling up a high stool and sitting down.

'It's a perfectly acceptable aperitif,' he said.

'You like a drink, don't you Mr Something?'

'I'm not the only one,' he replied, gesturing towards Kate's pint.

'Comes with the territory,' she said. 'They give you a pint on your first day of work in journalism, don't they?'

'Yes, they do. And a packet of fags if you're lucky.' Danny lit a cigarette, largely for effect.

'What are you after Danny Something? You're in Oldham more than me at the moment.'

'I'm looking for something else, another angle on the reservoir kid. Your dad gave me a fresh interview, but it was all a bit…'

'Copperspeak?'

'Yeah. Copperspeak.'

A brief clip of DS Smithdown talking about the case – how they were working on the theory that the boy could have gone missing from a care home – had run on the afternoon bulletins. Once.

'He still got a right telling off for doing it by his DS,' said Kate. 'He's treading a bit of a fine line at the moment between keeping the story going and getting bollocked by his boss. You'd think they didn't want to catch the killer or something.'

'Not exactly top of their priority list at the moment is it?' said Danny, drinking a quarter of his pint in his first few gulps. 'No one's going to get a promotion by helping a dead kid that no one cared about in the first place. Keeping the Strangeways lot banged up nice and neat for the Home Office until the riot is over... that's where the silverware is.'

Kate went digging into her handbag and pulled out a bulging red Filofax. It was rammed with so many additional bits of paper, Kate had put a large elastic band around it to stop the catch from popping open. She removed it and flicked through the A to Z section. 'What about Peter Jeffries? Bet he could give you a different angle.'

Danny took the next quarter of his pint and let out a long, disappointed sigh. 'Paedo Pete? Really?'

Oldham MP Peter Jeffries was the kind of politician who boasted that he didn't count his votes come election time, he weighed them. Despite representing an overwhelmingly
working-class area,

Jeffries was an old school hang 'em and flog 'em Tory. He could be relied upon to provide a rent-a-quote response to any journalist with access to a pen and a bit of paper, particularly on his pet subject: paedophiles. He'd become so overexposed on the subject that Manchester Radio had an unwritten policy to avoid him after some of his more outlandish claims about local satanic abuse cults had proved to be completely without foundation. 'We tend to steer well clear of Jeffries wherever possible. He's round the twist.'

'Yes, I'll give you that,' conceded Kate. 'He is a bit round the twist. But he knows more about child-related crime than anyone I've ever met. He's actually trying to get the system changed to force the police to set up specialist child protection units in each area. He knows his stuff.'

'Apart from the whole Satanic business.'

'Look, I'm trying my best to help you here,' Kate said. 'I've got his contact details if you want them.'

'Everybody's got his contact details,' Danny said. 'He's in the papers more often than a page three girl.'

'I mean his home address. It's only a few miles away. I thought we could both go.'

'I'm not sure your dad would approve,' Danny said.

'Dad totally approves,' Kate said, reassuringly.

'You haven't mentioned it to him, have you?'

'Not as such, no,' Kate said. 'Danny, you've got nowt else, to be frank. What have you got to lose?'

Danny finished his lager and looked at Kate. He didn't quite understand her and was still concerned he was being taken for a ride with this story. On the other hand, if he still wasn't being allowed anywhere near Strangeways, then where was the harm?

'Okay. Can we have another drink first?' he said.

'It's your shout, Danny Something.'

Peter Jeffries' home was a good fifteen-minute drive out of Oldham, Kate had said, through a village-come-housing estate called Alt. 'Welcome to the real Oldham,' Kate said as they passed through several sets of grey, pebble-dashed terraced houses.

'Jeffries lives here?' Danny said, as he dropped gears to counter the uphill climb.

'No,' replied Kate. 'He lives up there.' She pointed to a detached farmhouse that overlooked the estate. As they pulled off the road onto a snaking dirt track, several hefty brown dogs appeared and proceeded to give them a noisy escort all the way to the front door. There were several classic cars parked outside – *hardly farm vehicles*, thought Danny. A sky-blue Jaguar in particular caught Danny's eye.

'A Manchester MP who actually comes back to his constituency on a Friday teatime instead of stopping in London?' asked Danny as they came to a stop. 'That's a new one.'

'Jeffries comes and goes as he pleases,' Kate said. 'He's never going to get a cabinet post, so he doesn't feel the need to suck up to the Prime Minister – although apparently she's a big fan of his.'

The front door opened and a large man in his late fifties stepped briskly out to meet them. He was wearing a slightly-too-tight three-piece suit and a vivid blue tie that matched the Jag parked in the driveway. His hair was cut brutally short and his neck bulged slightly around his collar. He looked more like a sergeant major turned bouncer than a Tory MP, but that, for many, was part of his appeal. 'Miss Smithdown, with a plus one. What an unexpected treat. You'll come in for a cheeky one, won't you?' His accent was vaguely local but with slightly forced hint – like someone who was putting on a more upmarket voice for effect. Or had decided they didn't like the way they spoke and had chosen to alter it. Jeffries put out his hand towards Danny and proceeded to crush Danny's fingers in a ludicrously firm grip.

'This is Danny from Manchester Radio,' said Kate.

'Ah. The same Manchester Radio to whom I appear to be currently *persona non grata?*' Jeffries asked, with a strange mix of bullishness and theatricality. 'Well step inside young Daniel and let's see if I can't persuade you that I'm not all bad.'

Danny and Kate went inside the house, passing a packed suitcase by the door. 'Go through to the lounge,' Jeffries shouted, heading towards the kitchen. 'I'm on my way to Westminster, but who's in a rush to get to that place?'

'Why are we here?' Danny whispered to Kate as they walked into the lounge. The walls were covered with photos of Jeffries standing next to an array of sportsmen, middle-of-the-road musicians and TV personalities. Some of the pictures went back to the 1970s; many were signed. Danny pointed to one photo of the MP with a famous DJ. 'This is why we don't use Jeffries,' he said quietly. 'He's a fame-chaser, not a proper politician.'

Jeffries came in with a bottle of red wine and three large glasses. He motioned for Danny and Kate to sit down as he sluiced the whole bottle into the glasses and handed them out. 'So,' he said, tugging up his trousers slightly as he sat down. 'Is this about the lad up at Black Moss? Absolutely monstrous business.'

Kate motioned for Danny to take the lead and talk to the MP. 'Yes. Yes it is,' he began. 'The case is getting ignored because of Strangeways. The police have got nothing. I was wondering – we were wondering – if any information had come your way. Given your sort of, interest in this area. As it were.'

'I've been thinking about this a great deal actually,' Jeffries said, taking a healthy glug of his wine. 'Would you like to hear my theory?'

Not really, thought Danny. 'Absolutely,' said Danny.

Jeffries pulled a coaster from a dispenser sitting on the coffee table in front of him. He placed it onto the table and carefully set his wine glass down on top of it. 'I've heard a lot of talk about the placing of this boy's body – that there is some great significance about it being placed on the border. I think that's nonsense. That's what people want us to think. It's not where it was found that matters, but *when*.'

'It was in the middle of the night,' offered Danny.

'No, I don't mean the time, I mean *when*. Right in the middle of the biggest news story we've seen round here for years and years. I think someone did that little lad in, using Strangeways as a cover. They realised that all eyes would be on the jail, especially the eyes of the media, and figured out it would be the ideal opportunity to do something truly terrible, truly heinous and avoid all the usual attention.'

Danny sipped his wine and looked at Jeffries. He was annoyed. Not at the MP, but at himself. There was no bullishness now. He was talking quietly and convincingly. The theatricality had all but gone too.

Jeffries looked directly at Danny. 'I know you lot think I'm just here to get my picture taken with the likes of Jimmy Savile,' he said, waving at his celebrity photo gallery. 'But I've been investigating the way children without worth are treated by society for decades. You've been at it a few days.'

'Would you be willing to go on the record with this, Mr Jeffries?' Danny asked.

'Of course! But will you run it? That's the question. There's a sickness in society and you lot are more interested in the easy stuff – the murders, the robberies, the riots. Are you willing to get your hands really dirty, young Danny Johnston?'

Danny looked at Kate. She returned his glance. 'They're quite filthy as it is Mr Jeffries,' he replied.

'Excellent! Then get your tape out and let's get at it then.'

'It's in the car. Give me two minutes.'

'Not a problem. Kate and I can catch up in the meantime.'

Danny walked towards the door. 'Do you want to know what else I think, young Danny?' Jeffries said. 'I think it was a try out. A test. Whoever did it was dipping a toe into the water up there at Black Moss, if you'll forgive the expression.'

The MP's tone became even firmer. Quieter. He wasn't showing off now. He was deadly serious 'There's more to come. Mark my words. The police are chasing their tails over Strangeways and so are all you media types. It's the perfect time to do something utterly terrible. It was hardly flawless – definitely room for improvement – so it would be silly not to try it again, wouldn't it?'

Jeffries leant back into his leather chair and smiled at Kate, then at Danny. 'Just a theory, of course.'

After swapping numbers and leaving Peter's house at around 6.30 pm – they'd managed to split another bottle of red three ways after the interview was done – Danny dropped Kate off in Oldham centre before heading home.

He then left his car off near his flat. Danny lived on a road called The Beeches where most of the media types lived in West Didsbury, south Manchester. Then he walked over to the nearby Roebuck pub. He didn't particularly like The Roebuck; it just happened to be the nearest pub to his flat. As Danny walked in he noticed that an actor from *Coronation Street* was holding court; he was drunk and loudly telling the people gathered around him about the drug habits and sex life of one of his female co-stars. Danny went to the other end of the bar, bought a pint but found he had no taste for it. He still finished it, though. Then he left and went to the nearby deli, bought four cans of super-strength foreign lager and took them home.

The flat was part of a 1970s block situated at the end of a Victorian cul-de-sac. Danny didn't know any of his neighbours other than to offer the occasional swift nod as he came and went. He let himself in, popped open a can of lager and checked his mail.

A dim red light flashed from the front room. It took Danny a moment to realise what it was: an answer machine message. He didn't get that many. *Probably work*, he thought. There were two messages. He pressed play; before the first voice spoke, he heard a quick snatch of Indian restaurant music: 'Danny, it's DI Smithdown.' He sounded like he'd had a drink or two. 'Listen, can you please not be dragging my daughter around Oldham on this case? I'd appreciate it. The whole point of involving you is to keep her away from it, you dickhead. I know you've spoken to Jeffries by the way – he's not as daft as he looks, you know. He's nearly as daft as he looks but still, you could do worse than listen to what he has to say.'

A pause. *He really sounds quite pissed,* Danny thought.

'Look. I know this is all a bit weird but stick with it. It's not right what happened to that lad. *Obviously,* it's not right but... yes *obviously*. But it's *more* than that.'

Again, a pause – more Indian music.

'I thought really, really hard before involving you in this, Danny. Really, very hard. I wanted you to know that I didn't do it lightly. I'm worried that... it might be a bit much for you. Bit much for anyone, frankly, but *especially* you. Perhaps it might help you in a funny way. I don't know. No. Forget that. It's bollocks. It's enough for *anyone* – leave it at that. So, anyway. Thanks for sticking with it. Yeah, right. Anyway. Ring me tomorrow. We'll see what's what. Okay? Good. Ignore my bollocks. You're doing great. Okay... Bye.'

Beep. Message two. 'Young Danny, it's Peter Jeffries here. I'm en route to London on one of these dreadful mobile phone things. You will not believe what I've found out. Give me a few days and I reckon we can go public. You won't believe who's in on this. What an absolute shower of shits. Speak later in the week. Over and out.'

EIGHTEEN

3.30am Monday 20th June 2016

Danny lay on his bed. *No point in getting in it,* he thought. *I can't sleep. I don't want to sleep.*

He looked around his bedroom. And thought. Since the crash – since he'd stopped drinking – he had started to think about things. *Really* think about things.

He never had much of a tendency towards introspection; that had changed, drastically. He'd started to think about things he'd never given space to before. He had always been aware that his tastes were a little sparse compared to most people, but now he noticed how bare and soulless his bedroom was: no photos, no keepsakes no nothing. A bed. A wardrobe. A rug. That's it.

The house was the same - four walls that contained some clothes and practical things, but no more. *It could be beautiful… a real showstopper. It was worth a fortune compared to the price I paid for it.* But Danny had done nothing to it since he'd moved in. It even had the same curtains and decoration that had been here when he'd first bought it. He'd put his everyday essentials inside the house, but nothing more. He'd bought a new oven but wasn't sure he'd ever used it. The awards he'd won were in a box under the stairs – they certainly weren't on display. There were no paintings or posters on the walls.

He'd never invited anyone round. Ever.

It was a shell. A box that contained a bed and his clothes. Nothing more.

Danny got up and opened his laptop. He booked a train ticket for the first available train to Manchester – it was leaving from Euston at sixteen minutes past six later that morning.

Danny checked his watch. He rang Jo McGuire and told her he was taking a break from their sessions for the time being. Then he began to pack.

PART II

NINETEEN

10.30am Monday 20 June 2016

In the old days, it was a reasonable morning's work to track down someone if you didn't know where to find them; you might have to plough through the phone book, apologetically ringing all the numbers that had the same initials and surnames as the person you were seeking. If all you had was a road – or even just a rough idea of an area – then you'd go 'on the knocker', calling in person and asking whoever answered the door if they knew the subject of your search.

Things were very different now. By the time Danny left Euston Station he had traced Kate Smithdown via her Twitter account and messaged her. She'd replied at 8.30 am as Danny passed through Wilmslow station and they arranged to meet later that morning at her office in Salford Quays. He spent the rest of the journey digging through the internet and matching names to various profile pictures on Facebook accounts and company websites. *My God,* he thought as he looked at some of those faces, *we're so fucking old now, aren't we?*

Danny had booked a hotel as he travelled too – it caught his eye because it was on the same site as the old Manchester Radio building near Piccadilly Gardens. When he arrived at Piccadilly train station, instead of getting on the Metrolink tram or ordering a cab, he walked down Piccadilly Approach and arrived at the hotel on foot. Danny hadn't been back to Manchester since his adopted parents' funeral. Things had changed. No local politicians would say it out loud, but the city had benefited greatly from being continually targeted by the IRA in the late 1980s and early 90s, before the detonation of the largest ever bomb on mainland Britain in 1996. The bomb – and the subsequent rush to rebuild – had cut through years of red tape and the centre of Manchester now looked very different to the city Danny remembered. Where there had been a few greasy spoon cafes and chip shops, there were mid-range chain restaurants, fashionable retro stores and street food outlets.

But Danny didn't remember the brutal, seemingly pointless thick strips of concrete that now curved around Piccadilly Gardens. Nor did he remember the sheer volume of homeless people that seemed to dot every corner as he walked from the station to his hotel.

Danny checked into the hotel and went to his room. He dumped his small suitcase onto the bed. He paced the room then checked out the toiletries in the bathroom – Danny was a big believer in judging a hotel by its toiletries. They were okay. He opened his case and decided he couldn't be bothered to unpack. Instead he changed into a clean white t-shirt to complement his black Harrington jacket and expensive-looking jeans. He looked at himself in the mirror. He pushed a hand through his hair. He looked again, then went back to the bathroom and brushed his teeth. Then looked at himself again. He took a complimentary pen and a notepad from the small desk in the corner of his room and tucked them into the inside pocket of his jacket.

Then Danny looked out of the window and cast a glance across the skyline – there were cranes dotted across the west side of the city towards Salford. Lots of them.

He put the hotel key card into his wallet and headed out into the adjoining city of Salford. Kate Smithdown's office – her *building* – was a fifteen-minute tram ride away in Media City, the shiny temple to the area's newfound status as a magnet for all things TV, radio and internet. Danny remembered the former Salford dockland area as previously being home to nothing. The docks had long gone by the time he was born and the area had been a blank canvas for years, with only a taste of the impressive deco-style dock company buildings left standing. Kate's building, tucked between the BBC and an achingly hip supermarket, was called KSM House.

A very young, very fashionable young man with an impressive collection of piercings, facial hair and tattoos was manning the reception and said hello to Danny by name. 'Kate's expecting you, Mr Johnston,' the young man said. 'Great to have you here. Big admirer. Take a seat.'

Danny gave the receptionist a smile and sat down on a geometric set of brightly-coloured foam blocks that seemed to be the seating area. Retro ashtrays on stands stood next to the blocks. They had sweets in them. Retro sweets. *I hate all this shit,* thought Danny. *Hipster bollocks. She's just showing off. Couldn't we just have met at a cafe?*

As Danny cast a disapproving eye over the lollies and chews in the ashtrays, a well-dressed, very striking looking woman in a slim-fitting black trouser suit and white t-shirt walked towards him. She had jet-black hair with a white streak rising from her hairline at the front and she wore expensive-looking black-rimmed glasses. Apart from that, Kate Smithdown had changed very little in the intervening decades. 'Danny Something,' she said, smiling.

Danny wasn't quite sure what to do – they hadn't seen each other for more than twenty-five years. As he hesitated, Kate pressed her cheek against his. Her hands gripped the top of his arms and she held him there for a few seconds. Then she pulled back and looked him in the eye. She smiled. 'Now,' Kate said. 'Where *were* we…?'

TWENTY

4pm Monday 16 April 1990

After several missed calls were exchanged between DI Smithdown and Danny, the detective left a message for him at Manchester Radio, telling him they should meet that afternoon at an address near to Alt, the area he and Kate had passed through on their way to Peter Jeffries' house. He pulled up outside a grey, pebble-dashed semi on the edges of a sprawling council estate. Kids were running through the streets – some with fearsome-looking dogs – and every other house seemed to have a household item in its front garden: a fridge, a sofa, an armchair.

Throughout the day, Danny had been to-ing and fro-ing the question of whether he should mention the answerphone message the DI had left him. At first, he thought: *maybe he was just pissed – just rambling. He didn't mean anything by it.* Then he thought: *he may have been pissed but he's nobody's fool. What did he mean by it?*

Danny's internal debate was immediately silenced when he saw that DI Smithdown was accompanied by DC Jan Cave. As before, she didn't seem too pleased to be there. *No way am I asking him when DC Chuckle Pants is around,* he thought. *It can wait.*

Danny approached the officers and nodded a greeting. DC Cave looked directly at Danny and held eye contact. When DI Smithdown began to speak, Danny felt like she was still staring at him. 'Danny, lad. Glad you could make it.' Unlike his female colleague, DI Smithdown seemed to be having difficulty looking Danny in the eye. He shifted a cigarette end on the pavement with his foot and stared at it as he spoke. 'Right, so. This is one of two dozen care homes in the area – this is the biggest. It's a pair of semi-detached houses that have been knocked into one big house. The staff here… they're good people… they want to help.'

'Have they ID'd the kid?' Danny asked, adjusting the strap of the Marantz recorder that tugged at his shoulder.

'No. No they haven't.'

Danny felt a tinge of disappointment. 'But they know of a kid who fits the description of the lad. They want to help. One of the staff is willing to talk to you.' The DI finally looked at Danny – he made a twirling motion with his finger. 'With your tape rolling.'

Danny nodded, glanced at DC Cave, noticed she was still staring at him and followed DI Smithdown to the front door. The DI pushed the door and shouted a hello, identifying himself, DC Cave and Danny. A female voice shouted: 'Kitchen!' and they walked through the narrow hallway, following the direction of the voice. The kitchen was large, as if a wall had been knocked down to accommodate it. It was cluttered to the point of being chaotic; a dozen different brands of cereal were lined up across the main kitchen surface next to the sink, which was full to the brim and beyond with dirty dishes. Every horizontal surface was covered in schoolbooks, comics, clothes empty biscuit and sweet wrappers, bottles of juice and fizzy drinks. Danny noticed DC Cave's face was set to slightly-more-disapproving than usual.

A woman in her forties wearing an oversized, colourful jumper and black leggings beckoned them over to the large wooden table that stood in the middle of the kitchen. She was cradling a mug of coffee with both hands. 'Sit down, sit down,' she said. Her voice was soft and warm; there was a hint of Irish in her accent – not unusual in Manchester.

'Brenda this is Danny Johnston, the journalist I was telling you about. Danny, this is Brenda Graham, she runs this place.'

'Ha!' Brenda exclaimed, offering her hand to Danny. 'I wouldn't kid myself. No one runs this place. Anarchy rules here.'

She put down her mug and started work on a roll-up cigarette. Danny could sense a dozen pairs of young eyes, watching him. There were kids everywhere, though none were actually in the kitchen. They hovered and floated at the edges, in doorways or by the stairs. Watching. Listening. Danny caught the eye of a small boy of about ten with hair cut back as short as possible; the boy turned towards the stairs.

'Mr Smithdown thought you might be able to shed some light on this case up at Black Moss?' Danny said. 'The police think it might have been a care home kid. I've also spoken to Peter Jeffries…'

The voice of a teenage boy interrupted them from somewhere beyond the kitchen. 'Pete the Perv? He gives me the creeps. Fuckin' weirdo.'

'Shut it, Brian, you don't know what you're talking about,' Brenda admonished with a smile. 'He's done a lot for us has Mr Jeffries. Won't have a word said against him.'

'Have you got a missing kid at the moment, Brenda?' Danny asked.

'Every kid here is what we call a "persistent missing", Danny,' she replied. 'That's why they're here. They do more runners than Sebastian Coe. They go missing so often the police can't be arsed looking for them.' She nodded at DI Smithdown. 'Present company excepted, of course.'

DC Cave strummed her fingers on the back of the kitchen chair she was standing behind but said nothing.

'We did have a lad of ten go missing around the time the kid's body was found up at the Moss,' Brenda continued. 'But he turned up safe and well about an hour ago.' Brenda turned to look at a boy sitting on the stairs, looking at them through the wooden spindles. 'Didn't you Little Paul? Ya wee shit.'

The boy with the brutally short haircut, that Danny had noticed as he came in, flicked a v-sign in their general direction and then ran up the stairs.

Brenda returned the boy's v-sign with one of her own. She turned to DI Smithdown. 'Sorry John, I should have let you know. You know what it's like here. In and out like nobody's business. I can't chain them to their beds you know?'

'Have you any other children missing Brenda?' Danny asked.

'Here's the thing,' she said, licking the edge of her roll-up to seal it and then lighting it. 'Every single kid who is supposed to be here… is actually here. Normally, we'd expect about a third of them to be out and about, on their toes and missing in action, only to turn up a few days later. Not at the moment. Don't you see – they're *all* present and correct. All accounted for. All where they should be. All *here*.'

'And why do you think that is?' asked Danny. In the background, he was vaguely aware of a heavy-handed knock at the door. Footsteps immediately followed it – no waiting for an invite with this visitor.

A smartly-dressed figure appeared in the kitchen. He looked out of place in the kids' home. 'A word *please* DI Smithdown,' said Detective Superintendent James Pym. 'Now.'

The two policemen walked out of the kitchen. Brenda looked at Danny. 'Who's pissed in his chips?' she whispered loudly to Danny.

'You can't go behind a senior officer's back and expect there to be no repercussions,' said DC Cave, quietly. It was the first time she'd spoken since they'd arrived.

From his chair at the kitchen table, Danny had a clear view through the hallway and out into the street through the open front door. DS Pym had his back to him, but Danny could see DI Smithdown's face. He was just as angry as his boss, but his eyes were on the floor. He spoke intermittently, as if he was being continually cut off by the senior officer. After less than a minute, DC Pym left. The DI stood for a moment then came back into the house. 'We'd best be off Brenda. Now we know the lad's safe. We'll leave you and Danny to chat. DC Cave? Keep me posted, Danny.'

The two police officers left. They didn't speak. Danny watched them through the window. They didn't speak as they walked to their car either.

Several of the children who had been waiting and listening around the periphery of the kitchen, now came in and helped themselves to snacks and drinks. Chatter started. Whispers. Laughter.

'As we say in Oldham,' began Brenda, 'what the fuck was all that about?'

'Absolutely no idea,' said Danny. 'No idea at all.'

'I think he's a good man that John Smithdown,' Brenda said, smiling as a young girl of about thirteen leant across her and took an apple from a bowl on the kitchen table. 'But his boss doesn't seem to agree with me.'

'I sense that too.'

'He's done a lot for kids round here, has John. More than anyone will ever know.'

'What about these kids, Brenda,' Danny asked. His hand gestured towards the youngsters in the kitchen. There was now about ten of them, aged between about nine and sixteen. 'You were telling me that they're all present and correct at the moment. Why?'

Brenda finished the last of her tea and put out her roll-up. 'I think it's because they're shit scared of being *out there,'* she tilted her head in the direction of the window. 'They might hate it here, but right now they're more afraid of whoever or whatever is outside of these four walls.'

'Have they said anything specific?'

'No, but these kids know when something isn't right – *really* not right – and they stay well away from it. That's why we have a full house right now. Nothing scares these kids, they've seen it all. But for the first time I can remember, these kids are *afraid.'*

TWENTY-ONE

10.10am Monday 20 June 2016

Kate's office was on the top floor of KSM House – in fact, it *was* the top floor. The walls were bare bricks with some original and expensive-looking modern art attached to them. They were softly lit with industrial-style lamps attached to the exposed beams of the ceiling. The few items of furniture that were present were pure white and looked very uncomfortable. She motioned for Danny to take a seat at a u-shaped sofa at one end of the room. At the other end was her desk. She tapped a few words into her laptop – virtually the only thing on the desk apart from a photo in a frame – and went over to join Danny. The sofa was huge, but she sat close to him.

'So how are you then?' Kate said, taking off her glasses and putting them on top of her head. 'I heard about your accident. Maybe we should take you on as a client. We do a bit of image management work.'

'I think my image is beyond redemption,' Danny replied. 'Is that what you do here?'

Another fashionable young man brought in a tray filled with a variety of fruity and exotic teas and some tiny bottles of water. Danny opted for a water.

'Digital marketing, social content, viral campaign, that sort of thing. We're doing pretty well. You didn't think I'd still be on the *Messenger*, did you?'

'No not at all – thought you might have gone into radio or telly. You'd have been a natural.'

'I did.'

'Really?'

'Yes – and I've got you to thank, in a funny way.'

'How do you mean?'

'I got your old job at Manchester Radio. When you left I stuck in a CV and Mike Sharston gave me a job. Your job, in fact. I did a few years there, then a bit of telly, realised it was a mug's game and set up a little PR firm. Then it grew. And grew. We've got this office, one in Chester and a new place just opened in London. Not bad for a girl from the wrong side of Oldham. What did you used to call it? *Deliverance* country...'

'Did I say that?'

'Yes, you did.' Kate crossed her eyes, just to make the point.

'Well, I was an idiot in those days.'

'Yeah. You *were* an idiot in those days. Mind you, wrapping your car around a tree a few weeks back wasn't too clever either.'

'Can't argue with that.'

'You look different – from when I last saw you on the telly, I mean.'

'I am different. I stopped drinking for a start.'

Kate sipped her fruit tea. 'Wow. Things have changed. Mind you, we all used to drink a lot in the old days.'

'We did,' Danny agreed, smiling. 'You could pack away the pints with the best of them.'

'True. But you never seemed to take any… pleasure from it. Like it was something you had to do, rather than wanted to do. Sorry, I'm speaking out of turn. It's not my business.'

'It's fine. Not a problem.'

A pause. 'Wife, kids?' Kate asked.

'No and no. Too busy, I suppose. Too busy pratting about on the telly and getting pissed, mainly. How about you?'

Kate got up from the sofa and fetched the framed photo from her desk; she showed it to Danny. He saw the smiling face of a dark-haired boy aged about ten. 'That's my man right there: Jonathan. He's nearly eleven. He's all I need.'

'Dad not around?' Danny asked. He immediately wished he hadn't.

'Not very often. IT entrepreneur. That's what he calls himself, anyway. Lives in London. Too busy to see his son most of time. Dickhead.'

Danny felt slightly ashamed of the fact he was pleased about this bit of news. *Change the subject.* 'Jonathan? John was your dad's name. Is he…'

'Oh yes. Still with us. Couple of heart attacks, bit of cancer, a stroke, but still battling on. He always liked you.'

'I'd like to see him. Is that possible?'

'Why?' Kate asked.

Danny looked out of the window. He saw a Salford he didn't recognise. *Things have really changed. Perhaps this was a mistake,* he thought.

'Do you remember that kid that was found up at Black Moss?'

Kate face changed from puzzlement to surprise in an instant. She leant back in the sofa and put her hands to her head. 'Danny Something, you are such a walking, talking cliché! Don't tell me: *I fucked up my life in the here and now, so I want to go back and sort out the one thing that's been eating me up for years. Then everything will be all right.* Jesus Christ!'

'It's not like that…'

'What is it then?'

'Okay, it is, to some degree, like that…'

'Don't get me wrong – it's very admirable, in a way. God. I remember now… Dad didn't want me to have anything to do with it. He was dragging you here there and everywhere trying to get publicity for it. Strangeways! That was it. The only thing anyone cared about was bloody Strangeways.'

'Haven't you thought about it?' Danny asked. 'A little lad with his teeth and fingers gone, face down on the moors. All strapped up with weights ready to sink him in the Moss.'

Kate went back to her desk and carefully replaced the photo of her son in exactly the same spot where she'd taken it from. 'Weights? Christ. I don't remember that coming out.'

'It didn't. Only me and your dad knew about it. Christ, so much weird stuff went on back then,' added Danny.

'Like what?'

In a whisper – *why am I whispering?* – Danny said: 'Peter Jeffries. That stuff. The Peter fucking Jeffries' stuff.

TWENTY-TWO

9.05am Tuesday 17 April 1990

Danny walked into the newsroom in the middle of what appeared to be a noisy argument. News editor Mike Sharston and chief reporter Robert Crane were at the centre of it. Danny watched and listened.

He lost interest when he realised they were arguing about the best way to format a display board showing sweepstake entries for when the riot would end. There were now about a dozen prisoners left inside the jail and Manchester Radio reporters were being invited to put in a pound and guess the exact time and date the disturbance would finally come to a conclusion. Sharston seemed to favour a series of vertical columns displaying names and their corresponding guesses. Robert Crane was lobbying for a timeline, so each entry could be voided as the time of their guess elapsed. Crane had done well out of the riot: he'd been doing interviews with foreign TV and radio stations about the latest from the jail and there was talk of him getting a telly job when the incident was over. It was a case of when, not if, he'd be leaving Manchester Radio.

Danny found an empty desk just as Beth returned from the news booth. She caught Danny's eye and he pulled out a notebook and pretended to be looking for something in it as she spoke: 'Danny!' she cried, in a very loud voice. 'Message for you from a Mr Peter Jeffries, Member of Parliament for Paedophile Central.'

Robert Crane tapped the news editor on the arm and motioned that he should listen to this. Danny turned to Beth with a polite smile as she continued. 'He says he's coming in tomorrow first thing to give you the full story on the Oldham kid case. He says – and I quote – that you should hold onto your hat, because this is the big one.'

'Paedo Pete is going to give you the big one, Danny,' cried Robert Crane. 'Thought you were a bit old for him but, any port in a storm.'

'Any *reporter* in a storm,' added Mike Shartson, with a laugh. The news editor turned to Danny. 'I thought you knew the deal with Jeffries. He's not a serious politician, he's a grandstander, a rent-a-quote. I want nothing to do with him after that Satanic business.'

Beth waved a piece of paper in their direction. 'He left a number, Danny. It's Oldham 666…'

Some of the newsroom staff were really laughing now. 'He says he's really got something on the case,' Danny protested. 'I can't stick my fingers in my ears and pretend he isn't talking. He is an actual Member of Parliament, you know.'

'Well it will need to be pretty sensational stuff for it to go on air,' said Sharston, walking back to his office. 'Sorry – correction. As well as being sensational, it will need to be *true*.'

The sports journalists had their own area at the far end of the newsroom. They were chanting 'Paedo Pete, Paedo Pete, Paedo Pete' in the style of a 'Here We Go' football chant. One was blowing kisses at Danny. *God, I hate those guys. What do you call a failed journalist? A sports reporter.*

An A4 envelope appeared in front of Danny's face. It clinked with money as Gary Keenan shook it vigorously. 'Putting a quid in, Danny boy?'

'Why not,' said Danny, fishing a pound coin from his pocket.

'You need a precise time and date for when you think the riot will be over,' explained the engineer. 'That means when the very last prisoner gives up.'

Gary had a small notebook and the stub of a pencil to make a note of Danny's guess. As he pondered, Beth passed Danny's desk and handed him a piece of paper. 'Jeffries really is coming in tomorrow, Danny. There's his number. I'll leave it with you.'

'What time?'

'Half eleven,' she replied.

'There you go, then. Eleven thirty am, on the 18th of April. That's when I think the riot will end.' Danny put the coin into the envelope. 'And not a moment too soon.'

'Do you think he's really onto something, Danny?' asked Gary. Danny wasn't sure how to respond. Gary had shown him nothing but kindness – in his own, rude sort of way – but the sight of him out near Black Moss still unnerved him.

'I don't know, mate,' Danny said, picking up a phone and glancing up at the emergency numbers on the wall. 'But if there's a chance of moving this case on, I'll take the risk.'

TWENTY-THREE

10.20am Monday 20 June 2016

'You honestly think that Jeffries was involved in Black Moss?' asked Kate. She was off the uncomfortable sofa now, pacing up and down her office.

'Somehow, yes.'

'Based on what?' cried Kate, waving her hands in frustration. 'He was harmless – just a colourful MP with a liking for the limelight. There's never been any evidence there was any wrongdoing. Just rumour and innuendo.'

'It'd be interesting to know what your dad thinks.'

Kate turned around, leant over the stairwell and shouted: 'Ryan! Emergency supplies! Pronto!'

One of the fashionable young men Danny had seen earlier – *not sure which, everyone under thirty looks the same to me* – came into the office having clearly run up the stairs. He handed Kate a single cigarette and a cheap plastic lighter with something approaching disapproval. 'I know, I know, Ryan. Don't give me the look. Thanks. Now piss off.'

Kate lit the cigarette and inhaled with an eye roll of pleasure. Danny was about to ask if she was allowed to smoke indoors, then remembered that it was her building. She resumed her pacing. 'Dad doesn't really like talking about that case. He never has. He'll go on about the old days with the best of them – can't shut him up – but mention Black Moss and he just clams up. Like he's ashamed of it or something.'

'He must have had concerns about Jeffries, though. Didn't you?'

'It was so long ago, Danny. There was so much else going on at the time. I suppose it did seem weird at the time. Everything about it was weird. But maybe we didn't look hard enough. Maybe we should have gone at it harder, asked more questions. We weren't Woodward and Bernstein – we were just kids. Local reporters doing our best. I was barely twenty-three years old.'

'We were young, but we weren't stupid. The whole thing with Jeffries just stunk and we knew it. I bet your dad knew it too. He was nobody's fool, your dad – and not in the habit of being told what to do or think. If there was a bad smell around the whole Jeffries thing, then he would have known about it.'

Danny took the cigarette from her and took a drag. 'Absolutely filthy habit this. We should know better at our age.'

Kate took the cigarette back and drew the smoke in deeply. 'Fucking hellfire,' she whispered. 'Okay. When do you want to go and see Dad, then?' she asked.

TWENTY-FOUR

6.59am Wednesday 18 April 1990

Danny's alarm came on just as the last bars of 'Strawberry Fields Forever' by Candy Flip merged into the Manchester Radio news jingle.

He'd dreamed hard during the night and his bedsheets were a damp, tangled mess – *should have had more to drink, that normally blocks it out.*

Beth started to read the news – she had her extra serious voice on. 'The news at seven o'clock, I'm Beth Hall. The flamboyant Oldham MP Peter Jeffries has died in a road traffic accident just a few miles from his home in the Alt area of the town. His car left the road and plunged forty feet into a ravine in the early hours of this morning. It's believed that no other vehicles were involved in the incident. Mr Jeffries was known for his high-profile campaigns against child sex offenders – and recently lent his voice to a campaign calling for an investigation into claims of Satanic abuse in Oldham – claims that were later revealed to have been unfounded. In other news, the Strangeways riot has entered its…'

Danny leapt from his bed. He stood very still for nearly a minute. *I've jumped out of bed like I know what to do – but I don't. What the fuck do I do? I'll ring Kate. Too early. Is it, though? Probably. Maybe the DI. Ring him. And tell him what? That the notorious, self-promoting exaggerator Peter Jeffries had the biggest scoop ever and would have been giving it to Mr Danny Johnston later this morning… had he not died out on the moors before he could reveal all? Died. Or been killed? Come on. Grow up.*

The news was coming to end. Danny waited one minute – pulling his trousers on and finding a shirt as he counted off the time he knew it would take for Beth to get from the news booth back – and rang the Manchester Radio news desk. 'Hello, News,' she said.

'Beth, it's Danny.'

'Daniel. Thought it might be you. I take it you've heard about Jeffries?'

'Yes. Yes, I have.'

'Took a lot to knock Strangeways off the lead slot,' she admitted. 'But it finally happened. He always liked being in the news, I suppose. He would have liked it that he was the lead story.'

'He was supposed to be coming in today. To see me.'

'Here we go…'

'What does that mean?'

'Here comes the conspiracy theory.'

'He told me he had a massive story about the kid at Black Moss. Don't you think it's a *bit* of a coincidence?'

'Danny, I've been working for this radio station for five years. I've lost count of the number of times Peter Jeffries told us he had a massive story, including that time he claimed kids were being sacrificed in Satanic rituals out on the moors. It was all bollocks and Mike Sharston nearly got the boot. So, forgive me if I'm slightly sceptical about the big scoop that was coming your way.'

'But, to just swerve off the road like that for no reason…'

'Well, according to the Oldham cops, there was a perfectly sound explanation as to why he crashed,' Beth replied, her tone was now even sharper than usual. 'He was pissed. Your mate went off the road full of booze – he literally didn't feel a thing. It's a miracle he got as far down the road as he did. Even more of a miracle that he didn't kill anyone else in the process. I know someone on the force up there – they're working on the theory he did it on purpose. Guilty conscience. Can't be a coincidence it was so close to where your dead kid was found? How's that for a theory? Unlike yours, it hasn't just been pulled from thin air. It's from a very reliable source at Oldham nick. So, forgive me Danny for not shedding a tear for dear departed Paedo Pete.'

'No, Beth. Tears were the last thing I would expect from you.'

'Glad I didn't disappoint. You aren't on shift today – you were only coming in to interview Jeffries – so we won't expect to see you.'

The line went dead.

Danny, still wearing his trousers and unbuttoned shirt, lay down on the crumpled bed sheets. He stayed still and thought for no more than fifteen seconds, then headed for the shower.

As he'd left home in the middle of rush hour, the commuter traffic meant it took Danny more than an hour and a half to get to his destination. A call to the duty sergeant at Oldham Police station had given him the location of the crash site – a fierce bend in the Huddersfield Road. Black Moss was less than a mile from the spot.

Danny parked his car in a layby close to the scene; on foot he weaved through the traffic that had built up near the bend. The road was down to one lane and temporary traffic lights were controlling the traffic as a tow truck from a local firm worked to retrieve the vintage blue Jaguar from the hefty drop on the inside of the bend. The safety barrier was split in two, the metal curled back from the impact. *He must have been going at a hell of speed to smash through there*, Danny thought. *A hell of speed driving away from Black Moss.*

There were several uniformed officers at the scene; at the centre of the activity was the smartly-suited figure of DS James Pym. He appeared to mouth the words 'fucking Nora' as Danny made his way to where he was standing.

'Hello, Mr Pym. Terrible business. An accident, do you think?'

'Yes, I fucking well *do* think that, as it happens. So, don't you come here spinning a bastard yarn saying otherwise. We've got enough on our plates as it is without you making things worse. RTA, no other vehicle involved. End of.'

DS Pym was about to turn away from Danny, but then seemed to change his mind. 'Why? What do you know that would make me want to think any different?'

'I was due to see him this morning. He was coming into the radio station.'

DS Pym's tone and attitude changed. He stepped close to Danny. 'Why was he coming to see you?'

'I don't know, he didn't say.' Danny was getting very adept at lying to people about how much he knew. He had no intention of telling the DS anything beyond the basics at this stage.

'Then why would you think this was suspicious?' asked DS Pym, not unreasonably.

'I'm a journalist, Mr Pym. I think everything is suspicious. Do you think there's any link to the boy up at Black Moss?'

'Fuck off, Danny.' The detective turned away.

'Any witnesses, Mr Pym?'

The officer turned back. He had a slight smile on his face. 'As it happens, yes. Couldn't ask for a better one.'

DS Pym motioned towards a woman leaning against a police van parked on the other side of the hole in the road's crash barrier. Kate Smithdown was wearing a leather jacket over her pyjamas and had tartan slippers on her feet. Danny walked towards her; he'd never seen her without make-up on before. Nor had he seen her looking so upset. *She looks about twelve.* Danny wanted to put an arm around her shoulder. He didn't.

'You're the witness?' Danny said. 'What the hell were you doing out here, in your pyjamas?'

Kate turned and nodded towards a double-fronted Yorkshire stone house about a hundred yards up the road. 'That's our house.'

'You saw the whole thing?'

'Not exactly. I heard a crash and ran outside to see if I could help. I had to slide down the hillside to get to him. He was about fifteen feet away from his Jag. He'd been thrown from the car – didn't look like he was wearing a seatbelt. Classic Jeffries.'

Danny thought about what Beth had said. 'Had he been drinking?'

Kate looked puzzled. 'How should I know? He was a mess. I've never seen a dead body before.' She looked as though she was about to cry, but quickly stopped and wiped her nose on the cuff of her pyjama top. 'Big, tough journalist, huh?'

'I'd never seen a dead body either – up until the other week,' Danny replied. 'Where's your dad? This is literally on his doorstep.'

'He's… not here. He's with my mum. She's in the hospital.'

Kate began to cry properly this time – full-on sobbing. Danny didn't know what to do. He looked around; the police and recovery team were occupied with controlling the traffic and getting Peter Jeffries' car up from its last resting place down in the roadside valley. It looked to be down to Danny to help Kate. *Why am I so shit at things like this?* 'Maybe we should get you off this road. Shall we go to your house? Pym knows where to find you if he needs you. He clearly doesn't want to speak to me.'

Kate nodded. She rubbed both her eyes with the sleeves of her jacket. She was still crying but the intensity of it was dimming slightly. They crossed the road and walked up the drive. Kate pushed the door – it wasn't locked – and threw her coat on the floor. As they went into the kitchen she pulled a portion of kitchen roll from a wall-mounted dispenser, wiped her face with it, then loudly blew her nose. 'Oh God. *Grow up, Kate.* Do you want a cup of tea Danny?'

'Yes. Sure.' He looked around the kitchen; it was all rustic woods and reassuring brickwork. There were photos on the walls and on nearly every available surface. Weddings, anniversaries, birthdays, holidays, award ceremonies, graduations – every aspect of a happy family life photographically chronicled and displayed with affection and pride. It was clear Kate was an only child and that she'd been showered with love and attention. Danny ached as he looked at the photos. *God, what a lovely family to grow up in,* he thought. It was strange to see DI Smithdown's face *smiling* out from many of the frames. Very few smiling opportunities had presented themselves in the short time that Danny had known Mr Smithdown. As well as Kate and her dad, most of the pictures featured a slim, very attractive woman; the photos charted the myriad of hairstyles and dresses that she'd worn over the years. 'Your mum looks nice,' Danny said as Kate handed him a cup of tea in an Oldham Athletic mug.

The words seemed to set Kate off crying again and another section of kitchen roll was yanked from the holder. 'Yes. She is. Very nice. She's really not well at all at the moment. That's why Dad isn't here. He's with her at hospital.'

'Which one?'

'It's quite near where you live. The Christie.'

Everything dropped neatly and unpleasantly into place. The Christie was in Withington, the next area along from where Danny lived in West Didsbury. He passed it every day when he drove to work. The Christie was one of the largest cancer care facilities in Europe. 'I see,' said Danny. 'Sorry.'

'Don't be sorry. Not your fault.'

'No, I mean I'm sorry *for* you. And your dad. Still, they say if you're going to get cancer, get it in Manchester. It's world famous…'

'It's a cancer hospital, Danny, not Lourdes,' Kate interrupted. 'They have lots of machines and plenty of medicines. But sadly, no miracles.' She sipped her tea. 'Not for Mum, anyway.'

'Is she going to be okay?' Danny asked and immediately regretted it.

'No.'

'I never realised – your dad must be worn out with it all. No wonder he looks so tired.'

'Yes, he is. Very tired. Maybe that's why he's been so keen to get you to help on the Black Moss case. He can't do anything to help Mum – it's past that stage now. But if he can find out what happened to that kid…'

Kate started to cry again. Stepping forward, she put her head on Danny's shoulder. Again, he didn't seem to know what to do and didn't move. No arm round her, no comforting words. They stood there for half a minute. Kate lifted her head and rubbed her eyes. 'You're a cold fish, Danny Something.'

'Sorry,' he said. 'Maybe I should go.'

TWENTY-FIVE

Noon Monday 20 June 2016

'Now', was the answer that Danny gave when Kate asked when he'd like to see her father. She'd grabbed her keys, told one of the fashionable young men she was going out and she and Danny were headed for the M60 outer ring road that encircled Greater Manchester within minutes. In less than twenty minutes they'd turned off the motorway at junction 22 for Oldham. As they headed for the town, past Werneth Park, Danny saw the grey pebble-dash of the police building. 'Not changed a bit, has it?' she said as they skirted past the centre and began the uphill climb out of town.

'No,' he said. 'It really hasn't.'

Kate's car – a brand-new four-by-four that was far more expensive than the one Danny had owned before the crash – hugged the bends of the moorland roads easily and made quick work of the journey. As they got further into the hills and the moorland opened up around them, Danny noticed what he thought might be the spot where Peter Jeffries' car had left the road back in 1990. He glanced over at Kate, but she didn't respond. *Leave it,* he thought. Then they turned off the road and arrived at the detached, cottage that overlooked the moors. *Same house as in 1990. Beautiful spot. Never really noticed before.*

Kate unbuckled her seatbelt and turned to Danny. 'Let me go in first. Don't want to give him another heart attack,' she laughed. Then a pause. 'He's not what he was Danny. He had a stroke last year and it nearly finished him off. It affected his ability to speak, but he manages. He refuses to move to a care home – stubborn old bastard. I have help that comes in a few days a week. Me and Jonathan are here at weekends. We make it work.'

Kate went to the front door and let herself in. A few minutes later, she came to the door and gestured for Danny to come. She took his arm and led him through to the lounge. The photos he'd remembered from his last visit seem to have multiplied. The pictures of Kate's mother faded with age, but they were displayed just as prominently as they had ever been. John Smithdown was sitting with his back to Danny in a high-backed armchair – the kind with a sprung seat that gave you a boost when you needed to stand up. But the ex-detective remained seated. He was dressed in a pastel, v-necked jumper and an open-necked white shirt and had a blanket over his legs. He turned and smiled at Danny. It was a slightly lopsided affair; the left half of his face drooped slightly. But it was still a friendly, open smile nonetheless.

'DI Smithdown. Look at you… Lazing about in your retirement, you idle old bugger.'

John Smithdown's smile got bigger as Danny knelt down next to the older man's chair. He placed his hand on Danny's arm and lightly squeezed it.

'It's great to see you, Danny. Smashing. It really is.' There was a slight slur to his voice and the grip on Danny's arm was weak.

'Danny wants to talk about Black Moss, Dad,' said Kate. 'The boy… from all those years back. Do you remember?'

John Smithdown nodded slowly. He cocked his head slightly, indicating that Danny should lean a little closer. 'Fuckin' Strangeways,' he said.

'Dead right, Mr Smithdown. Fucking Strangeways. That's what screwed us over. Absolutely.'

The retired policeman looked at his daughter, nodded towards Danny and made a gesture with his hand close to his mouth. 'He wants to know if you're still drinking, Danny,' said Kate, slightly embarrassed..

'No, I'm not, you cheeky bastard,' Danny said. 'How about you?'

John Smithdown tilted his hand left and right as if to say, sometimes yes, sometimes no. *The old Mr Smithdown is still with us,* thought Danny. *Laid low, not quite what he was, but still there.*

The uneven smile ebbed away from John Smithdown's face. 'Black Moss,' he said, serious now. He jabbed at Danny. 'I knew. *One day*. I knew.'

Again, he pointed at Danny. 'You knew I'd come back wanting to ask about the kid, Mr Smithdown? Well *I* didn't, that's for sure.'

The retired policeman leant towards Danny and looked him in the eye. He tapped Danny on the chest and nodded. 'Nah. I knew. Always. Here, Danny. *It's in here.'*

Danny felt stinging heat behind his eyes. He wasn't going to cry – but he was pretty close to it. *He knows me better than I know myself, this bloke.*

'The thing is, it never felt right – the answers we were given at the time, I mean. The explanations – they seemed too easy, too convenient. If nothing else, it doesn't seem right that the boy was never ID'd. I've got a bit of time on my hands at the moment – you may have heard – and I thought I'd go back to the story. Look at it again with fresh eyes. What do you think, Mr Smithdown?'

'Best idea y'ever had, Danny.'

'It's a thumbs up from dad, then,' Kate said.

Danny nodded and produced his iPhone from his pocket. 'I've been looking online,' he said, flicking through some bookmarked pages. John Smithdown motioned to his daughter, who fetched a pair of glasses from the mantelpiece and gently placed them on her father's face. The old man nodded as if to say, *okay, carry on.*

'There isn't much out there on the case. It's pre-internet, obviously and I know a lot of older stuff still hasn't been archived on most local newspaper websites. But other than a few of Kate's old articles, it's mainly anniversary stuff.'

Danny showed Mr Smithdown a small item dated April 2010: *Appeal For Help To Solve Black Moss Mystery 20 Years On.* The sub-headline added: *Police ask public to 'search their consciences' over youngster's death.* 'This is straight-from-the-police-press-release stuff,' Danny said. 'All unsolved cases generate this stuff, there's nothing to it really. I wanted to know if there was anything that had surfaced over the years to identify the lad.'

John Smithdown shook his head and looked at his daughter. 'Dad knew he was always clutching at straws with the case,' she said. 'That's why he got you involved. He was desperate. No database match for a boy of that age and there was no DNA on his body. So, the only way to establish his ID was via a DNA match of someone who entered the system. That was only going to happen by a flukey bit of good luck, arresting someone who was related to him and matching them to the boy. That never happened. So… nothing.'

'Mr Smithdown…' Danny began.

'John,' said the old man, hesitantly. For the first time, Detective Inspector John Smithdown was telling Danny to use his first name.

'I'll try. No promises.' Danny had a dig into his jacket pocket and found the pad and pen he'd taken from his hotel room. 'Look, I want to track down all the officers involved in the case. Just to see if anything was missed, maybe there's some way of bringing the case back out into the open. Is there anything I could look at? Anything that seemed too weird or too difficult to examine at the time?'

John Smithdown looked questioningly at Danny and then his daughter.

'What do you mean, Danny?' Kate asked.

'I don't know. Other than you… *John*, no one seemed to care that much about the kid in 1990. I'm not saying they blocked your investigation, but you didn't get a lot of support, did you? What about your old boss, DS Pym? Remember he bollocked you for bringing me into it?'

John Smithdown shook his head. 'DS Dickhead,' he whispered.

'Dad always felt that Pym was a career man,' said Kate. 'He had his eye on being assistant chief constable, maybe more. Pym knew the best way up the ladder was doing a good, high-profile job supporting the Strangeways situation, not digging around up at Black Moss.'

'What 'bout your lot?' asked John Smithdown. 'Where were your mates when it mattered?'

Again, Danny struggled to catch what the old man was saying. 'Dad's pointing out that the local media didn't exactly cover themselves in glory,' Kate said. 'Every journalist with a pad and pencil to their name wanted to use Strangeways to further their career. No one cared about the kid. Except maybe you.'

Smithdown nodded. Then he gestured towards one of the many framed photos on the book case. Danny went over to them and pointed at individual pictures – *so many of them* – until he got to the one that John Smithdown wanted him to bring over. It was a picture from what looked like the early nineties. It showed Kate with an oversized 'Good Luck' card. Her hair was bleached into a nineties-fashionable quiff, but it was still unmistakably her. Drinks were being raised in the direction of the camera. *A leaving party?* She was surrounded by friendly, laughing faces that were familiar to Danny. He couldn't put a name to everyone in the line-up, but he certainly recognised the majority of the people in the photo. It had clearly been taken in the newsroom of Manchester Radio, some years after Danny had left.

'It's an interesting point, Dad. Okay. Why did no one support you Danny? All that work you did and you could barely get the story on the bulletins. Who would benefit from that?'

Danny thought about seeing Gary Keenan all those years ago, driving past Black Moss. He'd given him the opportunity to explain why he was driving past the scene, but he hadn't taken it. *Why would he do that? What did he have to hide?*

'This is all getting a bit conspiracy theory for my taste,' said Kate, tucking the blanket in around her father's legs.

Slowly, John Smithdown raised his hand and pointed at Danny. He spoke. It took Danny a few seconds to decipher what he'd said. *At least one person really didn't like what you were up to, Danny boy. Remember?*

TWENTY-SIX

1.30pm Wednesday 18 April 1990

Danny had driven home to Didsbury after he'd been to Kate's house. He listened to the Manchester Radio news as he drove. Peter Jeffries' death had been pushed into second place by the latest from Strangeways: that the jail was due to be stormed to take out the final set of protestors, whom the tabloids had dubbed *The Dirty Dozen.*

He passed the Christie hospital on the way back and wished he'd done more to comfort Kate. *Shit, what's wrong with me?*

Dropping his car off outside his flat he headed straight to the Roebuck pub nearby. He knew enough people in there to be able to stroll in and find a drinking companion or two within a matter of minutes. He drank through the afternoon, blathering and bullshitting with a changing roster of out-of- work cameramen, journalists and resting actors. He was glad of the chance to talk about nothing for a few hours; no Black Moss, no Peter Jeffries, no cancer, no Kate. *Bar room bollocks, that's all I want to talk about for the rest of today.*

By seven o'clock he was very drunk indeed. *If I don't go home sharpish I'll be too pissed to walk. Better go now.*

He managed to navigate his way out of the pub and down the road to a nearby row of takeaways. He ordered a burger and chips then took an age to find and count out the money from his pockets. He left and started on the five-minute walk back to his flat. Despite going to the toilet before he left the pub, he soon realised he needed to go again and lurched into an alleyway between two sets of Victorian terraces. It was edging towards darkness now: *no one will see me here.*

Leaning against the wall at one side of the alley, he put down his food and fumbled for his fly. The plastic bag came over his head with shocking speed and aggression; it gave him no time to protect himself. He inhaled with shock, in the process pulling the bag even tighter across his mouth. The artificial taste of the plastic made him retch. He tried to reach behind but felt nothing. He tried to twist away but that pulled the bag even tighter around his neck. He clawed at his face, but the plastic was like a second skin. There was no air in his lungs to form a shout. He kicked out but only found his takeaway food on the floor, scattering it across the ground. Slipping, he felt himself being swung to the left and his head connected violently with the wall. Once, then twice. His ears buzzed, his eyes fizzed with speckles of black and white light. *I can't fight this. Too drunk. No air. Please. Why are you doing this? Please.*

As Danny was thinking this, he was dragged to the other side of the alley and his head was banged fiercely against the right-hand wall too. This was enough to make his knees buckle and he dropped to the ground. This at least loosened the plastic bag. Instinctively, he curled into a ball just as the kicks began. None were aimed at his body. Every one of them was aimed at his head. Every one of them found its target.

A shout came from across the street and Danny heard heavy footsteps coming towards him – accompanied by another set running away. The feedback whine in his own head – as a result of the kicks and the lack of air – added to the din. More shouts. More running. The bag was pulled from his face and the air rushed into Danny's lungs as he looked around, panicking, as if expecting more blows to come his way. None came. There was, however, a man shouting at him, asking if he was alright. The man was telling Danny he was going to be okay and he should breathe slowly and steadily. Although Danny now felt surprisingly sober, he also felt very sick and turned over to threw up violently onto the ground.

'Christ, Danny,' said DI John Smithdown. 'Even by your standards, you've really upset some fucker this time.'

Then Danny was sick again. And everything went black.

When the light came back to eyes, Danny saw another figure. DC Jan Cave was also standing over him. 'He'll live, sir,' she said. 'From the smell of him he probably felt very little pain.'

'What the hell are you doing here, Mr Smithdown?' Danny slurred.

'I've been at the hospital, down the road,' he replied, quietly. Danny remembered that The Christie was barely a mile away. 'I was heading for the motorway when I saw some drunk in distress. That drunk being you. Did they get anything?'

'No. I don't know. I don't think so.' Danny looked around and saw a plastic Kwik Save bag lying on the floor. 'I don't think they were after money. I've spent it all anyway.'

The police officers pulled Danny to his feet. 'Do you want us to drive you around to Didsbury police station? It's only around the corner. I know the lads there. They could take a statement, get a description.'

'No point,' Danny said, brushing the dirt from his clothes. 'I didn't see anyone. I just want to go home.'

The DI looked at his colleague: 'DC Cave, could you possibly escort this young man to his lodgings? I need to get on my way.'

'I suppose so, sir,' she sighed, smiling slightly.

'Well you make sure you look after him DC Cave. He clearly shouldn't be out on his own – especially after he's tried to drink south Manchester dry.'

The DI nodded at Danny and headed swiftly towards his car; he'd left it double-parked with his hazard lights on and some of the other drivers were letting him know that they didn't care for this manoeuvre with their horns. 'Fuck off, I'm moving it,' Smithdown shouted and started the engine. With a small wave to Danny and DC Cave, he was gone.

'Right then, let's get you home,' said the DC. Even off duty and out of uniform, she still looked like a police officer. Her hair was still pulled back in a stern bun and her clothes were steadfastly black and white.

'I'll be fine,' Danny said. He was still drunk, but the shock of the attack had shaken much of the alcohol out of his system. 'I'm only around the corner.'

'The boss said I was to make sure you got home okay. So that's what I intend to do.'

Danny felt his way along the alley wall and turned into the street. DC Cave walked alongside him. 'Why would someone want to put a bag on your head, Danny? Do you have any enemies around here?'

'No – apart from the people at the pub I don't really know anyone. Maybe someone doesn't like me looking at the Black Moss case.'

'That's a bit over-dramatic, isn't it? Drunk guy, walking home alone, you're fair game for someone trying to grab your wallet. I'm sure there's no more to it than that.'

'What are you doing here, anyway? Were you with the DI at the hospital?'

'No, I've got relatives nearby. I was on my way home too.'

'Terrible about Mr Smithdown's wife, isn't it?'

'Yes. Yes, it is terrible. He's got a lot on his plate at the moment. I think he should spend less time worrying about that boy at Black Moss and more time looking after his wife. And himself. But that's between you and me, okay?'

'Sure,' nodded Danny. 'Absolutely.'

'His boss, Mr Pym, is really worried about the DI – and he's worried that you're not helping the situation.'

'I get it. Of course.'

Danny crossed the road and turned into The Beeches – his flat was down a dead-end street and he and DC Cave were the only ones around. He got to the front door and fumbled for his keys.

'I think this case is getting too much for Mr Smithdown. He's under a lot of strain. Mr Pym thinks so too. I wonder if it might be best to just leave it be for a while. Until things work themselves out with Mrs Smithdown. Do you know what I mean?'

Danny found his keys. He looked at DC Cave. She was slightly taller than he remembered – taller than him by an inch or so. She was also standing surprisingly close to him. She smelt very clean; a no-nonsense, soapy kind of smell. 'I do… I do know what you mean,' said Danny. 'It' just that I don't agree with you. I think this case might be the only thing keeping him going, actually. And I'll do anything I can to help him.'

He managed to get the key into the lock at the second attempt but didn't turn the lock. 'Thanks for the police escort, DC Cave. I'll be seeing you, yeah?'

'Absolutely, Danny,' she replied with a small smile.

He still didn't turn the lock. He waited. She took a step back from the door. 'Look after yourself, Danny. Any problems, let us know. But think about what I said, okay?'

'Will do.'

She turned, quickly took the steps down the front path and walked away. As she went, DC Cave said: 'We'll keep an eye out for you, Danny. The DC knows where you live.'

He turned the lock and quickly stepped inside. Danny ricocheted up the stairs and somehow ended up outside the door of his flat. His head felt like it was being inflated from the inside. He fell through the door, steadied himself on the other side, then locked it. His answer machine was flashing red. He pressed play and fell back onto his settee. 'Sean, it's Karen. Sorry to be the big sister, but I'm just checking in with you. Mum and Dad are worried. We've not heard from you for ages…'

'I hate it when she calls me Sean,' Danny said. He didn't hear the rest of the message. He passed out.

TWENTY-SEVEN

1.45pm Monday 20 June 2016

Danny and Kate didn't speak much as they headed back down to Oldham and then onto the motorway back to Manchester. A few minutes after leaving the house, Kate asked: 'Why did you never mention getting attacked that night?'

'I never knew for definite it was connected to the case,' Danny replied. 'It could have just been a coincidence.'

'It becomes a bit less of a coincidence when you know it happened within hours of Jeffries' crash,' she said. Kate's voice had become louder, more insistent. 'Who knows what might have happened if Dad hadn't helped you? Christ, Danny. You could have been killed.'

'Like Jeffries was?'

'Maybe, yes. God, what else don't I know about this?'

'I think that's something you need to speak to your dad about,' Danny replied, regretting it almost immediately.

'So, there *are* things I don't know? Christ.'

'Your dad wanted you to be kept away from it at the time. He was worried something might happen to you.'

'The kind of thing that happened to you?'

'Well, yes.'

'And Jeffries…'

'I suppose. Potentially.'

'You didn't answer my question,' Kate said. 'What else don't I know?'

Danny thought for a few moments. Then he told Kate everything. The weights on the child's body; the deliberate, expert disfigurement; the concerns over Peter Jeffries and the off-the-record line from the police about how he may have killed himself wracked with guilt over the Black Moss boy; the visit to the children's home; the conversations with DI Smithdown about keeping her out of it. Everything he could remember.

Everything he'd been thinking and dreaming about over the last few weeks.

After he'd finished, there was silence in the car as it cruised down the M60 towards the Salford turn-off. Danny was searching the internet on his phone. 'Sexist dickheads, the pair of you,' she finally muttered. 'I suppose I should be grateful that you were both concerned enough to lie to me. But you're still sexist dickheads.'

'Quite possibly, yes.' Conceded Danny. 'But it was such a strange time. I was completely paranoid – I thought at one stage your dad was testing me, seeing how much I'd be willing to tell you after he'd revealed something to me in confidence. I didn't know who to trust. Sorry. I thought I was doing the right thing. I still do, actually.'

By now, Kate's car was pulling into Salford Quays. More silence. They stopped close to her building. 'Okay,' she said. 'What now?'

'Well, I'm going to try the number for DS Pym that your dad gave me. In the meantime, a quick Google shows me that at least one person who used to work at Manchester Radio is still working there today. So, I'm going to pay them a visit.'

'Luckily for you, their new building is quite handy.'

Kate nodded towards a nearby converted dockside building with a red, neon MRFM logo attached to the outside wall. 'Just a brisk walk around the dock. Can you manage that, or do you need a lift?'

'No, I'll manage.'

Danny got out of the car. 'Danny?' said Kate. 'Come to my house tomorrow evening for dinner. Meet my son. Six thirty? I'll text you the address.'

'That would be really nice, thank you,' he said.

'Don't mention any of this, obviously.'

'Obviously. Got to protect the children. It's a parent's natural instinct. Your dad will tell you that.'

'Piss off, Danny,' said Kate. 'See you tomorrow.'

As he walked around the jetties and piers towards the MRFM building, Danny watched the bubble machines that aerated the water in the dock's basins. According to banners attached to the dock railings, the water was so clean these days they held swimming competitions in it. The force of the system meant that any rubbish floating in the water was pushed neatly to the corners of the basin; footballs, crisp packets, take away cartons and bits of polystyrene were all to be seen wobbling at the water's edge, waiting to be scooped out and disposed of. Danny stopped and stared at the detritus – then he realised he'd been standing there for at least five minutes.

The MRFM building was a tastefully converted dockside factory unit. Many of the old pullies and winches on and around the unit had been preserved to retain a period feel. Looking through the glass security door, Danny could see that another period feel had been maintained inside. The reception was very brightly lit – primary colours surrounded scores of framed, signed discs from recording artists and photos of the station' main presenters. *Radio stations, they never change,* he thought.

He pressed the security buzzer. 'Reception,' said a bright, young-sounding voice.

'Hi. My name's Danny. I'm here to see Gary Keenan.'

The door buzzed and Danny went in.

TWENTY-EIGHT

11am Thursday 19 April 1990

Danny tottered over to the bathroom and looked at his face in the mirror over the sink. It was the only mirror in his flat. The right side of his face was red and scratched where the plastic bag had torn and his head had hit the wall the second time. His left eye was swollen. And he was well and truly late for work. *Fuck work*, he thought, going back to his small and sparse living room. He punched the news desk number into his phone. Beth answered. Danny wanted to talk to Mike Sharston. One of the drawbacks of working in radio is that everyone's voice is instantly recognisable to their colleagues, so there was no point in Danny pretending it wasn't him.

'Hi, Beth,' he said.

'Danny. You're so late you're in danger of missing tomorrow's shift. Sharston's in a fury.'

'I see. I'd better speak to him.'

'He's in a meeting. What shall I tell him?'

'I'd rather tell him myself.'

'You're not doing yourself any favours here.'

'Look, I got hit by a car last night. I'm in a bad way. My face is all smashed up. I'm not up to work, so that's why I'm not in.'

There was a pause. 'So, RTA with one person injured,' Beth said, in a sing-song voice that suggested she didn't particularly believe him but was writing it down anyway out of politeness. 'Did you report it to the police?'

'No. No I didn't, I just went home. I didn't realise how bad it was until this morning.'

'Are you *going* to report it to the police?' asked Beth.

'I'll be fine, Beth. Thanks for your concern though. Tell Sharston I'll be back next week. Hopefully the riot will be done with by then and we can start getting back to normal.'

'Sure. Bye, Danny.'

The phone went dead. Danny took some painkillers and went back to bed.

Danny wasn't usually in the habit of sleeping during the day, but with his face aching nearly as much as the inside of his head, it seemed like a good idea. Without the protection of alcohol, the dreams came quickly. And they came with a clarity he wasn't used to. He dreamt of that plastic bag over his head – but when he took it off there was no DI Smithdown to save him. He was in a filthy bed, the legs of which were half submerged in slate grey water. Despite the water, the bed was in a dark attic room. Rubbish floated on the water. He rolled off the bed and fell for what seemed like minutes before hitting the surface. The cold shock of it woke him.

He showered, forced down a slice of toast and headed out towards Oldham.

Danny felt odd knocking on the door of the children's home without the police being there. *This is so dodgy*, he thought. Interviewing children was a delicate matter at the best of times; children in the care of local authorities were, journalistically, completely off limits. But Danny wasn't here to interview anyone. He just wanted to talk.

He knocked. Almost immediately, the door opened and a teenage girl appeared. She'd only opened the door enough to create a slim gap. She had spiky hair wrapped in a bandana. She wore a dirty, Reynolds Girls t-shirt. She looked at Danny's swollen face and scrunched her nose in disgust. 'Brenda!' she shouted, without taking her eyes off Danny. 'It's that reporter guy. He looks all fucked up. Should I let him in?'

An older voice came from inside the house. 'All fucked up you say? He'll fit right in then. Let the poor sod in.'

The door opened a little further – just enough to let Danny squeeze through – then it was closed very quickly behind him. Danny followed the girl through to the kitchen; she turned and looked at him several times as they walked, checking on him. Brenda was sitting at the kitchen, in the same spot she'd occupied when Danny was last there. *Maybe she hasn't moved,* he thought.

'Oh dear,' Brenda said, waving Danny towards a chair. 'You really are fucked up aren't you, Mr Reporter? Who have you been annoying this time?'

'I have no idea, Brenda. But I'd like to find out.'

She laughed and popped a roll-up cigarette between her lips. Brenda lit it with a Zippo lighter, shutting the flip top lid with a loud clack. 'Well I don't think you'll find them here, love,' she said.

Danny looked around the kitchen and at the doorways to the adjoining rooms. Just as they had done last time, the home's young residents hovered and floated around the edges of the room, but they seemed closer this time. A little bolder.

'No, I don't suppose I will,' Danny conceded. 'But I'd still like to talk. Not interview – just talk.' Danny lit a cigarette. Holding it between his lips hurt his mouth. 'I'm just trying to make sense of what's going on,' he said, blowing out smoke with a sigh. 'A kid gets found dead up the road and no one knows who he is. What's more, no one seems to care. Your local MP tells me he knows what's going on and he has a car crash the night before telling me. The cops seem to suggest to my colleagues at the radio station that he killed himself in some drunken guilt trip. I'm not buying that. Then someone bounces my head off a wall. Two walls, actually. And no one gives a shit about any of it because all eyes are still firmly fucking fixed on the rioters at Strangeways. So, I'm at the stage now where I don't know who to trust, who to believe or what the fuck is actually going on. Everyone strikes me as either being a lying fucker or, at the very least, having something shitty to hide, to be honest. Apart from you lot. So, I thought I'd come here.'

Danny looked around the room. A dozen kids were now fully in the room. Some looked as though they were about ten years old. 'Sorry for the language,' he added. 'Sorry.'

'They've heard a lot worse, let me assure you,' Brenda reassured him. 'Now. You and I know you can't interview these kids. They're wards of the court. You couldn't print or broadcast what they said even if you wanted to. You'd be prosecuted. You shouldn't even be here. But, there you go. You're here. So, what is it you want to ask?'

Danny turned in his chair and looked around the room. He examined the faces of the dozen or so kids present. They were very close now – within touching distance. Some whispered to each other. Most just stared at him. Danny addressed them directly: 'Last time I was here, Brenda said that some of you were frightened – *really* frightened – about what was going on outside the home. That you'd stopped going walkabout. Why? What's got you so scared?'

The young residents said nothing. They exchanged glances but said nothing. The room was quiet, except for the thin sound of a television in another room. Then Danny heard a whisper. He turned and saw a boy of about ten with his hand cupped around his mouth, saying something into the ear of the teenage girl who'd let Danny in. Her eyes were closed, concentrating on what the child was saying. The boy's hair was very short; he wore jeans that were too small for him and a dirty white t-shirt that was too big. He spoke for about ten seconds. Then, he ran off, clumping up the stairs. One by one, the other children slipped away. Only one stayed behind: the teenage girl. She looked at Danny directly – and she didn't seem too pleased. The only people left in the kitchen were Brenda, Danny and the girl. Brenda motioned for the teenager to take a seat. She did so, but her displeasure was very clear. 'This is bollocks, this is,' she said, helping herself to Brenda's pouch of tobacco and dumping it onto a Rizla cigarette paper. Danny was going to offer her one of his, but she'd already rolled one and lit it while he was digging around in his pocket to find his packet. Danny had never seen anyone roll a cigarette so quickly or expertly. *How old is she? Fifteen, tops?*

'Honestly,' said Danny, in what he hoped was his reassuring voice. 'This is in complete confidence. I won't repeat what you tell me, I won't tell anyone you spoke to me. I was never even here.'

Danny looked at Brenda, hoping she'd provide some form of back up or reassurance. 'Up to you, Jenny. No pressure, love. Entirely up to you.'

There was a long pause. The girl stared at her cigarette. 'Something happened to Little Paul the other week,' she eventually said. 'Something horrible. Us older ones are stopping in to make sure the young 'uns are okay. If we go out, we go out together. If we stay in, we stay in together. We all look out for each other at the best of times. And the worst. This is up there with the worst.'

'Christ, Jenny, why didn't you say anything?' said Brenda, pulling her chair closer to the table.

'Because Little Paul didn't want me to, Brenda. End of.'

'I know but –'

Danny cut in. This might be his only chance. 'What happened to Paul?'

'Little Paul,' Jenny corrected. 'He likes to be called Little Paul. It avoids confusion with Big Paul, one of the other kids.'

'Fair enough,' conceded Danny. 'What happened to Little Paul?'

Jenny stubbed out her roll up and started to roll another. This time, she did it slowly. 'He was grabbed in town,' she said quietly.

'Christ almighty,' cried Brenda.

'Look, Bren. Do you want me to talk to this bloke or not?'

'Sorry,' said the older woman. 'I'll keep it zipped.'

'Who grabbed him, Jenny?' Danny asked.

'If we knew that we wouldn't be sat here wondering about it, would we, clever bollocks?'

'Sorry. I mean, what happened?'

'He was in Oldham, just dossing about, cadging fags off people coming out of the pubs. It was pretty late. Someone grabbed him from behind, took him down a side street and tried to put him in a car. He was kicking and screaming like mad. He's tough as nails is Little Paul. Anyway, whoever done it tried to tie him up, but he was making that much of a din they sacked it off and left him. Then he came back here. Shaking like a shitting dog, he was. White as a sheet. He told me not to tell anyone. Didn't want to get moved to another home if the council found out he was out and about late at night. He likes it here, does Little Paul. He likes you, Brenda. Fuck knows why.'

The older woman smiled and made as if to speak, then thought better of it and made a zipping motion across her lips.

'Does he remember anything about whoever grabbed him?' Danny said. 'Anything at all?'

'They didn't say anything. Not a word.'

'What about their faces?'

'Nope. Couldn't see 'em.'

'Why not?'

'The bastards banged a plastic bag on his head. He couldn't see nowt. Poor little shit.'

Danny tried to avoid letting that piece of information distract him. Brenda looked away. Her eyes had tears in them now, but still she kept silent. 'Does he remember anything else? A smell? A noise? Anything?'

'Just a sort of… *skrawking* noise.'

'Sorry. How do you mean?'

'Like… *skrawking*. You know. Like when you pull off a big piece of tape when you're wrapping a present and it makes that noise. Don't know what the proper word is. Maybe there isn't one.' Jenny mimed pulling out a long strip of tape. '*Skrawk!*' she said.

'Sure,' said Danny. 'I get it.'

The room went quiet. Danny heard footsteps. Little Paul was standing at the kitchen doorway, listening in. Brenda got up and walked slowly towards the child. She knelt down and put out her arms, as if to ask if it was okay to hug him. He nodded. 'Oh, Little Paul,' she said. 'You daft sod. You lovely, daft little sod.'

Brenda held the boy tightly. 'I'd better go,' said Danny. He got up from the table, looking across at Brenda and the boy. 'I'll see myself out.'

Danny paused in the hallway. 'Thanks, Little Paul,' he said. The boy, his face buried in Brenda's jumper, said nothing. As Danny reached the front door, Jenny appeared behind him. 'Hey,' she said. 'What happens now?'

'Honestly? I'm not sure,' said Danny.

'There's no way Little Paul will talk to the police. I still can't believe he let me tell you about what happened. If he's frightened, then there must be something really scary out there. He's a tough nut, is Little Paul, but he's still just a kid.'

'Until Strangeways is finished it's hard to see how I can convince anyone that this is a really important story. So, it's down to us, I suppose.'

'No one gives a shit about us at the best of times.' Jenny scowled. 'Right now, it's like we don't even exist. Who cares if something that doesn't exist gets snatched in the street? Nobody, that's who.'

Danny pulled out his notebook and scribbled down the Manchester Radio newsroom number. Then he scribbled it out and wrote out his home number. He tore out the sheet and handed it to the girl. 'Look, if Little Paul says anything else give me a ring. In the meantime, keep doing what you're doing. Look out for each other.'

'You need to look after yourself too,' Jenny said. 'Whoever did that to your face wasn't messing about.'

'No,' said Danny. 'No, they weren't messing about, were they? Bye, Jenny.'

Danny walked to his car and drove just a few hundred yards to a corner shop nearby. He bought some cigarettes, a bag of peanuts and two overpriced bottles of Holsten Pils. *Lunch,* he thought. Slinging the bag onto the back seat of his car, he drove out towards Black Moss. When he got to the parking area he pulled a sharp right and tucked his car into the bottom corner. He was shielded from the road by a grass verge. He switched on the radio: they were playing 'Step On' by Happy Mondays. The song had become the unofficial anthem of the revitalised Manchester music scene and seemed to be currently unavoidable. Danny was already sick of the record so he turned the volume down, so he could barely hear it. Using a penknife on his keyring he popped open one of the bottles and took a drink; then he waited. And watched. And waited. *What kind of person comes here?*

Sliding down low in his seat, Danny took another sip of his beer. There was a police van parked at the far end. Two officers chatted by the rear doors, closed them and made off. *Nice of them to take an interest in the dead kid,* Danny thought, taking some pleasure in the fact that he was sipping his beer in full view of the policemen. Then he watched as a couple in their 70s parked up and slowly, methodically put on their walking boots and outer layers, then pack some food into a small rucksack before setting off down the Pennine Way. They held hands as they went. *That's nice.*

He saw a group of rowdy teenagers arrive in a van; they tumbled out, laughing and joking as a harassed teacher tried to corral them into staying together. He shouted at them and made several vague threats. That seemed to work and the teenagers finally formed into a group and also headed along the path. *That's going to spoil the peace for the old folks,* Danny thought.

He then watched a middle-aged man in a suit park his car, look around warily, drop a plastic bag into a bin, then leave. *That's weird.* Five minutes after he'd gone, Danny walked over to the bin to take a look. The bag had three empty vodka bottles in it. *Disgraceful.*

After finishing his second bottle of lager, Danny's eyes began to flicker and close. The sleep was light but welcome; half sleep rather than the real thing. Occasionally, Danny's eyes would open and he'd see different people arrive at the car park: a runner warming up before crossing the road and heading up the Pennine Way in the opposite direction towards Standedge. Then two people in their thirties arrived in separate cars; the woman got into the man's car. *Aye aye,* Danny said to himself. He watched their silhouettes as they spent the next ten minutes talking, kissing and embracing before the woman went back to her car. The two cars left several minutes apart but headed in the same direction. *Forbidden love in the office.*

The scenes played out before him as Danny slipped in and out of his sleep. He watched and snoozed, snoozed and watched. Then he saw something that made him snap out of his restful state very quickly indeed. A white van pulled into the car park a little faster than the other vehicles; so fast a little gravel flew off as he came to a stop. The driver turned off the engine but stayed in his seat and looked out towards the moors. Danny could only see his outline, but he seemed agitated; he banged the steering wheel with the flat of his hand and bit his thumb at the point where the nail meets the skin. He looked at something out of Danny's view then stepped sharply out. Danny slid a little further down in his seat.

Gary Keenan walked over to the bin with some pieces of paper in his hand. He was tearing them into pieces as he walked. Then he put them in the bin, returned to his van and drove off.

Danny waited a good ten minutes before going to see what the engineer had put there. He looked at the pieces then pulled several out. They were photos of a young child, happy and smiling at a birthday party.

Danny took as many of the pieces as he could gather before another car pulled into the parking spot. He put them in his pocket and drove back down the hill towards Oldham Police station.

TWENTY-NINE

2.20pm Monday 20 June 2016

'Danny boy!' cried Gary Keenan as he opened the door behind the MRFM reception and wedged it open with his body. 'Walk this way.'

Gary's ponytailed hair was as white as chalk. He'd put on a few stones in weight since Danny had last seen him, but he appeared to be wearing exactly the same combination of jeans, grey sweatshirt and keys that he'd worn in 1990. He stuck out his hand. Danny shook it, gasping slightly at the unnecessary firmness of the engineer's grip. 'Can't Stop the Feeling!' by Justin Timberlake accompanied them down a corridor then through an open-plan office. On one side, sales staff – some wearing headsets – talked to potential clients on the phone. On the other, journalists – about four of them – silently edited digital recordings on their laptops, quietly tapping in their scripts as they went. The sound of clattering typewriters was nowhere to be heard. Nor was there any shouting and swearing. Danny was shocked at how clean the new MRFM was compared to the coffee stains and fag burns of the old station. It looked and felt more like a call centre than a radio station.

'How are you then, Danny boy?' boomed Keenan, pushing his teardrop glasses up his nose as they walked. 'I hear you've been doing a bit of landscape gardening with your motor down in London.'

'Yeah, you could say that. Thanks, as ever, for your warmth and concern, Gary.'

'That's what I'm here for,' the engineer replied as he pushed open the door of his office. A sign on the door read: THE ANSWER'S FUCK OFF – NOW, WHAT'S THE QUESTION? Although they were in a different building in a different century, Gary's office seemed largely unchanged. There were wires, soldering irons, plastic tubs full of batteries and boxes of tiny, discarded earphones. As Gary motioned for him to take a seat, Danny's eye caught an upright pole on the engineer's desk. It was the kind normally found in a bathroom to hold multiple toilet rolls. Instead, it was stacked with rolls of different-coloured gaffa tape.

The engineer cleared away a small stack of electronics magazines and tool catalogues and gestured for Danny to take a seat. 'Don't wish to be rude, Gary,' said Danny. 'Which obviously means I'm about to say something really rude, but how the hell are you still at Manchester Radio? You should be retired by now, surely?'

'Cheeky bastard, I'm not even sixty yet. Not much older than you. I've always looked old, that's my problem. Dealing with shit from journalists for decades has aged me prematurely.'

'Sorry. It always felt like everyone was older than me back then. Like everyone knew what they were doing. And I didn't.'

'We were all just making it up as we went along, mate.' The engineer laughed. 'Still am, to be honest. Mind you, very different world now, Danny boy. No tape recorders, radio cars or razor blades any more. It's all done with iPhones, mate, by a handful of journos. Most of the bulletins are pre-recorded nowadays. So are loads of the programmes. No live reports any more, it messes with the timings. Hardly any cock-ups but equally, hardly any fun. All the mayhem has gone out of it, all the fizz and energy has disappeared. It's processed, fast-food news – McNews I call it. It's bollocks, but there you go. Anyway. What the fuck are you doing here?'

'Well, I'm kind of in between jobs at the moment – thanks to the tree remodelling you so kindly mentioned. So, I'm looking into something from the old days. Seeing if there's anything in it.'

Keenan leant forward in his chair. 'Tell me more.'

'It's a murder from 1990. A kid that was found out near a reservoir in the hills above Oldham. Nobody gave a shit at the time because everyone was too busy trying to win awards with their Strangeways coverage. Ring any bells?'

The engineer leant back in his chair and put his feet up on the cluttered table. 'Not sure. We had so many murders in those days. Which reservoir?'

Danny felt his heart beating. *Can he hear that? Can he hear how much noise it's making?* 'Black Moss.'

'It rings a bell, definitely. I know it well up there though. I've driven up and down that road many, many times. Too many bleedin' times.'

'Why's that, Gary?'

Gary looked over Danny's shoulder and checked the small window set into the door. No one was about. *What is he up to? Why so shifty?* The engineer opened a drawer on his desk. He pulled out a packet of cigarettes and offered one to Danny. 'You definitely can't smoke in here, Danny boy,' Keenan said, lighting up and offering the flame of a cheap plastic lighter to Danny. 'Sacking offence. Apparently. Like I give a shit.'

Keenan switched on a desk fan which sent a blast of air across the desk. 'Anyway. Yes. Black bloody Moss. Brings it all back.'

'Does it?'

'Yes, it most definitely does. I spent months driving up and down that road past the Moss.'

'Why?'

Keenan blew a jet of smoke straight into the fan. 'Because of the kids.'

Danny wasn't sure what he was hearing. 'What do you mean, Gary, the kids?'

'It was terrible, mate. Just the worst thing ever.'

'Gary, is there something you want to tell me?'

Gary took off his glasses and cleaned them with his sweatshirt, pinching the lenses through the material. He placed them back on his nose. 'Not especially, but it's all a very long time ago now, so I can't see the harm. I didn't tell anyone at the time. But it was the wife. Early 1990, she fucked off to Huddersfield with the kids. That's where she's from. I'd been working all the hours God sent in those days. When I wasn't in the radio station, I was in the pub. Not unlike yourself, Danny boy. She decided she'd had enough. Don't blame her wanting to be away from me. But Huddersfield? That's taking the piss. So that entailed months and months of schlepping back and forward between Manchester and Huddersfield to see the kids.'

'So that's why you were up and down the Huddersfield road?'

'Yeah. Grim it was. That MP crashed his car up there, didn't he? Dangerous bit of road, that. Then that murder. You got really involved with it, didn't you? Hang on, Danny-fucking-boy.' Gary turned off the prog rock that had been playing in his office. 'What the fuck do you think I was doing up there?'

'Sorry. Look. I saw you out at the Moss,' Danny said quietly. 'Twice. I asked you about it at the time and you said you hadn't been there. That's a bit suspicious, don't you think?'

'It was private!' Gary shouted. 'I didn't want you nosey bastard journalists knowing my business, thank you very much. I was in danger of losing contact with my kids. I didn't want anything to jeopardise that. So, I told no one. I cut down on the drinking, cut back on the long hours, sorted things out with the wife and we were back together by Christmas. Seriously, what the hell do you think I was doing up there? Come on I want to know.'

'It was a really weird time, Gary,' said Danny. 'To be honest, I didn't know what was going on or who to believe. No one was interested in the dead kid; I was up and down to Oldham all the time and could barely get a story on air because of Strangeways. Peter Jeffries, the MP you mentioned, he died in completely bizarre circumstances. I got done over down a back alley in Didsbury after digging about in places I clearly shouldn't have been digging about in. Then I spot you up at the murder scene – twice – and you tell me you've never been there.' Danny was matching Gary for volume now. 'So, excuse me for being mildly fucking curious about what you were up to!'

There was a good twenty seconds of quiet between the two men. The strains of a song could be heard from the adjoining offices. *Is that Justin Bieber?* thought Danny. *I don't know these songs anymore. What's more, I don't care.*

'Love Yourself,' said Gary. Picking up a foam microphone cover from his desk and putting it into a drawer.

'What?'

'Love Yourself,' repeated Gary. 'The song that's playing. Justin Bieber. I fuckin' hate Justin Bieber. It's the curse of working at a radio station – all the songs burrow into your brain, regardless of how much you hate them. In the old days we had proper songs from proper bands that were from round here. The Mondays, The Roses, New Order, James –'

'Tim Booth of James is from Yorkshire, if I remember correctly,' countered Danny.

'You know what I mean. Fucking Bieber! Christ, it's like everything around here these days. Processed crap. McMusic interspersed with McNews. All safe and processed. McBollocks.'

There was quiet again. Gary opened the drawer, took out the microphone cover and put it back on his desk. 'So, Danny boy. Apart from accusing me of being a kiddie murderer, what are you actually here for?'

Danny pulled his chair a little closer to Gary's and took out the hotel notepad and pen he had in his inside jacket pocket.

THIRTY

1.15pm Thursday 19 April 1990

Danny parked his car as close to Oldham Police station as he could and half walked, half ran inside. A collection of people whose lives weren't going quite as they'd hoped for were standing and sitting in the waiting area close to the desk. The duty officer, a harassed-looking man in his forties with his hair combed over to hide his obvious baldness, was standing behind the front desk with his hand shielding his eyes. On the other side of the chest-high counter, a young man of about nineteen wearing a multi-coloured shell suit was explaining a complex-sounding situation involving his girlfriend, another man and the other man's dog.

Danny couldn't wait for the story to unfold fully. 'I'm really sorry to interrupt, but is it possible to see DI Smithdown please?'

'Did the last bloke ya interrupted do that to ya face?' the young man asked Danny. 'Don't fookin' mind me mate – got all fookin' day, me.'

The front desk officer lifted his hand from his eyes and looked at Danny. Without speaking he held up a single finger to the shell-suit complainant, as if to say *you…wait.* He pointed at Danny and then indicated a vacant chair. He opened a door at the back of the desk area, put his head through the gap for a few seconds and returned. He put up five fingers to Danny, indicating how long he'd have to wait. Then he pointed at the shell-suit man and gestured that he should continue. The officer's hand found its original position, shielding his eyes with ease, and the young man continued his story.

Danny waited. *If it's all bollocks, DI Smithdown will know for sure,* he said to himself. *There's probably a perfectly reasonable explanation why Gary was up there. Twice. But what about those photos? That was creepy.* Danny pulled out the photos and looked at the pieces. He hadn't found them all, but there were enough to make out the faces involved.

After two minutes a side door opened – DC Jan Cave motioned for Danny to follow her. She headed down a grey corridor towards a row of offices. 'Alright, Danny. That face of yours still looks sore. Have you put anything on it?'

'Nah. I like it as it is. It's an icebreaker wherever I go. Causes a stir.'

'Yes, that's very much your thing, isn't it?'

'It's my reason for living, DC Cave.'

The Detective Constable tapped on the glass window of one of the offices. A voice half shouted, 'Come.' In they went. Behind the desk of the small office sat DS James Pym. Danny looked at DC Cave, puzzled. She closed the door behind them and stood by the door, as if standing on guard duty. 'Danny, hello. Take a seat. I hear you took a tumble last night. How are you feeling?'

'Surprisingly perky, Mr Pym, but a little confused,' he replied, lowering himself gently into the plastic chair he'd been offered. 'I was looking for DI Smithdown, is he about?'

'Not today Danny, no,' the DS replied. There was something about his manner that irritated Danny even more than usual.

'There's something I want to talk to him about. When will he be back?'

'Not for a while, Danny. Can I help?'

Danny could feel the heat of anger make his face even more painful than it already was. 'What do you mean, *not for a while?*'

'He's on leave, Danny.'

Danny stood up sharply. The chair skidded back. 'Leave? On *leave*. What the fuck are you lot up to? Have you knobbled him now as well? Got him out of the way? Jesus Christ, you must think I'm stupid! It's almost as if you bastards don't want anyone to know what happened up at the Moss. Every time someone gets a sniff of what might be going on, something shitty happens to them. Now the DI's mysteriously gone on leave? Fuck that.'

'Danny,' said DS in a quiet and reassuring voice. 'No one is getting Mr Smithdown out of the way of anything…'

'I wouldn't be surprised if you're in on it too, you greasy bastard.'

DC Cave took a step towards him and put a hand to his arm. 'Danny, please…'

'Get the fuck off me,' he shouted, shaking free of her hand.

'Danny,' DS Pym said, quietly. 'DI Smithdown's wife died this morning. The leave he's on is compassionate leave.'

The heat Danny had felt fill his face a few moments earlier slipped away quickly, to be replaced by a cold, exposed feeling. The images of Mrs Smithdown that he'd seen in dozens of photos and the DI's house snapped into his head. He looked at DS Pym and DC Cave and returned to his seat.

'I know you've had a bit of a time of it, so we'll let this pass, shall we?' DS Pym offered. 'DI Smithdown is exactly where he should be – at home with his daughter.'

Danny couldn't look directly at either of the officers, so he looked out of the window instead. 'Sorry,' he said. 'It's all been a bit… I'm sorry.'

'It's forgotten about,' DS Pym. 'Isn't it DC Cave?'

'Absolutely. In the past already,' she added. Her voice was gentle and reassuring. Kind. It made Danny feel worse than he already did.

'Please, Danny,' said the DS. 'Leave them be, lad. We haven't even told him about the body up at the Moss. He'll be delighted, but now's not the time.'

Danny looked at the DS now. 'I don't understand,' he said. 'You've lost me.'

The senior officer took an A4 notepad from a three-tier desk tidy and turned over several pages until he found what he was looking for. 'It's been on the news already. Your radio station included. Early hours of this morning, body of a white male aged approximately thirty years, found close to Black Moss reservoir. No suspicious circumstances. I can confirm we are not looking for anyone else in connection with the find.'

DS Pym looked at Danny as if expecting him to be somehow pleased. 'Sorry, Mr Pym. You've found another body? At the Moss?'

'Indeed. Good news for all concerned.'

Danny looked at DC Cave. She was smiling. 'Another body?' he asked again.

'Yes, Danny. I was hoping I wouldn't have to spell it out. A suicide at the same spot the kid was found. Local guy. Vincent Canning. He was well known to us. Persistent nuisance, anti-social behaviour, mental health issues, that kind of thing. He'd taken himself up the Moss with a bottle of whisky. After he'd finished it he'd smashed the bottle and cut his own throat with it. Right there on the path. He left a note. Shortest one I've ever seen – and I've seen a fair few. *Sorry*. That's all it said. *Sorry*.'

'Christ. Are you sure, Mr Pym?'

'Yes, Danny. We're sure. We found items on him that linked him to the lad.'

'What kind of items?'

'Let's just say, items linked to the way the boy's body was found that only the killer could have known.'

Danny hesitated, then he said: 'Like tape? Like the gaffa tape that was used to strap weights to the little lad's body?'

DS Pym's face changed from sympathetic to annoyed very quickly indeed. He closed the pad and put it back onto the sorting tray. 'I have absolutely no comment to make about that. But at another time, when things have cooled down a little, I will make it my business to find out why you just said what you just said.'

'I know more about this case than a lot of people realise, Mr Pym,' Danny offered, leaning forward in his seat.

'Well I'm sure Mr Smithdown had nothing but good intentions in involving you – what's done is done…'

'What about Peter Jeffries? I'd heard you were blaming him at one stage.'

DS Pym looked at DC Cave. He seemed genuinely perplexed: 'That's news to me. I don't know where you heard that, but it wasn't from me and it wasn't from any of my officers. We never considered Peter Jeffries a suspect in this case. We suspected he was an old drunk who shouldn't have been driving around the moors while he was pissed up, but there's no way we thought he was connected to the boy's death. Ever. I'd like to know where that story came from… something else for me to take a look at when this has all settled down.'

'So, what happens now?' Danny asked.

'Well, the main thing is that an individual who posed a major threat to children in this area is a threat no longer,' said DS Pym, leaning back in his chair and putting his hands behind his head.

Here comes the copperspeak, thought Danny.

'Clearly Mr Canning felt that the net was closing in and that taking his own life was the only option left open to him. Tragic, in many ways. There are no winners here, Danny.'

Pure copperbollocks.

'So, beyond the inquest into Mr Canning's apparent suicide, the ongoing priority for Oldham Police will be in identifying the young victim of this terrible crime. That remains our focus.'

'So, that's it?' said Danny.

'Publicly we have to be seen to be keeping an open mind until it's official, but essentially, yes. You should be pleased, Danny. This is what it's all been about, hasn't it? Finding out the truth. Trust me, I will leave no stone unturned until we identify the young victim. We'll also be liaising with colleagues from other divisions and forces to look at other unsolved missing persons cases involving young males. We want to know if this man has struck before.'

DC Cave spoke too. Danny had forgotten she was there. 'Do you have your recording equipment with you Danny? Perhaps DS Pym could do an interview for you. Give you the scoop. You deserve it.'

'Yes. That's the least we can do. Good thinking DC Cave. More than happy to do that. I know we've had our differences, but I can't help but admire the way you've put your heart and soul into this. Very commendable. Get your gear and let's do it.'

Yeah, so you can claim the credit. 'Sure,' said Danny. 'Give me a minute. Work will be very impressed. I'm supposed to be off sick.'

Danny went to his car, retrieved his Marantz and returned to the police station. DS Pym essentially repeated the same words he'd already used in largely the same order: *Terrible crime; no stone unturned; other unsolved crimes; tragic case.*

It took just over three minutes – Manchester Radio interviews rarely stretched to any longer than that – and when it was done, Danny did as he always did: stopped and checked that the recording was okay. It was. 'Thanks very much, Mr Pym,' Danny offered. 'That's all I need. I'm not in the radio car, but I'll try to get it back in time for the three o'clock news, then see if they'll run it in full on our main news at five. It's not been easy to get stuff on air, thanks to Strangeways.'

'Well,' said DS Pym, putting his hand on Danny's shoulder. 'I hear we're on the final push there. It's nearly over. Then we can start getting back to normal.'

DS Pym put out a hand to Danny. They shook. He smelled of Paco Rabanne. 'Sorry for what I said earlier,' Danny said. 'It was way over the top. I was out of order.'

'Sure. It happens. This has been difficult for all concerned - us as well as you. So, it's no wonder that feelings boil over sometimes. Just don't make a bloody habit of it, eh?'

'As if I'd do that, Mr Pym.' Danny's smile was thin, but he meant what he'd said. *Kind of.*

'Course not. DC Cave will see you out. Take care, Danny.'

Danny drove slowly back to Manchester. *No rush,* he thought. *Not as if they're going to lead on it. I'll be lucky if they find space for it at all.*

After he'd found a parking space on the roof, he walked slowly across the piazza towards the reception. His head still throbbed. Pauline buzzed him through the door. 'Blue Savannah' by Erasure greeted him as he stepped inside. 'Danny Johnston, what on earth has happened to you? You look like you've been hit by a bus.'

'No, just a car, Pauline. Still hurts though.' *Are you sticking with the car story? Might as well. Makes no difference now, does it?*

'You shouldn't be in work, Danny. You should be at home, resting. Or in hospital. My goodness, look at the state of you.'

Danny waved his Marantz in Pauline's direction. He felt a little unsteady on his feet. 'Got the scoop right here, Pauline,' he said.

'Is it that awful business up at Oldham? Tell me it's all over.'

'It's all over.'

'And tell me you have the scoop.'

'I have the scoop.'

'Good lad,' she smiled. 'I knew it.'

Pauline buzzed the second door. 'Please take care, Danny.'

The corridors were clogged by the usual mix of sales people, smokers and visitors. Erasure segued into 'Vogue' by Madonna. Danny's swollen face attracted glances, but not that many, considering. *Hard to surprise anyone around here,* he thought.

Inside the newsroom, heads turned as Danny entered. 'It's alive,' one of the sports reporters shouted from across the room. Chief reporter Robert Crane was editing tape at one of the Studer machines along the far wall. He pulled off his headphones; he did this carefully so as not to disrupt his hair. 'Mike!' he shouted. 'Johnston's escaped from the secure unit. And it's not a pretty sight.'

Beth Hall was at the news desk, handing over to the afternoon reader. 'Danny, my God, look at you,' she said. 'You're not even supposed to be here. Do you need first aid or are you going to tough it out?'

'I will keep going on a mixture of adrenaline and spite, Beth,' he replied.

Mike Sharston came out of his office. 'Danny. Bloody Nora, what a state. Why are you here?'

'Black Moss murder/suicide, boss. I've got an interview with the Detective Superintendent about the second body found up at Black Moss. And a good line for later about them possibly linking it to other missing kid cases.' Danny tapped his Marantz. 'It's all here.'

'Bloody good stuff, lad,' Sharston said. 'I think we'll lead with that on the next bulletin.'

Then everything went grey and white and Danny Johnston passed out cold onto the floor of the Manchester Radio newsroom.

THIRTY-ONE

3.15pm Monday 20 June 2016

After leaving MRFM Danny called a local mini-cab firm and booked a 'wait and return' ride. The driver seemed interested as to why Danny wanted to go to a reservoir car park in the middle of nowhere, but he didn't get very far with his queries. 'I just want to take a look,' was all Danny offered.

Danny stared out of the car window as the housing estates of Salford faded into the M602 and the M60. He saw the unchanged exterior of Oldham Police station, then the town centre thinned out and the hills took over. The outlying communities seemed largely as he remembered them: grey and red estates, takeaways and mini-markets that gave way to farms and country pubs before the moors opened up and filled the horizon in all directions.

'I think we're in Yorkshire here, mate,' the driver said as the mini-cab pulled into the car park. 'That's extra.'

'No, we're not,' Danny replied. He pointed towards the Pennine Way path. 'The border's right there. Look on Google Maps if you don't believe me. I'll be back in twenty minutes.'

A few improvements here and there, but pretty much the same, he thought, as he walked quickly along the path away from the car park, past Redbrook, then out towards Black Moss. The weather was fine, the wind gentle yet warm and the sky was a blast of blue. But, as ever, Black Moss clung to its favoured grey. The water level was low, and the size and shape of the sandy area had changed considerably, but he knew he was in roughly the right spot. He thought about how cold it had been that morning; how his head had throbbed from being woken up to come to this lonely place; he thought about the young cops; he thought about that piece of plastic sheeting. *If it hadn't been caught by the wind, it would have been just another story. And I wouldn't be here now.*

Danny found his iPhone in the back pocket of his trousers and took several individual landscape photos: the path, the water, the 'beach'. Then he turned the phone upright and took a panorama shot, shuffling in a circle on the paving slabs to take in as much of the area as possible. The panorama shot looked striking, beautiful even. The area was surprisingly free of walkers – just two women on the brow of the hill, shielding their eyes from the sun to take in the view. Then they left and he was alone.

Danny retraced his steps, returned to the cab and got in the back seat. He gave the driver an address in Wythenshawe, south Manchester, a good forty-five-minute drive, more if they were to catch the rush hour traffic. 'Not another reservoir is it, mate?' the driver said, punching the details into his navigation app. 'No,' said Danny. 'No more reservoirs for today.'

He slept during the journey. He'd forgotten he'd been up most of the night. The driver woke him as they turned into a crescent-shaped street. Children played on a grassy semi-circle surrounded by identical red brick ex-council houses. Not a wealthy area, but one that clearly was well maintained by proud residents. Danny gave the driver sixty pounds – more than he was asked for – and thanked him for his patience.

He waited for the cab to go before spotting the house he wanted and walking to the door. The doorbell sounded 'The Bells of St Clements' and a woman in her late fifties answered the door. Her hair was short and grey and she was wearing a black top, leggings and slippers.

'Hi Karen,' Danny said. 'How are you?'

'I am… surprised to see you, that's how I am,' she replied.

'Sure, I don't blame you. I should have rung but I thought I'd just swing past and see if you were in. On the off-chance, you know.'

'Sure. Well, I am. In, that is.'

A man's voice came from a back room: 'Who is it, Karen?' he said.

'It's our Sean,' she shouted back.

'Who?'

'Me brother, Sean!' she shouted. She kissed Danny on the cheek as he passed. Her voice dropped to its previous level. 'Come inside, Sean. It's lovely to see you.'

THIRTY-TWO

5.40pm Saturday 21 April 1990

Visiting hours at the Manchester Royal Infirmary didn't officially start until 6.30 pm, but DI Smithdown's police ID allowed him to smooth his way past the staff. He passed Kate off as a police colleague. As Danny saw them, he put down the magazine he'd been reading – a copy of *Q* with David Bowie on the cover – and straightened out his bed. He pushed himself up straight, smiling.

'Here he is,' the policeman said. 'I might have to arrest you for loitering – there's nothing wrong with you, lad.'

'Christ. I don't think I've ever seen you two together before. Actually being father and daughter,' Danny replied. 'Have you honestly come to see me?'

'Yes, we have, Danny.' She leant in and kissed him on the cheek. 'I've brought you these.' Kate placed a copy of *Empire* magazine and some chocolates on the table next to his bed.

'How are you, anyway?' asked the DI. He seemed genuinely concerned.

'I'm fine. Really. Mr Smithdown. I'm so sorry to hear about your wife. Truly I am. Such a difficult time for both of you, that's why I'm so surprised to see you here. I feel a bit embarrassed that you've come to check on me when you've got so much going on. It's very thoughtful. I mean it.'

Smithdown pulled up a chair and sat next to Danny's bed. 'Well, we were going a bit stir crazy at home weren't we, Kate? So, we thought we'd come and see how you're getting on. So, what's the damage?'

'Concussion, dehydration and third-degree embarrassment after passing out in the newsroom,' Danny answered.

'Dehydration? That must be a first for you, Danny lad,' said Mr Smithdown.

'If you're just here to take the piss…'

'We're here to see how you are, Danny,' said Kate.

'And take the piss, obviously,' added her father. 'Look, we won't stay too long – we told a little white lie to get in here – we were worried about you. Mainly Kate, obviously. I wasn't that worried.'

'Well, it's much appreciated. Do you mind if I ask you something, Mr Smithdown?'

'I think I can guess what it is,' the detective replied, folding his arms.

'The suicide up at Black Moss. What do you think? Honestly.'

'I've had my mind elsewhere Danny, if I'm honest,' the DI replied. 'But I've spoken to DS Pym and DC Cave and it seems pretty cut and dried. The note, the location, the items at the scene.'

'What items?' asked Kate.

'Items that connect it to the child's body, let's leave it at that, Kate,' suggested DI Smithdown to his daughter. 'This is a hospital visit, not a press conference for the *Messenger*.'

'You two – such a bloody boys' club. Why do I get the feeling I'm not wanted. Danny, can I get you anything?'

'A tea would be nice. Ask one of the auxiliary nurses. Sorry. Don't blame me, blame this guy.'

As his daughter walked away, DI Smithdown pulled his seat closer to Danny's bed. 'Make it quick, lad.'

'Yes or no – was it him?'

'I only spoke very briefly…'

'Yes or no?'

'Look.'

'I'm really sorry Mr Smithdown, I feel awful asking you at a time like this, but I'm going mad with this. Yes or no?'

'Yes. It's all there.'

'But? It sounds like there's a "but" coming.'

'But nothing. It's all there. There's nothing to suggest it wasn't him. Having said that…'

'What.'

'It's a very big leap. The suicide – Vincent Canning – he was known to the police. I had a few dealings with him over the years. Bits of this, bits of that. Nothing special. To go from being a medium-level pain in the arse to child abduction and murder, well, that's a big leap. But, that's where some of the worst crimes come from. Great big leaps.'

'So, you're not one hundred percent sure.'

'It's done with Danny,' sighed the DI. 'When you're feeling up to it and it all goes quiet over at Strangeways, we can talk about getting some publicity aimed at identifying the lad. I think he deserves that, don't you?'

'A kid at the children's home says someone tried to snatch him too. Plastic bagged him, just like me. Are you saying your man Canning did that too?'

The DI dropped his voice to a whisper. 'I'm saying that we'll follow up on the lad from the home, but I bet you a tenner he won't talk to me. Or anyone else. The plastic bag thing might be a coincidence, or maybe the kid overheard it and use it to get attention. Or to mess you about. It wasn't Little Paul, was it? Now, there's a kid that's going to end up in Strangeways. He's a little shit is Little Paul.'

Kate returned with a cup of tea and placed it on the small table next to Danny's bed. 'When are you getting out then, Danny Something?'

'I'm just waiting for the head specialist to sign me off, then I'm away. Hopefully tonight. They've run out of tests to do on me.'

'I suppose you won't be up in Oldham quite so much,' said Kate. 'Now they've found the kid's killer.'

'No. I suppose not,' Danny conceded. 'There'll still be the inquest to cover to confirm the suicide, but we tend to pinch that kind of stuff from the local reporters. Like you.'

'Charming.'

DI Smithdown stood up from his chair. 'Danny's welcome anytime, Kate. Anytime. Can't fault the effort you've put into this, lad. You were there at the start and you got the scoop with the DS when Canning's body was found. Your bosses at the radio station must be chuffed. I see they've sent you a little something.'

DI Smithdown nodded towards the oversized, padded card on the cabinet next to the bed – a teddy bear with a thermometer sticking out of his mouth was on the front. *Sending Hugs To You To Make You Feel Better*. Some of the messages written inside were a little less wholesome: *Get off your arse and back into work, all the best Gary,* said one. *Not sure who the fuck you are but get well soon anyway. Robert C (Number One Reporter).*

'Yes,' said Danny. 'Very moving.' He took a sip of his tea. It was scalding hot; he put it to one side. There were a few beats of silence.

'I'll tell you what,' said DI Smithdown. 'The car is parked across the other side of the hospital. I'll go and get it and see you at the front reception, Kate. Okay?'

'Sure, Dad. See you in a few minutes.'

The DI shook Danny's hand: 'Ring me when you're better. Let's get that poor lad identified.'

Kate waited for her father to go – she heard him explain that *my colleague just has a few more questions* to a member of staff, then he pushed his way through the swing doors leading out of the ward. 'You don't think this Canning guy did it, do you?' she said.

'No. I don't. There's just something not right about it.'

'Fucking hell, Danny,' Kate cried. 'How come you know better than anyone else?'

'I'm not saying that. But, I know one thing. In his heart of hearts, I don't think your dad thinks that guy did it either. But his hands are tied. Mine aren't.'

'So, what's your big plan then? How do you plan to succeed where the massed ranks of Greater Manchester Police have failed?'

'I have absolutely no idea.'

She paused and looked down the corridor, checking that her father was gone. 'I'll help if I can,' she said. 'Got to go.'

Kate leant to kiss him on the cheek. She banged Danny's head slightly in the process. 'Sorry. Bye. Sorry.'

Danny watched her go. He waited a few minutes, in case she returned. Then he pulled his sheets aside slowly and swung his legs out of the bed. *Brilliant! I've always wanted to check myself out of a hospital,* he thought. *Just like in a film.*

THIRTY-THREE

3.30pm Monday 20 June 2016

In the kitchen of Karen Doyle's house in Wythenshawe, Danny watched as his sister rattled cups and opened cupboards. 'I see you've had a bit of mither down in London, Sean,' she said, placing a teapot, two mugs and a plate of biscuits onto the small kitchen table pushed up against the wall. 'It was in the papers.'

'Yes, it was, wasn't it?' Danny's accent had changed since he walked into the house. It was broader, more nasally Mancunian. 'I don't suppose I'll ever convince you to call me Danny, will I Karen?'

'No, Sean. You won't. I've never liked that name – it doesn't suit you. Never has.'

She took a third mug into the living room. 'Alright, Sean?' came the man's raised voice through the wall. 'Came by taxi, I see. Off the road at the moment, are we?'

'For the time being Brian, yes,' Danny shouted. 'Try not to fret about it though. You take it easy. Still between jobs?'

'Thankfully, yes.'

'Good on you. Me too.'

Danny's voice dropped back to conversational level as his sister came back into the room. 'How have you been, Karen? Sorry, it's been a while.'

'A while, he says. Seven years, Sean. Maybe more. Before that, it was probably Mum's funeral. You never made it to Dad's. Sorry. I'm not having a go. I'm glad you're here. I'm glad you're safe. And I'm glad you didn't die in that bloody car crash. I'm even more glad you didn't kill anyone else while you were at it. Tell me you're not still drinking.'

'No, I'm not. I stopped after the crash.'

'Did you get help?'

'Yes. Drugs and a bit of therapy. Then I decided to come here for a bit of alternative therapy.'

'How is it going? Not drinking, I mean. Do you still think about it?'

'Yes, I do. A lot.'

'I can't bear it. Alcohol,' she said, sipping at her tea. She pushed the plate of biscuits towards her brother. He didn't take one. 'I think that's why I married Brian. 'Cos he's a teetotaller. I won't have it in the house. The smell of it makes me retch. *Looking* at it makes me retch. You went the other way, didn't you? Couldn't get enough of it. Where's the sense in that? Never understood it.'

'Do you know Karen, I'm not sure I understand it either. I was really young when we were taken into care. I don't remember much about it. It's not like we've ever really talked about it.'

'Is that why you're here then Sean, to talk about it?'

'I don't think so. But at some stage, I suppose we should.'

Karen cradled her tea with both hands. Tears looked like they were about to come. Just as quickly, she seemed to send them away. 'Yes… yes we should. Anytime, Sean. Anytime.'

'Danny. I prefer Danny.'

'I know you do. But you'll always be Sean to me. *My* Sean.' Like a gentle tide, the threat of tears came and went once again. Karen pushed a long, whistling breath out through her teeth. 'I'm not ashamed of who I am,' she said. 'Or what happened to us. I'm fine with it. Really, I am. You should try it some time.'

'Yes. You're right. I should. I *am* trying.'

She took the hands from around her mug of tea and placed them around Danny's. They felt very warm. They sat there like that for several minutes. No words, just warm hands. 'You've come so far. No one I knew growing up went to college, let alone university. But you did it. And became a famous journalist to boot. Amazing. But you've never been any use at looking after yourself. Stopping drinking – that's a start, isn't it? Progress, I'd say.'

Danny got up and emptied the remainder of his tea into the sink. He washed the cup and put it on the draining board. 'I need to be going,' he said.

'Why are you here, Sean?' Karen said after a few minutes. 'Apart from the pleasure of my company, obviously. Why have you come back after all these years?'

'There's a case I covered years back. A child murder up at Oldham. It's always bothered me. I thought I'd take a look at it again. They never identified him. It would be good to put it to rest.'

Karen joined him at the sink. She washed her mug too. 'So, it's the past you're visiting, rather than me?'

'The two aren't mutually exclusive.'

'No, you're right. They're one and the same, love. Will you come again?

Come for tea. You need fattening up a bit – you look skinny.'

'Yes, of course. I've got a lot of people to see – people involved in the case – but I'll make time, definitely.'

'Please do. I'll even try to call you Danny, if that helps.'

'It's fine, Karen. Call me what you like. It's up to you.'

She placed a hand on his shoulder as they walked towards the front door. 'See you, Brian,' Danny shouted. 'Don't overdo it.'

'Not going to happen, Sean lad.'

Karen hugged him. He left. She walked to the living room front window and waved. 'What was Sean after, love?' asked her husband. He was watching snooker on TV.

'I don't think he knows, to be honest.'

'Is he back permanently?'

'Depends.'

'What on?'

'He's digging around in something from years back. I suppose it's whether he finds what he's after.'

Brian paused the television, stood up and embraced his wife. 'Never ceases to amaze me that you and him are brother and sister. You've got nothing in common.'

'That's where you're wrong, Brian. We have plenty in common. Unfortunately.'

THIRTY-FOUR

7.45pm Saturday 22 April 1990

From the expression on her face when she walked into the Alt children's home, DC Jan Cave wasn't expecting to see Danny having a cup of tea at the kitchen table. 'Aren't you supposed to be at death's door in hospital, Danny?' she asked.

'I didn't care for their tea, DC Cave. So, I thought I'd pop round here for one.'

'Can I tempt you, officer?' said Brenda, tapping the teapot with her lighter.

'Not just now, Brenda. Thanks all the same. I'm following up on some information from, well, from Danny here, actually. Apparently one of your kids was the subject of an attempted abduction. A lad called Paul? I wanted to speak to him about it, if possible?'

'Little Paul's not here I'm afraid,' Brenda said. 'One of the older ones, Jenny, has taken him out to the pictures. *Bill and Ted's Excellent Adventure*. Have you seen it, DC Cave? It's about a couple of eejits that don't know their arses from their elbows. You might like it. Can I take a message in the meantime?'

'I'd like it if you'd could bring him down to the station, Brenda.'

'I'll do my best, but he's not overly keen on the police isn't Little Paul. Some of your lot tore him from his mammy's arms a few years back, you might recall. The vice lads didn't like the way she was providing for him and dragged social services into it. She *was* providing for him – she was a great mum. Dead now, of course. Overdose. She wasn't even on drugs until Little Paul was taken off her. Terrible business, Danny.'

'It sounds like it.' Danny sipped his tea, keeping his eyes on DC Cave across the rim of the mug.

'So, sure, I'll speak to Little Paul,' Brenda offered. 'But I'd be very surprised if he would want to talk to you. Stranger things have happened, though.'

'We can't help them if the kids won't talk,' DC Cave said.

'And they won't talk if they don't trust you,' Brenda replied. 'Trust comes first, DC Cave. Every time.'

'Well, trust works both ways, doesn't it?'

'Sometimes. Sometimes. But not very often as far as these kids are concerned. I'll be in touch. You'll see yourself out, yes?'

'Definitely.'

Brenda waited for the front door to close, then shouted for a teenage boy to check that she'd gone. He looked out of the front window and confirmed that she had. Jenny and Little Paul came slowly down the stairs. 'I don't get it, Brenda,' Jenny said, taking a seat at the table. 'One minute you're all lovey dovey with the cops and the next minute we're blanking them. I wish you'd make your mind up.'

'There's cops and then there's cops, Jenny,' Brenda said. 'DI Smithdown is okay. He's sound. I don't know much about that one, old frosty arse that was just here, but her boss DS Pym is a slippery shite and I don't trust him. It's up to Little Paul who he talks to. Not you, not me.'

Little Paul, his head barely clearing the height of the table, came alongside Jenny. He put his head in her lap and looked up at Danny. 'Don't you like that copper, Little Paul?' he asked. The boy shook his head.

'Little Paul hates 'em all, don't you mate?' said Jenny, stroking the short bristles of his hair. The boy nodded. 'Every last fookin' one of them,' she added.

Brenda turned to Danny. 'So. You're not buying this whole Black Moss thing, then? Bit too cut and dried for you is it?'

'Just doesn't feel right. Little Paul gets a plastic bag on his head, and so do I? That's a bit of a coincidence, isn't it? DI Smithdown is out of the way dealing with personal issues and a body turns up at the Moss? Life's just not like that.'

'I knew him, you know,' Brenda said. 'Canning, the poor lad up at the Moss.'

'Everyone did, didn't they Bren?' added Jenny.

'There was a lost soul if ever there was one,' Brenda agreed. 'There's one in every town just like him. Went through the care system just like this lot. When he got chucked out the other end he never found his feet. Stumbled his way through life and then ends up like this. Awful. Nice and neat for the police though. They can crack on with sucking up to the Home Office while they're dealing with the Strangeways lads. That's where the brownie points are right now.'

Jenny spoke to the boy – his head was still on her lap. 'God, Vince Canning stunk, didn't he, Little Paul? What did you used to say? *Stunk like a fookin' polecat!* Fook knows how Little Paul knows what a polecat smells like, but that's what you used to say, didn't you little man?'

'Do you think he was the one who tried to grab you, Little Paul?' Danny asked.

Little Paul shook his head. 'You would have whiffed him, wouldn't you, mate?' stated Jenny. 'No disguising that stink. He always seemed harmless to me, though. He stunk, and he was a nuisance. But harmless enough.'

'I think this whole thing still stinks,' said Danny. 'He didn't say it to me outright, but DI Smithdown didn't seem one hundred percent convinced of it either. Until they identify the boy up at the Moss and everything is sorted properly, then I think the kids should carry on being ultra-cautious. Stay in and stay out of harm's way. Especially you, Little Paul.'

The boy climbed up onto Jenny's lap. He whispered in her ear and then slid down and walked off, taking the stairs two at a time before disappearing upstairs. Jenny leaned closer to Danny. 'Little Paul says he's stopping in until you say otherwise, Danny.'

'Christ Almighty!' exclaimed Brenda. 'I've never known Little Paul to pay a blind bit of notice to anyone but Jenny here. You've a friend for life there, Danny.'

'Lost souls, Brenda,' Danny said with a smile. 'We always stick together.'

THIRTY-FIVE

11.45pm Monday 20 June 2016

Danny finished his room service steak and chips and placed the tray out in the hallway. He lay on his bed, fully clothed. It had been a long day and he was physically exhausted, but his mind raced, leaping between all the new pieces of information he'd come across. The hotel room was a good one, with plenty of space and a view across Manchester's city centre, but something inside the room was beginning to bother him: the light buzzing sound from the mini-bar fridge underneath the flat screen TV. He got off the bed and sat cross-legged on the floor in front of it. Then he opened the door and itemised what was inside:

Four bottles of Hildon still water
Four bottles of fizzy Pellegrino water
Two small cans of Schweppes Tonic water
Two cans of Diet Coke
Two full fat Cokes
Two cans of Fanta
Two tubs of plain Pringles
One Snickers bar
One Cadbury's Dairy Milk
One Green & Black's dark chocolate bar
One Green & Black's milk chocolate bar

Then it was onto the main event:

Four bottles of Heineken
Two double measures of Bacardi
Two double measures of Johnny Walker Black Label whisky
Two double measures of Jack Daniels
Two double measures of Stolichnaya vodka
Two double measures of Bombay gin
One half bottle of white wine

Danny stared at the contents. He shook the door very gently, listening to the clank and clatter of the bottles inside. There was, he calculated, just enough to get fairly solidly drunk if he were to tackle the whole lot. *Start with the lagers, onto the wine, then work your way through the spirits, saving the Stolichnaya for last. Pringles will keep you going if you get peckish. Leave the chocolate, bit fattening.*

He pulled out one of the Heinekens and held the bottle against his cheek to test how cold it was. It was okay. *Hotel fridges never get really cold,* Danny thought. He kept it pressed against his face for twenty seconds, then returned it to its slot, closed the fridge door and put a chair in front of it. Then he found the fridge's plug and pulled it from the wall. The thrum of the fridge stopped.

When sleep came, it was a fearful business for Danny Johnston, formerly known as Sean Doyle. He was running down a path through open countryside. It was cold and dark and he wasn't wearing a shirt. The path was filled with rubbish, slowing him down. There was a gate ahead but the closer he got, the bigger the gate appeared to be. He tried to climb it, but he was too small. Or the gate was too large. Maybe both. He looked around. The fence stretched left to right as far as he could see in both directions. Something was rushing towards him from behind, shouting his name. It was coming so fast it was moving the air forwards. Danny could feel the air pressing onto the back of his neck as he turned to see what was there. It slammed into him and woke Danny up.

THIRTY-SIX

5pm Tuesday 24 April 1990

Mike Sharston was fussing and moving papers from one area of his desk to the another when Danny walked to the doorway of his office and tapped on the frame of the open door. He'd been told to stay away for at least a week, but with the Black Moss case seemingly dealt with, he had nothing to occupy him.

Sharston's normally flushed complexion appeared to have been moving up to a purple-tinged colour chart of unhealthiness over the last few weeks; his collar seemed even more strained against his neck and his gut pushed further over his trouser belt. *A pending heart attack in a sports jacket,* thought Danny. 'Yes. Right. Come in,' Sharston said, still seemingly engrossed in his ongoing paper migration task. 'Danny. Yes. How's that head of yours?'

Danny used both hands to feel up and down his face. 'Largely intact. Sorry about the whole passing out in the newsroom thing. I feel a bit of an arse.'

'Well, we were concerned about you, weren't we Beth?' The newsreader had quietly appeared at Danny's shoulder.

'I've barely slept, Mike,' she said with a very small smile.

'Yes. Right. Steady, Beth. Try and keep those emotions in place, will you?'

'I'll do my best,' she replied. *They can't resist it,* Danny said to himself. *They're still taking the piss.*

'Look,' said Sharston. 'Joking aside, I do actually have a responsibility to protect you from yourself here. I can't have reporters getting their heads mashed in and keeling over in my newsroom. But the fact you were clearly in a mess, yet still brought in that interview about the Oldham murder-suicide speaks volumes to me. Fair play to you, Danny.'

'Thanks, Mike.' *An actual compliment. Jesus Christ.*

'Even though you're still a dickhead for coming in with a concussion,' added Beth.

'Quite. Well, don't be fooled by Beth's eternally frosty demeanour. She's been very impressed by the way you've kept at it with this kiddie murder thing. It was a thankless task, as far away from the action of Strangeways as it's possible to get. But you stuck at it without moaning.'

'He moaned quite a bit, Mike. To be fair,' Beth added.

'Alright, Beth,' said Danny. 'Mike's doing just fine, thanks.'

'Anyway,' the news editor continued. 'The post-mortem has confirmed – it was definitely suicide. So, barring the inquest to dot the i's and cross the t's, it's done with. So, when you're feeling a bit better, we should get you down to Strangeways before it all finishes. It's down to the absolute hardcore now, about seven of them, so it can't be long. Though, to be fair, I've been saying that since the start of the month.'

'I'm happy to go now, Mike, really I am,' Danny offered.

'That might be a bit premature,' the news editor said. 'Your face still looks like a dog's been at it. Maybe in a day or two.'

Beth was about to speak but she was interrupted by a shout from the other side of the newsroom. 'Mike! Lord's been snatched. It might be game on.'

Alan Lord, a convicted murderer serving a life sentence, had been seen as the second in command amongst the rioters, likely to be the last to give up after 'ringleader' Paul Taylor. If he'd gone, then the end could be very near. 'Right, who have we got?' asked the news editor. He stood up and scanned the newsroom. Three sports reporters, a cleaner, a secretary and a university placement student whose name no one could remember.

'Where the fuck is everyone?' Sharston shouted. 'I mean, seriously. This is supposed to be the biggest independent radio station newsroom outside of London. I ask again. Where the fuck is everyone?'

'Robert Crane is at the scene – has been since day one. The night time crew are asleep,' itemised Beth. 'We've got three off sick with stress, whatever that is. The day reporters have just finished and are in the pub – so at the moment, the only people free are the sports reporters and that placement student over there.'

'What's her name?'

'I have no idea,' replied Beth.

'Danny. Looks like you're on.'

Fucking hell!

THIRTY-SEVEN

11.45am Tuesday 21 June 2016

'Mr Pym?' Danny asked as the cottage door opened. The house was small but clearly expensive and well maintained, sitting at the edge of the village of Prestbury in the Cheshire commuter belt. An equally well-maintained man in his sixties looked at Danny with a slightly annoyed expression on his face. A waft of potpourri and croissants came with him.

'It is,' confirmed the older man. 'Look, there's a sticker on the door that says we never buy anything from cold callers…'

'I'm not selling, Mr Pym. 'It's help I'm after. Your help.'

'Do I know you?'

'Hopefully, you'll remember me. My name's Danny Johnston. I'm a journalist. I used to be, anyway.'

A woman's voice came from inside the house. 'Who is it, Jim?' She approached the door and stopped just behind the former DS. She was also in her sixties and just as well turned out as her husband. 'Oh, my goodness, Daniel Johnston,' she said. 'Jim's always mentioning you, aren't you Jim? Every time he sees you on TV it's always, *I remember him when he was at Manchester Radio*.'

Danny extended a hand towards the woman. 'That was a very long time ago. It's Mrs Pym, I presume? Nice to meet you. Please call me Danny. Everyone does. Though you used to have a few other names for me, didn't you Mr Pym?'

'One or two Danny, yes. One or two. Jean, I'll take our guest to the summer house. Tea?'

'Yes. That'd be lovely… Jim.'

The ex-detective winced slightly when Danny used his first name. He led him down the side of the house to a path across an immaculately trimmed lawn. Under a willow tree was a top-of-the-line summer house. Pym produced a key and opened the door. The key, attached to an elastic fob, snapped back onto his belt once the door had been opened. Pym gestured towards a rattan armchair and Danny settled into the chair's floral cushions. He looked at the dried flowers, photos and figurines inside the summer house. 'Very nice. Retirement seems to be treating you well, Mr Pym.'

'Yes. It's nice out here. Nicer than Oldham, that's for sure.'

'They call it the Golden Triangle, don't they?' said Danny. 'Prestbury, Wilmslow and Alderley Edge. You can barely move for all the four-by-fours and footballers.'

Pym stared at Danny. 'What do you want?' he asked, quietly.

Mrs Pym arrived with a tray of tea and biscuits. She smiled at Danny as she put it on a small table between the two men. She seemed to sense her presence wasn't required and walked back towards the house. 'I often think I should have joined the police,' Danny said. 'You only need to do thirty years then you cash in your chips and retire with a lovely pension. Especially when you leave on an assistant chief constable's salary.'

'You have to put up with thirty years' worth of shit though. I'll ask again, what do you want, Danny?'

'I'm looking at an old case. One that's never been quite resolved for me.'

'And which case might that be?'

'The Black Moss kid. Remember that one, Mr Pym?'

'Yes, I do. Very much. You might find this hard to believe, but I've thought about that kid a lot over the years. I really have.'

'Can I cut to the chase?'

'Please do.'

'Why didn't you give a shit about that kid back in 1990?'

Pym poured himself a cup of tea. He didn't pour Danny one. 'That's not true, Danny. It's not true and you know it.'

'I don't. I don't know it at all, Mr Pym. It felt like me and Mr Smithdown were the only people who thought that boy was worth anything. Worth going the extra yard for. Worthy of *anything*. It seemed like that kid was an inconvenience for you while you were seen to be mopping up the mess at Strangeways. Got you that promotion you wanted, didn't it? ACC Pym. Lovely. Just what you were after.'

Danny poured himself some tea and took two biscuits. Then a third. Pym stared at him; he was leaning forward now, tense in his seat. 'Listen, I appreciate you've experienced not so much a fall from grace as a fucking skydive in recent weeks, but you've got no right coming here making accusations to try to make yourself feel better. Don't lecture me about not caring. I saw that kid laid out on slab, Danny. I saw what had been done to him. We did our best with what we had at the time. It was chaos not conspiracy. I wouldn't have put DI Smithdown and DC Cave on it if I didn't want it solving. Our best people, no question about it. Was it ideal? No, it wasn't. A combination of Strangeways, DI Smithdown's wife being so very ill and… other factors made it a very difficult case. We did our best.'

'What other factors?' asked Danny.

'DI Smithdown's decision to involve you for a kick off. He was a good cop. A great cop. But he used you, Danny. He used you to get at me. Leaking stuff to you, getting you to run stories that he knew were just guesswork on his part. Sending kites up to see if the wind would catch them. That's all it was. At the time you probably thought you were something special. He'd done it loads of times with different reporters. He'd even used his daughter, for fuck's sake. Encouraged her to become a journalist so he could undermine me. His own daughter! How low is that?'

'He's a good man. A better one than you.'

'Grow up, lad.'

'I'm nearly fifty, Mr Pym.'

'Then fucking act like it,' he shouted. 'Coming here with your pious act. You were as bad as him. You were trying to make a name for yourself, coming up to the hill country, giving us the benefit of your journalistic wisdom. Fuck off. You were just a kid, you didn't have a clue and it appears you still don't. If you want to do some good – and I assume that's what this is all about, trying to ease your conscience about pissing your life and what talent you had away – then try to identify that kid. Do that. Find out who that kid was and provide a bit of closure for his family.'

'The only way to ID the kid is to ID the murderer, Mr Pym.'

'We know who the fucking murderer was! That sad sack of shit they found up at the Moss with a broken bottle of whisky and a suicide note. Cut and dried. I know it might have seemed too easy from the outside, but it was bang to rights.'

'Really? At one stage you were trying to pin it on Peter Jeffries.'

'That's an outright lie, Danny. Where the fuck did you get that from?'

'One of my colleagues at the radio station said they'd been briefed, off the record, that Jeffries topped himself after killing that kid. Drove off the road on purpose. That could have only come from you.'

Pym leant even further forward. 'It. Did. Not. Come. From. Me,' he stated his finger hitting the tea tray with every punctuation point. 'Jeffries was a gobshite who loved the sound of his own voice, but he was no danger to kids. I'm sure of that. He'd been drinking that night, no question of it. But nothing suggested he was involved or that he'd crashed on purpose.'

'Then why would someone smear his name after his death?'

'I have no idea. Honestly. No idea whatsoever. That's the first I've heard of it in twenty-five years. You seem to have cooked up quite a conspiracy theory here, Danny. I don't believe in conspiracies. I really don't.'

'What do you believe in?'

'Silence, Danny. That's how bad things happen. Through silence.'

'Did you keep silent about anything connected with this, Mr Pym?'

Former Assistant Chief Constable James Pym leant back in his seat. 'No, I didn't. Did you?'

THIRTY-EIGHT

5.50pm Tuesday 24 April 1990

Rather than wait for a cab in the rush hour, Gary Keenan volunteered to take Danny down to Strangeways. It was, the engineer said, the right time to do a gear check and swap the radio car's battery again. 'Don't want the biggest story we've ever had to go tits up at the last minute now, do we?' Gary asked as they drove at high speed though Manchester city centre.

'I'm going to treat that as a rhetorical question, Gary,' Danny said, gripping the side of the car seat as they jumped a red light, crossed the main Deansgate road and headed down Blackfriars Street towards Strangeways.

'You can treat it to a slap-up meal at the Midland Hotel as far as I'm concerned, kidder. No point in you covering the end of the riot if no one can hear you 'cos of faulty gear and a battery that's flatter than a witch's tit.'

The hoppy tang of the Boddington's brewery next door to the prison caught Danny by surprise, as did the log jam of traffic around the approach roads to the jail. Gary pulled into a side street and got out of the car. He popped the boot and lifted a new car battery out. 'Come on, soft bollocks,' he said. 'We're walking.'

'You'll get a ticket there,' Danny said, glancing at the double yellow lines Gary had parked on. 'I couldn't give a flying shit – stick it on the pile with all the others,' Gary replied, slamming the boot shut. For a big man he moved surprisingly quickly across the road towards the jail. Danny struggled to keep up. There seemed to be a general movement of people towards the prison; the word was clearly out that some kind of end point was near. Danny and Gary became part of the flow. The crowd was five deep at the perimeter fence and the pair had to push their way through to get to the radio car. Robert Crane was pacing up and down alongside the vehicle. His usually dapper appearance was no more: his suit was crumpled, his normally slicked-back hair had tumbled into his face and his eyes were underscored with dark semi-circles. He smelled of cigarettes and stale sweat. 'I think Bobby has gone feral on us,' Gary said to Danny in a stage whisper. 'He looks like a shit in a bucket.'

Crane waved to Gary, but his face clouded with disappointment when he spotted Danny. 'Are you the cavalry, then?' he asked sipping from a can of Coke.

'It would appear so,' Danny replied, glancing at the inside of the radio car and seeing the piles of drink cans, food cartons, crisp packets, sweet wrappers and newspapers that were inside. *Makes my car look like a palace.*

Gary Keenan was looking at the mess too. 'Christ, we're going to have to burn this radio car when this story is over and done with. Right, let's get this battery swapped before the seven o' clock news. You kids play nicely while I sort this out.'

The chief reporter pushed a hand through his hair and looked at Danny. 'Did you bring anything for me?' he asked.

Danny had a plastic carrier bag in one hand; the placement student whose name no one could remember had given it to him. From it he produced a new shirt, still folded and shrink-wrapped. It was dark brown with heavy black stripes and was branded with a name Danny had never heard of before. It was, by anyone's estimation, a cheap and unpleasant-looking shirt. 'Where the fuck did you get that? Shit Shirts R Us? It's a monstrosity.'

'It's what I was given. Don't shoot the shit shirt messenger,' said Danny, quietly pleased with his response.

'Christ alive,' Crane said. He pulled the wrapping away, shook out the myriad clips and pins holding it in place and held it up to the fading, early evening light. 'It'll have to do, I suppose.' Crane took off his jacket and the shirt he was wearing. He bundled up his old shirt with the remaining packaging and shoved it into the plastic bag Danny was carrying. He put it on. It looked worse on him than it did in the packet.

'So, what's the plan?' Danny asked as he looked around for a bin to put the bag into.

'The plan, young Daniel, is this,' said Crane. 'See those metal barriers over there? Any time now, some bod from the Home Office will pop out and give us an update on the situation inside. It's basically a numbers tally. Someone will ask if they plan to retake the jail by force, blah blah blah. Then we have our top line for the seven.'

'So, shall I go and wait for the Home Office bod to come out?' asked Danny.

'Will you fuck. I'm doing that. You never know, he might actually come out and say something interesting, in which case, I'm having it. You, on the other hand, will go among the crowd and vox pop them about whether they think it's all about to come to an end. After seven o'clock we have an agreement down here that all journos down tools and take a break. That way, no one scoops anyone else. We go to the Woolpack up there.' Crane pointed to an old-fashioned pub a hundred yards up the road from the jail. 'You can wait here just in case. I'll bring you back some crisps. Then, when I've had two, possibly three pints of Boddington's finest bitter, I will return, make sure all is well, use your vox pop for the eight, then I will fuck off home and you will stop here for the night. Any questions?'

'Just one.'

'Shoot.'

'Can I have nuts rather than crisps, please? And a couple of tins to see me through?'

THIRTY-NINE

1.30pm Tuesday 21 June 2016

As the tram travelled south from Manchester city centre, Danny looked at the list of people to track down that he'd scribbled on his hotel notepad. Robert Crane was now a political lobbyist, working back in London. He was reasonably far down Danny's list of people of interest anyway. *A suit full of fuck all. Always was, always will be.* Mike Sharston had died in 2005. Heart attack. *What a shocker,* thought Danny. Brenda from the care home had passed away in 2010. *Shame, she was a lovely person.* With her gone it would be very difficult indeed to track down the likes of Jenny and Little Paul.

He got off the tram. There had been no trams in Didsbury when he'd lived here. According to Gary Keenan, Beth Hall had also been 'not too well' but she'd seemed pleased to hear from Danny via Facebook Messenger the previous night and gave him her address. She now lived in West Didsbury, not far from Danny's old flat.

He followed Google Maps and turned into Beth's road as instructed by the apps' voice. Her house was an impressive three-storey detached affair tucked into the corner of a cul-de-sac. There was a ramp fitted to the front door to allow wheelchair access and large handles were attached either side of the front door. *She must still live with her folks. They're clearly getting on a bit.*

There was a video intercom at the door; he looked up at the camera and waved. *Her folks must be very security-conscious.* Danny went to push the buzzer, but he heard Beth's distinctive voice interrupt him before he could press the button. It annoyed him a little, but it was cheerier than he remembered: 'Danny Johnston! Come in, come in.'

The door buzzed open and Danny stepped inside. He noticed a stairlift attached to the wall running up the stairs and more handles attached to door frames along the hallway. He could smell fresh baking. There was also an undercurrent of another slightly harsh, medicinal smell that he didn't care for at all. 'In the kitchen,' instructed the voice, 'come through!'

Danny did as he was asked. There was a small ramp levelling off the step into the kitchen; Beth Hall was next to the oven, setting out a plate of chocolate brownies. With a deft movement of her right hand she manoeuvred her wheelchair 180 degrees so she faced the kitchen table. 'Sit, sit,' she instructed. 'It's brownie o'clock. Tea?

'Yes please, thanks.' Her manner was bright and undeniably cheery. Danny didn't quite know how to react. She was wearing a black polo neck jumper with her hair cut into a bob – the colour was much more vivid than he remembered. Her make-up was immaculate, with her lipstick especially bright and freshly applied.

'Bet you never knew I was such a domestic goddess, did you, Danny?'

'No, Beth. You have hidden depths.'

'Don't I just? How long has it been? No, don't! It's going to be some horrendous figure that will make me feel very old, isn't it?'

'A quarter of a century, I'd say. At least.'

'Noooo! I don't want to hear it,' Beth cried, laughing as she put her hands over her ears. 'You look great, Danny. Super healthy. I heard about your problems in London. Really sorry. But maybe it was a Godsend. Is that a bad thing to say? You know what I mean, I'm sure.'

'I know exactly what you mean. It's fine. You're probably right. Crashing into a tree – best thing that ever happened to me. How about you? How have you been?'

She poured tea for them both. The mugs were earthy, handmade and fashionable. 'I've been pretty good, actually,' she replied. 'I write, I do some radio consultancy stuff, I lecture at universities; can't complain. Apart from the whole wheelchair thing – I'm perfectly capable of complaining that. Otherwise, not bad at all.'

'Can I ask about the whole wheelchair thing? Sorry. I didn't know.'

'M.S.' she said, in a business-like way. 'Comes and goes. I don't always need the chair. A crutch is fine a lot of the time. No big deal. I don't let it get to me. Much. Anyway. Have a brownie. Have two – and tell me what brings you up here. Manchester Radio's brightest star. Mr Network!'

'Yeah, well, not anymore,' Danny said.

'You had a great run,' she insisted, her eyes shiny with pride. 'Lots of people at the station in the old days thought they were going to go all the way. But you *actually did it*. All the way. A fantastic achievement.'

'I don't remember anyone thinking I was very good back then. I was the runt of the litter. Mr Invisible. You were horrible to me!' Danny was laughing now, but inside he was serious.

'I never was!' Beth protested, with a wink. 'I was harsh but fair, at all times.'

'Fairly harsh, more like.'

'Really? I thought I was the model of encouragement and understanding.'

'That must have been on my days off.'

'We were all very young and ambitious and competitive and… it was an amazing time,' she said, leaning back in her wheelchair. 'It was like we were at the centre of the news universe. Moss Side, Madchester, Gunchester, IRA bombs, all the trouble at The Haçienda club, Strangeways – everyone was looking away from London and looking at us. In Manchester. Amazing. An amazing time and amazing stories.'

'There's one story I'm still interested in, Beth. One that I want to look at again.'

'I know!' she said, putting down her mug of tea. 'The Black Moss boy. Everyone's talking about it. Amazing. What a great idea. You should do a documentary or write a book.'

'Who's talking about it?'

Beth pointed to a battered laptop that was open on the kitchen table close to Danny. He slid it over to her. A few taps and she turned the screen around, so Danny could see it. It was a Facebook page called 'I Survived Manchester Radio'. The top post was entitled 'Danny Johnston Back in Manchester'. There were forty-five comments; one stated that Danny was a 'great guy, great reporter, good to see him back on his old stomping ground'. Another was more succinct: 'Let's hope he didn't drive back – silly old piss artist'. Both had plenty of likes. The second one had also garnered a few laughing emojis. He clicked on the post – the author was Robert Crane.

'Always nice to hear from old showbiz mates,' Danny said, pushing the laptop away. 'He was always a charmer, was our Bobby.'

'He was a glory hunter, out for himself the whole time,' added Beth. 'And he was a lazy bastard, ducking out of the jobs he thought were beneath him – the poor boy at Black Moss being a prime example.'

'What do you mean?'

'That morning the boy's body was discovered. I called Robert Crane to go out there. He called you out because he didn't fancy dragging his arse up to Oldham. He wanted to stay at Strangeways – where the prizes were. Or at least, where he thought they were. Don't you remember?'

'I've been pissed for the last thirty years, Beth. I can barely remember you, let alone the finer points of what happened in 1990. That's why I'm doing this. To try to fill in the gaps.'

'Well, I'm very offended you barely remember me, Danny.'

'Just a figure of speech, Beth. I very much remember you. Though it's fair to say I remember you a bit differently. I was frightened to death of you. Back in the day, I mean.'

'I'm sure you weren't.'

'I was. I really was.'

'Well, I'm not that frightening anymore, am I?'

'No, you're not Beth.'

'So, what are you going to do with the Black Moss story?' she asked, blowing across the surface of her tea. 'A book, maybe? I think it'd make an amazing book.'

Danny nodded. 'It's definitely crossed my mind. Sure. A book. Why not?'

'If you could identify the boy,' Beth offered. 'That'd be the scoop.'

'Indeed. Tall order, though.'

'Keep me posted,' she said. 'If I can help in any way, let me know.'

After saying his goodbyes to Beth, Danny texted Kate to ask about another name on his list: DC Jan Cave. Kate had already been through her father's notebooks and found a business card with her name on: *Jan Cave – Child Protection Consultant.* She'd sent Danny a photo of it.

He thanked her via text. More messages followed:

Still ok for dinner 2nite?

Sure. What shall I bring?

Just yourself. CU 6.30 ish.

Jan Cave's card didn't have an address but a swift internet search for her name and profession via the Companies House website showed that the business was registered in Old Trafford, halfway between Didsbury and the centre of Manchester. *Perfect. I'll just swing past. If she's there, she's there. Then back to the hotel, shower up and off to Kate's.*

The red brick mill building where the former DC's offices were situated was a twenty-minute tram ride away, then just a few minutes' walk from the station. The mill had been through many lives and uses over the years. Now, according to the huge map sign at the entrance, it was divided up into hundreds of businesses of every type, from indoor climbing to Cave Consultants.

Danny made his way around the site until he got to the unit he wanted, which was tucked away close to the canal that ran alongside the mill.

Climbing a small metal set of steps up to the front door, he found a panel full of buttons – many had handwritten cards signifying the business it connected to. He pressed the one next to a white card with Cave Consultants printed very neatly on it.

No reply. *Should have sent a message,* Danny thought. He pressed again. *No reply.* He turned on the steps; former DC Jan Cave was there right in front of him, her face slightly too close to his. 'Hi, Danny,' she said in a slightly amused monotone. 'Coming in or are you just going to hang around here?'

'Alright, err Jan?' Danny felt uncomfortable using her first name. *What am I supposed to call her, former DC Cave?* 'Sure. Thanks.'

Danny looked at her. She wore a smart black trouser suit and a white shirt. Her hair was still pulled back from her face – as it had always been in 1990 – but considering she must be in her late fifties, she was largely unchanged from the last time he'd seen her. 'I've been expecting you,' she stated, pressing a four-digit number into a security pad mounted next to the door. As she went in, she picked up some mail and motioned for Danny to follow her across the small hallway. There were four of five doorways; she headed to one tucked away underneath an iron stairway.

'Really?' Danny asked. 'How come?'

'They have this thing called the internet these days,' she pointed out. 'Even the police use it. You should try it sometime. We have ex-officers' forums, Facebook and WhatsApp groups – you name it. I know you've been to see Mr Pym – you got chucked out I hear. So now you're here to see me. Inevitable, really. Tea?'

'No thanks, I've had gallons today – my back teeth are floating.' Danny smiled to himself for using a Manchester expression he remembered from his childhood. He looked around the small office. It was well ordered and efficient looking. There were framed certificates on the wall and several photos, including one of her with DS Pym.

'Have a seat,' she said. Danny sat in a leather swivel chair; Jan Cave placed herself in a chair behind the modern grey desk, which dominated the tiny space.

'Do you mind if I record the conversation,' he asked, putting a hand into his inside jacket pocket. 'I'm thinking of writing a book.'

'Yes, I do mind,' she snapped. 'I don't want to obstruct you, Danny, but this is just a nonsense.'

'Oh. Okay. And why's that, then?'

She leant forward so she was even closer to him. He could smell soap. An old-fashioned, incongruous smell. 'Do you honestly think I'm going to assist you with some weird ego trip? So, you can write a book about how the police messed it all up back in 1990 and how you came back home to save the day? John Smithdown might buy into it, but I certainly won't. This seems to have very little to do with that kid up at Black Moss and everything to do with you trying to rehabilitate your reputation at our expense.'

'No, it isn't,' he insisted, surprised at how close he was to shouting. 'It really fucking isn't... *Jan.* It really is about that kid. The kid that no one gave a shit about. The kid that your bosses didn't think would get them a promotion and put their time and effort into Strangeways instead. So, don't lecture me about being in it for myself, because you really don't get it.'

'Look,' she explained, matching him for volume. 'No one claimed to be an expert in child protection back then, but we worked hard with what we had and we did our best. That kid was almost certainly a missing from home that had the misfortune to come across a very bad person indeed. Persistent, missing-from-home kids were considered a nuisance back then. The record-keeping by the homes they were dumped in was nonexistent. No one cared about the root of the problem – that families that can't cope with the most basic things in life can't be expected to cope with the responsibility of children. Family support units – the idea of properly organised police involvement in child protection – didn't even kick in until around 1991. After the Black Moss case, I dedicated the rest of my career to trying to stop things like that ever happening again. A dead child face down by a reservoir and we can't even identify him. Why? Because no one thought it was important to keep track of kids like that? In 19-fucking-90? A disgrace. *That's* why I do child protection work to this day.' She moved an arm around her office, indicating the meticulously framed certificates that trumpeted her child protection qualifications. 'You're not the only one who was changed by what happened at Black Moss, Danny.'

'Okay. You said you didn't want to obstruct me. Answer me one thing. Vincent Canning. The suicide. What was he like? Tell me about him. Did he have family?'

Jan Cave, for the first time since they had sat down, leant back in her chair. 'Never met him – I only knew him by reputation. Saw him a few times through the cell peepholes at Oldham nick. He was a sad case. To be honest, looking at his record, I was surprised that he did what he did. Not that he killed himself, but that he'd snatched and killed a kid. But the evidence was there. Undeniable.'

'What about Peter Jeffries?' countered Danny. 'Your station was putting it out that he was somehow involved… ran his car off the road on purpose.'

'News to me,' she said, shaking her head. 'Who told you that?'

Danny hesitated. 'Another journalist told me that Oldham Police were actively pushing that line after the crash. True?'

'Absolutely not. Which "other journalist" was this? Kate Smithdown, girl reporter? Can't imagine where she could have gotten that theory from. Look. Her dad was an amazing copper. One of the best. But he wasn't himself during the Black Moss investigation. And he certainly isn't himself now. Poor soul.'

'One more question, Jan.'

'Okay.'

'Is there any doubt in your mind that Vincent Canning killed that little boy?'

'Do you know what? John Smithdown did an absolutely thorough job on it. Astonishing really, considering everything else he had on his plate – with his wife in The Christie and everything. He still managed to do a very professional job with Canning. I would have helped but I kept getting dragged back into other cases – and Strangeways, of course. Barely a minute went by without something to do with Strangeways needing your attention back then. So, to answer your question, I have no doubts at all about Canning's death and that he was responsible for the boy's murder. None whatsoever. The tragedy is that the chances of ID-ing the boy died up on the Moss with Canning. Cowardly bastard.'

There was silence. Jan Cave had clearly said her piece and wasn't planning to say any more. Danny thanked her and left.

FORTY

6.15pm Tuesday 24 April 1990

After Robert Crane had received the latest head count from the Home Office and headed off in the direction of the pub, Danny went through the crowd outside Strangeways, looking for likely targets for vox pops. He hated doing vox pops. *Excuse me, sir/madam – can I garner your opinion on something completely hypothetical that you are clearly unqualified to speak about in any way, shape or form? Many thanks.*

Manchester Radio was unusually popular among the kind of people who would be hanging around Strangeways of a Tuesday evening, so it wasn't usually too difficult to get people to speak. Most were delighted at the chance of being on their favourite station. Danny looked hard at the people gathered around the jail. He quickly found a man whose friend – or at least the friend of a friend – was still inside the jail. Though he wasn't totally sure. He thought that the siege *has gotta end sometime, hannit? Can't go on forevoh, cannit?* He also asked Danny if he had any weed.

Danny then found some young women aged about twenty who were on their way into Manchester and thought they'd just take a look at what all the fuss was about before it all ended. Only one was prepared to speak – she believed the jail should have been stormed by the SAS on day one.

The Golden Rule of vox pops is that you need at least three. So, three was all that Danny had any intention of getting. He saw a woman in her forties her fingers gripping the mesh of the high-perimeter fence. She was staring at the roof. Two or three silhouettes could be seen, trotting nimbly across the roof top towards the main rotunda. Her hair, bleached white but with jet black roots, was pulled back from her face with a large elastic band. She wore an oversized black cardigan and had a clump of tissue in one hand. 'Hi,' said Danny. 'I'm sorry to bother you. I'm from Manchester Radio and I was wondering if I could ask you when you think the riot is going to finish?'

She didn't turn to look at Danny. 'Wouldn't you be better off asking how the riot started?'

'Sorry?'

'How it started,' she repeated, still looking at the jail. 'Rather than playing a stupid guessing game about when I think it will end, why not ask how it started? A prison built for nine hundred people, rammed with sixteen hundred souls. Three to a cell, shitting in a single bucket that's overflowing by morning. Locked in their cells twenty-three hours a day. Staff brutality. No grievance procedure. Food that a dog would cross the street to avoid. Why not ask about that?'

'I'm sure that will all come out once it's all over,' Danny said, slightly regretting his choice of interviewee.

'Are you sure?'

'Yes. So, when do you think the riot will finish?'

'It's not a riot. It's a protest.'

'Okay. When do you think the protest will finish?'

The woman looked at Danny. Her face was so pale it looked unreal, like she was wearing stage make-up. 'Tomorrow,' she stated and walked away before Danny could turn on his Marantz.

He watched her go, then found someone else who said they wanted it to carry on as long as possible as this was the best entertainment currently available in Manchester. Danny went back to the radio car, fed the clips back to the station and waited for Crane to return from the pub.

FORTY-ONE

6.25pm Tuesday 21 June 2016

Danny had debated long and hard about what to bring to Kate's house for dinner. He wasn't even close to the stage where he could buy alcohol – even if it wasn't for him. He'd opted for some upmarket soft drinks from a hipster deli in Manchester city centre; overpriced ginger beer and dandelion and burdock in bottles with complex-looking opening mechanisms – and some flowers. He wanted to get something for Kate's son too, so he opted for a very large bag of Skittles from a nearby twenty-four-hour mini market. *Think I've got it covered.*

A cab took him out to Kate's address in Uppermill: *Ah. The posh part of Oldham.* It dropped him down a winding path leading to a large, detached house backing onto the Huddersfield canal. The air was warm and filled with birdsong and reassuring chugs and chatter from the canal. As Danny approached the front door a young boy with a mop of jet black curly hair came skidding down the path on a mountain bike, flinging pebbles onto the front step. 'Hi. Are you Danny?' he asked, in a clipped, not-very-Oldham-sounding accent. He stepped off the bike and laid it onto the path in one smooth movement.

'I am. You must be Jonathan.' Danny put down the carrier bag of drinks and extended his hand towards the boy. They shook.

'Are those for my mum?' Jonathan asked, nodding at the flowers in Danny's other hand.

'They are. And these are for you.' Danny pulled out the bag of Skittles and waved them gently in the boy's direction.

'I'm not allowed those,' he said in a serious voice. His face immediately broke out onto a huge smile as he quickly took them from Danny. 'Thanks a lot! Mum's in the garden. See you.'

He tucked the sweets into the panniers attached to his bike and made off at great speed. Danny made his way around the side of the house. Kate was laying out plates and serving spoons onto a wooden garden table. She was wearing white shorts and a light blue polo shirt and smiled at Danny as he approached. 'Hi. You haven't seen Jonathan, have you?'

'About ten? Dark curly hair? Carrying a massive bag of Skittles? Yeah, he's just gone off on his bike.'

'Christ, Danny. You certainly know how to please a kid and annoy a parent, don't you? I'll be scraping him off the ceiling at bedtime. I'll text him.'

'I've brought a load more sugar in liquid form too,' he said, taking the deli bottles out of the carrier bag and placing them on the table. 'And I got these for you.' He put flowers on the table too.

'Aww, thanks Danny,' said Kate. 'We'll make a viable human being of you yet. The food won't be long. What do you want to drink? I wasn't sure what you'd want, so I bought every soft drink in the local shop. How's your investigation going? Any news?'

'It's not an investigation,' he corrected. 'It's more of a refresher – and it's making things more confusing than ever, to be honest. Things just aren't as I remember them. I suppose that's what being pissed all these years does for you. Your perception of things is totally unreliable. People I thought were horrible are being really helpful. People I thought would be helpful are no use at all – no offence.'

'Quite a bit of offence taken. But, continue,' she requested, pointing at some French bread and indicating that Danny should cut it.

'I know one thing: that people are a damn sight easier to track down now than they used to be. We used to have to go through all the Smithdowns in the Oldham phone book to find someone in the old days. Now everyone is just a social media click away.'

'And what are you planning to do with all these refreshers? You don't honestly think you can solve this and be the big hero? Put everything right?'

Danny didn't say anything. He carried on cutting bread then pushed back the top of one of the drinks he'd brought with him and took a sip. It was bitingly sweet. Kate stopped setting the table. 'You do, don't you? You think this is your ticket out of Shitsville, don't you? The redemption express.'

'It's funny – that's pretty much what the cops have said to me but it's a bit more complicated than that,' Danny said, setting aside his drink and pouring some iced water instead. 'I don't know. A book, maybe? Is it going to be like this all evening or are you just being horribly judgemental before your son returns?'

'No, I plan to be horribly judgemental without any pauses whatsoever.

Ah, speak of the Devil.'

Kate's son arrived in the garden and headed straight for the table. He grabbed a chunk of bread and bit it in half. 'Jonathan! Hands washed first please, you mucky bugger.'

'I'll bet you never asked Danny if he washed his hands,' the boy answered, brightly. 'Have you washed your hands, Danny?'

'Not washed 'em for years, mate. Never found the need to. It's a myth put about by mums.'

'Hands! Now!' said Kate, pointing at Danny and making a zipping motion across her mouth with her hand. Jonathan ran through the open French windows into the kitchen, ran his hands under the tap for a matter of seconds, then ran back out, wiping his hands on his jeans. Danny winked at him as the boy grabbed another piece of bread and sat down.

'How's your grandad, Jonathan?' asked Danny. 'I knew him when he was a policeman in the olden days when dinosaurs roamed the hills above Oldham and there were no mobile phones.'

'He wanted to come, but Mum says she wouldn't get a word in edgeways if he did and that you'd ignore her. So, he got banned.'

'Pass the salad to Danny, Jonathan,' said Kate. 'Before I chuck you in the canal.'

The table seemed to have enough food on it for a dozen people, let alone two adults and a ten-year-old. Danny helped himself to spiced chicken, cous cous, corn on the cob and salad. The freshness of it shocked his taste buds – he'd been living on train and hotel food since he'd arrived back in Manchester – but there was something else: *this is the first time I've eaten with people for quite some time. God, it's so nice.*

Danny didn't say too much. He watched as Kate and her son joked with each other as they ate, gently making fun without harm or malice. Jonathan coerced Danny into a little garden football – mother and son were shocked and amused at how awful he was. Afterwards, Danny asked about Jonathan's school – a private prep nearby. In return, Jonathan asked Danny about his school; Danny told him how he'd been given money from the local council to go to a fee-paying school as he'd been identified as being very bright while at his state primary school. 'Oh, like a bursary?' asked Jonathan.

'Yes, mate. Exactly like a bursary.' Danny looked at Kate and widened his eyes, as if to say: *he's cleverer than both of us put together, this one.*

'Do you have any siblings, Danny?' Jonathan asked. 'Brothers and sisters, I mean.'

Again, Danny smiled at Kate. 'Oh right. I see what you mean. Brother and sisters. No, I don't I'm afraid. Just like you, I'm a one-off.'

'You certainly are,' added Kate. 'Right! Time to get ready for bed, Jonathan. School night and all that. Say good night to Danny.'

'Good night. You coming again, Danny?' asked the boy.

'Possibly, mate. If I'm allowed.'

'Great. See you.'

'See you, Jonathan. Say hi to your grandad for me.'

'I will. He likes you,' the boy said as he walked towards the house. 'He says… now you're off the booze, you're sound as a pound.'

'Jonathan!' exclaimed Kate. 'Bed. Now!'

Danny laughed and gave the boy a thumbs up sign. Jonathan returned it and went inside. 'What a horrendous little monster,' he told Kate. 'You must be a terrible parent – shame on you.'

'I need to start keeping him and Dad apart. I'm so sorry.'

'Not at all. As ever, your dad is spot on in his assessment of the situation.'

They sat in silence for a moment. Danny looked across the garden and watched a barge go by through the trees. On the far side of the water, a few people could be seen. Some were walking along the towpath hand in hand. Kate and Danny were happy to sit in silence for a while. 'I should be getting off, Kate. Thank you so much. It was really nice. I'll call a cab.'

'No need. I'll take you down to the station. It'll only take a few minutes and there's a train to Manchester due soon. You'll be back in your hotel before the cab gets here and you'll save yourself a fortune.'

'Sure. Great idea. What about Jonathan?'

'He'll be fine for a few minutes. Don't worry. You're not in London now – safe as houses around here. Let me grab my keys and we'll be off. Then you can tell me what your next move is in the Great Black Moss Investigation.'

'I was hoping you'd have a few ideas.'

'Maybe I do.'

They got into Kate's car and headed up the drive, towards the tree-lined path that connected the house to the road. From a vantage point close to the canal their departure was watched. Their entire evening had been watched. Watched and duly noted.

FORTY-TWO

1.30am Wednesday 25 April 1990

Sitting in the front seat of the radio car, Danny watched as a group of young boys, aged around ten or eleven, chatted and laughed around a bonfire they'd started on wasteland close to the perimeter fence of the jail. Two of them pulled glowing batons of wood from the flames and began a play swordfight with them; sparks ricocheted around them as the swords clashed. *Kids out on their own this time of the morning. No wonder they go missing.*

Danny sipped the third of his four cans of lager. Crane had forgotten the nuts Danny had asked for, but the alcohol was keeping his hunger at bay. He was timing the cans so he could have one every hour; he'd sleep when they ran out.

He listened to the shouts and cries from the remaining prisoners on the roof as they shimmied across the rooftop. It would be strangely quiet for a while, then a shout of 'I love you!' or even 'Ken Dodd!' would cut through the night. Then quiet again. Then 'Mr Blue Sky' would start playing. While all this was going on, Green Goddess fire engines, borrowed from the army, were soaking the jail with water. The Home Office claimed it was to damp down fires started by the rioters; more streetwise observers believed it was to try to soak the inmates into submission. *I'm not surprised Crane looked like he'd just got back from the trenches – three weeks of this is enough to drive anyone mad.*

Danny decided to stretch his legs. As he stepped out of the car and locked it, he crushed the two empty cans underfoot and threw them onto the nearby bonfire as he passed. 'They won't burn, ya knobhead,' said one of the ten-year-olds.

'I'll bear that in mind, lads. Appreciate the info. Bit late to be out on a school night, isn't it?'

'Fook off!' several of them replied.

There were still about forty people milling around the jail – not including journalists. Small groups of men in their twenties went from camera crew to camera crew, volunteering to be interviewed about the latest from 'inside the jail', for fifty pounds. Sometimes, they accepted as little as ten. Danny watched as these lurid tales were spun, with the cameramen angling their shots so the interviewees faces couldn't be seen, as confident-sounding predictions were made about the occupation continuing until the end of the month. *I really hope not,* thought Danny.

He lit a cigarette as he walked around the site. The casual flow of people in and out of the area around the jail was constant. Taxis would swing past every now and then, dropping off people who wanted to take a look at *The Strangeways Rioters.* They'd stop, maybe ask someone if anything was happening. *Just the usual.* They'd hang around for a while, seemingly tire of it, then move on.

Danny did a loop of the area in front of the jail, heading back towards the radio car. As he walked up Southall Street to the right of the jail, he saw the peroxide blonde woman he'd seen earlier. She was standing at the same spot. She noticed Danny and began walking away. 'Still think it'll end today?' Danny called after her.

She turned, looked back for a few steps, nodded, then walked away. Danny watched her until she disappeared into the orangey haze of the street lights along the road. *Normally, that would be a bit weird. But not around here.*

He got back to the radio car. The two rear tyres were both flat. Crouching down to take a closer look, he noticed that both had a neat slit cut into them. He looked around. The kids around the bonfire had gone. *Little bastards.*

<u>FORTY-THREE</u>

11.30am Wednesday 22 June 2016

After Kate had dropped him off at the station the previous evening, Danny spent the train journey scanning Facebook groups that might help him find the next person he wanted to trace. He came across several sites that seemed to fit the bill: I HEART OLDHAM, OLDHAM IN THE 80s, OLDHAM MEMORIES all seemed the right kind of pages and he posted the same message on all of them.

Hi. Trying to trace anyone who remembers a local man called Vincent Canning. He was very well known in the town in the late 80s. He died in 1990. Those who were around at the time will know the circumstances – no need for me to repeat them here. I was wondering – could someone here put me in touch with anyone who knew him or was related to him? Thanks.

Replies and comments came in very quickly. A few were recounting things that Canning had done; two mentioned Black Moss; one asked Danny how the driving lessons were going; several tagged in the same name: *Sarah Lewis was Canning.*

Danny had messaged her. She replied. She was Canning's sister and she seemed keen to talk to him. Very keen indeed.

Danny's cab dropped him off on a steep street packed with two up/two down terraces, Glodwick just outside the town centre. The front doors of each house were separated from the street by a single, red step. The street was, he thought, how people in London imagined the whole of Manchester to look like. It certainly struck Danny as being how a lot of Manchester had looked like to him in 1990.

Sarah Lewis came to the door seconds after he knocked. From the information and photos on her Facebook page, Danny guessed that she was in her mid-forties. She looked at least ten years older. She invited him in and Danny went from the street into the living room with one step. The tiny living room floor was partially covered by carpet tiles which appeared to have come from several sources. Loud dance music thumped from an upstairs room and there were empty bottles of wine and super strength cider scattered on the floor around the furniture. There was a large brown sofa which sagged so deeply in the centre that the middle seat cushion touched the floor; the main armchair was a car seat. Sarah Lewis caught Danny's eye as he looked around the room. She looked a little ashamed. Danny felt the same and looked directly at her rather than at the surroundings. 'Thanks very much for seeing me Sarah. It must have been a little weird, me messaging you out of the blue.'

'A little bit, yeah.' Sarah pronounced little as 'lickle', an old Manchester habit that Danny hadn't heard for a very long time. 'No one's been interested in our Vinny for ages. We pretended for long enough that we wasn't even related to him. Terrible really. He were my brother – he were a fookin' nuisance at times, but I still loved him. Blood's blood innit? Do you want tea?'

'Sure. Thanks. Why did you pretend he wasn't your brother?' Danny asked, following her into the tiny kitchen.

'Why'd ya fookin' think? Because we was the child killer's family, weren't we? We had to move twice. Red paint chucked at the windows. Shit through the letterbox. All sorts. Lived over in Bolton for a few years 'til things calmed down a bit. Sorry. Dint mean to shout. Sorry.'

'No, I understand. It must have been hard for you.'

'People we thought were friends blanked us in the street. Invisible we were. Put our mum into an early grave. Speaking of which... DUANE! TURN THAT FOOKIN' MUSIC DOWN.'

Danny didn't notice any change in the volume. Sarah motioned for him to sit at the small table that was pushed up against one side of the kitchen and handed Danny some very dark tea in a mug advertising social housing helpline numbers. 'Look, Sarah, I'm not here to upset you, or pry or cause trouble...'

'Bet all three are gunna happen, though, eh?' she interrupted.

'Probably, yes,' Danny admitted. His accent had dropped several notches since he'd entered the house, mirroring the person he was talking to. *Just like the old days.* 'Do you mind if I record this on my phone? Just so I get everything right. It's not for broadcast or anything. Just for the record'

'Yeah, go on, then.'

He placed his iPhone on the table, switching on a recording app he'd downloaded. The app looked like an old-fashioned cassette player and two wheels began rotating to show Danny that it was recording. 'I was really involved in the murder of the kid up at Black Moss,' he explained.

'I saw his body the morning it was discovered. There was so much going on at the time, then when your brother's body was found, everything came to a halt. It left so many unanswered questions.'

'Tell me about it. I didn't believe what the police said at the time and I don't believe it now,' Sarah said, staring at the wheels on Danny's recording app.

'What did you tell the police at the time?'

'That no way our Vinny would do that to a kid. And that no way he'd top himself, either. No way. But they wouldn't listen. They treated me like shit, especially sending that copper round – they knew full well Vinny hated that copper.'

'Which one?'

'That DC Cave bint. She was always on our Vinny's back. Always hassling him around town. Trying to get him to act the snitch for her. He hated doing it, but sometimes he had to. She had him by the goolies. He was out of prison on licence half the time and she had the power to send him back inside just like that. He was frightened to death of her.'

Danny glanced down at his phone app to make sure the virtual wheels were still turning. They were. 'So, DC Cave knew Vinny before all the business up at Black Moss?'

'Course she fookin' did! She was on him all the time.'

'And did you tell this to the police at the time?'

'Yep. But who do you think they sent 'round to take me statement when Vinny's body was discovered? I said I didn't want to talk to her, but she reckoned she was the only one available. Short-staffed 'cos of Strangeways. She had shit on me as well. I never claimed I were an angel. Neither were our Vinny. But she told me if I kicked up a fuss I'd be inside again. So, I kept quiet. Fat lot of difference it would have made, anyhow. I even tried the local paper – they didn't wanna know either. That's the way it works, innit? No fooker listens to the likes of us. Not the police. Not nobody.'

'Well, I'm listening, Sarah. I really am. What do you think happened to Vinny?'

She lit another cigarette. 'You'll think I'm barmy. Everyone round here does.'

'I know the feeling. I won't think that. Not in the slightest.'

She sighed, exhaling smoke at the same time. 'The police. That MP up the hill who died in the crash. All powerful people, aren't they? All in it together. Looking after their own. Scratching each other's backs. I reckon our Vinny saw something he shouldn't have saw. Heard something he shouldn't have heard. And some fooker thought, "No one will miss this scrote. Let's get rid. But hang on a minute. Maybe he could be useful for one last thing. I can kill two birds with one stone here: sort out Vinny Canning and blame the death of that kid on him at the same time." And that's what did for our Vinny.'

'Do you have any proof of this, Sarah?'

'Absolutely none whatso-fookin-ever. But Vinny was scared before he died. Scared the cops were out to get him. Scared he was going to get the blame for something he didn't do. People thought Vinny was mad. Maybe he was, but he wasn't daft. You think I'm mad too, don't you?

Danny thought about Jan Cave's clear denial about knowing Vinny Canning. *She looked me in the eye and lied. It's happened. The first out and out lie. Right there.* 'No, Sarah, I don't think you're mad in the slightest.'

FORTY-FOUR

5.40pm Wednesday 25 April 1990

Danny had been outside Strangeways' prison for nearly twenty-four hours. Throughout the day, he'd been fully expecting Robert Crane to return so he could take a break, but so far, nothing. *I am in serious danger of entering into the hallowed halls of the Twenty-four-Hour Club, here,* he thought. *It would be just like that bastard Crane to turn up at the last minute to make sure I don't.*

He scribbled notes, preparing for the package he had been asked to do for the six o'clock news. He'd been doing items on the hour throughout the day, many of them live. Doing that many live reports had certainly cured him of any lingering nerves he had about speaking off the cuff. *Work out the first and last things you're going to say, plot three key points to make in the middle, then join them up – easy.*

As he wrote, he spotted Gary Keenan approaching in the rearview mirror. He was rolling two tyres up the street, had a Marantz tape recorder over one shoulder and a cigarette dangling from his lips. Danny got out. 'Danny boy!' the engineer cried. 'You read my mind. I'd rather not jack this car up with you still inside, if that's all the same. The local scrotes have been out again, have they? This is the third fresh pair of tyres since this started.'

Gary handed Danny the tape recorder: 'Got you a fresh Marantz too. Figure your one would be knackered.'

'Well, I have it on good authority that it's all going to end today, Gary.'

'Is that right?' said the engineer, spitting out his cigarettes and jacking up the radiocar to change the first tyre. Well if it does, you're on strict instructions to let Robert Crane know asap.'

'Strict instructions from who?' Danny asked.

'From Robert Crane, you dick. You don't think he wants you to get any of the glory for this, do you? They've put him in a hotel down the road to rest up, but it's only five minutes away, so he can dash over if it all kicks off and do the final report. You must contact him on pain of death, got that?'

'Got it, Gary.'

'Grand. You doing something for the six?'

'Yup.'

'You'd better crack on then.'

Danny took the cassette from his old Marantz and put it into the fresh recorder Gary Keenan had brought with him. He lined up a clip from an interview he'd done earlier in the day with a solicitor who represented several men who had been in the jail. The man had sought Danny out – the radio car was a giveaway – telling him his clients had asked him to put out their message about conditions in the jail via Manchester Radio. Standing next to the car as Gary worked on the tyres, Danny made a note of where the start of the clip was on the four-digit counter on the face of the Marantz. Then he did the same with some atmospheric sounds he'd recorded earlier in the afternoon – the noise of sirens and music being blasted at the remaining rioters. He fed the clips back to the radio station and prepared to feed his own voice down the line too. At ten minutes to six, he rang the newsroom. Mike Sharston answered. *Christ, we are short-staffed if Sharston's come out of his cave.*

'Hi, Mike. Piece for the six. Right, here's the cue,' he said. 'Ready? Okay.'

Danny said the words of the cue slowly so Sharston could type then: *The 24th day of the stand-off at Strangeways' Jail is drawing to a close with the authorities seemingly no closer to ending the longest prison disturbance this country has ever seen.*

Meanwhile, a solicitor for some of the inmates who've already given themselves up says he believes there's now just five rioters left inside the prison. Danny Johnston is outside the jail and sends this report.

'Okay? So, mix in a bit of the atmos at the start then bring in my voice after two seconds. Here we go. Three, two, one:

Day 24 of the riot has seen more sirens and more music blasted at the remaining inmates, neither of which seems to have made the slightest bit of difference to their resolve. They're still on the roof, still shouting defiant messages and still showing no signs of giving up their protest – despite the loss of a key figure, Alan Lord. He was snatched by prison officers yesterday. Mark Tarporley, a Manchester solicitor representing several men involved in the disturbances, says he believes just five inmates are left, including the so-called ringleader of the riot, Paul Taylor.'

Danny paused and said: 'Right, so the clip of Tarporley goes there; end it when he says, "my information is that the number is just five," then I'll round it up. Three, two, one:

It's hard to believe that just five men are still in control of Strangeways – what's even more incredible is that there doesn't seem to be a thing that the prison authorities, the Home Office or the British Government can do about it… other than wait. This is Danny Johnston, for Manchester Radio News, at Strangeways Jail.'

Danny waited a few seconds and then said: 'Okay, I'll assume that's fine unless I hear otherwise.'

The line went dead. He lit a cigarette and flicked on the radio. 'All I Wanna Do Is Make Love To You' by Heart segued into the news jingle, followed by the news and Danny's report. *I'm finally starting to enjoy this job.*

Danny watched as the TV reporters started and finished their live reports for their six o'clock bulletins. *I could do that. Might need a haircut and some better clothes. But, yeah. Why not?*

The radio car dropped slowly to its normal height as Gary loosened the jack. 'Very good that, Danny boy. Nice to hear a fresh voice on this. Getting sick of Crane saying the same things in a different order all day long.'

'Thanks Gary,' Danny replied, offering the engineer a cigarette with a smile. 'But, as I've pointed out before, I'm very much straight.'

'You may be straight, but you're not very observant.'

'How do you mean?'

'Look.'

Gary nodded towards the roof of the jail. The five remaining rioters were gathering at the left side of the roof. As they did so, a cherry picker rose slowly to meet them. There was a wave of raised voices across the site. 'Fuck me, it's ending,' shouted Danny. 'It's actually ending.'

'Right,' said Gary. 'You ring the news desk. I'll check the signal ready to go live and line up some extra cable in case you have to go walkabout. This is your big chance, Danny. Don't fuck it up.'

'But what about Crane? Strict instructions to call him, you said.'

The engineer opened the boot of the radio car and pulled out a large reel of microphone cable. 'Fuck him, Danny! There's no time. Go, go, go!'

Danny rang the news desk. A young woman answered. 'Err. Hello. Sorry. Manchester Radio newsroom, can I help you?'

'Hi, it's Danny at Strangeways. Who's that?'

'It's Michaela.'

Danny was thrown: 'Who?'

'Michaela. The work placement student.'

So THAT'S her name. 'Right, of course. Michaela, who else is there?'

'No one. They've gone to the pub.'

'What?' Danny couldn't believe what he was hearing. 'Shit me. Really?'

'Yes. Is anything wrong?'

'The riot. It's ending. Right now. I need you to ring Sharston, get him back here and tell whoever's on air that they need to be ready to take a live feed from the jail as soon as possible.'

'FUCK SHARSTON, DANNY!' shouted Gary. 'GO LIVE NOW!'

'But the protocol to break into the schedule is for it to be okayed by Sharston.'

'NOW, YOU TWAT, NOW!'

'Michaela,' said Danny. 'Patch a talkback feed up to the studio.'

'What?' the young woman said. 'I have no idea what you're talking about.'

'Shit. Okay. Forget it. Tell the presenter to take the outside broadcast feed in exactly thirty seconds. Start counting backwards from thirty in your head slowly. Keep the phone line open and run to the studio and keep counting. When you get to zero, tell him to slide up the OB fader. Whatever he says, don't take no for an answer. In thirty seconds. Add one-thousands to get real seconds. 1030, 1029, like that. Got it?'

'Yes.'

'Great Michaela. Now, start…'

'Okay… 1030, 1029…'

Danny listened as Michaela's voice faded away. He was counting too. The studio was fifteen seconds away, giving her another fifteen to convince the presenter to do as they were told. Tight. *But do-able.*

Gary Keenan handed Danny a set of headphones and a microphone as he unravelled a looped pile of cable at their feet. 'Slick idea that, Danny boy. Like your style.'

Danny nodded as he continued a whispered count.

'…1022, 1021, 1020…'

'Might, work, might not. Depends how thick the presenter is. Knowing our presenters, pretty thick…'

'Shut the fuck up Gary… *1015, 1014, 1013…'*

'Don't start turning into a diva on me. Ready?'

Danny put on the headphones but left one ear uncovered so he could hear what was going on around him. He could hear the station output: 'Dirty Cash' by The Adventures of Stevie V. He gave Gary a thumbs up.

'Good luck, our kid,' said Gary.

Danny watched as the first of the final five rioters on the roof of

Strangeways jail reached out towards the cherry picker cradle.
'1005, 1004, 1003, 1002, 1001...'

FORTY-FIVE

4.30pm Wednesday 22 June 2016

'She lied, Kate. Right to my face. I checked back with Canning's sister. Rang her and went through the whole thing a second time. Cave told me she didn't know Vincent Canning, yet his sister says he was her snitch and he was terrified of her. Why would she do that?'

Kate gestured for Danny to sit down, but instead he kept pacing across the open area of her office. 'I don't know,' she said. 'I really don't.'

'You must have come across her back in the day. Did Cave seem straight to you?'

'Too bloody straight. Never got so much of a sentence out of her for the paper. She played things absolutely by the book. She never seemed to have the common touch, could never connect with people like Dad could. But he won't have a word said against her. So, yeah, I don't know why she'd do that.'

'What about Canning's sister? She said she tried to get the local paper to look into it. Was that the *Messenger?'*

'I'm afraid it might very well have been, yes,' Kate confirmed, looking at the floor rather than at Danny.

'So, the paper knew there were questions about Canning's suicide and did nothing? They ignored her?'

'She'd turn up at the front desk, off her head, shouting and screaming,' admitted Kate. 'Every newsroom has them, Danny, you know that. Nutters claiming cover up this and conspiracy that. Whoever is the most junior in the office normally gets sent out to speak to them. I'd moved up the ranks by then, so it never fell to me.'

'And you didn't think to tell me?'

'It's was a bloody long time ago, Danny! You've haven't exactly got a photographic memory about this yourself, have you? You were pissed most of the time, I believe.'

'Great. Thanks for that, Kate.'

'Sorry. That was out of line. Apologies.'

'Forget it. Look… I really need to speak to your dad, Kate. Something isn't right about this. Is it okay if we ring him?'

'Of course. He's got Jonathan with him at his house. Mutual babysitting.'

Kate speed dialled the number on her desk phone and put it on loudspeaker. Jonathan answered. 'Hi, Johnny. How was school?'

'Fine, thanks. Can I have some biscuits? Grandad's got some Hobnobs and he says they are the greatest biscuits ever made.'

'He's probably right. Can you put Grandad on the phone please? Hold the receiver to his ear, it's easier for him.' A pause.

'Dad, it's me,' she said. 'I've got Danny with me and you're on the loudspeaker, so don't say anything libellous, okay?'

'Spoilsport,' said the former detective, eliciting a small smile from both Danny and Kate.

'John, it's Danny. Vincent Canning – the suicide up at Black Moss – I've been talking to his sister. Did you know he was a regular informant for Jan Cave?'

'No. No, I didn't. But cops kept grasses to themselves in those days.'

'His sister says that he was scared of DC Cave,' Danny continued. 'Frightened to death was the expression she used. Yet she was sent to get a statement from his sister when he died and there was no disclosure that DC Cave knew him at the time. That's not usual, is it?'

'Not usual. No. Didn't even know he had a sister.'

'I spoke to Cave about this and she denied ever knowing Canning. Yet his sister says she was on him constantly. Why would she do that?'

'Haven't got a clue, Danny. It was a very bad time, as you know. As Kate knows, too. Very bad.'

Danny looked at Kate and she indicated that he should carry on with his questions. 'I know John. I'm so sorry. You had so much to deal with – with your wife being so ill and having the Black Moss boy to investigate and then Canning's suicide.'

There was silence from the speakerphone. 'Not me, Danny.'

'How do you mean?' asked Danny.

'Dad had nothing to do with the Canning case,' said Kate. 'By the time Mum had died and he'd been given compassionate leave, it was all sorted.'

'Who sorted it?' Danny asked.

'DC Cave,' came the crackly reply from the speaker. 'I was very…' The old man struggled to get the words out. '… grateful at the time.'

'Of course, John. Completely understand. Listen, thanks very much. I'll speak to you later.'

'Okay Danny. Take care.'

Kate leant close to the speaker: 'I'll talk to you later, Dad,' she said and returned the phone to its normal setting. 'Okay. That's really, really strange,' she said.

'Cave told me your dad did all the work on the Canning case. He says he didn't. Well, I know who I believe. Cave said she didn't know Canning, but his sister says she definitely did. Again, my money is not on DC Cave. It's smells like shit to me.'

'You're not going to do anything weird, are you Danny?'

'No. I'm going to go back to the hotel and think it through. Don't worry. I just need to get my head around it… doesn't make sense.'

'Okay, I'll be picking Jonathan up from Dad's then heading home; call me later.' Kate stood up and gave Danny a hug.

'I will.'

'No weird stuff, Danny Something, okay?'

'No weird stuff, Kate.'

'Promise?'

'Promise.'

Danny made his way down the stairs. When he was out of earshot he made a call on his mobile: 'Gary? It's Danny. Great, mate. Listen… you're the master of all things electronic, aren't you? How easy is it to get into an office protected by a keycode, when you haven't actually got the keycode?'

FORTY-SIX

6.45pm Wednesday 25 April 1990

Danny talked live on air for more than twenty minutes as Glynn Williams, Martin Brian, John Murray, Mark Williams and Paul Taylor came down from the roof of Strangeways jail. The words flowed out of him and he decided he wouldn't stop until someone told him to. Eventually, a call came through to the radio car mobile phone from the studio. Gary took it, nodded and made a thumbs up sign, then made a cutthroat sign to Danny, who brought his live report to a close: *'Tomorrow morning – or maybe even tonight – the clean-up operation will begin at Strangeways jail. As that's happening, so will another task: that of finding out how this happened and most importantly, why it happened. This is Danny Johnston for Manchester Radio News at Strangeways jail in Manchester.'*

Danny waited a few beats, got the all clear and took off his headphones. Gary Keenan shoved a cigarette between Danny's lips and lit it for him. 'Well done, our kid,' said the engineer. 'Amazing.'

'Cheers, Gary. Don't know where it all came from. Doubt I could do it again if you paid me.'

'That was Sharston on the phone, by the way. He came out of the pub sharpish when he heard. Don't worry. He's cock-a-hoop. Says you were right to go straight to air; he loved the countdown bit with whassername the student…'

'Michaela, apparently.'

'I'll take your word for it. And he says it was the right call to go for it rather than wait for Bobby Crane. Which might prove helpful as I can see Bobby heading this way and he has a face on him like a tropical fucking thunderstorm…'

Danny turned just as Robert Crane pushed his forearm across his chest and forced Danny backwards against the side of the radio car. 'You sly little twat. You knew fucking well you were supposed to call me if it all went off and you deliberately took the tale for yourself.'

'It wasn't like that, mate,' countered Danny. 'Seriously.'

Gary Keenan grabbed Crane, spun him around and pushed him away with little visible effort. 'He did the right thing,' the engineer shouted. 'If he'd waited we'd have got nothing. And Shartson agrees. So, stop being a prick and calm the fuck down. Danny's got it covered for the seven, haven't you mate?'

'Yes, I do, Gary. Thanks.' Danny glanced up the road and saw prison officials putting up crash barriers. Journalists and camera crews rushed to get a good spot. The final government statement of the riot was about to be made. 'Look, the Home Office bod is coming out,' Danny said to Crane. 'This is it. The end. Robert, do you want to get the audio for that while I prep a piece for the seven? It can be a co-production – you and me - how about that?'

'Three and a half fucking weeks I've been here,' Crane muttered as he pulled a microphone out of his pocket, tested the Marantz and half walked, half ran towards the barriers.

'The mighty Robert Crane,' Gary said, shaking his head. 'Reduced to being your audio bitch. Why not get him to knock off a few vox pops while he's at it? Just to plunge the knife in even deeper?'

'Not a bad idea that, Gary. Will you tell him, or shall I?'

'Please, please! Can I? This has been a long time coming. Arrogant bastard deserves this. Very important lesson, Danny boy. Try not to be a twat to anyone on your way up. They're very likely to remember it on your way down.'

The engineer walked towards where Robert Crane was caught in a scrum with other reporters, surrounding an official from the Home Office, who was shaking his head a great deal. 'Gary?' Danny shouted after him. 'Thanks very much.'

'No worries, mate. Seize the day and all that.'

The statement from the Home Office to mark the end of the riot was clearly short and sweet. Robert Crane was already heading back towards them, checking the audio on his recorder. 'Oi, Bobby!' shouted Gary. 'While you've got your Marantz out, one more thing…'

FORTY-SEVEN

10.40pm Wednesday 22 June 2016

Danny had arranged to meet Gary in a side street across the road from the mill that housed Jan Cave's office. He'd walked there from the hotel rather than take a cab or a tram; although he wasn't in the habit of breaking and entering, he figured the less indication that he'd been anywhere near the site, the better. He'd also decided it would be best to meet away from the site to avoid any CCTV cameras around the mill.

Gary pulled up in a white van that looked remarkably similar to the one Danny remembered him driving in 1990. He'd advised Danny to wear nondescript clothes; not a problem for Gary as he was wearing the same jeans and grey sweatshirt combo he always wore. The night was warm and clear. The main road dividing them from the mill was busy with traffic heading into Manchester. 'Alright, Danny boy? Bit different for a Wednesday night out this, innit?'

'Gary, you don't have to do this if you don't want to – I'd completely understand.'

'Don't be daft. It's great, this is. Look. The kids are all grown up. The wife barely talks to me. I'm long past my sell-by date at work… this is the closest thing to excitement that's come my way for years. Bring it on.'

'As long as you're sure. Okay, this is what I know so far…'

The engineer held up a hand. His fingers were calloused, and the palm was peppered with tiny cuts and burns. 'I rather suspect that the less I know, the better, Danny boy. Has someone who might be bad 'un been lying to you?'

'Yes.'

'Might there be a few answers in this office that might catch aforementioned bad 'un?'

'Yes.'

'Then that's all I need to know – let's crack on, then.'

The inside of Gary's van was essentially a mobile version of his office at MRFM. It was awash with tools, electronica and a rainbow of electrical tape. Gary took a utility belt that bulged with small-scale tools and gadgets and wrapped it around his waist. He also produced a couple of old baseball caps, banging them against his leg to remove the dust. 'Put this on and pull it down over your face,' he advised Danny, who took the cap and glanced at the small logo on the front. 'Blue? The boy band, Blue? What kind of baseball cap is this?' he asked.

'A free one. Now shut the fuck up, turn it inside out, put it on and let's go.'

The two men crossed the road and walked around the outer edge of the mill car park, which was dotted with just a few cars. Danny led the way, showing the engineer the office entrance. 'Don't be tempted to look for cameras,' Gary said. 'There will definitely be cameras. Just keep your head down and your cap pulled low and keep going.'

They got to the front door. 'Just see if there's any security blokes about,' instructed Gary. 'These places share one bloke between several sites. They only come around every few hours. Just take a peek, will you?'

Danny turned on the step and looked around from under the rim of his cap. He heard a double clink, followed by a beeping noise and turned to see that Gary had already opened the main door. 'Christ, Gary. You don't mess about do you? Where did you learn to do that?'

'Lost count of the number of times I've had to break into the radio station over the years because the security system has ballsed up. It's simple enough. You just need to know how to do it.'

'Okay. How *do* you do it?'

'Never you mind. Where's the next door?'

As they headed towards the second door, Gary put a small LED torch into his mouth. 'I think I heard something,' Gary whispered.

Danny turned towards the outer door, looked around and saw it was all clear. Again, he heard a double clink and a beep. 'I fell for it again, didn't I?' Danny asked, rhetorically.

'You certainly did, Danny boy,' Gary replied, talking around the torch in his mouth as he pushed open the inner door. 'Now, let's not fuck about, please. In and out, okay? It might be helpful to know what we're actually looking for.'

'Yes, it would, wouldn't it?' Danny agreed, stepping gingerly into the small office and switching on the torch setting on his iPhone. Jan Cave's office was as neat and frugal as he remembered. A desk with minimal stationery – no computer – two chairs, a printer, framed certificates on the walls and a double-fronted metal cupboard; that was the full extent of *Jan Cave – Child Protection Consultant.* Danny and Gary looked at the cupboard, then at each other.

'I've been asked to open more metal filing cabinets by more radio station managers than you've had liquid lunches, Danny boy. So, yes, I can open it.' The older man took a small, sharp metal tool like a dentist's pick and applied it to the cupboard's padlock, which snapped open almost instantly. The pair shone their lights inside.

'She really likes stationery, doesn't she?' the engineer said, taking the torch from his mouth and casting its beam across neat shelves of sticky notes, pens, pencils, A4 sheaves of paper and highlighter pens. Beneath them were drop files filled with child protection consultancy cases going back to the early 2000s. Danny flicked through them: schools, sports clubs, youth organisations, dance schools and virtually every local council social services department in the area were represented.

'And she's been very busy since she cashed in her thirty-year ticket from the police,' added Danny. 'Very busy indeed.'

At the bottom of the cupboard was a large metal box. It looked old and out of place; it was also padlocked. The two men knelt down to take a closer look. Gary's joints clicked and cracked with the effort. 'Last peep, Danny boy, then we need to be on our way. We're pushing our luck, here. Not to mention the damage it's doing to my old bones.'

Gary popped the lock with the same ease he'd done previously. He pushed himself up from the floor and put his torch back in his mouth as he put away his lock-picking tool. A perfect circle of LED illumination wobbled and wavered across the box. Danny flipped up the hook-and-eye clasp that held it shut, then opened the lid and looked inside.

FORTY-EIGHT

10.15pm Friday 27 April 1990

'The free bar doesn't look like it's going to run out anytime soon, does it?' Danny was on his tip toes as he shouted into Gary Keenan's ear over the loud music being blasted out across the packed upstairs room of the city centre pub.

'There's a very good reason for that, Danny boy,' Gary replied. 'See Mike Sharston over there?' Danny glanced over at the head of news, who had an arm around Robert Crane's shoulders and was animatedly waving a bottle of beer in the air as he spoke. 'He's got a blank cheque in his pocket – literally, a blank cheque from management – to pay for us to get battered into next week. And it's largely thanks to you. So, drink up, mate, 'cos it'll never happen again.'

'Will do, Gary, will do.'

Danny ordered 'two very large vodka and oranges, please,' from one of the harassed-looking bar staff.

'Do you mean a double, sir?' she asked.

'No, he said a VERY large one,' clarified Gary.

Two triple vodka and oranges were delivered – no money changed hands and the two looked across the room. Around the edges of the room, two dozen people were shouting, screaming, laughing and arguing as a DJ played music at teeth-rattling volume. Beth Hall was dancing with one of the sports reporters, grinding her backside against him to De La Soul's 'The Magic Number' as several other journalists cheered them on. Pauline the receptionist was dancing on her own with a half-empty bottle of wine in one hand, until one of the studio producers began to do some grinding of his own against her. Pauline dropped her bottle and it smashed on the hardwood surface of the dance floor. A cheer went up.

'Things are about to go downhill very, very rapidly,' Danny offered.

'I know. Fucking great, isn't it?' added Gary, clinking his glass against

Danny's and heading off into the fray.

Danny leant on the bar, not wanting to lose his prime place as order after order came at the staff from those present. A woman, aged about twenty-one wearing a baggy 'Cool As Fuck' t-shirt, jeans and Doc Martens approached him with a huge vase-like glass of white wine. A hefty blob of wine seemed to spill over the rim with every step. 'Daaaaaanny!' she cried, giving him a hug and spilling more wine down the back of his shirt. 'Daaaaaanny The Champion of the World! Have you heard? I've been offered a job at the station. Newsroom assistant! Can you believe it? All because I could count to thirty backwards!'

'But more importantly, it's because you refused to take no for an answer,' he shouted. 'You convinced that presenter to do your bidding and slide up that fader with the power of your personality. That's what it's all about. Good for you.'

The music changed to 'Put Your Hands Together' by DMob. 'Come and have a dance,' Michaela shouted, tugging at the sleeve of Danny's shirt.

'Maybe later. Just finishing my drink,' he said, tapping his glass and smiling. She shrugged as if to say: *you're loss…* and tottered off towards the dance floor. As she went away, Danny saw that Mike Sharston and Beth Hall were heading his way. The news editor put a hand on Danny's shoulder and pointed in the direction of the exit. The three walked through the crowd. Sharston pushed open the function room door and walked through onto a landing. The noise level dropped significantly. The news editor put his pint glass onto a cigarette machine that was pushed up against a wall next to the toilets and Danny did the same. Beth stood next to Sharston, leaning slightly against his shoulder to steady herself.

'I'm not in trouble already, am I?' Danny asked, swaying slightly and making a mental note to buy some cigarettes when they were done.

'No, Danny. Definitely not,' said Sharston. 'Your stock is still very high. Too high, if anything.'

'I've no idea what that means, but if I'm not in the shit, that's good enough for me.' Danny made another mental note: *be careful… he's still your boss and you're really quite drunk.*

Beth spoke next: 'It means you were a bit *too* good at Strangeways the other night.'

'Still no idea what you're talking about, Beth,' said Danny. 'But it sounds vaguely like a compliment, so I shall give it a good home.'

'Listen, Danny,' said the news editor. 'You know that the TV guys are always sniffing around our reporters, picking off the best talent. It's happened for years. There's not a lot I can do about it, other than get something in return. For the last few years I've had a deal with ITV and the BBC: if you want reporters, don't go behind my back – come to me first. I'll tell you who's worth having and who's to be avoided.'

There's was a loud crash as Robert Crane came through the function room door. Danny gave him a smile; Crane gave him the finger.

'Danny, your contract's coming up…'

Oh, hello. Here we go…

'… and Beth has been telling me about how you've put everything into this dead kid out on the moors,' Sharston continued. An unpleasant thought snapped into Danny's head: *shit! What's wrong with me? I've barely given it a moment's thought since I was called out to Strangeways.*

'… doing stuff in your own time. Getting friendly with the local cops. Even carrying on with it after you got your face bashed in. Fair play.'

'I'm still baffled, Mike, to be honest…'

'We're letting you go, Danny,' interrupted Beth. She winked at Danny as she said it.

'What?'

'Letting you go to ITN. They're after fresh blood, and having spoken to Beth, we think they should go for you. We'd already decided, but this Strangeways thing put a cherry on it. We broke the story first because of your quick thinking. In fact, it made me want to keep hold of you… but that wouldn't be fair.'

Robert Crane came back into view at the other end of the hallway. Two other journalists were pushing him through the door back into the function room. He was pointing at Danny and shouting. 'Love Shack' by the B-52s drowned out what he was actually saying, but Danny felt he could still get a sense of it.

'So, it's down to you, Danny,' said Beth, ignoring the commotion. 'Do you want a job in network telly, or not?'

FORTY-NINE

10.54pm Wednesday 22 June 2016

'It's just a load of crap, mate, let's go,' Gary said, pointing the beam of his torch directly into Danny's face after they'd seen the contents of the locked box.

'Shine the light back on the box, Gary,' said Danny. 'Let me give it a proper looking at, then we can go.'

The cold LED circle flicked back to the bottom of the cupboard. Danny sat on the floor and looked at the contents. There were old copies of the *Manchester Evening News* and other local and regional newspapers, some going back nearly thirty years. Tucked in the top right corner was a shoe box. Danny opened it; inside were old cassette tapes. The brands were ones that Danny hadn't seen for a long time: AGFA, Memorex and even some with Boots logos on them. Each had an initial and a date on them, nothing else. 'Time's up, let's go,' whispered Gary.

Alongside the newspapers and the shoe box full of cassettes was a padded, fawn-coloured jewellery box. It had a tiny gold-coloured clasp on it holding down the lid. Danny opened the clasp and a ballerina on a spring popped up and did a slight turn, accompanied by a few plinking notes of music. Both were enough to startle him into dropping the musical box. 'You big soft arse, Danny. Out, now!'

Danny turned to Gary and grabbed his hand, guiding the beam of the light into the overturned music box. It had a false bottom underneath the ballerina mechanism. Inside it were a dozen or so tiny teeth, yellow and flecked with brown dots and smears.

'Jesus fuck, Danny!'

'I know, I know. Out!'

In a blur of movement, Danny shoved the lid back on the musical box, refitted the clasp and closed the lid of the metal box. At the same moment, a yowling, deafening alarm went off. 'What have you done?'

Gary shouted over the din.

'Nothing,' Danny yelled back. 'Finish up and let's go.'

Gary clicked shut the padlocks and the two men made their way out of the office, closing the door behind them. They did the same at the outer door. The alarm was even louder outside the office. Instinctively, Danny glanced around, and his eye caught the security camera tucked in the corner between the wall and the ceiling. He paused a beat, then took off his baseball cap, stared at the camera and gave it the middle finger.

FIFTY

10.15pm Friday 4 May 1990

Management at Manchester Radio quickly discovered that since joining the station in October of the previous year, Danny hadn't taken a single day of annual leave. There was no way they were going to pay him for the time he was owed, so the only solution was to reduce his four weeks' notice to five working days. Seven days after being told he'd been offered a job, he was gone.

One week after the post-Strangeways party, a smaller, quieter send-off was held for Danny at the same venue. No function room was required this time, just a low-key corner of the radio station's favoured pub. There'd been a few swift words from Mike Sharston, some gifts – a dictionary signed by everyone at the station plus a twelve-bottle case of red wine – and the usual cheery words of good luck and promises to stay in touch. Pauline the receptionist told everyone who would listen that she'd always believed in Danny; Michaela the former placement student got drunk quickly and became a bit teary, vowing that she would never, ever forget Danny; Beth was very complimentary and had even given him a hug and a swift kiss on the cheek. Robert Crane was the only person not to show a face.

In ones and twos, people drifted away; before too long, Danny and Gary Keenan were the only ones left. Eking out a pair of expensive and large whiskies that Gary had bought for them, they sat on stools at the end of the bar. Despite it being Friday night, the pub was nearly empty. Danny looked around at the tired, dated fixtures and fittings. 'Why do we use this pub?' he asked Gary.

'It's the only place that'll have us. You should have seen the mess in the upstairs function room after last week. Jesus wept. Anywhere else would have barred us for life.'

'I won't miss it, if I'm honest,' Danny offered.

'Don't give it a backward glance, mate,' the engineer said. 'Get yourself off to London and do your thing. You deserve it.'

'I don't know how you lot will survive without me, Gary.'

'We always do. They come and go, but the station always survives.'

'Ah. But they'll always remember me.'

'Course we will.' Gary drank the last of his malt and stepped down unsteadily from his stool. 'Here's one: Knock, knock…'

'What?'

'Try again. Knock, knock…'

'Who's there?' Danny asked with a sigh.

'Danny.'

'Danny who?'

'That's showbusiness, mate. See you sometime.'

Gary waved as he went but didn't turn around. Danny asked the landlord to call him a taxi and cradled his whisky until the driver came to the pub door. 'Taxi for Danny,' the driver shouted.

'Yeah,' Danny confirmed. 'Taxi for Danny.' He drained his glass and left.

When he got home, Danny's flat was even emptier than usual. The minimal possessions Danny owned were already boxed and ready to be driven south the following morning. His answer machine had yet to be packed away though, and the red light flashed to show he had messages. The digital display showed there were three of them.

Message One: *'Danny. John Smithdown. Hello. Just a belated thank you for your help with the Black Moss case. Obviously, I've had a lot on my plate with the funeral and everything, but DC Cave seems to have had things under control. I hear you finally managed to get yourself to Strangeways. Anyway, let's have a pint in my local, maybe even a curry.*

Message Two: *'Danny Something! Pick up, pick up. It's Kate here. Remember me? I know you're Lord Scoop of Strangeways now, but give me a call. We've got a real opportunity to do a proper job on the Black Moss kid, get him identified, but I need your help. Someone said you'd left Manchester Radio. That can't be right, can it? No, it can't be. Anyway. Call me back.'*

Message Three: *'Danny, it's Brenda from the kids' home. Hi. Look, I wanted to let you know that Little Paul has gone AWOL. He seemed to have taken a shine to you and I was wondering if you'd heard anything. Let me know as soon as poss.'*

Danny thought for a few moments. Then he deleted all three messages and went to bed. The next day he moved to London, leaving everything behind him.

PART III

FIFTY-ONE

12.05am Thursday 23 June 2016

Gary Keenan was sitting on the floor of Danny's hotel room with his head inside the mini-bar fridge. He came out with a bottle of lager, a whisky miniature and a can of Coke. Tossing the Coke to Danny he popped the top of the lager with a fitting on the Swiss Army knife attached to his belt. Half the lager went in one tilt. 'Mini-bar lager… it's never quite cold enough,' he muttered. The second half of the lager went as quickly as the first. The whisky followed it at the same pace.

Danny slid down the side of the bed and joined Gary on the floor, watching enviously as the engineer reached for a second lager. Danny opened his Coke and took a half-hearted sip.

'So, Gary,' he said.

'So, Danny.'

There was silence. 'I suppose we should talk about the whole teeth-in-the-box thing,' Danny said.

'It would seem sensible, yes. Might also be worth touching on something else while we're at it. That being… WHY THE FUCK YOU GAVE A FULL-FRONTAL FINGER TO THE SECURITY CAMERA!'

'I think it was pretty obvious that we were there anyway,' Danny offered. 'We didn't exactly cover our tracks like ninjas did we. Christ. It was creepy as fuck. Never heard a bloke scream like you did back there, Gary.'

'Is that what you journalists call gallows humour? Because it isn't funny. Not in the slightest.'

Silence again. Gary scraped at the label of his beer bottle with his thumbnail. 'I've seen some weird shit in my time, but that took the biscuit,' said the engineer. 'Souvenir teeth? That's trophy shit, that is. *Weird* trophy shit. What the fuck is this all about, Danny?'

'When I was first out on the moors in 1990,' Danny explained. 'That kid's body was out there in the sand. The cops were trying to hold a sheet up in the wind, trying to stop people from seeing what was going on. They seemed more concerned that people would notice what a mess they were making of it – more concerned about that than they were about the kid. It feels like that all over again. *That's* what the fuck this is all about, Gary. I always felt like they fucked up – now it feels worse than that. It's pretty clear the police have been covering something up all along. The only people involved in this – the only ones whose stories don't match up – are the cops. But what am I supposed to do about it – go to the police? How much good will that do, apart from *no* fucking good?'

The engineer finished his second beer and threw it into the bin, rattling it so hard it nearly toppled over. 'Understood, Danny boy. But prancing about in front of the camera wasn't perhaps the subtlest move you could have made at this stage of the game, was it?'

'Yeah, I know,' Danny conceded. 'I just wanted to let them know that I know they're lying and I'm not going anywhere. Not this time. It was fishy as shit back in 1990; it stinks even worse now. Keeping a box of teeth inside a locked cupboard – who the fuck does that?'

'I can honestly say, I don't know anyone who does that,' Gary conceded. 'So, what's the plan?'

'First thing in the morning, we're back to that office. If she's there, confront her. If she isn't, we'll break back in and take a few things from that cupboard.'

'Thought you might say that. Then what?'

Danny stared at the writing on his can of Coke. He thought for a few moments: 'Fucked if I know.'

'It's a work in progress, then,' Gary said, trying to sound positive. 'Right you are. Mind if I crash here?'

'Sure.'

'No funny stuff though, right?'

'I think it's fair to say I'm not especially in the mood for any funny stuff, Gary.'

'Be like that then,' smiled the engineer. He got up, took a spare blanket from the wardrobe and grabbed the suitcase stand from the other side of the room, putting it in front of the armchair tucked into the corner. He sat down, stretched his legs out across the stand, covered himself with the blanket and closed his eyes. Within two minutes the engineer was asleep.

Danny stayed awake for quite some time. It wasn't Gary's snoring that stopped him from sleeping – though it didn't help – it was the thought of the teeth. And how small they were.

At 7.30 am, Danny nudged Gary awake. He put a cup of tea into one of the engineer's hands and a pastry he'd taken from the hotel restaurant into the other. 'Come on, lazy arse. Let's be having you. We've got weird shit to sort out.'

After paying £28 to have Gary's van released from the hotel's underground car park – *'I'll pay it Gary, stop fucking moaning'* – they headed back towards the mill and Jan Cave's office.

No side streets and baseball caps this time; the two men parked in front of the office, close to a double set of industrial bins. A security guard was there, looking at the keypad system. His stomach bulged under a dark blue jumper that was too small for him. He looked tired and was distractedly rubbing his shaven head: 'You the locksmiths?' he asked as Danny and Gary walked towards the front door.

'Yes indeed,' replied Gary, surprising Danny with the swiftness of his answer and the effectiveness of his lie. 'We've just come to assess it first and then we'll put a quote together.'

'Not sure how they got in,' offered the guard, 'but the system needs resetting or replacing, one or the other.'

Gary looked sagely at the keypad. 'Right. Well, whoever broke in knew exactly what they were doing. Professionals. No question about it. But, yeah, you need a whole new system here, mate. It's so old the bloke who installed it was probably wearing a powdered wig. Get it updated and keep the scrotes out, that's what I reckon.' Gary turned to face Danny. 'You go and look at the internals and I'll get this priced up.'

Danny nodded and walked past the security guard. As he did, Gary asked the guard: 'Don't suppose there's any chance of a brew, is there, mate?'

While Gary distracted the guard, Danny headed straight for Jan Cave's office. The door was open. Everything was gone. Other than the carpet – which appeared to have been hoovered – and a cream-coloured lampshade on the light fitting, the office was completely bare. Gary joined him at the door. 'Well either someone burgled the place after we left, or your mate the ex-policewoman has cleaned up and moved out,' he said, quietly. 'She's very efficient I'll give her that. I'll bet there was a CCTV link to her house. She was probably watching us all the time – especially your one-fingered salute at the end. Don't suppose she's left a tooth or two behind, has she?'

'Not as such, Gary, no.'

'Too much to hope for, I suppose. What now, Danny boy?'

'I don't know. Let me think.'

The security guard arrived with two cups of very dark tea. 'Nice one,' said Gary, taking the less chipped of the two mugs. 'What's your name, mate?' he asked the guard.

'Tariq.'

'Listen, Tariq,' Gary said. 'This is going to be a bigger job than expected. Have you got any contact details for the occupant? Our boss is out and about and we need to contact them asap so we can okay the work and get this office secure.'

'So sorry, no,' replied the guard. 'I'm just a temp for the firm with the contract; we've got several sites around here. I don't know any of the businesses at all.'

'Could you ask, please, Tariq?' Danny said. 'It'd be a massive help.'

The guard walked away from them, tugging at the walkie talkie attached to his belt. As he went, Danny motioned for Gary to follow him out of the building and he headed straight for the bins near their van. They were gunmetal grey, with twin plastic lids on and were easily six feet tall. 'Give me your penknife a minute,' Danny said to Gary. 'And then give me a leg up.'

Gary easily hoisted Danny up the side and into the first metal container. Along with various broken lamps and bits of chipboard, there were a dozen tied black bin liners. He pulled out the main blade of the penknife and sliced a bag; it was filled with paper coffee cups, takeaway cartons and some mail. The second was filled for a sports trophy company. The next bag was full of fishing magazines. The third was office stationery – much of it still sealed and unused – and junk mail, addressed to Jan Cave Consulting. Danny threw the bag out of the bin, climbed out and upended it in the car park. He began kicking at the various items of post, office waste and food wrappers. 'Here we go,' Danny said, picking up an envelope that looked different to the others. It wasn't a letter that had been sent to the office – it was one that was ready to be posted, but the envelope had been torn in two. Danny looked inside. There were two halves of a newspaper cutting inside. There were also two halves of a compliments slip; on it was written: 'Danny J's an accident waiting to happen. Will you tell him, or shall I?' It was signed 'Jan'.

Danny walked away and read the cutting with his back to Gary. He was silent for several minutes. Then he walked back, showing Gary the two envelope halves. 'I know this address,' said Danny. 'Let's go.'

Danny tucked the torn envelope into the inside pocket of his jacket. 'You okay, Danny?' queried the engineer. 'You look a bit weirded out.'

'I *am* a bit weirded out,' Danny confirmed.

The security guard came back across the car park as they got into the van. 'It's all good, Tariq,' Gary said, cheerily. 'We've found an alternative address. In fact, we'll pop round there right now in person. Don't worry. We'll tidy this lot up later.'

'I've got to hand it to you lads,' Tariq said. 'You are the most conscientious locksmiths I've ever come cross. Definitely, definitely recommending you next time there's a break in.'

'Cheers, Tariq!' Gary cried with a wave, as they drove out of the car park. They headed though Salford towards the motorway.

'So, where are we headed?' asked Gary.

'Oldham,' Danny replied, putting the postcode into Google Maps and letting the app guide the engineer to their destination.

'Lovely,' sighed Gary. 'Fucking lovely.'

They drove against the tide of the worsening rush hour traffic heading towards Manchester, heading for the ring road, then north west, away from the city centre, towards Oldham. 'Can't Stop the Feeling!' by Justin Timberlake was the soundtrack as they passed the police station. 'My ears just popped, then,' said Gary as the countryside opened out and they reached higher grounded. Danny said nothing. He was thinking about the cutting in his jacket pocket – more than that, he was thinking about Jan Cave's note attached to it.

'So, Danny boy,' Gary asked. 'Remember, I'm just a thick old radio engineer. Are we heading for the address on that envelope?'

'Yes, we are,' Danny confirmed. 'It was the only bit of mail in the bin bag that didn't have the office address on it. It was outgoing mail – due to be sent but it never got posted. She clearly changed her mind.'

The female Google Maps' voice told Gary that their destination was coming up on the left. Danny saw Kate hurrying her son into the car parked in the driveway of her father's house. She was surprised to see him. 'Danny? Bit early, isn't it?'

Jonathan ran over to Danny's side of the van. He opened his smart school blazer on one side, showing Danny the bag of Skittles poking out of his inside pocket. He put his finger to his lips, urging Danny not to say anything to his mum. 'Ah, the breakfast of champions,' Danny whispered. 'Your secret's safe with me, mate.'

'Grandad's inside, Danny,' Jonathan shouted as he raced back to the car. 'See you later.'

'Oh wow, Gary Keenan!' Kate said. 'Christ, haven't seen you for years. Double surprise. Danny, I can't stop, I've got to get Jonathan to school. Is everything okay?'

'Sure, Kate,' Danny said in his most reassuring voice. 'All Good. Speak later.' As he stepped out of the van, Danny went around to the driver's window and spoke quietly to the engineer: 'Gary. Just drop me off. I've got stuff to sort out here. I'll ring you later.'

'Okay, Danny boy. Fucked if I know what's going on, but I'm sure you'll tell me in the fullness of time. Or not.' His voiced changed from a whisper to a shout: 'Bye, Kate. Looking more sensational than ever.'

Gary drove off and Kate pulled away in her car too; Jonathan waved from the back seat. Danny walked inside John Smithdown's house. He watched as the older man shuffled across the living room to his favourite chair. Each step was a measured effort. Danny knew better than to offer help. He waited until the older man lowered himself slowly into the chair, then made himself known. 'Danny!' Smithdown said. 'What you doing here?'

Danny pulled a chair next to the retired detective and pulled the torn envelope from his pocket. He took out the two ripped pieces of the newspaper article, placed them on the arm of John Smithdown's chair and pushed them together, smoothing them out as best he could. The clipping had been well kept and showed little sign of age or damage – up until being torn in two at Jan Cave's office. It had been cut carefully from a paper as if in preparation for a scrapbook or archive. It had '*Manchester Evening News* library copy, please return' stamped on it and was dated Saturday 3 February 1973. The headline read:

CHILDREN RESCUED FROM 'HORROR HOUSE'

Danny placed a third piece of paper next to them: the compliment slip with Jan Cave's neat writing on it. Danny looked at Smithdown – his gaze wasn't returned. 'John. You've never, ever shitted me. Please don't shit me now. I've a lot of things to ask you about, but this one goes first. What the fuck is this?'

The old man continued looking at the torn article. There was a slight gap between the two pieces. With a shaking hand he touched one half of the cutting and pushed it, so it touched the other half. Finally, he looked at Danny. Former DI John Smithdown's eyes were wet, but he blinked the tears away. Danny read the cutting out loud. His voice was just a whisper.

A boy and girl were rescued yesterday from what police are describing as a 'house of horror' in Salford.

The children, a girl aged nine and a boy of six, are thought to be brother and sister and were found tied to their beds in squalid conditions at an address in the Weaste area of the city. Police have asked that the exact address be kept secret to avoid identifying the youngsters.

A man and woman, thought to be their parents, have been arrested on suspicion of child cruelty. Police broke down the door of the house after a tip off from neighbours. One woman who lives on the street, who asked not to be named said: 'The mum and dad are notorious around here. Drunk all the time and screaming and shouting at those kids. Sometimes you'd hear the boy and girl crying too. You never saw them out and about. They never played out like the other kids do. It's just awful.'

The photo accompanying the story showed a police officer with two children, their backs to the camera. The policeman was holding his helmet in one hand; his other arm was around the boy and girl. The side view of the young policeman's face showed how handsome he was. His hair was dark, cut short yet curly. There was a look of pure anger on the PC's face. The photo caption read: *PC John Smithdown comforts the two crying children taken from the so called 'house of horror'.*

'I'd only been on the job a few months when we were called to that house...*your* house,' Smithdown said, looking at the clipping. 'I'll never forget it as long as I live. The stink of the place. Piled high with shit and rubbish. You and your sister tied up like dogs, so thirsty you were drinking dregs from beer cans. We got you out late morning and waited for them to return. I was there until half eleven at night. The bastards had been out all day and half the night drinking.'

'What's my name, John? Tell me. Do you know? What's my real name?'

'Sean,' the older man said. 'Your name is Sean Hargreaves. I'm so sorry that you had to find out like this.'

Danny chose his words carefully. 'I always knew things were bad before we were adopted. Really bad. But I'd always pushed it away. My sister, she always dealt with it better. I wanted nothing to do with the past. I even used to tell people I didn't have a sister – as if that would help cut the ties. But it's not that easy, is it?'

'No, Danny. It really isn't. I wish it was. How is your sister?'

'She lives down in Wythenshawe. Married to a nice bloke. Bone idle, but nice. Decent people.'

Smithdown squeezed Danny's arm. 'You're decent people too, Danny. I mean it.'

Danny touched the newspaper pieces, pushing them slightly apart. 'Years ago, John, you said something to me... something about feeling bad for involving me in Black Moss, didn't you?'

John Smithdown nodded.

'Did you know, John? In 1990… did you know me and the kid in the photo were one and the same?'

'Not at first, Danny, no. But there was something about you… so I did some digging. By the time I'd put two and two together, I'd already involved you. *You'd already involved yourself.* I thought… perhaps you were using it to try to wipe the slate clean. Trying to do right by that little lad at the Moss. I didn't want to pry. Maybe I should have. I'm sorry.'

Danny leant in close. 'I found teeth John, *fucking teeth,* at Jan Cave's office. Now the place has been cleaned out and she's disappeared.'

'I don't get it, Danny. I swear I don't. She was the best cop I ever knew. So hard working. She took over everything to do with Black Moss when my wife died. Everything. Now she's a child protection expert – that's not the CV of someone who means harm to children.'

'She's the only person involved in this case who isn't telling the truth,' Danny pointed out. 'Plus, she's the only one with a box full of kids' teeth.'

Smithdown shifted into ex-cop mode: 'Did you get any evidence of this Danny – a photo or anything?'

'No. No, I didn't. Jan Cave is trying to make out that I'm not to be trusted because of this.' Danny jabbed at the cuttings. 'That I'm round the twist. Who'd believe a drunk old journo like me? What's more, he's all fucked up because of his childhood. Perfect, isn't it? Your address is on the envelope. But she never posted it to you. Why's that?'

John Smithdown pulled a similar envelope from the pocket of his cardigan. 'Because she sent me this one instead,' he replied. 'It arrived this morning. It had been pushed through my letterbox.'

The cutting was again from the *Manchester Evening News* and the photo of John Smithdown was featured alongside two police mugshots of Danny's biological parents. *'HOUSE OF HORROR' MUM AND DAD JAILED FOR SICK ABUSE* said the headline. Jan Cave had written an identical message across the cutting as she had on her previous effort. 'She obviously thought that this one would drive her point home a bit harder,' Danny said, looking at the story but trying not to take too much of it on board. 'You know…*Danny's not right, he's not to be trusted.*'

'What now?' asked the older man. 'My connections with the force are long gone – most of my ex-colleagues are either dead or in care homes, Danny. What are you going to do?'

Danny thought for a moment. 'I'm going to walk into Oldham nick and tell them what I know. I had someone with me at her office – they can do the same. But before that, I'm going to stop and see someone.'

'Who's that, Danny?'

'My sister.' Danny pointed at John Smithdown's cutting. 'Can I have that?'

'Of course.' He handed Danny his cutting, then carefully scooped up the two halves of the other one. He looked at Danny as he passed it to him.

Danny put all the cuttings into one envelope and patted the ex-detective on the arm. 'Bye, John. I'll ring later. Don't tell Kate. No point in worrying her at this stage.'

'Sure, Danny. Story of my life, that is.'

Danny headed for the door. John Smithdown spoke: 'Danny?'

'Yes, mate,'

'I'm so sorry.'

'You saved us, John. *Saved us*. So, don't be so fucking stupid.'

Danny walked down the steep slope from the Smithdown's home, calling a local cab as he went. He wanted to walk for a while. Wanted to think, so he gave the firm a description of what he looked like and set off down the road towards Diggle.

Within minutes he reached a spot he recognised: the bend in the road where Peter Jeffries had crashed his car all those years ago. It looked safer now than it had then. More robust. Danny stood a moment and tried to remember the scene of the accident. As he waited a lone car went past, down the hill away from Black Moss. It was travelling too fast and there was a squeak as the driver pushed on his brakes a little too hard, panicking that they'd connect with the barrier on the outside of the bend. Danny watched as the car drove away. *But Jeffries' car didn't go through the barrier on the outside of the bend. It crossed into the wrong side of the road and crashed into the inside of the bend. Like he was trying to avoid something. Or he'd been sent in the wrong direction. Or both.*

Danny must have been standing on the bend for some time when he was snatched away from his thoughts by the beeping horn of the taxi driver, who'd pulled into a layby a few yards from where Danny was standing. Danny got into the cab and gave the driver his sister's address in Wythenshawe.

FIFTY-TWO

11.55am Thursday 23 June 2016

Treating them like precious artefacts, Danny placed the newspaper cuttings onto his sister's kitchen table. Karen didn't look at them. She looked at her brother instead. 'I've seen them,' she said, smiling and crying at the same time. 'Got copies upstairs. I know them off by heart. I wish I was more like you; young enough at the time to forget or at least, not fully understand.'

Danny looked around the kitchen, as if he'd find the words he was looking for. After a few moments, he did: 'It's like I *knew*… but *didn't* know. Remembered… but didn't really want to remember. The memory was there but it was easier to just not access it. That sounds like psychobollocks, I know, but it's true. What do you remember, Karen?'

Karen Hargreaves looked at her brother: 'They beat us. They left us tied up in our own filth. The only time they washed us was when they wanted to touch us. Or let someone else touch us. How long have you got, our Sean? How much do you *want* to know?'

'I've got all the time in the world, Karen. Not today, maybe. There's a *lot* going on today. But after today. Definitely. It's time.'

Karen looked at the clippings. Her eyes lingered on the story that showed the two mug shots. Their real parents. The man's eyes were downcast, reluctant to meet the camera lens. The woman was different – defiant and angry-looking. 'They must have had a terrible life before they had us,' Karen said quietly. 'Terrible.'

'They treated us like *animals*, Karen. How can you feel sorry for them?'

'I didn't say I felt sorry for them. I said something terrible must have happened to make them that way.'

She got up from the table and took down a framed photo from a shelf cluttered with mementos, letters, postcards and children's drawings. The instamatic tones and colours identified it as being from the 1970s or early 80s. In the photo, a couple smiled, their arms linked. He was around forty, dressed in a chunky brown jumper and jeans. He was broad and looked like he knew what a hard day's work meant. She was younger, wearing a lime green dress; she had blonde hair that looked like it had just had a shampoo and set. Karen took the photo and placed it on top of the cuttings. 'These people who took us in and raised us, the Johnstons. They were our real mum and dad.' She prodded the press clippings: 'Not these monsters.'

Danny took the photo from her hands. 'I never really appreciated them. Never really thanked them for what they did – they treated us so well, got me into a good school, pushed me, encouraged me. First thing I did when I got that newspaper job after college was move out and then I barely contacted them. Then they were gone.'

She reached out, putting her hands around his as he held the photo. 'They didn't blame you. They understood. They kept in touch via me. It made them sad, but they understood.'

They sat in silence at the kitchen table. Danny pushed the photo to one side and pointed at the newspaper picture of John Smithdown. 'I know him – PC Smithdown, there – I know him really well. He turned into a great cop – a detective. One of the best. He's helping me look at an old case – a child murder from when I was at the radio station.'

'Why wasn't it solved at the time?'

'Because no one cared.'

'That's when bad things happen, Sean.'

'Yeah. I know.'

'So, what are you going to do about it?' Karen asked.

'I think I've found the person who knows what really happened. I'm going to the police today. Right now, in fact. And I'm going to get them arrested.'

'Sounds like a plan,' Karen said.

Danny's text alert went off. *Hi Danny, it's Beth. Some mental ex-copper woman just turned up at my door, looking for you. She was screaming and shouting. I didn't let her in… but she was scary as hell. She says she's coming back. Come ASAP please!!*

'Change of plan,' said Danny. 'I've got to go. I'll let you know how I get on.'

Danny stood up and hugged his sister. Then she looked at him. 'I don't really know what you're up to but promise me you'll take care.'

'Of course.'

'Promise?'

'Promise.'

FIFTY-THREE

3.10pm Thursday 23 June 2016

It occurred to Danny that he might need to make his approach in a low-key way, so he asked the driver to stop a few streets away from Beth's house.

Although only a few miles from his sister's house, Didsbury was a far more upmarket affair, even more so than when Danny had lived there in 1990. The main road running adjacent to the cul-de-sac where Beth lived was peppered with a few cars, cyclists and pushchair-wielding parents, making Danny self-conscious about the way he was stealthily walking too slowly along the pavement. He made an effort to walk in a more normal fashion, which only made him feel even more self-aware of the strangeness of the situation. *What the fuck are you doing? This is mad.*

As he turned the corner into Beth's street, he noticed her front door was open – only slightly – but open nonetheless. *That's not right. She's so security minded. No way would she leave the door open. That's not right at all. Fuck, fuck, fuck.*

Danny picked up his pace as he approached the front door. He looked around. The dead-end street had six houses on either side. Beth's was tucked into the corner on its own. No one was around. He'd had plenty of doorstep encounters in his TV days, but they were always with a camera crew and a producer. Never on his own. Danny felt very exposed without the bravado that being in a group of people – especially one carrying a camera – can provide. He quietly took the three steps up to the front door and looked through the gap. And listened. 'Beth?' he asked. Then again. Louder this time. 'Beth? It's Danny. Is everything okay?'

He gently pushed the door wider and saw Beth's empty wheelchair in the hallway. Stepping inside the dark hallway and squeezing past the wheelchair, he heard a radio from what sounded like the kitchen. He made his way towards the only sound in Beth's house – the radio. 'Beth,' he said again. 'Don't freak out, it's just Danny. I got your message and was worried. You alright?'

He turned into the kitchen and saw Beth lying face down on the smooth lino floor. Her eyes were closed, and she looked so still, she didn't appear to be breathing. Danny took several quick steps towards her and bent down. As he did so, a strong arm slipped around his neck; a hand clamped onto the back of his head, locking him into a shockingly powerful choke hold. He felt the weight of the attacker's body force him to the ground, knocking what little breath he had in his lungs out of him. The side of his face was pressed hard onto the cold kitchen flooring as he struggled. He tried to push himself upwards, but the fight was draining out of him. Danny remembered a TV piece he'd done about self-defence. An expert had told him that trying to knock someone out by hitting them over the back of the head was a piece of Hollywood nonsense. You're more likely to enrage them – or even kill them outright. The chances of getting it just right were minimal. No. The best way to put someone into unconsciousness was a choke hold. *Good to know,* he thought.

Still struggling, Danny caught the shortest of breaths and the medicinal smell of soap rushed into his nostrils. The only part of his attacker he could see was their elbow, clad in a crisp, white shirt. *Fuck this.*

His face was close to Beth's on the kitchen floor. She opened her eyes and looked directly at Danny. And winked. As he whited-out into unconsciousness, Danny heard Beth speak. It was the same tone she'd used to him back in the Manchester Radio days: sneery, aloof and sarcastic. Very different to the cheery voice he'd heard her use two days earlier. She said: 'Danny Johnston. You are, without doubt, the stupidest cunt I have ever had the misfortune to come across.'

FIFTY-FOUR

5.30am Friday 6 April 1990

'Yeah? Umm… Hello?'

'Danny, it's Beth.'

'Oh, hi. Right. Hi. I haven't overslept, have I?'

'No. It's fine. We've got a suspicious body out near Oldham. It's the absolute back of beyond but you're the next reporter on shift. Sharston wants you to go and check it out. Please tell me you have a Marantz?'

'Right. Okay. Yes, I do. That couldn't be further away from where I live if you tried. It'll take ages to get there. Aren't there any reporters that live nearer? Robert Crane lives in Middleton, doesn't he? That's much nearer.'

'Two words Danny: STRANGE, WAYS,' Beth shouted. 'Robert and the rest of the good journalists are down at the jail and will be for some time. It's down to you.'

'Right. Sorry. I wasn't being unwilling – just thinking of the practicalities, that's all. Right. Have you got an address?'

'Yes, I have,' Beth confirmed. 'It's a bit of a weird one… It's Black Moss reservoir. I've got some directions. Got a pen? Right. Take the A62 out of Oldham. Pass through Diggle. Stop at Brun Clough Reservoir car park. No, not Burn, Brun. Clough as in Brian. There's a Pennine Way sign on your right. Walk the Pennine Way path until you reach a second reservoir, that's Redbrook. The next one is called Back Moss. There's a smaller reservoir next to it called Little Black Moss. Then look for a beach and police activity.'

'Beach?' queried Danny.

'Yes. Apparently, there's a beach there. Probably just the low water level exposing the sand around the reservoir. I don't know. Do I sound as if I work for the water board? That's the information that's come through.'

'Okay. Probably take me an hour to get there, if I get out sharpish.'

'Then you'd better get out sharpish then, hadn't you?' said Beth.

'Right you are.'

'Danny?'

'Yeah?'

'Don't fuck it up.'

FIFTY-FIVE

3.40pm Thursday 23 June 2016

There was a lot to take in for Danny as he came to in an alleyway close to Beth's house. Yes, there was the thumping, swollen feeling in his head as he regained consciousness and realised where he was. There was also the sight of two young police community support officers looking down at him: 'You alright, sir?' one said in the overly-loud, overly-slow way that someone might speak to an elderly relative. He was in his mid-twenties with a light beard and seemed very wary of the situation.

'Bit early for it sir, don't you think?' said the other, a woman who looked very disapproving indeed of Danny lying in an alleyway on a Thursday afternoon.

But the number one source of confusion was the explosive, orangey and utterly forbidden taste of vodka that filled his mouth and was busily setting fire to the inside of his chest. There was barely enough to wet the inside of his mouth, but it was mixing with his saliva and Danny had swallowed it as a reflex action. There was barely a shot's worth, but it was enough to knock his senses sideways.

As Danny sat upright, he noticed his light black t-shirt was wet through, so much so he could feel moisture seeping into his trousers and underwear. He *reeked* of alcohol. The smell of it, the taste of it, the feel of it against his skin, thrilled and shocked him in equal measure.

'We've had a complaint, sir,' PCSO number one said. 'Been causing a nuisance, have we?'

'*She* fucking sent me out there!' shouted Danny. 'Sent me out to the Moss, all those years ago. She's right – I am stupid! A stupid, stupid cunt. Jesus Christ Almighty what a mug.'

Danny tried to get to his feet but lurched sideways, leaning heavily into a hedge running down one side of the ally. 'Take it easy, sir,' said PCSO number two. 'And tone down the language – there's a police station just around the corner on Elizabeth Slinger Road. I'm sure our friends there would be happy to accommodate you if you persist in causing a public nuisance.'

Copperspeak. Never changes, thought Danny. *And they're not even real coppers.* Although distracted by the notion of the alcohol that had been poured over and into him, it was clear that Danny was going to get nowhere telling what he knew to the PCSOs. He pulled himself up straight, trying to shake off the effects of being choked into unconsciousness. 'Okay,' he said. 'I'll keep it down. Am I under arrest?'

'Well, we could detain you while one of the local officers get here, but let's hope it doesn't come to…'

'Good!' Danny turned around and sprinted unsteadily back towards Beth's house, half fell up the steps and banged on the door with his fist. The PCSOs were right behind him. He alternated between banging on the door with his fist and jabbing at the intercom button. 'Out!' he shouted. 'Come the fuck out, right now!'

Unsurprisingly, there was no reply. 'Please, sir,' said one of the PSCOs. 'We're happy to listen to your side of the story, but you're not doing yourself any favours here.'

Danny stopped banging and jabbing. Several people were now watching proceedings from a safe distance. Danny heard some of their chatter.

It's him off the telly.

The alkie?

Yeah, that's him.

Danny felt the fury drain away. He looked at the PCSOs. Both were in their mid-to-late twenties. Both seemed slightly frightened. They reminded him of the policemen out on Black Moss all those years ago. 'Really?' Danny said, the anger almost gone from his voice. 'My side of the story? You want to hear my side of the story? Somehow, I don't think you'd believe me.'

He held up both of his hands to the officers, palms facing them, in a peaceful gesture: defeat rather than surrender. 'It's probably best if I just get myself home. Sleep it off.'

'A grand idea, sir.'

Danny walked backwards from the scene, his hands still in the air. When he turned the corner, he started to walk quickly in the direction of the tram stop, pulling out his mobile phone as he went. A note was wrapped around the phone, secured with a thick elastic band. It was written in bland block capitals with a marker pen. It said:

BE ON THE TRAIN BACK TO LONDON BY SIX TONIGHT OR PEOPLE YOU KNOW WILL DIE

First, he rang Gary. Then he rang Kate. He asked both the same question. *How quickly can you meet me at my hotel?*

Then he started to run.

FIFTY-SIX

6.35pm Thursday 23 June 2016

'Right,' said Danny, raising his voice over the chatter that filled his hotel room. 'Can I get a fucking word in edgeways here, please?'

'Sorry, Danny,' said Kate, pointing at Gary. 'But I haven't talked to this bastard for twenty-odd years, we've got some catching up to do.'

'That's because you turned your back on a proper job in radio to become a zillionaire, you capitalist cow,' Gary replied, rifling through Danny's replenished mini-bar.

'Dead right. That was stupid of me, wasn't it?' she said.

'Shut the fuck up and listen.' Danny had spent the last half hour in the shower, trying to wash away the smell of alcohol from his skin and hair – and the sense of fear and lack of control that the small amount he'd swallowed had given him. He'd only stopped showering when Gary and Kate had arrived. His teeth and gums tingled from the scrubbing he'd given them with his toothbrush. He'd used half a tube but could still taste vodka.

Gary and Kate sat side by side on Danny's double bed and looked at him. 'Okay. Here's what I know. Beth and Jan Cave are tied into this together somehow. I don't know how, but they are. It was Beth that sent me out to the Moss that morning in 1990 when the kid's body was discovered, and it was Beth that conned me into going to her house today. I'm pretty sure it was Jan that choked me into next week back at the house and it was probably her that played basketball with my head against a couple of brick walls back in the day. Plus… she collects kids' teeth. Which is a bad thing, as far as I'm concerned.'

'Agreed,' said Gary.

'Plus,' Danny added, 'they doused me in vodka to make me look like a drunken headcase. Who's going to believe me? No fucker, that's who. I couldn't even convince a couple of volunteer community cops that I was worth listening to. So, as a great man once said – fuck the police.'

'It's getting really weird this,' Gary whispered to Kate. 'Really, really weird. I've known Beth most of my life. Okay, she was a cow in the old days but, covering up child killings? Jesus Christ. She's got M.S.'

'They also gave me this,' Danny said, throwing the note onto the bed.

Gary and Kate read it. 'I assume you aren't going?' Kate said.

'You assume correctly,' Danny confirmed.

Gary pushed his glasses up his nose. 'So, what's the plan? Whatever it is, I'm bang up for it. I'm serious. Heads need breaking here.'

FIFTY-SEVEN

1.25am Friday 24 June 2016

'There you go,' said Gary. 'I got the most expensive ones they had. I think you get what you pay for when it comes to baseball bats, I really do.'

Danny looked at the bat Gary had handed him.

'That's sixty quid's-worth of Louisville Slugger, that is,' Gary said, giving his bat a slow-motion swing through the air. 'Whammy,' he whispered. 'Fucking *whammy…*'

'Sure. Whammy,' Danny said in reply. *This is mad.*

'Here's the genius bit,' Gary added. 'I bought a ball and a glove too, so if we get stopped we can legitimately say we're just out for baseball practice.'

'At midnight?' queried Danny.

'We're very keen,' Gary countered.

'Of course we are. Kate, come on, what are you doing?'

'Just texting Dad with a few reminders about Jonathan for the morning. The pair of them are like two kids having a sleepover.'

She looked at the two men, testing out their baseball bats. 'Don't I get one?' she asked, stepping down from the front seat of Gary's van. 'Or are women not allowed to smash heads in, you sexist bastards?'

Gary handed Kate a bat. 'Of course I got you one,' he confirmed, speaking in a slow, patronising voice. He handed Kate a rounders bat that was half the size of the other two weapons. 'Not quite a Slugger, but you don't mind, do you?'

Kate looked at the bat. 'Wow. Had they run out of My Little Pony ones? I would have preferred something with a bit of glitter on it, but it'll have to do, I suppose.'

She briefly gave the bat a swing back and forward, then, slightly embarrassed, tucked it into the pocket of her overcoat. 'Okay,' said Danny, getting out his iPhone and switching it to video mode. 'I'm on camera. Kate, you're on lighting, but wait until we're at the door. We want every scrap of evidence we can gather. Gary, you're in charge of twatting anything that moves.'

'I can do that,' the engineer confirmed.

'Thought so,' said Danny. 'Let's go.' The three walked quietly to the front door of Beth's house. Danny, Kate then Gary. There was a warm breeze and the moon was bright, lighting their way along with the orangey glow of the street lights. Kate was tapping the bat against her leg and whispering something under her breath. Danny walked a little slower, holding back so he could hear: 'Shit. Shit. Shit. Shit. Shit,' she said.

'Okay, Kate?' he asked.

'Definitely,' she replied. Then the whispered chant started again.

They got to the door and the three of them huddled in the small porch of the house. They looked around. The road was empty. 'Give me a little space here, will you?' Gary said, gently shooing them off the steps. 'Kate, step back and give me a little light from your phone. Danny, you'd better start recording.'

Danny and Kate looked down and began changing the settings on their phones. There was a clunk and Beth's door opened with a quiet beep. 'How the fuck did he do that?' Kate asked. Danny shrugged.

Danny and Kate peered around Gary into the house. It was silent. It was dark. 'What if there's someone here?' Kate asked in the quietest voice she could manage.

Gary tapped the end of his bat. 'Whammy,' he replied.

'Jesus Christ,' she sighed, 'I would really like my old life back, if that can be arranged, please?' She turned on her phone light, shining it thorough the gap in the doorway. The cold, white LED beam made the hallway appear frozen like a museum exhibit. There were tasteful art prints on the wall and several framed awards, including at least two for "Beth Hall – Independent Radio Newsreader of the Year." There was a stairlift too, with the chair ready to take someone upstairs. The light cut through the dark, well into the rear of the house.

Danny turned on the video function on his iPhone. He held it out in front of him. 'Let's go.'

They searched the downstairs front room first. More prints, furniture with expensive-looking throws and cushions and more framed awards. Gary picked up a photo from the fireplace surround. It showed a group of people at a Christmas party, looking the worse for drink. He was one of them. 'I have no memory of that photo being taken,' he said, mainly to himself.

The kitchen next. Kate nearly slipped on the small ramp that smoothed out the step, allowing access for Beth's wheelchair. 'It's not here,' said Danny.

'What isn't?' asked Kate.

'Beth's wheelchair,' Danny said, allowing his voice now a little louder than before. 'It's not here. Unless she drags it upstairs every night, that must mean that she's not here either.'

'Unless it's in here,' Gary said, tapping on the cellar door that featured an electronic lock similar to one at the front door.

Danny and Kate both spoke at the same time: 'Let's find out, shall we?'

Gary's bulk covered their view of the cellar door. In a matter of seconds, the double click signalled that the door had been opened. 'Gary,' Kate said. 'If we manage to not get put in prison for this, please promise me you'll show me how you do that.'

'Don't waste your time,' Danny said. 'It's ancient magic passed down through generations of hairy-arsed radio engineers. They're sworn to secrecy.'

Gary pushed open the cellar door and the three of them looked down into the darkness – it seemed to absorb the iPhone light rather than be illuminated by it. It was unusually robust for an internal door and banged hard against the wall leading down into the cellar. The three winced at the noise it made and stood in silence for at least a minute afterwards. Nothing. They walked down the harsh, stone steps then banked right as the room opened up. The cellar was the size of a large living room with a small window at the far end providing a little weak light from the street outside. It was filled with tools, boxes, old paint tins and spare furniture. All were neatly stacked on metal shelving units. There was also a large first aid kit attached to the left wall. It looked out of place, more like it belonged in a factory or large office rather than a house. Underneath it was a tent-like shape – several sheets pulled over something low and oblong. Danny lifted one of the sheets. There was a single, metal-framed bed underneath it. The mattress on it was dusty and soiled. Danny stared at it, scrunching the section of sheet that was in his hand into a tight ball. Gary's voice dragged his eyes away, but his mind was still captured by the bed. 'Nothing here,' said the engineer. 'Upstairs?'

'Wait,' said Kate. 'There.'

She shone a light onto a dilapidated Welsh dresser that stood against the far right-hand wall. It was partially covered with another sheet and had been painted a sickly light green colour. Behind it was a door with another keypad lock. Kate and Danny gestured towards the door to Gary. They moved the dresser as quietly as they could as the engineer hunched over the lock. True to form, it popped open in seconds. 'Move the dresser a bit more, so I can open the door wider. I'm not as slim as you two,' he said.

Kate and Danny did as they were asked. Kate's light revealed a larger room, five feet wide and fifteen feet long. On one side of the room ran a shelf. On it were boxes of gear that reflected twenty-five years of technical advances in camera equipment. There were Polaroid cameras, camcorders, digital cameras, Hi-8 units and DV cams. There were several developments in mobile phone technology represented too: many of the boxes boasted of the mega pixel quality offered by the phone's camera capability. The boxes were creased and yellowed but in remarkably good condition, given how old some of them were. Each camera or phone had clearly been used, then neatly returned to its original packaging and then stored as the next new gadget had come along and superseded it.

On the opposing wall of the narrow space were framed newspaper front pages, their headlines going back more than a quarter of a century. The stories told of IRA bombings in Manchester and Warrington, the murder of a Manchester aid worker at the hands of ISIS, child sex abuse rings in Rochdale – story after story, about a dozen in all, demonstrated moments in time over the last twenty-five years or more when Manchester and its surrounding areas had been the centre of national and international attention. Each front page had been carefully mounted and framed. In the bottom left-hand corner of each frame was a photograph. The earlier pictures were Polaroids, the newer ones were digital pictures that had been printed off and cut to the same size. Each photo was dated with extremely neat handwriting. Each was of a child, looking directly at the camera, like police mug shots. They were mainly boys, but some were girls. Some looked smiling and hopeful. Others appeared scared. Very, very scared.

Danny looked at the children's faces. One frame in particular caught his eye. At the far end of the room was a headline from the *Manchester Evening News*' coverage of the Strangeways' riot – it said: "20 DEAD". Danny remembered it well, remembered it being passed around the newsroom. He walked towards the framed front page. Unlike the other pictures, there were two photos inside this one. He stared at the pictures, both were of young boys. The picture in the right of the frame was dated 5 April 1990. The boy looked dirty and distraught. His eyes were half closed; he appeared to be crying.

The second photo was also dated: 25 April 1990 – the last day of the Strangeways' riot.

Danny looked at this photo – a boy with brutally short hair stared defiantly at the lens. Danny touched the glass of the framed page. His eyes began to burn with tears. 'Little Paul,' he whispered. 'Oh, Little Paul, you poor bastard.'

'What the fuck am I looking at here?' demanded Gary, no longer bothering to keep his voice quiet.

'The dream team's trophy room, Gary,' Danny said. 'The fucking *dream* team. They figured out that the best way to steal something and not get caught is to steal something nobody wants… Care home kids that no one gives a shit about. And just to make sure you can do as you fucking well please, you take control of the way it's seen by the outside world too. So, a cop to manipulate the cases and a journalist to manipulate the coverage. Oh, they fucked it up the first time, out at the Moss. Dropped that kid before they could sling him in the water. Probably panicked or got disturbed. But they got better, lessons were learned, they *refined* it, for fuck's sake. Somebody gets in your way like Peter Jeffries? Send them off the road and twist the coverage to suit your purpose. Make it look like he had a guilty conscience. Need a scapegoat when things start getting a little too close for comfort? Get a local grass, fill him with drink and guide his hand to cut his own throat up on the moors – make it look like he killed a kid at the same spot. Need a diversion? Do it all during the biggest stories of the last twenty-five years while the media is looking elsewhere.'

'Christ All-fucking-mighty,' Kate whispered. 'I can't take this in. I really can't take this all in.'

Danny looked at Gary. The engineer pulled a dirty hankie from his pocket and wiped his eyes. 'Jesus wept, Danny. Jesus fucking wept. Those vile, murdering fucking cunts.'

Danny rubbed his eyes. He spoke more quietly this time: 'Oh yes. One more thing. And this one's a belter. Need to be seen to be covering a murder while the really big story is unfolding elsewhere? Send the shittiest reporter you've got out there – he's *bound* to fuck it up.'

'Danny…' Kate began.

He was smiling now. 'A cop and a journalist,' he said. 'What better team could you ask for? It's perfect. The fucking *dream team.*'

Danny continued to stare in wonder at the framed front pages as Gary reached for one of the camera boxes and took it down from the shelf. He opened it and pulled out a clunky camcorder. He tried the power switch, but the battery was unsurprisingly dead. He moved on to a newer model and flipped open the DV cam playback screen – the camera came alive, but the power level was very low. Danny and Kate heard the slight whirring noise the unit made as the power kicked in. They looked at each other. Then at Gary. Then at the screen. They gathered around it.

They saw a bed – it appeared to be the same one as the room behind them – and there was a sheet over it. Nothing happened. Just a bed with a sheet. Gary put the camera into rewind and the picture went into reverse, showing them what was on the footage in reverse. They saw the sheet appear to be pulled back to show a child with a pillow on their face. They saw a desperate struggle – skinny arms and legs shaking and waving uselessly against the attack. They saw the pillow come away from the child's face. And they saw a boy, aged about ten, his face bruised and bloody, cry and plead and shake his head. All in reverse. Then the battery died and the screen went blank.

All three were still – unable to move – for at least a minute. Finally, Danny looked at Kate. She was weeping, head down, shoulders moving almost imperceptibly. Danny looked at Gary. The engineer was staring at the ceiling, breathing heavily.

Danny broke the silence. 'Grab a camera box and a picture frame each and let's go,' he said.

Silently, they did as Danny asked. They didn't bother to tidy up after themselves; Gary knocked several boxes from the shelf. He didn't pick them up and put them back, he left them there. They didn't even bother to put the dresser back in its place. There seemed to be no point in pretending that they hadn't been here. Gary went upstairs and half-heartedly checked the bedrooms – he wielded his bat as if hoping, praying, that he would bump into someone, but all three seemed to know that the house was empty.

As they headed towards the front door, Danny noticed an iPhone taped to the side of the door frame. He pressed the home button and it came out of energy saving mode. It was eavesdropping on what had been happening via Facetime video. Danny looked at the screen. The person at the other end appeared to be driving a car, but he couldn't make out any faces. Then the connection was ended. 'We need to go,' Danny instructed, pulling the phone from the wall and jamming it into his pocket.

'Go where?' asked Kate.

'To Oldham Police station. Right now. There'll probably only be a duty sergeant and a few drunks there, but we need to go now. Looks like we're going to be in the twenty-four-hour club before the night's done. Just like the old days.'

'Sure,' Gary replied. 'Just like the old days, mate.'

'Can we go via my dad's? Just to make sure everything's okay.'

'Absolutely,' Danny said, putting a hand on Kate's shoulder. She pulled him close and hugged him.

'Those poor kids,' she said.

All three got into Gary's van. Danny took the frames and cameras and placed them carefully behind the seats. He took care not to look at the faces in the photos, especially the one he had grabbed, dated 5 April 1990 that showed the boy from Black Moss.

Gary pulled away from the kerb and the van headed down Princess Parkway, the main connecting dual carriageway from south Manchester to the city centre. All three sat in silence. After a few minutes, the engineer spoke: 'I didn't even vote,' he said.

'What?' asked Kate, still in a daze.

'Fucking Brexit. Completely forgot to vote.'

FIFTY-EIGHT

3.25am Friday 24 June 2016

'The lights are on,' cried Kate as Gary's van pulled into the driveway of her father's house. 'Shit, shit, shit. No, no, no. It's half past fucking three in the morning and all the lights are on.'

As Gary came to a stop, Kate pushed Danny out of the way and climbed out of the van. She hit the gravel drive running and dashed straight to the front door, which was already open. 'Dad!' she shouted. 'Jonathan!'

Danny and Gary were right behind her. Both had their baseball bats. 'I'm going to use this thing tonight if it fucking kills me,' Gary shouted as they barrelled their way through the front door. Kate was still shouting for her father and her young son as she ran upstairs. Danny headed for the living room. John Smithdown was lying face down on the carpet, with the shattered remains of a glass coffee table surrounding him. Chips and shards of glass were stuck to his bloodied face and he was perfectly still. Danny stared at him, unable to make a decision about what to do next. He heard Kate shouting in a state of pure fury from upstairs, followed by the sound of her stomping down the stairs. 'Johnny's not here, Danny,' she shouted, taking the stairs two at a time. 'Those fucking bitches. He's gone.'

The sight of her father turned Kate's shouts into roars. Gary was moving John Smithdown's body into the recovery position, shifting the old man's arms and legs with surprising gentleness. 'Ambulance,' the engineer said. 'Now.'

As Kate dialled 999, Danny's mobile pinged. He didn't recognise the number but there was no doubt in his mind as to who it was. The message read: *Bring the pictures and equipment you stole – plus all mobile phones – to postcode OL3 6LF. Do not copy or send any footage, the phones will be checked. We will know if you call the police. It's the time for this to end. Everyone can walk away if you do exactly as you are told.*

As soon as he'd finished reading it, a second message arrived. A video file this time. Danny looked at Kate and tried to give her a reassuring smile. He walked out of the room and turned down the volume before opening the video. It was Jonathan Smithdown. Danny didn't need the sound to know that the boy was hysterical. The video was a close-up of his face – an arm was wrapped firmly around his throat, he was hitting the arm ineffectually, clawing at the pure white material of his abductor's shirt. The video lasted just a few seconds before freezing on the final frame of the boy's face.

'Danny!' shouted Gary. 'Where are you? Get the fuck in here, now.'

Danny returned to the front room. 'Was that them?' Kate asked. 'On the phone, was it them?' She seemed calmer now; the shouts and screams had been replaced with a quiet rage.

'Yes. They've got Jonathan. They want the evidence – the pictures, the camera gear and our phones – and they say they'll let Jonathan go. We've got to meet them – fuck knows where it is – but they've given me a postcode.'

'Punch it into Google Maps,' said Gary, still on his knees tending to John Smithdown.

Danny did as he was asked and showed it to Kate and Gary. 'It's a lane out towards the Yorkshire border,' Kate said. 'It goes for miles past some old shooting lodges then just fades out into the moors. Danny, we can't leave my dad here. He's in a bad way. But I've got to go to Jonathan.'

Gary unclipped the keys that seemed to have been welded to his belt since at least 1990 and tossed them to Danny. He followed it with his phone. 'Take the van, take the gear and go where they ask. Do whatever they say and get your lad back, Kate. We'll figure something out when he's safe. I'll wait here with your dad until the ambulance arrives.'

'That's a better plan than anything I've come up with,' admitted Danny. 'We'd better go.'

As they got to the van, Danny handed the keys to Kate, remembering he wasn't allowed to drive. She looked at him as if he were mad. 'You're right. Fuck it.'

FIFTY-NINE

4.45am Friday 24 June 2016

Coming off the main Huddersfield to Manchester road, Danny turned the van into a series of lanes and tracks, each narrower and bumpier than the last. Street lighting had ended a good ten minutes earlier. There was the slightest sense that sunrise was on its way from across the edge of moors, but the retreating darkness was being backfilled by a heavy mist that the van's fog lights were struggling to cut through.

Danny and Kate had barely spoken since leaving her father's house. At one point she'd asked him why Gary hadn't text her about John Smithdown's condition. Then she had answered her own question, remembering that they had Gary's phone, along with the rest of the items they'd been told to bring. Danny idly flicked on the radio. The local all-night radio host was fielding calls about Brexit. 'Fucking hell,' said Danny. 'We're out. That's all anyone will be talking about today. And the next day.'

'Perfect, isn't it?' Kate said, staring at the ever-diminishing lane in front of them. 'Who will be interested in a missing kid on a day like today?'

Danny looked at her: 'They've got this diversion thing down to a fine art, you've got to give them that.'

'Danny? What are we going to do when we get there? It doesn't seem right to just let them disappear. Not after what they've done.'

He thought for a moment. 'Gary's right. Get Jonathan then worry about it later.'

'It's not right,' she repeated, glancing to the back of the van at the picture frames they'd taken from Beth's house.

'No,' agreed Danny. 'It's not right at all.'

The lane passed through a series of wooden buildings that they assumed were part of the shooting range; then it went down to almost nothing. A strip of grass ran down the middle of the track; it led the way and demonstrated how little traffic came through the route. The track continued to shrink until the hedgerows running alongside it touched the van on both sides, scratching the exterior as if the branches were trying to get inside the vehicle.

In the distance they saw a figure. Jan Cave stood at the end of the track, one hand in the air telling them to stop. She was wearing a dark overcoat, but the fog lights caught the white of her shirt and illuminated her. The look on her face chilled them both; totally calm and business-like without a trace of emotion.

Danny brought the van to a halt but kept the motor going. Jan made a cutting motion across her neck with her thumb and he killed the engine. 'Yes, that's a good idea, you bitch,' whispered Kate. 'Let's see if we can get that throat cut before all this is done.'

The ex-policewoman walked away from the van and motioned for them to follow her. She walked slowly towards a disused concrete bunker-like building at the very end of the track. Danny gathered up the frames, held them flat and asked Kate to pile the camera boxes on top of them. She took the phones and they walked towards the bunker. Danny was starting to panic. *Look at us. Like we're taking presents to a party. It just gets weirder and weirder. I'd do anything to be back in London now. Anything. I'd even do that skiing reality show my agent talked about. Please let me be anywhere. Anywhere but here.*

He looked across at Kate. He envied her calm. She was staring at Jan Cave's back as she slipped into the darkness of the abandoned building. As she stared, she moved her lower jaw slowly left to right in a series of tiny movements. Danny could hear the click-click noise she was making as she ground her teeth together.

Jesus Christ, we're fucked. Really, really fucked. No one is coming out of this tonight. Not one of us.

He was about to tell Kate to turn back but she'd quickened her pace and was now ahead of him. The blackness of the bunker took her too. For a second Danny was all alone. He looked around – the moors gave nothing back. He went inside.

Dressed all in black and using a single forearm crutch to support herself, Beth Hall stood inside the building. All of the windows had long since been smashed and Danny could see the stars through the roof – a third of the tiles were missing. Bird droppings, discarded bottles and the burnt remains of a small bonfire were the dominant features, along with some old car seats arranged in a semi-circle. Jonathan Smithdown was sitting on one of them. He was conscious but was struggling to stay awake, as if he'd been drugged. Both of his hands had been bound together at the wrist with shiny grey tape. Jan Cave stood next to him. In her hand was a huge kitchen knife. She stroked Jonathan's black, curly hair, gently at first. Then she took a handful of it and pulled his head to one side. She put the knife to his throat. Danny heard Kate whisper her son's name. The pain in her voice pushed away the panic Danny had been feeling and replaced it with guilt and shame. *We wouldn't be here if it wasn't for me and my great big fucking ego trip. Kate was right. Go back and sort out the one thing that's been eating me up for years? Then everything will be all right. What a walking, talking cliché.*

'Let's crack on, shall we?' said Beth. 'Danny, it's very important that you do as you're told, understand?' She spoke with calm and clear authority. It was her newsreader's voice.

'Yes,' he confirmed.

Beth glanced over at Jonathan. 'And it's very important that you answer my questions concisely and honestly. Do you understand that too?'

'Yes, I do.'

'Grand. Danny, have you brought everything that you took from my house with you?'

'Yes.'

'Have you got all three phones with you?'

'Yes.'

'Have you sent any messages or footage from them?'

'No.'

'Have you been in touch with the police, Danny?'

'No.'

'Does anyone know you're here?'

'Just Gary,' Danny replied. 'He wanted to come, and he sends his best, but he's busy tidying up the mess you left at John Smithdown's house.'

'Maybe we'll pop down to the hospital later, just to say hello. We'll see. Danny, put the frames and cameras on the floor please.'

He did as he was told. 'Good. Now then. Kate. Hi. Long time no see and all that.' Beth took a roll of tape from the pocket of her long, dark coat and threw it to Kate, who caught it, instinctively. 'You need to tape Danny's hands together please.'

Kate didn't move. 'Fuck this,' she said under her breath. Jan grabbed Jonathan's hair tighter and shook his head backwards and forwards. She was smiling.

'Now!' screamed Beth. Kate jumped with shock. 'Now! Now! Fucking now! Or she'll cut his fucking head off. Now!'

Kate moved forward. She seemed unable to look at Beth. She certainly couldn't look at Jan and Jonathan. She was staring at the compacted soil that served as a floor in the lodge. Her eyes looked up for the briefest of moments, then she crossed the room, pulling out a length of tape as she went. It made a *skrawking* noise. She bit it and tore off a two-foot-long piece. Danny put out his hands and gave her the merest nod, to let her now that it was okay. She wrapped the tape around his wrists as Beth looked on.

'You know what I'm going to ask you Beth, don't you?' asked Danny. He kept his eyes locked on Kate's trying to work out what she was thinking. Trying to read her thoughts. *I haven't got a clue,* he thought.

'Oh, fuck off, Danny,' shouted Beth. 'Oooh... Why did you do it?' Her tone was whingey and sarcastic. It was the 'cry baby' voice that she used to use in the Manchester Radio newsroom. 'Why, why, why oh fucking why?'

Kate finished strapping Danny's hands and put the tape into her coat pocket.

Beth looked at him. She was breathing heavily. 'Because we could. That's why. Because we fucking *could.* And because we fucking wanted to. That's it. Nothing more. Just that. Happy now? All nice and neat and resolved for you, Danny? Lots of lovely closure? What a dickhead you are. We don't all need some convoluted backstory to justify what we do – not like you. You fucking cry baby. Oooh, I'm all messed up and drunk all the time because of what happened to me and my sister in the past. But I can make it all better. No, you can't, Danny. You *can't* make it better, not for you, not for Kate here and not for your sister out in Wythenshawe either. We don't all need the past to justify what we do, Danny. Some of us just fucking *are.*'

Danny looked through the roof at the sky. The stars were fading. Dawn was coming. Jan spoke now. 'And some of us are actually close to our sisters, Danny. Not like you.'

Danny looked from Beth to Jan. And back again. *They have the same eyes. Jesus Christ. Sisters?*

Beth nodded at him. And winked. 'Kate. Come here please and bring the tape that you put in your pocket with you, please. Your turn now. Then it'll be time – and it'll *all* be over.'

Kate hesitated, then did as she was told and approached Beth, putting her hand into her pocket as she walked. She stopped and stood in front of Beth, who was still smiling. Then, for the first time since they'd arrived, Kate looked directly at Beth. There was silence for a moment.

Then Kate took her hand from her pocket, pulled out the rounders bat and smashed it across Beth's jaw with a single backhanded stroke. She brought it back and hit Beth's face again from the opposite side; the woman's jaw wobbled slackly, free of its broken hinges on both sides. Kate hit her a third time, higher now, across the side of the head. Beth's crutch fell away and she dropped to the floor as blood splashed from her mouth and head.

A heartbeat after Kate's first strike, Danny ran directly at Jan who was shouting her sister's name. She'd loosened her grip on Jonathan's hair, but only slightly. Danny put his shoulder forward and tucked his head down, preparing to put his full weight behind knocking her off her feet and away from Jonathan. Just as Danny's shoulder was about to connect, she spun him round with shocking ease, slammed him against the wall and jabbed the knife twice into his shoulder and upper torso. Kate ran towards them both, swinging the bat wildly. Jan met it with the point of the huge knife, which stuck into the bat. She yanked the bat from Kate's hands, sending it across the room, then lifted her foot and kicked Kate square in the chest, sending her backwards. Jan picked Jonathan up by the tape that bound his wrists, put him over her shoulder in a fireman's lift and ran out the lodge through the rotten remains of the back door. As she went she turned and looked at Danny; she motioned with her head as if to say: *come on. Come and get me.*

Kate was still gasping for breath but managed to get to her feet. She staggered towards Danny and began unwrapping the tape from his hands. He pulled his wrists inwards and shook the remainder of the tape free. Although he was fully aware that he was bleeding heavily, he wasn't in as much pain as he'd expected. Kate bent double, her hands on her knees, fighting for breath. She pointed at the doorway. Danny headed off onto the moors. Kate followed as best she could.

The light was slowly spreading across the eastern edge of the moor. Through the mist, Danny could see Jan Cave in the distance. She was half walking, half running through the clough that stretched north of the shooting lodge. Jonathan was on her shoulder. The boy's head lolled from side to side. He was starting to move. Then he began screaming.

Danny followed them as quickly as he could. Kate was moving more slowly behind him, shouting her son's name. The moorland peat was soft and wet with dew under their feet. The depth of the terrain varied wildly; sometimes Danny's foot would drop into a wet and muddy hole. Next, he'd be jumping over mounds covered in sharp moorland grass. He was tiring quickly, but he was gaining ground. He looked ahead. Jan passed by a small reservoir. *Little Black Moss,* thought Danny. *She's heading for the Pennine Way and then the main road.*

As she passed the small reservoir, Danny saw her let the boy slide from her shoulder. He landed unsteadily on his feet. His knees buckled slightly but he stayed upright. Jan then dragged him onwards towards Black Moss itself. He screamed and screamed.

When she got to the path she stopped and turned. She slipped an arm around the boy's neck and held up the knife; its point was tucked behind his ear. 'FUCKING STOP!' she screamed. 'Do not take another fucking step. Come an inch closer and I'll slit his throat.'

Danny stopped. Kate came up behind him and they grabbed onto each other. 'Please,' Kate said. 'Please.'

Jan walked backwards up the Pennine Way path, the knife still threatening the boy's throat. Danny and Kate stayed where they were, afraid to make even the slightest movement, fearful it would be interpreted as a step forwards.

Jan edged away from them. As she got close to the brow of the hill, with the Manchester Road behind her, Gary Keenan ran at her from behind. Jonathan was knocked to one side of the path, Jan to the other. Gary landed on top of the woman, his weight pinning one arm behind her back. She yelled in pain as her arm snapped above the elbow. Her free hand moved with astonishing speed as she stabbed at Gary with her knife. Four times, five times the knife went into his side and neck before Danny and Kate got to them. Danny kicked the knife from her hand. Shouting and swearing, Gary rolled to one side and Jan twisted around on to her front and crawled free. Gasping to replace the air that Gary had knocked out of her, she pushed herself upwards, but her hands sank into the wet sand around the edge of Black Moss. Kate jumped on her back and put her knees across Jan's upper arms. The ex-policewoman screamed in pain. Kate then put both hands to the back of Jan's head and began pushing her face into the sand at the water's edge of Black Moss.

Danny watched them, transfixed. The fight was draining from Jan Cave as Kate suffocated her. Her face had disappeared into the sand up to her hairline. The sun broke over the edge of the moors and the three of them were flooded with light.

I suppose I could do the right thing and stop her, Danny thought. *But fuck me I want that woman to die right now. I've never wanted anything more in my whole life. Die. Die. Fucking die.*

EPILOGUE

10.30am, six weeks later

Danny was quite enjoying his Community Payback work. He didn't especially care for the orange vest he had to wear, or the toots he and the rest of the six-strong clear-up team would occasionally get from passing motorists. But there were worse ways to spend a summer's day. The sun was shining, he was out in the fresh air and clearing rubbish from the roadside seemed like a reasonably worthwhile task. He wasn't about to kid himself that the exercise was going to wipe out decades of heavy drinking, but it certainly wasn't doing him any harm. He felt healthy and strong. Picking up the roadside litter with a grab-stick was good exercise for his shoulder too. The sheer weight of the knife that he'd been stabbed with had caused more damage than the sharpness of the blade, but the fracture on his collarbone was healing reasonably well.

Another driver bibbed his horn and waved. 'They never get tired of doing that, do they?' Danny said to one of his fellow workers, a teacher in her thirties who'd punched a sixth-former who had been beating up another pupil.

'No,' she said, smiling at Danny as she grabbed at some takeaway cartons before popping them in her bag. 'They seem to get endless pleasure from it.'

The court had initially wanted Danny to do his community service near the site of his car crash in London, but Danny's lawyer had successfully argued that he would be more use here on the outskirts of Oldham, where he could continue to help the police build their case against Bethany and Janet Cave.

Though he'd been commended by the judge for his actions, Danny was still a convicted drink driver and as such had another 130 hours of litter picking and graffiti scrubbing to do.

The initial charges that came about as result of what happened in the early hours of the 24th of June – one count of murder, two counts of attempted murder and one of child abduction – didn't receive as much attention as they normally would have done. Everyone was initially too busy looking at the Brexit result to care too much. But as the weeks went by – and more children were identified – the media's interest began to grow. The tabloids had even given the case its very own nickname. Danny winced every time he heard a mention of the 'Twisted Sisters'. *That's a terrible, terrible name for a case. Awful.*

He was also slightly annoyed that he hadn't thought of it himself, particularly as his publishers were adamant that his book about the case should have that very same name.

Beth and Jan still weren't cooperating with the police. After her face was put back together, Beth had been placed at Bronzefield prison in Surrey; Jan was at Foston Hall in Derbyshire. Little Paul had been identified by the teeth found at Jan's office, but there was still no word as to who the boy was that Danny had seen on the 'beach' at Black Moss in 1990.

Danny thought about the boy a lot. He was thinking of him as he cleared away rubbish when a voice from a passing car that had slowed down next to him snapped Danny out of it. 'Put your back into it, you lazy fucking bastard,' said John Smithdown, leaning out of the window.

'Dad!' Kate cried from the driver's seat. 'Language in front of Jonathan, please.'

The boy gave Danny a thumbs up from the passenger seat. Danny returned it.

Kate pulled the car to a stop. 'Shall I pick you up at five?'

'Yes please,' said Danny. 'Gary's wife is expecting us. I know we've been to see her already this week, but she was in a bad way at the funeral. Of course she would be. Stupid thing to say. So yes, five would be perfect.'

As the car pulled away, John Smithdown dropped an apple core onto the verge in front of Danny. 'You missed a bit,' he shouted as the car headed off.

Danny gave John Smithdown the middle finger and watched them go. It was a hot and hazy day and the moors seemed to shimmer. He saw some children head down the Pennine Way path. They were probably going to take a paddle in the cool waters of one of the reservoirs. One kid pulled his t-shirt off and waved it around his head, shouting at his friends as he ran bare-chested towards the water. Danny knew that going into reservoirs wasn't allowed, but there were more dangerous things in the world.

He took a swig from the water bottle attached to his belt and caught up with the rest of the community payback team as they made their way steadily up the Manchester Road and away from Black Moss reservoir.

An official report has found fundamental deficiencies in the way the police deal with child abuse and the sexual exploitation of children. The Inspectorate of Constabulary found unacceptable delays in obtaining evidence, a failure to take certain cases of missing children seriously and a lack of awareness among local officers about registered sex offenders in their area.

BBC Radio 4 News Friday 25 November 2016

THE END

THE BALLAD OF HANGING LEES

The following is an extract from the book *Twisted Sisters - The Inside Story of Manchester's Most Notorious Child Killers Since the Moors Murderers* by Danny Johnston.

I first came across the terrible handiwork of Beth Hall and Jan Cave at Black Moss Reservoir on the outskirts of Oldham in April 1990. I saw the body of a little boy face down in the sand, weights taped to his tiny chest in a failed attempt to sink his body into the dark waters of the reservoir. The child had been tortured and killed by the two women, one a journalist, the other a police officer. The press later dubbed them the 'Twisted Sisters'.

He was their first victim. But not their last.

At the time, it seemed like no one cared about this poor little boy. A few miles away, rioters had taken over Strangeways Jail, occupying the roof of the prison for 25 days. They provided a show that the whole world seemed very keen to watch.

Thanks to the media, it was the only story that people were offered at the time. The commercial radio station I worked for in 1990 - Manchester Radio - very quickly worked out which side their broadcasting bread was buttered. Strangeways was a listener magnet, and more listeners meant you could charge more for advertisements. Therefore, the more Strangeways we give them, the more money we'll make.

That boy at Black Moss was never identified. To this day I still think about him. I feel ashamed that I didn't try harder to get people interested in his story. But in 1990 every journalist in Manchester saw Strangeways as their ticket to glory. Me included.

Maybe if we had given more airtime to that boy, then Beth Hall and Jan Cave wouldn't have been able to carry on with a killing spree that lasted until 2016. Twelve children died at their hands. *Twelve.*

The two-pronged trick they used to commit then cover up their crimes was ghoulishly simple: wait until the attention of the police and the media was diverted elsewhere by a riot, a bomb or a political scandal... and then strike. Plus, they made sure they targeted kids that had no one to speak on their behalf: care home kids.

They'd worked out that the best way to steal something and not get caught is to steal something nobody really wants. They took children that no one missed - what dreadful words they are to write - while everyone was looking in the other direction.

As well as killing all those poor children, Beth Hall and Jan Cave drugged and kidnapped the son of my friend Kate Smithdown. They attacked and nearly killed her father, former Detective Inspector John Smithdown. They murdered my friend and former colleague at Manchester Radio, Gary Keenan. And they tried to kill me.

But why did they do it?

Because they wanted to. And because society let them.

What they did was evil.

But shame on us for letting it happen right under our noses.

PROLOGUE

Before tonight, Barry Mortimer had never heard Darkthrone's 'Fuck Off and Die'. He was more of a Simply Red man. But now 'Fuck Off and Die' was being sung - *screamed* - right into his bruised and bleeding face by his captors as they cranked the song up to a teeth-rattling level. It must have been the twentieth time they'd played it in a row. Maybe the fiftieth. Hard to tell.

Every time it got to the chorus, the gang members crowded round him and bellowed the words directly at him: 'FUCKOFFANDDIE! FUCKOFFANDDIE!' Even through the skull face bandanas that covered their faces, he could smell the sour, acidic blast of super strength cider on their breaths. Several of the gang even pulled down their masks as they screamed the song into his face, as if removing the thin strip of material would mean that Barry would be able to hear them more clearly.

'FUCKOFFANDDIE! FUCKOFFANDDIE!'

Some of them aren't even bothering to hide their faces now, he thought. *Shitting hell.*

Barry moved a little. The plastic back of the old car seat he was tied to stuck to his sweaty, bare skin. His wrists, attached with plastic ties to the metalwork underneath the seat, were purple and raw. One of his eyes was swollen shut and the other wasn't far behind.

The song came to an end. Barry waited for the grinding, metallic introduction to start again. This time it didn't. Two of the group - something about the way they carried themselves made it clear they were in charge - had called for quiet.

One of the leaders produced a claw hammer and then squatted down, pointing the head of the tool at Barry's face. It touched his skin just above the eyes. Leader Number One pulled a sponge - the kind you'd use to wash your car - from Barry's mouth. Leader Number Two also came down to Barry's level; in his hand was Barry's phone. He waggled it close to the captive man's eyes: 'Passcode,' Number Two said. 'Now.'

There was a pause. Only a few beats but the hesitation caused the hammer to be brought down sharply onto Barry's nose. The cartilage made a cracking sound and blood came spilling down his chest and onto his trousers. 'Passcode. Now.'

Barry was crying now. 'One, eight, one, two,' he said. 'Please. Leave me be. I'm sorry. Really, I am. I've been stupid. I know I have. It won't happen again. But, no more. Please.'

Leader Number Two unlocked the phone, opened the Facebook Messenger app and scrolled through the messages. 'Dear oh dear, Barry,' he said. 'This is properly disappointing. It really is.'

Number Two showed the phone to his compatriot. They both shook their heads. 'Not nice, Barry,' Leader One offered. 'Not nice at all. You haven't just let us down; you've let yourself down.'

Number One produced a marker pen, pulled the top off with their teeth and spat it out. 'What was that number again? One… eight… one… two? That was it.' Each number was written on Barry's forehead in the largest letters that the space could accommodate. 'There you go. Lovely.'

Number Two then pulled a roll of gaffer tape from his pocket and strapped the phone to Barry's chest. He smoothed the tape down, so it stuck to the injured man's clammy skin.

Leader One stood up, turned to the rest of the gang and handed one of them the hammer. 'Hands only, okay?' Number One stated. 'Elbows and arms if you must. Leave his legs. I mean it. We'll need him to walk up to the farm. I'm not carrying this cunt. When we get there, feel free to do his feet and shins. We'll save the head to last.' 'Shall we gag him?' one of the gang asked. The others stood perfectly still; their concentration was fixed firmly on Leader Number One. 'Nah,' said Number One. 'Let the fucker scream.'

ONE

Maggie Ormrod stepped out of the Bull's Head pub and into the warm moorland breeze that swept up the sandstone hills of Piethorne Valley on the border between Oldham and Rochdale. To her right, the lights of Denshaw village; to her left, the ever-present low hum of the M62 motorway that crossed the divide between Greater Manchester and Yorkshire.

Last orders had been called some time ago, but she'd been even more reluctant to leave the pub than usual. Everyone knew Maggie. And everyone knew she preferred the low-ceilinged friendliness of the Bull's Head to her tiny, terraced cottage just a few hundred yards down the Ripponden Road.

That Sunday night though, her requests for one last pint had been more insistent, the need to tell just one more tall tale more pressing. The eventual goodbye hugs were firmer, more flamboyant than ever, and they lasted a few seconds longer than usual. *I wouldn't mind,* the landlord thought, *but she'll be back in tomorrow. You can set your watch by Maggie.*

Outside the pub she undid the plum-coloured jumper that had been wrapped around her waist since she'd arrived at teatime and pulled it over her head. It took a while for her to find the arms and complete the task; she was drunk, but no more drunk than usual.

'Bye Maggie,' the other regulars shouted. 'Mind the road, you're pissed! See you tomorrow.'

She waved to them then dug her hands deep into the pockets of her combat trousers and tipped her face into the wind. She felt it brushing and caressing her face and it made her smile. Maggie sat on a nearby wall out of sight and waited until the last of the pub-goers had left. Then, instead of walking down the A872 towards her house, she turned and took the path that ran behind the pub. In front of her the moonlight bounced off the series of reservoirs that ran through the valley below the road. In the far distance was Ogden Reservoir. Before that, Kitcliffe. Just off to Maggie's right, Piethorne Reservoir. To the left, Rooden. Then up above her to the right, was Norman Hill Reservoir. But she wasn't interested in any of them; Maggie headed to the reservoir that was dead ahead of her: Hanging Lees.

The path down to the triangular reservoir wasn't designed to be walked in the dark by someone who had spent all evening drinking, but Maggie knew every pothole and rock it had to offer and got to the outer wall of Hanging Lees without so much as a stumble. She looked at the ornate metal gate that stopped the public getting access to the cold, grey water. She touched the butterflies and dragonflies that adorned the gate and ran her fingers over the letters and numbers that had been welded into it. She sounded them out as she touched them:

H. A. N. G. I. N. G. L. E. E. S. 1. 8. 7. 0.

Maggie used a large rock to step up to the top of the wall next to the gate, pushed herself upwards, rolled over and slid down the other side.

Easy.

She walked towards the water. Of all the Piethorne Valley reservoirs, Hanging Lees was her favourite. People didn't notice it, it was tucked away to one side and had no path around the back to tempt walkers, so most people just passed it by. Not Maggie. She often came here at night to watch the surface ripple and sway. And to think.

And cry.

Maggie sat down by the water's edge and listened to the sounds of the moors; the hissing of the grass as the wind pushed against it, the left to right arc of bird calls above her, and even the drone of the motorway traffic to the north. She listened to the sounds of the night, and she loved them all.

After a few minutes she took an envelope from the buttoned-up thigh pocket of her combat trousers. She'd wrapped the envelope in a plastic bag, the thin kind you get fruit in at a greengrocer. It fluttered and crackled in the breeze as she rummaged in her other pocket. Maggie lay back on the grass so she could get right to the bottom. Finally, she produced a safety pin and attached the bag with the envelope inside to the front of her jumper. *Just in case it rains. It's forecast. That's thinking ahead, that is.*

It took several goes before she was satisfied with the way it was pinned. She spread it flat with both hands, nodded her approval, then rolled up both sleeves of her jumper. She took out her favourite knife – the one she'd bought at the Army and Navy shop in town - and, with a series of upward strokes, opened up the veins in both arms. Then Maggie lay back in the mossy grass and closed her eyes.

The following morning Maggie's rain-soaked body was found by two walkers, a married couple from Slaithwaite. They'd argued about whether they should look at the envelope pinned to her jumper or leave it to the police. He said leave it. She said they should look, as the poor woman might be from nearby. If the letter had her details, they could contact her family, she pointed out.

After some debate they agreed to leave the envelope where it was. There was no mobile signal out there by the reservoir, so the husband headed off to find the phone box which their map said was up near the pub. 'Which service do I require?' the man had asked when his 999 call was connected. 'Police, I suppose,' he said. 'And ambulance. Bit late for the second one through.'

While her husband was away, the woman carefully released the safety pin and read the note attached to Maggie Ormrod's jumper. Then she wept.

First up, can I say sorry to the person what found me. It can't have been nice for you at all. I have tried to do things neat so as not to terrify you too much. Don't have no nightmares, please.

Sorry also to the ambulance staff what will have been called out. I know its your job and that but no one would want to see a thing like this. You do a great job + I love the NHS.

Any road. Here we are.

My name is Maggie. Everyone who knows me would think I were just fine. Always been happy on the outside me. Inside, I was totally NOT + haven't been right for years.

When I was a kid I was in care. Look up my name. I was at a kids home in Greenacres. The things what were done to me weren't right. Sexual abuse + worse. I was messed with when I were young, just a kiddie. It fucked up my head + I hate them all for letting I happen.

But there's one person who were the worst. I hate him the most.

He should have helped us but he never. His name is John Smithdown and he were a detective with Oldham Police. He abused me/raped me. Said he would kill me if I said owt.

Well he cant kill me now can he?

Sorry again to the ambulance people + the person what found me.

MAGGIE

TWO

<There's a dead body next to Hanging Lees Reservoir. Cops are there now. Looks like a suicide.>

'Body found near reservoir,' muttered Danny Johnston, peering over the top of his glasses to read the Twitter direct message he'd been sent from an anonymous account. 'Absolutely my four favourite words in the whole world, no question about it.'

Danny Googled Hanging Lees Reservoir, then he messaged back:

<technically over the border into Rochdale, that is.>

Danny was a stickler for borders. Always had been.

<Could take a look though. Any pix?>

The reply came within seconds:

<There's a note pinned to her jumper that fingers one of your Oldham cop mates as a paedo. Stick that on your fucking website.>

Charming. Danny took a screenshot of the message just in case the sender had second thoughts, deleted their account and the words were lost forever.

It was a good thing he did, because a few seconds later @rambo536448 was no more, taking their faceless account and their zero number of followers with them.

Danny's DMs were always open - as editor of news website *Oldham Now* he got his stories any way that he could. Most of the tip offs he received centred on traffic problems, illegal dumping of rubbish and local charity events, so this one stood out a little. He did a quick social media search to see if there were any photos or video clips of the scene. Nothing. *Way too specific to be a prank, it must have just happened.*

He got the directions to Hanging Lees - *24 minutes despite heavier than usual traffic* - and headed out of his tiny, rented cottage in the village of Friezland in Saddleworth.

When Danny had opted to move to Oldham, he'd decided quite quickly that he wanted to live in the slightly upmarket area of Saddleworth, although Danny's run-down terrace was probably the least upmarket property in the area. He didn't care. He rather liked the mix of wild countryside and the nearby frou-frou shops and restaurants, but he told people it was for purely practical reasons: *it's easy to get around Oldham rather than fighting your way out of the town centre all the time, plus the phone signal's pretty good.*

He liked the village's name: Friezland. *Sounds like some Nordic crime series on BBC4.*

He was about to close the front door when he remembered that he'd forgotten the two most important pieces of equipment in his job, his mobile phone plus a portable charger. A mobile was all he needed these days. Not only was Danny the editor of *Oldham Now*, but he was also the owner, chief reporter, photographer, videographer and researcher - a journalistic one-man band. 'Hyper Local News' they called it. *Cheap as fuck and the only job I could get, more like.*

The novelty of driving himself around Oldham hadn't quite worn off yet. He'd finished the driving ban and community service order he'd received in 2016. He'd refused a breath test at the scene and because of the seriousness of the incident… *driving into a tree while pissed, don't dress it up as anything else*… the community service order had been a welcome alternative to the custodial sentence that had been talked about in court.

He loved driving through the hills around Oldham. The villages peeled away as the countryside opened up to its full, stark beauty. This was not a place for tree-lovers; when the rounded, brown hills met the slate grey sky, there was little or nothing to break up the stark, straight border between them. Sky at the top. Land at the bottom. *That's the way it is out here. And it's beautiful.*

Google Maps told him that the quickest route to Hanging Lees was to park at the Bull's Head pub and then walk. *Your destination is on the left.* But Google didn't take into the account the fact that the pub car park was cordoned off with police tape, as was the path behind it. As Danny slowed down to get a better look, he was waved on by an angry-looking police officer in a high vis jacket who was muttering to himself and shaking his head. Danny was no lip reader, but he was sure two of the words the officer had used were 'daft' and 'twat'.

Danny gave the officer a cheery wave, carried on up the road and pulled into the first layby he came across. He checked social media again for any mentions of the incident; he did a geo-located search via Tweetdeck, looking for tweets sent within a 10-kilometre radius of the scene that contained photos or video. It was a good way of shutting down the noise of Twitter and zeroing in on exactly what he was looking for. Still nothing.

Danny had been forced to become a reluctant expert in the art of social media since setting up on his own, but there was one thing he refused to let go of from the previous century: maps. Proper actual physical, dog-eared, tea-stained maps. He preferred them because they were very useful when it came to public rights of way - those little dotted lines that showed you the way to get around police tape while still claiming you were just out for a leisurely stroll. He didn't care for Ordnance Survey maps - too much information that he didn't need and way too pricey. He preferred Philip's *Street Atlas* and there was no finer copy than their Greater Manchester edition. Full colour, large scale sections for town centres and all the footpaths you could wish for, especially out here in the sticks. *Bloody lovely.*

A quick flick through his atlas to pages 32-33 showed him that there was a footpath 100 yards up the road that veered off to the left, following a stream through Cold Greave Clough; and what's more it delivered him directly to the other side of Hanging Lees Reservoir. Danny put on a fleece and the walking boots he kept in the boot of his Honda - *just out rambling officer, honestly* - and trotted down the path.

There were three figures on the other side of the clough as Danny got closer. Two Scenes of Crime Officers stood out against the browney greens of the landscape around the reservoir with their bright, ultra-white 'scene' suits. They were standing next to a pop-up crime scene preservation tent, and one was taking photographs. Close to them was a man whose personal colour scheme also clashed dramatically with the environment. He was dressed in well-worn but expensive-looking neon outdoor gear and his curly red hair was rippling in the moorland breeze. Danny was faintly disgusted as to how young he looked. *A teenage detective. Fucking Nora.* Then Danny reminded himself that the red-haired man was probably well into his 30s. *It's not that he's young, Danny boy, it's that you're fucking OLD.*

With his arms tucked firmly to his sides to minimise camera wobble, Danny started taking video of the scene on his phone. He did two wide, left to right panning shots; on the second pass he noticed another figure had joined the scene. To the right of the police activity, someone was doing exactly what Danny was doing - filming the scene. That included filming Danny himself. The difference was that the other videographer was wearing sunglasses and a baseball cap, plus their face was covered with a bandana that had a grinning skull pattern on it.

While still filming with one hand, Mr. Skull Face waved to Danny. Instinctively, Danny waved back. Then Skull Face gave him the finger and disappeared over the lip of the clough.

That's nice.

Danny found a vaguely comfortable looking rock, sat on it, and then trimmed the video clip he preferred and posted it to the *Oldham Now* Twitter page:

> *Breaking: reports of a body on the #Oldham #Rochdale border close to #HangingLees Reservoir. Here's the scene right now as @gmpolice search the scene. More details as we get them, rt and follow @oldhamnow for updates.*

He posted slightly altered versions on both Facebook and Instagram; his aim was to push people to his website rather than have them linger on any of the social media platforms: *I'd like to see a bit of traffic on this come my way, rather than just Mark Zuckerberg benefitting from my hard work.*

When the story had been posted Danny headed down his side of the clough, stepped over the stream at the bottom and headed up towards the site where the body was. The young-looking detective stepped forward to meet him. 'No closer please, sir,' he said. He didn't sound like he was from Oldham. His accent was flatter, maybe Derbyshire.

'Hi there,' Danny said. 'You the Detective Constable here?'

'Detective Inspector,' he replied.

Fucking Nora. You really are old, Danny.

He went into his patter: 'Sorry, Detective Inspector. I know you're busy. I'm Danny from *Oldham Now.* Just wondering if I could get a few words from you about what's going on?'

'Nothing to say at this time,' the Detective Inspector said. 'Please contact the Press Office. Thanks very much.'

Danny persevered, nodding towards the white-suited Scenes of Crimes Officers: 'You've got SOCOs out, so you must be treating this as suspicious.'

'They're going home,' the detective replied. 'Police Coroner's Officers will be taking over. It's not suspicious… there's nothing for you here.

But I'm sure the Press Office will help you, sir. Please. Contact them.'

Danny tried a different tack. 'The top road is getting pretty busy,' he pointed out. 'It might help keep it clear if you can tell people to stay away from the scene. I can get that message out.'

The detective checked that Danny wasn't filming him: 'More likely it'll bring a load of dickheads with packed lunches out here, just to have a nosey at what's going on,' he said. 'The Press Office is your best bet.'

'You know as well as I do that the GMP Press Office is a glorified email account these days,' Danny countered. 'I'll be lucky to get a reply by the end of the week.'

'Move along sir or I'll do you for obstruction,' the detective said.

'Obstruction?' Danny shouted, indignantly. He stretched out both arms, drawing attention to the wide open space of the moors. 'Out here?'

'It was a joke sir,' the detective said with a smile that suggested he felt a bit sorry for Danny. 'Press Office. Please.'

Young, ginger and a comedian. Wow.

The detective turned away. *I'm not having this,* Danny thought. 'Will the Press Office be able to help me with the note that was found with her body?' he asked in a deliberately loud voice. The two Scenes of Crime Officers standing next to Hanging Lees reservoir heard what he said and stopped what they were doing. They looked at the detective and then at Danny.

'Her?' the detective asked.

'Yes,' Danny replied. 'Her.' *Might as well take a swing at this and see what happens. I've got a 50/50 chance at being right.* 'There's a woman under that tent with a note pinned to her jumper.'

'Mr. Johnston,' the detective said, pointing towards a pair of large flat stones by the side of the path. 'Please, take a seat.'

Danny did as he was asked. 'How did this information come your way?' the Detective Inspector asked.

'A direct message on Twitter,' Danny replied. 'I get them a lot. Not many like this one, though.'

'Can I see it?'

'No, you can't. Sorry. Not yet anyway. But the DM also said that the note mentioned a cop. A *paedo* cop.'

'I see. Was there a name attached to that?'

Danny was again going to decline to answer - *make him think I know the name* - when his phone pinged with a WhatsApp message. It was from Kate Smithdown:

<Danny. There are police at the house. They've come for my dad and they're doing a search. Please come ASAP. There are people here and it's all over social media.>

THREE

Danny drove past the end of the driveway to former Detective Inspector John Smithdown's detached home on the Huddersfield Road. It always took him slightly by surprise how close it was to Black Moss Reservoir. He pulled into a small layby just beyond the house. He'd always liked Smithdown's home, a double-fronted stone cottage with views across the small towns and villages that peppered the valleys and hills down towards Oldham town centre. Flower tubs and hanging baskets added to its moorland charm. But today, the outside of the retired detective's home looked very different.

Outside the house, a crowd of about 40 people had gathered. Many were holding up their phones to record what was going on. Most of them were men in their 30s or early 40s. There were several women too and a couple of school age children. The atmosphere was like a slightly raucous party. A man in a skull bandana mask was shouting into the narrow end of an orange and white traffic cone. *Is that the same guy I saw out on the moor?* Danny thought as he got out of his car. Then he noticed that nearly all the people in the crowd were wearing similar skull face bandanas to prevent them from being identified.

'WHO ARE YA?' the man shouted into his makeshift loudhailer.

'JOHN SMITHDOWN,' the crowd shrieked back at him.

'WHAT ARE YA?' he asked.

'BEAST!' the crowd replied.

'WHERE ARE YA?'

'RIGHT! FOOKIN! THERE!' The crowd pointed at the house with each word. 'BEAST! BEAST! BEAST, BEAST, BEAST' they added.

Then the chant began again: 'WHO ARE YA?...'

This is some proper organised shit, Danny thought as he approached the front of the short drive. Several police officers were leaving the house with plastic bags containing DVDs, several cameras, a laptop and dozens of VHS cassettes. Through the milky plastic of one of the bags Danny could see that one was marked in faded red marker pen.

'WEDDING SUPER 8 FOOTAGE DO NOT RECORD OVER THIS PLEASE!!'

'Don't you need a warrant to do this?' Danny asked to any of the officers willing to listen, realising as he spoke that he didn't really know what he was talking about. *You sound like some character in a shit TV cop show.*

'Under the Police and Criminal Evidence Act we can search at the point of arrest to look for supporting evidence, sir,' said a male detective at the doorway. He was dressed in a black suit and white shirt - both contrasted sharply with the shock of bright red curly hair that was piled on top of his head.

'Arrest?' asked Danny. 'John Smithdown is in his 80s; he's had a stroke. Is this all entirely necessary? More importantly… the man's a fucking hero - a decorated *police* hero - worth more than you lads all rolled into one.'

'It's Mr. Johnston, isn't it?' the officer said. 'I believe you were waving your iPhone about up on the moors earlier. We'll be checking your Twitter feed at some point.'

'Check it all you want, mate,' Danny said. 'That's what it's there for.'

'Yes, I'm afraid we have arrested Mr. Smithdown…' the officer continued, noticing that Danny was staring at his hair. 'And no sir, Oldham Police do not have a policy of only employing gingers. Just me and my brother. I assume you met him out on the moors?'

'We did meet. He's a comic too.' Danny looked around the detective and through the open door of the cottage. 'Can I see him? Can I talk to John?'

Before the detective could speak, Danny heard Kate Smithdown's voice from inside the house. 'Danny! Get in here, now. Fuck what ginger bollocks says.'

The detective formed his lips into an *ooooh* of mock offence as Danny stepped into John Smithdown's cottage. Smithdown was sitting in his favourite armchair in the lounge with Kate kneeling next to him. She'd clearly been crying but that had now passed. Now she just looked angry. Very angry.

The stroke John Smithdown had suffered several years earlier had dampened the movement in his face a little, but Danny was still able to clearly see the hurt on his old friend's features. Smithdown didn't acknowledge Danny's arrival. He was staring at a set of photographs on a bookcase next to the open fireplace. The photos were mainly of Jean Smithdown, the retired detective's wife and Kate's mum. Jean had died in 2016. Cancer.

'Dad, Danny's here,' Kate said, rubbing her father's arm reassuringly and forcing a smile. 'Look. It's Danny. Here to help. Like always. Oh, Danny thanks for coming.'

'Of course, Kate. No problem. John, how are you, mate?'

Smithdown carried on staring at the photos of his late wife. 'What a woman, she was,' he said, quietly. 'By Christ. Oldham's answer to Audrey Hepburn. Thank God she's not around to see this.'

'John, we need to speak,' said Danny. He looked around and saw the detective was talking to a uniformed officer in the front doorway. 'I had a message this morning, about a woman found dead over at Hanging Lees Reservoir.'

'Oh aye?' was all that Smithdown said in reply; he was still looking at the photographs of his wife.

'She had a note pinned to her,' Danny continued. 'A suicide note. It named you, John.'

'So, I believe,' Smithdown said, still seemingly distracted by the photos.

'That's all Ron Weasley out there would tell us,' Kate added, nodding towards the red-haired detective.

'John, I'm really sorry,' Danny said. 'We're short of time here and you need to know. It said you abused her as a kid.'

'Danny, what the fuck are you talking about?' interrupted Kate.

'Kate, please,' Danny urged. 'John, do you understand me?'

Smithdown looked at Danny, then at his daughter. Before he could reply, the detective stepped into the living room: 'Right, Mr. Smithdown. You've had your usual cautions and explanations. I believe your solicitor is on their way to Oldham police station. It's time you came with us, I reckon.'

Smithdown looked out of the window of his cottage and saw the crowd outside. 'Kate, Danny… what about those people?'

'It's not safe for him,' Kate said. 'Please. Can't you clear them away first?'

'Don't worry, we'll make sure he's alright,' the detective said to Kate. 'He's in good hands.' He turned his attention to Smithdown, making a point of speaking much louder: 'WE'VE GOT TO GO NOW, MR SMITHDOWN. LET'S GET YOU TO OLDHAM STATION. BET IT'S BEEN A WHILE SINCE YOU'VE BEEN THERE, ISN'T IT?'

'TURN THE VOLUME DOWN, LAD… I'M NOT DEAF,' Smithdown shouted back. 'I'M NOT A CHILD MOLESTOR,

NEITHER. Help me up, Kate. Let's get this sorted.'

She grabbed a coat for her father as they headed for the door. Danny helped him on with the light brown windcheater. Smithdown looked at Danny, then he did something that he'd never done in the four decades that Danny had known him - the retired detective gave him a hug. 'I'm *scared*, Danny lad,' he whispered.

Then former Detective Inspector John Smithdown was led away by officers from Greater Manchester Police. Danny watched as two uniformed officers cleared a path so Smithdown could get in their unmarked car. As he walked along the gravel path, the crowd ramped up their shouts as he passed: 'WHO ARE YA?'

'JOHN SMITHDOWN!'

'WHAT ARE YA?'

'BEAST!'

Everyone in the crowd seemed to be pointing a camera phone in Smithdown's direction. Danny held Kate's hand as her father bent his head to get into the back seat of the police car. Danny watched the face of the young officer who was helping keep the crowd back. He was sure he saw him smile and give a wink to one of the ringleaders. Just before the door closed, a young woman holding a child of about three in her arms, got close enough to spit in Smithdown's face.

'BEAST! BEAST! BEAST, BEAST, BEAST!' the crowd sang.

FOUR

BODY FOUND AT HANGING LEES RESERVOIR

Danny Johnston - Oldham Now

Police in Oldham are investigating after the death of a woman at a local beauty spot.

The body was discovered at Hanging Lees Reservoir in Piethorne Valley by a couple out walking early this morning. The woman hasn't been named by police, but it's believed she was in her 50s and lived locally.

Detectives are examining a note that had been left at the scene - it had been pinned to the woman's body.

The moors around the reservoir close to the A627 Ripponden Road have been sealed off and a search of the area is taking place.

Police initially thought that the circumstances surrounding were not suspicious but in a new development, a man in his 80s has been arrested following the discovery.

It's believed he is helping police with their inquiries into what's been described as a 'non-recent abuse' case.

It's expected that the woman will be named later today.

FIVE

When Danny's phone thrummed and 'Kate Smithdown' appeared on the display, he knew he was in for a pretty harsh conversation inspired by his *Oldham Now* story.

He'd written it while sitting in his car outside John Smithdown's house, but he'd done what he always did when covering 'death' stories; he'd left out the code that told WordPress to insert adverts into the story. Despite the fact that doing this cost him money, it had always been Danny's policy. It was one thing to get 15 pence a click thanks to a story about school dinner ladies going on strike or a missing dog being reunited with its owner, but it was quite another to profit from someone's death. This was financially unfortunate for Danny, as the site always experienced a noticeable analytic spike with death stories. *If you weren't so self-righteous, Danny Johnston, you wouldn't be so skint.*

'What the fuck is that piece all about?' Kate shouted. 'Why would you post that? I mean, seriously. Dad's your fucking friend, for Christ's sake. My fucking son will have seen it too, Danny. Did you think about Jonathan's feelings before you wrote it, or do you just not care?'

Danny took a breath before he answered: 'It's exactly what I would have written if I didn't know your dad. Word for word. I can't ignore what's happened just because it involves John Smithdown. Plus, I didn't name him.'

'You don't need to name him, Danny,' Kate said, her anger seemed to have gone up a notch. 'Have you looked on social media? There are videos of him being arrested everywhere. They're chanting his name, for God's sake. Hashtag fucking BEAST is trending locally.'

'Well, there you go,' Danny pointed out. 'It looks like I'm the responsible one, then, doesn't it? That's the difference between a journalist and someone with access to the internet. We adhere to the rules. Look, I did what I had to do - bare minimum, no more. Where are you now?'

'I'm at Oldham Police Station,' Kate said. 'And it would be quite nice if my friend Danny Something would get himself down here and offer a bit of fucking support.'

Danny always knew he was in trouble with Kate when she called him Danny Something - the name she'd used when they'd first met nearly thirty years earlier. He'd been a reporter for Manchester Radio; she was a journalist on the *Oldham Messenger*. 'Jimmy Something, isn't it?' she'd asked in 1990, struggling to remember the person she'd heard on the radio. 'Danny Something,' he'd corrected her, as a joke. And it had struck.

'You want support?' he said. 'Not a problem. Whatever you want. I mean it. What do you want me to do?'

'Get your arse down here, sharpish. Dad's just gone in for questioning. I'm freaking out and I want you here.'

'Of course. I'm literally on my way. I'll be there in 20 minutes.'

There was a pause. A few beats. 'We first met at a police station, didn't we Danny?' she said.

'Yes, we did, Kate.'

'It was a press conference after the kid's body was found at Black Moss. There was only you and me there, do you remember?'

'I do, indeed.'

'God, it was so long ago. Hard to believe I'm in my late 40s now.'

'It's been several years since you were in your 40s, Kate Smithdown. Let's do the maths, shall we…?' '

'Just shut it, will you?' Another moment of quiet. 'I'm scared, Danny,' Kate said. '*Really* scared. I need to ring the school - speak to Jonathan. He needs to find out what's going on with his grandad from me, not from social fucking media.'

'How do you think he'll take it?' Danny asked; he regretted it immediately.

'He's fifteen, he's in a special school for kids with extreme emotional difficulties and his grandad is all over the internet as Oldham's answer to Jimmy Savile. How do you think he's going to take it?'

'It'll be alright,' Danny said, summoning up his best reassuring voice. 'I'm sure it will. I'll be there as soon as I can.'

'Good. Be as quick as you can. And no stopping off to write any more stories. Understood?'

'Understood.'

SIX

'Which one are you again?' Smithdown asked as he neatly hung his jacket on the back of a chair in the interview room. 'You two ginger lads look the same to me. No offence, obviously.'

'None taken, Mr. Smithdown,' the DI said, pulling up a chair. 'I'm Detective Inspector Patrick McIntyre. This is Detective Constable Karl McIntyre. Yes, we are related. You might have guessed that already.'

'Where's the tape machine?' Smithdown said. He looked at his solicitor as she took out a notepad and pen from her shoulder bag. 'Paulina, this should be being taped.'

'It's Digital Interview Recording now, Mr Smithdown,' the DC replied. 'DIR. All recorded evidence goes to a central server. No more sticking pencils into C90 cassettes. Easier for all concerned.'

'It's fine John,' Paulina said. 'Don't worry. We'll soon sort this out.'

'Right then,' DI McIntyre said. 'I'll be asking the questions; DC McIntyre will be observing. Shall we make a start?'

RECORD OF INTERVIEW
Person interviewed: SMITHDOWN, John (11/1/39)
Place of interview: Oldham Police Station
Time commenced: 1340 hours
Interviewer(s): DI3716 McIntyre, Patrick DC2184 McIntyre, Karl.
Other person(s) present: Paulina Scorer - Solicitor from Blanco & Harkness Solicitors.
Usual introductions, cautions and advice.
This is the first interview with JOHN SMITHDOWN - SMITHDOWN confirms that no questions have been asked before the recording begins.
DI MCINTYRE: Mr Smithdown, the person I want to talk to you this afternoon is Margaret Jane Ormrod, known as Maggie Ormrod. Does that name mean anything to you?
SMITHDOWN: I suppose that's the name of the poor woman found out at Hanging Lees this morning?

DI MCINTYRE: That's correct. Did you know that name before today?
SMITHDOWN: I did not, no.
DI MCINTYRE: Are you absolutely sure about that?
SMITHDOWN: Yes, I am. That's why I said it.
DI MCINTYRE: You formerly worked for Greater Manchester Police - when did you become a police officer, Mr Smithdown?
SMITHDOWN: I'd retired by the time you'd worked out where your dick was, lad, put it like that.
DI MCINTYRE: For the benefit of the recording, Mr Smithdown's solicitor Ms Scorer just very quietly advised him to answer the question, though she does seem to find what he said quite amusing. What year, Mr Smithdown?
SMITHDOWN: 1965.
DI MCINTYRE: What dealings did you have with children during the 60s and 70s? In particular, I'm meaning children that were in the care of the local authorities.
SMITHDOWN: Well, in those days you'd basically round them up, take them home, then repeat. There were no child protection units in those days. It wasn't very touchy feely… if you'll excuse the expression. You'd just scoop them up and put them back where they were supposed to be. If they'd done something that they shouldn't have done while they were out and about, then we'd deal with it accordingly.
DC MCINTYRE: You had quite the career, didn't you Mr Smithdown? Commendations left, right and centre. Mentioned in dispatches in 1973 for pulling two kids out of an abusive household. Mum and Dad were proper wrong uns, weren't they? Commended again for saving a teenage lad and a young girl in '88 over at Kinder Scout. You were involved in the Black Moss murder case in 1990 as well, I see. All those kids killed by the two women. Sisters, weren't they? Those poor children. Terrible. But there's a pattern here, isn't there? A common thread. Children, Mr Smithdown. Time and again. Have you noticed? I have. There always seems to be children involved in your heroics. Every time. For the benefit of the recording, Mr Smithdown has just mouthed the words 'Fucking Nora' in response. Have you ever had any sexual interest in children, Mr Smithdown?
MS SCORER: Oh, come on.
SMITHDOWN: DI McIntyre, really? What do you lads call it these days? ABE? Achieving Best Evidence? And this is your idea of Achieving Best Evidence, is it? No, lad. I have zero sexual interest in children.
DI MCINTYRE: You were suspended in 1988 for harming a child

though, weren't you? A child in your custody. You split her lip open, I believe?

SMITHDOWN: I was cleared of any wrongdoing.

DI MCINTYRE: Don't see any record of you denying that you did it, though? In fact, it looks like you admitted it at the time.

SMITHDOWN: I was cleared.

DI MCINTYRE: Okay, Mr Smithdown. Can we talk about events up on the moors today, please? At Hanging Lees.

SMITHDOWN: If you want to. Fine. Not sure if I can be of any use though.

DI MCINTYRE: As a result of a note we found at the scene, we removed a variety of items from your house today, Mr Smithdown.

SMITHDOWN: I'm old, but I'm not stupid. Yes, I did happen to notice your lads stomping about the place this morning. I want everything back exactly as it was, some of that stuff is irreplaceable.

DI MCINTYRE: Well, we're examining those items at the moment. They're in safe hands. Are we likely to finding anything that would incriminate you in any way?

SMITHDOWN: Yes… crimes against fashion from my wedding videos. Guilty as charged, but it was the 70s after all. Other than that, no. Nothing incriminating.

DI MCINTYRE: Are we likely to find any material of a sexual nature, Mr Smithdown?

SMITHDOWN: Just me in my Speedos in Benidorm in 1973, if that's the kind of thing that gets you going.

MS SCORER: John, let's keep the answers to the point, shall we, then we can get you home.

DI MCINTYRE: Thank you, Ms Scorer. I agree. I don't think we're finding this quite as funny as you are, Mr Smithdown. A woman has taken her own life. She opened both her arms up from top to bottom. I've spent the morning looking at her body.

SMITHDOWN: You're right. It isn't funny. It's horrible. I'm sorry. But I don't know this poor woman. I never heard about her until Danny… until now.

DI MCINTYRE: That's Danny Johnston, the gentleman who was at your house earlier. Is he your daughter's boyfriend?

SMITHDOWN: No. Everyone thinks that, but they're just friends.

DI MCINTYRE: Mr Johnston is a journalist, isn't he?

SMITHDOWN: He is.

DI MCINTYRE: And he runs the *Oldham Now* website, is that correct?

SMITHDOWN: Yes, he does.
DI MCINTYRE: Mr Johnston was spotted out on the moors at Hanging Lees this morning, filming the scene where the body was found. He was also asking questions at the scene. He seemed to have a surprising amount of knowledge about what had gone on. Amazing really, how much he seemed to know. How did he come by that information?
SMITHDOWN: I don't know. He's a journalist. A very good one as it happens. He's been ahead of you lads more than once. And me, for that matter.
DI MCINTYRE: You have a very long connection with Mr Johnston, don't you? He was one of the kids you pulled out of that abusive household in '73, wasn't he? I read his book, the one he wrote about the Black Moss case. They called it the house of horrors in the press, didn't they? You probably saved his life, is that fair to say?
SMITHDOWN: Now then, which of the many questions that you've just fired at me do you want me to answer, Detective Inspector? Remember - ABE.
DI MCINTYRE: How does your friend Danny Johnston, who you've known since the 1970s, know so much about the body found at Hanging Lees?
SMITHDOWN: I don't know. Why don't you ask him? Like I say, he's very good at his job.
DI MCINTYRE: For the benefit of the recording, I'm now showing Mr Smithdown a cutting from the *Manchester Evening News* dated the third of February 1973. The article is headlined 'CHILDREN RESCUED FROM HORROR HOUSE'. The article is accompanied by a photograph of a police officer with two young children. I believe the photo is of Danny Johnston and his sister being rescued from the aforementioned house. Is that you in the photograph with them, Mr Smithdown?
SMITHDOWN: Yes, it is.
DI MCINTYRE: I'm now showing Mr Smithdown another photograph. This is a colour photograph, looks like it was taken on a domestic type of camera. It's a bit creased but the people in the picture are clearly discernible. It's of a man with his arm around a young girl, aged about 11 or 12 years. Is that also you in the colour photograph?
SMITHDOWN: Okay… Let's have a look. Right. Well it certainly looks like me, yes.
DI MCINTYRE: It does, doesn't it? Do you know the girl in the photograph, Mr Smithdown?

SMITHDOWN: I'm afraid I don't. Look, where is this is going?
DI MCINTYRE: This photo was found at Maggie Ormrod's house this morning. I believe that's you in the picture and I believe the young girl with you is Maggie.
SMITHDOWN: Right, so that's why you were bagging up my photo albums this morning, was it? Looking for more pictures? You've got one photo as a piece of evidence and that gives you the okay to take every picture of mine that you can lay your hands on. Right you are. I don't know this girl. And that's that.
DI MCINTYRE: I believe that despite what you have told us you did know Maggie Ormrod, Mr Smithdown. I believe you had a sexual interest in her and that you acted on that sexual interest. I believe that what happened to Maggie has played on her mind for 40 odd years. It tortured her, in fact. And I believe that's why she took her own life this morning. Anything to say, Mr Smithdown? You're very quiet all of a sudden.
MS SCORER: I think we should stop, Mr McIntyre. I think Mr Smithdown is unwell.
DI MCINTYRE: For the recording, here's the letter that Maggie had pinned to herself before taking her own life. In the letter she states: 'He should have helped us but he never. His name is John Smithdown, and he were a detective with Oldham Police. He abused me/raped me. Said he would kill me if I said owt.'
MS SCORER: Please, we need to stop. John, are you okay?
DI MCINTYRE: 'His name is John Smithdown… He abused me/raped me.' That's what it says. Did you, Mr Smithdown? Did you abuse that little girl? What do you have to say? Mr Smithdown? Can you hear me? Right. Okay. We should stop. Mr Smithdown doesn't look right. Okay, let's stop.

End of recording: 13.58

SEVEN

After Smithdown had been taken away from his house, Danny had talked to a few of the more reasonable-looking members of the mob outside and discovered where Maggie Ormrod had lived. He felt bad that he'd lied to Kate about going straight to the police station but justified it in his own mind: *I'm of more use here trying to find out what the fuck has happened. Sitting about like a spare part in the waiting area of Oldham nick isn't going to help John.*

Maggie's terraced house on the outskirts of Denshaw stood out from the others. Not just because there was a policeman stood outside it - though that certainly helped - but because, compared to its slightly upmarket neighbours, it looked ramshackle and uncared for. Denshaw had changed in recent years with incomers and newbuilds taking the area into a higher price bracket. Maggie Ormrod's house had stayed defiantly ungentrified.

The tiny front garden was almost filled with a single, battered sofa that had a large scorch mark on one of the cushions. Several old paint tins and a toy pram accompanied it. The path from the battered gate to Maggie's door was barely ten feet long. There was a hand-written sign taped onto Maggie's door:

BELL NAKKERED, KNOCK REELY HARD!

Danny stood at the gate and looked at the policeman. The policeman looked at Danny and shook his head. 'Good day, officer,' Danny said with a smile. 'You're doing a cracking job.'

Danny changed direction, swung open an altogether less battered-looking gate and knocked on the house to the right of Maggie's. He winked at the police officer as he waited. A man in his 60s opened the door; Danny got as far as… 'Hi, I'm from *Oldham Now…*' when the door was quickly closed again.

'That's a shame,' the officer said, quietly, as Danny walked past

Maggie's house and went to the house to the left. 'Not your day, is it?'

'Least I don't spend all my time standing around like Piffy on a rock bun doing nowt,' Danny replied with a smile. "Piffy on a rock bun" was an old Mancunian expression he'd picked up from John Smithdown. It meant hanging around, doing nothing. *My God, I'm actually turning into the old bastard.*

At the second house, the door was opened by a woman of Danny's age holding a cat. Danny smiled and introduced himself; he was braced for the same treatment, but the door stayed opened and the woman listened to what he had to say. 'I was wondering if I could ask you about the woman who lived next door... Maggie Ormrod, I believe that was her name. Did you know her?'

'Yes, I knew Maggie,' the neighbour said. Her accent was only lightly Mancunian, almost non-existent. *Not from round here. Trendy incomer? Bit like yourself, Danny boy.* 'Hard NOT to know people when you live next door to them in little terraced houses like these.'

'That's a fair point,' Danny admitted. With as little fuss as possible, Danny took out his phone. 'I assume you've heard about what happened up at Hanging Lees... Sorry, do you mind if I record you? Is that okay?'

'I suppose so,' she said. Her eyes darted for the slightest moment towards the policeman who was just a few feet away from them. 'What do you want to know?'

'What was Maggie like?' Danny said, instinctively going for an open question - who, what, when, where, why, which, how - that invited the other person to speak.

The woman thought for a moment. There was a slightly awkward silence. Danny's experience told him to wait... *never interrupt silence, let them think. Wait. The less the journalist speaks the more the interviewee might say.*

'She was alright...' the woman began, hesitantly. 'She had a good heart did Maggie. Yes. A good heart. She was a bit of a... character, you might say. Always cheery and happy. But very much her own person. I'd help her out sometimes. She'd do the odd job for me. Yeah. She was a good un. So sad to hear about what's happened.'

Danny nodded and pulled a gently sympathetic face. He created another few beats of silence and waited to see if she was going to say something else. He was about to ask when the woman had last seen Maggie, when she unexpectedly spoke again: 'Never had any trouble with her. Good as gold. Until recently that is.'

'How do you mean?' asked Danny. Another open question - Danny left some silence. Again, she gave the slightest of looks towards the police officer.

‘She always… God, people always say this in these kinds of situations, don’t they? She kept herself to herself. That was Maggie. She was very self-contained. But lately, there were more people about next door. Pretty noisy people, to be honest. Making a din late at night. Partying. You know the kind of thing. I had to have words. We didn’t fall out, but I did ask her to keep it down a bit.’

‘How would you describe these people?’ Danny asked.

‘Sorry, I just thought you wanted a few nice words about Maggie,’ the woman said, sounding slightly annoyed. She motioned towards the officer outside Maggie’s door. ‘You seem more like a policeman than he does.’

‘Sorry. Last thing I’d want to do is sound like that. Can I ask your name?’

‘I’d rather not give my name thanks,’ she said. ‘Look, I’ve got things to do. That’s enough, isn’t it?’

‘Sure. I really appreciate it, thanks.’

She closed the door. The police officer was staring directly at him now; he seemed to want Danny to know that he’d been taking in everything that had been said. Danny paused and saved the recording on his phone. He marked it as MAGGIE NEIGHBOUR. He noticed a text had come in while he’d been interviewing the woman. It was from Kate Smithdown:

<Danny I know you’re probably on the knocker asking questions, you predictable bastard, but you really need to come now. Dad’s in a bad way. He’s in the Royal Oldham Hospital. I mean it, come now.>

EIGHT

'It must be handy if there's trouble at the football stadium,' Danny said as he looked at the grainy remains of his tea that was stuck to the bottom of the paper vending machine cup.

'What are you on about?' Kate asked as she prodded at her phone.

'This hospital. It's right next door to Oldham Athletic's ground. If it all kicks off, as it were, then it's not far to come. For the wounded and that. No need for ambulances. The walking wounded can literally just walk around the corner.'

'When was the last time you went to a football match?' Kate asked.

'Do you know what?' Danny replied. 'I don't think I've ever actually been to a football match.'

'Exactly,' Kate said. 'It's not the 1970s, Danny. Nobody does hooliganism anymore. The football fans all work at PC World and have mortgages. The world's changed. It's not all Angel Delight and The Magic Roundabout out there anymore, you know. We have Thai food and Amazon Prime nowadays. You live in the past, that's your problem.'

'I wouldn't say I *live* in the past,' he huffed.

'Well, you've certainly got a holiday cottage there, put it like that.'

'It was a genuine loss to comedy when you decided to become a… whatever it is you are now,' Danny said.

'I'm a lady of leisure…' she pointed out. Kate took great delight in reminding Danny of her 'retired' status. The media businesses she'd built up over the years had all been bought out, meaning she never had to work again. 'But what I really am right now is pissed off about waiting here for news about Dad,' Kate added. 'It's been over an hour.'

A woman of about 60 wearing a volunteer's badge approached them with a trolley; she put a hand gently on Kate's shoulder and smiled. 'How are you two doing? It's awful just waiting isn't?'

'Was I moaning?' Kate said and smiled back. 'Nobody likes a moaner, do they? Not in a hospital anyway. We're just waiting for someone to tell us how my dad is. Sorry.'

'Don't be - they'll be back to you as soon as they can,' she said. 'Promise.'

Her voice was quiet and calming. Danny liked to listen out for accents; hers wasn't from around Oldham. *Derbyshire maybe. Not sure. Either way she must be from a factory where they make really nice volunteers. Why can't everyone be like that?*

'I've got some biscuits and a spot of cordial spare if you want it,' the woman said. 'Teas and coffees have all gone. Would you like a bit to keep you going?'

'Oh, yes please,' Kate said, as if she'd been offered the finest champagne. 'Got any Vimto?'

'I have indeed. Two Vimtos, coming right up.'

The woman handed them two plastic cups of juice and two mini packs of digestive biscuits. 'Thank you so much,' Danny said.

'I'll be back round later on,' the volunteer said, pushing her trolley. 'Hopefully, I won't see you… if you know what I mean. Everything will be fine, you'll see. By the time I'm back you'll be on your way home. Best of luck with your dad.'

'Thank you,' Kate said as the woman left. 'She was so nice. God, I fucking love Vimto.'

Danny spotted a doctor walking towards them in the waiting area. 'Is that the guy who admitted your dad?' he asked.

'Yes, that's him,' Kate confirmed. 'He's Spanish. Christ, it must have been a shock for him ending up in Oldham...'

'He's very young-looking,' Danny pointed out. 'Fuck. That's exactly the kind of thing your dad would say.'

'Oh shit, Danny, look at him. His face is so stern.' Kate wiped her eyes then took hold of Danny's hand and squeezed until it hurt. Danny could feel that she was shaking.

They both stood up. The doctor smiled: 'Hello. Hi. Please. Don't be worried. Please. He's doing okay. He's doing good.' His accent was an eccentric mix of Spain and Oldham. 'Please, won't you sit down?'

'Do you know happened?' Kate asked. She had slightly loosened her grip on Danny's hand, but it still hurt.

'He had a stroke in the past, correct?' the doctor checked.

'Correct,' Danny and Kate said at the same time. *He's not your dad you know, he's Kate's,* Danny reminded himself.

'Well, your dad has had a Transient Ischaemic Attack - a TIA. That's a kind of mini stroke. The symptoms are the same, but the difference is that they pass. No lasting harm. His arm and face were numb when he arrived, but that's fading now. His speech hasn't degenerated. He's doing okay. He's upset. A bit confused. But all in all, not too bad.'

'Oh, thank you,' Kate said, freeing her hand from Danny's and touching the doctor's arm. 'Thank you so much. Can I see him?'

'I would like you to see him very much,' the doctor said. 'Because I think it would be a very good idea if he were to stay here tonight. Your father, on the other hand… he disagrees.'

'Stubborn old bugger,' Kate whispered and rolled her eyes at Danny.

'Maybe you could help convince him for me?' the doctor added.

'Bloody right I will,' Kate confirmed. 'Lead the way.'

'Of course,' the doctor said. He took Danny and Kate through a set of double doors, down a corridor and into the Stroke Unit. Lying in bed, John Smithdown mouthed the words 'fucking' and 'Nora' when he saw his daughter approach and pulled himself slightly upright.

'Mr Smithdown,' the doctor said introducing Kate as if she was entering a stage. 'I'm afraid you are in very serious trouble now…'

'Don't you fellahs take an oath or something, promising not to cause harm to your patients?' Smithdown said. He nodded at his daughter: 'You've put me right in harm's way here.'

The doctor held up his hands as if to indicate there was nothing he could do.

'Dad,' Kate began. 'This lovely doctor is too polite to say it, but I'm not. Stop being a silly twat and do as you're told. I mean it. If he says you need to stop here, you need to stop here. There's no reason for you to go home, we need you at your best to fight this Hanging Lees bollocks. Am I making myself clear? You're staying put and that's final. DO YOU UNDERSTAND?'

'Yes,' Smithdown said quietly.

'Good. Any more of this crap and I'll smack your legs, understand?'

'Fully,' her father confirmed. Danny smiled. He knew that Kate's mum used to use that expression when she was being troublesome as a child. She never actually smacked her legs - that's why it became a family joke. *God, imagine growing up like that.*

'I'd say that was very much settled then,' the doctor said. He looked at Kate. 'Go home, you and your husband need rest too.'

'Oh, he's not my husband,' Kate said, winking at Danny. The doctor flashed what Danny had to admit was a very winning smile at Kate. *She's practically old enough to be your mum, mate,* Danny thought. *Pack it in. These lads can't help themselves when Kate's around, can they?*

'Danny,' Kate said. 'We need to go and see Jonathan. Tell him what's happened. Will you come with me?'

'Yes, of course I will,' Danny confirmed.

'It's my son,' Kate explained to the doctor, unnecessarily, in Danny's opinion. 'He's at a residential school. We have to treat news like this very carefully.'

The doctor nodded sympathetically. 'You do what you need to do. We'll take good care of your father.' Inside his head, Danny repeated the doctor's words back, only in a whiny voice. *You do what you need to do. Meeeh, meeh, meeh I'm so caring.* The moment he'd done it he felt bad. He looked around just in case he'd accidentally said it out loud.

'Hey… Danny,' John Smithdown said, indicating that Danny should come closer with a weak wave of his hand. 'Here a minute.'

Danny squatted next to Smithdown's bed and looked at the retired detective. Close up, the jokiness wasn't as apparent. His eyes were grey and watery, and he looked afraid. 'What is it, John?'

'Too good looking for my taste, that doctor,' Smithdown said in a whisper.

'Dead right, mate,' Danny winked. 'Fucking Antonio Banderas with a stethoscope. Coming over here, being all professional and handsome. Bollocks to him.'

Smithdown smiled for a brief moment. Then it slipped away: 'Listen to me,' he said quietly. 'I'm being serious, now. I'm no angel. Never said I was. I've done some things that wouldn't be tolerated in this day and age. I accept that. But I'm telling you now, I don't know that woman up at Hanging Lees. And I certainly didn't know her as a kid. You must believe me. You do believe me, don't you, lad?'

'Of course I do, John,' Danny said. 'Totally. Don't worry. We'll put this right.'

NINE

30 March 1975

Maggie Ormrod slipped a finger into the coin return holder of the pinball machine and scooped out a ten pence piece. *Ace!*

She paused a moment and looked at the machine's flashing lights; a cartoon drawing of a confident-looking man with light brown way hair was on the main upright panel alongside a flashing red, white and blue NUMBER 1. The boys at the care home had been talking about the man the other day after there'd been a piece about him on *John Craven's Newsround.* The boys said he was mad - *not John Craven, he's not mad, he's nice* - and that he'd broken every bone in his body. They'd been arguing about how to pronounce his name and John Craven had settled it when he said: *Evel Knievel.*

Maggie looked at the man's image on the pinball machine: *fancy being called Evel! It must cause all sorts of mither… No one would believe a word you said! If you got stopped by the police and they said, 'right, what's all this then? You were going right fast on that bike, sir… what's your name, then?' And then you said, 'Evel', they'd be like, 'right then, smart arse, you'd better come with us.' You'd never get NOWT done being called Evel.*

Maggie slipped the coin into the flapped pocket on the front of her dungarees and fastened the button to secure it. She gave it a little pat and the coins inside made a satisfying tik tak sound. She watched the flashing lights of the pinball machine for a few moments more. Pinball machines didn't interest Maggie. *Just a load of noise and lights and what do you get at the end? Nowt. Another go if you're lucky. Waste of money.*

No. What Maggie liked was Penny Falls. Now THAT was a game worth playing. *I'll have to go next door for that. Just daft pinball in here.* Maggie sorted out her 'shiny coins' from her 'not shiny coins'; the 'not shiny' ones went back into her special pocket. Then she crossed the arcade tent, stood on her tiptoes and pushed her 'shiny coins' across the counter of the change booth. The man behind the counter barely looked at her as he swapped them for two pence pieces, the accepted currency of the experienced Penny Falls player.

Maggie left the pinball 'arcade' - in reality a canvas rectangle supported by scaffolding poles - and stepped outside into the warm, Spring air. The pinball area smelled of boys: cigarettes, sweat and cider. *Yuk! Have a bath now and again yer mucky buggers.*

But outside was different. Outside had all the best smells ever all rolled into one: doughnuts, candy floss, popcorn, hot dogs, onions and that difficult-to-pin-down oily odour that seemed to hang over every travelling fair. Maggie wasn't sure what was better: the smell of the fair or the fact that no one knew that she was here smelling it. For a moment she thought about spending a few of her precious coins on a burger - she'd barely eaten all day - but decided to be cautious. *I'll have a double burger with my winnings. With chips n'all!*

The rides added a wonderful soundtrack to the smells. The Cyclone, the Mad Mouse and the Walzters; each had its own special set of clanks and rattles, sending out a message that expressed the possibility of real danger and genuine mishap. Maggie heard the cries of the fairground workers too: 'Readyboyzangirlz?' a man shouted over the Waltzer's fuzzy PA system, dipping the pounding music slightly to make sure his slurry words of warning could be heard. 'I SAID... AREYOOREADYBOYZANGIRLZ?'

'YEAH!' came the replies from the excited teenagers who were bracing themselves for the ride to start.

'OKAYTHEN... HEREWEGOHOLDTIGHT!'

Then the ride lurched into life and there were screams. Lots of screams.

Maggie looked beyond the rides and out towards the huge expanse of dark water next to the fairground site. She watched as the cascading, spinning funfair lights danced across the surface of the Alexandra Park boating lake; the skittering reflections made the fair seem twice the size that it really was. Maggie didn't like the lake. It's featureless sheen uneased her. She didn't like water full stop - lakes, ponds, pools and reservoirs all gave her chills. But she also felt weirdly excited by them too; the same fear that she imagined people experienced when they went on fairground rides. Maggie didn't like fairground rides much either; she liked Penny Falls.

As she headed for the slot machine arcade, Maggie made a point of staying as close to the tents as possible, brushing the canvas with her hand as she walked past. The touch of the heavy-duty material made her feel safe. Safe from the water. Safe from anyone who might spot her and wonder why such a young girl was on her own. Just... safe.

As she entered the tent there was a new smell to add to the already heady list - the coppery smell of coins. Lots of coins. *There must be millions... no, BILLIONS of them,* she thought.

Inside were at least twenty variations of her beloved penny machines. Each one had a slightly different theme and design to entice the player: some were six-sided, some had four, others two. One had a surfer theme, another had cartoon lumberjacks riding logs over waterfalls. They all shared the same simple idea: put your coins in and - if you timed it right - the electric pushers and paddles would slide your money into the teetering pile of coins left by other, less skillful players and force it towards the edge. Then gravity would do its work and a great chunk of cash would tumble into the chutes below. *And then it's all mine. All for little Maggie.*

With an expert eye, Maggie walked around the machines, looking for especially vulnerable piles of coins that were ripe and ready to be released. After a lap of the tent, she decided on one machine, a multi-sided unit designed to look like a spaceship. *Penny Planet! That's so ace...*

Maggie unbuttoned her special pocket and dug out a handful of two pence pieces. She watched intently as the pushers moved backwards and forwards and waited until experience told her the time was just right time, then she pushed three coins very quickly into the same slot. They tumbled down, and then fell into line, guided by the paddle; then they snuggled up against the existing money. Maggie's coins then helped push the coins already inside the machine forward towards the edge. They were close, but not quite close enough to tip them over. She repeated the action in exactly the same way; three coins, one after the other, pushed into the same slot. Nothing. She did it again. And again. By now the money at the edge - much of it prized, shiny ten and five pence pieces - seemed to be defying all logic by clinging on and refusing to budge.

Maggie looked at the wobbling mass of money and checked what she had left... *three coins. Bloody Nora.*

As she debated whether to change her strategy there was a bang on one corner of the machine and a large pile of money fell into the chute nearest to Maggie. She looked up. A man in a beige raincoat had bumped the machine with his hip. He smiled and made a 'oops' face as if it had been a terrible accident and he hadn't actually meant to send all those coins down the chute and into the collection point right near where Maggie was standing.

'Mister!' she said, her eyes wide with shock and pleasure. 'Yer can't do that, the fairground lads will call the police!'

The man smiled again. 'I wouldn't worry about that,' he said. He looked around then bent down to Maggie's eye level. *He smells of beer and mints.* His voice dropped to a friendly whisper. 'I *am* the police.'

TEN

It wasn't hard to tell that Hunter's Hollow Residential School on the outskirts of Diggle had, in a previous life, been a hotel. As a child, Danny - along with his older sister - had spent six months in a care home while they waited to be fostered. That home had been nothing like this.

Set back from the road by a 200-yard driveway, Hunter's Hollow and its various add-ons and extensions through the decades fanned back from an impressive former coaching inn that now served as its main entrance. Behind the main doors were former conference areas that now served as classrooms, an ex-health club that was now the school gymnasium and hotel rooms that could accommodate up to 70 pupils aged eight to eighteen. Behind the site were extensive grounds, including tennis courts and climbing walls, that stretched into the distance before a craggy ridge known as Hunter's Edge took over.

Danny had looked at the school's website on the way there. The care home he'd been sent to had been little more than a holding pen for kids that people either didn't want or couldn't handle. Hunter's Hollow had carers, teachers, therapists and clinical psychologists to help pupils overcome their problems and learn at the same time. One of the school's specialties was helping young people who'd suffered 'adverse childhood experiences'; Kate's son Jonathan had certainly had more than his fair share of those.

At the front entrance a woman dressed in slightly muddy softshell trousers and a hoodie was waiting for them: 'Kate! Hi. I'm so sorry to hear about your dad. How's he doing?'

'They're keeping him in overnight,' Kate replied as she and Danny stepped from her Mercedes and climbed the steps to the main entrance. 'He's comfortable I suppose. That's the word they use, isn't it? Comfortable? Sorry, Susan, this is my friend Danny Johnston. Danny, this is Susan Matlock. She's the manager here.'

Susan smiled at Danny. 'Hi, Danny. Nice to meet you. I've read your book.'

'Oh dear,' Danny said. 'I don't like the sound of that…'

'No, it's all good,' Susan said, reassuringly. 'It's great, in fact.

Fascinating. Terrible title though. *Twister Sisters*? Bet the publishers forced that on you, didn't they?'

'They did,' Danny admitted. 'I wanted to call it *Black Moss*, but I got overruled. That's showbiz.'

'We should get you into the school sometime,' Susan said. 'You could talk to the pupils about journalism and writing. You up for that?'

'Sure,' he said. 'Why not?'

Susan made Danny shake on it: He looked at her: *Late forties but looks younger. Sporty. Super confident. No messing about. Not what I imagined… I was expecting someone in dungarees.*

'Done!' Susan exclaimed. 'You heard him, Kate? That's a binding contract, right there.'

'I did indeed,' Kate confirmed, pointing a finger at Danny then at Susan as if to indicate… do as you're told. 'Best to sort it on email,' Susan said. 'The phone signal is shit out here.'

'How's Jonathan?' Kate asked as they went through the reception and into the main body of the school. Susan used her electronic identity card to open up multiple, secure doors as they went.

'Do you know what?' Susan said. 'Considering what's been flying about on the internet today, he's not too bad at all.'

'It's all crap,' Danny said. 'I've known John Smithdown since I was seven. Trust me. He's innocent.'

'Yes, I read about that in your book. He saved you and your sister, didn't he? Very brave of you to write about it. You've had quite the journey Danny, haven't you?'

'You make me sound like I'm on my way out,' Danny replied.

'Not at all,' Susan replied, again she was smiling at Danny. 'You never know what excitement could be waiting for you just around the corner, do you?'

'You really don't,' Danny agreed. *Did I just blush a bit then? Fucking Nora.* He looked at the artwork on the corridor walls as they walked and tried to avoid eye contact with Kate.

Susan led them into a medium-sized room with soft furnishings and low-key lighting; there were posters on the wall with uplifting messages on them about achievement, potential and determination. 'Jonathan has said that he'd prefer to meet in one of these quiet areas rather than in his room,' she said. 'His choice. Really important we respect that. If you'll both just wait here, I'll go and get him.'

Danny walked around the room, looking at the positivity posters; he was still trying to avoid Kate's look. *Don't you dare, Kate Smithdown. Don't.*

You. Fucking. Dare.

Kate waited for Susan to leave the room. 'Danny Something,' she sighed. 'Was that your attempt at flirting back there? God, I think I'm going to be sick.'

Danny ignored her and leant in to examine one of the posters more closely: 'Do you know what it says on this poster, Kate?'

'What does it say, Danny?'

'It says… shut your cakehole,' he replied, tapping the poster that was actually about life goals with the knuckle of his forefinger. 'Right here. Shut your cakehole. That's what it says. Those are very wise words and I think you should take them to heart.'

'Danny Johnston, flirting,' she said quietly. 'Christ Almighty, I've seen it all now.'

Susan came back into the room with Jonathan, relieving Danny of the need to say something clever in return. Kate's son had been 10 years old when Danny first met him - a tiny ball of energy, all curly hair and smiles, charging about on his bike. Now it looked like he'd been on some kind of teenage stretching machine; his arms and legs seemed 20 percent too long for his torso, and his face had lost every trace of its youthful roundness. He wore ultra-skinny black jeans that had been strategically ripped in key places and a red t-shirt with a Soviet Coca Cola logo on it. He raised a hand, smiled at Danny and sat down. The seat he chose was nearer to Danny than to his mum.

'Right, I'll leave you guys to it,' Susan said.

'Actually,' Jonathan said, his voice took Danny by surprise. It was deep, calm and insistent. 'Can you stay, Susan? Is that okay?'

Susan looked at Kate before she answered: 'Of course, not a problem.' She perched herself on the windowsill facing them, crossing her arms and looking at her feet.

'Right… okay… Jonathan,' Kate began. 'It's about your grandad. He's in hospital. He's had a very minor sort of stroke. Just a mini one, honestly. He's okay, but he's been told to stay at the Royal tonight so he can rest and get his strength back.'

Jonathan said nothing. He looked at the ends of his fingers as if they were the most fascinating thing imaginable.

Kate sighed and carried on: 'You may have seen some stuff about him on social media. Or in the local press.' There was a darting look towards Danny when she said that. 'It's not true. I'm telling you now, it's all fake. You know that I'm sure you do. But until we can clear things up, your grandad is better off in hospital where he can rest and stay out of the way. Okay?'

Jonathan played with the skin on the edge of his fingernails. There was silence. 'Jonathan,' Kate said, her voice was wobbly with tiredness and emotion. 'If you're still angry at me for placing you here at the school... I get it. I understand.'

'You don't get it though, do you?' the teenager said, looking at his mother for the first time since he'd entered the room. 'I'm not angry at you. Not for that, anyway. I actually like it here. I feel safe. Protected. That's a nice feeling, that is. The feeling of being... protected.'

'Jonathan, please...' Kate said; she was struggling now to keep from sounding upset.

'Danny gets it,' Jonathan said. 'You know what it's like to be uncared for as a kid, don't you, Danny?

'Mate, come on,' Danny pleaded quietly. 'There's no need for this.'

Jonathan then turned his attention towards Susan: 'When I was 10, my mum let me be kidnapped, Susan. You know that don't you? Of course you do. It's all there in my records. We've talked about it in group sessions. I was drugged and kidnapped. By two fucking weirdos. The twisted fucking sisters. They were going to kill me, Susan. Just like they'd killed all those other kids. If it hadn't been for Danny, I'd be at the bottom of Black Moss Reservoir instead of being here. So, you're wrong, Mum. I like it at Hunter's Hollow. I feel safe. I AM safe.'

'Jonathan,' Danny said, speaking despite the strong feeling that it wasn't really his place to talk. 'It was your mum that saved you, don't you remember? I was no use. One of them, Jan Cave, had banged a knife in me. Your mum took care of Beth Hall with a bat - took her jaw clean out of its hinges - then she just about drowned Jan in Black Moss. It was her, Jonathan. Your mum. My friend Gary Keenan helped too. He died trying to help you. But it was her,' he jabbed his forefinger in Kate's direction. 'She was the one that saved you. She protected you like no one has ever protected a kid before. She's the reason you're alive. Her. Right there.'

'She's the reason I was taken in the first place,' Jonathan muttered. 'Her. *Right there.*' His voice was harsh and sarcastic now. He looked at Susan. 'Are we done?'

'You're free to go to your room at any time, Jonathan,' Susan confirmed. 'You know that.'

Jonathan jumped up from his seat, nodded to Danny and left. A few moments after the door closed behind him, Kate began to cry.

ELEVEN

That night, for the first time in several years, Danny dreamt about The Shirtless Boy.

He'd become aware of The Shirtless Boy after he'd stopped drinking. The Boy had been one of many unpleasant side effects. Danny often wondered if The Boy had always been there, and that alcohol had just taken away his ability to remember his presence.

The boy he saw face down in the sand at Black Moss in 1990 had no shirt on. He had weights strapped to his chest, admittedly, but no shirt. When he'd crashed his car in 2016, he was sure he'd seen a boy with no shirt on just before he'd hit the tree that had stopped his car, his career and his drinking all in one instant.

He even thought he'd seen such a boy out on the moors; it was while he was doing his community service after his drink driving conviction. Danny had always convinced himself that the boy with no shirt that he'd seen that day, the boy at Black Moss, the boy at the crash scene and The Shirtless Boy in his dreams were all very separate things. *Different boys with no shirts on. Coincidence. Not connected. No way*

Danny's dreams were always harsh and unpleasant when The Boy made an appearance; the waking was inevitably sweaty, cold and jarring. Even within a dream, Danny was able to think… *oh fuck*… when The Boy showed up. He wasn't the kind of person who would attempt to trying to 'interpret' a dream, but even Danny had to admit - to himself, never to anyone else - that things were usually about to take a bad turn when he dreamt about The Shirtless Boy.

In his dream that night, his car had broken down in a layby out on the moors. *Have I run out of petrol? Not sure. You never are in a dream, are you? Anyway, the car definitely won't start. Hazard lights on? Yes.*

It was late at night but the moon and the tangerine glow of lights from a distant town provided just enough illumination for him to see down the curving moorland road. It stretched away from him and seemed to get longer and longer the more he looked. The inside of the car was cold - *really* cold - and Danny could see his own breath wisping upwards in front of his face.

As Danny's hazard lights clicked on and off, he saw The Shirtless Boy through his windscreen; no shirt as ever but wearing grey shorts and holding something in his hand. Each time the lights flashed, The Boy got a little closer to the car, though his legs never seemed to move.

Danny looked at his face. He couldn't see his features. The Boy definitely had features, it's just that Danny could never quite see them, no matter how hard he tried to make them out.

He could definitely see what was in The Boy's hand though: a candyfloss on a stick. There was no doubt in Danny's dream-mind that this was the biggest, brightest and best candyfloss he'd ever seen in his life. It was fluffy, pink and beautiful. He felt jealous that The Shirtless Boy had it. *Lucky little bastard. Why can't I have one? Wonder if he'll give me a bit?*

Although Danny couldn't see his mouth, The Boy was clearly eating the candyfloss and really enjoying it. *That must be the best candyfloss in the world and that tight little twat is hogging it all for himself.*

With every flash of the hazard lights, The Boy got closer and closer, and the candyfloss got smaller and smaller.

Flash. Closer. Flash. Closer. Flash. Closer.

Then the lights flashed again but The Boy wasn't there. Danny leant forward and stared though his windscreen. It was misty from his breath and he wiped the inside of the glass with the sleeve of his jumper. The Shirtless Boy was gone.

Then Danny heard a tac tac sound. The Boy was by the driver's window. He stood there for a moment; then he tapped the glass with his empty stick and motioned for Danny to lower the window. Danny shook his head. The Boy tapped again.

Absolutely no fucking way, you little bastard.

They looked at each other through the car window. The Shirtless Boy then pulled his arm back and pushed the stick through the glass as if it wasn't there and straight down Danny's throat.

Danny woke up. His mobile was ringing. *Unknown caller. Maybe it's the hospital. Oh God.*

'Hello?'

'Lad's Grave.' The voice was male. There were other voices in the background. They sounded like they were running.

'What?' queried Danny, still fuzzy from being woken from his dream. 'What are you on about?'

'LAD'S GRAVE MOOR,' the voice shouted. Look it up. That's where you need to be, right now.'

TWELVE

Danny passed Hanging Lees Reservoir and the Bull's Head pub, eased up the moorland Ripponden Road and saw the huge, skeletal frame of the Windy Hill transmitter up ahead. It stood guard next to the M62 motorway at the border between Greater Manchester and Yorkshire. Lad's Grave lay ahead, just as the road cut across one of the bleakest sections of the moors. *Lad's Grave? Seriously? Why the fuck do they give places names like that around here?*

The pre-dawn light showed the elegant silhouette of the Pennine Way footbridge on Danny's left as he drove under the M62 and out onto the other side. He pulled into a layby; behind him, lorries clattered up and down the motorway between Manchester and Leeds. *The highest bit of motorway in England, this is. There's a fun fact to distract you from being scared out of your fucking mind, Danny boy.*

In front of him were the moors. Layer after layer of peaty bogland with only patchy sheets of heather, crowberry and cottongrass to break it up. The land dipped, swooped and disappeared into the darkness; there were no trees to interrupt the bleak dominance of the land. Not one. In any direction. There was only one vertical that broke up the endless lines of moorland horizontals - a lone wind turbine whooshing a circular beat on the crest of the second or third rolling hill of Lad's Grave Moor.

Shit. I suppose I've got to go up there, haven't I? Brilliant.

Having learned some hard lessons in relation to inappropriate footwear and the moors around Manchester many years earlier, Danny was prepared. He pulled a pair of walking boots from the box in the boot of his car and took a torch too. He closed the boot and took a look around; all he could see was that very special brand of nothing that was the only true defining feature of the moors. Once he was booted up, he headed off across the open land towards the turbine.

As a young man, the hills and moors that curved around Greater Manchester had baffled Danny. It was an alien landscape that didn't welcome the likes of him. Now, in his mid-50s, he understood the landscape a little better. He knew the hags that could trip him, the gullies and hidden streams that might take hold of his ankle and the cloughs that could distract him and lead him astray. He liked the reliable nothingness that the moors provided, and he was wise to the dangers that lay hidden underneath its mossy folds.

He moved quickly and efficiently across the terrain, zig zagging his way up the moor towards the turbine. The lone unit up ahead was only about 40 feet high, no match for the 200-foot monsters to the west at the Scout Moor Wind Farm. There were no actual farms on this section of the moors - the landscape was far too harsh for that; the wind farms had taken over that responsibility now.

Danny guessed that the turbine was probably to provide emergency power for the motorway or the nearby Green Withens Reservoir; perhaps it was a test unit to feed energy into the National Grid with an eye on a fully-fledged wind farm in the future. Either way, it looked strangely alone, quietly fulfilling its purpose on there on the moors without any company.

As he got closer, Danny shone his torch and noticed what looked like a sack or a bin bag at the turbine's base. The light shak shak shak sound of the blades as they cut through the chill air got louder as he approached. The dawn light was just starting to creep across the top edge of the moors that surrounded him.

Shak shak shak.

The sack at the bottom of the turbine was bent at the middle as if it had been tied to the base of the unit.

Don't be a person, don't be a person, don't be a person.

Danny was about 20 feet from the turbine now and he could see that it was indeed a person. Or at least, what was left of one. Danny could tell it was a man because he had no shirt on; his hairy arms, chest and shoulders were all matted with blood. His jaw hung loose, and his cheekbones were now dents in the remains of his face; there were holes and parallel gouges in his balding head. Underneath the blood and around the holes, the numbers '1812' were just about visible on the man's forehead. What looked like a mobile phone was strapped to his chest; the grey tape holding it there was also streaked in blood.

There was an A4 sign between his legs, printed out in a strangely jaunty, knockabout typeface and pinned down by rocks at each corner.

HERE LIES BARRY 'THE BEAST' MORTIMER
CHECK HIS PHONE.

LET THIS BE A WARNING TO ALL PAEDOS.
NONCE AND YOU WILL DIE.

Danny stood and stared. He looked around the moors. 'Just you and me then, Barry,' he whispered. 'Christ Almighty, what the fuck did you do?'

He looked at the phone strapped to the man's chest and the four-digit number on his forehead. He thought for a moment about activating the screen and putting the number into it. *Don't be a tit, Danny. For once in your life, don't be a tit.*

Taking out his own phone, Danny rang 999, told the operator what he knew and then rang off. He then sat on a large rock nearby and stared at the man's body. Then he searched Facebook for the name Barry Mortimer. It didn't take him long to find what he suspected was the man's account. *Local guy. Family man. Wife and three kids. Holidays in Spain and Florida. Happy, happy, happy. Fucking Nora.*

The latest post on the man's page - put there two hours ago - was certainly eye-catching:

STAND BY FOR A MAJOR ANNOUNCEMENT… I,
BARRY MORTIMER, AM A MASSIVE NONCE.
DETAILS TO COME LATER TODAY!

So that was what was 'on your mind' when you were on Facebook at 2.10 am this morning was it, Barry? I suspect you didn't actually post that yourself, did you?

Underneath the post, some of the man's friends had already added likes, laughing emojis and comments: 'Think someone's been at your phone, Baz!' one said. 'Don't tell me, you've been hacked. Ha! Ha! Ha!' said another. 'Always suspected it Bazza!'

Danny took screen grabs of the page and saved copies of Barry's photos, then he scrolled through his 'about' information to find his place of work. He also took note of a Strava post showing that the man had managed a 5K run earlier in the year. There was a photo of a tired and sweaty-looking Barry wearing running gear; he had his hands in the air in triumph. *Looking to drop a few pounds there, Barry?* The looped Strava route highlighted where the run had started and ended. *That's probably his home address, right there in Delph. People give so much information out; in the old days I would have had to ring every B. Mortimer in the phone book. Not anymore. You need to think more about your privacy settings, Barry. Bit late now, I suppose.*

Danny took several photos of the scene, including the sign, but was careful to keep anything gruesome out of the frame. Then he started writing. He didn't care for doing stories on his phone; he couldn't do that double-thumb thing that everyone under 35 seemed able to do with ease. After ten minutes and a few tweaks, he was ready to post the story; then he hesitated. *If you weren't so self-righteous, Danny Johnston, you wouldn't be so skint.*

Danny looked at the body and the sign. The wind pushed across the moor and rattled the paper. He added the code that inserted adverts into the story and pressed 'publish'.

THIRTEEN

'VIGILANTE' FEARS AFTER MUTILATED BODY FOUND NEAR MOTORWAY

Danny Johnston - Oldham Now

Murder squad detectives, investigating the discovery of a man's body on moorland near the M62, fear he may have been subjected to a vigilante-style attack.

The grim discovery was made in the early hours of this morning at an area known as Lad's Grave. It's close to the motorway underpass on the A672 Denshaw to Ripponden road. Police were alerted after an anonymous tip off to *Oldham Now*.

The badly mutilated body had been strapped to a wind turbine and a note found at the scene suggested that the man had been targeted as an alleged paedophile. The note said:

'LET THIS BE A WARNING TO ALL PAEDOS,
NONCE AND YOU WILL DIE.'

The note named the man, but *Oldham Now* is withholding his identity until relatives can be informed.

A post-mortem examination is expected to be carried out later today to establish the exact cause of death. Police will also spend the day examining a phone found at the scene. A four-digit passcode had been written on the victim's head, indicating that those responsible were keen for police to look at the dead man's online activity.

It's the second body to be found in the area in the last 24 hours. On Monday morning, the body of a woman was found at Hanging Lees Reservoir, which is also just off the A672 road. The woman has since been identified as Maggie Ormrod, aged 57, of Ripponden Road, Denshaw.

It's not yet known if police are linking the two finds, but Detective

Inspector Patrick McIntyre and his brother Detective Constable Karl McIntyre are believed to be leading both investigations.

Danny checked how the story looked via Facebook. Nearly all the traffic to his website came via Facebook, so it was always his priority. *Twitter is just noise. FB is where the engagement comes from. Hook them there, then get them onto the website sharpish. That's how to make money in this game.*

He watched as the comments, shares and angry emojis began to grow, even though it was barely six o'clock in the morning.

The first comment was from Jill from Coldhurst (Love my hubby, my two beautiful boys and nites out with my Girl Squad): 'Good fookin riddance. Scum,' it said.

Jill's comment began racking up likes and laughing emojis straight away. 'Spot on, Jill'… 'You go, Jill'… 'No arguments from me, one less nonce to lock up. Whoever did this… good on them I say!'

Danny flicked through some more of the comments and reactions that his story was provoking:

Royton Ray: 'About time someone started tackling this head on. Cops have got their hands tied. A dead nonce can't nonce again. Fact.'

Juliepops: 'Made my day this. Get in!!! If they need a hand getting rid of anymore give me a shout!!!'

Jake and Janet's Mum: 'Someone should set up a fund to buy these vigilantes a pint. Good work lads!'

Like after like. Laughing emoji after laughing emoji. Heart after heart.

The sun began to rise behind Manchester city centre. Danny could see the sharp silhouette of the Beetham Tower at the end of Deansgate from his vantage point next to the wind turbine. It was cold and he wanted to go back to his car, but it seemed wrong to leave Barry Mortimer out there alone strapped to the wind turbine. Danny wasn't sure why it felt wrong - no one had less sympathy for the likes of Barry than he did - but it just didn't feel right. He managed to justify staying for entirely practical reasons: *I'll get some video of the cops when they arrive. That's good content, that is.*

Plus, Danny reasoned, he felt obligated to be on standby to shout a warning to any early morning walkers or joggers who might go by… *What should I say? I wouldn't go this way if I were you, mate. There's a nonce with his head caved in. You're welcome!*

So, Danny sat down, pulled his jacket tight around his neck and waited. Down the M62 motorway he saw flashing lights bouncing off the slopes that hemmed in the carriageway on the westbound carriageway. The sound of the sirens came seconds later. *By God, that was quick. Maybe I wasn't the first person to call.*

Across the other side of the motorway, close to the Windy Hill transmitter, he saw two figures in the morning light. One was holding out an arm as if holding up a phone. Both seemed to have their faces covered. Danny stood up to get a better look. There was a growling, mechanical sound and then they were gone. *I can hear motorbikes; is that from the moors or the motorway?*

Down the moor he saw the police pull up into the layby next to his car; he waved to them and pointed at the turbine.

Five minutes later the McIntyre brothers arrived at the scene: 'Mr Johnston,' Detective Constable McIntyre said. 'Always a pleasure.'

The two detectives looked at Barry Mortimer's battered body and the sign in front of him. 'Well, I don't like to jump to conclusions,' his older brother said,' But I suppose you're going to say it was like this when you found him?'

'That's exactly what I'm going to say, because that's what happened,' Danny confirmed.

'…And that you absolutely haven't touched anything,' DC McIntyre added. 'Especially the phone that's strapped to his chest.' The two brothers were like a double act, almost finishing each other's sentences.

'Again, correct,' Danny said.

'Are you familiar with the expression "helping police with their inquiries" Mr Johnston?' DI McIntyre asked.

'I am indeed,' Danny replied, blowing into his cupped hands to keep warm.

'Good,' the DI said. 'Well, how about me and my brother here get you out of the cold, get a nice mug of Oldham police station hot chocolate down you and then you can do just that.'

FOURTEEN

RECORD OF INTERVIEW
Person interviewed: JOHNSTON, Daniel (12/7/66)
Place of interview: Oldham Police Station
Time commenced: 0810 hours
Interviewer(s): DI3716 McIntyre, Patrick. DC2184 McIntyre, Karl.
Other persons present: Paulina Scorer - Solicitor from Blanco & Harkness Solicitors.
Usual introductions, cautions and advice. JOHNSTON has been informed that he is not under arrest and that he is free to leave at any time. JOHNSTON has opted to have a legal representative with him (Ms P Scorer).
This is the first interview with DANIEL JOHNSTON - JOHNSTON confirms that no questions have been asked before the recording begins.

DI MCINTYRE: Mr Johnston, I want to talk to you about two matters today. One is the discovery of a woman's body - a Maggie Ormrod - at Hanging Lees Reservoir. But I'd like to start with some questions about the discovery of another body, that of Barry Mortimer, which was found at Lad's Grave Moor in the early hours of this morning. Did you know Mr Mortimer at all?
JOHNSTON: I didn't. I spent a bit of time with him out on the moor in the early hours of this morning. He didn't say much. So…no, it's fair to say that I didn't know him.
DI MCINTYRE: Can you tell me how you came to be out on the moors at that time?
JOHNSTON: I got a call telling me to get myself out to Lad's Grave. They do love spooky names for places around these parts, don't they? So, the call said go there… and that's what I did.
DI MCINTYRE: Do you know the identity of the caller?
JOHNSTON: No. I don't. It was anonymous. You don't kill someone then call a reporter and leave your name and number, do you?
DI MCINTYRE: What can you tell me about the person who called you?
JOHNSTON: Male. Not young, not old. Northern accent, not strong.

Might have been from round here, maybe not. He just told me to get myself out to Lad's Grave, sharpish. When I tried to get more out of him, he told me to Google it and hung up. That's it.

DI MCINTYRE: Did you recognise the voice?

JOHNSTON: No.

DI MCINTYRE: And where were you when you got the call?

JOHNSTON: At home. On my own.

DI MCINTYRE: And prior to that?

JOHNSTON: I'd been to Hunter's Hollow School to see John Smithdown's grandson…To tell him what's been happening with his grandad. Left there about nine. Called in for a takeaway at Valentino's on the main road near my house. Took it home. Ate it. Watched the news. Updated my website. Went to bed. That's it. I've got a receipt. For the pizza, I mean. I had a thin crust with anchovies by the way. In case you need to know. For the record and that. It was nice. Not everyone cares for anchovies on pizza, but I do.

DI MCINTYRE: Let's stick to the matter in hand, shall we? What happened then?

JOHNSTON: I went up onto the moor and… well, there was Barry. He was in a bit of a state, to say the least. Yeah. Quite a sight.

DI MCINTYRE: There was a note left at the scene, wasn't there?

JOHNSTON: There was indeed.

DI MCINTYRE: The note read: HERE LIES BARRY 'THE BEAST' MORTIMER. CHECK HIS PHONE. LET THIS BE A WARNING TO ALL PAEDOS. NONCE AND YOU WILL DIE. You know that because you rather unhelpfully put a picture of it on your news site. What did you take that note to mean?

JOHNSTON: Well, I'm not a detective like you and your brother are, but I took it as a warning. Someone's out to get paedophiles. And whoever did this had clearly fingered Barry. If you'll excuse the expression.

DI MCINTYRE: So, you took this to be a threat to paedophiles?

JOHNSTON: They'd caved his head in. So, yes… a little bit of a threat.

DI MCINTYRE: Did you notice anything else about the body?

JOHNSTON: A phone was taped to his chest… I assumed it was his. A four-digit code had been written on his forehead. Very thoughtful of them, I thought. Clearly a better class of vigilante - a cut above.

DI MCINTYRE: Did you touch the phone?

JOHNSTON: Absolutely not. I looked at his Facebook page from my own phone. They'd obviously posted something on there on his behalf,

too.
DI MCINTYRE: I'm a massive nonce.
JOHNSTON: I think we should stick to talking about Barry, don't you?
DI MCINTYRE: Hilarious, Mr Johnston. You know exactly what I mean. That was the message they posted. Why do you think they wrote the number on his head?
JOHNSTON: I'd be guessing.
DI MCINTYRE: What would be your guess?
JOHNSTON: My guess would be that the code was for Barry's phone. Then you lot could unlock it and scroll through all Bazza's slickest chat up lines aimed at the younger end of the market. Then you could see that he was, as the note so eloquently stated, a nonce. One less for you to worry about, I suppose. The youngsters of Oldham are safe. Facebook is loving it. Everyone's happy. Apart from Barry, of course.
DI MCINTYRE: That's a rather cynical way of looking at it, Mr Johnston. A man's been murdered. We will be putting every resource we have at our disposal to see that those responsible for this are caught and prosecuted.
JOHNSTON: Of course. Every resource. Right you are. Anything else?
DI MCINTYRE: Well, you were also at the scene of the body found at Hanging Lees Reservoir on Monday morning. Could you tell me how that came about?
JOHNSTON: Similar scenario. Got a message via an anonymous Twitter account that disappeared immediately afterwards. Advised me I should get myself to Hanging Lees. So, I did. I saw you out there. That was nice. Took a few photos and a bit of video. That's it.
DI MCINTYRE: Was there any mention of anyone else in the message?
JOHNSTON: No.
DI MCINTYRE: No name?
JOHNSTON: No.
DI MCINTYRE: Any mention of anyone you might know?
JOHNSTON: No names, like I said.
DI MCINTYRE: Did you screenshot the message?
JOHNSTON: No.
DI MCINTYRE: You're normally a very chatty sort of man, Mr Johnston. Now it's all one-word answers.
JOHNSON: That's not a question. Try a question.
DI MCINTYRE: Did you know Maggie Ormrod, the woman found at Hanging Lees?
JOHNSTON: See, that's a closed question. Did you, were you, are you

- all closed questions. It just invites me to offer a one-word answer. So here it is. No.
DI MCINTYRE: Did Mr Smithdown ever mention the name Maggie Ormrod to you?
JOHNSTON: Closed question again. Come on. No.
DI MCINTYRE: What's the nature of your relationship with John Smithdown?
JOHNSTON: Open question. That's better. Well done. We're making real progress. John Smithdown saved me and my sister's lives when we were kids. Got us out of our parent's house and into a care home. The house of horrors the newspapers called it at the time. I met up with him again during the Black Moss murder investigation in 1990, then again when I moved up here from London in 2016.
DI MCINTYRE: After your arrest for drink driving?
JOHNSTON: That's correct, as you well know. These days, I help his daughter look after him. I see him several times a week. He's like a father, uncle and best mate to me, all rolled into one. Look at your police records. He's a hero, too. The real deal.
DI MCINTYRE: You mentioned your sister - did she continue her friendship with John Smithdown?
JOHNSTON: You're back on the closed questions again, but I'll let you off. No, she didn't. She didn't feel the need, plus she died of cancer recently and that tends to limit your social life. And if you're mentioning my sister to have a little dig around about whether John Smithdown liked young girls or not, then fucking shame on you.
DI MCINTYRE: I wasn't, but I have to ask. Have you ever known John Smithdown show an interest in young girls?
JOHNSTON: Absolutely not.
DI MCINTYRE: Okay, let's leave it there.

End of recording: 0831 hours.

Danny put on his jacket and smiled at his solicitor. 'That okay, Paulina? I told you I'd be on my best behaviour.'

'I was pleasantly surprised,' she said cheerfully, packing her notebook into a briefcase. 'Well done.'

'Did you get everything you want?' Danny asked the Detective Inspector.

'That's a closed question, Mr Johnston,' the DI replied. 'As a special treat I'll give you the benefit of a two-word answer. For now.'

‘Can I ask you a question?’ Danny said. Paulina gave him a warning glance and shook her head.

‘You can ask,’ the detective said. ‘Whether I can give you a reply, that’s a different matter.’

‘It’s a closed question,’ Danny said. ‘Based on what you’ve presumably seen on his phone… private messages and so on… do you think Barry Mortimer was a paedophile?’

DC McIntyre got up from his chair and stood alongside his brother: ‘We can’t answer that, as you well know.’

‘I rather think that you just have. Here’s another one. Do you think he was trapped and killed by vigilantes?’

‘You definitely know we can’t answer that,’ the DI said.

‘Again, you kind of just did…’

‘Mr Johnston, we’re all on the same side here, as far as I know,’ DC McIntyre said.

‘That depends whether you seriously think John Smithdown harmed that poor woman up at Hanging Lees when she was a kid,’ Danny said. ‘If you do, then we are definitely not on the same side.’

‘We have to investigate it,’ the DI said. ‘Non-recent abuse cases are a big deal right now, and rightly so. You know that better than anyone. As soon as we can get this sorted out, the better it’ll be for all concerned.’

‘Can I go now?’ Danny asked.

‘You were free to go at any time,’ the DI responded. ‘We appreciate your help. Here’s my number. If you think of anything else - or get any similar messages - please get in touch.’

Danny took the detective’s card and made an ‘after you’ gesture to Paulina Scorer.

‘Mr Johnston,’ DI McIntyre said. ‘One other thing. Please stay away from Barry Mortimer’s family, okay?’

‘Absolutely,’ Danny replied. He smiled at his solicitor.

‘We mean it,’ the DC added, firmly. ‘Don’t go near them.’

‘Absolutely,’ Danny said.

FIFTEEN

From the woods that peppered the streets on the outskirts of Delph, Danny spotted the back garden of Barry Mortimer's new-build house. *Trampoline in the garden. Built-in barbeque. Living the suburban dream. You had it pretty good, Barry. Until you fucked it all up.*

He saw a woman in her 40s leaning on the sliding patio doors smoking a cigarette. Danny had spotted the police standing outside the front of the house - along with a removal van - and decided to take the more scenic route around the back. He'd noticed another thing about the front of the house too: it had the word NONCE written across the front window in white paint.

Danny knew the woman was likely to be alarmed by his presence as he approached the low back fence behind the house, so he had to work quickly. She spotted him straight away: 'What the fuck are you doing?' she said, shielding her eyes from the thin morning sunshine with her hand.

'Mrs Mortimer, I'm so sorry to disturb you. My name's Danny from *Oldham Now*. Can we talk please?'

'Why exactly should I talk to you?' she said, stubbing out her cigarette and heading indoors.

Her accent was strong, typical of people from areas of Oldham close to the Yorkshire border. Using a technique he'd been taught many years before Danny tweaked his nondescript accent so it more closely reflected hers. 'Because it was me who found him out on the moors,' Danny replied. 'I was there. I saw him. And I want to know why someone would do that to him.'

The woman stopped. She looked through the house to the silhouette of the police officer at her front window. Then she closed the patio doors and walked over to the fence. 'I'll bet you do,' she whispered.

'As I said, my name's Danny... what's your first name, Mrs Mortimer?'

'It's Christine,' she replied and lit another cigarette. Danny had given up the previous year. *God, I could murder a ciggie.*

'How are you doing, Christine?' he asked.

'I'm muddling through,' she said with a tinge of sarcasm in her voice.

Danny thought about the photos he'd seen on Barry Mortimer's Facebook page. 'What about your kids, how are they doing? Two girls, yes?'

'How d'you know that?'

'It's all on your Barry's Facebook page. No secrets anymore, Christine. A 20 second glance at someone's social media tells you everything you want to know about them these days.'

'Yeah,' she agreed, sending a jet of exhaled smoke in Danny's direction. He really wanted a cigarette. 'Well, he did like a bit of Facebook did our Barry. My daughters aren't doing too well, as you can imagine. They're at my sister's. We're leaving. Have you seen the front of our house? Our neighbours seem to have gone off us a bit. They were here drinking our wine on Saturday night, now they're redecorating our front windows. People can be funny like that, can't they? Anyway, what do you want then Mr Danny Johnston from *Oldham Now*?

'The police know more than they're letting on, Christine,' Danny said. His voice was soft and reassuring. 'Two bodies have turned up in 24 hours. Your Barry and a woman up at Hanging Lees. A friend of mine has a saying, Mrs Mortimer. TFC. When more than one strange thing happens at about the same time, he says…TFC. It stands for That's a Fucking Coincidence. When the woman died up at the reservoir, I got a message telling me that it had happened. I got there just after the police did. Then I get a similar call about your husband. This time I get there *before* the cops. Two bodies and I get a tip off about them both? TFC if ever I heard it.'

'You reckon?'

'I do, Christine.'

'You saw my Barry up at the moor, did you?'

'I did,' Danny replied.

'Bit of a state, was he?'

'I'm afraid so.'

'Do you reckon he suffered?' the woman asked.

Danny paused, not sure how to answer. 'I think it's fair to say he did, Christine.'

She looked across at the woods, flicked her ash and scratched at some invisible mark on the fencing. *Looks freshly creosoted, that fence,* Danny thought. *Say what you will about Barry, he kept on top of the jobs around the house.*

'There was a sign there I hear,' she said. 'Telling everyone my Barry was a nonce.'

'There was. I don't know where all that came from. That's why I wanted to talk to you. Do you know why someone would leave a note like that?'

'Well, I've got a theory,' the woman said. 'Would you like to hear it?'

'I would, Christine,'

'Well, this might sound a bit harsh Mr Danny Johnston from *Oldham Now*...But there's no way to sugar-coat this. I reckon he WAS a fucking nonce.'

SIXTEEN

ONLINE OBSESSION OF 'VIGILANTE' VICTIM
Danny Johnston - Oldham Now

The wife of a man found battered to death close to the M62 motorway says she had fears over what her husband was doing online in the months leading up to his murder.

A post-mortem examination on Barry Mortimer, 44, from the Delph area of Oldham has revealed he'd been repeatedly hit with a blunt instrument, possibly a hammer. His body was found strapped to a wind turbine on Lad's Grave Moor. He'd been missing for several days and it's thought he'd been tortured for some time before he died.

The discovery of Mr Mortimer's body was made after a tip off to *Oldham Now*. His mobile phone had been left at the scene and the code to unlock the device had been written on his forehead. A sign had been placed nearby stating:

'LET THIS BE A WARNING TO ALL PAEDOS. NONCE AND YOU WILL DIE.'

Mr Mortimer's wife, Christine, says she thinks her husband was targeted by online vigilantes who set up fake profiles online to ensnare paedophiles. 'I had my concerns about what he was up to online,' she told *Oldham Now* in an exclusive interview. 'He seemed to be obsessed with it. He'd spend hours chatting to people late into the night. He said he was contacting old mates from school, but I knew that wasn't true. I thought he was contacting women, then a friend's daughter told one of my kids that Barry had been messaging her. She's only 15. It's not right. He promised he'd stop, then he started going out at night. Said he was looking at new business premises, but he was meeting girls. Young girls. Looks like he arranged to meet someone, and that it wasn't a young girl at all. It was these vigilantes.'

Mrs Mortimer has now moved out of the area, fearing for her safety and that of her children.

Detective Inspector Patrick McIntyre, who's leading the hunt for Mr Mortimer's killers, has refused to comment. But he confirmed that police are now looking at Facebook groups dedicated to exposing people they believe to be paedophiles. There's been a huge rise in such groups in recent years. Some have resulted in prosecutions but there's mounting concern over people going one step further and taking the law into their own hands.

Meanwhile, police are appealing for anyone who knows Barry Mortimer's whereabouts in the days leading up to his death to come forward.

<u>SEVENTEEN</u>

Danny was at home, listening to music and calculating how much money he had made in the last 36 hours. Engagement on his social media was up and so was the number of hits on his website. He was being offered block bookings for adverts on the *Oldham Now* site stretching into next year. The money that was coming his way was at a far higher rate than he was used to. *Two grand from a chain of nurseries, three from a double-glazing company, five grand from a betting firm. Fuck.*

When he'd established *Oldham Now,* Danny had gone on a seminar to find out how to make money from local news. He remembered what he'd been told: *good content makes people stay longer on the website. That means more eyeballs on the adverts. That makes for better analytics for the advertisers. Then you can charge them more for the adverts.*

He also had a growing pile of messages from TV companies and news outlets wanting to interview him about the vigilante murder. He had ignored them all. *Why should I help them put eyeballs on their adverts? Fuck 'em. This is my story.*

He carried on adding up the money - he kept messing it up and having to start again - when his phone rang; it was Jonathan.

'Hi mate,' Danny said. 'Where are you?'

'I'm up in the hills near the school. It's about the only place you can get a signal around here. I'm sure they built the school here on purpose. What's that music you're listening to?'

'It's an album called *Adventure*, by a band called Television.' Danny held his phone up so Jonathan could hear it better.

'Nice,' the teenager said. 'Is it new?'

'It came out when I was your age. Younger than you, in fact. Steal it off the internet and have a listen. Now then, something makes me think that you didn't ring me just to talk about music.'

'Yeah. Okay. You're right. I want to go and see Grandad in hospital. Will you come with me?'

'Of course,' Danny said. 'When are you and your mum free?'

'Thing is,' the teenager said. 'I don't want Mum to go.'

'Bloody hell, Jonathan,' Danny said. 'You're putting me in a tricky situation here. I don't get why you've got it in for your mum at the moment. She's amazing and she only wants to protect you. That's all she's ever wanted. Honestly.'

'I just want to do this without any drama,' Jonathan said. 'There's always drama with Mum. I just want to see Grandad… that's reasonable, isn't it?

'I suppose it is,' Danny admitted. 'But I don't think I'd be allowed to take you out of the school, even if I wanted to. I'm not family, am I? Not actual family, anyway.'

'Susan from the school can come along too, then it's all fine.'

'Oh right. Susan? Yeah. Course.'

'Thought that might change your mind.'

Danny scratched on his phone with his fingertips and whistled into the microphone: 'Sorry, Jonathan. The signal's really bad. I can't make out what you're saying…'

'Yeah, right. I'll get Susan to email you. Thanks, Danny. Got to go. Time to do healthy, outdoor stuff. See ya.'

'See you, Jonathan.'

God, Kate's going to kill me when she finds out.

Danny sat back down and looked at the Adventure album sleeve. He had very few possessions when he moved to Friezland and Kate had harassed him into buying some 'stuff'. One of his few purchases had been a proper record player and he'd been buying up old vinyl, mainly stuff from the 70s and 80s. Music was one of the few things from the past that didn't make him feel unhappy. Television singer Tom Verlaine was shouting 'Foxhole, Foxhole' from the song of the same name when there was a knock at Danny's front door.

When people go to someone's house they tend to knock and take a step back; DC Karl McIntyre was right in Danny's face when he unlocked the cottage's battered front door. 'You fucking dickhead, Johnston,' he said.

Danny took a step back. 'And a very good evening to you too, officer,' Danny replied. 'I'd invite you in, but I don't want to, so I won't. Does your big brother know you're out this late on your own?'

'What did I tell you? It was literally the last thing I said to you; stay away from Barry Mortimer's family. What's the first thing you do? Go and interview his missus, for fuck's sake.'

'Well, with the greatest respect, DC McIntyre… and you can probably tell that I'm going to say something rude now, because I've prefaced it by saying with the greatest respect… but I don't need your fucking permission to do an interview with someone. As it happens, Mrs Mortimer was happy to talk. More than happy, in fact. So, with the greatest respect, fuck off.'

Danny went to close the door, but the DC had his foot in the way. 'Then you go and splash it all over your shitty little website,' the detective added. 'You honestly don't know what you're messing with here. Not a fucking clue.'

'I think you should go,' Danny said. The DC was 20 years younger and fitter than he was; if he wanted to push his way in, he could do it very easily. Danny reached into his pocket. 'I like your feisty policing techniques, though. Very energetic. Let me get them on video for posterity.'

With his weight still on the door, Danny pulled out his phone and unlocked the screen. The DC stepped away. His tone immediately changed. 'Good night, Mr Johnston. Thank you for your assistance.'

Danny watched as the young DC marched off down the street. 'Well, you're very welcome,' he replied. 'I suppose.'

Without turning around, DC McIntyre waved a hand: 'We'll be in touch, Mr Johnston. You can rely on it.'

EIGHTEEN

Danny arrived at the Hunter's Hollow reception to find Susan Matlock and Jonathan already waiting for him. With them was a tall, well-built man in outdoor gear who looked too old to be a student. Susan clasped Danny's hand with both of hers: 'Danny, lovely to see you again. Sorry I've got to act as chaperone. But as Jonathan didn't want his mum to come and you're not actually a relative… Rules are rules and all that.'

'Of course,' Danny said. 'Kate's not going to be happy, I reckon.'

'The child takes priority here at Hunter's Hollow,' Susan said. 'Always.'

Danny realised that Susan was still holding his hand; she let it go. 'Oh, sorry, Danny, this is my son, Ben. He works here too. He does the rufty tufty out and about stuff… climbing, quad bikes, orienteering and all that. But his main job is to be everyone's big brother. Isn't it love?'

'Hi, Danny,' Ben said, putting out a hand. 'Great to meet you. I wondered why Mum was all dressed up.'

'Not wearing a tracksuit doesn't qualify as getting dressed up, Ben!' she laughed. 'Be aware that I'm not just your mum, I'm also your boss. I'm quite happy to sack you, right now.'

Danny laughed and shook Ben's hand. He had always adhered to John Smithdown's theory about handshakes: they had to be the correct kind. Not too firm - *a bullshitter's handshake, no thanks.* Not too weak - *like a wet lettuce, a vicar's handshake, no thanks either.* Ben Matlock's handshake was just right.

'Did you hear that, Danny?' Ben said. 'Workplace bullying! I'm going to have to take that up with our HR department.'

'I am the HR department, Ben,' Susan said. 'So, shut it. I'll see you later.'

Ben held up his hands in mock surrender: 'Nice to see you, Danny. Hope your grandad's on the mend, Jonathan.'

'Thanks, Ben,' Jonathan said. Danny put an arm around the teenager's shoulder.

'Don't be home late, Mum,' Ben added as they walked away. 'You know how I worry!'

'I swear I will kill him,' Susan muttered.

When they got to the six-bed ward at the Royal Oldham Hospital, Danny peaked around the corner to double-check if Kate was there. She wasn't.

Smithdown was dozing in his bed, so Danny quietly pulled up three chairs for him, Johnathan and Susan and they just sat quietly by the retired detective's bedside. A few photo frames had been placed on the cabinet next to the bed; one was of Smithdown with Kate and Jonathan at what looked like a fair; another was of Jean Smithdown, looking glamorous at a party from the 1980s.

Danny felt a hand on his shoulder. The volunteer who had given him and Kate cups of Vimto last time was there. She put a finger to her lips and handed Danny a cup of tea in a proper cup and saucer. She smiled and Danny took the tea. He noticed the name on her volunteer badge: 'Thanks Jennifer,' he whispered. Susan whispered, 'coffee, please' and Jonathan pointed to the bottle of Vimto. When all three had a drink she once again put a finger to her lips, gave Danny the thumbs up and left.

'You'll never be accepted into the SAS, Danny,' Smithdown said a few moments later with his eyes still closed. 'I could hear you coming from halfway down the Manchester Road. Have you brought me anything or are you just here for the free tea?'

'Largely for the tea if I'm honest,' Danny replied. He put a box of Maynard's Wine Gums on the cabinet. 'There, you old sod. Hope they choke you.'

'Lovely to see you too, Danny,' Smithdown said. 'Oh, Jonathan. Come here, lad. If ever your grandad needed a bloody big hug, it's right now.'

The teenager bent over and held Smithdown tightly. Danny thought for a moment that Jonathan was about to start crying, but the young man buried his face in his grandad's shoulder to hide it. By the time he let go, the tears had largely gone.

'And who's this, then?' Smithdown said, nodding in Susan's direction. 'Is this your new lady friend, Danny?'

'Jesus Christ, don't you start,' Danny sighed.

'Hello, Mr Smithdown I'm Susan Matlock from Hunter's Hollow School. I'm just here to accompany Jonathan. Hope that's okay?'

'It's more than okay, love. It's a pleasure. Lovely lady like this and you brought her to a hospital, Danny? Not my idea of a romantic location...'

'Shut it,' Danny said. 'Or I'll euthanise you, right now.'

Danny sat back and let Jonathan and his grandad talk. He smiled as they chatted about school, football, and why Jonathan had deliberately torn holes in the knees of his trousers. Susan leant over and whispered in Danny's ear: 'It's such a shame that Kate's not here.'

'I know,' Danny whispered back. 'But I'm sure he'll come around.'

'Maybe it's Kate that needs to come around, Danny. Not Jonathan.'

'Right,' Smithdown announced. 'Sorry to interrupt you two lovebirds, but it would be nice to get an update about what the fuck is going on out there, Danny lad. Excuse my language love.'

'I hear a lot worse on a daily basis, Mr Smithdown. Trust me.'

Smithdown started to pull himself further up in his bed; Danny helped him. He could feel the retired detective's bones through his hospital issue bed shirt.

'It's all happening,' Danny said. 'Paedo vigilantes… torture… murder. You'll be pleased to hear that you're yesterday's news, mate.'

'I wish I was,' the old man said. 'I had one of the flying ginger brothers in here earlier on. My case is pending further inquiries. They'll be looking for other victims, I suppose. But there aren't any victims in the first place, so that'll go nowhere. Plus, there's all this other caper going on.'

'The damage is already done though, isn't it?' Danny said, picking up the Wine Gums and helping himself to a few. 'Your name is already shitted up, whatever happens. That's the power of the internet, John.'

'Do you want us to go?' Susan asked.

'No, it's fine, love,' Smithdown said. 'I've nothing to hide. Give me a Wine Gum, Danny, you tight get. They're supposed to be mine, you know.'

Danny offered the sweets to Susan and Jonathan first, then gave the box to Smithdown. There was quiet for a few moments. 'I don't like those two detectives,' Smithdown finally said. 'There's something off about them.'

'I don't like them either,' Danny agreed. 'The DI is alright, I suppose, but his little brother is a headbanger.'

'You don't like any cops, Danny,' Smithdown pointed out.

'Apart from you, John. You're just about bearable.'

'Thanks for those kind words, lad. Proper moving, that is.' Smithdown shook the box of Wine Gums. 'Don't take the black ones. They're my favourites.'

There was silence again. 'I don't want to die with this hanging over me, Danny,' Smithdown said. Jonathan reached out and held his grandad's hand.

'You're not going to die, John,' Danny said. 'It was a mini stroke, that's all.'

'I am going to die, Danny. In case no one's told you, we all are. It doesn't matter if I die when I'm 103 or a week on Tuesday, I don't want this on my name. Understood?'

'Understood,' Danny confirmed. 'It's not going to be easy. There's the note. The photo too. It all points to you. What should I do?'

'Go back to the start,' Smithdown said. 'Look at it afresh with your…'

'I know,' Danny said, remembering what the detective had once told him. 'With my eyes open and my gob shut.'

NINETEEN

'Oh... It's you again,' Maggie Ormrod's neighbour said as she opened her front door to Danny. The weather had taken a turn for the worse after he had dropped Jonathan and Susan back at Hunter's Hollow. It was raining heavily now and the woman's tiny, terraced cottage opened directly onto the street, offering him no shelter. 'I suppose you think I'm going to ask you in because it's raining, don't you?' she said.

'It would be nice,' Danny said, pulling the collar of his jacket tightly up.

'Well, I'm not going to,' she said. 'What do you want? I've been reading your website. You're a proper trouble magnet, you are, aren't you?'

'I'm not here to cause trouble,' Danny said. 'I'm not after an interview or anything. Just information. No phones, no recording. Just help. Something's not right and I want to make it better. For Maggie if nothing else.'

The neighbour looked at Danny, then glanced up and down the street. 'Go on then,' she said. 'I must be mad. Take your shoes off.'

Danny did as he was told and followed the woman into the kitchen. It was deliciously warm from an AGA cooker. Art prints covered the walls and an old, contented-looking cat was curled up on a cushion-covered seat at the wooden table. 'Your house is really nice,' Danny said. 'Mine's an old cottage like this but it's a tip compared to yours.'

'Hmm. Flattery now. You're trying all the tricks, aren't you? Take a seat, but mind the cat. Do you want tea?'

'I'd love a tea. Thank you.'

'I'm Joy, by the way. Joy Pritchard. It's Danny Johnston, isn't it?'

'It is.'

'Well, allow me to throw a little flattery your way,' Joy said. 'I read your book about those child murders. Amazing story. Hard to believe that Smithdown guy is a wrong un, to be honest.'

'He isn't. That's why I'm here. He's in hospital; he's had a mini-stroke but he's still cracking on and the least I can do is put this right while he's getting better.'

'Okay,' she said, cautiously. 'He's lucky to have a friend like you, I suppose. But… what if he actually is a wrong un? What would you do then?'

'I'd wheel his hospital bed into Oldham cop shop myself,' Danny stated. 'And that's a promise.'

The cat next to Danny made a light snoring sound. 'What do you want to know?' Joy asked.

'You said that Maggie was a character. How did you mean?'

'It's a polite way of saying she was piss artist, I suppose,' Joy replied with a smile. 'What little money she had, she spent in the pub. The Bull's Head up the road, mainly. She'd been barred from most of the other local places.'

'Why?' asked Danny, sipping his tea from a rustic-looking mug that looked hand made.

'The pubs around here have gone a bit upmarket, and they like it quiet. Maggie was loud and could be a bit of a handful. She upset the diners having their sea bass and crushed potatoes, that kind of thing. Have you spoken to anyone at The Bull's Head?'

'I've just come from there. They didn't want to know. I'm a so-called journalist, apparently and they don't want my sort in their pub. Did she drink at home?'

'Not really. She craved company. She'd sit here with me sometimes and have a few glasses of wine. Well, I had wine, she preferred Carlsberg Special Brew. But she knew I wouldn't put up with any nonsense, so she was always on her best behaviour.'

'You also said before that things had changed at her house. Noisy parties, that kind of thing.'

'Yeah, maybe she was short of money. She hadn't been working very much and supermarket tins of beer are cheaper than pub pints, aren't they?

'They are indeed, Joy. I can vouch for that. What did she do for money?'

'Cleaning, mainly. Wherever would have her. She went here and there. Offices, schools, that kind of thing. She cleaned at the police station for a while last year.'

'She was a cleaner at the police station?' Danny asked. 'The main Oldham station in town? The cops never mentioned that.'

'Yes, she did. Used to cycle there and back first thing in the morning.

Had to push her bike up halfway up the hill to get home.'

'A cleaner at the cop shop… Fucking Nora. Sorry Joy. No need for that, is there?'

'I've heard worse, Danny.'

'Fucking cops. Why is it always the bastard fucking cops?'

'Okay, I think you've used up all your swearing tokens now.'

'You're right. Sorry. Did Maggie ever talk about her childhood?'

'She'd been in children's homes, I knew that. You could tell she was damaged. No question about it. It was clear she'd really been through it. A few times when she was really drunk, she'd take out a photo of her and a guy from the 70s. Rant and rave about it. I rescued the picture from the bin a few times after she'd screwed it up and thrown it away in a rage.'

'Do you still have it?'

'No. She'd taken it back for the umpteenth time. The police have got it now. But I took a photo of it just in case she destroyed it. Thought it might come in useful one day. I suppose it has, in a way.'

Joy pulled out her phone and flicked the screen until she found what she wanted. She showed it to Danny. Little Maggie Ormrod with a young, smiling John Smithdown. Danny looked at the detective's arm around her slim shoulders. It gave him a cold feeling. 'Could you send that to me?' he asked. 'I'll show you how to Airdrop it if you like?'

Danny's phone pinged with an Airdrop notification. 'I know how to Airdrop,' Joy said. 'I'm not that past it. I've got a recent picture of Maggie too, if you want it?'

Before he had time to say yes, a second alert hit Danny's phone. This time it was of a much older Maggie. Her eyes were closed in pleasure as she nuzzled Joy's cat. 'You're very much on the ball, Joy,' Danny said, saving the pictures. 'Why do I get the impression you know what you're doing?'

'Kind of,' she confirmed. 'I used to work in telly, like you. Down the road at Granada TV. I worked in the gallery on the news, so I know the importance of a good picture.'

'One last thing,' Danny said. 'Do you know why she stopped cleaning at the police station?'

'I don't. Sorry.'

'Don't be. You've been really helpful, Joy.'

'I have?'

'Yes. You really have. It'd be interesting to know why she stopped cleaning at the nick, wouldn't it?'

'I suppose it would,' she agreed. 'How do you propose to find out?'

'Well, it just so happens that I'm going to Oldham Police Station tomorrow.'

TWENTY

DEATH AT HANGING LEES - DID YOU KNOW MAGGIE ORMROD?

Danny Johnston - Oldham Now

Oldham Now is trying to trace anyone who knew local woman Maggie Ormrod, whose body was found on Monday morning at Hanging Lees Reservoir.

Police say there are no suspicious circumstances surround her death and are not looking for anyone else in connection with the find. That is the usual statement police put out when there has been a suicide, pending an inquest.

In a separate development, a man in his 80s, who was being interviewed by detectives about allegations made in a note left at the scene, has been told he won't have to answer further questions about the matter for the time being. He fell ill while helping police with their inquiries at Oldham police station.

Do you know Maggie? A recent picture shows her cuddling a neighbour's cat. She was a familiar figure in the area near her home on Ripponden Road, Denshaw.

She worked locally as a cleaner and was known to frequent several local pubs, including The Bull's Head, which is close to Hanging Lees Reservoir. Staff at the pub declined to comment when asked about Maggie earlier today.

It's believed that she spent time in children's homes in the 1970s. Were you in care at that time? Do you remember Maggie? If so, please contact **danny@oldhamnow.net**

TWENTY-ONE

Danny set up a tripod with his iPhone clamped to the top, focussed it on the top table and set it to record. He attached a note to one of the legs with the word TV people use for tripod.

MIND MY STICKS

He then placed another iPhone on the top table next to the nameplate that said:

DETECTIVE INSPECTOR PATRICK MCINTYRE.

He set that one to record audio via the Voice Memo app; he'd synch the two up later. Then he took a seat on his own; he wanted to sit away from the other journalists who were waiting for the police press conference to start.

He looked around the large conference room at Oldham Police Station. *Decent turn out.* The usual faces were here from the regional news operations: *Manchester Evening News,* BBC North West, ITV Granada, Press Association, local news agency Cavendish Press and Kate's old paper the *Oldham Messenger.* But there were network TV reporters here too, and Sky News were also in attendance. *This story is definitely taking off.*

An onscreen TV reporter he knew from when she was a researcher on his ITV show mouthed, 'Hello Danny' from across the room. She then pointed to herself and then at Danny and made the internationally recognised sign for 'talking' with her thumb and second finger. Danny mouthed back, 'Later' and gave her the thumbs up. He had absolutely no intention of talking to her afterwards and had already worked out how he could slip out of the room at the end of the press conference without answering any questions from the other journalists. *Fuck 'em. This is my story.*

DI Patrick McIntyre then entered the room, accompanied by a

Greater Manchester Police Press Officer. Danny noticed DI McIntyre's brother Karl standing to one side of the room. He was looking right at Danny. The 'look' went on for what Danny felt was a rather strange amount of time. *Is he trying to intimidate me? Really? What a massive weirdo.*

After a little thought, Danny came up with a way to diffuse the situation - he stood up, waved to the DI and shouted: 'Karl! Hey, Karl! How are you mate? Nice to see you last night. Drinkies later, yeah?'

Everyone in the room stopped and looked; first at Danny, then at Karl McIntyre. *I do believe he went a bit red there.* The DC walked over, crouched down and leant in to talk quietly into Danny's ear. 'You're a witness in this case, Mr Johnston. Not sure it's appropriate for you to be here.'

'Well, you know what I'm not sure about?' Danny replied, not bothering to speak quietly at all. 'I'm not sure GMP is telling the whole story here. Not about this and not about the suicide at Hanging Lees either. And I'll bet you a tenner that what we are about to witness here is your brother talking a load of copperspeak bullshit that will add fuck all to what you've released already. So don't come the big bollocks with me. I've had coppers ten times more frightening than you have a pop at me in the past. Trust me.'

The detective stared at Danny; his face was close, and his breath was deep and slow. 'You shouldn't be here,' the DC repeated. As he walked away, he gave Danny's sticks a kick, tipping it over. Danny caught it just before it hit his chair.

'Bye Karl,' Danny shouted. 'I am single, actually. Thanks for asking.'

Standing next to the top table, the Press Officer spoke: 'Right then. Morning all. Thanks for coming today. This is Detective Inspector Patrick McIntyre. He has an appeal that we hope you can help with - it's in connection with the discovery of a man's body close to the M62 motorway. Before we start, as you may know there has been a certain amount of information about this case that's already appeared online.' Several of those present turned to look in Danny's direction. *Oh, okay, it's going to be like this is it?*

The Press Officer continued: 'We are going to give you the correct version this morning. We would ask you to ignore what you may have seen and heard and stick to the details you are about to get from DI McIntyre. The purpose of the exercise here is to find the person or persons responsible. I think we can all get behind that, yes? Okay. Great. DI McIntyre, over to you.'

'Thank you very much,' the detective said. 'Yes, good morning, everyone. The reason we've called this press conference is to make some specific appeals in relation to the death of Barry Mortimer. Mr Mortimer was 44 years of age and he was from the Delph area of Oldham. His body was found at a wind turbine at an area known as Lad's Grave Moor. He'd been subjected to a sustained and brutal attack that we believe had lasted for many hours before he was found dead. Mr Mortimer ran a printing business in the centre of Oldham and security footage shows him leaving work early at 4pm on Saturday afternoon. We believe he then headed east towards the Greenacres area. His wife reported him missing at 9pm that evening. We are keen to trace anyone who saw Mr Mortimer in the Greenacres area after 4.30pm on Saturday.

'Secondly, we also want to speak to anyone who saw anything suspicious close to the Junction 22 turn off of the M62 on the night Mr Mortimer's body was found. So that's Monday night or the early hours of Tuesday morning, some two days after he was last seen. This is a very remote section of the motorway, surrounded by open moorland. Despite this, it's a hugely busy section of the motorway, with thousands of cars and lorries passing, even in the middle of the night. We'd ask any motorists or lorry drivers who were in that area on Monday night or the early hours of Tuesday to think hard. Did you see anything out of the ordinary that night on the motorway?

'Thirdly… I'm appealing to anyone involved in the so-called online vigilante community, particularly those based on Facebook, to examine their consciences and come forward with any information they might have. They can do so anonymously if they like via Crimestoppers. The number, as ever, is 0800 555 111. I know there's been a lot of speculation about why Mr Mortimer was murdered and what kind of person he was. I know there's a lot of anger out there, which can sometimes boil over. But the legal system is the best way to deal with criminals, whatever type of crime they may or may not have committed. So, I'm appealing for calm. Let us do our job. Please.

'And finally… I know there has been some reporting on this case so far that can, at best, be described as unhelpful to this investigation. Mr Mortimer's background will obviously form part of this inquiry. Mr Mortimer was a family man and his family want to know what happened to him; we are committed to finding that out. The key thing here is that he was the victim of an horrific attack. The worst I've ever seen. Whoever did this needs to be caught quickly before they do it again. That's our focus. That's why we need your help. I'm very happy to take any questions; please be aware though that there will be certain aspects of the case I can't talk about.'

'Thank you, DI McIntyre,' the Press Officer said. 'Right then. Please tell us who you are and what organisation you represent before asking your question, thank you.'

Danny leant back in his chair and folded his arms. He watched as the other journalists asked their questions. It was all perfectly orderly. *Not like in the TV dramas where the journalists attending the press conference all stand up and shout questions at the same time. Absolute bollocks.*

The BBC asked about the sign found next to Barry Mortimer's body. DI McIntyre politely declined to comment, repeating his key appeals and asking for people not to speculate. ITV Granada wanted to know more about what kind of person Barry Mortimer was. The DI talked about the murdered man's wife, his children and his business. Sky News went straight to the point and asked: 'Was Barry Mortimer a paedophile?' DI McIntyre said largely the same words he'd already spoken but delivered them in a slightly different order. Again, he mentioned irresponsible reporting and repeated his appeals.

The Press Officer held up his hand: 'Okay. Any other questions?'

One by one, all the journalists in the room turned and looked at Danny. He did nothing. Eventually he stood up, walked over to where DI McIntyre was sitting and stood right in front of him. They looked at each other. 'You need to keep a tight leash on your brother, Detective Inspector,' he said. 'He's a bit excitable.'

Then Danny picked up his iPhone from the top table, collected his other phone on the sticks and walked out.

He got as far as the reception doors when he heard a shout behind him: 'Danny, Danny, Danny! Wait, please!'

Danny kept walking but the TV reporter who he used to work with - try as he might, he couldn't summon up her name - quickly caught up with him. 'Come on Danny, wait a sec,' she said. 'I'm in heels here, they're not made for running.'

'I'm in a rush, sorry,' he said. 'Can't stop.'

'Come on. I just need a few minutes with you for our package. You know me… help me out here.'

'I do kind of know you,' he said. 'But to be honest I can't remember your name. Sorry, but it was during my pissed years, so don't take it personally.'

'It's Carrie!' she cried indignantly. 'Carrie O'Connor. Oh my God. You don't even remember my name? I groped you at a Christmas party once!'

'I definitely don't remember that,' Danny muttered, quickening his pace across the car park. 'Look, I'm not doing any interviews, Carrie and that's that. Journalists interviewing other journalists… it's a load of crap. Plus, there's nothing in it for me. Thanks, but no thanks.'

'Course there is,' she said. 'It'll be great exposure for your website.'

Danny stopped walking and looked straight at her: 'Exposure? Fucking Nora! Oh, well that's different. Print me off a bit of that lovely exposure so I can spend it on rent for my house. My landlord much prefers exposure to cash. For fuck's sake… *exposure*. That old chestnut. The answer's no, Carrie. Lovely to see you again. Thanks for the grope, although I genuinely don't remember it. But the answer is most definitely… no.'

TWENTY-TWO

THE FIVE KEY THINGS WE DIDN'T FIND OUT FROM TODAY'S 'VIGILANTE' MURDER PRESS CONFERENCE

Danny Johnston - Oldham Now

Greater Manchester Police held a press conference today to appeal for information about the murder of Oldham man Barry Mortimer - but refused to talk about why the 44-year-old was targeted.

And that isn't the only thing the police aren't talking about.

Mr Mortimer's body was found strapped to a wind turbine close to the M62 motorway. He'd been tortured for some time before he was discovered on a stretch of moor known as Lad's Grave.

The person who found him was me. I went to the moor after getting an anonymous tip-off. I got a similar alert about the death of Maggie Ormrod at Hanging Lees Reservoir.

Let me tell you something: these press conferences are pantomimes. The detective in charge, Detective Inspector Patrick McIntyre said nothing of any note and declined to answer anything about what is really going on. His brother, Detective Constable Karl McIntyre was openly hostile towards me, almost threatening in his manner.

So much that goes on between journalists and the police in this country is done behind closed doors. I should know, I've been a journalist for 35 years. So, I've decided to be completely transparent and publish the questions I have for Greater Manchester Police right here to see what *Oldham Now* readers think of them. If officers from Greater Manchester Police want to respond, they know where to find me.

1.Why was Barry Mortimer targeted?

Mortimer's wife confirmed to me that she had real concerns about what he was doing online. *Oldham Now* reported this earlier in the week. Yet, police seem to be pretending that this information isn't out there. It definitely is out there, so they need to take their fingers out of their ears and start listening. Mrs Mortimer seems convinced that her husband was a danger to young people online. Why don't GMP?

2.Why won't the police discuss the sign found at the scene?

As reported earlier this week a sign was found at the scene close to Barry Mortimer's body. As our exclusive pictures show, it features a chilling warning:

HERE LIES BARRY 'THE BEAST' MORTIMER. CHECK HIS PHONE. LET THIS BE A WARNING TO ALL PAEDOS. NONCE AND YOU WILL DIE.

The whole of Oldham has seen this sign via *Oldham Now;* yet the police seem to be pretending it doesn't exist. It does.

3.Why have Oldham detectives kept their connection with the Ormrod case a secret?

Maggie Ormrod's body was found in the early hours of Monday morning at Hanging Lees Reservoir. She was a cleaner at Oldham Police station, yet detectives have kept this vital fact a secret. Why did they do that?

4.Who is contacting *Oldham Now* with details of these incidents?

Twice now, I have received tip-offs about serious incidents in the area from anonymous but extremely well-informed sources. Where is this information coming from?

5.Why do masked 'vigilantes' keep appearing at the crime scenes?

I was the first person at the spot where Maggie Ormrod's body was found. I was also the first person on the scene of the Barry Mortimer murder. At both places I saw one or more masked people filming the scene. What do the police know about these people and why were they in attendance at both of these apparently unconnected incidents? These masked people also turned up at the house of a man in his 80s who was being taken in for questioning about historic abuse allegations. Who is feeding these people such detailed information?

The Oldham Division of Greater Manchester Police has a grim record of being involved in the most serious of crimes. Officers from Oldham were involved with murders and incitement to cause a race riot in the town in the late 1980s after the so-called 'Mermaid's Pool murder'. An Oldham detective was also responsible for the horrific 'Twisted Sisters' killing spree that started with the discovery of a child's body at Black Moss reservoir in 1990.

Promises of change have always followed these terrible crimes. Assurances of inquiries, recommendations and new practices, followed by root and branch removals of so-called 'rogue' officers.

The problem isn't an institutional one, we are told, it's just a few 'bad apples'. We've heard the excuses and explanations before. But did anything really change after Black Moss and the Mermaid's Pool? Or are we witnessing a new breed of bad apple in the famously rotten barrel known as Oldham Police?

It's starting to look like the bad old days are back. With a vengeance.

TWENTY-THREE

31 March 1975

'Flippin eck Maggie, you proper frightened me then,' Alma Richards said from under the covers of her bed in the Greenacres Children's Home. 'Where've you been? It's really late.'

'To the fair,' Maggie whispered, taking off her clothes as quickly as possible and getting into bed in just her pants and vest. 'Shurrup and go back to sleep.'

'How can I go back to sleep with you banging about like a baby elephant?' Alma moaned.

Maggie closed her eyes for all of ten seconds then threw back the covers and leant out of bed so far that she was almost upside down.

'What you after now?' Alma pleaded in a hushed voice.

Maggie was digging around in the pockets of her dungarees that were on the floor by her bed. She found what she was looking for, pulled herself back upright and tucked the precious item under her pillow. She closed her eyes for another ten seconds, then opened them again and lay on her back, staring at the ceiling.

'What's up with you?' Alma whispered. 'You're driving me mad.'

Maggie rolled over, propped herself up on her elbow and looked at Alma: 'If you could have any treat, I mean anything, what would you have?'

'Oh God, stop mithering me!' Alma said, covering her face with her blanket.

'Go on,' Maggie said. 'What would you have?'

Alma turned to face Maggie; their beds were just feet apart. 'Anything at all?' she asked.

'Anything,' Maggie confirmed.

'A Wimpy Special Grill…' the girl began.

'Oh!' Maggie interrupted. 'The one with the sausage that bends around the tomato!'

'A Wimpy Special Grill, a Knickerbocker Glory and a banana milkshake.'

‘Not strawberry?’ Maggie queried.

‘No, definitely banana,’ Alma confirmed.

There was silence. Maggie smiled: ‘I’ll get it for you. On Saturday in town. My treat.’

‘Don’t be daft,’ Alma sighed. ‘A Special Grill is 49p on its own. With the other stuff as well, it’d be nearly a pound!’

The two girls lay quietly in their beds. ‘Can you keep a secret?’ Maggie asked.

‘I’m no grass, Maggie Ormrod,’ Alma pointed out, slightly indignantly.

Maggie reached under her pillow and took out a blue piece of paper. She unfolded carefully then held it up so Alma could see it. ‘Bloody Nora!’ the younger girl cried, then slapped a hand across her mouth to keep herself silent. ‘A fiver! Where did you get that? Did you nick it?’

‘No, I did not!’ Maggie said. It was her turn to sound indignant now. ‘It’s mine. My new friend gave it to me. Not nicked. All mine. And I was going to treat you to a Wimpy, but if you’re going to be rude…’

‘I’m sorry!’ Alma squealed. ‘Oh God. Are you serious? I’ve looked at the menu of the Wimpy that many times, I could tell you everything on it by heart.’

‘You and me, Saturday dinner time,’ Maggie said. ‘The Special Grills are on me.’

TWENTY-FOUR

For the next few days, Danny kept a low profile and watched as the police tried to rattle as many cages as possible in the online vigilante community, largely centred on Facebook.

He saw how carefully invited journalists accompanied police officers on early morning raids to arrest 'people of interest' in the Barry Mortimer case. Doors were kicked in for the benefit of the cameras and sallow-faced men in shell suits were taken away for questioning. The raids made the lead story on both *Granada Reports* and *North West Tonight* and some of the clips got big numbers on social media *Nice PR for the police, good ratings for the news. Everyone's happy.*

Danny wasn't surprised that there was an underground digital hub dedicated to baiting, catching and exposing men with fake profiles and promises of underage sex. But he was stunned by the sheer size of it. He was also very disappointed by the lack of creativity that had gone into naming the various Facebook groups dedicated to it.

He'd lost count of the sheer numbers of 'Noncebusters' there were, though 'Paedohunters' ran a close second. A few bucked the trend: he quite liked 'Pae-DON'T' for its brutal simplicity; he'd slowly developed a soft spot for 'Molester Testers'; but his firm favourite was 'Nonce Upon a Time in the West (of Oldham)'. It had a winning mix of fairy tale and western film references, along with a pun no one else had so far thought of. The sheer levels of interaction that each page generated was also staggering - thousands of angry emojis, positive comments and likes for every video. *With engagement like this no wonder I've been skint for so long. These guys are hoovering up all the online traffic. Looks like they're in it for the likes as much as the noncebusting.*

The contents of the Facebook pages were depressingly repetitive. A middle-aged man - usually white, but not always - would be confronted in a car park, bus station or occasionally at his own home. This was normally done by some slightly younger white men. The confrontation would be filmed as the target discovered that the liaison they'd set up online wasn't quite what they had expected. Some denied all knowledge, even as the proof was shown to them. Others were struck mute by a strange mix of shame and bafflement. Some ran away, only to be chased and caught by the younger, fitter hunters with their cameras still rolling. As an ex-television reporter, Danny was impressed with some of the production values; many had a reasonably professional air, using graphics, music and even animation to 'sell' the sting. Most were shot on single iPhones but some were multi-camera affairs that had been well edited and even sound mixed.

He watched one video that showed a man identified as Paul being approached in his car at a McDonalds in Chadderton. The video team approach him and ask who he was waiting for. 'My brother-in-law,' Paul said. 'What's with the cameras?'

'Is your brother-in-law called Briony, mate?' the lead vigilante sneered, off-camera. "Cos that's who you're actually waiting for, isn't it?'

'No idea what you mean, sorry.' Paul's face clearly showed that he knew he'd been found out, despite his denials.

The vigilante affected a sarcastic, singsong tone of voice: 'Briony, I will treat you right. You're first time is precious... once in a lifetime... and should be with someone who will respect you and make sure you feel like a princess and a lady…'

The camera zoomed in on Paul's face: 'Ring any bells, mate?' the vigilante continued. 'Remember messaging those words to Briony? Little 14-year-old Briony? Do ya, Paul? Beautiful words, mate. Genuinely. Shame you were actually messaging us, Paul, ya fookin paedo.'

Paul tried to move his car, but he was now pinned in from all sides by the video team. 'Now, if anyone else wants Paul to write them some beautiful words like these, here are his contact details, starting with his home address...'

Paul had started to cry now. 'Please. Oh God, please, I'm sorry. So, so sorry. I've never done this before. Swear to God. It was stupid. Absolutely fucking stupid. It'll never happen again. I swear. Please can you delete this? Please?'

'Too late for that mate. So here we go. Paul's a local lad, from right here in sunny Chadderton and can be found at 23a Montague Close. That's near the chippy, yeah? Thought so. So yeah, that's the place to meet up with Paul to discuss anything you've seen or heard here tonight. It's a good chippy too, so you can get some grub after you've put his windows in. If you want to pre-book a visit to Paul, no problem. Just call him on 07913...'

Danny watched as Paul started up his car and tried to nudge it past his tormentors. They cheered and jeered as his pulled out of the car park, throwing stones and takeaway milkshake cups at the back of his car. As he pulled away the camera zoomed in and then focussed on his number plate.

Danny looked hard at each video to see if he could find anyone claiming responsibility or knowledge of either the murder of Barry Mortimer or the death of Maggie Ormrod. Nothing.

These are exactly the kind of people who were outside John's house. Definitely. But are they the same kind of people who'd kidnap and torture Barry Mortimer? That's a stretch. The cops are looking in the wrong place, I reckon. These guys want likes. They want comments. They want people to follow what they're up to. The other lot… they don't give a shit about Facebook and all the online clout. They're probably not even on Facebook. They don't need to be. They're a straight up execution squad.

TWENTY-FIVE

Danny didn't really have the time to do a talk for pupils at Hunter's Hollow School. The Barry Mortimer murder and the Hanging Lees suicide were two of the biggest stories he'd ever had on *Oldham Now*.

His Twitter following had gone up by 25 per cent; the *Oldham Now* Facebook group page had been liked by an extra thousand people and he was getting a lot of 'Hi Danny, can you follow me back so I can DM you?' messages from other news organisations wanting to use his pictures and videos. He had bypassed the usual 'sure, if you give me credit' response; he'd written up a rate card and had started charging for them.

Plus, requests to advertise on *Oldham Now* were still coming in. Another six local firms had offered him four thousand pounds each to run ads for the next twelve months. Revenue from banner ads, filler ads, job ads and the financial kick back from the analytic spike on all his stories was really starting to add up, especially now that he'd added the code to accept adverts on all the 'death stories' in his archive.

So, Danny was far too busy to give a talk to a bunch of teenagers at the Hunter's Hollow School. But Susan Matlock had emailed him, saying how much it would mean to the students if he came. So, instead of politely declining he'd said... *yes, absolutely, love to, when do you want me to be there?*

Danny had worked in TV for years so expressing himself to an audience was in his bones. But as he buzzed the main entrance door to the school, he felt a tug of nerves. *That's weird. I can talk to anyone. Maybe it's because of Susan. It's almost as if I really want to please her. Which is weird because I don't normally give a shit about pleasing anyone.*

He had even invested in a new, white tee-shirt at his local supermarket while he'd been doing his weekly shop. And he'd ironed it too.

Danny buzzed through the main door and Susan Matlock met him in the reception. *Jeans, white shirt, fancy pumps. Definitely no outdoor gear today… Why am I even noticing this stuff?*

'Danny, thanks so much for doing this,' she said with a smile. 'The pupils are really looking forward to listening to you.'

'No problem at all,' Danny said, trying not to smile too hard in return. 'It's going to be good.'

'How long can you give us?' she asked.

'Do I need to keep it clean?'

'If possible, yes,' Susan replied.

'I'll do you two minutes then.'

Susan laughed and very lightly touched Danny's forearm; it was like he'd experienced a tiny static shock on the spot where her fingers had connected with his skin.

Ben Matlock joined them and shook Danny's hand. 'Aright, Danny?' he said with a grin. 'Nervous?'

'It's fine, I've done loads of talks in my time,' Danny replied.

'No, I meant nervous about seeing Mum again… it's technically a date this, isn't it?'

'Ben!' Susan cried. 'For Christ's sake, shut it! Sorry, Danny. Let's get you signed in and badged up, then we can get cracking before I punch Ben in the throat…'

With the paperwork done, Danny was taken down a long corridor lined with certificates and awards and into a conference room that was clearly a leftover from the school's time as a hotel. There were forty teenagers waiting for him; three-quarters were boys. The room had that blunt, musky smell that comes with large groups of lads: *Hair gel, body spray and laddishness. Oh, to be young.*

Danny spotted Johnathan sitting at the back of the room. He nodded towards the teenager, and he got the smallest of nods in return. *Can't be seen to be too friendly when you're with your mates. Not cool.*

'Right then!' cried Susan, putting both hands in the air and waving them to get the group's attention. 'Bums on seats, please. Let's be having you.'

Susan pointed to a pale-faced teenage boy who had two hoods over his head. 'Josh… are you staying?' she asked. 'You are? Then take your coat off then, you're making me nervous. At least take one of your hoods down. You look like a bank robber. Thank you. So! As promised, this is Danny Johnston. He's a journalist and an author and he runs the *Oldham Now* news website. So as there's no news at all currently happening in the Oldham area, he had nothing better to do… so he's come here to talk to you lot.'

Susan winked at Danny and motioned for him to step forward. He stood at the front of the meeting room and took out a small bottle of sparkling water, opened it and then had to shake his hand dry when it bubbled over and splashed onto the floor. 'That was a good start,' he muttered, wiping his hand on the back of his trousers. 'Okay. Right. My name is indeed Danny Johnston and Susan has asked me to come and talk to you about being a journalist.'

He paused and looked around the room. Forty pairs of young, slightly puzzled eyes were trained on him. He noticed at least twenty pairs of folded arms too. 'So… I think being a journalist is a calling: like being a doctor. Or a teacher. Or a nun.'

He'd done talks before and that line usually got a small laugh. Not today. He took another sip of water. 'Being a journalist has totally changed. When I started you were sent out with a pad, a pen and a bag of two pence pieces.'

Danny noticed some puzzled faces: '…So you could phone your story into the news desk from a phone box. That's what the coins were for. Now all you need is a mobile phone. You can write on it, film on it, edit on it and publish on it. What's more, everyone's got a phone. Everyone. Doesn't make everyone a journalist, though. So, what's the difference? Well, accountability for one thing. A journalist doesn't just stick something online anonymously. A journalist puts their name to their story and stands by it. They take responsibility for it. They understand the law and how to stay on the right side of it while still holding people to account. They appreciate the importance of consent and how vital it is to respect it when people agree to talk to you. They get the fact that to be given a platform to tell stories to other people is a privilege. It's the best job in the world but it's also a massive responsibility. You've got to get the balance right; make sure you talk to plenty of people who don't have much of a voice… and at the same time, challenge as many people as possible who maybe have too much of a voice. That's what being a journalist is.'

Danny looked at the pupils. The same number of arms were still folded. *I'm dying on my arse here.*

He decided to try a different approach: 'Look. To be honest, I'm not sure what being a journalist actually is any more. It's become very confusing in recent years, for me anyway. I do know this, though. I got really lucky. I didn't have the nicest start in life when I was a kid. Me and my sister were taken away from our parents because they were shit at looking after us. We were in care - not for long, but long enough to know it was better than where we'd come from. We got lucky that we were adopted by two amazing people who did their best to give us a better life. I didn't like school and school didn't like me, but I did better at college and fluked a job on a local paper. Then I fluked another job at what used to be called Manchester Radio. I think it's called All The Fucking Hits now, or something shit like that.'

There was a small ripple of laughter in the room. 'Sorry, Susan,' Danny said. 'I promised to keep it clean. Anyway, when I was working at Manchester Radio, I found a story - literally stumbled across it - that changed my life. A kid's body had been dumped on the edge of Black Moss Reservoir. It's only a few miles from here. No one cared about the kid because there was a much bigger story down the road that was sexier and more high profile. The Strangeways Riot. Look it up. Not now, obviously. Later. Anyway, no one gave a shit about this kid apart from me and a policeman called John Smithdown. A really good man… don't let anyone tell you otherwise. I didn't know it at the time, but John Smithdown was a hero. Still is. He stopped Oldham going up in a race war in the 1980s. Seriously. He did. Then I got lucky again and got a job in London with the national TV news and then my own current affairs series. I was in showbiz! Then I fucked it all up because I was pissed all the time and crashed my car into a tree. I got sacked because everyone saw what I did. Do you know why? Because someone filmed me with their phone and put it on the internet. Oh, the irony. So, I came back up here a few years ago. Me and John Smithdown managed to find out who killed that kid, you've probably heard about that. But we never found out who the kid actually was. One day I will though. That's a promise. So maybe that's what being a journalist is all about. Wanting to put things right and never giving up until you do. I don't know. Does that make sense? Sorry. I went off on one there, didn't I? I probably shouldn't have sworn as much either. Sorry. Any questions?'

There was a silence - quite a long one - then Josh, the boy in the coat and hoodie, put up his hand and asked: 'How much do you earn?'

'Fuck all,' Danny replied. That got a laugh too, and the room relaxed a little bit more. He felt the need to mouth 'sorry' again to Susan. 'Seriously, not very much at all, I'm afraid. It's Josh, isn't it? Well, Josh… I turned over about 15 grand last year. You can earn more at McDonald's. I won't starve and I've got a few quid stashed away from the old days, but if you want to go into journalism for the money, you're in for a big surprise. And not a nice one either, I'm afraid. Yes, you?'

Danny pointed at a girl of about 15 in a shell suit: 'Hi. What's your name?' he asked.

'It's Carly. Hi. How many people work for you?'

'Ha! None, Carly. Zero. I'm it. A one-man band. I do everything myself. Everything. But, on the plus side, no one tells me what to do. And not many people can say that.'

Josh put up his hand again: 'What was it like seeing that dead paedo guy out on the moors?'

There were a few sniggers. Susan was about to say something, but Danny answered: 'It was horrible, Josh. One of the worst things I've ever seen. No one deserves to die like that.'

'Not even paedos?' Carly asked.

'Not even *alleged* paedos,' Danny confirmed. 'The law is there to decide things like that, not vigilantes. Anyone else?'

Josh put his hand up again. *Josh is in an inquisitive mood tonight,* Danny thought.

'You said you only made about 15 grand, yeah? But how do you actually make that money?'

'Advertising,' Danny replied. 'I get paid to include adverts on the website.'

'So, the more people go on your site, the more money you make?'

'Correct.'

Josh looked at his phone: 'I'm on your site now. There's a sidebar showing this week's top stories. The top three are about the paedo murder, the fourth and fifth are about the woman who did herself in at Hanging Lees.'

'I haven't looked since this morning,' Danny said. 'I'll take your word for it.'

'So, the more people die - preferably in really nasty ways - the more money you make?'

'Technically, yes. I'd love to be funded by the public like the BBC or by some rich benefactor… but I'm not. The reality is that without me there'd be little or no local accountability around here. Local newspapers have all but fizzled out. Local radio stations are essentially national franchises with shared news content. No one goes to council meetings or covers the courts like they used to. That world is gone. Someone needs to tell local stories that hold local organisations to account, otherwise it's all just clickbait bollocks about celebrities. I wish that my top five stories weren't the ones you mentioned. But that's not under my control. The public decides that, not me. The popular stories pay for the unpopular ones. What I do and the way I do it isn't perfect, but it's probably the least worst way of doing it, put it like that.'

There was quiet. 'Right then,' Susan said. 'Any more questions? Preferably ones that don't contain the word paedo.'

Danny fielded a few more questions. They asked about reading an autocue on TV (*I never used one, I only ever did short pieces to camera when I was out and about filming stories and I memorised the words I had to say. I had a go once and I was rubbish at it*); they asked about the most famous person he'd ever met (*Probably Margaret Thatcher, but she probably isn't that famous to you, I'd imagine. Fame is generational, isn't it?)* and they asked about the most embarrassing thing that had ever happened to him (*went out on a tip off that there was a riot in Rusholme, South Manchester. Lot of South Asian people. Turned out to be Eid. Still, I thought it was a great story, so I interviewed loads of lads, the police, shopkeepers, everything. Turned out the whole time I thought I was recording I was on pause. When I thought I was on pause I was actually recording. So, I got nowt but the sound of my own footsteps. When I got back to the radio station, I was so embarrassed I lied and said that when I got there, there was no one about so I'd just left. I still cringe myself to sleep about it*).

After half an hour Susan smiled and looked around the room: 'Right, if there's no more questions, let's thank Danny, please.' A medium strength ripple of applause came from the audience. He tried to catch Jonathan's eye but he was already on his way out of the room, talking to Josh, who's hoodie and coat were now back in their original positions.

'Was that alright?' Danny asked, finishing his water. 'I'm not sure that was any use to anyone.'

'It was great,' Susan said. 'What was that you said? *Trying to put things right and never giving up until you do*. Those are golden words, right there.'

'Well, that's very kind. Josh is a character, isn't he?'

'Clever lad,' Susan smiled. 'He wants to be a journalist.'

'He's got the charm, that's for sure,' Danny said.

'You need charm to be a journalist?' she asked with mock incredulity. 'How did you get under the wire then?'

'Oh, that's nice…'

'I'm only messing. I really appreciate you coming. And by way of a thank you, I'd like to buy you lunch sometime. Somewhere local. Saddleworth, maybe? Could you pick me up from here? Ben needs the school Land Rover most days. What do you think?'

Danny felt slightly flustered and didn't do a very good job of hiding it: 'Well… I…I think that's the least you can do after hurting my feelings like that,' he said.

'Ha! Great. Thursday alright?

'Thursday is very alright,' he said with a smile.

‘That’s settled then. I’ll show you out.’

Danny and Susan walked across the room and through the reception and he returned a wave and a thumbs up from Ben. As they walked, Danny turned his phone back on. There was a text message from a number he didn’t recognise.

<MIDNIGHT ON THE M62 FOOTBRIDGE.>

‘Everything okay?’ Susan asked.

‘Cracking, yes,’ he replied. ‘Just a potential new story. See you Thursday.’

TWENTY-SIX

Danny looked at Kate's outfit as they headed up the foggy path past the Windy Hill transmitter. She was sporting hiking boots and a slightly shabby looking faux leopard skin coat. 'You look like Richey Edwards on a Duke of Edinburgh expedition,' he said.

'What are you on about?' Kate said, sounding annoyed and out of breath.

'The coat. The boots. You look like the guy from the Manic Street Preachers. But on an outward-bound course. Absolutely bizarre choice of gear.'

'The boots are Jonathan's from years ago,' Kate pointed out. 'The coat is the warmest thing I could find at short notice. It's fucking freezing out here. No wonder they call it Windy Mountain.'

'Hill,' Danny corrected. 'It's Windy Hill. You're telling me the warmest jacket you could find was that thing? Who left it at your house, Bet Lynch off Coronation Street?'

'Sorry, Danny,' she said, looking at Danny's outdoor clothing. 'I didn't have time to get properly kitted out in all the weekend warrior gear like you're wearing. Next time you get another weird tip off from Paedo Killers R Us, I'll make sure I'm better prepared. Where the fuck are we going, anyway?'

'The Pennine Way bridge. It goes over the M62. You'll have driven under it a thousand times. It's very distinctive. It's called a parabolic arch.'

'This whole thing is parabollocks if you ask me,' Kate added. 'Why am I here, exactly?'

'I need a witness,' Danny said. 'Plus, you're my only friend. Apart from your dad. And he's a bit old to be knocking about on the moors at this time of night.'

'I'm genuinely touched,' she said. 'How far is it?'

'Just over this ridge. Can you hear the motorway? It can't be far now.'

As the path crested the hill, the noise suddenly increased and the rolling landscape was crudely interrupted by the M62. Cars and lorries thundered past in both directions below them, fog lights pushing through the late-night haze.

Connecting the gap across the east and westbound lanes was a strangely elegant footbridge, curving more than 60 feet above the carriageways.

'Such a weird bridge to be plonked out here in the middle of nowhere,' Kate muttered, pulling her coat around her for warmth. 'It's wasted on ramblers and Boy Scouts. It's too fancy, isn't it?'

'Apparently the transport minister at the time was a keen walker and insisted on something a bit special,' Danny offered. 'Quite European, isn't it?'

'Très chic, Danny, I'm sure.' Kate looked across at the empty bridge. The far end of the structure over the eastbound carriageway almost faded away into the fog. 'There's no bugger here anyway,' she pointed out. 'Another fun night out, Danny. Nice one. You should ask Susan Matlock out, see if she fancies coming up here. Very romantic.'

'She's already asked ME out,' Danny said. 'Get with the times, Grandma, this is the modern world and Susan is a very modern woman.'

'She's a very strange woman if she's asked you out,' Kate replied.

As they got closer to the eastern entrance to the narrow bridge, two groups of figures scurried onto it from either end. They gathered into two separate huddles and then stopped. There were four people in each group, and they were all looking directly at Danny and Kate. One person from each of the groups then waved to them. 'Okay, that's a bit freaky,' she said. Danny took out his phone and started filming. *It's like they really want me to record it.*

Danny and Kate walked slowly toward the edge of the footbridge. It was surprisingly narrow; two people coming in opposite directions would struggle to pass each other. The traffic below the bridge seemed to push and pull at the fog, making the figures clear one minute and indistinct the next.

'Oh good,' Kate added as they got closer still and the lights from the traffic below revealed more about the people on the bridge. 'They're all wearing masks too. Nice touch.'

'Not quite,' said Danny. 'Look.'

The two gangs all sported variations on the skull bandanas Danny had seen before, but there were two people without masks. Instead, they each had a strip of gaffer tape across their mouths. Danny couldn't see the gagged man at the far side of the bridge too well because of the fog, but the one closer to him clearly had dried blood caked onto his bare chest and his hands were tied behind his back.

One of the masked figures held out a hand, motioning to Danny and Kate that they shouldn't come any further.

'Are we stopping?' Kate asked.

'I reckon we are,' Danny replied.

Danny and Kate stood still. The masked figures stared at them. After 20 seconds they seemed satisfied that their instruction was being followed. Then, with very deliberate, exaggerated movements, two of the group produced mobile phones, held them high and then taped them to the upright spokes of the bridge railings close to where the two shivering, shirtless figures were standing.

'What the actual fuck are we watching here, Danny?' Kate asked. 'This is beyond weird.'

'You know the guy I found over at the wind turbine? It can't have been more than a mile from here. Barry Mortimer was his name. They'd taped Barry's phone to his body to make sure it was found. Not sure why they're taping these phones to the railings.'

Then Danny got his answer. Two people from both of the groups grabbed an ankle each and tipped both men head-first off the bridge.

'Shit, Danny!' Kate cried. 'What the fuck!'

One of the men hit the roof of a passing lorry with a terrible clattering sound before bouncing off the top and crashing onto the carriageway. He was then hit by a series of cars and vans as his body was flipped and battered this way and that before landing in some bushes by the westbound carriageway. The other man somehow managed to find a gap between the traffic as he fell; he went straight down onto the motorway before a gravel truck flattened the top half of his body. The downward force of the truck made his crushed and bloodied figure stick to the road surface, then it was hit by a series of vans, lorries and cars. Over and over and over again.

'Fucking Nora,' Kate whispered. Then she shouted: 'I mean, Fucking Nora, Danny! Jesus Christ Almighty, what the fuck just happened?'

The masked gang raised their fists in triumph and ran towards the far end of the bridge. The foggy night took them and they disappeared from view. But Danny could hear the sound of revving engines - *motorbikes? God, they came on motorbikes* - which roared away as the sound was swallowed up by the moors.

Danny and Kate opened their mouths at the same moment; both were about to scream a warning to the drivers below. No sound came out.

Danny realised there was no point; there was no question that both the men were dead.

They stood and watched as the Manchester bound side of the motorway started to slow down. Not before two lorries and a car had skidded through the side crash barrier and onto the steep grass verge to avoid the vehicles up ahead. Then a motorcyclist rear-ended a car and somersaulted the rider onto its roof. It took at least two minutes for the traffic to come to a complete halt on the westbound carriageway. On the eastbound side, where the dead man's body was still stuck to the motorway, the vehicles kept hitting what was left of his body for another three minutes.

Traffic on both sides finally came to a stop; drivers were getting out of their cars to see what had happened. When they saw the bodies, several of them took out their phones to call the police. Others took out their phones and began filming the scene.

On the bridge above the chaos, all that was left were the two mobiles strapped to the railings.

'On second thoughts, Danny,' Kate said. 'Don't bring Susan here. Ever.'

TWENTY-SEVEN

THE VIGILANTES ARE IN CHARGE NOW AND OLDHAM POLICE KNOW IT

Danny Johnston - Oldham Now

It's usual when covering stories like last night's double motorway murder to use expressions like 'execution-style' or 'so-called vigilantes'. It protects the journalist from any comeback as they are essentially guessing at what actually happened.

Not this time.

What happened on the M62 footbridge was a double execution, pure and simple. I know. I saw it with my own eyes.

The two men murdered last night, were put to death because the vigilantes decided that they deserved to die. Simple as that.

They were thrown onto the M62 because a new breed of vigilante has declared themselves to be judge, jury and executioner in their fight against online sexual predators.

They made it very easy for the police to see what they wanted them to see. The victim's phones had been left at the scene attached to the footbridge railings close to the Windy Hill transmitter. The passcodes had been written on the mobiles in fluorescent white marker pen.

The deliberate placing of the victims' phones at the scene - so police can see what the two men had been doing online - is identical to the method used in the murder of Barry Mortimer less than a mile away. His body was found close to the motorway at Lad's Grave Moor last week. He'd been beaten to death and strapped to a wind turbine alongside a sign threatening more murders:

'NONCE AND YOU WILL DIE'

It looks like at least two people in Oldham didn't listen to that warning. Now they're dead.

It's the third time in less than a week that a message sent to this website has led to the discovery of a dead body or bodies. Last Monday a Twitter message alerted *Oldham Now* to the apparent suicide of local woman Maggie Ormrod. This was followed by another tip off concerning the murder of Barry Mortimer.

Last night I was told to be at the M62 footbridge at midnight. The vigilantes waited for me to arrive before putting on their vile show. I believe they want as many people as possible to know what they're doing and why they are doing it. That's why the tip-offs are being sent to me and that's why they are giving police access to their victims' phones.

Their message is clear: online groomers are fair game. But it's no longer about being named and shamed on a video that gets sent to the police or posted on social media. The rules have changed: online paedophiles are in their sights and if they get caught by the vigilantes, they'll be killed.

A quick look online shows that there's a huge amount of support for the vigilantes. Social media is awash with praise for the killers and there are reports that the usual 'paedophile hunters' - using fake profiles to trap and film suspects - may soon be out of business. Oldham's sexual predators are now in hiding, too scared to ply their sick trade.

I wonder if Oldham Police are secretly delighted by the actions of this new breed of vigilante.

<u>TWENTY-EIGHT</u>

RECORD OF INTERVIEW
Person interviewed: JOHNSTON, Daniel (12/7/66)
Place of interview: Oldham Police Station
Time commenced: 0940 hours
Interviewer(s): DI3716 McIntyre, Patrick DC2184 McIntyre, Karl.
Other persons present: Paulina Scorer - Solicitor from Blanco & Harkness Solicitors.
Usual introductions, cautions and advice. JOHNSTON has been informed that he is not under arrest and that he is free to leave at any time. JOHNSTON has opted to have legal representative with him.
This is the second interview with DANIEL JOHNSTON - JOHNSTON confirms that no questions have been asked before the recording begins.

DI MCINTYRE: Mr Johnston, can you tell me how you and Ms Smithdown came to be out on the moors last night?
JOHNSTON: I'd been out at Hunter's Hollow giving a talk to the pupils. I got a text telling me to go to the bridge. I didn't recognise the number. I guess it was from a chuckaway phone. We parked up near the transmitter and the rest is on the video… which I have very helpfully provided for you so as not to be accused of getting in the way of justice and all that. I don't really have anything else to say. For now.
DI MCINTYRE: And why was Ms Smithdown there?
JOHNSTON: As an extra pair of eyes. And back up. And a bit of company. Its scary out on the moors and she's tough as fuck.
DI MCINTYRE: What did you see on the bridge when you got there?
JOHNSTON: It's on the video.
DI MCINTYRE: Just run though it for me.
JOHNSTON: Well, as you can see on the video… some well-organised, masked men executed two people that they probably thought were paedophiles. They made a proper show of it too, real pantomime stuff.
DI MCINTYRE: Did you hear any voices? Any accents?
JOHNSTON: No one actually spoke. Like I said… a pantomime. It was

all acted out for the benefit of my camera phone. Like… Ooh, look at this… it's some very bad men. What's that, children? Should I throw them off the bridge? All of that. But no one spoke. Not a word. Then over they went…splat, splat. Then they took off on motorbikes. Then you lot miraculously turned up.
DI MCINTYRE: Did you see the motorbikes?
JOHNSTON: No, I didn't. I just heard them.
DI MCINTYRE: Could you identify what type of bike you heard?
JOHNSTON: Not really. I don't know much about motorbikes. What kind of bikes do the police use? Maybe ones with Greater Manchester Police Paedo Death Squad written on them.
DI MCINTYRE: I don't know what that means.
JOHNSTON: Of course you don't. You and your brother are a pair of choirboys, aren't you? Little angels, the pair of you.
DI MCINTYRE: Are you saying that the police are somehow involved in these killings?
JOHNSTON: Are you saying that they aren't?
DI MCINTYRE: Okay, I think we'll leave it at that for the time being.

End of recording: 0949 hours

'Was that alright, Paulina?' Danny said to his solicitor as he put on his jacket. 'I didn't want to come across as rude or sarcastic or anything.' He winked at Detective Constable Karl McIntyre who'd been observing while his brother took Danny's statement.

'Let's just go, Danny,' Paulina said, gathering her things. 'I think you've said quite enough.' She turned to the two detectives. 'I assume you'll be naming the men killed at some point today?'

'After relatives have been informed, yes Ms Scorer,' the DI replied.

'That was quite the piece you posted on your website, Mr Johnston,' DC McIntyre added as they were leaving. 'I particularly liked the bit where you suggested we were dead chuffed about people being chucked off bridges. Made my day, that did. Such insight.'

'Come on, Danny,' Paulina said. 'You've given a statement, let's leave it at that.'

'It's okay,' Danny replied. 'Perhaps the McIntyre lads are just annoyed that they didn't manage to put me in hospital with their line of questioning… like they did with John Smithdown.'

'Danny, please,' Paulina said. 'You have told the DI what you saw. That's what we came for. Time to go.'

They headed for the door of the interview room, but Danny couldn't stop himself from talking: 'These dirty bastards are up to something, Paulina. If there's a trail of slime stinking the place up in Oldham, there's always a cop at the end of it. Every time.'

'Speaking of which,' DC McIntyre said. 'How is Mr Smithdown doing?'

Danny turned and kicked his chair in the detective's direction. It clattered against the edge of the table separating them. 'Hey, Danny!' Paulina said, grabbing the arm of Danny's jacket and pushing him towards the door. 'Out. Right now!'

'You and your brother are wrong uns,' Danny said, pointing at both of the detectives as Paulina coaxed him in the direction of the door. 'I know it and John Smithdown knows it. This is just as much a panto as that shit out on the bridge. Maggie Ormrod killing herself… That's all part of the show too, I reckon. I'm being played for a prick here. Not anymore. That's it. This is the last time I'll be coming in here. Unless it's to watch you two dickheads being arrested for whatever it is you're up to. Because I'm going to fucking well find out. And that's a promise.'

TWENTY-NINE

Danny had been sitting in the café with Paulina for 20 minutes, eating toast and laboriously tapping his story into his phone, when Kate finally arrived from giving her statement.

'How was it?' Danny asked. 'Did you confess?'

'Yes,' Kate confirmed. 'I'd admit to anything to get out of being in the same room as those tools. Especially the younger one. He's an arse.' Kate pulled up a chair next to Paulina; she nodded at Danny. 'And did this lad behave himself?' she asked.

'He did really well,' Paulina said. 'Until right at the end. Things went downhill, you might say. Kicking a chair at the DC was probably a low point.'

'Oh dear, Danny,' Kate sighed. 'Not like you to antagonise the police.'

'It would break my heart if I thought I'd upset them in any way,' Danny said; he didn't look up from writing his story.

'Speaking of you annoying people,' Kate continued. 'I believe you took Jonathan to see Dad at the hospital the other night.'

Danny slowly looked up from his phone: 'You can't kill me in a public place in front of a solicitor, Kate.'

'I'm sure Paulina would look away for a few moments, wouldn't you, mate?'

'Justifiable homicide…' the solicitor smiled.

'Oh, don't worry… I forgive you,' Kate said. 'Me and Jonathan would probably would have gotten into a massive argument anyway. I'll go and see Dad myself later.'

'How did you find out?' Danny asked, completing his story in draft form; he'd left a gap where the dead men's names could be inserted when they'd been positively identified.

'Susan told me,' Kate said, taking a piece of Danny's toast. 'The future Mrs Johnston.'

'Shit! I'm supposed to be seeing her at lunchtime. I'd better get home and clean myself up.'

THIRTY

As Danny waited in the Hunter's Hollow reception for Susan Matlock, he spotted her son Ben talking to a group of teenagers. Danny decided that he felt slightly uncomfortable with the idea of making small talk with a man just before taking his mother out to lunch, so he pretended to be on his phone to avoid eye contact. It didn't work. Ben saw him and shouted across the reception area: 'Hey, Danny!'

Please, don't.

'I hear you're off on a hot date with my mum?' Ben added, walking towards Danny but still speaking in a very loud voice.

Oh fuck.

'Hope you're going to behave yourself,' Ben said with a grin; he playfully punched Danny on the arm.

Shit, it just gets worst.

'Ben, pack it in,' Susan Matlock shouted as she appeared from a side meeting room. *She looks nice. I should have made more of an effort. Shit.* 'We're just going for bite to eat,' she continued in a slightly louder voice than Danny cared for. 'You don't have to start calling him Dad or anything.' She smiled and winked at Danny. 'Not yet anyway.'

Jesus Christ, take me now.

'Sorry to keep you waiting, Danny,' Susan said and pressed her cheek against his. 'And sorry about that dickhead. Try not to set fire to the place while I'm out, Ben!'

'Can't promise,' Ben said as Danny and Susan walked towards the door.

'It's alright,' Danny said. 'Could be worse, I suppose. It's not like he wants to beat me up or anything. He doesn't want to beat me up, does he?'

'Not as far as I'm aware,' she said. 'Depends if we have a nice time or not, doesn't it?'

As they reached the door, Ben shouted one last time: 'Oh Mum… don't be back late or I'll lock the front door.'

'Fuck right off, Ben,' Susan muttered.

As the main security door closed behind them, Danny heard a barrage of laughter. 'Well, that wasn't awkward in the slightest,' he said.

'I'm so sorry,' Susan offered as she got in Danny's car. 'Looks like they've practically married us off before we've had so much as a packet of crisps. Ben shows off a bit for the pupils sometimes. He doesn't mean any harm. Like I said before, he's like their big brother in a lot of ways.'

'It's okay,' Danny said, starting the car. 'I'll live. I think. I could do with a laugh at the moment.'

'I'll bet you could,' Susan said. 'That stuff out on the motorway bridge. Just unbelievable. Are you okay? Kate was there too, right?'

'I'm fine. She's fine too. It was some really weird stuff, that's for sure. This town seems to be going mad at the moment.'

'Who do you think is doing all this vigilante stuff?' she asked as Danny headed off down the school's driveway.

'I don't know. I have a few ideas… let's see how they pan out. Can we talk about something else, is that okay? I just want a break from it all for an hour.'

'Of course,' she said. 'Sorry. That was insensitive of me. I should know better, shouldn't I?'

'Not a problem,' Danny said. 'Right, where are we going? You're paying, aren't you? So, hopefully somewhere really expensive.'

Susan had chosen a café that backed onto the Huddersfield Narrow Canal in Uppermill. It was far from expensive, but the bacon rolls and thick slabs of tray bakes that they served were just the kind of thing Danny would have chosen himself. As they watched the canal boats chug past in the light sunshine, Danny felt happy and relaxed; similar to the ease he experienced when talking with Kate, but subtly different. They discussed the canal (nice and clean on this section), whether either of them could see themselves living on a boat (Susan, yes; Danny absolutely no chance), the cake (they swapped when they saw what the other had ordered) and Kate (all the young guys get goo-goo eyes when they see her - how does she do that?).

'It's quite a place, your school,' Danny said when the talk turned to work. 'Imagine if there were places like Hunter's Hollow when I was a kid. Maybe I wouldn't be so screwed up.'

'You seem pretty together to me,' Susan said. 'You're right. It is an amazing place. But no one would be happier than me if it were to be closed down.'

'How do you mean?' Danny asked.

'Wouldn't it be great if we didn't actually need places like Hunter's

Hollow? If there weren't any kids with SEMH needs?'

'You've lost me now,' Danny pointed out.

'Sorry. Social, Emotional and Mental Health... kids who've been abused and damaged. Kids who need protecting from the outside world just to give them a chance, just a *chance*, to claw something back of themselves so they can function. We can't keep up with demand for places. We're overwhelmed. One kid once said to me - he'd been horribly abused - he said... it's like I've got a black hole inside me instead of a heart. He was 11. A kid that age with a *black hole* where his heart should be, Danny. I never get used to hearing things like that. Never. So, yes... it's an amazing place and Ben and the other staff do fantastic work. But I'd love to be thrown out on my ear and told that I was no longer needed. Does that make sense?'

'Yes, it makes total sense,' Danny nodded.

Danny got an alert on his phone. He looked at it. 'Can you excuse me for one minute while I just do this?' he asked.

'Of course.'

'The police have just named the two guys killed on the bridge. I just need to put it into my story and then publish it. Bit of cut and paste... Nearly got it... aaaaaaand there. It's done.'

'Who were they?' Susan asked. 'Sorry. You said you didn't want to talk about it.'

'Bit late now that I've just interrupted our lunch to publish a story about it. Two South Asian guys. That'll go down a storm on Facebook.'

'The whole thing just freaks me out,' Susan said dabbing up the last of her cake crumbs with her finger.

'I know. It's mad. But pretty clever too, in a terrible sort of way.'

'In what way is it clever?'

'It's going to be very hard to trace the victims' movements before they were killed, because they had gone out of their way to hide where they were going before they were snatched,' Danny pointed out. 'Of course they did... they were up to no good.'

'Never thought of that. Good point.'

'Another thing... You can forget about CCTV. Any cameras on the M62 are going to be pointed at the motorway not at the moors. And if the evidence on their phones shows they really were paedos, which it will, then the great British public are going to be right behind the killers. Have you seen the *Oldham Now* Facebook page? It's already 99.9 per cent behind the vigilantes. Same with Barry Mortimer out at Lad's Grave. No one is going to come forward with information that'll catch the killers...

because no one wants them caught. Keep going lads, you're doing a cracking job… that's the feeling in Oldham right now. I hate to say it, but it's almost perfect.'

'They're perfectly insane, more like. They're not the only mad ones… what were you thinking, taking Kate out onto the moors with you like that? God knows what might have happened.'

'She was a proper journalist once, you know. Tougher than me any day of the week. Not the first time she's dealt with horrible shit out on the moors. Plus, she's my friend. When you need help you ask your friends, don't you?'

'I suppose so,' Susan agreed. 'She's so great. I love her. Coolest kid in the class. Everyone thinks you're a couple, you know.'

'Well, we're not,' Danny said with a smile. 'Never have been. Just mates.'

'Is that right?'

'Yep. Mates. Nothing more.'

'I see.'

There was quiet for a moment. Danny looked at the light on the surface of the canal. He was just about to say something when Susan spoke first: 'Look at the time! I should get back. Ben will be reporting me missing!'

THIRTY-ONE

VIGILANTE VICTIMS NAMED AFTER M-WAY DOUBLE KILLING

Danny Johnston - Oldham Now

Police have named the two men thrown from the M62 footbridge by vigilantes in the early hours of yesterday morning.

They were 42-year-old Kabeer Sajid and Adil Aziz aged 35. Both were from the Glodwick area of Oldham and are believed to be brothers-in-law.

Both died after being tied up and thrown from the Pennine Way footbridge by a gang of masked vigilantes. The killings were captured on video by *Oldham Now*, but we are not showing the moment when the two men were actually killed.

After the double execution, the gang are believed to have made off from the scene on motorbikes.

Both the men's mobile phones were left at the bridge, taped to the railings. It's thought that detectives are currently examining the phones to see what online activity the pair had been engaged in before they were killed.

The M62 has now been re-opened after the carriageway was closed in both directions while forensic teams carried out fingertip searches of the area around the scene. The footbridge across the M62 remains closed and the public has been asked to stay away.

Many questions remain about the police's handling of this case so far. *Oldham Now* would like to hear from anyone who knew the two men and has any information about how they got out onto the moors. I'm also interested in any information from serving police officers or support staff who can shed any light on the case that hasn't so far been revealed by Greater Manchester Police.

THIRTY-TWO

Danny got a smile from Kate and a thumbs up from John Smithdown as he entered the ward at the Royal Oldham Hospital. 'How was your hot date, Danny lad?' Smithdown said as he approached the bed.

'Oh, for fuck's sake,' Danny sighed. 'Not you as well. Any more of this and I'll wheel you down to the morgue and leave you there.'

'Come on, Danny,' added Kate. 'We want all the gossip.'

'I'll take you down there with him in a minute, Kate,' warned Danny. 'We had bacon rolls, some cake and a nice chat. That's it.'

'Bacon rolls, eh?' Kate said, raising her eyebrows. 'You dirty bastard…'

'Shut it, the pair of you. I mean it. I don't suppose that nice volunteer lady is about with a cup of tea?'

'He's changed the subject, Kate,' said Smithdown. 'Did you notice that?'

'I did indeed, Dad. Classic technique. The dirty bastard. Honestly.'

'That's enough, you pair. Jesus. First things, first. How are you, John?'

'I'm not too bad actually,' Smithdown replied. 'They reckon I can go home later. Any joy with that appeal story you did about anyone who knew Maggie Ormrod?'

Danny checked his email: 'Nowt so far, sorry. I'll keep plugging away at it, though. The woman next door was very helpful. The picture she gave me of Maggie with her cat should create a bit more interest, too. You never know. Everyone loves cats, don't they?'

'We appreciate it, Danny,' Kate said. 'We know you won't give up. You never do.'

Danny looked to see if there were any Wine Gums left in the box next to Smithdown's bed. It was empty. 'I'll tell you what, John. Those two cops are getting to me. There's something not right about them. It's making my teeth itch, know what I mean?'

'I do, Danny lad.'

'When I'm 60, John, will you stop calling me lad?'

'Probably not,' Smithdown said. 'You'll always be a young pain in the arse to me.'

'So, what's the plan?' Kate said.

'Well, we need some more Wine Gums, that's for sure,' Danny said. He stared into the empty carton. 'The vigilante victims aren't just being lifted off the street at random. They're being targeted. The cops are concentrating on Facebook, but it's got to be cleverer than that. They're laying bait somewhere; I need to find out where they're putting it.'

'Why do I get the feeling something dodgy and dangerous is on its way?' Kate sighed.

'Meet me at my house later if you fancy getting a slice of it,' Danny said with a wiggle of his eyebrows. 'After you've settled John back in at home.'

'Surprised you've got time to do that,' Kate said. 'What with your commitments as Oldham's number one ageing gigolo…'

'Oh, do fuck off,' Danny said, a little louder than he intended to. The other hospital visitors and a few of the staff turned to look in his direction.

'Right, I'm off before I get chucked out,' he said. 'See you later, Kate. I'll get a takeaway; I'll save you some if you like.'

'See, those are the kind of slick lines that make him such a hit with the ladies, Dad.'

Danny showed her his middle finger, then placed a hand on John Smithdown's shoulder. 'Take it easy, mate.'

Smithdown nodded and smiled: 'Danny?' he said. His voice was hoarse and tired sounding. He motioned for Danny to come close. Danny leant in. The retired detective signalled for him to come even nearer. Danny put his ear close to the old man's mouth. He could feel his breath on his neck and his heart went a little faster, fearful of what he might hear: 'You're a dirty bastard,' Smithdown said.

After a few words with the staff, Danny and Kate went their separate ways at the car park. Danny waited until Kate's blue Mercedes with its KTS1 number plate pulled away. He pulled a packet of John Player cigarettes from his jacket pocket and lit one up. He knew she'd be furious with him if she knew he was sneaking the odd smoke behind her back - they'd given up together less than a year ago. *There's something about getting stuck into a story that makes me need a cigarette. God, smoking was compulsory in newsrooms back in the old days.*

He looked around the car park and caught the eyes of a few more guilty smokers. *I know. Smoking outside a hospital. Ludicrous.*

As he finished his cigarette, he spotted Jennifer the volunteer outside the hospital doors. He was about to wave to her, but she spotted someone else and stepped off the pavement as a car pulled up next to her. She got in and gave the driver a peck on the cheek. As the car pulled around the waiting zone and out towards the main road, Danny saw the driver. It was DC Karl McIntyre.

THIRTY-THREE

Several times during the half hour drive, Danny lost sight of the car with DC McIntyre and Jennifer inside. But the ebb and flow of the traffic through Lees, Mossley and then Stalybridge seemed to favour him, and each time he thought they had slipped away, the car came back into view. After Mottram in Longdendale they headed towards the outskirts of Glossop before stopping at a neat, detached house on a new build estate in Simmondley. *That's a fucking long way to come just to volunteer at a hospital.*

Danny watched and waited as the Detective Constable escorted the woman to her door while carrying her bag. They chatted for a moment and the woman touched the detective's face and gripped his hand. Danny took a few photos, making a note of the address. The detective kissed her on the cheek; then she went inside and McIntyre drove off.

Danny sat in his car trying to make sense of what he'd seen. *As a great man once said... TFC. The cops are investigating Smithdown and one of them knows a volunteer who's hanging around his hospital bed? That really is a fucking coincidence.*

He thought about the situation for a moment then sent a text to Kate: 'I'll be a bit late. Get me a sweet and sour chicken. I'm buying. Got some weird stuff to tell you.'

'Okay, just leaving the hospital now with Dad,' Kate replied.

Danny then sent Kate several of the photos he'd taken.

*<Know her? She's that nice volunteer at the hospital.
Mrs Vimto. She seems to know the Oldham DC that's
looking at Maggie's suicide.>*

Kate replied:

<Hang on a sec>

A minute later a photo came back. It was a clear, closeup picture of

Jennifer. She was smiling and wearing her volunteer's badge.

<Yes, that's her…Where did you get that?'>

<Her pic's on the wall with all the other volunteers.
Clever, aren't I?>

A few seconds later, another text from Kate:

<I just showed your pix to Dad and he's freaking out.
Come to his house ASAP.>

Danny put his phone on the passenger seat and started his car; a second after he'd put it into first gear the driver's side door opened and he was grabbed by the open zip of his jacket. As he was yanked from the car his foot came off the clutch, stalling the vehicle and jerking it forwards. The attacker stumbled as the car jolted and momentarily loosened his grip on Danny's jacket. Twisting his position in his seat, Danny brought his foot up and kicked DC Karl McIntyre square in the chest, sending him stumbling backwards into the road. *Oh shit. I've just assaulted a police officer.*

Danny stepped quickly out of the car and raised both his hands in apology. *Why are you saying sorry? He attacked me.* McIntyre was back on his feet and on him within a moment; his forearm slammed across Danny's throat and his hand gripped his shoulder. 'What the fuck are you doing here?' the young detective shouted. 'Answer me, right now. And it better be fucking good.'

Danny felt the pressure on his throat increase. *He's younger, fitter and better trained than me. Plus, I'm in the top three of the shittest fighters in the world. So, it's probably best to think of another way out of this.*

While Danny tried - and failed - to think of something, a hand reached out from behind the detective; his arm was pulled firmly away, allowing Danny to step away from the car. Danny watched as the detective's arm was expertly pushed up his back and he was firmly shoved to one side. The detective lost his footing and had to put a hand out to stop himself from falling. It was all done in one very quick, efficient move. It was only then that Danny saw that the person responsible for this impressive physical display of man management was Jennifer, the hospital volunteer.

'Leave it, Karl,' she said, using the same calm, pleasant voice Danny had heard in the hospital. 'It's not necessary.'

'He shouldn't be hanging about outside your house, Mum,' the detective said, holding his shoulder in obvious pain. 'He's a fucking dickhead.'

'He may well be a dickhead, son,' Jennifer agreed. 'But this isn't the time or the place. So, let's try and play nice boys, shall we? It's Danny, isn't it? You okay?'

'I'll live,' Danny said, straightening his jacket. 'I was just about to take him down… you saved me the bother. You've got some pretty good moves yourself, Jennifer. I wouldn't want to fight you for the last Wagon Wheel on the hospital tea trolly.'

'I think that's very wise, Danny,' she said. 'Very wise indeed. I think it's probably best if you leave now.'

'It's a bit weird, you being their mum and all that,' Danny said. 'A mate of mine has a saying…'

'Is it… that's a fucking coincidence, by any chance?' Jennifer offered.

'Yeah,' Danny said. 'TFC. The very same. You're not making this any less weird, you know. Quite the reverse, in fact.'

'I can imagine what you're thinking,' she said with a sweet smile that Danny found rather unnerving. 'But, honestly, what's going through your head right now isn't the truth. Really, it isn't. So, I'd suggest you put your energy elsewhere.'

'Oh really?' Danny shouted. 'What am I thinking, exactly? That you're spying on John Smithdown so that your lads can fit him up as a child molester? That? Well, it's fucking tempting to think it, isn't it?'

'Bye Danny,' Jennifer said, beckoning the DC to come into the house. 'Take care.'

THIRTY-FOUR

When Danny arrived at Smithdown's house, he could hear the retired detective shouting from the kitchen. 'Danny! Here! Now!'

Sitting at the kitchen table and surrounded by untouched Chinese takeaway cartons, Smithdown was holding Kate's phone and jabbing at the screen with his finger. 'I never saw her at the hospital, but I know who this is,' Smithdown said, showing Danny the photo on Kate's phone.

'Calm down, Dad,' Kate said. 'Please.'

'Do you know who this is, Danny?' Smithdown shouted, as if he were the only person with any sense in the room.

'It appears to be the ginger cops' mum, John,' Danny said.

'It's Jenny fucking Seddon! That's who it is!'

'Remind me, John,' Danny said. 'Remember, I was pissed for 25 years; my recall isn't as good as yours.

'Jenny Seddon!' Smithdown shouted, as if he couldn't believe how stupid Danny was being. 'Mermaid's Pool Jenny Seddon... Kinder Scout Jenny Seddon... ex-Detective Constable with Derbyshire Con-stab-u-lary Jenny Seddon. THAT Jenny fucking Seddon! She had three kids when I met her back in the 80s. Little ginger sods they were, always charging about the place. Those detectives must be two of her lads. Once a ginger sod, always a ginger sod. DI Patrick and DC Karl McIntyre.... McIntyre was her fellah's name. They weren't married. Very fucking modern for Glossop in the 80s, that was.'

'He's been like this all the way home,' Kate said. 'Effing and jeffing all the way up the Huddersfield Road. Detective Constable Jenny Seddon. Look her up.'

Danny Googled DC Jenny Seddon; when he didn't produce a result straight away, Kate pulled out her phone: 'Come on, Danny,' Kate said. 'It's the internet. How difficult can it be?'

'You've been watching too many films, Kate,' he pointed out. 'Only a tiny percentage of information and press articles from before the internet properly kicked in are actually online. *Manchester Evening News* pieces before the year 2000 are practically non-existent. No one can be bothered archiving them. I'm looking for anniversary pieces, follow ups, stuff like that.'

Then Danny found what he was looking for.

MERMAID'S POOL HEROINE COP RETIRES EARLY
Glossop Chronicle - 9/7/2001

A Glossop police detective who helped foil a terror plot by Far-Right extremists has retired from the Derbyshire Constabulary.

Detective Constable Jenny Seddon received a commendation for her part in the arrest and conviction of neo-Nazi thug Tom Lennon at the Mermaid's Pool near Kinder Scout in 1988. Greater Manchester Police Detective John Smithdown was also honoured at the time for his bravery.

Lennon was the leader of a hate group known as the White Wolves, based in an abandoned shooting lodge in the moors close to Kinder Scout. He plotted to start a race war in the Oldham area as a means of seizing political power on the local council.

The plot was uncovered after Oldham Councillor Sharmeen Chowdhury and sex worker Naomi Wells both went missing in April of 1988. Both later died as a result of events at the Mermaid's Pool.

Lennon was charged with multiple killings, including the machete murder of DC Seddon's partner, Brian McIntyre. Mr McIntyre was a teacher and local mountain rescue volunteer and had three children with Ms Seddon.

Tom Lennon died in prison in 1993, the victim of an apparent revenge attack by South Asian inmates.

His co-conspirator, Bob Donaldson, a former detective with Greater Manchester Police, is still in jail, serving a 'life means life' sentence for his part in the conspiracy.

Ms Seddon was today thanked for her service at a special ceremony at Derbyshire Constabulary headquarters in Ripley. She says she now plans to spend more time with her teenage children, Jordan, Patrick and Karl.

Danny, Kate and Smithdown had formed a huddle to read the article. They broke away and looked at each other. 'That deserves a fucking Nora I think, John.'

'Dead right it does, Danny,' Smithdown agreed. 'Fucking... Nora.'

'So, a woman whose husband was murdered after he'd helped Dad at Kinder Scout in 1988 has been hovering around him at the hospital?' Kate said. 'And two of her sons are trying to fit dad up with historic sex abuse crimes against this poor Maggie Ormrod woman? Allow me to join in... Fucking Nora!'

'I'd save your fucking Noras if I were you,' Danny said, showing them his phone again. 'Look at this.'

CORONER: SON OF MERMAID'S POOL HERO TOOK HIS OWN LIFE
Glossop Chronicle - 5/6/1998

A promising law student - whose father was killed during an incident at the Mermaid's Pool beauty spot in 1988 - died after hanging himself nearby, a coroner has concluded.

The body of Jordan McIntyre was found at the Bowden Bridge car park at the foot of Kinder Scout on the 5th of April this year, ten years to the day after the murder of his father.

Glossop teacher and mountain rescuer Brian McIntyre had been hacked to death by neo-Nazi Tom Lennon during an incident at Kinder Scout. Brian McIntyre's partner, Detective Constable Jenny Seddon, later arrested Lennon at the scene and gave evidence at his trial. Lennon died in prison in 1993 after being stabbed to death by other inmates.

Jordan McIntyre, the eldest of three brothers, had never come to terms with his father's death, the inquest heard. He had often struggled around the anniversary of his father's death. According to family and friends, these feelings had intensified as he got older.

Jordan had gone to Leeds University to study law, but on the night of the 5th of April, he told fellow students he had to return home to Glossop because of a family emergency. It's thought he drove instead to Kinder Scout, stopped at Bowden Bridge and hanged himself from a tree in the car park.

Recording a verdict of suicide, Assistant Coroner Deirdre Castle said: 'Jordan had clearly made the decision to take his own life, hence the remote nature of the spot he chose. There was nothing anyone could have done to stop him or to save him. He was resolute in his decision. My heart goes out to his family, especially his mother and two younger brothers.' Verdict: Suicide.

There was quiet in Smithdown's living room. Kate prodded at her takeaway with a fork, then pushed it away. There was a variety of 'Oh my Gods', 'Jesus Christs' and the inevitable 'Fucking Nora'.

'So, those two cops investigating Dad have quite the axe to grind, don't they?' Kate said. 'I'm not being unreasonable when I say that, am I? Their dad's dead, their brother went and topped himself…. All because of DI John Smithdown. In their minds, anyhow. Christ Almighty. You said they made your teeth itch, didn't you, Danny?'

'All cops make my teeth itch,' Danny said. He nodded at Smithdown: 'Present company excepted.'

'I'm touched,' Smithdown said, quietly.

Kate continued: 'And if they're keeping secrets like these, fuck knows what they're hiding when it comes to these vigilante murders. Danny, you've got to stay away from this, it's gone too far and it's getting too dangerous.'

'You're absolutely right, Kate,' he said sarcastically. 'I'll call the police immediately. I'm sure they'll be a massive help.'

'See, it's that stupid attitude of yours that causes half the problems, Danny,' Kate shouted, banging the table and knocking over a tray of noodles.

She got up to fetch a cloth. As she was away from the table, Danny received an anonymous WhatsApp message. He tried his best to maintain a blank expression as he read it. Kate came back to wipe up the mess; he waited 20 seconds before saying: 'I'm not hungry, to be honest. You finish mine. I can't take all of this in. My mind's like a tub of mushy peas. I think I need to sleep on it. I'll ring you in the morning.'

Danny was aware that Smithdown was staring at him; he avoided the retired detective's suspicious eyes. *Nothing gets past that old bastard.*

'Why don't you stop here with us, Danny?' Kate asked. 'The spare room's already made up, you can stay the night.'

'No, I need to get home,' he said. 'Clear my head. We can't just go charging in with this. We need to be clever. And calm. Let's speak tomorrow and decide what to do then.'

Kate stacked the takeaway cartons and moved them to the draining board. Smithdown looked at Danny and whispered: 'Be… fucking… careful.'

THIRTY-FIVE

I need to move somewhere where every single place isn't called after something weird-sounding, Danny said to himself as he slowed down close to the path leading to Crow Knowl. *It's like the Ordnance Survey people are deliberately trying to freak me out. Hanging Lees, Lad's Grave… now Crow Knowl.*

Danny parked his car in a layby at the point where the Huddersfield and Rochdale roads met and looked at his map. There was a service track that wound a steady path through Crompton Moor and up to Crow Knowl - the highest point on the moor - but it was gated and locked.

Yes, that's another thing for the list. As well as going to places that aren't called something scary, it would at least be nice to be able to drive there. Just once.

He stepped over the stile next to the gate and headed up the track. Behind him was the Windy Hill transmitter and Piethorne Valley. To his left he saw the lights of houses, farms and pubs marking out the small village of Denshaw. On his right were the moving illuminations of the M62, with Rochdale and the Scout Moor wind farm beyond it. Danny could see the lights on top of the giant turbines; some winked and blinked as the rotor blades whizzed past and momentarily blocked them from view.

Ahead of him was the blank moorland canvas of Crompton Moor. There was little to see but as he got higher the view beyond opened out. The sharp rise of Oldham Edge hill and the town centre appeared first, then in the distance, Manchester. He recognised the tall yet bizarrely slim structure of the Beetham Tower at the end of Deansgate. Then he saw the faint outline of the Arndale Centre. To the right was the unmistakable tower and rotunda of Strangeways jail. The sun had nearly set now - silhouetted on the horizon were the towers of the Fiddler's Ferry power station, way out west in Warrington.

Danny realised he was running through the geography of the area in his mind for one reason only: he was very scared. *I can't involve Kate in this one, it's not fair and it's too dangerous. I can't call the cops, don't trust them. For all I know, it's the cops sending me these tip offs… they could be waiting for me right now at the top of Crow Knowl. If only you were 30 years younger John Smithdown, we'd be out here together. Christ we'd be the same age. You'd know what to do, John, wouldn't you? I'm just making it up as I go along.*

The track began to curl in on itself as it snaked around the summit of Crow Knowl. At the top, three transmitter stations, 20 yards apart, came into view. All three had single storey redbrick bases of varying sizes depending on the height of the mast; two had metal chain link fencing around them to protect the buildings and the telecoms masts that stood next to them.

Next to the first and largest of the masts was the remains of an ancient boundary; all that was left was a wall of crossed stones just a few feet high and barely six feet in either direction. Not a huge wall, but just about big enough to prop up the body of a man. Danny stopped and stared at the body. His head had a series of two-pronged jagged holes in it - *claw hammer by the looks of it* - and was covered in blood.

A sign was on the man's lap and his hands were curled around its edges, like he was holding an advert.

PAUL DOCHERTY.
PAEDOPHILE.
GOOGLE HIM.

No threats, no abandon-hope-all-ye-that-nonce style threats. Just a name and job description. That's weird.

Danny took out his phone and did as the sign suggested and carried out an internet search for Paul Docherty. When that provided too many results he added the word paedophile. A series of local news articles came up detailing the man's abuse of children. *Oh dear, Paul. Can't argue with this one. You really were a very nasty piece of work, weren't you?*

Danny took several pictures of the scene, even though he knew he'd probably be unable to publish them. *I suppose I'd better call the police then. Maybe they already know. Wouldn't surprise me in the slightest.*

He was about to publish the details as a breaking news alert on his social media when he heard a noise from the other side of Crow Knowl. Accompanying the low growl of the motorway traffic in the distance and the light wind from the moors he heard a crackling sound. *Like someone's eating a giant bag of crisps.*

He walked around the second transmitter; the building at its base was derelict and open and he could hear birds moving around inside. The crackling noise was further away.

He moved on to the final mast; it was taller and slimmer than the other transmitters and had no protective fencing. It stood on a brick building the size of a domestic garage that had a large and ornate graffiti tag on it. There was something lying next to the mast base, covered in a plastic sheet that crunched and crackled in the wind. *This isn't right. This really is different. It's still fucking horrible, but it's definitely different.*

In the distance he could hear the sound of motorbikes fading then disappearing into the moorland. Then nothing. Just the sound of the M62, and the wind pushing and pulling at the plastic sheeting.

A message had been gaffer taped to the wall next to the sheeting; it looked different to the other sign, and to the one left next to Barry Mortimer's body. There were no shouty, upper case letters making a declaration this time around; the letters were smaller, more low-key.

We are sorry.
This was not supposed to happen.
This is a war and casualties are inevitable.
Do not interfere like he did. Leave us to our work.

Danny looked at the sheeting; the corners had been pinned down by rocks, but it still moved and rippled in the moorland breeze, as if something was moving underneath.

Don't touch it. Leave it be. Do… not… touch… it.

Danny knelt down and pulled the sheet aside. It crackled as it moved. He looked at the bloodstained face staring up at him. The side of the man's head was misshapen and dented inwards, like someone had scooped a section of it away; blood pooled around the upper part of the body and was making its way down the slope of Crow Knowl away from the transmitter. Danny looked at the face - the jaw was open and slack, and the eyes were wide open. Despite the severity of the injuries, there was no doubt in Danny's mind who this was. It was Detective Constable Karl McIntyre.

So much for your theory about the cops being in on it, Danny boy.

THIRTY-SIX

PAEDO KILLERS SAY 'SORRY' OVER COP DEATH

Danny Johnston - Oldham Now

Vigilantes thought to be responsible for the murder of at least four suspected paedophiles have apologised for the death of an Oldham detective investigating the case.

The body of Detective Constable Karl McIntyre was discovered on Crompton Moor last night after another anonymous tip off to *Oldham Now*.

A note was left at the scene, saying that the vigilantes were sorry for his death and that police shouldn't interfere with their murderous campaign. 'Let us get on with our work,' the killers stated.

Another body found at the scene is thought to be that of 46-year-old Paul Docherty. Unlike the previous victims who had no criminal records, Docherty was a convicted sex offender. He was out on licence after serving half of a nine-year sentence for abusing two girls in the Coldhurst area in 2014.

DC McIntyre was the brother of Detective Inspector Patrick McIntyre, who is also working on the vigilante case.

The brothers come from a policing family: their mother, former Detective Constable Jenny Seddon, received a bravery award for her part in foiling a plot to start a race war in Oldham in the late 80s.

It's not the first time the McIntyres have had to deal with tragedy in their family. Their father, Glossop teacher and mountain rescue volunteer Brian McIntyre, was murdered on Kinder Scout near Hayfield in Derbyshire in 1988. Their brother Jordan later took his own life nearby on the 10th anniversary of his father's death.

The McIntyre brothers had also been working on the death of local woman Maggie Ormrod, who committed suicide at Hanging Lees Reservoir ten days ago. It's still not known if the death of Maggie Ormrod is linked to the vigilante killings.

THIRTY-SEVEN

After Danny had given his account of what happened at Crow Knowl, DI Patrick McIntyre turned off the DIR and leant back in his chair. He looked at Danny. 'I think we're done,' he said. 'You can go.'

'I'm very sorry about your brother,' Danny said. 'I'm sorry about both your brothers. I didn't know. How's your mum doing?'

'Since when do you give a fuck about us?' the DI said, quietly. He stared into the bottom of the plastic cup of tea he was holding. He swirled the last remains around then decided not to drink it. 'My mum is really quite upset, seeing as though you've asked, Mr Johnston. Yes, she's really quite put out by the whole situation… what with her son being murdered and all that. Plus, there's the small matter of another one of her sons committing suicide, of course. Oh yes. Then there's her husband… my fucking dad… let's not forget him. He was murdered too. Had his head just about cut off with a machete up at Kinder Scout. Is that all of it? Yeah, I think so. So, apart from all that… she's muddling through, thanks for asking.'

'I saw the articles,' Danny said. 'Just terrible. I'm very sorry. I didn't really look into it when I did my book. I was just focussing on Black Moss. What your mum did was astonishing. No wonder she can take care of herself.'

'You don't like the police,' McIntyre continued, ignoring what Danny had just said. 'I get it. But did it occur to you… just for a moment… that maybe other people want to catch these killers as much as you do? Oh… something's wrong in Oldham… it must be the cops. It's always the cops. You don't have the monopoly on virtue, Danny Johnston. There's room in the world for other, perfectly decent people, as well as you.'

Danny's solicitor Paulina spoke: 'DI McIntyre, I'm sure Danny wants to help in any way that he can. He's here of his own accord. He wants to do the right thing, don't you Danny?'

'Of course I do,' Danny nodded. 'We're all on the same side, after all, aren't we?'

'Wow. Very big of you to acknowledge that, Danny. Do you know what my brother had been doing? Spending every hour of every day trying to stop the abuse of children in Oldham. Look at this…'

The DI produced his phone and showed Danny an article from the *Manchester Evening News*:

THESE ARE THE PERVERTS WHO TRIED TO FIND VICTIMS ONLINE - INSTEAD THEY WERE LURED INTO A TRAP.

'See this Danny?' McIntyre said, jabbing at the screen with his finger. 'Sting operations to catch paedophiles… 63-year-old man meeting what he thought was a 13-year-old for sex. A guy in his 50s arranging to meet two girls of 12 at McDonalds so he could give them money. Man in his 30s arrested in Morrisons car park after sending pictures of himself to what he thought was a girl of 14. All caught by my brother posing as a kid online. He didn't even have to try that hard. They were on his fake profiles like flies on a lolly. Can you see now why he was so annoyed about you sticking your oar in? No one did more than my brother to stop this plague. So it really warms my heart to know that we are all finally on the same side.'

'Sure, I understand,' Danny said. 'It's just looked weird from my perspective… who wouldn't want paedos permanently out of the frame? Everyone's a winner, right?'

'The people doing this are murderers, Danny,' the DI stated, leaning across the table. 'Barry Mortimer hadn't been convicted of any crimes. Neither had Kabeer Sajid and Adil Aziz, the guys on the bridge. Okay, their phones painted a pretty grim picture of what they had in mind, but they had all been tortured for days before they were killed. No investigation, no report to the CPS, no court case… just straight to the toolbox and out with the claw hammers. I have two daughters, Danny. Do you think I like the idea of people like them trying to contact my kids? It turns my stomach. But the people who are killing these men aren't vigilantes. They're murderers. Last time I checked, murdering people is against the law. And we can't just ignore the law just because the victims themselves make us feel sick.'

'Okay,' Danny said, holding up his hands. 'I get it. I'm sorry. Do you know what actually happened to your brother before I found him?'

'Not yet,' McIntyre replied. 'I know he was digging about in his own time. Maybe even posing as a potential groomer online to see what he could flush out. He'd definitely gone somewhere after you'd had your little encounter at my mum's. And he definitely headed back towards Oldham. After that… we don't know. He had his phone taken off him at some stage. And his Fitbit watch.'

'So, no way of tracking his whereabouts,' Danny offered.

'Exactly. We're looking for them but… well, you know the moors around here, they could be anywhere. Whoever did this isn't daft.'

'Doesn't sound like some dickheads with an I Hate Nonces Facebook page, does it?' Danny said.

'No, it doesn't,' the DI agreed.

'I do, genuinely want to help, Detective Inspector. Can I ask a question?

The DI nodded: 'The first three victims had no criminal records, is that right?' Danny asked.

'Correct.'

'Then why target Paul Docherty? He was known to the police, served time for sex offences and was out on licence.'

'Good PR, I reckon,' the detective said. 'Keep the public onside. Offer up a known offender to show that they're the good guys. But my brother must have gotten too close to them. That's why he ended up under a plastic sheet up on Crompton Moor. It could have been you.'

'Why are you telling me this?' Danny asked. 'You've shared nothing so far.'

'Because, whether I like it or not, you're the only person the killers are in contact with,' DI McIntyre said. 'There's no other trace of them. They're like ghosts. Gives me no pleasure to say this, Danny Johnston, but it looks like I need you.'

'Fucking Nora,' Danny said with a weak smile. 'You must be desperate.'

'My brother's getting a post-mortem as we speak. Of course I'm fucking desperate.'

THIRTY-EIGHT

'In the big, long list of your all-time stupid fucking ideas, Danny,' Kate said, pacing up and down in Danny's tiny living room, 'That is, without doubt, the fucking stupidest.'

'I think that's a bit harsh,' Danny replied. 'It might work. DC McIntyre was apparently trying a similar approach.'

'And look where he is now… dead! Pretending to be a paedo and waving it about on Facebook - that's your idea of a GOOD plan, is it? If you're lucky, you'll only get battered. The more likely scenario is you'll end up dead with a claw hammer sticking out of your head out on... Lonely Skeleton Hill or something.'

'There's no such place as Lonely Skeleton Hill,' Danny pointed out. He thought for a moment. 'There isn't, is there?'

'You... are… an... idiot, Danny,' Kate said. 'That cop tried the same thing and he got himself killed. Doesn't that give you a clue that it might just be a slightly shit idea?'

'It must have worked to some degree, otherwise they wouldn't have snatched him.'

'Stunning logic, Danny,' Kate sighed, sitting down and lighting up a cigarette.

'I thought you'd quit,' Danny said, also lighting up.

'I thought you had, too. Maybe if you could quit being a total arsehole too, you'd be really getting somewhere.'

'Look, Kate. The cops are totally stuck. The public are actually supporting the killers. The internet is awash with Noncebusters and Paedopouncers - it was only a matter of time before things got out of hand, and now they well and truly have. Maybe the best way to break the deadlock is to stir things up a bit. It could really help find these vigilantes and put them behind bars.'

'Oh, so Detective Inspector McIntyre is right behind this scheme, is he?'

'Not as such…'

'Fucking Nora, Danny!' Kate exclaimed, flicking ash onto the carpet. 'No, no, no!'

'Admittedly, there's potential for things to go a little bit wrong,' Danny said. 'But it's got to be worth a go. It might even do a bit of good.'

'It might do your analytics a bit of good, more like...' Kate muttered.

'What's that supposed to mean?' Danny asked.

'You know exactly what it means,' Kate stated. 'I've seen all the money spinners suddenly popping up on your site. Didn't you used to refuse ads in death stories? Not any more it seems. Saint Danny Johnston! Defender of the oppressed! Saviour of the abused! It appears things have changed a little. You're just another clickbait bollocks bandit like everyone else.'

'Where the fuck has all this come from?'

'You're doing this for clicks,' Kate continued. 'You're no better than these paedo pile on merchants on Facebook. They don't care about child protection. They just want the online attention. But at least they're not selling ad space on the back of it. These murders are making you money. I'd have more respect for you if you admitted it.'

'I have to eat, Kate. I'll admit that. I have to light this house and put petrol in my car. Guilty as charged. If I don't get income into the site, then it'll die... and any kind of independent local scrutiny dies with it. You're a businesswoman, surely you must understand that?'

'I understand that you're going to get your head caved in if you carry on like this. And that's just not worth it. It's not worth a couple of grand of ad revenue from a double fucking glazing firm in Greenacres.'

Danny felt anger and resentment bubble up and overtake him; he stood up from his chair and shouted at Kate. 'Maybe you should worry a bit less about me and a bit more about your dad, who the whole of Oldham thinks is an old nonce... and maybe give a bit of thought to your kid, who thinks you rather carelessly let him be abducted and can barely even bring himself to look at you.'

As soon as the words had come out of Danny's mouth, he wished he could gather them up and put them back where they'd come from. Kate's face was a hurt mixture of shock and anger. She put out her cigarette into the remnants of her cup of tea. 'You're right Danny. I should definitely stop worrying about you. In fact, I'm not going to give you another fucking thought.'

'No change there, then,' Danny said, his tone shifting down several gears as he thought of a way to diffuse the situation.

Kate said nothing. She stared at Danny; she checked that her car keys were in her bag, then put the strap over her shoulder as she got to her feet. There were tears in her eyes. 'Apart from Dad, I'm your only friend. Now you've only got Dad. Congratulations. Hope you're happy, Danny Something. You stupid fuck.'

THIRTY-NINE

The Shirtless Boy and Danny were standing at the top of Crow Knowl. It seemed five times as high this time. Despite being fully aware that this was a dream, Danny could still feel the breeze coming off the moors.

Danny and The Boy seemed like friends this time. *Thank fuck for that.*

It was as if the landscape around the hill had been ironed flat. The hills and valleys looked like a two-dimensional hand-drawn map and Danny could see everything in all directions for mile after mile: there was Black Moss and next to it, Little Black Moss. He could see Hunters Hollow and Maggie Ormrod's house, with Hanging Lees just behind it. Danny had never been to the Mermaid's Pool, but he knew he could see that too, because right over there was dark oval of water with actual mermaids swimming in it. They didn't look like the mermaids he'd seen in films or cartoons though. They were grey and emaciated and their hair was greasy and matted. *Those are the worst-looking mermaids I've ever seen, absolute shockers.*

Down below Crow Knowl, Danny could see a group of men in skull face masks climbing up the hill towards them. He looked at The Shirtless Boy; he didn't seem to be too worried, but Danny was getting more panicked the closer they came. There were dozens of them, clawing their way up Crow Knowl.

No. There were hundreds. Thousands, maybe.

Danny looked at The Shirtless Boy for help. The Boy was nodding downwards towards Oldham. It was clear to Danny what he was suggesting: jump.

The gentle slopes of Crow Knowl were now sheer cliffs. Danny was really scared now, but The Shirtless Boy was adamant.

We have to jump.

So they did.

FORTY

After three days of pretending to be a paedophile on the internet, Danny's first face-to-face attempts to flush out the vigilantes didn't go quite to plan.

He'd made various fake profiles and had attempted to engage with accounts that looked like they could be the vigilantes in disguise. Different platforms generated very varied results. He found TikTok to be too time consuming; Reddit - particularly subreddits about exam advice and divorce - generated some responses but there were too many levels for him to feel like he was getting anywhere. By way of contrast, joke accounts - particularly on Instagram - like 'Oldham Incel-ectuals' and 'Memes Only Oldham High Schoolers Will Understand' were very fertile ground.

But the corner of social media that generated the best results were the places where young people were asking for things for free. He was inundated with responses. *Could one of them be the vigilantes in disguise?*

As a result of one such post, he'd arranged to meet up with a girl that he'd found remarkably easy to engage with online; the agreed meeting place was 5pm outside the Greggs in Oldham town centre. It was nestled in the familiar company of Home Bargains, Primark and McDonald's in the precinct behind Oldham Police Station.

The bakery was already closing by the time he arrived at 4.45. He was expecting a fruitless hour waiting around trying not to look suspicious before heading home. *Kate was right. I hate it when that happens. Bloody stupid idea.*

Then he heard a voice behind him; it was frail and hesitant: 'Are you Danny?'

Danny had decided to use his real first name to avoid any suspicion that he really was up to no good. *Be upfront... it'll look better later.* He'd sent emails to himself, explaining his thinking about trying to lure the vigilantes into the open that, with the hope that their date and times of sending would prove his intentions were good.

He'd also sent a good old-fashioned letter to DI Patrick McIntyre at Oldham Police station, explaining his plan, his thinking behind it and his intention to write a story about it afterwards.

He was prepared for vigilantes masquerading as young girls online to turn up. He'd even bought a small hammer from a hardware shop just in case; he could feel it banging against his hip from its resting place inside his shoulder bag. What he wasn't prepared for was the sight of a small, frightened-looking girl in an oversized sweatshirt and jogging pants. *Oh God, a real kid has turned up… She'd said online she was 'nearly 16'. She looks all of 13.*

'Have you got me phone?' the girl asked. 'I can't stop. My boyfriend is waiting for me. Have you got it or not?'

Danny had researched some of the techniques used by groomers; one was to search through social media for young people looking for something for free. In this case: a mobile phone. The girl had broken hers and didn't want her mum to find out. If someone could give her a replacement it would 'save me life' she'd posted. *It's exactly the kind of trick the vigilantes would use.*

Danny had engaged the girl in online conversation, switched over to private messaging and offered her a phone. He was surprised at how easily she'd agreed to meet him. *Maybe it's really them.* He was stunned that she'd actually turned up.

'Well?' she demanded, 'Have you got it?'

'It's Jasmine, isn't it? Or is that not your real name?'

'It is, actually. Why, are you not really called Danny?'

'I am. I didn't think you were real… that you'd really show up, I mean.'

'Well, I am real and I'm here now,' she said. 'Come on, stop messing. Me mam will batter me if she finds out.'

Danny looked at the girl. It was a warm early evening, yet she hugged herself as if she were freezing. Her hair was scraped back harshly from her head, and she wore large, hooped earrings. On her feet were Vans, but they were battered and worn with what looked like a cigarette burn hole near one of the toes. He felt stupid and embarrassed at himself over what he'd done; and he felt terribly sorry for her.

'I don't actually have one on me…' Danny explained.

'Whoah, then why get me here then, you waster?' Jasmine cried. 'You a nonceman? Is that ya game?'

'Look. Sorry. I wasn't sure if you were you… or if you'd show up or… Sorry. Maybe I could come and talk to your mum? I'm sure she'd understand.'

'Would she fook!' the girl exclaimed, as if what Danny had made the stupidest suggestion in history.

'Let's find a phone repair shop and I'll buy you one.'

The girl thought for a moment. 'No bollocks, right? If you go weird on me, I'll scream the joint down.'

'No bollocks. Promise.'

'Okay then. There's a CEX round the corner.'

They walked. Danny made a point of staying as far away from the girl as possible. They entered the CEX shop and she pointed to an iPhone in the long glass case near to the counter. Danny paid and tucked the receipt into his wallet. As he thanked the shop assistant the girl ran.

Not your finest hour that, Danny. At least it stopped her from getting a battering from her mum. For now at least.

Danny's second attempt at kicking the nest of Oldham's paedophiles was also not quite what he had hoped for.

He had thrown his net far and wide on many platforms; he'd lost count of the number of profiles he'd set up and conversations he'd initiated. But try as he might, Danny couldn't quite work out how he had managed to arrange a meeting outside the Subway outlet in Chadderton with a very nervous looking man in his late 40s called Charlie. *This man is not a vigilante. No chance. And why has he brought me flowers?*

After five minutes of standing next to each other, punctuated by the odd nod and awkward smile, Danny had said: 'Look, I know this might sound a bit weird… But you're not Charlie, are you?'

'I am actually,' the man said. He had a bunch of flowers with him and a rucksack.

'I'm Danny.'

'Really?' the man said. 'I was expecting a D.A.N.N.I.'

'Were you know? And how O.L.D is this D.A.N.N.I. you were expecting?' Danny asked. 'About F.I.F.T.E.E.N?'

The man looked scared and worried for a few moments. Then his face cleared, and a slight smile appeared: 'And how old was this C.H.A.R.L.I.E that YOU were expecting?'

'You can fuck right off now,' Danny said. 'I'm here trying to trap paedophiles… well, not paedophiles as such… What I'm really after is…look, never fucking mind what I'm doing, what's in that rucksack?'

'Never YOU fucking mind,' Charlie shouted, seeming to take genuine offence at the suggestion that he was up to no good. 'And what room have you got to talk? Hanging around Chadderton looking for…

whatever it is you're looking for.'

'I think you'd better be on your way, mate,' Danny said. 'Before I call the police.'

Charlie looked as if he was about to come up with something desperately clever, but instead he gave Danny the finger and dumped the flowers in a bin outside the Subway. 'Four quid those flowers cost me,' he muttered as he walked away.

Danny watched Charlie cross the dual carriageway road that ran through Chadderton. Halfway across he gave Danny the finger again then crossed to the other side. Danny took his picture. 'Fuck off!' the man shouted as he waited for the crossing lights to change.

Charlie got into a car at the edge of the Costco car park that skirted the main road and quickly drove off. *The sooner I can go back to missing dogs and traffic delays on my website the better,* Danny thought.

Attempt number three had felt different right from the start. Instead of a takeaway or a bakery, the meeting place that 'Alice' had chosen to meet Danny was Oldham Edge, the ominous-looking lump of land that overlooked Oldham Royal Infirmary. Over the years it had been used as farmland, a quarry and even a Ministry of Defence facility thanks to its prominent position. Now it was a mix of woodland, criss-crossed pathways and abandoned shopping trolleys. The sun was already close to setting by the time Danny got there. He parked his car near to an abandoned radio station at the top of Henshaw Street. He'd been here a few years earlier promoting his book, but the building was now boarded up.

Danny made his way up the concreted MOD 'tank road' that climbed steadily up through the woods towards a radio mast at the top of the Edge. Housing estates and old mills stretched out on all sides. He could see the lights of a scrapyard below and, in the distance, the Seven Sisters tower blocks in Rochdale.

This is way too similar to the locations where the bodies were found... Windy Hill... Crompton Moor... Go back. Go back right now.

But Alice had asked him to meet her near the mast. So, the mast is where he headed. *This is the plan, isn't it? This is why you bought the phone for Jasmine and met up with Charlie, Oldham's most hopeless nonce. You wanted to flush the vigilantes out... Well, you've well and truly pulled the handle now. Danny lad.*

As the path levelled out and more of the mast came into view, Danny saw a slight figure in the distance. There was Alice, wearing black skinny fit jeans and a hoodie. He relaxed a little. As he got closer, he saw how tiny she looked: *all spindly arms and cocktail stick legs... out here on her own, just as it's getting dark.*

Alice waved to him, then stepped into a gap between the trees that led to the base of the mast. Danny slipped a hand inside his shoulder bag and touched the rubber handle of the hammer he'd bought with him. The weight of it calmed him down a little. *Don't kid yourself. It'll be fine for waving about a bit, but it's hardly a .44 Magnum, is it?*

Danny turned into the clearing. Alice was standing directly in front of him now and pulled back her hoodie as she spoke: 'Yer in the shit now, ya fookin' wrong un,' the young man said. 'Alice' was in his early 20s with a see-through moustache and cropped hair.

Bingo!

Danny took his hand away from his hammer and reached for his phone instead: 'I think even I can take you on, you little turd,' Danny said. 'Smile for the camera. How about a few words for *Oldham Now* about being a shit vigilante?'

Danny unlocked the phone and was about to press the camera icon when the force of three people charging him from behind sent him staggering forward. He slid face down across the grass; the air was pushed out of him by three sets of knees on his back. 'Showtime lads,' he heard one of the gang shout.

The knees came off his back; he turned, and several smartphone torch lights snapped on. The glare made it difficult to see who had rushed him, but it looked like there was at least half a dozen of them and they all had scarves over their faces. It was dark now and Danny was quite willing to accept that Kate had been right: *in the big, long list of your all-time stupid fucking ideas, this is without doubt, the fucking stupidest.*

He looked around for his phone; he couldn't see it. *Fuck the phone, where's that hammer?*

The bag - with the hammer hopefully still inside it - was six feet in front of him. Danny readied himself to jump towards it, just as one of his attackers picked the bag up and threw it into the bushes.

'Right then!' a voice said from within the main group. 'Nonce target identified and subdued! Weapons at the ready, lads!'

Danny saw they all had backpacks and each of the silhouetted figures was reaching inside. He twisted around on the grass and sat up, putting his hands in the air to show he knew he was outnumbered: 'Listen, please. My name's Danny. I'm not a nonce...'

'Oh Danny,' the leader laughed. 'I have to say that 100 per cent of our subjects say those exact words. Literally! Word for word! I suspect young Alice here will disagree with you. Wouldn't you, Al?'

'I'd definitely disagree with his assessment on non-noncery, mate,' the skinny young man in the hoodie answered with a smile. 'Violently disagree, in fact.'

'Please,' Danny persisted. 'Hear me out. I've got a website…'

'Here that, lads?' the ringleader shouted. 'He's got a website. I'LL BET YOU FOOKIN' HAVE, MATE!'

Each person in the group walked towards Danny, phone in one hand, contents of their backpacks in the other. They formed a semi-circle, cutting off his escape. Behind him was the fence surrounding the transmitter at the top of the Edge. The semi-circle became a circle.

'Right then, let him have it,' the leader said.

Surrounded, Danny put up his hands to protect his head, just as six cartons of rotten milkshake were emptied onto him. 'Danny the nonce… You have been milkshaked by Nonce Upon a Time in the West of Oldham! While you're busy washing cheesy lumps of milky banana goodness out of your hair, we'll be sending these videos to the police!'

'Don't bother,' DI Patrick McIntyre said from behind the group. He was flanked by two uniformed officers. 'He's not a nonce. He's just a fucking idiot.'

FORTY-ONE

'You still smell like bin juice,' McIntyre said after Danny had used the showers at the police station.

'I think it's these clothes you've given me,' Danny replied, pulling at the baggy jumper and ragged combat trousers that he'd been given from a box stashed in a storeroom by the Duty Sergeant's desk. He gave the jumper's sleeve a sniff. 'Genuine dead bloke apparel, this is.'

'Idiots can't be choosers, Danny,' the DI said. 'If that had been the real vigilantes instead of those Nonce Upon a Time comedians, I could be scraping you off the M62 by now.'

'Well, it seemed like a good idea at the time,' Danny offered.

'Please, just stay away, Danny. We've already had one person die trying to find these murderers, we don't want another one.'

'How come you were up on Oldham Edge?' Danny asked. 'Following me? I'm not complaining. Just wondering.'

'Don't flatter yourself,' the detective said. 'We've been monitoring the Nonce Upon a Time lads for a while. We were following them, not you.'

'Oh, so you haven't seen the letter I sent you?'

'What letter?'

'Never mind. How's your mum doing?'

'She's putting a brave face on it,' McIntyre said. 'Just like she always does. But inside… that's a very different matter. Karl was her golden boy. He could do no wrong in his mum's eyes. Now he's gone, she's just stuck with me.'

'Your mum is a pretty amazing person,' Danny said.

'She is. And she seems to quite like you. Can't think why. So I don't want anyone else getting hurt. Even you.'

'You don't have to worry about me.'

'I'm not, to be honest, but every minute I spend saving your stupid arse is a minute I could spend eliminating another gang of Facebook attention seekers from the inquiry. You're really not helping, Danny. Go home. Please. When something happens that you can write about, I'll let you know. I promise.'

'So, you're getting close to finding out who the vigilantes are?'

'Put it like this, we know who they *aren't*. They aren't milkshake marauders like the Nonce Upon a Time lot. That much we do know.'

'I could have told you that a week ago.'

'Look, you've got my number. If you get another call from the vigilantes, let me know straight away. No running about the moors on your own. No involving the likes of Kate Smithdown...'

'No chance of that…'

'…just call me straight away, understand?'

'Okay.'

Danny headed for the door. 'How's John Smithdown doing?' the DI asked.

'He's keen to clear his name, that's how he is.'

'Maybe you should concentrate on that.'

'Maybe I will.'

FORTY-TWO

6 April 1975

Maggie waited on the street corner and looked up and down the steep road; terraced houses huddled around a chip shop in one direction, more terraces and a hardware store in the other. *Come on, I haven't got all day.*

As she looked up the road, she felt a tap on her shoulder. She turned. No one there. She looked down the road. No one there either. She looked back up the road and there he was, smiling. 'Can't believe you fell for that one, Maggie Nuisance,' he said. 'Oldest trick in the book that. Tap and move. I got you, just like that. Blimey. Good job I'm here to look out for you, isn't it?'

'Spose it is,' Maggie said with a smile. Her smile got bigger when he gave her a Bar Six and a pack of Rainbow Drops. With a tilt of his head, he indicated that Maggie should follow him. She did. He placed a hand lightly on her shoulder. As they walked, a woman pushing a large, battered looking pram passed them from the opposite direction. She smiled at them and carried on. The pair walked down the street for a few yards then into a side road which petered out into a ginnell between two warehouses. Maggie began to open the Rainbow Drops. 'Hey, save them for later,' he said.

'Later? Where are we going?' She tucked the sweets onto the bib pocket of her dungarees.

'Not sure yet. Pictures, maybe?'

'I've got no money.'

'Don't worry about that,' he said. 'I've got money. Got a car too.'

'Is it one of them police panda cars?' Maggie asked.

'No,' he laughed. 'I don't use those. Too obvious. We don't want the baddies to know who we are until it's too late.'

'Oh right,' Maggie said. 'Sneaky!'

'That's right. Got to be. Baddies are sneaky, so we've got to be even sneakier. I'll take you into the police station sometime, if you like, so you can meet a few. Then you can see how bad some of them really are.'

'I'd be too frightened to do that.'

'You'd be safe. As long as you were with me.'

He stopped and crouched down until he was at her eye level. 'I worry about you, Maggie. You're out and about on your own at places like the fair. It's not safe for a girl of your age. Anything could happen. That's what I wanted to talk to you about.'

'Oh right. Am I in trouble?'

'No Maggie, you're not in trouble. Like I say, I'm worried about you. Girls like you go missing all the time. And I'm afraid the police haven't got time to look for all of them. Some of them just have to stay missing. And I don't want that to happen to you.'

'Thank you,' Maggie said quietly.

'There's no point in just taking you back to the children's home, you'll be on your toes again before I get to the end of the drive, won't you?'

'Maybe...'

'Definitely, more like. So that's why I'm making you my personal project. I'm going to make sure that nothing bad happens to you. There are some terrible people out there, Maggie. Trust me, I know. I've locked enough of them up. But I can't lock them all up. I do my best, honestly, I do. But it's just not possible. So, here's my plan. If you're going to be out and about, you're better being out and about with me rather than being on your own. Then I can protect you. What do you think?'

'I think… that's great. Thanks, Mr Smithdown!

'Call me John,' he corrected. 'I'm your friend, after all.'

FORTY-THREE

Danny pulled into Smithdown's driveway hoping to see Kate's distinctive dark blue Mercedes. Instead, there was a small Ford Fiesta that he didn't recognise. He knocked and opened the door with the key he'd had for the last two years. 'John, it's Danny,' he shouted. 'I've got the Dignitas lads with me… get your stuff, we're off to Switzerland.'

'In the front room, Danny,' Smithdown shouted back. 'You rude bastard.'

In the living room, Smithdown was in his favourite armchair. Sitting next to him on a dining room chair was Jenny Seddon. Danny saw that Jenny was holding Smithdown's hand. She smiled at him.

'Here he is,' Smithdown said. 'Oldham's biggest trouble-causer. I believe you've had a bit of a falling out with our Kate?'

'Just a touch, yes,' Danny said. 'I'm lying low at the moment. Has she cooled off a bit?'

'Not as such, lad. Not as such. I believe you've met Jenny Seddon, formerly of the Derbyshire Con-stab-u-lary.'

'I met Jennifer the volunteer at the hospital, yes. Then I got a little glimpse of Jenny Seddon Supercop outside her house. Watch your arm there, John. She'll have it up your back before you can say unnecessary force.'

'He's safe from me, Danny,' she said, patting Smithdown's hand. 'It's nice to meet you properly.'

'I'm so sorry about your son Karl,' Danny said. 'I think that under different circumstances, me and him would have got on pretty well. He couldn't let things go, could he? I get that.'

'Thank you,' Jenny said. 'That's kind. I'm sorry for all the… you know… cloak and dagger malarkey. When I spotted John at the hospital, I was worried how it would look… with the family connection to the Hanging Lees investigation. So, I thought I'd just keep an eye on him from a distance. I've been volunteering at hospitals for years. Since I retired from the police, in fact. And like a pair of old dafties, we haven't spoken properly in ages, have we, John?'

'We haven't,' he said. 'Stupid, really. After all the stuff we went through in the 80s, we just…I don't know. I thought she wouldn't want to see me after what happened to her Brian out on Kinder. I thought she blamed me.'

'I never did, John,' she replied. Both her hands were now tightly gripped around Smithdown's. 'Not once. Not ever. I know who killed my Brian. It wasn't you. You saved lives that night out on Kinder. I know you had your own battles to fight. GMP wanted you gone. You fought them and won. I left you to it. I thought I was doing the right thing. I wasn't. We were both as daft as each other.'

'That's not true, Jenny,' Smithdown said. 'You're far dafter than I am.'

'Right, well I'm sorry to break up this *Cocoon* sequel, but there's a few things I want to ask you, John. You can probably help too, Jenny.'

'I'll try,' she said.

'One thing I've learned in the last few days is that there's quite enough nonces in Oldham as it is, without adding the name John Smithdown to the list. As it happens, I'm having a little rest from the vigilante murders. So, I'm going to use my time wisely and do some more digging on Hanging Lees. I'll have another crack at some people who knew Maggie Ormrod. Find out more about her. I also need to find out more about you, John.'

'I don't like the sound of that,' Smithdown said.

Danny took out his phone and showed them the picture of Smithdown and Maggie Ormrod. 'It's definitely you, John,' Jenny said, looking at the photo. 'That's not terribly helpful, is it?'

'It is, actually,' Danny said. 'We know *who* is in the picture: John and Maggie. That means the remaining questions are… *where*, *when* and *why*. Plus, *what* the hell drove Maggie Ormrod to take her life now? Just before all this vigilante stuff kicks off. That is what's known as…'

'… a fucking coincidence,' Jenny and Smithdown said together.

'TFC. Exactly. We need to know more about this photo, more about where it was taken and why.'

'There's another "who" to add to your list, Danny,' Jenny said. That's… who took the photo.'

'And why,' agreed Danny.

'I've tried and tried,' Smithdown said. 'But I can't remember anything about that picture. It's obviously me. I accept that. But I just can't recall it being taken.'

'I brought this,' Jenny said, showing Danny a shoebox on the table next to Smithdown's armchair. 'I thought it might get his old brainbox working a bit.'

'Good idea, Jenny.' Danny looked inside the box. In it were press cuttings about the Mermaid's Pool case, along with several audio cassettes.

'Has it worked?' Danny asked.

'Not so far,' Jenny sighed. 'Why don't you take it, Danny? See if anything is of use.'

'I will. Thank you, Jenny. See, John? That's what a proper copper looks like. Watch and learn.'

'Fuck off with you,' Smithdown said.

Danny smiled at Jenny. 'The charm never fades, does it? Thanks for this. I'll take a look. I'll leave you to it.'

'I'll see you out, Danny,' Jenny said.

'Great. See you later John.'

'Danny?' the retired detective said as he headed for the door. 'You smell like a dead tramp, by the way.'

'So I believe, John. Long story. Speak to you tomorrow.'

As they got to the front door, Jenny placed a hand on Danny's arm. 'I know one person you could speak to. I didn't want to mention it in front of John. Didn't want to upset him. It'll take a while to get to him but if anyone knows what went on at Oldham Police back in the day, it'll be him.' She took a cutting from the box and showed it to Danny, placing a finger on a yellowy photo from the *Manchester Evening News*. 'Him. Speak to him. It won't be easy. But try. If anyone knows about John Smithdown's past, he does.'

FORTY-FOUR

It had taken Danny a good 20 minutes to find the cassette player he knew was stashed in a box of unwanted chargers and TV scart leads in his loft. It was an ugly red twin-deck and until he plugged it in, he wasn't entirely convinced it would actually work.

He took the audio tape from the shoebox Jenny had given him. The neat handwriting on the inlay card said:

9am Manchester Radio News, Sunday 1 April 1990.

Well, I certainly remember that date. It's the day the Strangeways riot started. The biggest British prison disturbance of the 20th century. But the trouble didn't start until lunchtime.

He put the cassette in and pressed play. The tape wobbled and wowed then settled:

"Radio Manchester News at nine, this is Beth Hall.

A policeman, hailed a hero after his part in exposing the neo-Nazi infiltration of Oldham Police, is set to return to work tomorrow after spending nearly two years on suspension.

Detective Inspector John Smithdown was told to step down from his duties over allegations that he harmed a child in his custody. But an internal Greater Manchester Police inquiry has found that there is no case to answer.

The investigation had to be put on hold until the end of the so-called 'Nazi Cops' trial. Several Oldham police officers, including Detective Constable Bob Donaldson, were finally jailed on Thursday for their part in a string of murders and racist attacks.

Danny Johnston reports…"

"What started as a murder inquiry into the disappearance of sex worker Naomi Wells in April 1988, turned into one of the biggest police scandals Manchester has ever seen.

Officers from Oldham Police were found to have conspired with neo-Nazi groups to seize power on the local council by any means possible - that included murder, kidnapping and inciting a riot. Their aim was to provoke a race war to push an extremist, racist agenda. Nine people are now serving life sentences for their parts in the plot - six were serving police officers, including Mr Smithdown's former colleague, Detective Constable Bob Donaldson.

Donaldson, along with neo-Nazi activist Tom Lennon, staged a series of murders and attacks to further their aim of generating a backlash against South Asian communities in Oldham. Their ultimate goal was grabbing political power and making money from land sales brought about by forced repatriation.

DI Smithdown is now in line for a police bravery award for his actions in exposing the plot, alongside DC Jennifer Seddon of the Derbyshire Constabulary.

After the initial arrests of DC Donaldson and several of his colleagues, Greater Manchester Police promised what was described as a 'root and branch' investigation into further links between its officers and neo-Nazi groups. So far, no other officers have been suspended and GMP describe the 'Nazi Cops' case as a one-off incident.

Danny Johnston, Manchester Radio News, at GMP Headquarters in Old Trafford."

My God, I sound about nine years old. I don't even remember doing that story. It was probably just a script shoved under my nose. Voice that up, Danny, we've got no one else to record the script, you'll have to do. The day the Strangeways riot started; the day before the boy's body was found at Back Moss. Half a lifetime ago.

FORTY-FIVE

That night, Danny did something he hadn't done for a very long time: he dreamed he was back at Strangeways Prison.

The Home Office preferred the jail to be known as Her Majesty's Prison Manchester, but no one used that name. It was and would always be called after the area of Manchester it was housed in… Strangeways.

It was dark and Danny was standing next to the perimeter fence. He could hear the prisoners inside the jail shouting; they were knocking down walls, smashing their way towards E Wing where the sex offenders were housed. They chanted as they got closer and closer: 'BEASTS! BEASTS! BEASTS, BEASTS, BEASTS!'

Two or three silhouettes could be seen, trotting nimbly across the roof of the jail towards the main rotunda. There were helicopters above and jets of water shot across the buildings as a series of fires burned brightly in the night sky. The riot was in full swing. It was 1990 but Danny wasn't young. He was middle-aged.

He saw a woman in her late 30s. Her hair, bleached white but with jet black roots, was pulled back from her face with a large elastic band. She wore an oversized black cardigan and the fingers of one of her hands were gripping the mesh of the fence and she was staring at the roof. The other hand was holding onto a boy of about ten. Danny didn't look at him. He didn't need to. He knew who it was.

'Hi,' Danny heard himself asking the woman. 'I'm sorry to bother you. I'm from Manchester Radio and I was wondering if I could ask you when you think this is all going to end.'

She didn't turn to look at Danny. 'Wouldn't you be better off asking how it all started?' she said.

'Sorry?'

'How it started,' she repeated, still looking at the jail. 'Rather than playing a stupid guessing game about when I think it will end, why not ask how it started. Why not ask about that?'

'I'm sure that will all come out once it's all over,' Danny said, slightly regretting his choice of interviewee.

'Are you sure?' the woman asked.

'Yes. I'm sure. So, when do you think this will end?'

The woman looked at Danny. Her face was so pale it looked unreal, like she was wearing stage make up. 'Not long now,' she stated as if it was the most obvious thing in the world. 'It'll soon all be over. I think so, anyway. What do you think?'

'Yes, I think so too,' Danny agreed.

Danny could hear a rattling sound; the perimeter fence was shaking. Just slightly to start with, but the rattling was getting louder and louder.

'I wasn't asking you,' the woman pointed out. 'I was asking the boy. He knows. Don't you?'

The Shirtless Boy stopped shaking the fence. Then he turned and smiled at Danny. A terrible, eyeless smile.

FORTY-SIX

Danny was led into the wigwam-shaped visitors centre at Strangeways and his fingerprints were scanned. His ID was checked - he'd spent a good 20 minutes looking for his passport that morning - and his clothes were given the once over. *No watches, sunglasses, fluorescent tops, key chains or ripped clothing; no clothes with football or gang slogans or clothes with racist or bad language on them; no diaries, bank cards or sunglasses; no see-through or revealing clothing, or crop tops that reveal the stomach. Those are the rules.*

Danny was allowed to take his passport, his locker key and £20 in cash into the main body of the jail, plus the appropriate clothing he was standing up in. Everything else was stashed in a locker.

He went through an airport-style scanner, putting his jacket and shoes into a tray. He was hand-searched - very thoroughly - got a stamp on the back of his hand like he was getting a pass out of a nightclub and then a prison search dog gave him a thorough sniffing before moving on to another visitor. His hand stamp was checked under an ultraviolet light, then he pressed his finger onto a biometric scanner before the last gates opened and Danny finally gained access to the visitors' hall.

It was large and relatively new looking; there were tables with chairs attached to them that were bolted to the floor. On the walls were examples of prisoners' art. There was a canteen and a shop as well as a children's play area; no children today though, that was only at weekends.

Danny sat and waited at one of the tables. He nodded to a middle-aged couple on the next table. 'First time is it?' the man asked him. Danny nodded. 'How are you liking it so far?'

'Not the best hotel I've ever been to,' Danny replied. 'The security's a bit over the top, isn't it?'

'You'll get used to it,' the man laughed.

I bloody hope not, thought Danny.

The prisoners arrived; dressed in various combinations of jeans, jogging trousers, plain t-shirts and sweatshirts, their pale, dejected-looking faces lit up just a little when they saw their loved ones. One face, however, remained defiantly unchanged - that of John Smithdown's former colleague, ex-Detective Constable Bob Donaldson.

He walked slowly but steadily towards Danny's table. He compared what he saw in front of him with the faded pictures he'd studied from Jenny Seddon's box of cuttings. For a man in his 80s he moved and looked reasonably well. His face was gaunt, pinched and expressionless; he'd lost his hair on top, but it was long at the back and sides, and he was wearing large, black-rimmed glasses.

Donaldson sat down: 'Tea with two sugars, a couple of Mars bars and a comfort pack,' Donaldson stated.

Danny looked at him. 'Chop chop, I haven't got all day, you know,' Donaldson said, as if Danny was a child having to be shown the most basic of tasks. Then he did something that Danny didn't like one little bit - he winked and smiled.

Danny did as he was asked and returned a few minutes later.

'The comfort pack gets delivered to you later, I believe,' Danny said.

'It does indeed,' the old man muttered. 'A few sweet treats and home comforts. I'll be thinking of you when I open it later.'

Then Donaldson opened both of the Mars Bars and ate them each in two bites. 'Tiny these are,' he complained. 'Not like they used to be. A Mars a day helps you work, rest and play. That was the old slogan. Remember that? Barely big enough to get stuck between your teeth these days.'

'Thank you for seeing me, Mr Donaldson,' Danny said, trying to keep his tone quiet and business-like. 'I know you didn't have to.'

'I was intrigued,' Donaldson said, screwing up the Mars wrappers into one, tight length then tying it into knot. 'Bored, obviously. Boredom is the *lingua franca* in here. Not a lot to occupy my time. And, as I'm sure you're aware, I've been inside for a great deal of time. But intrigued too.'

'An ex-cop inside Strangeways?' Danny said. 'I'm amazed you've lasted this long.'

'Well, you'd be surprised,' Donaldson said, putting out his hands in a friendly, open gesture. 'Yes, there has been the odd person that's taken slight offence to me being a former police officer. People can be a bit sniffy about that sort of thing in here. But there's also been plenty of others who have wanted to protect me. And it's thanks to them that I'm still here today… having a lovely chat with you.'

'What kind of people? Racists? Neo Nazis?'

'I'd prefer to think of them as like-minded souls. Anyway, the first ten years inside were… tricky. Yes, that's fair to say. Challenging they were… on a day-to-day basis. I was stabbed on three separate occasions in one year. Three times, eh? That's persistence for you. But after that, things calmed down a little. I've had no bother for a long time. We've got our own little bit of the jail, you know, us senior citizens. Our own little slice of OAP paradise in H Wing. It's a bit different to the rest of Strangeways. It's like an old folks' home. Less stairs, but more toilets. Ha ha! The staff, the gen pop… that's the wider prison population to you… they just leave us to it. They don't really bother with us. We're invisible. What do they think we're going to do… start a riot?'

'That's been done,' Danny pointed out. 'Prison riots are a bit like Mars bars. Better in the old days.'

'True. Very true. So, I got your message and approved your visit via the Unilink system. And here we are. So… what do you want?'

'I wanted to ask you about John Smithdown,' Danny said.

'John Boy! Is he still with us?'

'Yes, he is. Very much so. A great dad, a wonderful grandad, and a fantastic friend… a proper, decorated police hero too. He's loved Mr Donaldson. In fact, he's all the things you're not.'

'Less of the attitude, lad, if you don't mind.'

'You're a racist murderer, Mr Donaldson. You'll forgive me if I don't treat you like Nelson Mandela.'

Donaldson slurped his tea. 'What do you want, Mr Danny Johnston?'

'I sent you a picture in advance,' Danny said. 'Did it clear security?'

Donaldson produced a folded piece of paper. It was a printout of the picture showing John Smithdown with his arm around Maggie Ormrod. Donaldson waved it at Danny then placed it on the table.

'Who took that picture?' Danny asked.

Donaldson barely glimpsed at it. 'I did,' he smiled. 'I remember it well.'

'What can you tell me about it?'

Donaldson looked again. 'It was taken at Oldham nick. Mid-70s by the look of it. All shiny and new it was, look how white the walls are. John was showing this young girl around and he wanted a snap taking. He asked me to take it. So… I took it. In those days we got the police photographic unit to develop all our pics for free; perk of the job, if you like.'

'Did you know Maggie, the girl in the picture?'

'Didn't know she was called Maggie until you told me just then,' Donaldson replied.

'You're in prison, not on a desert island, Mr Donaldson. You have access to news.'

'News doesn't really interest me, Danny Johnston. Very one-sided in my experience.'

'Maggie Ormrod. Ex-care home kid. I've been trying to trace her records, but everywhere I go, her file is missing. Or there's been a fire. Funny that. She killed herself out at Hanging Lees reservoir the other week. She left a note saying she'd been abused as a child. I want to know who did it to her. John Smithdown says it wasn't him. And I believe him.'

'Do you, now? Well, John asked me to take that picture, so I did. That's all I know. He seemed to like showing people around. Mainly kids. Waifs and strays, that sort. I never pried. Perhaps he thought taking them around the police station and showing them the cells was better than giving them a clip round the ear. Personally, I've always been a big fan of a good clip round the ear, but there you go. What's your interest?'

'I'm interested because John Smithdown is my friend,' Danny said. 'And I want to make sure I've covered every possibility when it comes to investigating the real story behind this picture. Even coming here to see you.'

'No one's stopping you from leaving, lad. You know where the door is. Don't forget to shut it on your way out.'

Danny stood up and searched for his locker key. 'Kate's doing well, by the way… John's daughter. You remember Kate. The one you tried to kill in the 80s. That Kate.'

For the first time since he had entered the visitors' area, Danny provoked a real reaction from Bob Donaldson. His grey face flushed and he bared his uniform, false-looking teeth.

'Yeah, sold off her businesses for a fat load of cash,' Danny continued. 'Lady of leisure now. She's just like her dad, though… a proper hero. She saved my arse out at Black Moss a few years back, I can tell you.'

'Black Moss, eh?' said Donaldson. He was smiling again now. 'There are some real secrets out there, Danny Johnston, believe you me. If only those moors could talk.'

'Maybe they can, Mr Donaldson,' Danny said. He snatched the photo from the table and put it in his pocket. 'Have a nice life.'

FORTY-SEVEN

6 April 1975

'I've never seen an AH-AH film before,' Maggie said as they found a seat in the semi-darkness of the cinema.

'Double A,' he said. 'It's called a Double A film. And I should think not, you're supposed to be fourteen to see one. They only let you in because you're with me.'

He took off his overcoat, folded it several times and placed it on Maggie's seat. She looked at him, puzzled. 'Sit on it… It'll make you little a bit taller,' he whispered, tapping the side of his nose as if he was passing on a vital piece of information she could use again at a later date.

She smiled and sat down: 'It's not gunna be dead scary, is it?'

'No. I don't think so. Not really. Maybe bits of it.'

The familiar brassy stabs of the Pearl and Dean music blasted across the speaker, signalling the start of the pre-film advertisements. 'I love this tune,' Maggie said, jigging in her seat. 'It makes me happy. Pa-Pa Pa-Pa Pa-Pa Pa-Pa Pa Pa Paaaar…'

'Shhh. Not so loud. Here, have one of these.' He pulled out three packets of Payne's Poppets and shook them. The small, rectangular packets made a satisfying little chik chik sound as the small, round chocolates rattled around. 'Orange, toffee or mint?'

'I like toffee,' Maggie said. 'And I like the orange ones too. I like all of em.'

'Well, you might as well have them all, then,' he said with a sigh.

'Ta very much,' she said in a loud, excited voice.

He put a finger to his lips to indicate she was being too loud again. 'Do you know why they sell these in cinemas?' he asked, handing her all three of the pocket-sized boxes of Payne's Poppets.

'I 'spose cos they're right tasty.'

'Well, yes. There is that. But there's another reason… listen.'

He cupped a hand to his ear. All around them were the sounds of people eating snacks in the cinema. Cellophane-wrapped packets of sweets were being tugged open; boiled sweets were being unwrapped, crisps were being munched and Butterkist popcorn bags were being dug into and crunched.

The policeman took one of the packets from Maggie's lap and popped open the hatch at the corner of the box. He took hold of Maggie's hand and tipped several of the chocolates into her hand. 'See? No noise…These are the best kind because they're dead quiet.'

He smiled, took one of the sweets from Maggie's hand and popped it onto his mouth.

FORTY-EIGHT

Danny looked at the poster he had made. The two faces of Maggie Ormrod looked back at him: Maggie as an adult holding her neighbour's cat, and Maggie as a young girl at Oldham Police station. He'd cut John Smithdown out of the 1970s photo, then put both of the pictures of Maggie side by side above the text he'd written:

DID YOU KNOW MAGGIE ORMROD?

MAGGIE WAS IN CHILDRENS' HOMES AROUND OLDHAM IN THE 1970S.

SHE LIVED ON DENSHAW ROAD CLOSE TO HANGING LEES RESERVOIR.
SHE WORKED AS A CLEANER

.

DID YOU KNOW HER - PARTICULARLY WHEN SHE WAS A GIRL?

CONTACT DANNY JOHNSTON AT OLDHAM NOW

danny@oldhamnow.net
www.oldhamnow.net

Danny had already been to Hanging Lees Reservoir, taping posters to the car park sign that housed a map to the footpaths and waterways of the Piethorne Valley. He'd also attached one to the ornate metal gate at Hanging Lees itself, just yards from where Maggie's body was found. They seemed to be the logical places to put them.

But something pulled at him. Partly it was the dreams he'd been having, the terrible visions of The Shirtless Boy. But some of it was Bob

Donaldson's reaction back at Strangeways. *Winding him up about what a loser he was, that seemed to make him drop his guard a little… There are some secrets out there, Danny Johnston, believe you me. Fuck me, some real secrets. If only those moors could talk… that's what he said.*

Danny took his remaining posters and drove over to Black Moss Reservoir.

He pulled into the car park at Brun Clough and headed up the path that formed the Pennine Way. Danny was fond of pointing out to people that it had been a journalist who'd come up with the idea of the Pennine Way, the 268-mile path that connected the Peak District with the Scottish borders. *Tom Stephenson… he wrote an article about the idea in the Daily Herald in 1935. Thirty years later it was opened. See, journalists are good for something.*

Standing on the paved footpath that led past Redbrook Reservoir and onto Black Moss, he remembered being on the same spot in 1990, trying to interview a very reluctant DI John Smithdown. He remembered how cold he'd been in his thin shirt and cheap jacket. He remembered the way the two uniformed officers had let the sheet slip in the wind, revealing the puffy white body of a little boy dressed in a pair of shorts. And he remembered the piece he'd filed for Manchester Radio.

"A child's body has been found close to a reservoir on the outskirts of Oldham. The grim discovery was made in the early hours of this morning. Murder squad detectives have sealed off the area close to the main A62 road at Diggle. From the scene Danny Johnston has this exclusive report.

The body of the child, thought to be about nine years old, was found at the edge of Black Moss Reservoir a few miles outside of Diggle. Officers are now sealing off the scene. Detective Inspector John Smithdown is in charge of the operation… 'At approximately 5.30 am this morning the body of a juvenile male was discovered by a man out walking his dog. The area is currently being sealed off and a fingertip search of the scene will commence shortly. The age and identity of the juvenile male are not yet known, and I have no further details to give at this present moment in time.'

Forensic teams have arrived at the scene, and murder squad officers are now overseeing the removal of the child's body before a postmortem examination can reveal the cause of his death.

Danny Johnston, Manchester Radio News, at Black Moss Reservoir."

Danny taped a poster to the gate which led to the reservoir itself, took a photo of it and walked down the slope. The mini beach at the water's edge looked smaller than he remembered. The day was bright and the sky a clear blue, but Black Moss stubbornly refused to shift from its favoured tone of dull, peaty grey. Danny looked around; there was nothing to attach any more posters to. No trees, no signposts, no information boards. Nothing. Just a cold slab of water called Black Moss.

The light moorland wind moved the surface of the water in a series of tight zig-zags. Danny looked around; he saw someone across the other side of the water. A lone figure in a light brown anorak. No one else.

He'd always loved the bleakness of the moors, the nothingness that allowed you to fill in your own version of beauty. But today the very emptiness that normally drew him in made him feel uneasy and unwelcome.

Danny found a rock and used it to weigh down his remaining posters on the path that stretched across the flat, front end of the reservoir. Then he left as quickly as he could.

FORTY-NINE

Danny sat in his at the reservoir car park, clumsily entering text and pictures into his phone. Using the photos he'd taken of his DO YOU KNOW MAGGIE ORMROD? posters, Danny pressed 'publish' on the appeal story for the *Oldham Now* website when he received a text from an unknown number. *Fuck. Here we go again.*

But the message wasn't another vigilante tip-off; it was a plea for help.

<Danny. It's Jenny. You'd better come to the hospital ASAP. Ward T4. There's trouble and you might be able to help before the police are called.>

What the fuck is that all about?

He had learned several things about Jenny Seddon in the week that he'd known her. One of them was this: she was a woman to be taken seriously. *If she thinks I can help, then I'd better get my arse down there sharpish.*

Visiting hours were just ending as Danny made his way through the last of the people who'd come to see friends and relatives. He saw Jenny standing next to the admissions desk. She raised a hand to him and then pointed to her ear, then down the corridor that ran to her left, indicating that he should keep quiet and listen.

'WILL YOU FUCKING LISTEN TO ME?' a voice screamed. 'PLEEEEEEASE? THE FUCKING PAIN! I CAN'T STAND IT ANY MORE. I MEAN IT. GIVE ME SOMETHING OR FUCKING KILL ME. I MEAN IT. I CAN'T STAND IT. PUT ME OUT OF MY FUCKING MISERY. JESUS CHRIST! I THOUGHT THIS WAS A HOSPITAL! PLEASE, WILL SOMEBODY HELP ME?'

Danny looked around the corridor corner; the shouting was coming from behind a screened-off bed. Then he heard another voice: quieter, calmer, more familiar. 'Please, mate… let's just go. Come on. Let's get you back.'

Danny put a hand on Jenny's shoulder. 'What's going on?'

'Hospital jumper,' she said.

'What?' Danny asked, as something crashed to the floor behind the curtain with a metallic clang.

'Jumpers,' she repeated over the noise. 'They go from hospital to hospital, trying to get prescribed painkillers… Putting it on that they're in terrible pain and that they're dying. He's probably already been to Fairfield or to Tameside.'

'PLEEEEASE GOD, JUST GIVE ME SOMETHING. ANYTHING. YOU PEOPLE ARE SUPPOSED TO HELP, FOR FUCK'S SAKE! I'M DYING HERE AND YOU'RE DOING NOWT!'

'I see,' Danny said, raising his voice over the din. 'That's a new one on me. Not sure how I can help though.'

The curtain was pulled back and a harassed-looking nurse in her mid-20s appeared. Through the gap Danny could see there were two young men in the cubicle. One was Josh, the aspiring journalist from Hunter's Hollow; he was doing all the shouting. The other was Jonathan Smithdown. He was doing the peace-making. The teenager made eye contact with Danny just before the curtain swished closed again.

'Oh, for fuck's sake,' Danny sighed.

'Exactly,' Jenny said. 'I recognised Jonathan from all the photos of him at Smithdown's house. If they don't leave in a minute the police will get called. And young Jonathan seems to be a bit of a bystander here. So, if you could help get them both out of here, we might avert a bit of a situation. The last thing the Smithdown family needs at the moment is for the lad to get banged up.'

'I can but try,' Danny said. 'But Josh seems pretty amped up.'

'All jumpers seem pretty amped up, Danny,' she said. 'That's the idea.'

Jenny spoke to the nurse, pointed to Danny and then at the cubicle; then she waved him over. He passed through the curtains; Josh was lying on the bed holding his sides around his lowers ribs and moaning and swearing.

'Hey, Josh,' Danny said, trying to be heard over the shouting. 'What's all the commotion?' Jenny and the nurse were standing just behind him.

'You a fucking doctor?' Josh asked, his face buried in a pillow.

'No, I'm the fucker who's going to try to stop you pair of dickheads getting arrested,' Danny said. 'Jonathan, what are you playing at?'

'Danny… shit,' Jonathan said. 'Josh, it's not a doctor, it's Danny.'

Danny expected Jonathan to be angry or defensive, or in denial. Instead, the teenager looked almost relieved that he was here. 'I didn't know he was going to go mad, Danny,' Jonathan said. 'He told me he just had bad guts. Then we got in here and he went mental.'

'Bad guts?' Danny queried. 'Well, he's definitely full of shit, Jonathan, I'll give him that. Okay, we need to knock this on the head right now.'

Danny kneeled down so his face was level with Josh's. The young man's face was knotted with apparent pain, his eyes were closed and a low howl came from his lips. 'Listen to me, Josh,' Danny said. 'You have three seconds to get your arse off this bed and out of the door. Otherwise I'll take Jonathan here back to Hunter's Hollow and leave you here. Do you know what'll happen next? Well, that woman there with the grey hair - she's called Jenny - she will push your arm so far up your back you'll be able to wave to yourself. Then she'll fucking Ninja you from here to Chadderton and back. Then she'll hand you over to the cops. Her son's a cop… so him and all his cop mates will be really rather cross with you. So they'll probably take great pleasure in kicking your kidneys out down at the local police station. If you think you're in pain now, just imagine what you'll feel like then...'

Josh looked at him. The grimace fell quickly from his face. The moaning stopped. 'What do you think?' Danny whispered. 'Back to Hunter's Hollow right now, or watching your kidneys flopping about on the cell floor of Oldham nick?'

Jonathan spoke: 'He's right, Josh. Come on, let's go. Please.'

'Listen to him, Josh,' Danny said. 'He's clearly the brains of the operation. I'll even give you a lift back if you like. Then we can let these good folks get on with helping people who are really sick. Rather than throwing pills at the likes of you… just to make you shut the fuck up.'

Josh looked at Danny and then at Jonathan. Then he leant to one side to see the expression on Jenny Seddon's face. She nodded her confirmation that everything that had just been said would definitely happen.

Josh sat up and swung his legs around to the edge of the bed: 'Can we stop for a McDonald's on the way back?' he asked.

FIFTY

'Danny, thank you so much for what you did,' Susan said as she and Ben Matlock walked Danny to his car outside the school. 'And thank Jenny from the hospital for us as well.'

'Absolutely,' Ben agreed. 'That was a tricky call, but we're so glad she made it.'

'I'll tell you what, Josh deserves a BAFTA for his acting work tonight,' Danny said. 'He pretty much convinced me he was on his way to Oldham Crematorium. A stellar performance. Hospital jumpers, eh? You learn something new every day.'

'We've tried so hard to keep Josh out of the criminal system,' Ben explained. 'He's 16, for God's sake. Another product of adult abuse. That's why he's here. He's a victim and his problems are too complex for the mainstream structure to understand. Criminal detention would probably be the end of him. You and Jenny probably saved his life tonight. I mean it.'

'What about Jonathan?' Danny asked.

'Oh, he's about to get a punishment far worse than mere incarceration,' Susan said as Kate Smithdown's car came up the Hunter's Hollow driveway. 'I wouldn't wish it on my worst enemy…'

Kate's car stopped. She got out and gave the door a very robust slam. 'Where is he, Susan?' she asked, ignoring Danny completely.

'He's inside,' Susan said. 'Me and Ben were just thanking Danny for what he did. You would have been visiting Jonathan at Oldham Police Station if it weren't for him.'

Kate still didn't look at Danny and made no response. 'Right, well I'll take you to him, Kate,' Ben said with a smile. 'He's fine. Bit shaken up, but fine. I think he's definitely learned something tonight, hasn't he Mum?'

'Oh yes. We all have, haven't we Danny?'

'Yes,' Danny agreed. 'I should do a piece about it, show the kind of stuff that hospital staff have to put up with.'

Again, Kate ignored him. 'I'll see you inside, Susan,' she said. 'Lead on, Ben.'

'You're welcome, Kate,' Danny said as Kate and Ben walked towards the main entrance.

'I'm still not taking to you, dickhead,' Kate shouted. She carried on walking.

Danny tried again: 'Kate, you'll never guess who I went to see…'

'Don't care!' she said and went through the main doors of the school.

Danny smiled awkwardly at Susan. 'That went better than I was expecting if I'm honest,' he said.

'Hate to see what things would be like if it went badly,' Susan replied. 'Can't work out who she's more annoyed with… you or Jonathan. What on earth went on between you two?'

'Just me being an insensitive arsehole,' he sighed. 'As usual. It'll all blow over. Nothing that a bit of time won't heal. About 90 years should do it.'

'Oh dear,' Susan said, rubbing Danny's arm. 'Listen, I'd better go. Thanks again for what you did. I mean it. You're a good un, Danny Johnston.'

Susan leant in, apparently to hug Danny and press her cheek against his as she had done before. Danny did the same. At the last second, she turned her head and kissed him very quickly on the lips. Danny was so shocked he stepped back sharply and almost slipped on the gravel path.

'Okaygottagobye,' Susan said, and half walked, half ran to the school's main entrance. Danny watched as she punched in the key code on the front door and went inside. Then, Susan looked back, pulled an 'Ooooh' face at him and then gave a smile and a wave. Then she was gone.

Fucking Nora.

Danny made his way back to his car; it looked very battered next to Kate's gleaming Mercedes that was parked next to it. As he dug around in his pockets for his keys, he heard a tapping sound. John Smithdown was sitting in the passenger seat of Kate's car, trying to get his attention. As Danny approached the car, the electric window slid down: 'You dirty bastard,' Smithdown said. 'I saw you.'

'I think it's fair to say it's YOU who's the dirty bastard in this scenario,' Danny pointed out. 'Spying on people in the dark… I should call the police.'

'I believe the police were narrowly avoided this evening, thanks to you and Jenny,' Smithdown said.

'Looks that way. Not that I'll get anything resembling a thank you from your daughter, though. It appears that I'm still very much on the shit list. Anyway, what are you doing, sitting here like Piffy on a rock bun?'

'I just thought I'd let Kate get on with bollocking young Jonathan. Plus, I don't care for all the stairs in there.'

'Fair enough. Not going to be pretty, is it?'

'Fucking brutal,' Smithdown said. 'What've you been up to?'

Danny wanted to tell him about his encounter with Bob Donaldson but thought better of it. Nothing that Smithdown's former colleague said during their encounter had really helped matters. In some ways, it had made things worse. *He's never coming out of Strangeways, he's got nothing to gain from lying. But, all that stuff Donaldson said about Smithdown and his waifs and strays. Grim.*

'I've been putting posters up at Hanging Lees about Maggie Ormrod,' Danny said. 'That's what I've been up to. Not everyone's on the internet. You never know. I left some at Black Moss as well.'

'Why did you do that?' Smithdown asked.

'Honestly? Not sure. It just seemed like… I don't know, a good idea.'

'Hmm… I think you're going a bit weird in your old age, Danny.'

'Coming from you, that's quite the observation. What about you?'

Smithdown didn't reply. His attention seemed to have wandered off elsewhere; he seemed to be transfixed by something in the rear-view mirror of Kate's car.

'Helloooo? Danny calling space cadet Smithdown. Are you receiving me?'

'I am, Danny. Loud and clear.' Smithdown tapped the mirror. 'I was just wondering what these fuckers are up to…'

Danny turned to see what Smithdown was looking at in the mirror. On the ridge to the east of the school was a fast-moving line of lights. From down below they looked like a shiny snake, swerving and bouncing across the edge of the moor. They were shimmering their way west towards the motorway. 'Motorbikes, John?' Danny asked.

Smithdown thought for a moment. 'Looks like it, Danny lad. Scramble bikes, maybe. Good way to get across the moors. You don't have to worry about roads and paths. You can just go straight from A to B. No messing.'

'Absolutely, John,' Danny said, following the lights as they ran parallel to the school. 'No messing. I'll speak to you later.'

Danny got into his car and drove as fast as its worn-out engine would take it. He left the road that led up to the school, clipping the stone-mounted sign on the way out with his front wing. He cut across the busy

Standedge Road, then drove at high speed through the village of Diggle, winning himself a cheer from a group of teenagers outside the local chip shop for driving so fast.

The bouncing line of moorland lights was still clearly visible on his left; Danny took out his phone and managed to get a few seconds of video just before he crossed the small bridge over the Huddersfield canal with a harsh clang. *What the fuck are you lot doing?*

The village road gave way to lanes and then tracks as the hedgerows on either side of the car got closer and closer to Danny's windows. Any ambient light had now disappeared; the car's headlights were the only thing cutting through the darkness of the moors. As he passed what looked like a derelict hunting lodge Danny realised he had absolutely no idea where the track led to. *You didn't really think this through, did you?*

He looked to his left as he slowed and then came to a stop; the dancing lights had disappeared. The track ended at what looked like some abandoned reservoir workings. The moor rose steadily ahead of him and there was little by way of turning room. As he turned in his seat to start manoeuvring his way backwards out of the dead end, he saw a bank of lights behind him; the bikes were blocking his exit. *Fuck!*

He waited.

One by one, the engine noises he could hear cut out and fell silent. There were just the lights now, dazzling him so he couldn't see who was on the bikes. Then the lights were extinguished.

Danny looked left and right across the moors that surrounded him on three sides. The silent stand-off continued for another 30 seconds. 'Bollocks to this,' he said and was about to put his car into reverse when a cluster of bricks, held together by concrete, came flying towards him and crashed through his rear window, hitting the back of his seat. The headrest took most of the force but the remaining impact on the side of Danny's face was enough to make him shout out in pain.

He drove backwards as quickly as he could back up the track towards the bikes. He got within 20 feet of where he thought they were before he slid backwards into a ditch, tilting the car at a 45-degree angle as it came to a stop. The driver's side door was now blocked by the hags and broom bushes that ran alongside the track. Danny could hear the sound of shouts and laughter; he could also hear feet scrambling across the side of his car. The passenger side door was now above him; Danny looked up just as another lump of brick and concrete smashed through the window. Thousands of tiny chunks of glass showered down onto him. He covered his head with his hands to brace against the impact of the bricks and concrete he expected to follow the glass, but it didn't come. The side window was too small, and the lump had jammed in the frame.

Danny unfastened his seatbelt, twisted himself around and clambered into the back seat. Above him, one of the attackers was now jumping on the concrete block, trying to stamp it through the window frame. He looked around for something to defend himself with. There were plenty of takeaway cartons, empty cans of coke and bits of paper, but not much else. The best he could find was a can of de-icer spray.

He climbed up the back set and managed to push open the rear door that was now facing the starless night sky. Danny leant through his car's door frame and rammed the end of the de-icer tin into the shin of the biker who was standing on his car. A highly satisfying scream resulted, and the attacker fell forwards, hit his face on the side of the car and then bounced into the ditch on the other side of the path.

Danny pulled himself through the open car door and ran into the dense gorse that surrounded the path. Just as he got clear, a shower of half bricks and concrete lumps rat-a-tatted onto his car, breaking the remaining windows and wing mirrors and peppering the bushes around him like gunfire. He lay on the ground and waited for a few beats before moving forwards on his elbows. The jaggy gorse thorns pulled and pinched at him as he crawled along the damp ground. He could hear random, indistinct shouts and instructions all around him; the biker he hit with the can was still screaming.

Danny worked his way away from his car on his belly before turning left; he was now moving parallel to the path, trying to get behind his attackers as they swarmed around his car. The sound of his car being comprehensively trashed grew louder, then suddenly stopped. There was silence for a few seconds, then a few shouts. Danny sensed the bushes behind him moving with increasing energy. Then the gorse shook either side of him. And then stopped. Everything was still. *They've sussed me out. Fuck.*

Danny found a piece of brick and a small chunk of concrete. He took them in his hands, tapped them together for good luck - *ridiculous thing to do* - and got to his knees. *Time to find out if you really are one of the world's worst fighters, Danny lad.*

Danny then stood up and shouted, 'FUCKING COME ON THEN!' Just as he did this the track and surrounding moor was lit up by two powerful beams of light coming from down the track. Danny was blinded by the light but could hear shouts and commands, plus the sound of revving engines.

Then the lights dipped to a more manageable level, allowing him to see what was going on. There was now a Land Rover parked near to where his car had gone into the ditch. Susan got out of the driver's side; Kate put her head out of the passenger window. Both looked at him as if he'd just crash landed from another planet.

Danny, his face dirty and scratched, was standing waist-high in a gorse bush with lumps of brick and concrete in each hand. His eyes were wide with fear and confusion.

'Oi, Rambo,' Kate shouted. 'What the fuck are you doing?'

FIFTY-ONE

'Oh, that's nice,' Danny said, sipping on the mug of hot chocolate that Susan had given him.

'How come he's got little marshmallows in his?' Kate asked looking at her mug with a sigh. 'He fell into a ditch; he didn't storm the beach at Normandy.'

'Come on now, Kate,' Susan said, pulling up a chair and sitting next to Danny. 'Anyone would think you're letting the fact that you're still pissed off with Danny effect your normally very high levels of human compassion.'

'Yeah, Kate,' Danny agreed, giving the marshmallows a little stir with his spoon. 'Anyway, I fell into a bush. It was my car that went into the ditch.'

'Mard arse…' Kate muttered.

'So did you get any idea of who it was, Danny?' Ben Matlock said, leaning against the wall of the school meeting room.

'No really, it was either totally dark or it was blindingly light from the headlights of the motorbikes. Either way you couldn't see anything. So… no idea at all, I'm afraid.'

'So, you reckon they were on motorbikes?' Ben asked.

'Sounded like it, yes,' Danny confirmed.

'Mum?' Ben asked. 'Did you see them?'

'I must confess I didn't actually see anyone,' Susan said. 'I heard something that sounded quite like motorbikes. Scramble bikes are quite common on the moors, we all know that.'

'What about you Kate?' Ben continued. 'You were there with Mum.'

Kate nodded towards Danny: 'I saw Jason Statham there shouting his head off. That's about it. There could have been motorbikes. Or it might have been the sound of Danny reversing up the track at a hundred miles an hour. Not sure. Didn't see any kind of gang, though. Certainly nothing like the vigilantes we saw out at the M62 bridge. Sorry.'

'I saw them,' Smithdown pointed out. 'Looked like five or six lads on bikes to me.'

'From the car park, Dad…' Kate pointed out. 'That's bloody miles away, that is.'

'I know what I saw, Kate,' Smithdown said. 'And if Danny says they attacked him that's good enough for me.'

'Absolutely,' Susan said. 'I'm sure Danny is right. We just didn't see what he saw, that's all.'

Jonathan Smithdown appeared at the doorway: 'Hi. Is everything okay?'

'It's all fine, Jonathan,' Ben Matlock said. 'Danny had a bit of car trouble out on the moors. We're just sorting out getting it towed away.'

'Oh, right… you look a bit messed up, Danny.'

'I just fell on my arse, Jonathan,' Danny said. 'Nothing that a cup of hot chocolate won't sort out.'

'Yes, Susan's doing a grand job of warming Danny up,' Smithdown said. Susan narrowed her eyes at the ex-detective and shook her head. She couldn't stop herself from smiling, though.

'Can I make a suggestion?' Susan said. 'Kate, you've barely had a chance to see Jonathan yet. I'm sure you've still got plenty more to say to him after tonight's other little escapade. Ben, you need to have a proper session with Josh as well. We need to know if he managed to get any pills from anywhere else. How about we have a quick word now, then let them both sleep it off. Then we can reconvene in the morning when we're all a bit calmer… how about that?'

'Sure,' agreed Kate, finishing her hot chocolate. 'Seems sensible. Danny, you stay here with Dad, then let's get home. I suppose you'll be needing a lift?'

'I suppose I will,' Danny agreed. 'If only I knew someone nice who'd help me out in my moment of difficulty…'

'Now, now,' Susan said with a smile. 'Play nice you two. Come on Ben, let's get this over with. Lovely to see you, Mr Smithdown. Take care.'

'You too, love,' Smithdown said with a wink. 'You'll need a good rest after all tonight's excitement, won't she Danny?'

'I'm sure she can handle it, John,' Danny said, not rising to the bait.

'Absolutely, Mr Smithdown,' Susan agreed. 'Night, Danny. Thanks again for what you did for Jonathan and Josh.'

Susan placed a hand on Danny's shoulder as she stood up. Then she led Kate and Ben out of the room, giving Danny a smile as she left. Danny and Smithdown were left alone in the room. There was silence for a few moments. 'Not a fucking word, John Smithdown.'

'I'm sure I don't know what you mean, Danny,' the old man said.

'It WAS the vigilantes,' Danny said. 'I know it was. It's weird, though. One minute they're inviting me along to their little parties, next thing they're attacking me. Something's changed.'

'He's a funny bugger, that Ben,' Smithdown observed. 'He seemed very keen to know what you did and didn't see. Proper nosey.'

'Yeah, I noticed that too,' Danny agreed. 'Kate and Susan seemed to get the same treatment too.'

'Oh, and one other thing,' Smithdown added. 'There's one aspect of this that no one seems to have noticed yet.'

'What's that?'

'That you're a dirty little bastard.'

'Thanks for that, John. Much appreciated.'

FIFTY-TWO

'VIGILANTE BIKERS' ATTACK *OLDHAM NOW* REPORTER

Danny Johnston - Oldham Now

A motorbike gang, thought to be connected to the killings of several men in recent weeks, attacked *Oldham Now* reporter Danny Johnston during the night.

The gang were spotted at around midnight on moorland close to Diggle. Video footage shows at least six bikers heading over the moors towards the M62. They then carried out the attack on a track close to the disused firing range near Diggle Reservoir. They used bricks and stones to smash in the car's windows. The vehicle ended up in a ditch next to the track and is due to be removed this morning.

Motorbikes have been heard close to the scene of all the recent killings. Barry Mortimer, Kabeer Sajid, Adil Aziz and Paul Docherty were all killed by vigilantes claiming they were ridding the area of paedophiles.

Oldham police officer Detective Constable Karl McIntyre also died at the hands of the gang; it's thought he got close to discovering the gang's identities and was killed to keep him quiet.

Since DC McIntyre's death there have been no more killings, but murder squad detectives - led by Mr McIntyre's bother Detective Inspector Patrick McIntyre - seem no closer to catching the gang.

Did you see anything suspicious on the moors last night? Please contact Danny Johnston at *Oldham Now* if you have any information. Email: **danny@oldhamnow.net**

FIFTY-THREE

That night, Danny saw The Shirtless Boy skimming towards him across an icy slab of dark reservoir water.

Danny wasn't sure if he was at Hanging Lees or Black Moss; either way it was a bizarre, elongated version of one of the reservoirs he'd seen earlier that day. It was longer, wider and deeper looking. It looked so deep he felt it was trying to pull him in. It tugged at his clothes and skin like it had a gravitational force.

Come on, Danny. Join us. Just a quick dip. It'll make you feel so much better.

The Shirtless Boy's toes just touched the surface of the water as he moved closer and closer to the sandy bank where Danny was standing.

Sandy bank? It's a beach. Manchester has everything apart from a beach. That's what they say. It's clearly not true…

The Boy came near to Danny then moved away in an elegant arc across the water. Danny realised that he was now following The Boy, floating across the surface behind him like an upright bird. They travelled for hours. Or maybe seconds.

Danny blinked then looked around. They weren't at the reservoir anymore; they were in the doorway of a tiny bedsitting room. It felt cold and damp, much more so than out on the moors.

The Shirtless Boy stepped inside and waved a hand, inviting Danny to join him.

In the corner of the room a woman was nursing a baby. Her back was turned so Danny couldn't see her face. The baby was crying but it wasn't the kind of noise you'd expect a baby to make; it was a horrible metallic sound, like an aluminium can being ripped in two.

Skrawk.

Skrawk.

Skrawk.

Then the tearing sound stopped. All was still in the room. The Shirtless Boy's hand was outstretched, as if to say… *come on, step inside.*

Danny didn't want to. He was happier where he was. Reluctantly, he took one small step. He was almost clear of the door frame.

Skrawk.

Skrawk.

Skrawk.

He couldn't bear the noise anymore and closed his eyes. When he opened them, he was above the water again. He hovered for a moment, then dropped into the darkness.

FIFTY-FOUR

The next morning Danny rolled over in bed to answer his phone. DI Patrick McIntyre's number came up on Danny's phone. *He's unlikely to be pleased.* 'Hi, Patrick. You don't mind if I call you, Patrick, do you? Don't shout at me. I'm very sore. Please remember, I'm the victim here.'

'You're a pain in the arse, Danny,' the DI said. 'That's what you are. When were you planning to report what happened last night to us? Or was it more important to get the hits on your website first?'

'There's no way I'm going to sit on a video that shows the very gang that your lot seems unable to track down,' Danny said. 'I did you lot a favour; every news outlet in the country is carrying the story. I should be charging you for acting as your Press Officer.'

'Yeah,' the detective agreed, sarcastically. 'Every news outlet in the country. Which means that I'll be getting calls from Weymouth to Wick from nutters who think they know something, when what I really need is proper information from around here. Still, as long as it drives traffic to your site, Danny. That's the main thing, isn't it?'

'Is there a wider reason for your call, or is it just to question my journalistic ethics? There's a bottle of paracetamol in the cupboard that's got my name on it.'

'Did you film anything else last night?' the DI asked.

'No. What's on the site is all I have. That's literally every second of it.'

'Is there anything else that you saw or heard that might help us? You must have gotten pretty close to them.'

'Well, they got pretty close to me is probably a fairer way to put it,' Danny pointed out. 'It was all pretty chaotic.'

The detective pressed Danny for more: 'Anything at all, Danny. Anything unusual. Anything that struck you as out of place.'

Danny thought for a moment. He debated whether to mention something that had been on his mind. 'Maybe. Possibly. I'm not sure.'

'Anything, Danny. No matter how small or weird.'

'Well speaking of small and weird… I did actually hit one of them. With a can of de-icer. I know, proper Crouching Tiger Hidden Dragon stuff.'

'What about it?'

'It's just that... he went down like a sack of spuds. I barely touched him, and I still managed to knock him clean off his feet. I'm literally the least hard person in Oldham and I took him out with minimal effort. Plus, he... screamed.'

'How do you mean?'

'I mean... he really screamed. Proper high-pitched stuff.'

'Okay. That is a bit weird. But you never know, it might come in useful. Can you send me the full clip please? For evidence. Include any shaky stuff at the beginning and the end too. We'll overlook the whole driving at high speed through Diggle while using your phone stuff. For now.'

'That's very decent of you,' Danny said. 'Give me your email and I'll WeTransfer it to you now.'

McIntyre gave Danny his GMP email. 'Okay, thanks. Oh and Danny... Let me know when anything else happens that might be of help to us. You remember us, right? Oldham Police. The ones that are apparently NO CLOSER TO CATCHING THE GANG according to your piece. No fucking wonder, is it? Maybe we will actually catch them if we get a bit more co-operation from the likes of you. Just a crazy thought.'

'Okay. Will do. It was a spur of the moment thing; I spotted them and just sort of went for it. It wasn't like before... they didn't contact me. I don't actually think they'll be contacting me again anytime soon. I seem to have been dropped from their Christmas list, for some reason. Maybe I've served my purpose. Not sure.'

'Just let us know, Danny. That's all I ask.'

Danny thought about mentioning his visit to Strangeways to see Bob Donaldson. *Think I'll keep that to myself for the time being.* 'I'll keep you up to date at all times, Detective Inspector,' he said. 'Guaranteed.'

FIFTY-FIVE

Danny's afternoon wasn't the most exciting he'd ever spent. Painkillers, ignoring requests for interviews from other news organisations and being kept waiting on the phone - that was the main thrust of it. *They never show people on hold to insurance companies in films, do they? There are crashes and mayhem and all that, but you never see people listening to light jazz whilst being told, 'you are currently 49th in the queue... your call is very important to us,' after their car's been trashed by the bad guys. Never happens.*

He put his landline on speakerphone, took another couple of painkillers and listened to the voicemail messages on his mobile:

> 'Hi Danny, it's Mike from *Granada Reports*. We were at Strangeways together, remember? Those were the days mate! Can you give me a call please? It's about the vigilantes, obviously. Love to get your eyewitness account to go with the video. Cheers. Bye.'
> *<Message deleted>*

> 'Danny it's Carrie O'Connor from Sky. Been trying you since the murder presser. My editor is going to kill me if we don't get you on. He knows we're mates! We are still mates, aren't we? Ha ha! Anyway, please call. Thanks.'
> *<Message deleted>*

> 'Danny, it's James from GB News. Really keen to speak to you about those vigilantes. Our viewers are 100 per cent behind them, no surprise there! Anyway, would really like to get you on air to debate with one of our tame Lefties about why killing paedos is actually the way forward. It'll be brilliant. Give me a call, ASAP. Cheers.'
> *<Message deleted>*

'Alright, dickhead. It's Kate here, in case you've deleted me from your contacts list. Or you've forgotten what I sound like. I don't care either way, but I'm just seeing if you're alive and stuff. If you are then… fine. Well done. That video's taken off, hasn't it? Your analytics will be going bingo bango bongo, won't they? Anyhow, glad you're not dead, assuming you're not dead, that is. Call me if you like. Not bothered, obviously. Bye.'
<Message saved>

'Danny, it's Susan. Just checking in and seeing how you are. Bit sore I imagine. Nothing that a bit more hot chocolate with marshmallows won't sort out, eh? Anyway, give me a call and I'll come round and see you if you like. Okay? Give me a call. Bye.'
<Message saved>

'Danny, it's Susan again. Sorry. I was just thinking… hope you didn't mind that I gave you a little extra goodbye last night. Did Mr Smithdown see us? Anyway, hope you didn't mind. I thought it was nice. Give me a call. Bye. Again.'
<Message saved>

'Danny… Hiya. Yes. It's Joy Pritchard, Maggie's neighbour. Well, not anymore obviously. Anyway… you know what I mean. If you're passing, give me a knock. Something a bit weird is going on here, thought you'd want to know. Ok. Bye.'
<Message saved>

<You have no new messages>

FIFTY-SIX

Danny looked out of the rear first floor window of Joy Pritchard's house and into Maggie Ormrod's garden. Amid the tangle of overgrown bushes and discarded household goods, a figure in a beige coat was sitting on an upturned beer crate. It was raining and they had what appeared to be a plastic carrier bag on their head to keep them dry.

'How long has he been there?' Danny whispered, realising almost straight away that he probably didn't need to whisper.

'Half an hour or so,' Joy said. 'It's the fourth time they've been in Maggie's garden in the last day or so. It's a she, by the way.'

'Oh right. Have you spoken to her?'

'The first time I saw her I knocked on the window and she left straight away. Second time, I opened the window and said hello - same result. Off she went. Third time I went down to see if she was okay. She spotted me from the path around the back and made off. So, no… I've not actually spoken to her yet.'

'She must want something, otherwise she wouldn't keep coming back.'

'Well, it's clearly not me she wants,' Joy pointed out. 'Maybe it's someone else. Maybe it's you.'

Danny looked at Joy then back down at the woman in the garden. 'How do you get to Maggie's garden?'

'There's a ginnel at the end of the terraces. Walk down there and it'll take you round the back.'

'Okay, I'll give it a go.'

'Danny?' Joy said. 'Take care, alright?'

'It's a woman with a bag on her head sitting on a crate,' he said. 'How dangerous can it be?'

'I don't know, just take care, okay?'

The rain made the ginnel cobbles slippery underfoot as Danny made his way through the back of the terraced houses. Each had a small backyard; the narrow alley separated each house's yard from a series of tiny, gated gardens. Most were modern and neat, with pricey-looking outdoor furniture and fire pits. But not Maggie's. Her garden looked messy and out of place. Danny could imagine some of the neighbours looking down their noses at Maggie and her raggle taggle patch of unkempt grass. Thinking about it made him angry.

Danny stood at the gate and waited. The woman hadn't moved. Danny saw the crate she was sitting on was clearly from a pub; it had a Skol lager logo on it. 'You okay?' he asked. No answer. 'Did you know Maggie? This was her house. I'm Danny, by the way. I've been trying to find out more about her. Do you think you could help me?'

Danny noticed he was speaking in a loud voice and saying his words LIKE THIS AS IF THE PERSON COULDN'T UNDERSTAND HIM. *Don't do that.*

'Yeah… I knew Maggie,' she said. Her voice was quiet with a West Yorkshire accent, more pronounced than its Oldham equivalent. 'You're that journalist fellah, aren't you? I'm not deaf, by the way. I'm wet, but I'm not deaf.'

'Why don't you come in?' Danny suggested. 'Joy next door will make us a brew. She's nice. We can get in out of the rain. What do you think?'

'I think I like it out here,' the woman said. 'I don't like inside. I prefer outside. Maggie was the same. She didn't like being shut in. If there was a chance to get herself out and about, she was away.'

She turned to Danny and smiled. She looked thin and exhausted; the bag on her head was from Kwik Save. *I thought Kwik Save had gone out of business years ago.*

'You're Danny Johnston, aren't you? You used to be on that Manchester Radio years and years ago. MAN-CHEST-AH RAY-DEEE-OOOH… FIRST WITH NEWS! Funny how you remember stuff like that. Can't remember what I had for tea last night, but I can remember your radio station's daft jingles.'

'Yeah, they sort of worm their way into your brain, don't they? What's your name?'

'Alma. Alma Jane Richards… care of the Greenacres Children's Home, Oldham.'

The woman shuffled slightly on the crate and moved to the right. She patted the space she'd vacated. The rain was easing now, barely spitting, so she took the bag from her head, folded it and put it in the pocket of her coat.

Danny did as he was asked. The two sat for a moment in silence. 'What was Maggie like?' he asked. 'I never met her. I feel like I know her a bit.

But not enough.'

'She was nice,' Alma said. 'A bit older than me. She was like our big sister. She looked out for us younger ones.'

'In the care home? I tried to find the records but every time I tried the files were missing or there'd been a fire and the paperwork had been destroyed.'

'Yeah, funny that, isn't it?' Alma smiled. 'All these… what do they call them? Agencies! All these agencies that are supposed to look after kids. They often do the opposite, don't they? Different now though. Better. That's why she liked doing cleaning work at kids' homes and that. Sort of comforted her. Knowing things had changed. She loved that one up past Diggle.'

'Which one?' Danny asked.

'Hunter's Hollow,' Alma said. 'Said that the things they did for the kids there was amazing. Taking them rock climbing and quad biking and all that. Amazing place, that's what she said.'

'Maggie worked at Hunter's Hollow? I know people there. They never said anything.'

Alma was adamant: 'Well, she did. On and off. And she loved it.'

The rain had stopped now. The crate felt wet under the seat of Danny's trousers. 'When they found her at Hanging Lees, Maggie had left a note,' he said. 'She named someone she said had harmed her when she was young.'

'Harmed her?' Alma laughed. 'Ha! That's a good one. Very polite talk, that is, Danny Johnston. Harmed her… that's brilliant. There's that other one they use these days, isn't there? Groomed. It sounds quite nice, doesn't it? Like he was brushing her hair or something. Groomed? Abused her… raped her… got her pregnant… got rid of her kid… abandoned her… drove her to kill herself out on them moors. Yeah. He harmed her alright. That fucking bastard John Smithdown.'

'Smithdown… that was his name?'

'She used to talk about him all the time. Like he was her boyfriend or something. He'd come and pick her up and the people at the care home would just let him. Sick.'

'And it was definitely John Smithdown?'

'Definitely. She told me all about it.'

Danny took out his phone and showed Alma the photo of Maggie Ormrod with John Smithdown. 'The man in this photo… is this him?'

She looked at the screen. 'I have no idea who that is, at all. Is he one of Smithdown's mates?'

'No, it's him. John Smithdown. The police found this picture in Maggie's house. It's Smithdown. I know him.'

'No idea who that is, but it isn't John Smithdown,' Alma said, emphatically.

Danny pulled a newspaper clipping from his pocket: 'What about this man. This picture is from 1988. Do you recognise him?'

Alma looked at the story: 'Yeah. THAT'S John Smithdown. I'd recognise the slimy twat anywhere.'

'Come inside, Alma,' Danny said. 'Please. And tell me everything you know.'

Inside, Danny introduced Alma to Joy. They put her wet coat over a radiator and gave her tea and toast.

Then Alma Jane Richards - formerly care of the Greenacres Children's Home - told them everything she knew about Maggie Ormrod.

Danny listened to what she said. Then, finally, Danny understood. And then Danny wept.

FIFTY-SEVEN

16 April 1975

Maggie sang along to the theme song at the end of the TV programme: 'B… O… B.O.Y.S… boys to entertain yoooo!'

The policeman switched off the television set and pointed to his watch. 'Look at the time, Maggie! It's way past your curfew. The people at Greenacres will be going mad. You'll get in big trouble if you go back now. I knew I shouldn't have let you talk me into watching another programme.'

'Well, you should have told me what time it was, John!' she said, indignantly. 'Why is it always my fault?'

'I don't know Maggie Nuisance,' he said, leaning across the sofa to tickle her. 'Why IS it always your fault?'

'Gerroff!' she screamed, laughing so much she could barely speak. 'I'll scream, gerroff!'

'Go on then,' he said. 'Scream all you like. I dare you.'

She looked at him for a moment; then let out a scream so loud it hurt her own ears. She put a hand to her mouth, embarrassed at what she'd done.

'It's fine. You can't disturb the neighbours here. I haven't got any.'

He got up and stood at the window. The curtains were open, and the sun had set across the moors. The wind scraped at the windows, giving them a playful rattle. 'That's the beauty of this house. Nobody either side. Nobody at the front, nobody at the back either. Just the moors. We can't bother anyone, and no one can bother us.'

'But what about the home?' Maggie asked. 'If I get in trouble again, I'll get shipped off to Borstal.'

The man stood up and paced around the front room, apparently deep in thought. For a moment it looked like he had an idea, but then he shook his head, dismissed it and returned to pacing the floor. Maggie tried to say something, but he shushed her to stop his train of thought being disturbed. Then he clicked his fingers. 'I've got it,' he said. 'You can stay here tonight. I'll take you back in the morning and we'll tell them you were being chased by some older kids and hid because you were so frightened. I found you and brought you back. I'll tell them it wasn't your fault and that I'll get the kids that did it. How about that?'

'Great,' Maggie said. 'Yeah. If that's okay?'

'Of course,' he replied, reassuringly. 'Not a problem. So, it's settled. You can stay here tonight.'

FIFTY-EIGHT

John Smithdown was watching *Pointless* on the TV when Danny ran up his driveway, banged on his window and then let himself into the house.

'What's up with you?' Smithdown asked as Danny came into the room. 'Have you been crying?'

'I'm so sorry, John,' Danny said and knelt beside the old man's armchair. 'I mean it, I'm sorry.'

Danny's face was already wet with tears; he started crying again. 'Come on, lad,' Smithdown said. 'Whatever it is that's upset you, it can't be as bad as all this.'

'It is, John. I have to tell you… I thought you might have done it. I thought you might have hurt Maggie Ormrod. I hate myself for saying it, but it's true. I definitely thought it. I'm sorry for doubting you, even for a second. After everything you've done for me as well. Now I know you didn't do it, and I can prove it.'

'Well, that's great then… isn't it?'

'But now everything is coming crashing down. It's like I've been digging and digging all this time and now everything has caved in on me all at once. Black Moss, Mermaid's Pool, Hanging Lees, the whole stinking lot.'

Danny was now crying so hard he couldn't speak. Smithdown seemed unsure of what to do; he went to put a hand on Danny's shoulder. Then he seemed to change his mind and held his hand instead. Initially that made things worse; Danny cried even harder. Slowly, he calmed down and the tears lessened.

'That's better, Danny,' Smithdown said. 'Simmer down.'

Danny wiped his face on his sleeve. 'Fucking Nora,' Danny said. 'Look at the state of me. What a mess. Sorry. But I don't know what to do, John. It's too much to take in. There's so much to sort out, so much to put right. I don't know where to start.'

'Now you know what it's like being a policeman, Danny. So much shit to deal with and not enough shovels.'

Danny had regained his composure by now: 'So, how did you manage it, then?'

'An old boss of mine used to say: save a life today, change a life tomorrow.'

'Sounds like the kind of thing they'd put on a poster up at Hunter's Hollow,' Danny said, still sniffing and rubbing at his eyes.

'Yes, I used to think it was corny old shite, but he was spot on. Like getting you and your sister out of that house when you were kids. That was the priority. The other stuff can wait. The other stuff happened BECAUSE we prioritised what was important. Same with this. I know I didn't harm Maggie Ormrod. Now you do too. But sorting that can wait until tomorrow. It sounds like there's shit that needs shovelling before that.'

Danny laughed and wiped the last of his tears away: 'I think that's fair to say, John.'

'Then never mind about me,' Smithdown said. 'Get your shovel out.'

FIFTY-NINE

Danny had called Susan Matlock several times already, but thanks to the poor phone signal at the school, every attempt so far had gone straight to voicemail. On the fourth go, he got through: 'Hi, Susan, it's Danny.'

'I know, you daftie,' she laughed. 'I've got one of those up-to-date phones where the caller's name appears. Very modern here, you know… apart from our 1980s phone signal.'

'Yeah, of course. Listen, I wanted to ask you something about Maggie Ormrod, the woman that was found up at Hanging Lees. Why didn't you tell me she'd worked at Hunter's Hollow?'

Susan's tone changed; the good-natured cheeriness slipped away a little: 'Not being funny Danny, but I assumed you knew. I didn't want to talk about it in front of Kate for obvious reasons… all that stuff with her dad. And to be honest, I only met her once or twice. She tended to be on site really early. She was nice, though. I remember that. It was so sad what happened.'

'Did you ever talk to her?' Danny asked.

'Just to say hello, mainly.'

'That's it?'

Susan paused. Danny waited. 'She did ask me about the work we did at the school. It was literally while she was cleaning one of the classrooms. She seemed quite interested.'

'In what way?'

'Well, she asked me a question that I get asked a lot. The question I'm asked more than any other, in fact.'

'Which is?'

'She asked me… what should someone do if they'd been hurt by someone in the past?'

'And what did you tell her?'

'I told her what I tell everyone; that it's important to hold them to account for what they did and to get justice.'

'Justice?'

'Justice, yes. Always. It's the bedrock of everything we do here. Is everything okay, Danny.'

'Sure. Everything's fine. One more thing… Why was Maggie let go from her job?'

'I'm not sure I should say,' Susan replied.

'Please. It's important.'

Danny heard Susan let out a long breath. Then she spoke: 'She'd been buying booze for some of the pupils. She was letting them drink it at her house too. That's just not acceptable, especially as some of the kids have addiction issues. We had to let her go.'

'I see.'

'Danny, where are you now?' she asked.

'I'm at home, Susan. Why?'

'I was going to come round and see you. Make sure you're okay.'

'I'm fine. Pretty tired, though. And sore too. I'm going to get an early night.'

'Sure. We can speak tomorrow, yeah?'

'Definitely. Bye, Susan.'

Danny hung up and tightened the fasteners on his jacket to keep out the cold moorland breeze that was pushing its way across the valley. He watched and waited in his position on the ridge opposite Hunter's Hollow School. Fifteen minutes later he saw a line of bikes appear on a ridge to the north. Their lights dipped in and out of the curved landscape until they reached the hills to the right of the school. Then the bikers turned off their lights and travelled the last mile in darkness. Then they went out of sight behind the final ridge that curved around the back of the school. Danny heard the engines stop one by one. A few minutes later a line of five bikers walked down into the hollow behind the school, helmets in their hands. The hills behind acted like a natural amplifier and Danny could hear them laughing and chatting; he was too far away to make out any faces. A sixth person was clearly having too much fun to stop; they circled around the group and then did a wheelie across the top of the hill. For the first time Danny got a good look at the transportation the group was using to zip across the moors. *Not motorbikes at all. Quad bikes. Kids on fucking quad bikes.*

The lone quad biker got a telling off from someone; the gang waited until he put his bike away over the ridge and joined the group. Lights came on at the back of the school as they entered through the rear doors.

Danny pulled out his phone again and called up a stored number: 'Detective Inspector McIntyre…? Danny Johnstone here. Are you still keen to catch those vigilantes? Thought so. Well, get your boots on. I think I've found the little fuckers. Oh, and John Smithdown's innocent. And what's more, I can prove it.'

SIXTY

'Where's the back up?' Danny asked as he and DI McIntyre took a wide route on foot to the right of the school. 'Not that it isn't a pleasure to see you, but I was expecting back up. You know… big lads from the Tactical Aid Unit with body armour and guns. Where the fuck are they?'

Danny's mind was tumbling with everything he now knew. But he was trying to maintain some level of normality in front of the detective as they half walked, half ran up a steep path hemmed in by a dry-stone wall and an ancient-looking hedgerow. The wall provided cover for them as they passed the school; it was dark now and the pew-pew-pew sound of moorland curlews punctuated their steps.

'The Tactical Aid lads will be in the pub, if they've got any sense,' the DI replied, stepping nimbly over a stile and then a small stream that crossed their path as their route eased its way up the moors. 'I'm only here out of the kindness of my heart, Danny. That sort of stuff takes time. And money. And paperwork. I'd need to get an operational order, not to mention a risk assessment. All we've got to go on at the moment is you seeing some kids on quad bikes near the school.'

'It's a bit more than that,' Danny insisted. 'I know fuck all about motorbikes, but I know the sound I heard out on the moors after the murders; and it sounded just like those quads. The bikers that attacked me seemed small and light. I knocked one over and I barely tried. Kids, Patrick. They're just kids. And I think that arrogant twat Ben Matlock knows all about what's going on.'

'Let's just calm down a little, Danny,' the detective said. 'Let's just have a look over this ridge and then take it from there. Okay?'

'Sure. Okay. I've got something to tell you about Maggie Ormrod too that'll do your nut in. I've already texted Kate. She's going to freak out.'

'Danny! One thing at a time, please. Let's stick with the job in hand. Kate's son, Jonathan might be one of them… you know that don't you?'

'Yes, I do,' Danny said, reaching out a hand to steady himself as the land around them got steeper and steeper. 'I'm trying not to think about it.'

They crested the brow of the hill and lay on their bellies; the quad bikes were there; half a dozen of them had been stashed under a corrugated iron shelter. Beyond that was a battered caravan; it looked like a 1970s model, long with mouldy-looking net curtains and moss growing up the brown and white side panels. 'Oh shit, I hate them,' Danny said, his voice dropping to a whisper. 'Fucking abandoned caravans. There's literally nothing creepier in the world than rancid old, abandoned caravans out in the middle of nowhere.'

'Oh yes there is something creepier… look,' McIntyre said. 'An abandoned caravan in the middle of nowhere with a light on inside.'

The curtains were closed and there were newspapers stuck to the insides of the windows, but a few thin strips of light could be seen between the sheets. Danny rolled onto his back. 'Caravans with bit of light coming from inside. Fucking Nora. They're the worst kind!'

'We can go back if you like,' McIntyre said. 'God forbid that you get freaked out by the sight of a manky old caravan with a light on. Get your big boy pants on, Danny and let's go and check it out.'

The pair got up and walked down the other side of the hill, keeping low as they crossed the field towards the caravan. They stopped outside the door and listened. All they could hear was the sound of the moors.

McIntyre took out his phone and used the torch to examine the door. Two u-shaped clamps had been screwed into the panels on either side of it and a plank of wood had been slotted into them, barricading the door. 'I don't think it's to keep people out,' the DI pointed out to Danny. 'I reckon it's to keep someone in.'

'Oh, that's welcome news,' Danny said. 'Just what I was hoping for, a scary caravan with something locked inside. I suppose we'd better go in then, hadn't we?'

'I suppose we had.'

Danny looked around; the orangey glow of lights from the school gently lit the edge of the hill behind them. He could hear cattle in the distance, but they were definitely alone. 'Fucking Nora,' Danny muttered. 'Absolutely Fucking Bloody Nora...'

He gently lifted the plank that was keeping the door closed. The caravan wasn't level and it tilted slightly in their direction, so when the door came free it swung open towards them, taking both men by surprise. They stepped back and waited. There was silence apart from the squeaking of the door as it swung to and fro.

'You big mard arse,' the DI said. 'In you go.'

Danny took out his phone, swiped on the torch and stepped inside; *why am I going in first?* The caravan smelled of beer and stale sweat. Most of the fixtures and fittings had been ripped out and the floor was littered with empty lager cans. In the small kitchen area there was a bunch of flowers standing upside down in the sink. Further inside a few cushions and an old car seat could be seen on the floor. Then they saw the light that they'd spotted from outside. It was coming from the rear bedroom; there was also a tikka-tikka-tikka-tikka sound coming from the other side of the door.

The two men glanced at each other and then looked at the door.

Tikka-tikka-tikka-tikka.

Without a word being exchanged they both began to look around for some form of weapon. DI McIntyre kicked over some takeaway containers and discovered a stave of wood the size of a cricket bat; the best Danny could find was an old milk bottle.

'Really?' the DI whispered. 'Is that all you can find?'

'It's either that or the bunch of flowers,' Danny replied. 'Come on, are we going into this bedroom or what?'

They stood close to the door with their improvised weapons raised; the detective pulled at the magnetic catch and the door swung open.

The tikka-tikka-tikka-tikka noise got a little louder.

In the middle of the caravan's bedroom was a topless man taped to a chair. There was blood smeared across his chest and arms; several of his fingers were pointing in the wrong directions and were clearly broken. His mouth was covered with gaffer tape and a pair of headphones had been taped to his head. They were attached via a curly lead to an old cassette player. The song that was being played had clearly been set at a deafening volume; the sound of the drums could be heard leaking from the headphones from across the room: tikka-tikka-tikka-tikka.

Danny pulled at the tape and loosened it enough to free the headphones: 'FUCKOFFANDDIE!' could be heard before DI McIntyre stopped the cassette. The man looked up and made eye contact with Danny; there was a pleading look in his eyes. 'Oh, for fuck's sake,' Danny sighed, lowering his milk bottle. 'Not you.'

'Do you know this guy?' the detective asked. He dug around in his pocket and then used the serrated edge of his car keys to saw at the tape around the back of the man's head.

'Yeah, I'm afraid I do,' Danny replied. 'It's Charlie, at least that's what he told me his name was. He's officially the stupidest nonce in the whole of Oldham. We had a hot date outside the Subway in Chadderton the other week.' Danny helped the DI remove the tape from the man's mouth. 'Still going with the whole flowers thing, Charlie? Classy. Who did this to you?'

Charlie opened his mouth; he made a moaning sound and two of his teeth fell out. 'Kidsss,' he slurred. 'Fucking kidsss.'

'We need to get him out of here,' the DI said. 'Those kids could come back at any time.'

'There's plenty of people out there who'd say we should leave him here,' Danny said.

'Well, I suppose right now is the perfect time for you to decide which side you're on, isn't it?' the detective responded, pointing his car keys at Danny. 'Are you the kind of person who turns a blind eye and lets someone be tortured and murdered because they disgust you? Or are you genuinely trying to put an end to this? It's as simple as that. Decide, Danny. Because I can't carry this fucker on my own and I'm getting a bit tired of you sitting on the fence. You wanted to get the vigilantes. Now's your chance. Or was this just a story to you? A bit of clickbait for your website? Because I'm a police officer, and I don't have a choice. I have to protect this man whether I like him or not.'

'Alright, Captain Self-Righteous, keep your halo on,' Danny said. 'What about if we bust the door off and use it as a stretcher?'

'Perfect. Let's do it.'

The two men went to the bedroom door. They put down their weapons; Danny held the bottom and DI McIntyre grabbed the top. They braced themselves. 'I get it,' Danny said in a whisper. 'I know you're right. But me and my sister… We were both done over when we were kids. Passed around like sweets. It fucked up our lives. She died last year. Cancer. This shit is hard. Really hard.'

'I know, Danny,' the detective said. 'I'm sorry. Nobody would like to change the past more than me. But I can't. All I can do is deal with what's happening right now… and right now we need to get this door off these hinges so we can get that nonce out of this caravan. Okay?'

'Okay. How come you're about 20 years younger than me, yet about 20 years better at dealing with this shit than I am?'

'Absolutely no idea, Danny. Ask my mum. Right. Are you ready? After three…'

On three, the two men pulled at the door; it came away in one go but the effort put both of them on their backsides. As they got to their feet the caravan flooded with light from three powerful head torches. Ben Matlock entered with a hammer in his hand; with him were two teenage pupils, Josh and Carly. They had hammers too. Danny noticed that the teenage girl who'd asked him how much he earned during his talk, was limping and one side of her face was puffy and bruised. The three faced off against Danny and the detective with just four or five yards of caravan floor between them.

'Detective Inspector McIntyre, meet Ben,' Danny said. 'He's the nasty bastard who's been getting these kids to do his dirty work. Ben, meet Detective Inspector McIntyre. He's the man who's going to arrest you… Something I'm very much looking forward to. And this is Carly… That leg must be proper sore. Nothing worse than a can of de-icer right in the shin, is there Carly? And finally, here's Josh; pill popper and hospital jumper extraordinaire. Is that how Ben gets you to do stuff, Josh… by limiting your pills? That's lovely, that is.'

'Ha ha!' Ben said. 'Brilliant! Let me have a turn, this is fun: Josh and Carly, you've already met Danny. He's the self-righteous hypocrite who makes money from writing stories about all the nasty things that happen in life. But unlike us, he isn't prepared to actually do anything to try to stop them. He's all talk and no action.'

'They're kids, Ben,' Danny pleaded. 'Vulnerable, damaged kids. They need to be helped, not filled with vengeance and hate. You've groomed them.' He nodded towards, Charlie, who was moaning and crying behind them. 'You're as bad as him over there. Maybe worse.'

Ben ignored him and carried on with his introductions: 'Now then Ben… Carly… this is Detective Inspector McIntyre. You've already met his brother, out at Crow Knowl. That didn't end well, did it? Look at him… he's more interested in saving that sick fucker Charlie who tried to nonce on Carly than he is in protecting the children of Oldham. I've said it before and I'll say it again: the law doesn't care about kids. The law only cares about making sure that Charlie the Paedo's precious rights aren't violated. That's why we have to do what we do.'

'Oh, shut the fuck up,' McIntyre said, picking up one end of the bedroom door. 'I'm not listening to this shite. I fancy our chances here, Danny. We'll make light work of these three and then get on our way. Because what are we dealing with here? One pill head, one girl with a gammy leg and one BIG MOUTHED TWAT THAT'S ABOUT TO GET THIS DOOR IN HIS FUCKING FACE.'

Danny took hold of the other end of the door and steadied himself. The two men bent their knees, ready to charge across the caravan. There was silence for a few moments, then Danny heard a banging noise on the side of the caravan. It got louder and more frequent; it started to their left and moved to the right. The banging was all around them now, the sound of metal clanging on the outside panels on all sides. DI McIntyre reached out and pulled away several sheets of newspaper that were taped to the window nearest to him. Danny did the same on his side. The caravan was surrounded by Hunter's Hollow pupils; they all had hammers and were banging them on the outside of the caravan. Then the banging stopped.

Susan Matlock stepped into the caravan. Charlie, still strapped to the chair behind Danny and the DI, began to cry and moan and plead even louder. He shook his head and begged for mercy through his broken teeth. 'Not her. Please. Not her!'

'Oh, Danny…' Susan said with a disappointed smile. 'It shouldn't have turned out like this. Makes me very sad, it really does. We should all be on the same side. You, me, the police, the kids. All fighting the good fight against the common enemy. I honestly believed that you'd join us. I read your book and thought… this guy is one of us.'

'So that's why you sent me the tip offs about the bodies?' Danny said. 'Fucking hell, Susan, couldn't you just film them in a car park and stick it on Facebook like everyone else? Surely naming and shaming is a pretty good deterrent?'

'If doing shit like that was such a good deterrent, why doesn't it seem to deter them?' Susan snapped. 'They just keep on coming. Wave after wave of online predators. Then it's down to the likes of me and Ben to pick up the pieces after the abuse has already happened. Mopping up the mess isn't the way forward. I've been doing that for years. I've been through all the social care systems there are - worked in every single one of them - and none of them do any good. None of them… no matter how hard people like me try. And what's more, coppers like your friend here have looked down their noses at us for years. Do-gooders... Hippies... Tree huggers. I'm sick of it. So, we tried a different method. And this one very clearly works. Online grooming incidents in Oldham have almost entirely stopped. Amazing! And why? Because the predators are in hiding. They're the ones living in fear. Makes a nice change. All apart from that prick behind you, of course. He was too stupid to listen to the warnings. Which is why he's here to face a little bit of instant justice.'

'This is no way to help children, Ms Matlock,' DI McIntyre said. He looked at Josh and Carly. 'They've already been abused. That's bad enough. Now you've turned them into murderers.'

Carly laughed and shook her head: 'He just doesn't get it, does he? It'd be funny if it wasn't so pathetic.'

'You're so wrong, Detective Inspector,' Josh said. 'We're not murderers, we're warriors. Me, Carly and the others are doing this so that young people in the future can be safe. And the best way to keep kids safe is to go to the source of the danger and cut it off. And that's exactly what we're doing.'

'What about my brother?' the detective said, firmly. 'Did you all have a meeting and just decide that he should be cut off too?'

'That was very unfortunate,' Susan admitted. 'But we are at *war*, Mr McIntyre. You and your brother had your chance to fight it and you lost. You can't stop this, and you know it. So, now you need to stay out of our way. I'm afraid your brother didn't do that. I'm sorry. But this is more important.'

'Was Maggie Ormrod in the way too?' asked Danny.

For the first time, Susan's resolve seemed to falter. 'Maggie was another victim. Abused by someone she trusted when she was just a child. More proof that we can't trust the so-called authorities. I told you the truth about my dealings with her, Danny, I really did. I told her that it's important to hold abusers responsible for what they did and to get justice. Taking her life was the way she chose to do that. She held her abuser accountable for her life and her death. She's a heroine.'

'Christ Almighty, Susan,' Danny said. 'This is madness. You can't seriously think that you can keep all this secret and just bury it, can you?'

'Depends how far you're prepared to dig, Danny,' Ben Matlock said with a smile. 'The moors around here can be very accommodating.'

Susan held up her hand as if she was in a classroom silencing her pupils: 'Okay… I'm done with this. Look. Danny… DI McIntyre. Let's be practical here. There's too many of us. If you want to fight us, fine. Have a go… smash a few kids' heads in with your stupid bit of caravan door. But you'll lose anyway. This is over.'

Danny looked at Charlie and then shook his head: 'We can't let you take him, Susan. I hate myself for saying it, but we can't.' Danny picked up his milk bottle again, while still holding onto the corner of the door. He looked at DI McIntyre. 'It's wrong.'

Then half a dozen more teenagers with hammers stepped inside the caravan. 'Well, that's disappointing to hear, Danny,' she sighed. 'Very disappointing indeed. I'd expect that kind of nonsense from Detective Inspector Dickhead over there, but not you. Oh well.'

She turned to face her pupils: 'Take them,' Susan said. Then she pointed her hammer at Charlie: 'Then we'll rip that fucker apart.'

'I'm telling you now, I'm shit at this,' Danny whispered to DI McIntyre; he felt slightly foolish holding the milk bottle above his head.

'I'll go for Ben, you go for Susan,' the detective said. 'Maybe the kids will take fright and run. Maybe not. Worth a go.'

'You want me to bottle her, is that what you're saying?' Danny asked.

'Fine. You take Ben. He'll knock you into next Friday but at least you won't have the indignity of Susan kicking your arse.'

'Fucking Nora,' Danny muttered. 'We'd best take a run up, I suppose.' He looked around; there was hardly any space. They'd edged backwards so far that they were almost pressed against Charlie. Danny could feel the injured man's bloodied, wet skin against the back of his hand. *Even if we did just step aside and let them take him, they'll kill us anyway.*

Fuck it.

Danny and McIntyre readied themselves to dash forwards just as the whole caravan lurched violently to the left, accompanied by a metallic crashing sound. The front end, where Susan and Ben were standing, crumpled inwards and sent them and the pupils violently across to the opposite wall. The outer shell of the caravan tore open; Danny heard the sound of an engine revving and then the caravan spun sideways for a second time. It was now facing the opposite way and the back end of the caravan had been completely sheared off. Danny could see that the damage had been caused by the school's Land Rover; Jonathan Smithdown was at the wheel. Danny and Jonathan looked at each other for a moment; then he gave the teenager the thumbs up. 'Fucking nice one,' he mouthed to him.

Danny couldn't see Susan, Ben and the other pupils; it appeared they'd been knocked out of the caravan with the impact. 'Right,' said McIntyre, grabbing the back of Charlie's seat with his left hand and tipping him backwards. 'We haven't got time to untie him - grab the chair legs and let's take this twat out of here as he is.'

Danny did as he was asked, and the two men half-carried and half-dragged Charlie through the hole in the end of the caravan. The detective was clearly struggling with the weight; then Danny noticed that McIntyre's right arm appeared to be the wrong way round; it was bent outwards and there was blood and bone visible around the DI's wrist. 'That's going to be a bit sore in the morning,' Danny pointed out.

He got no answer; McIntyre's eyes were unfocused, and he looked like he was struggling to breathe. *Don't pass out you bastard, I need you to be conscious.*

They managed to get Charlie out of the caravan; Jonathan pulled the

Land Rover close to them, nearly hitting Danny in the process. 'I didn't know you could drive, Jonathan,' Danny said.

'I can't, really,' the teenager said, stepping out of the vehicle just as McIntyre let go of the chair and dropped Charlie on his back. There was shouting and screaming all around them. Some of the pupils were running back to the school, but others were regrouping and pointing at them. Danny started pulling at the gaffer tape that was securing Charlie to the chair.

'Jonathan… you help the policeman and I'll get the paedo,' Danny shouted. 'There's a sentence I didn't think I'd be saying when I got up this morning.'

Jonathan helped McIntyre get to his feet and then pushed and pulled him onto the back seat of the car. The detective immediately keeled over and lay flat across the seats. Danny was still struggling with the tape; the more he pulled, the tighter it seemed to get. He looked up and saw half a dozen pupils coming towards him.

'Right fuck this,' Danny said. 'Jonathan, open up the boot. Then grab the chair legs. We'll just chuck him in as he is.'

The pair opened the rear of the car; they got Charlie as far as the lip of the boot before Jonathan lost his footing in the muddy ground and let go of the chair. Charlie let out a cry as he fell on his side. The pupils were getting closer to them now. 'Danny, please,' Jonathan cried. 'Leave him and let's just go. Trust me. I know them. We need to get out of here right now.'

'No,' Danny stated. 'Grab the chair legs and get him in. He's a prick, I know. But we can't leave him. They'll tear him apart. I mean, fucking literally tear him apart.'

'Fucking Nora,' Jonathan said and grabbed the chair legs again. This time, Charlie went into the back of the Land Rover with one lift. He was face down in the boot, but he was in. 'Probably best if I drive,' Danny said as they ran to the front of the vehicle. They slammed the doors closed. The pupils were nearly on them. Danny recognised some of their faces from his talk; Josh and Carly were at the front of the pack. 'Jonathan, have you got your phone?' Danny said. 'Call the police. Now.'

'There's no signal,' Jonathan cried. 'We need to be out of this valley and away from the school.'

Josh then appeared at the driver's side window and smashed it in with his hammer; Danny was peppered with tiny cubes of glass as he shoved the gear stick into reverse. He heard a bang at the rear. *That could have been a kid hitting the car with a hammer… or I could have hit a kid. Hard to tell.*

Danny had never driven a Land Rover before and struggled with the gears; he finally managed it and reversed up the hill behind the school at high speed. The further up the slope he got, the faster he seemed to be going. 'Signal, Jonathan?' Danny shouted. 'Come on, there must me a signal!'

'No, nothing!' the teenager said. 'Shit. Keep going higher.'

Danny saw the dry-stone wall at the top of the field getting closer and closer. 'I'm running out of field, mate. There must be something.'

'Nothing! Still no signal!'

'Typical fucking Oldham,' Danny said. 'It's like a Third World country.'

They reached the top of the field and Danny stopped. The wall was five or six feet high and there was no gate or break in the stones. The pupils were lined up in front of them now.

'Did you know?' Danny asked quietly, watching the teenagers as they walked towards them.

'What the fuck are you talking about?' Jonathan shouted. 'We need to go, now!'

'Did you know what Susan and Ben were doing?'

'No!' Jonathan cried. 'Well, not really. I mean, a bit, I suppose… but I don't KNOW know, if you know what I mean. Josh was talking about it at the hospital. Ranting about how we had to stop people harming kids, take them out and all that.'

'You seemed pretty happy to leave Charlie behind.'

'I wasn't… *happy.* I was just… I don't know. It's fucking complicated, Danny. You must know that better than anyone.'

'Yes,' Danny admitted. 'I suppose I do.'

'Now, can we go, please!' Jonathan cried. 'Go around them, past the school and head for the main gate.'

Danny put the car into first gear and shot off down the hill. He did his best to avoid the pupils as several hammers came flying at them. One cracked the windscreen making it difficult for Danny to see. He heard a heavy clunk to his left and the vehicle lurched briefly upwards. *Was that a rock in the field or a kid? I don't give a fuck, to be honest.*

They passed the caravan and saw Susan Matlock lying on the ground; her face was covered in blood. 'Looks like Susan will be calling in sick tomorrow,' Danny muttered as the Land Rover went up the hill on the other side of the valley and then headed down the other side towards the main school building. As they passed the side entrance, two more hammers hit the rear windscreen; the first cracked it, the second smashed it in. In the back, Charlie moaned as the glass covered him. Some of the glass hit DI McIntyre too, but he didn't make a sound.

'Any signal?' Danny shouted as the moorland wind came blasting through the car.

'No. Wait, yes. No, it's gone again.'

The car sped through the school car park and out onto the main drive towards the exit. A sign said:

THANK YOU FOR VISITING HUNTER'S HOLLOW SCHOOL. THANK YOU FOR BELIEVING IN US!

Twenty yards from the main road Danny saw a car heading towards the entrance from the main road. It was Kate's blue Mercedes.

'Yes!' Danny cried. 'It's your mum! God love her! Now we're talking.'

Danny waved at Kate through his broken window as they both approached the narrow exit at the same time. Danny waved at her to move back but instead Kate pulled her car across the drive and blocked it. 'Kate, shift yourself, we need to go,' Danny shouted as the Land Rover came to a halt. He looked around. Several pupils were coming down the school drive towards them on quad bikes.

'Kate, stop dicking about and move your arse!' Danny shouted.

Kate stepped out of the car. She looked at Danny. There were tears in her eyes as she shook her head.

'Kate, please. Jonathan's in the car. Come on!'

'Jonathan will be fine,' she said, hugging herself from the chill air. 'You've decided which side you're on, Danny. So have I.'

'FUCKING NORA!' Danny shouted. He banged his fist onto the steering wheel. He looked around and saw that the lead quad biker was close to them now. It was Ben Matlock; he came to a skidding stop with a hammer held high over his head and was about to throw it at Danny. 'FUCKING FUCKING NORA!' Danny shouted. He jammed the Land Rover into reverse and backed up sharply, straight into Ben's quad bike.

Danny saw the bike fly to the right and Matlock go to the left. He drove forwards again, right up to Kate's car. 'Move yourself, Kate.'

She shook her head. 'You stood by and fucking let them do it, Kate,' Danny shouted. 'You fucking knew what was going on and you did nowt.'

'Not at first,' she said. 'I suspected, but I didn't know. We had to do *something* to stop them. Nothing else works, Danny. Stupid videos on the internet don't make a difference. You can't name and shame someone who's not ashamed of what they're doing.'

'But you can't just kill people just because you hate them, Kate. It'll never end.'

'You should have helped us, Danny. That's why Susan gave you all those stories. To get you onboard. You didn't mind what they were doing when you were making money out of it, did you?'

'What they're doing is sick, Kate. It infected poor Maggie Ormrod's mind and look what happened to her. Look how it pulled in your dad too. Nothing good has come from this. Your Jonathan can see this is wrong and he's just a kid. Yet somehow, you can't. Now move your car or I'll ram it out of the way.'

Kate stood her ground. A group of quad bikers were now grouped behind the Land Rover, unsure of what to do. Susan Matlock was walking up the drive towards her son. He was lying by the drive and wasn't moving. 'What are you waiting for, you stupid fucking kids,' she screamed. 'Stop him!'

'Fuck this,' Danny said. Danny banged the Land Rover into reverse, accelerated hard and smashed it straight into Kate's car.

'Danny!' Jonathan cried. 'Mind my mum, please!'

'I'll do my best,' Danny said, reversing again. He smashed into the car twice more until he'd battered Kate's Mercedes halfway across the road and there was enough space for the Land Rover to get by. Kate and Danny looked at each other as they passed; then he drove as fast as he could away from Hunter's Hollow School. Behind them, Danny could hear her screaming: 'Jonathan, please. Come back! I'm so sorry. Please.'

They were 100 yards down the road when Danny heard Jonathan's voice next to him: 'Hello? Yes! Police, please…'

SIXTY-ONE

CHARGES MADE OVER 'VIGILANTE' KILLINGS

Danny Johnston - Oldham Now

A mother and son have been charged with a series of murders after police were called to an award-winning school on the outskirts of Oldham.

Emergency crews found what eyewitnesses describe as a 'scene of carnage' at the Hunter's Hollow School near Denshaw. Many of those arrested required hospital treatment before they were taken in for questioning.

Susan Matlock, aged 47, and her son Ben, 25, have both been charged with multiple counts of murder. The charges follow the deaths of Barry Mortimer, Kabeer Sajid, Adil Aziz and Paul Docherty in alleged 'vigilante' killings.

The Matlocks have also been charged with the murder of Detective Constable Karl McIntyre. His body was discovered on Crow Knowl on Crompton Moor, accompanied by a note apologising for his death. He's the brother of Detective Inspector Patrick McIntyre who was also badly injured during the events at Hunter's Hollow. He's currently in the Royal Oldham Hospital but is expected to make a full recovery.

The Matlocks also face kidnapping, false imprisonment and grievous bodily harm charges in relation to another person, Charles Morris of Chadderton. Mr Morris also sustained serious injuries at Hunter's Hollow; it's alleged he'd been tortured. He's now in hospital but his injuries aren't thought to be life-threatening.

Nineteen other people face conspiracy charges in connection with the incidents; they can't be named for legal reasons because of their ages.

Another person, local businesswoman Kate Smithdown (52) has also been charged with conspiracy. She's been released on police bail on the understanding that she doesn't contact anyone connected with the school or members of her own family.

Susan and Ben Matlock have both been remanded in custody and will appear before Oldham Magistrates tomorrow morning. The teenagers connected with the case have all been taken into the care of Oldham Social Services and are being held in secure units across the town.

SIXTY-TWO

'Painkillers are all well and good,' Danny said, looking at the metal rods and pins that were clustered in and around DI Patrick McIntyre's arm. 'But there's only one thing that will really get you on the mend. And that's these fellahs.'

Danny put a box of Wine Gums onto the cabinet next to the detective's hospital bed and made a dramatic hand gesture towards them, like a magician drawing his audience's attention to a thing of great wonder.

'Thank you very much, Danny,' McIntyre said. 'If my arm didn't feel like an elephant was sitting on it, I'd give you a great big manly hug.'

'Speaking of your horrifically mangled arm, young Jonathan asked me to say hello,' Danny added. 'And to say sorry, of course. Sorry for driving into the caravan and breaking your arm in 97 places and all that. He's concerned he's going to be charged with assaulting a police officer. I told him not to worry about it.'

'That's very Christian of you,' McIntyre said. 'How's he doing?'

'All things considered, not bad,' Danny replied. He smiled at Jenny as she approached with her drinks' trolly. She handed him a cup of Vimto and a Tunnock's Teacake. 'Me and him are staying at Smithdown's house for the time being. Until we get things sorted out.'

'You, Smithdown and Johnathan all under the same roof,' Jenny laughed. 'What's it like looking after that pair, Danny?'

'It's not easy,' Danny replied with a shake of his head. 'He's moody, answers back all the time and plays his music way too loud. Jonathan can be a pain in the arse as well.'

'Very funny,' Jenny said. 'That poor boy. He's been through so much. He's lucky to have you as a friend, Danny. Anyway, I need to get on. Can't have people thinking I'm giving my son preferential treatment, can I? You take care, Danny. Don't take any nonsense from this one.'

'I won't, Jenny.' He gave her a hug. She smelled of Vimto. Just for a moment, Danny thought he might cry. *Not everyone's a bad un.* It was as if Jenny could sense it, so she held him just a few moments longer.

'I mean it,' she whispered. 'Take care, Danny. People forget how much you've been through too.'

'Thank you, Jenny. I will.'

Danny watched as she went out of the ward, then took a seat next to DI McIntyre's bed. 'She's lovely, your mum.'

'She could still knock the shit out of you, though,' the detective replied.

'I know, but who doesn't appreciate a highly protective mum? Wish I'd had one.'

'Some mums can take being protective a bit too far though, can't they?' McIntyre pointed out. 'Is Kate sticking to her bail conditions?'

'So far, yes,' Danny said. 'I think it's only a matter of time until she tries to contact Jonathan though. It's just the way she is. I think she genuinely believes she was doing the right thing. I bet the courts might disagree with her, though.'

'And how's Smithdown doing?' McIntyre asked.

'He's putting his stoic, old school Oldham face on things but I think he's pretty devastated that Kate could side with what was going on at Hunter's Hollow. I don't blame him – I am too.'

McIntyre scratched at the small area of skin on his hand that wasn't covered by plaster, bandages and steel rods. 'You were going to tell me about how you could prove Smithdown was innocent,' he said. 'You know, before I got my arm twisted backwards by a kid who can't drive.'

'I've found a friend of Maggie's who was in a care home at Greenacres with her. She'll give a statement confirming that it wasn't Smithdown who abused her.'

'Then what are you doing here? Get her down to Oldham Police Station sharpish.'

'I will,' Danny said. 'Definitely. But there's something I need to do first.'

SIXTY-THREE

'No care package?' Bob Donaldson asked as he sat down opposite Danny in the Strangeways visitors' area.

'No, Mr Donaldson,' Danny replied. He gripped his hands together under the table. They were shaking. 'No care package, I'm afraid. Not today.'

'Hardly worth coming then, was it?' he stated. 'I hear Kate Smithdown's been a bit of a naughty girl. Very disappointing. You can't be taking the law into your own hands, I always say. It's just not right.'

'Well, it's a good job you're here to provide us all with a bit of moral guidance, Mr Donaldson.'

'Have you come all this way just to take the piss, Danny Johnston? Wish I hadn't okayed your visit request now, to be honest.'

'Well I for one am very glad you did,' Danny said.

'Why's that then?'

'I met Alma Richards the other day. Do you know her?'

'I don't, I'm afraid,' Donaldson said. 'Is that it?'

'She was in a care home out at Greenacres with Maggie Ormrod. She certainly remembers you. For some reason, she thought your name was John... John Smithdown. I showed her a photo of you, and she identified you as the person that was always taking Maggie out of the care home back in the 70s. Treating her to the pictures, giving her money... all of that. They didn't call it grooming in those days, did they? But that was exactly what you were doing. You took your time too. No rushing, nice and steady. You've got to cover your tracks too, haven't you? Making sure her files all went missing; you even took that photo of Smithdown and Maggie, didn't you? When you were giving her a tour of the police station. Even then, all those years ago, you were covering your arse. Just in case.'

Donaldson stared at Danny. He didn't move. He just listened.

'Alma told me how you got Maggie pregnant,' Danny said, leaning in. 'Raped her then kept her and the kid hidden away in some ratty bedsit in Royton. By the time Maggie was old enough to realise how wrong the situation was, it was too late.'

'It's good stuff this, Danny Johnston,' Donaldson observed. 'Riveting. Do go on.'

'Sitting in here after you'd been done for the Mermaid's Pool murders, you knew you had to get rid of the kid, didn't you? Did you get some of your skinhead mates to snatch the lad? Doing it at the start of the Strangeways riot was the perfect cover, wasn't it? Being in here, you would have known trouble was brewing. I wouldn't be surprised if you actually started it. You arranged to have that kid given to Jan Cave and Beth Hall. And they tortured him and killed him. Then they dumped him out at Black Moss. You handed that kid over to them like a piece of meat. That poor little lad, face down in the sand at Black Moss. All these years and I never knew his name. Now I do. Alma told me. Robbie Ormrod. His name was Robbie Ormrod. Maggie's son. *Your* son.'

Though the visitor's room was noisy, there was total silence between the two men. Donaldson continued to stare at Danny. Then he clutched his chest and grimaced in agony. Danny flinched and jumped to his feet. Then Donaldson's face changed to a smile. 'Ooh, you got me. You're so fucking clever… you got me,' he laughed. 'You're right! So… fucking… what. Nobody gave a shit about the kid then. Nobody gives a shit about him now. You and John Smithdown on your high horses. Fuck the pair of you.'

'It's always been you, hasn't it?' Danny said, raising his voice. One of the guards glanced in his direction. 'Every truly terrible thing that's happened in Oldham for decades has your stink attached to it. Black Moss, the Mermaid's Pool, Hanging Lees. All covered in Bob Donaldson's shit. Even while you were in here you were still infecting the whole town with it. Well not any more. You're done.'

'It's not like the films this, you know,' Donaldson said, jabbing at the table with his finger. 'This is real life. You can't suddenly whip out your phone and show me you were recording the conversation the whole time. That's the beauty of this place. No phones allowed. It's on the list, along with see-through clothing and crop tops that reveal the stomach. No phones. You can't prove anything, Danny Johnston. And even if you could, what's the worst that could happen? I'm never getting out of Strangeways. I'm in here until I die. Good luck with making things worse for me than they already are. There's literally fuck all you can do to me.'

Danny was quiet for a moment. He thought about Maggie Ormrod, lying next to Hanging Lees Reservoir. He thought about the deaths at the Mermaid's Pool and how Oldham had come close to a race war thanks to Bob Donaldson. And he thought about little Robbie Ormrod, lying face down in the sand on the edge of Black Moss in 1990.

Then he thought about standing outside Strangeways during the riot in 1990. He remembered hearing the mainstream prisoners breaking down walls to get to E Wing, where the sex offenders were. From the perimeter fence he had listened to the prisoners shouting as they smashed their way towards the section of the jail where the lowest of the low were housed. They chanted as they got closer and closer: 'BEASTS! BEASTS! BEASTS, BEASTS, BEASTS!'

One remand prisoner in E Wing had later died after getting an horrific beating from the mainstream prisoners. Danny even remembered his name. Derek White. Beaten to death because he was in E Wing. Where the sex offenders were.

Bob Donaldson wasn't in the sex offenders wing. Because as far as the prison was concerned, he wasn't a sex offender.

'You're wrong, Mr Donaldson. There is something I can do.'

'Oh, fuck off, you self-righteous prick,' the old man said.

'Goodbye Mr Donaldson.'

Danny stood up, put a foot onto his seat and got up onto the table. He looked across at the other visitors. And the prisoners. He could see that he'd caught the attention of the guards immediately. They shouted at him to get down.

He didn't have much time. 'HEY!' he shouted. 'LISTEN! LISTEN TO ME! THIS MAN IS A PAEDOPHILE.' He pointed down at Donaldson. 'HE GROOMED A YOUNG GIRL CALLED MAGGIE ORMROD AND RAPED HER. HE RAPED A LITTLE GIRL AND SHE HAD A KID. A BOY CALLED ROBBIE. WHEN HE THOUGHT HE WAS GOING TO GET FOUND OUT HE ORGANISED FOR ROBBIE TO BE KILLED. THIS MAN, RIGHT HERE. HE'S A CHILD RAPIST. HE'S CALLED BOB DONALDSON. AND HE'S IN H WING.'

Danny heard someone shout: 'Control and restraint!' The guards dragged him from the table, and he was pulled firmly to the floor. Three guards were on his legs and arms immediately; they pushed the left side of his face firmly onto the floor. 'We're going to keep your head down, so you don't hurt yourself or bite one of us,' one prison officer said. 'Then we're taking you out of here. Please don't struggle, understand?'

Danny confirmed that he understood; from his position on the floor he still was facing Bob Donaldson and could still talk. 'It's one thing to be an ex-cop in prison, Bobby lad,' he shouted. 'But it's quite another to be a paedophile. A child raping, murdering fucking paedophile.'

The prison officers picked him up and carried him away, headfirst towards the exit. As he was transported through the visitor's area, Danny carried on shouting as loud as he could: 'BOB DONALDSON! H WING!'

Danny was at the door now: 'BEAST!' he cried. 'BEAST! BEAST! BEAST, BEAST, BEAST!'

SIXTY-FOUR

That night, Danny dreamed about The Shirtless Boy.

Robbie Ormrod.

The two were standing on a metal walkway. Robbie had no shirt on. As ever. Danny gave him a parcel wrapped in brown paper, tied up with string. The boy opened it, excitedly. It was a V-necked jumper; the kind that gave the impression the wearer was sporting another top underneath it. Danny remembered wearing them when he was a kid.

Despite Robbie having no facial features, Danny knew the boy was pleased with it; he put it on and looked at it admiringly. Then Danny took the boy by the hand, and they headed along the walkway.

They were at Strangeways… *inside* Strangeways.

The prison was a ruin. Danny had seen footage of the jail after the riot in a documentary on Granada TV. The riot had clearly ended, and the jail looked empty. Toilet paper hung down from the balconies like streamers; rubble and rubbish filled the safety netting that hung below the balconies; the walls were covered in graffiti. Danny and Robbie stopped to look at one of the paint-daubed walls. Someone had written:

WE WONDER WHY?

Still holding hands, the pair walked on. At the end of the walkway a slit of light could be seen from under one of the cell doors. They stood outside and Robbie looked up expectantly at Danny.

I don't know what you want. Tell me.

Robbie nodded towards Danny's pocket. For the first time Danny noticed that there was something heavy there. He reached in; it was a key. A large, metal key. Danny handed it to Robbie; he took it and put it into the cell door. It took both hands for the boy to turn the lock. There was a satisfying loud *thunk* when the mechanism shifted.

A strip of moonlight stretched across the walkway as the cell door swung open. Bob Donaldson was asleep in his bed.

Danny and Robbie looked at him and then at each other.

Robbie put a finger to his face where his lips should have been, then waved his hand at Danny to say goodbye.

Bye Robbie.

Then the boy stepped inside and closed the cell door.

SIXTY-FIVE

KILLER COP FOUND DEAD IN STRANGEWAYS

Danny Johnston - Oldham Now

Bob Donaldson, the former police detective who was behind the Oldham race riots of the 1980s, has been found dead in his cell at Strangeways Jail.

Donaldson, who was 84, was given a 'life-means-life' sentence for his part in a brutal string of murders that were part of a plot to kickstart a race war in Oldham.

The former Detective Constable conspired with neo-Nazi groups to stage a series of murders and racist attacks in Oldham in 1988. Among his victims was Oldham Councillor Sharmeen Chowdhury, who was burned to death at the Mermaid's Pool beauty spot in neighbouring Derbyshire. Mountain rescue volunteer Brian McIntyre also died at the same spot, along with Oldham woman Naomi Wells.

Donaldson's co-conspirator, racist murderer Tom Lennon, also died in prison in 1993. He was stabbed to death, the victim of an apparent revenge attack. The cause of Bob Donaldson's death isn't yet known.

Meanwhile, Donaldson's former colleague, retired detective John Smithdown, has been cleared of any wrongdoing in connection with the recent death of Oldham woman Maggie Ormrod. She's believed to have taken her own life at Hanging Lees Reservoir; a note left at the scene said she'd been abused as a child by an Oldham police officer. That officer is now known to have been Bob Donaldson.

SIXTY-SIX

Danny tucked the sandwiches he'd made into a rucksack, added a water bottle and some fruit and zipped it up. 'Ready?' he asked Jonathan.

'Ready,' the teenager replied. 'See you later, Grandad.' He leant in and kissed John Smithdown on the head.

'See you in a bit, lad,' Smithdown said. 'Take care out on those moors.'

'See you John,' Danny said. He also moved in to kiss the ex-detective.

'Fuck off, Danny, you weirdo,' Smithdown said, swatting him away.

'We'll make a metrosexual of you yet, mate,' Danny said. 'Right, got the flowers, Jonathan?'

'I have,' the teenager said. 'I've taken all the cellophane off them too. There's enough rubbish out on the moors without us adding to it.'

'That is very true,' Danny agreed. 'Jenny, are you sure you won't come with us? You know the hills better than anyone.'

Jenny Seddon came through from the kitchen with mugs of tea for herself and Smithdown. 'No, I'll stop here and look after His Lordship,' she said. 'But I wonder if you would do me a favour?' She went to her shoulder bag and pulled out two small bunches of tulips. They'd been tied together with a natural raffia ribbon. She gave them to Jonathan. 'Danny will know where to place them,' she said.

'Yes, I do, Jenny,' Danny confirmed. 'It'll be an honour.'

Danny and Jonathan drove away from Smithdown's house and headed up Huddersfield Road towards Black Moss Reservoir. Jonathan had Jenny's box of newspaper cuttings on his lap and was leafing through them as they went.

As he drove, Danny could clearly remember the directions he'd been given in 1990 when he'd been sent out to Black Moss when all the good reporters were busy covering the Strangeways riot:

> *Stop at Brun Clough Reservoir car park. There's a Pennine Way sign on your right. Walk the PW path until you reach another reservoir, (Redbook). The next one is Black Moss Reservoir, with Little Black Moss next to it. Look for a beach and police activity.*

After they'd parked up, Danny and Jonathan set off down the windy Pennine Way path. The gravel soon gave way to paving slabs, which rocked and squelched under their feet; the ground below was soaked through with water. The path forked right at the first reservoir and then headed upwards, following the soft, rolling flow of the moorland. The slabs that formed the path were drier here, the slope of the route allowing the moisture to drain off the watershed. Danny looked right; down through the valleys he could see the growing skyscrapers of Manchester. He looked left; over there were the neighbouring moors of Yorkshire.

Even after all these years he was still surprised by the sheer unrelenting *nothingness* of the area. It was like the world had been horizontally cut in two - sky at the top, moor at the bottom, with nothing to provide any form of relief from the two themes. *Not even a tree. Not one. In any direction. Bleak.*

As they crested the hill, Danny could see a second reservoir; the wind pushed tiny, quick waves across the surface of the water. Danny saw a dark, yellowy strip that separated the mossy moorland from the reservoir. Next to the reservoir - there was no other word for it - was a beach.

They stood quietly for a while, then Jonathan took out two bunches of flowers. Danny laid them on the sand close to the water's edge; one for his old friend from Manchester Radio, Gary Keenan, the other for Robbie Ormrod. 'How old would Robbie have been now?' Jonathan asked.

'I've never thought of it like that,' Danny said. 'My God, he'd be about 40. Old enough to be your dad.'

'Fucking Nora, as Grandad would say,' Jonathan replied.

Danny smiled. 'Yes, he probably would say that, wouldn't he?'

The pair stood still for a few moments. Then Jonathan spoke: 'Let's go, shall we? Lots to do.'

They retraced their steps, returned to Danny's car, then headed south past Bury and Ashton and then through Glossop before cutting through the village of Hayfield. Smithdown had told Danny that in the 80s, the local mountain rescue team had been based in an old stable building behind a pub. It still was, and Danny pointed it out to Jonathan as they drove through the village and up Kinder Road.

They parked up at Bowden Bridge next to the plaque that marked the start of the Kinder Scout Mass Trespass in 1932. Danny explained to the teenager how young ramblers and communists had taken it upon themselves to organise a mass invasion of the moors around Kinder Scout in 1932, a place that they were forbidden to walk on by moneyed landowners.

Then they took out a bunch of Jenny's flowers and placed them in the rocks below the plaque. Danny told Jonathan about Jordan McIntyre and how he'd taken his own life here in 1998, ten years after the murder of his father. For the second time that day they took a moment to think about what had happened at this spot. Then, once again, they moved on.

Danny and Jonathan headed up a cobbled path, past Kinder Reservoir and across the moors towards a walled plantation of trees. They saw scorch marks on the rocks from the fire that had been set there in 1988. Jonathan read out a cutting from the *Manchester Evening News* that detailed the bravery award that his grandad had received for his actions that night. Danny pointed out that Jenny Seddon of the Derbyshire Constabulary had also received one.

'Grandad says it's pronounced Con-stab-u-lary,' Jonathan said.

'If that's what he says, then it must be true,' Danny agreed.

They passed through the plantation and over a steep brow; in front of them was the Mermaid's Pool. It seemed strangely unimpressive; brown and shallow-looking, with a few rocks and reed banks scattered around the perimeter. It was about 40 feet long and less than 20 feet wide in the middle. It was uneven, shaped not unlike a map of Ireland. Behind the pool, the ground rose up sharply to meet the edge of the Kinder plateau above. Blue dragonflies flitted and swooped around the water's edge.

Jonathan found another cutting that told of how Councillor Sharmeen Chowdhury had been murdered here, set on fire by a racist gang led by Bob Donaldson and Tom Lennon. Jonathan got upset after reading it and took a walk around the water's edge to recover. They left flowers at the place where her body had been found and moved on.

Then they walked under the edge of Kinder Scout and went to bottom of Red Brook, the ravine that stretched up to the lip of the Kinder plateau high above them. They left two bunches of flowers; one for Naomi Wells, who'd sacrificed her life to save her daughter here in 1988 and another for Jenny's partner Brian McIntyre.

Having read the cuttings in Jenny's box, Jonathan convinced Danny to make another, unplanned stop. They called in at a florist and left flowers at the boating lake of Alexandra Park in Oldham town centre. 'They're for all the people killed and hurt in the race riots in 1988,'

Jonathan said. 'We shouldn't forget them.'

'You're right,' Danny said as they stood next to the boating house next to the lake. 'As usual.'

Finally, they returned to John Smithdown's house to pick up the retired detective. Jenny made sure Smithdown was wrapped up warm but declined their offer to come too. 'It should just be you three, I reckon,' she said. 'I'll see you when you get back.'

There was no way Smithdown could have walked to Black Moss, and the Mermaid's Pool would have been totally impossible. But Hanging Lees had a wide path running up to it and Danny was able to drive right up to the reservoir, despite annoying some of the walkers who were crossing the Piethorne Valley.

When they got there, Jonathan handed his grandfather the last bunch of flowers and Smithdown attached them to the metal gate at Hanging Lees. He tucked it between a fish and a dragonfly on the ornate metalwork. 'Maggie Ormrod, that poor woman,' Smithdown said. 'She had no chance, did she, lads? Right from the start. No chance at all.'

'We'll come back again another time, Grandad,' Jonathan said. 'With more flowers. We won't forget her.'

'That's a lovely thought, lad,' Smithdown said, cupping Jonathan's face with his hands. The old man looked across the water. 'What are you going to do then, Danny?' Smithdown asked. 'Your website has gone a bit quiet. There's been nothing new since your story about Bob. What's the plan?'

'My heart's not in it anymore,' Danny said. 'Not in the way it works now, anyway. Making money off people dying, writing stuff that's just designed to get clicks and put eyes on adverts. It seems wrong. Maybe I'll turn *Oldham Now* into a subscription service. Charge people a few quid a month. That way I can write longer, more in depth stuff, not just snappy headlines about death and destruction. Proper stories that could make a real difference. I'd like to investigate hospital jumping, those addicts going from hospital to hospital blagging pills. That kind of thing.'

Danny looked across at Jonathan: 'Maybe I could take an apprentice on, who knows?'

'I'd rather he got a proper job than be a journalist,' Smithdown said with a wink. 'That's a job for dickheads, that is.'

The wind was gathering now. It moved the surface of the reservoir left and right. The sky was blue but the reservoir was stubbornly grey. 'Hanging Lees…' Danny said. 'Who the fuck calls a reservoir Hanging Lees? It sounds like a Nick Cave song, doesn't it? *The Ballad of Hanging*

Lees.'

'Who's Nick Cave, Grandad?' Jonathan asked.

'I don't bloody know,' Smithdown said. 'One of those modern singers I suppose. Sounds a bit depressing.'

'Right,' said Danny. 'Let's get ourselves off home.'

'Can we go to the chippy on the way back?' Jonathan asked.

'That sounds like a great idea, what do you say John?'

'It's a resounding yes from me, Danny,' the ex-detective said. 'Steak pudding, chips, peas and gravy please. You're buying. Jonathan, call Jenny and see what she fancies.'

Danny took one last look at the dark, choppy waters of Hanging Lees. 'Fucking reservoirs,' he said. 'They creep me out.'

'They're just lumps of water, Danny. They can't do anyone any harm. It's people that do that.'

'Maybe. But I'll tell you what, John. I'm never going near a reservoir ever again.'

THE END

About the author

David Nolan is a multi-award-winning author, television producer and former crime reporter.

He has written a dozen books including *Tell the Truth and Shame the Devil,* the true story of the largest historic abuse case ever mounted by Greater Manchester Police. He presented a BBC Radio 4 documentary based on the book called *The Abuse Trial* . It won both the Rose D'Or and the New York International radio awards in 2016. He was also given a Royal Television Society award for his documentary *Riot! - Strangeways Ten Years On.*

He lives in the hills overlooking Manchester.

Author's Note

The events of this book are fictional, but like all the stories in the Manc Noir series, they are based on fact. In 2021 the National Society for the Prevention of Cruelty to Children (NSPCC) carried out freedom of information requests on police forces in England and Wales. They found that online grooming crimes recorded by police jumped by around 70% in the last three years reaching an all-time high in 2021.

There were 5,441 Sexual Communication With a Child offences recorded between April 2020 and March 2021, an increase of around 70% from recorded crimes in 2017/18.

Almost half of the offences used Facebook-owned apps, including Instagram, WhatsApp and Messenger.

Instagram was the most common site used, flagged by police in 32% of instances where the platform used was known.

Snapchat was used in over a quarter of offences, meaning the big four platforms were used in 74% of instances where the platform used was known.

Andy Burrows, Head of Child Safety Online Policy at the NSPCC, said: 'Year after year tech firms' failings result in more children being groomed and record levels of sexual abuse. To respond to the size and complexity of the threat, the Government must put child protection front and centre of legislation.'

The Perception of Dolls by Anthony Croix

"It's almost as if history is trying to erase the whole affair." - Anthony Croix

The triple murder and failed suicide that took place at 37 Fantoccini Street in 2001, raised little media interest at the time. In a week heavy with global news, a 'domestic tragedy' warranted few column inches. The case was open and shut, the inquest was brief and the 'Doll Murders' - little more than a footnote in the ledgers of Britain's true crime enthusiasts - were largely forgotten.

Nevertheless, investigations were made, police files generated, testimonies recorded, and conclusions reached. The reports are there, a matter of public record, for those with a mind to look.

The details of what took place in Fantoccini Street in the years that followed are less accessible. The people involved in the field trips to number 37 are often unwilling, or unable, to talk about what they witnessed. The hours of audio recordings, video tapes, written accounts, photographs, drawings, and even online postings are elusive, almost furtive.

In fact, were it not for a chance encounter between the late Anthony Croix and an obsessive collector of Gothic dolls, the Fantoccini Street Reports might well have been lost forever.

Cash Rules Everything Around Me by Rob Gittins

Morrissey Jarrett is fresh out of prison and back on the streets of his hometown Cardiff.

During his enforced absence the city has been re-developed to within an inch of its life and a disoriented Morrissey falls back into old habits as he scams, schemes, and steals whatever he needs to survive.

Morrissey has big dreams though. Dreams of making one last huge score, dreams of leaving his life of crime behind, dreams of reuniting with the love of his life and dreams of walking off into the sunset with her. Happy. Ever. After.

All he needs is a plan.

Luckily, the circles Morrissey frequents provide ample opportunities for ill-gotten gains and soon the perfect job literally falls into his hands.

And so, along with a hastily assembled crew of misfits, Morrissey embarks on planning the perfect heist. With all their eyes fixed steadily on a payday that could change their stars forever - all they have to do is keep their heads down, play it cool, and follow the plan to the letter.

What could possibly go wrong?

Printed in Great Britain
by Amazon

54088482R00381